F9910 45

Lineberger Memorial

Library

LUCIAN

V

LCL 302

LUCIAN

VOLUME V

WITH AN ENGLISH TRANSLATION BY

A. M. HARMON

HARVARD UNIVERSITY PRESS
CAMBRIDGE, MASSACHUSETTS
LONDON, ENGLAND

First published 1936
Reprinted 1955, 1962, 1972, 1996

ISBN 0-674-99333-0

Printed in Great Britain by St Edmundsbury Press Ltd,
Bury St Edmunds, Suffolk, on acid-free paper.
Bound by Hunter & Foulis Ltd, Edinburgh, Scotland.

CONTENTS

NOTE

In the constitution of this volume *Peregrinus*, *Fugitivi*, and *Toxaris*, which in Vat. 90 (Γ) follow *Abdicatus*, are placed before *Saltatio*; i.e. at the beginning of the volume instead of the end. *Amores*, which in that MS. follows *Astrologia*, is omitted here for inclusion in Volume VII, and *Pro Imaginibus*, which follows *Amores*, has already been published in Volume IV, following *Imagines*.

In editing the Greek Text, rotographs of Γ and N have been used throughout, except for the *Peregrinus*, now lacking in N. Rotographs of U, P, and Z have been used for the pieces contained in those MSS.: for *Astrology*, Z; for *The Parliament of the Gods*, P and Z (but Z has only the *prephisma*); for *The Tyrannicide* and *Disowned*, U and Z.

LIST OF LUCIAN'S WORKS

SHOWING THEIR DIVISION INTO VOLUMES IN THIS EDITION

LIST OF LUCIAN'S WORKS

THE PASSING OF PEREGRINUS

An account of the life and death of a Cynic philosopher
who for a time in his early life went over to Christianity,
practising it to the point of imprisonment under a very
tolerant administration, and after returning to Cynicism
became in his old age so enamoured of Indic ideas and precedents that he cremated himself at Olympia, just after the
games of A.D. 165, even as Calanus had done at Susa in the
presence of Alexander the Great and as Zarmarus had done
at Athens, after initiation into the mysteries, in the presence
of Augustus.

Writing soon after the event, of which he was a witness,
Lucian makes his main theme the story of what went on at
Olympia. The earlier life of Peregrinus is portrayed incidentally in a speech attributed by Lucian to someone whose name
he did not know, but clearly made by Lucian himself (p. 8,
n. 2).

Lucian believes himself to be exposing a sham, whose
zeal was not at all for truth but only for applause and renown.
Many notable modern critics, including Zeller, Bernays,
Croiset, and Wilamowitz, dissent from his interpretation,
discerning in the man an earnest seeker after truth; for to
them thirst for glory is not an adequate explanation of his
final act. This point of view hardly embodies sufficient
recognition of the driving force of that motive with Greeks,
and particularly Greeks of the second century (Nock, *Con-
version*, p. 201). Greek writers recognised it as a possible
explanation of the behaviour of Calanus and of Zarmarus.
In this case, Lucian not only knew the man but knew others
who knew him : for instance, Demonax. Assuredly, the
interpretation that he gives is not his alone. Perhaps it is
not so far wrong after all. Certainly there are authentic
features in it, like the attempt of Proteus to get back the
inheritance he had previously renounced and bestowed upon
his native city, which make it impossible to see in him the
"earnest and steadfast man" that Aulus Gellius thought him.

I

ΠΕΡΙ ΤΗΣ ΠΕΡΕΓΡΙΝΟΥ ΤΕΛΕΥΤΗΣ

Λουκιανὸς Κρονίῳ εὖ πράττειν.

1 Ὁ κακοδαίμων Περεγρῖνος, ἢ ὡς αὐτὸς ἔχαιρεν
ὀνομάζων ἑαυτόν, Πρωτεύς, αὐτὸ δὴ ἐκεῖνο
τὸ τοῦ Ὁμηρικοῦ Πρωτέως ἔπαθεν· ἅπαντα
γὰρ δόξης ἕνεκα γενόμενος καὶ μυρίας τροπὰς
τραπόμενος, τὰ τελευταῖα ταῦτα καὶ πῦρ ἐγένετο·
τοσούτῳ ἄρα τῷ ἔρωτι τῆς δόξης εἴχετο. καὶ νῦν
ἐκεῖνος ἀπηνθράκωταί σοι ὁ βέλτιστος κατὰ τὸν
Ἐμπεδοκλέα, παρ' ὅσον ὁ μὲν κἂν διαλαθεῖν ἐπει-

This piece is wanting in N and several other MSS. because
it was in the *Index Librorum Prohibitorum*. It has been
edited separately by Lionello Levi, with the readings of
eight MSS., chief of which are Γ, X (Pal. 73), and M (Par.
2954).

---

[1] The greeting here employed (its sense might perhaps be
more adequately rendered by "Good issues to all your
doings") marks Cronius as a Platonist. Lucian himself
(*Lapsus*, 4) ascribes its origin to Plato, and he employs it in
addressing the philosopher Nigrinus (I, p. 98). A Platonist
named Cronius is more than once mentioned by Porphyry,
but to identify the two would contribute next to nothing to
our knowledge of either.

[2] Cf. Aulus Gellius, XII, 11 : philosophum nomine Pere-
grinum, cui postea cognomentum Proteus factum est, virum
gravem et constantem, etc. Lucian calls him Peregrinus
Proteus in *Demonax*, 21 (I, p. 156), but simply Proteus the
Cynic in *adv. Indoct.*, 14 (III, p. 192), and he is Proteus to

THE PASSING OF PEREGRINUS

BEST wishes from Lucian to Cronius.[1]

Unlucky Peregrinus, or, as he delighted to style himself, Proteus,[2] has done exactly what Proteus in Homer did.[3] After turning into everything for the sake of notoriety and achieving any number of transformations, here at last he has turned into fire; so great, it seems, was the love of notoriety that possessed him. And now your genial friend has got himself carbonified after the fashion of Empedocles, except that the latter at least tried to escape

the Philostrati (cf. *Vit. Soph.* II, 1, 33 and for the elder Philostratus the title of his lost work *Proteus the Cynic ; or, the Sophist*), to Tatian (*Orat. ad Graecos,* 25), and to Athenagoras (*Legat. de Christian.,* 26). The name Peregrinus is used in Aulus Gellius, VIII, 3, Ammianus Marcellinus, XXIX, 1, 39, Tertullian *ad Martyres*, 4, and Eusebius, *Chron.,* Vol. II, p. 170, Schöne. From the passage in Gellius cited above we can infer only that he did not hear the sobriquet Proteus when he was in Athens. The manner of its employment by Lucian is sufficient evidence that it did not originate with Lucian, or after the death of Peregrinus. It was probably applied to him towards the close of his career. That it bears a sense very like what Lucian attributes to it is clear from Maximus of Tyre, VIII, 1. In § 27 Lucian professes to have heard that he wanted to change it to Phoenix after his decision to immolate himself.

[3] The transformations of the sea-god in his effort to escape from Menelaus, who wanted to consult him, are told in the *Odyssey,* IV, 454–459.

ράθη ἐμβαλὼν ἑαυτὸν εἰς τοὺς κρατῆρας, ὁ δὲ
γεννάδας οὗτος, τὴν πολυανθρωποτάτην τῶν
Ἑλληνικῶν πανηγύρεων τηρήσας, πυρὰν ὅτι
μεγίστην νήσας ἐνεπήδησεν ἐπὶ τοσούτων μαρ-
τύρων, καὶ λόγους τινὰς ὑπὲρ τούτου εἰπὼν
πρὸς τοὺς Ἕλληνας οὐ πρὸ πολλῶν ἡμερῶν τοῦ
τολμήματος.

2 Πολλὰ τοίνυν δοκῶ μοι ὁρᾶν σε γελῶντα
ἐπὶ τῇ κορύζῃ τοῦ γέροντος, μᾶλλον δὲ καὶ ἀκούω
βοῶντος οἷά σε εἰκὸς βοᾶν, " Ὦ τῆς ἀβελτερίας,
ὦ τῆς δοξοκοπίας, ὦ—" τῶν ἄλλων ἃ λέγειν
εἰώθαμεν περὶ αὐτῶν. σὺ μὲν οὖν πόρρω ταῦτα
καὶ μακρῷ ἀσφαλέστερον, ἐγὼ δὲ παρὰ τὸ πῦρ αὐτὸ
καὶ ἔτι πρότερον ἐν πολλῷ πλήθει τῶν ἀκροατῶν
εἶπον αὐτά, ἐνίων μὲν ἀχθομένων, ὅσοι ἐθαύμαζον τὴν ἀπόνοιαν τοῦ γέροντος· ἦσαν δέ τινες
οἳ καὶ αὐτοὶ ἐγέλων ἐπ᾽ αὐτῷ. ἀλλ᾽ ὀλίγου δεῖν
ὑπὸ τῶν Κυνικῶν ἐγώ σοι διεσπάσθην ὥσπερ ὁ
Ἀκταίων ὑπὸ τῶν κυνῶν ἢ ὁ ἀνεψιὸς αὐτοῦ ὁ
Πενθεὺς ὑπὸ τῶν Μαινάδων.

3 Ἡ δὲ πᾶσα τοῦ πράγματος διασκευὴ τοιάδε
ἦν. τὸν μὲν ποιητὴν οἶσθα οἷός τε ἦν καὶ ἡλίκα
ἐτραγῴδει παρ᾽ ὅλον τὸν βίον, ὑπὲρ τὸν Σοφοκλέα
καὶ τὸν Αἰσχύλον. ἐγὼ δὲ ἐπεὶ τάχιστα εἰς τὴν
Ἦλιν ἀφικόμην, διὰ τοῦ γυμνασίου ἀνιὼν[1] ἐπήκουον
ἅμα Κυνικοῦ τινος μεγάλῃ καὶ τραχείᾳ τῇ φωνῇ
τὰ συνήθη ταῦτα καὶ ἐκ τριόδου τὴν ἀρετὴν
ἐπιβοωμένου καὶ ἅπασιν ἁπαξαπλῶς λοιδορου-
μένου. εἶτα κατέληξεν αὐτῷ ἡ βοὴ ἐς τὸν

---

[1] ἀνιὼν Sommerbrodt.: αὐτῶν MSS.

[2] "Up" means to Olympia (cf. § 31).

4

observation when he threw himself into the crater,[1] while this gentleman waited for that one of the Greek festivals which draws the greatest crowds, heaped up a very large pyre, and leaped into it before all those witnesses; he even addressed the Greeks on the subject not many days before his venture.

I think I can see you laughing heartily at the old man's drivelling idiocy—indeed, I hear you give tongue as you naturally would: " Oh, the stupidity! Oh, the vainglory! Oh "—everything else that we are in the habit of saying about it all. Well, you are doing this at a distance and with far greater security, but I said it right by the fire and even earlier in a great crowd of listeners, angering some of them—as many as admired the old man's fool-hardiness; but there were others beside myself who laughed at him. However, I narrowly missed getting torn limb from limb for you by the Cynics just as Actaeon was by his dogs or his cousin Pentheus by the Maenads.

The complete *mise en scène* of the affair was as follows. You know, of course, what the playwright was like and what spectacular performances he presented his whole life long, outdoing Sophocles and Aeschylus. As for my part in it, as soon as I came to Elis, in going up [2] by way of the gymnasium I overheard a Cynic bawling out the usual street-corner invocations to Virtue in a loud, harsh voice, and abusing everyone without exception. Then his harangue wound up with Proteus, and to the best

---

[1] Of Aetna; it was said that the manner of his death remained unknown until the mountain cast up one of his golden sandals.

Πρωτέα, καὶ ὡς ἂν οἶός τε ὦ πειράσομαί σοι
αὐτὰ ἐκεῖνα ἀπομνημονεῦσαι ὡς ἐλέγετο. σὺ δὲ
γνωριεῖς δηλαδή, πολλάκις αὐτοῖς παραστὰς βοῶσιν.

4 " Πρωτέα γάρ τις," ἔφη, " κενόδοξον τολμᾷ
λέγειν, ὦ γῆ καὶ ἥλιε καὶ ποταμοὶ καὶ θάλαττα
καὶ πατρῷε Ἡράκλεις—Πρωτέα τὸν ἐν Συρίᾳ
δεθέντα, τὸν τῇ πατρίδι ἀνέντα πεντακισχίλια
τάλαντα, τὸν ἀπὸ τῆς Ῥωμαίων πόλεως ἐκβλη-
θέντα, τὸν τοῦ Ἡλίου ἐπισημότερον, τὸν αὐτῷ
ἀνταγωνίσασθαι τῷ Ὀλυμπίῳ δυνάμενον; ἀλλ'
ὅτι διὰ πυρὸς ἐξάγειν τοῦ βίου διέγνωκεν ἑαυτόν,
εἰς κενοδοξίαν τινὲς τοῦτο ἀναφέρουσιν; οὐ γὰρ
Ἡρακλῆς οὕτως; οὐ γὰρ Ἀσκληπιὸς καὶ Διόνυσος
κεραυνῷ; οὐ γὰρ τὰ τελευταῖα Ἐμπεδοκλῆς
εἰς τοὺς κρατῆρας;"

5 Ὡς δὲ ταῦτα εἶπεν ὁ Θεαγένης—τοῦτο γὰρ
ὁ κεκραγὼς ἐκεῖνος ἐκαλεῖτο—ἠρόμην τινὰ τῶν
παρεστώτων, "Τί βούλεται τὸ περὶ τοῦ πυρός, ἢ τί
Ἡρακλῆς καὶ Ἐμπεδοκλῆς πρὸς τὸν Πρωτέα."
ὁ δέ, " Οὐκ εἰς μακράν," ἔφη, " καύσει ἑαυτὸν
ὁ Πρωτεὺς Ὀλυμπίασιν." " Πῶς," ἔφην, " ἢ
τίνος ἕνεκα;" εἶτα ὁ μὲν ἐπειρᾶτο λέγειν, ἐβόα
δὲ ὁ Κυνικός, ὥστε ἀμήχανον ἦν ἄλλου ἀκούειν.
ἐπήκουον οὖν τὰ λοιπὰ ἐπαντλοῦντος αὐτοῦ καὶ

---

[1] The cases of Dionysus and Asclepius were not quite
parallel. Zeus could not have Asclepius raising the dead,
and so transferred his activities to a higher sphere by means
of the thunderbolt. It was Semele, the mother of Dionysus,
whom his other bolt carbonised; but as it certainly effected,
even if only incidentally, the translation of Dionysus, and as
one of the epigrams in the *Anthology* (XVI, 185) similarly
links Dionysus with Heracles as having achieved immortality
by fire, it is hard to see why so many editors have pruned

THE PASSING OF PEREGRINUS

of my ability I shall try to quote for you the very
words he said. You will find the style familiar, of
course, as you have often stood near them while
they were ranting.

"Does anyone dare," he said, " to call Proteus
vainglorious, O Earth, O sun, O rivers, O sea, O
Heracles, god of our fathers!—Proteus, who was
imprisoned in Syria, who renounced five thousand
talents in favour of his native land, who was banished
from the city of Rome, who is more conspicuous
than the sun, who is able to rival Olympian Zeus
himself? Because he has resolved to depart from
life by way of fire, are there people who attribute
this to vainglory? Why, did not Heracles do so?
Did not Asclepius and Dionysus,[1] by grace of the
thunderbolt? Did not Empedocles end by leaping
into the crater?"

When Theagenes [2]—for that was the bawler's
name—said that, I asked a bystander, " What is the
meaning of his talk about fire, and what have Heracles
and Empedocles to do with Proteus?" "Before
long," he replied, " Proteus is going to burn himself
up at the Olympic festival." " How," said I, " and
why?" Then he undertook to tell me, but the
Cynic was bawling, so that it was impossible to hear
anyone else. I listened, therefore, while he flooded

the exuberance of Theagenes by excising mention of Dionysus
from his remarks. Cf. *Parl. of the Gods*, 6 (p. 425).
[2] We learn elsewhere in this piece that Theagenes lived
in Patras and had property worth fifteen talents, obtained
by lending money. Bernays (*Lucian und die Kyniker*, pp.
13–18) is very likely right in thinking this to be the man
whose death in Rome is described by Galen (*Meth. Med.*, 13,
15 : X, 909 Kühn), but he makes rather too much of that
passage as an endorsement of Theagenes.

7

THE WORKS OF LUCIAN

θαυμαστάς τινας ὑπερβολὰς διεξιόντος κατὰ τοῦ
Πρωτέως· τὸν μὲν γὰρ Σινωπέα ἢ τὸν διδάσκαλον
αὐτοῦ ᾿Αντισθένη οὐδὲ παραβάλλειν ἠξίου αὐτῷ,
ἀλλ᾿ οὐδὲ τὸν Σωκράτη αὐτόν, ἐκάλει δὲ τὸν Δία
ἐπὶ τὴν ἅμιλλαν. εἶτα μέντοι ἔδοξεν αὐτῷ ἴσους
πως φυλάξαι αὐτούς, καὶ οὕτω κατέπαυε τὸν
6 λόγον· " Δύο γὰρ ταῦτα," ἔφη, " ὁ βίος ἄριστα
δημιουργήματα ἐθεάσατο, τὸν Δία τὸν ᾿Ολύμπιον
καὶ Πρωτέα· πλάσται δὲ καὶ τεχνῖται, τοῦ μὲν
Φειδίας, τοῦ δὲ ἡ φύσις. ἀλλὰ νῦν ἐξ ἀνθρώπων
εἰς θεοὺς τὸ ἄγαλμα τοῦτο οἰχήσεται, ὀχούμενον
ἐπὶ τοῦ πυρός, ὀρφανοὺς ἡμᾶς καταλιπόν."
ταῦτα ξὺν πολλῷ ἱδρῶτι διεξελθὼν ἐδάκρυε μάλα
γελοίως καὶ τὰς τρίχας ἐτίλλετο, ὑποφειδόμενος
μὴ πάνυ ἕλκειν· καὶ τέλος ἀπῆγον αὐτὸν λύζοντα
μεταξὺ τῶν Κυνικῶν τινες παραμυθούμενοι.

7 Μετὰ δὲ τοῦτον ἄλλος εὐθὺς ἀναβαίνει, οὐ
περιμείνας διαλυθῆναι τὸ πλῆθος ἀλλὰ ἐπ᾿ αἰθο-
μένοις τοῖς προτέροις ἱερείοις ἐπέχει τῶν σπονδῶν.
καὶ τὸ μὲν πρῶτον ἐπὶ πολὺ ἐγέλα καὶ δῆλος ἦν
νειόθεν αὐτὸ δρῶν· εἶτα ἤρξατο ὧδέ πως· " Ἐπεὶ
ὁ κατάρατος Θεαγένης τέλος τῶν μιαρωτάτων
αὐτοῦ λόγων τὰ Ἡρακλείτου δάκρυα ἐποιήσατο, ἐγὼ κατὰ τὸ ἐναντίον ἀπὸ τοῦ Δημοκρίτου
γέλωτος ἄρξομαι." καὶ αὖθις ἐγέλα ἐπὶ πολύ,
ὥστε καὶ ἡμῶν τοὺς πολλοὺς ἐπὶ τὸ ὅμοιον

---

[1] Diogenes.
[2] Evidently the Cynic had spoken from a high place
(perhaps the portico of the gymnasium) to which the new
speaker now ascends. What Lucian has previously said (§ 2),
together with his failure here to say a word about the identity

THE PASSING OF PEREGRINUS

us with the rest of his bilge-water and got off a
lot of amazing hyperbole about Proteus, for, not
deigning to compare him with the man of Sinope,[1]
or his teacher Antisthenes, or even with Socrates
himself, he summoned Zeus to the lists.   Then,
however, he decided to keep them about equal, and
thus concluded his speech: " These are the two
noblest masterpieces that the world has seen—the
Olympian Zeus, and Proteus; of the one, the creator
and artist was Phidias, of the other, Nature.   But
now this holy image is about to depart from among
men to gods, borne on the wings of fire, leaving us
bereft."   After   completing   this   discourse   with
copious perspiration, he shed tears in a highly
ridiculous way and tore his hair, taking care not to
pull very hard; and at length he was led away,
sobbing as he went, by some of the Cynics, who
strove to comfort him.

    After him, another man went up at once,[2] not per-
mitting the throng to disperse, but pouring a libation
on the previous sacrificial offerings while they were
still ablaze.   At first he laughed a long time, and
obviously did it from the heart.   Then he began
somewhat after this fashion: " Since that accursed
Theagenes terminated his pestilential remarks with
the tears of Heraclitus, I, on the contrary, shall
begin with the laughter of Democritus."   And
again he went on laughing a long time, so that he

or personality of the author of these remarks, puts it beyond
doubt that the "other man" is Lucian himself, and that he
expects his readers to draw this inference. The device is so
transparent that its intent can be regarded only as artistic.
It is employed also in *The Eunuch*, 10 (p. 341). Somewhat
similar is his borrowing a Prologue from Menander to speak
for him in *The Mistaken Critic* (p. 379).

9

THE WORKS OF LUCIAN

8 ἐπεσπάσατο. εἶτα ἐπιστρέψας ἑαυτόν, " Ἡ τί
γὰρ ἄλλο," ἔφη, " ὦ ἄνδρες, χρὴ ποιεῖν ἀκούοντας
μὲν οὕτω γελοίων ῥήσεων, ὁρῶντας [1] δὲ ἄνδρας
γέροντας δοξαρίου καταπτύστου ἕνεκα μονονουχὶ
κυβιστῶντας ἐν τῷ μέσῳ; ὡς δὲ εἰδείητε
οἷόν τι τὸ ἄγαλμά ἐστι τὸ καυθησόμενον, ἀκού-
σατέ μου ἐξ ἀρχῆς παραφυλάξαντος τὴν γνώμην
αὐτοῦ καὶ τὸν βίον ἐπιτηρήσαντος· ἔνια δὲ παρὰ
τῶν πολιτῶν αὐτοῦ ἐπυνθανόμην καὶ οἷς ἀνάγκη
ἦν ἀκριβῶς εἰδέναι αὐτόν.

9 Τὸ γὰρ τῆς φύσεως τοῦτο πλάσμα καὶ δημιούρ-
γημα, ὁ τοῦ Πολυκλείτου κανών, ἐπεὶ εἰς ἄνδρας
τελεῖν ἤρξατο, ἐν Ἀρμενίᾳ μοιχεύων ἁλοὺς μάλα
πολλὰς πληγὰς ἔλαβεν καὶ τέλος κατὰ τοῦ τέγους
ἁλόμενος διέφυγε, ῥαφανῖδι τὴν πυγὴν βεβυσμένος.
εἶτα μειράκιόν τι ὡραῖον διαφθείρας τρισχιλίων
ἐξωνήσατο παρὰ τῶν γονέων τοῦ παιδός, πενήτων
ὄντων, μὴ ἐπὶ τὸν ἁρμοστὴν ἀπαχθῆναι τῆς Ἀσίας.

10 " Ταῦτα καὶ τὰ τοιαῦτα ἐάσειν μοι δοκῶ·
πηλὸς γὰρ ἔτι ἄπλαστος ἦν καὶ οὐδέπω ἐντελὲς
ἄγαλμα ἡμῖν δεδημιούργητο. ἃ δὲ τὸν πατέρα
ἔδρασεν καὶ πάνυ ἀκοῦσαι ἄξιον· καίτοι πάντες
ἴστε, καὶ ἀκηκόατε ὡς ἀπέπνιξε τὸν γέροντα,
οὐκ ἀνασχόμενος αὐτὸν ὑπὲρ ἑξήκοντα ἔτη ἤδη
γηρῶντα. εἶτα ἐπειδὴ τὸ πρᾶγμα διεβεβόητο,
φυγὴν ἑαυτοῦ καταδικάσας ἐπλανᾶτο ἄλλοτε
ἄλλην ἀμείβων.

---

[1] ἀκούοντας . . . ὁρῶντας Γ: ἀκούοντα . . . ὁρῶντα XMF.

---

[1] The proportions of the statue of a naked youth carrying
a spear (the *Doryphorus*), made by Polyclitus, were analysed

drew most of us into doing likewise. Then, changing countenance, he said, " Pray, what else, gentlemen, are we to do when we hear utterances so ridiculous, and see old men all but standing on their heads in public for the sake of a little despicable notoriety? That you may know what manner of thing is this 'holy image' which is about to be burned up, give me your ears, for I have observed his character and kept an eye on his career from the beginning, and have ascertained various particulars from his fellow-citizens and people who cannot have helped knowing him thoroughly.

" This creation and masterpiece of nature, this Polyclitan canon,[1] as soon as he came of age, was taken in adultery in Armenia and got a sound thrashing, but finally jumped down from the roof and made his escape, with a radish stopping his vent. Then he corrupted a handsome boy, and by paying three thousand drachmas to the boy's parents, who were poor, bought himself off from being brought before the governor of the province of Asia.

" All this and the like of it I propose to pass over; for he was still unshapen clay, and our 'holy image' had not yet been consummated for us. What he did to his father, however, is very well worth hearing; but you all know it—you have heard how he strangled the aged man, unable to tolerate his living beyond sixty years. Then, when the affair had been noised abroad, he condemned himself to exile and roamed about, going to one country after another.

by the sculptor himself in a book called the *Canon*, and universally accepted as canonical for the male figure.

11   " Ὅτεπερ καὶ τὴν θαυμαστὴν σοφίαν τῶν
Χριστιανῶν ἐξέμαθεν, περὶ τὴν Παλαιστίνην τοῖς
ἱερεῦσιν καὶ γραμματεῦσιν αὐτῶν ξυγγενόμενος.
καὶ τί γάρ; ἐν βραχεῖ παῖδας αὐτοὺς ἀπέφηνε,
προφήτης καὶ [1] θιασάρχης καὶ ξυναγωγεὺς καὶ
πάντα μόνος αὐτὸς ὤν, καὶ τῶν βίβλων τὰς μὲν ἐξη-
γεῖτο καὶ διεσάφει, πολλὰς δὲ αὐτὸς καὶ συνέγραφεν,
καὶ ὡς θεὸν αὐτὸν ἐκεῖνοι ᾐδοῦντο [2] καὶ νομοθέτῃ
ἐχρῶντο καὶ προστάτην ἐπεγράφοντο, μετὰ [3]
γοῦν ἐκεῖνον ὃν [4] ἔτι σέβουσι, τὸν ἄνθρωπον τὸν
ἐν τῇ Παλαιστίνῃ ἀνασκολοπισθέντα, ὅτι καινὴν
ταύτην [5] τελετὴν εἰσῆγεν ἐς [6] τὸν βίον.

12   " Τότε δὴ καὶ συλληφθεὶς ἐπὶ τούτῳ ὁ Πρωτεὺς ἐνέπεσεν εἰς τὸ δεσμωτήριον, ὅπερ καὶ
αὐτὸ οὐ μικρὸν αὐτῷ ἀξίωμα περιεποίησεν πρὸς
τὸν ἑξῆς βίον καὶ τὴν τερατείαν καὶ δοξοκοπίαν
ὧν ἐρῶν ἐτύγχανεν. ἐπεὶ δ᾽ οὖν ἐδέδετο, οἱ
Χριστιανοὶ συμφορὰν ποιούμενοι τὸ πρᾶγμα πάντα
ἐκίνουν ἐξαρπάσαι πειρώμενοι αὐτόν. εἶτ᾽, ἐπεὶ
τοῦτο ἦν ἀδύνατον, ἥ γε ἄλλη θεραπεία πᾶσα οὐ
παρέργως ἀλλὰ σὺν σπουδῇ ἐγίγνετο· καὶ ἕωθεν
μὲν εὐθὺς ἦν ὁρᾶν παρὰ τῷ δεσμωτηρίῳ περι-
μένοντα γράδια χήρας τινὰς καὶ παιδία ὀρφανά,
οἱ δὲ ἐν τέλει αὐτῶν καὶ συνεκάθευδον ἔνδον μετ᾽
αὐτοῦ διαφθείραντες τοὺς δεσμοφύλακας. εἶτα
δεῖπνα ποικίλα εἰσεκομίζετο καὶ λόγοι ἱεροὶ
αὐτῶν ἐλέγοντο, καὶ ὁ βέλτιστος Περεγρῖνος—
ἔτι γὰρ τοῦτο ἐκαλεῖτο—καινὸς Σωκράτης ὑπ᾽
αὐτῶν ὠνομάζετο.

---

[1] καὶ MF: not in ΓΧ.
[2] ᾐδοῦντο Cobet, Fritzsche: ἡγοῦντο MSS.
[3] ἐπεγράφοντο, μετὰ Cobet: ἐπέγραφον· τὸν μέγαν MSS.

" It was then that he learned the wondrous lore of the Christians, by associating with their priests and scribes in Palestine. And—how else could it be ?—in a trice he made them all look like children ; for he was prophet, cult-leader, head of the syna-gogue, and everything, all by himself. He inter-preted and explained some of their books and even composed many, and they revered him as a god, made use of him as a lawgiver, and set him down as a protector, next after that other, to be sure, whom [1] they still worship, the man who was crucified in Palestine because he introduced this new cult into the world.

" Then at length Proteus was apprehended for this and thrown into prison, which itself gave him no little reputation as an asset for his future career and the charlatanism and notoriety-seeking that he was enamoured of. Well, when he had been imprisoned, the Christians, regarding the incident as a calamity, left nothing undone in the effort to rescue him. Then, as this was impossible, every other form of attention was shown him, not in any casual way but with assiduity ; and from the very break of day aged widows and orphan children could be seen waiting near the prison, while their officials even slept inside with him after bribing the guards. Then elaborate meals were brought in, and sacred books of theirs were read aloud, and excellent Peregrinus—for he still went by that name—was called by them ' the new Socrates.'

[1] The sense of the unemended text here is " protector ; that great man, to be sure, they still worship," etc.

---

4 ὃν Harmon: not in MSS.
5 ταῦτα ΓΧ.   6 ἐπὶ ΓΧ.

13   "Καὶ μὴν κἀκ[1] τῶν ἐν Ἀσίᾳ πόλεων ἔστιν
ὧν ἧκόν τινες, τῶν Χριστιανῶν στελλόντων ἀπὸ
τοῦ κοινοῦ, βοηθήσοντες καὶ συναγορεύσοντες καὶ
παραμυθησόμενοι τὸν ἄνδρα. ἀμήχανον δέ τι
τὸ τάχος ἐπιδείκνυνται, ἐπειδάν τι τοιοῦτον
γένηται δημόσιον· ἐν βραχεῖ γὰρ ἀφειδοῦσι
πάντων. καὶ δὴ καὶ τῷ Περεγρίνῳ πολλὰ τότε
ἧκεν χρήματα παρ' αὐτῶν ἐπὶ προφάσει τῶν
δεσμῶν, καὶ πρόσοδον οὐ μικρὰν ταύτην ἐποιήσατο.[2] πεπείκασι γὰρ αὐτοὺς οἱ κακοδαίμονες τὸ
μὲν ὅλον ἀθάνατοι ἔσεσθαι καὶ βιώσεσθαι τὸν ἀεὶ
χρόνον, παρ' ὃ καὶ καταφρονοῦσιν τοῦ θανάτου καὶ
ἑκόντες αὐτοὺς ἐπιδιδόασιν οἱ πολλοί. ἔπειτα δὲ
ὁ νομοθέτης ὁ πρῶτος ἔπεισεν αὐτοὺς ὡς ἀδελφοὶ
πάντες εἶεν ἀλλήλων, ἐπειδὰν ἅπαξ παραβάντες
θεοὺς μὲν τοὺς Ἑλληνικοὺς ἀπαρνήσωνται, τὸν
δὲ ἀνεσκολοπισμένον ἐκεῖνον σοφιστὴν αὐτὸν[3]
προσκυνῶσιν καὶ κατὰ τοὺς ἐκείνου νόμους βιῶσιν.
καταφρονοῦσιν οὖν ἁπάντων ἐξ ἴσης καὶ κοινὰ
ἡγοῦνται, ἄνευ τινὸς ἀκριβοῦς πίστεως τὰ τοιαῦτα
παραδεξάμενοι. ἢν τοίνυν παρέλθῃ τις εἰς αὐτοὺς
γόης καὶ τεχνίτης ἄνθρωπος καὶ πράγμασιν
χρῆσθαι δυνάμενος, αὐτίκα μάλα πλούσιος ἐν
βραχεῖ ἐγένετο ἰδιώταις ἀνθρώποις ἐγχανών.

14   " Πλὴν ἀλλ' ὁ Περεγρῖνος ἀφείθη ὑπὸ τοῦ τότε
τῆς Συρίας ἄρχοντος, ἀνδρὸς φιλοσοφίᾳ χαίροντος,

---

[1] κἀκ Jacobitz, Dindorf: καὶ MSS.
[2] ἐποιήσατο X[2] (Faber): ἐποιήσαντο X[1], cett.
[3] αὐτὸν X, Sommerbrodt: αὐτῶν ΓΜ.

THE PASSING OF PEREGRINUS

" Indeed, people came even from the cities in Asia, sent by the Christians at their common expense, to succour and defend and encourage the hero. They show incredible speed whenever any such public action is taken; for in no time they lavish their all. So it was then in the case of Peregrinus; much money came to him from them by reason of his imprisonment, and he procured not a little revenue from it. The poor wretches have convinced themselves, first and foremost, that they are going to be immortal and live for all time, in consequence of which they despise death and even willingly give themselves into custody, most of them. Furthermore, their first lawgiver [1] persuaded them that they are all brothers of one another after they have transgressed once for all by denying the Greek gods and by worshipping that crucified sophist himself and living under his laws. Therefore they despise all things indiscriminately and consider them common property, receiving such doctrines traditionally without any definite evidence. So if any charlatan and trickster, able to profit by occasions, comes among them, he quickly acquires sudden wealth by imposing upon simple folk.

" However, Peregrinus was freed by the then governor of Syria, a man who was fond of philosophy.[2] Aware of his recklessness and that he

---

[1] From the wording of this sentence the allusion is so obviously to Christ himself that one is at a loss to understand why Paul, let alone Moses, should have been suggested. For the doctrine of brotherly love cf. Matt. 23, 8 : πάντες δὲ ὑμεῖς ἀδελφοί ἐστε.

[2] The Roman governor of the province of Syria is meant. Identification is impossible because the date of the imprisonment of Peregrinus cannot be fixed.

ὃς συνεὶς τὴν ἀπόνοιαν αὐτοῦ καὶ ὅτι δέξαιτ'
ἂν ἀποθανεῖν ὡς δόξαν ἐπὶ τούτῳ ἀπολίποι,
ἀφῆκεν αὐτὸν οὐδὲ τῆς κολάσεως ὑπολαβὼν
ἄξιον. ὁ δὲ εἰς τὴν οἰκείαν ἐπανελθὼν καταλαμβάνει τὸ περὶ τοῦ πατρῴου φόνου ἔτι φλεγμαῖνον
καὶ πολλοὺς τοὺς ἐπανατεινομένους τὴν κατηγορίαν. διήρπαστο δὲ τὰ πλεῖστα τῶν κτημάτων
παρὰ τὴν ἀποδημίαν αὐτοῦ καὶ μόνοι ὑπελεί-
ποντο οἱ ἀγροὶ ὅσον εἰς πεντεκαίδεκα τάλαντα.
ἦν γὰρ ἡ πᾶσα οὐσία τριάκοντά που ταλάντων ἀξία
ἦν ὁ γέρων κατέλιπεν, οὐχ ὥσπερ ὁ παγγέλοιος
Θεαγένης ἔλεγε πεντακισχιλίων· τοσούτου γὰρ
οὐδὲ ἡ πᾶσα τῶν Παριανῶν πόλις πέντε σὺν αὐτῇ
τὰς γειτνιώσας παραλαβοῦσα πραθείη ἂν αὐτοῖς
ἀνθρώποις καὶ βοσκήμασιν καὶ τῇ λοιπῇ παρα-
σκευῇ.

15 " 'Αλλ' ἔτι γε ἡ κατηγορία καὶ τὸ ἔγκλημα
θερμὸν ἦν, καὶ ἐῴκει οὐκ εἰς μακρὰν ἐπαναστήσε-
σθαί τις αὐτῷ, καὶ μάλιστα ὁ δῆμος αὐτὸς ἠγανάκτει,
χρηστόν, ὡς ἔφασαν οἱ ἰδόντες, γέροντα πενθοῦντες
οὕτως ἀσεβῶς ἀπολωλότα. ὁ δὲ σοφὸς οὗτος
Πρωτεὺς πρὸς ἅπαντα ταῦτα σκέψασθε οἷόν τι
ἐξεῦρεν καὶ ὅπως τὸν κίνδυνον διέφυγεν. παρελθὼν
γὰρ εἰς τὴν ἐκκλησίαν τῶν Παριανῶν—ἐκόμα δὲ
ἤδη καὶ τρίβωνα πιναρὸν ἠμπείχετο καὶ πήραν
παρήρτητο καὶ τὸ ξύλον ἐν τῇ χειρὶ ἦν, καὶ ὅλως
μάλα τραγικῶς ἐσκεύαστο—τοιοῦτος οὖν ἐπιφανεὶς
αὐτοῖς ἀφεῖναι ἔφη τὴν οὐσίαν ἣν ὁ μακαρίτης

16

would gladly die in order that he might leave behind
him a reputation for it, he freed him, not considering him worthy even of the usual chastisement.[1]
Upon returning to his home, he found that the matter
of his father's murder was still at fever heat and that
there were many who were for pressing the charge
against him. Most of his possessions had been
carried off during his absence, and only his farms
remained, amounting to fifteen talents; for the
entire property which the old man left had been
worth perhaps thirty talents, not five thousand as
that utterly ridiculous Theagenes asserted. Even the
entire city of Parium,[2] taking along with it the five
that are its neighbours, would not fetch that much,
including the men, the cattle, and all the rest of
their belongings.

"However, the charge and complaint was still
aglow, and it was probable that before long somebody
would appear against him; above all, the people
themselves were enraged, mourning over a good old
man (as he was called by those who had seen him) so
impiously slain. But observe what a plan our clever
Proteus discovered to cope with all this, and how he
escaped the danger. Coming before the assembly
of the Parians—he wore his hair long by now, dressed
in a dirty mantle, had a wallet slung at his side, the
staff was in his hand, and in general he was very
histrionic in his get-up—manifesting himself to
them in this guise, he said that he relinquished to the

---

[1] "The usual chastisement" (Allinson's phrase) was
scourging.
[2] A small (but not really so contemptible) Greek town on
the Hellespont, site of a Roman colony since Augustus. See
Sir W. Leaf, *Strabo on the Troad*, pp. 80–85.

πατὴρ αὐτῷ κατέλιπεν δημοσίαν εἶναι πᾶσαν.
τοῦτο ὡς ἤκουσεν ὁ δῆμος, πένητες ἄνθρωποι καὶ
πρὸς διανομὰς κεχηνότες, ἀνέκραγον εὐθὺς ἕνα
φιλόσοφον, ἕνα φιλόπατριν, ἕνα Διογένους καὶ
Κράτητος ζηλωτήν. οἱ δὲ ἐχθροὶ ἐπεφίμωντο,
κἂν εἴ τις ἐπιχειρήσειεν μεμνῆσθαι τοῦ φόνου,
λίθοις εὐθὺς ἐβάλλετο.

16   " Ἐξήει οὖν τὸ δεύτερον πλανησόμενος, ἱκανὰ
ἐφόδια τοὺς Χριστιανοὺς ἔχων, ὑφ' ὧν δορυφορού-
μενος ἐν ἅπασιν ἀφθόνοις ἦν. καὶ χρόνον μέν τινα
οὕτως ἐβόσκετο· εἶτα παρανομήσας τι καὶ ἐς
ἐκείνους—ὤφθη γάρ τι, ὡς οἶμαι, ἐσθίων τῶν
ἀπορρήτων αὐτοῖς—οὐκέτι προσιεμένων αὐτὸν ἀπο-
ρούμενος ἐκ παλινῳδίας ἀπαιτεῖν ᾤετο δεῖν παρὰ
τῆς πόλεως τὰ κτήματα, καὶ γραμματεῖον ἐπιδοὺς
ἠξίου ταῦτα κομίσασθαι κελεύσαντος βασιλέως.
εἶτα τῆς πόλεως ἀντιπρεσβευσαμένης οὐδὲν ἐπρά-
χθη, ἀλλ' ἐμμένειν ἐκελεύσθη οἷς ἅπαξ διέγνω
μηδενὸς καταναγκάσαντος.

17   " Τρίτη ἐπὶ τούτοις ἀποδημία εἰς Αἴγυπτον
παρὰ τὸν Ἀγαθόβουλον, ἵναπερ τὴν θαυμαστὴν
ἄσκησιν διησκεῖτο, ξυρόμενος μὲν τῆς κεφαλῆς
τὸ ἥμισυ, χριόμενος δὲ πηλῷ τὸ πρόσωπον, ἐν
πολλῷ δὲ τῶν περιεστώτων δήμῳ ἀναφλῶν τὸ

---

[1] The phrase is F. D. Allinson's.
[2] In Acts 15, 29 the apostles and the elder brethren prescribe abstaining " from sacrifices offered to idols, and from
blood, and from things strangled " (εἰδολόθυτα καὶ αἷμα καὶ
πνικτά). Probably what Lucian has in mind is pagan sacrificial meats. This may be just a guess, from the way he
puts it; but if so, it is highly plausible on account of the

state all the property which had been left him by his
father of blessed memory. When the people, poor
folk agape for largesses,[1] heard that, they lifted their
voices forthwith: ' The one and only philosopher!
The one and only patriot! The one and only rival
of Diogenes and Crates!' His enemies were
muzzled, and anyone who tried to mention the murder
was at once pelted with stones.

" He left home, then, for the second time, to roam
about, possessing an ample source of funds in the
Christians, through whose ministrations he lived in
unalloyed prosperity. For a time he battened himself thus; but then, after he had transgressed in some
way even against them—he was seen, I think,
eating some of the food that is forbidden them [2]—
they no longer accepted him, and so, being at a loss,
he thought he must sing a palinode and demand his
possessions back from his city. Submitting a peti-
tion, he expected to recover them by order of the
Emperor. Then, as the city sent representatives to
oppose the claim, he achieved nothing, but was
directed to abide by what he had once for all determined, under no compulsion from anyone.

" Thereafter he went away a third time, to Egypt,
to visit Agathobulus,[3] where he took that wonderful
course of training in asceticism, shaving one half of
his head, daubing his face with mud, and demonstrating what they call ' indifference ' by erecting his

notorious indifference of the Cynics towards what they ate.
Peregrinus may have signalised his relapse to Cynicism by
sampling a " dinner of Hecate " at the cross-roads.

[3] In *Demonax*, 3, Lucian alludes to Agathobulus as one of
those with whom Demonax had studied. The teacher of
Peregrinus was therefore reputable as well as famous.

αἰδοῖον καὶ τὸ ἀδιάφορον¹ δὴ τοῦτο καλούμενον
ἐπιδεικνύμενος, εἶτα παίων καὶ παιόμενος νάρθηκι
εἰς τὰς πυγὰς καὶ ἄλλα πολλὰ νεανικώτερα
θαυματοποιῶν.

18 "Ἐκεῖθεν δὲ οὕτω παρεσκευασμένος ἐπὶ Ἰτα-
λίας² ἔπλευσεν καὶ ἀποβὰς τῆς νεὼς εὐθὺς ἐλοιδορεῖτο πᾶσι, καὶ μάλιστα τῷ βασιλεῖ, πρᾴότατον
αὐτὸν καὶ ἡμερώτατον εἰδώς, ὥστε ἀσφαλῶς
ἐτόλμα· ἐκείνῳ γάρ, ὡς εἰκός, ὀλίγον ἔμελεν
τῶν βλασφημιῶν καὶ οὐκ ἠξίου τὴν³ φιλοσοφίαν
ὑποδυόμενόν τινα κολάζειν ἐπὶ ῥήμασι καὶ μάλιστα
τέχνην τινὰ τὸ λοιδορεῖσθαι πεποιημένον. τούτῳ
δὲ καὶ ἀπὸ τούτων τὰ τῆς δόξης ηὐξάνετο, παρὰ
γοῦν τοῖς ἰδιώταις, καὶ περίβλεπτος ἦν ἐπὶ τῇ
ἀπονοίᾳ, μέχρι δὴ ὁ τὴν πόλιν ἐπιτετραμμένος
ἀνὴρ σοφὸς ἀπέπεμψεν αὐτὸν ἀμέτρως ἐντρυφῶντα
τῷ πράγματι, εἰπὼν μὴ δεῖσθαι τὴν πόλιν τοιούτου
φιλοσόφου. πλὴν ἀλλὰ καὶ τοῦτο κλεινὸν αὐτοῦ
καὶ διὰ στόματος ἦν ἅπασιν, ὁ φιλόσοφος διὰ τὴν
παρρησίαν καὶ τὴν ἄγαν ἐλευθερίαν ἐξελαθείς,
καὶ προσήλαυνε κατὰ τοῦτο τῷ Μουσωνίῳ καὶ
Δίωνι καὶ Ἐπικτήτῳ καὶ εἴ τις ἄλλος ἐν περιστάσει
τοιαύτῃ ἐγένετο.

19 "Οὕτω δὴ ἐπὶ τὴν Ἑλλάδα ἐλθὼν ἄρτι μὲν
Ἠλείοις ἐλοιδορεῖτο, ἄρτι δὲ τοὺς Ἕλληνας
ἔπειθεν ἀντάρασθαι ὅπλα Ῥωμαίοις, ἄρτι δὲ
ἄνδρα παιδείᾳ καὶ ἀξιώματι προὔχοντα, διότι καὶ
ἐν τοῖς ἄλλοις εὖ ἐποίησεν τὴν Ἑλλάδα καὶ

---

¹ ἀδιάφθορον MSS.: corrected in ed. Flor. (1496).
² Ἰταλίας ΓΧ : Ἰταλίαν MF, edd.
³ τὴν XF : τὸν ΓΜ.

yard amid a thronging mob of bystanders,[1] besides giving and taking blows on the back-sides with a stalk of fennel, and playing the mountebank even more audaciously in many other ways.

" From there, thus equipped, he set sail for Italy and immediately after disembarking he fell to abusing everyone, and in particular the Emperor,[2] knowing him to be mild and gentle, so that he was safe in making bold. The Emperor, as one would expect, cared little for his libels and did not think fit to punish for mere words a man who only used philosophy as a cloak, and above all, a man who had made a profession of abusiveness. But in our friend's case, even from this his reputation grew, among simple folk anyhow, and he was a cynosure for his recklessness, until finally the city prefect, a wise man, packed him off for immoderate indulgence in the thing, saying that the city had no need of any such philosopher. However, this too made for his renown, and he was on everybody's lips as the philosopher who had been banished for his frankness and excessive freedom, so that in this respect he approached Musonius, Dio, Epictetus, and anyone else who has been in a similar predicament.

" Coming at last to Greece under these circumstances, at one moment he abused the Eleans, at another he counselled the Greeks to take up arms against the Romans,[3] and at another he libelled a man outstanding in literary attainments and position because he had been a benefactor to Greece in many

[1] The allusion is to that variety of " indifferent " action (*i.e.* neither good nor bad) ascribed to Diogenes himself by Dio Chrysostom VI, 16–20 (pp. 203–204 R).

[2] Antoninus Pius.

[3] The life of Antoninus Pius (*Script. Hist. Aug.*), § 5, notes suppression of a rebellion in Achaia.

ὕδωρ ἐπήγαγεν τῇ Ὀλυμπίᾳ καὶ ἔπαυσε δίψει
ἀπολλυμένους τοὺς πανηγυριστάς, κακῶς ἠγόρευεν
ὡς καταθηλύναντα τοὺς Ἕλληνας, δέον τοὺς θεατὰς
τῶν Ὀλυμπίων διακαρτερεῖν διψῶντας καὶ νὴ
Δία γε καὶ ἀποθνήσκειν πολλοὺς αὐτῶν ὑπὸ
σφοδρῶν τῶν νόσων, αἳ τέως διὰ τὸ ξηρὸν τοῦ
χωρίου ἐν πολλῷ τῷ πλήθει ἐπεπόλαζον. καὶ
ταῦτα ἔλεγε πίνων τοῦ αὐτοῦ ὕδατος.

" Ὡς δὲ μικροῦ κατέλευσαν αὐτὸν ἐπιδραμόντες
ἅπαντες, τότε μὲν ἐπὶ τὸν Δία καταφυγὼν ὁ
20 γενναῖος εὕρετο μὴ ἀποθανεῖν, ἐς δὲ τὴν ἑξῆς
Ὀλυμπιάδα λόγον τινὰ διὰ τεττάρων ἐτῶν συν-
θεὶς τῶν διὰ μέσου ἐξήνεγκε πρὸς τοὺς Ἕλληνας,
ἔπαινον ὑπὲρ τοῦ τὸ ὕδωρ ἐπαγαγόντος καὶ
ἀπολογίαν ὑπὲρ τῆς τότε φυγῆς.

" Ἤδη δὲ ἀμελούμενος ὑφ᾽ ἁπάντων καὶ μηκέθ᾽
ὁμοίως περίβλεπτος ὤν—ἕωλα γὰρ ἦν ἅπαντα καὶ
οὐδὲν ἔτι καινουργεῖν ἐδύνατο ἐφ᾽ ὅτῳ ἐκπλήξει[1]
τοὺς ἐντυγχάνοντας καὶ θαυμάζειν καὶ πρὸς
αὐτὸν ἀποβλέπειν ποιήσει, οὗπερ ἐξ ἀρχῆς δριμύν
τινα ἔρωτα ἐρῶν ἐτύγχανεν—τὸ τελευταῖον τοῦτο
τόλμημα ἐβουλεύσατο περὶ τῆς πυρᾶς, καὶ διέδωκε
λόγον ἐς τοὺς Ἕλληνας εὐθὺς ἀπ᾽ Ὀλυμπίων τῶν
21 ἔμπροσθεν ὡς ἐς τοὐπιὸν καύσων ἑαυτόν. καὶ
νῦν αὐτὰ ταῦτα θαυματοποιεῖ, ὥς φασι, βόθρον

---

[1] ἐκπλήξει MF, edd.: ἐκπλήξειε ΓΧ.

ways, and particularly because he had brought water to Olympia and prevented the visitors to the festival from dying of thirst, maintaining that he was making the Greeks effeminate, for the spectators of the Olympic games ought to endure their thirst—yes, by Heaven, and even to lose their lives, no doubt, many of them, through the frequent distempers which formerly ran riot in the vast crowd on account of the dryness of the place![1] And he said this while he drank that same water!

When they almost killed him with stones, mobbing him with one accord, he managed to escape death at the moment by fleeing to Zeus for sanctuary (stout fellow!), and afterwards, at the next Olympiad, he gave the Greeks a speech which he had composed during the four years that had intervened, praising the man who had brought in the water and defending himself for running away at that time.

" At last he was disregarded by all and no longer so admired; for all his stuff was stale and he could not turn out any further novelty with which to surprise those who came in his way and make them marvel and stare at him—a thing for which he had a fierce craving from the first. So he devised this ultimate venture of the pyre, and spread a report among the Greeks immediately after the last Olympic games that he would burn himself up at the next festival. And now, they say, he is playing the mountebank over that very thing, digging a pit,

---

[1] The man was the famous Herodes Atticus. For the aqueduct built by him at Olympia see Frazer's Pausanias, Vol. IV, pp. 72 ff. Philostratus (*Vit. Soph.* II, 1, 33) records that Herodes was often berated by Proteus, to whom on one occasion he hinted that it might at least be done in Greek.

ὀρύττων καὶ ξύλα συγκομίζων καὶ δεινήν τινα
τὴν καρτερίαν ὑπισχνούμενος.

" Ἐχρῆν δέ, οἶμαι, μάλιστα μὲν περιμένειν τὸν
θάνατον καὶ μὴ δραπετεύειν ἐκ τοῦ βίου· εἰ δὲ καὶ
πάντως διέγνωστό οἱ ἀπαλλάττεσθαι, μὴ πυρὶ μηδὲ
τοῖς ἀπὸ τῆς τραγῳδίας τούτοις χρῆσθαι, ἀλλ' ἕτερόν
τινα θανάτου τρόπον, μυρίων ὄντων, ἑλόμενον[1]
ἀπελθεῖν. εἰ δὲ καὶ τὸ πῦρ ὡς Ἡράκλειόν τι
ἀσπάζεται, τί δή ποτε οὐχὶ κατὰ σιγὴν ἑλόμενος
ὄρος εὔδενδρον ἐν ἐκείνῳ ἑαυτὸν ἐνέπρησεν μόνος,
ἕνα τινὰ οἷον Θεαγένη τοῦτον Φιλοκτήτην παραλαβών; ὁ δὲ ἐν Ὀλυμπίᾳ τῆς πανηγύρεως πληθού-
σης μόνον οὐκ ἐπὶ σκηνῆς ὀπτήσει ἑαυτόν, οὐκ
ἀνάξιος ὤν, μὰ τὸν Ἡρακλέα, εἴ γε χρὴ καὶ τοὺς
πατραλοίας καὶ τοὺς ἀθέους δίκας διδόναι τῶν
τολμημάτων. καὶ κατὰ τοῦτο πάνυ ὀψὲ δρᾶν
αὐτὸ ἔοικεν, ὃν ἐχρῆν πάλαι ἐς τὸν τοῦ Φαλάριδος
ταῦρον ἐμπεσόντα τὴν ἀξίαν ἀποτετικέναι, ἀλλὰ
μὴ ἅπαξ χανόντα πρὸς τὴν φλόγα ἐν ἀκαρεῖ

---

[1] ἐλεύθερον Γ[1].

---

[1] Thanks to Paul Graindor, the date of the Olympiads
mentioned in connection with Peregrinus can now be determined. He has deduced from the apparent ages of the children
represented in the exedra erected by Herodes on the completion of his aqueduct that this took place in A.D. 153
(*Hérode Atticus et Sa Famille*, pp. 87–88). His deduction
finds support in the text of Lucian as soon as we recognise
that Lucian is talking about four different Olympiads, not
three. The first is that on which Peregrinus criticised the
aqueduct, which will be the year of its completion, A.D. 153.
At the *next* (τὴν ἐξῆς, A.D. 157) he withdrew his criticism.
The Olympiad just after which he announced his intention
of cremating himself need not and cannot be identical with

collecting logs, and promising really awesome fortitude.[1]

" What he should have done, I think, was first and foremost to await death and not to cut and run from life ; but if he had determined to be off at all costs, not to use fire or any of these devices out of tragedy, but to choose for his departure some other form of death out of the myriads that there are.   If, however, he is partial to fire as something connected with Heracles, why in the world did he not quietly select a well-wooded mountain and cremate himself upon it in solitude, taking along only one person such as Theagenes here for his Philoctetes ?[2]   On the contrary, it is in Olympia, at the height of the festival, all but in the theatre, that he plans to roast himself—not undeservedly, by Heracles, if it is right for parricides and for atheists to suffer for their hardinesses.[3]   And from that point of view he seems to be getting about it very late in the day ; he ought long ago to have been flung into the bull of Phalaris [4] to pay the fitting penalty instead of opening his mouth to the flames once for all and expiring in a trice.   For

the one of A.D. 157; it is called by the speaker the *last*, or *previous* (τὴν ἔμπροσθεν), and the text clearly implies a lapse of time. It must therefore be the one of A.D. 161.   Then comes the fourth, on which the cremation took place, dated by Eusebius in A.D. 165.

[2] Philoctetes had helped Heracles to cremate himself on Mt. Oeta by kindling the pyre for him.

[3] As the cremation actually took place at Harpina, two miles away from Olympia, and on the day after the festival closed, it may be that religious scruples (cf. § 26) caused Peregrinus to modify an original plan which involved its taking place at Olympia itself while the festival was in progress.

[4] See *Phalaris I*, 11–12 (Vol. I, pp. 17 ff.).

τεθνάναι. καὶ γὰρ αὖ καὶ τόδε οἱ πολλοί μοι
λέγουσιν, ὡς οὐδεὶς ὀξύτερος ἄλλος θανάτου
τρόπος τοῦ διὰ πυρός· ἀνοῖξαι γὰρ δεῖ μόνον τὸ
στόμα καὶ αὐτίκα τεθνάναι.

22 "Τὸ μέντοι θέαμα ἐπινοεῖται, οἶμαι, ὡς σεμνόν,
ἐν ἱερῷ χωρίῳ καιόμενος ἄνθρωπος, ἔνθα μηδὲ
θάπτειν ὅσιον τοὺς ἄλλους ἀποθνήσκοντας. ἀκούετε
δέ, οἶμαι, ὡς καὶ πάλαι θέλων τις ἔνδοξος γενέσθαι, ἐπεὶ κατ' ἄλλον τρόπον οὐκ εἶχεν ἐπιτυχεῖν
τούτου, ἐνέπρησε τῆς Ἐφεσίας Ἀρτέμιδος τὸν
νεών. τοιοῦτόν τι καὶ αὐτὸς ἐπινοεῖ, τοσοῦτος
ἔρως τῆς δόξης ἐντέτηκεν αὐτῷ.

23 "Καίτοι φησὶν ὅτι ὑπὲρ τῶν ἀνθρώπων αὐτὸ
δρᾷ, ὡς διδάξειεν αὐτοὺς θανάτου καταφρονεῖν
καὶ ἐγκαρτερεῖν τοῖς δεινοῖς. ἐγὼ δὲ ἡδέως
ἂν ἐροίμην οὐκ ἐκεῖνον ἀλλ' ὑμᾶς, εἰ καὶ τοὺς
κακούργους βούλοισθε ἂν μαθητὰς αὐτοῦ γενέσθαι
τῆς καρτερίας ταύτης καὶ καταφρονεῖν θανάτου
καὶ καύσεως καὶ τῶν τοιούτων δειμάτων. ἀλλ'
οὐκ ἂν εὖ οἶδ' ὅτι βουληθείητε. πῶς οὖν ὁ
Πρωτεὺς τοῦτο διακρινεῖ καὶ τοὺς μὲν χρηστοὺς
ὠφελήσει, τοὺς δὲ πονηροὺς οὐ φιλοκινδυνοτέρους
καὶ τολμηροτέρους ἀποφανεῖ;

24 "Καίτοι δυνατὸν ἔστω ἐς τοῦτο μόνους ἀπαντή-
σεσθαι τοὺς πρὸς τὸ ὠφέλιμον ὀψομένους τὸ
πρᾶγμα. ὑμᾶς δ' οὖν αὖθις ἐρήσομαι, δέξαισθ'
ἂν ὑμῶν τοὺς παῖδας ζηλωτὰς τοῦ τοιούτου γενέσθαι; οὐκ ἂν εἴποιτε. καὶ τί τοῦτο ἠρόμην,

---

[1] Herostratus, in 356 B.C. The Ephesians sought to
defeat his object by forbidding anyone for all time to mention
his name (Valerius Maximus, VIII, 14, 5). The prohibition,

people tell me that no other form of death is quicker than that by fire; you have only to open your mouth, and die forthwith.

"The spectacle is being planned, I suppose, as something awe-inspiring—a fellow getting burnt up in a holy place where it is impious even to bury the others who die. But you have heard, no doubt, that long ago a man who wished to become famous burned the temple of Ephesian Artemis, not being able to attain that end in any other way.[1] He himself has something similar in mind, so great is the craving for fame that has penetrated him to the core.

"He alleges, however, that he is doing it for the sake of his fellow men, that he may teach them to despise death and endure what is fearsome. For my part, I should like to ask, not him but you, whether you would wish malefactors to become his disciples in this fortitude of his, and to despise death and burning and similar terrors. No, you would not, I am very sure. How, then, is Proteus to draw distinctions in this matter, and to benefit the good without making the bad more adventurous and daring?

"Nevertheless, suppose it possible that only those will present themselves at this affair who will see it to their advantage. Once more I shall question you: would you desire your children to become imitators of such a man? You will not say so. But why did I ask that question, when even of his disciples them-

---

which very likely was accompanied by a curse, was far from ineffective, for nearly all ancient authors who mention the story, including Cicero and Plutarch, omit the name just as Lucian does.

ὅπου μηδ' αὐτῶν τις τῶν μαθητῶν αὐτοῦ ζηλώ-
σειεν ἄν; τὸν γοῦν [1] Θεαγένη τοῦτο μάλιστα αἰτιά-
σαιτο ἄν τις, ὅτι τἆλλα ζηλῶν τἀνδρὸς οὐχ ἕπεται
τῷ διδασκάλῳ καὶ συνοδεύει παρὰ τὸν Ἡρακλέα,
ὥς φησιν, ἀπιόντι, δυνάμενος ἐν βραχεῖ παν-
ευδαίμων γενέσθαι συνεμπεσὼν ἐπὶ κεφαλὴν [2] ἐς
τὸ πῦρ.

" Οὐ γὰρ ἐν πήρᾳ καὶ βάκτρῳ καὶ τρίβωνι ὁ
ζῆλος, ἀλλὰ ταῦτα μὲν ἀσφαλῆ καὶ ῥᾴδια καὶ
παντὸς ἂν εἴη, τὸ τέλος δὲ καὶ τὸ κεφάλαιον χρὴ
ζηλοῦν καὶ πυρὰν συνθέντα κορμῶν συκίνων
ὡς ἔνι μάλιστα χλωρῶν ἐναποπνιγῆναι τῷ καπνῷ·
τὸ πῦρ γὰρ αὐτὸ οὐ μόνον Ἡρακλέους καὶ Ἀσκληπιοῦ, ἀλλὰ καὶ τῶν ἱεροσύλων καὶ ἀνδροφόνων,
οὓς ὁρᾶν ἔστιν ἐκ καταδίκης αὐτὸ πάσχοντας.
ὥστε ἄμεινον τὸ διὰ τοῦ καπνοῦ· ἴδιον γὰρ καὶ
ὑμῶν ἂν μόνων γένοιτο.

25 " Ἄλλως τε ὁ μὲν Ἡρακλῆς, εἴπερ ἄρα καὶ
ἐτόλμησέν τι τοιοῦτο, ὑπὸ νόσου αὐτὸ ἔδρασεν,
ὑπὸ τοῦ Κενταυρείου αἵματος, ὥς φησιν ἡ τραγῳδία,
κατεσθιόμενος· οὗτος δὲ τίνος αἰτίας ἕνεκεν
ἐμβάλλει φέρων ἑαυτὸν εἰς τὸ πῦρ; νὴ Δί', ὅπως
τὴν καρτερίαν ἐπιδείξηται καθάπερ οἱ Βραχμᾶνες·
ἐκείνοις γὰρ αὐτὸν [3] ἠξίου Θεαγένης εἰκάζειν,
ὥσπερ οὐκ ἐνὸν καὶ ἐν Ἰνδοῖς εἶναί τινας μωροὺς
καὶ κενοδόξους ἀνθρώπους. ὅμως δ' οὖν κἂν
ἐκείνους μιμείσθω· ἐκεῖνοι γὰρ οὐκ ἐμπηδῶσιν
ἐς τὸ πῦρ, ὡς Ὀνησίκριτος ὁ Ἀλεξάνδρου κυβερνήτης ἰδὼν Κάλανον καόμενόν φησιν, ἀλλ'
ἐπειδὰν νήσωσι, πλησίον παραστάντες ἀκίνητοι

---

[1] γοῦν Bekker : οὖν MSS.

selves not one would imitate him? In fact, the thing
for which one might blame Theagenes most of all is
that although he copies the man in everything else,
he does not follow his teacher and take the road
with him, now that he is off, as he says, to join
Heracles; why, he has the opportunity to attain
absolute felicity instanter by plunging headlong into
the fire with him!

"Emulation is not a matter of wallet, staff, and
mantle; all this is safe and easy and within anyone's
power. One should emulate the consummation and
culmination, build a pyre of fig-wood logs as green as
can be, and stifle one's self in the smoke of them. Fire
itself belongs not only to Heracles and Asclepius,
but to doers of sacrilege and murder, who can be
seen enduring it by judicial sentence. Therefore it
is better to employ smoke, which would be peculiar
and belong only to you and your like.

"Besides, if Heracles really did venture any such
act, he did it because he was ailing, because the blood
of the Centaur, as the tragedy tells us, was preying
upon him; but for what reason does this man throw
himself bodily into the fire? Oh, yes! to demonstrate his fortitude, like the Brahmans, for Theagenes
thought fit to compare him with them, just as if
there could not be fools and notoriety-seekers even
among the Indians. Well, then, let him at least
imitate *them*. They do not leap into the fire (so
Onesicritus says, Alexander's navigator, who saw
Calanus burning), but when they have built their
pyre, they stand close beside it motionless and en-

---

² ἐπὶ κεφαλῆς MSS.: corrected by Jacobitz.
³ αὑτὸν ς, Faber: ἑαυτὸν ΓΩΧΜΦ.

THE WORKS OF LUCIAN

ἀνέχονται παροπτώμενοι, εἶτ᾽ ἐπιβάντες κατὰ
σχῆμα καίονται, οὐδ᾽ ὅσον ὀλίγον ἐντρέψαντες [1] τῆς
κατακλίσεως.

"Οὗτος δὲ τί μέγα εἰ ἐμπεσὼν τεθνήξεται
συναρπασθεὶς ὑπὸ τοῦ πυρός; οὐκ ἀπ᾽ ἐλπίδος
μὴ ἀναπηδήσασθαι αὐτὸν καὶ ἡμίφλεκτον, εἰ μή,
ὅπερ φασί, μηχανήσεται βαθεῖαν γενέσθαι καὶ
26 ἐν βόθρῳ τὴν πυράν. εἰσὶ δ᾽ οἳ καὶ μεταβαλέσθαι [2]
φασιν αὐτὸν καί τινα ὀνείρατα διηγεῖσθαι, ὡς
τοῦ Διὸς οὐκ ἐῶντος μιαίνειν ἱερὸν χωρίον. ἀλλὰ
θαρρείτω τούτου γε ἕνεκα· ἐγὼ γὰρ διομοσαίμην
ἂν ἦ μὴν μηδένα τῶν θεῶν ἀγανακτήσειν, εἰ
Περεγρῖνος κακῶς [3] ἀποθάνοι. οὐ μὴν οὐδὲ ῥάδιον
αὐτῷ ἔτ᾽ ἀναδῦναι· οἱ γὰρ συνόντες κύνες παρορ-
μῶσιν καὶ συνωθοῦσιν ἐς τὸ πῦρ καὶ ὑπεκκάουσι
τὴν γνώμην, οὐκ ἐῶντες ἀποδειλιᾶν· ὧν εἰ δύο
συγκατασπάσας ἐμπέσοι εἰς τὴν πυράν, τοῦτο
μόνον χάριεν ἂν [4] ἐργάσαιτο.

27 "Ἤκουον δὲ ὡς οὐδὲ Πρωτεὺς ἔτι καλεῖσθαι
ἀξιοῖ, ἀλλὰ Φοίνικα μετωνόμασεν ἑαυτόν, ὅτι
καὶ φοῖνιξ, τὸ Ἰνδικὸν ὄρνεον, ἐπιβαίνειν πυρᾶς
λέγεται πορρωτάτω γήρως προβεβηκώς. ἀλλὰ
καὶ λογοποιεῖ καὶ χρησμούς τινας διέξεισιν παλαιοὺς
δή, ὡς χρεὼν εἴη [5] δαίμονα νυκτοφύλακα γενέσθαι
αὐτόν, καὶ δῆλός ἐστι βωμῶν ἤδη ἐπιθυμῶν καὶ
χρυσοῦς ἀναστήσεσθαι ἐλπίζων.

---

[1] ἐκτρέψαντες Faber, accepted by Jacobitz, Bekker, Dindorf, Fritzsche. But cf. *Fugit.* 7; also Schmid, *Atticismus*,
I, 393, citing *Hist. Conscr.* 15, *Pseudol.*, 7, 14. The genitive
depends on ὀλίγον.
[2] μεταβάλλεσθαι X², F², edd., mistaking the meaning.
[3] κακῶς MSS. (except κακὸς X¹): κακὸς κακῶς Fritzsche.

30

dure being toasted; then, mounting upon it, they cremate themselves decorously, without the slightest alteration of the position in which they are lying.

" In this man's case, what great thing will it be if he tumbles in and dies in the sudden grip of the fire? It is not beyond expectation that he will jump out half consumed, unless, as they say, he is going to see to it that the pyre is deep down in a pit. There are people who say that he has even changed his mind, and is telling certain dreams, to the effect that Zeus does not permit pollution of a holy place.[1] But let him be assured on that score; I would take my oath to it that no one of the gods would be angry if Peregrinus should die a rogue's death. Moreover, it is not easy for him to withdraw now; for his Cynic associates are urging him on and pushing him into the fire and inflaming his resolution; they will not let him shirk it. If he should pull a couple of them into the fire along with him when he jumps in, that would be the only nice thing about his performance.

" I have heard that he no longer deigns to be called Proteus but has changed his name to Phoenix, because the phoenix, the Indian bird, is said to mount a pyre when it is very far advanced in age. Indeed, he even manufactures myths and repeats certain oracles, ancient, of course, to the purport that he is to become a guardian spirit of the night; it is plain, too, that he already covets altars and expects to be imaged in gold.

[1] See above, p. 25, and n. 3.

---

4 ἄν Jacobitz: ἐργάσεται X, perhaps right.
5 εἴη Bekker: εἶναι MSS.

28 "Καὶ μὰ Δία οὐδὲν ἀπεικὸς ἐν πολλοῖς τοῖς
ἀνοήτοις εὑρεθήσεσθαί τινας τοὺς καὶ τεταρταίων
ἀπηλλάχθαι δι' αὐτοῦ φήσοντας καὶ νύκτωρ
ἐντετυχηκέναι τῷ δαίμονι τῷ νυκτοφύλακι. οἱ
κατάρατοι δὲ οὗτοι μαθηταὶ αὐτοῦ καὶ χρηστήριον,
οἶμαι, καὶ ἄδυτον ἐπὶ τῇ πυρᾷ μηχανήσονται,
διότι καὶ Πρωτεὺς ἐκεῖνος ὁ Διός, ὁ προπάτωρ
τοῦ ὀνόματος, μαντικὸς ἦν. μαρτύρομαι δὲ ἦ
μὴν καὶ ἱερέας αὐτοῦ ἀποδειχθήσεσθαι μαστίγων
ἢ καυτηρίων ἤ τινος τοιαύτης τερατουργίας,
ἢ καὶ νὴ Δία τελετήν τινα ἐπ' αὐτῷ συστήσεσθαι
νυκτέριον καὶ δᾳδουχίαν ἐπὶ τῇ πυρᾷ.
29 " Θεαγένης δὲ ἔναγχος, ὥς μοί τις τῶν ἑταίρων
ἀπήγγειλεν, καὶ Σίβυλλαν ἔφη προειρηκέναι περὶ
τούτων· καὶ τὰ ἔπη γὰρ ἀπεμνημόνευεν·

᾿Αλλ' ὁπόταν Πρωτεὺς Κυνικῶν ὄχ' ἄριστος
    ἁπάντων
Ζηνὸς ἐριγδούπου τέμενος κάτα πῦρ ἀνακαύσας
ἐς φλόγα πηδήσας ἔλθῃ ἐς μακρὸν ᾿Ολυμπον,
δὴ τότε πάντας ὁμῶς, οἳ ἀρούρης καρπὸν
    ἔδουσιν,
νυκτιπόλον τιμᾶν κέλομαι ἥρωα μέγιστον
σύνθρονον ῾Ηφαίστῳ καὶ ῾Ηρακλῆϊ ἄνακτι.

30 " Ταῦτα μὲν Θεαγένης Σιβύλλης ἀκηκοέναι
φησίν. ἐγὼ δὲ Βάκιδος αὐτῷ χρησμὸν ὑπὲρ

---

[1] Athenagoras reports that Parium, where Peregrinus was
born, cherished a statue of him from which oracles were
derived (*Leg. de Christ.*, 26).

THE PASSING OF PEREGRINUS

" By Zeus, it would be nothing unnatural if, among all the dolts that there are, some should be found to assert that they were relieved of quartan fevers by him, and that in the dark they had encountered the guardian spirit of the night! Then too these accursed disciples of his will make an oracular shrine, I suppose, with a holy of holies, at the site of the pyre, because the famous Proteus, son of Zeus, the progenitor of his name, was given to soothsaying.[1] I pledge my word, too, that priests of his will be appointed, with whips or branding-irons or some such flummy-diddle, or even that a nocturnal mystery will be got up in his honour, including a torch festival at the site of the pyre.

" Theagenes, as I have been told by one of my friends, recently said that the Sibyl had made a prediction about all this; in fact, he quoted the verses from memory :

But when the time shall come that Proteus, noblest
    of Cynics,
Kindleth fire in the precinct of Zeus, our Lord of
    the Thunder,
Leapeth into the flame, and cometh to lofty
    Olympus,
Then do I bid all alike who eat the fruit of the
    ploughland
Honour to pay unto him that walketh abroad in the
    night-time,
Greatest of spirits, thronéd with Heracles and
    Hephaestus.

" That is what Theagenes alleges he heard from the Sibyl. But I will quote him one of the oracles of

τούτων ἐρῶ· φησὶν δὲ ὁ Βάκις οὕτω, σφόδρα
εὖ ἐπειπών,

'Αλλ' ὁπόταν Κυνικὸς πολυώνυμος ἐς φλόγα
πολλὴν
πηδήσῃ δόξης ὑπ' ἐρινύι θυμὸν ὀρινθείς,
δὴ τότε τοὺς ἄλλους κυναλώπεκας, οἵ οἱ ἕπονται,
μιμεῖσθαι χρὴ πότμον ἀποιχομένοιο λύκοιο.
ὃς δέ κε δειλὸς ἐὼν φεύγῃ μένος 'Ηφαίστοιο,
λάεσσιν βαλέειν τοῦτον τάχα πάντας 'Αχαιούς,
ὡς μὴ ψυχρὸς ἐὼν θερμηγορέειν ἐπιχειρῇ
χρυσῷ σαξάμενος πήρην μάλα πολλὰ δανείζων,
ἐν καλαῖς Πάτραισιν ἔχων τρὶς πέντε τάλαντα.

τί ὑμῖν δοκεῖ, ἄνδρες; ἆρα φαυλότερος χρησμολό-
γος ὁ Βάκις τῆς Σιβύλλης εἶναι; ὥστε ὥρα τοῖς
θαυμαστοῖς τούτοις ὁμιληταῖς τοῦ Πρωτέως περι-
σκοπεῖν ἔνθα ἑαυτοὺς ἐξαερώσουσιν· τοῦτο γὰρ
τὴν καῦσιν καλοῦσιν.''

31   Ταῦτ' εἰπόντος ἀνεβόησαν οἱ περιεστῶτες ἅπαντες, '' 'Ήδη καιέσθωσαν ἄξιοι τοῦ πυρός.'' καὶ
ὁ μὲν κατέβη γελῶν, '' Νέστορα δ' οὐκ ἔλαθεν
ἰαχή,'' τὸν Θεαγένη, ἀλλ' ὡς ἤκουσεν τῆς βοῆς,
ἧκεν εὐθὺς καὶ ἀναβὰς ἐκεκράγει καὶ μυρία κακὰ

---

[1] Lucian gives the Cynic a Roland for his Oliver. Bacis
was a title rather than a name, and in early Greece prophets
who bore it were little less numerous than the Sibyls.
Naturally it was a convenient tag for a spurious oracle,
whether composed with fraudulent intention or, as often in
Aristophanes, for fun.
[2] Below (§ 33), Proteus speaks of being '' commingled with
the ether.''

Bacis dealing with these matters.[1] Bacis expresses himself as follows, with a very excellent moral :

> Nay, when the time shall come that a Cynic with names that are many
> Leaps into roaring flame, soul-stirred by a passion for glory,
> Then it is meet that the others, the jackals that follow his footsteps,
> Mimic the latter end of the wolf that has taken departure.
> But if a dastard among them shall shun the might of Hephaestus,
> Let him be pelted with stones forthwith by all the Achaeans,
> Learning, the frigid fool, to abjure all fiery speeches,
> He that has laden his wallet with gold by the taking of usance;
> Thrice five talents he owns in the lovely city of Patras.

What do you think, gentlemen ? That Bacis is a worse soothsayer than the Sibyl ? It is high time, then, for these wondrous followers of Proteus to look about for a place in which to aerify themselves —for that is the name they give to cremation." [2]

When he had said these words, all the bystanders shouted : " Let them be burned right now ; they deserve the flames ! " And the man got down again laughing ; but " Nestor failed not to mark the din : " [3] I mean Theagenes. When he heard the shouting he came at once, took the platform, and fell to

[3] *Iliad*, XIV, 1.

THE WORKS OF LUCIAN

διεξήει περὶ τοῦ καταβεβηκότος· οὐ γὰρ οἶδα
ὅστις ἐκεῖνος ὁ βέλτιστος ἐκαλεῖτο. ἐγὼ δὲ
ἀφεὶς αὐτὸν διαρρηγνύμενον ἀπήειν ὀψόμενος τοὺς
ἀθλητάς· ἤδη γὰρ οἱ Ἑλλανοδίκαι ἐλέγοντο εἶναι
ἐν τῷ Πλεθρίῳ.

32 Ταῦτα μέν σοι τὰ ἐν Ἤλιδι. ἐπεὶ δὲ ἐς τὴν
Ὀλυμπίαν ἀφικόμεθα, μεστὸς ἦν ὁ ὀπισθόδομος
τῶν κατηγορούντων Πρωτέως ἢ ἐπαινούντων τὴν
προαίρεσιν αὐτοῦ, ὥστε καὶ εἰς χεῖρας αὐτῶν
ἦλθον οἱ πολλοί, ἄχρι δὴ παρελθὼν αὐτὸς ὁ
Πρωτεὺς μυρίῳ τῷ πλήθει παραπεμπόμενος κατόπιν τοῦ τῶν κηρύκων ἀγῶνος λόγους τινὰς διεξῆλθεν
περὶ ἑαυτοῦ, τὸν βίον τε ὡς ἐβίω καὶ τοὺς κινδύνους οὓς ἐκινδύνευσεν διηγούμενος καὶ ὅσα πράγματα φιλοσοφίας ἕνεκα ὑπέμεινεν. τὰ μὲν οὖν
εἰρημένα πολλὰ ἦν, ἐγὼ δὲ ὀλίγων ἤκουσα ὑπὸ
πλήθους τῶν περιεστώτων. εἶτα φοβηθεὶς μὴ
συντριβείην ἐν τοσαύτῃ τύρβῃ, ἐπεὶ καὶ πολλοὺς
τοῦτο πάσχοντας ἑώρων, ἀπῆλθον μακρὰ χαίρειν
φράσας θανατιῶντι σοφιστῇ τὸν ἐπιτάφιον ἑαυτοῦ
πρὸ τελευτῆς διεξιόντι.

33 Πλὴν τό γε[1] τοσοῦτον ἐπήκουσα· ἔφη γὰρ
βούλεσθαι χρυσῷ βίῳ χρυσῆν κορώνην ἐπιθεῖναι·
χρῆναι γὰρ τὸν Ἡρακλείως βεβιωκότα Ἡρακλείως
ἀποθανεῖν καὶ ἀναμιχθῆναι τῷ αἰθέρι. "Καὶ
ὠφελῆσαι," ἔφη, "βούλομαι τοὺς ἀνθρώπους

[1] τό γε Gronovius: τότε MSS.

36

ranting and telling countless malicious tales about the
man who had just got down—I do not know what
that excellent gentleman's name was. For my part,
I left him splitting his lungs and went off to see the
athletes, as the Hellanodicae were said to be already
in the Plethrium.[1]

Well, there you have what happened at Elis; and
when we reached Olympia, the rear chamber [2] was
full of people criticising Proteus or praising his
purpose, so that most of them even came to blows.
Finally, Proteus himself appeared, escorted by a
countless multitude, after the contest of the heralds,
and had somewhat to say about himself, telling of the
life that he had led and the risks that he had run,
and of all the troubles that he had endured for
philosophy's sake. His speech was protracted, though
I heard but little on account of the number of
bystanders. Afterwards, fearing to be crushed in
such a throng, because I saw this happening to
many, I went away, bidding a long farewell to the
sophist enamoured of death who was pronouncing his
own funeral oration before his demise.

This much, however, I overheard; he said that he
wanted to put a tip of gold on a golden bow; [3] for
one who had lived as Heracles should die like Heracles
and be commingled with the ether. " And I wish,"
said he, " to benefit mankind by showing them the

[1] According to Pausanias (VI, 23, 2), a place in the Gymnasium of Elis where the officials of the games (Hellanodicae)
determined by lot the matching of the athletes.
[2] Of the temple of Zeus; as it was open at the end, it
formed a sort of portico. Cf. *Runaways*, 7; *Herodotus*, 1.
[3] Pandarus the Trojan (*Iliad*, IV, 111) put a tip of gold on
the bow he had fashioned of horn. The golden bow ($\beta\iota\tilde{\omega}$) of
Peregrinus is his life ($\beta\iota\omega$).

δείξας αὐτοῖς ὃν χρὴ τρόπον θανάτου καταφρονεῖν·
πάντας οὖν δεῖ μοι τοὺς ἀνθρώπους Φιλοκτήτας
γενέσθαι." οἱ μὲν οὖν ἀνοητότεροι τῶν ἀνθρώπων
ἐδάκρυον καὶ ἐβόων " Σώζου τοῖς Ἕλλησιν,"
οἱ δὲ ἀνδρωδέστεροι ἐκεκράγεσαν " Τέλει τὰ
δεδογμένα," ὑφ' ὧν ὁ πρεσβύτης οὐ μετρίως
ἐθορυβήθη ἐλπίζων πάντας ἕξεσθαι αὐτοῦ καὶ
μὴ προήσεσθαι τῷ πυρί, ἀλλὰ ἄκοντα δὴ καθέ-
ξειν ἐν τῷ βίῳ. τὸ δὲ " Τέλει[1] τὰ δεδογμένα "
πάνυ ἀδόκητον αὐτῷ προσπεσὸν ὠχριᾶν ἔτι
μᾶλλον ἐποίησεν, καίτοι ἤδη νεκρικῶς τὴν χροιὰν
ἔχοντι, καὶ νὴ Δία καὶ ὑποτρέμειν, ὥστε κατέπαυσε τὸν λόγον.

34 Ἐγὼ δέ, εἰκάζεις, οἶμαι, πῶς ἐγέλων· οὐδὲ
γὰρ ἐλεεῖν ἄξιον ἦν οὕτω δυσέρωτα τῆς δόξης
ἄνθρωπον ὑπὲρ ἅπαντας ὅσοι τῇ αὐτῇ Ποινῇ ἐλαύ-
νονται. παρεπέμπετο δὲ ὅμως ὑπὸ πολλῶν καὶ
ἐνεφορεῖτο τῆς δόξης ἀποβλέπων ἐς τὸ πλῆθος τῶν
θαυμαζόντων, οὐκ εἰδὼς ὁ ἄθλιος ὅτι καὶ τοῖς ἐπὶ
τὸν σταυρὸν ἀπαγομένοις ἢ ὑπὸ τοῦ δημίου
ἐχομένοις πολλῷ πλείους ἕπονται.

35 Καὶ δὴ τὰ μὲν Ὀλύμπια τέλος εἶχεν, κάλλιστα
Ὀλυμπίων γενόμενα ὧν ἐγὼ εἶδον, τετράκις
ἤδη ὁρῶν. ἐγὼ δέ—οὐ γὰρ ἦν εὐπορῆσαι ὀχήματος
ἅμα[2] πολλῶν ἐξιόντων—ἄκων ὑπελειπόμην. ὁ
δὲ ἀεὶ ἀναβαλλόμενος νύκτα τὸ τελευταῖον προειρή-
κει ἐπιδείξασθαι τὴν καῦσιν· καί με τῶν ἑταίρων
τινὸς παραλαβόντος περὶ μέσας νύκτας ἐξαναστὰς
ἀπῄειν εὐθὺ τῆς Ἁρπίνης, ἔνθα ἦν ἡ πυρά. στάδιοι
πάντες οὗτοι εἴκοσιν ἀπὸ τῆς Ὀλυμπίας κατὰ τὸν

---

[1] τὸ δὲ τέλει Fritzsche: τὸ δὴ τελεῖν MSS. (δὲ X²).

way in which one should despise death; wherefore
all men ought to play Philoctetes to me." The
more witless among the people began to shed tears
and call out: " Preserve your life for the Greeks! "
but the more virile part bawled " Carry out your
purpose! " by which the old man was immoderately
upset, because he hoped that all would cling to him
and not give him over to the fire, but retain him in
life—against his will, naturally! That " Carry out
your purpose " assailing him quite unexpectedly
caused him to turn still paler, although his colour was
already deathly, and even to tremble slightly, so
that he brought his speech to an end.

You can imagine, I expect, how I laughed; for it
was not fitting to pity a man so desperately in love
with glory beyond all others who are driven by the
same Fury. Anyhow, he was being escorted by
crowds and getting his fill of glory as he gazed at the
number of his admirers, not knowing, poor wretch,
that men on their way to the cross or in the grip of the
executioner have many more at their heels.

Soon the Olympic games were ended, the most
splendid Olympics that I have seen, though it was
then the fourth time that I had been a spectator.
As it was not easy to secure a carriage, since many were
leaving at the same time, I lingered on against my
will, and Peregrinus kept making postponements, but
at last had announced a night on which he would
stage his cremation; so, as one of my friends had
invited me to go along, I arose at midnight and took
the road to Harpina, where the pyre was. This is
quite twenty furlongs from Olympia as one goes past

---

² ἅμα MF: ἀλλὰ ΓΧ.

ἱππόδρομον ἀπιόντων πρὸς ἔω. καὶ ἐπεὶ τάχιστα
ἀφικόμεθα, καταλαμβάνομεν πυρὰν νενησμένην
ἐν βόθρῳ¹ ὅσον ἐς ὀργυιὰν τὸ βάθος. δᾷδες
ἦσαν τὰ πολλὰ καὶ παρεβέβυστο τῶν φρυγάνων,
36 ὡς ἀναφθείη τάχιστα. καὶ ἐπειδὴ ἡ σελήνη
ἀνέτελλεν—ἔδει γὰρ κἀκείνην θεάσασθαι τὸ κάλλιστον τοῦτο ἔργον—πρόεισιν ἐκεῖνος ἐσκευασ-
μένος ἐς τὸν ἀεὶ τρόπον καὶ ξὺν αὐτῷ τὰ τέλη
τῶν κυνῶν, καὶ μάλιστα ὁ γεννάδας ὁ ἐκ Πατρῶν,
δᾷδα ἔχων, οὐ φαῦλος δευτεραγωνιστής· ἐδαδο-
φόρει δὲ καὶ ὁ Πρωτεύς. καὶ προσελθόντες
ἄλλος ἀλλαχόθεν ἀνῆψαν τὸ πῦρ μέγιστον ἅτε
ἀπὸ δᾴδων καὶ φρυγάνων. ὁ δέ—καί μοι πάνυ
ἤδη πρόσεχε τὸν νοῦν—ἀποθέμενος τὴν πήραν καὶ
τὸ τριβώνιον καὶ τὸ Ἡράκλειον ἐκεῖνο ῥόπαλον,
ἔστη ἐν ὀθόνῃ ῥυπώσῃ ἀκριβῶς. εἶτα ᾔτει λιβανω-
τόν, ὡς ἐπιβάλοι ἐπὶ τὸ πῦρ, καὶ ἀναδόντος τινὸς
ἐπέβαλέν τε καὶ εἶπεν ἐς τὴν μεσημβρίαν ἀποβλέπων—καὶ γὰρ καὶ τοῦτ' αὐτὸ² πρὸς τὴν τραγῳδίαν
ἦν, ἡ μεσημβρία—" Δαίμονες μητρῷοι καὶ πατρῷοι,
δέξασθέ με εὐμενεῖς." ταῦτα εἰπὼν ἐπήδησεν
ἐς τὸ πῦρ, οὐ μὴν ἑωρᾶτό γε, ἀλλὰ περιεσχέθη
ὑπὸ τῆς φλογὸς πολλῆς ἠρμένης.
37 Αὖθις ὁρῶ γελῶντά σε, ὦ καλὲ Κρόνιε, τὴν

---

¹ βόθρῳ Fritzsche: βάθει MSS.
² τοῦτ' αὐτὸ Harmon: τοῦτο τὸ ΓΧ¹ΜF: τοῦτο τῶν Χ²
(Fritzsche). Cf. below, c. 39.

---

¹ C. R. Lanman (in Allinson, *Lucian : Selected Writings*,
p. 200) thus explains the mystic allusion to the South : " It
is to be noted that Yama—the first man who died and found
out for all men the pathway ' to a distant home, a dwelling-
place secure '—conducts souls to the ' Blessed Fathers ' in

the hippodrome towards the east. As soon as we
arrived, we found a pyre built in a pit about six feet
deep. It was composed mostly of torchwood, and
the interstices filled with brush, that it might take
fire quickly. When the moon was rising—for she
too had to witness this glorious deed—he came
forward, dressed in his usual fashion, and with him
the leaders of the Cynics; in particular, the gentleman from Patras, with a torch—no bad understudy.
Proteus too was bearing a torch. Men, approaching
from this side and that, kindled the fire into a very
great flame, since it came from torchwood and brush.
Peregrinus—and give me your close attention now!—
laying aside the wallet, the cloak, and that notable
Heracles-club, stood there in a shirt that was downright
filthy. Then he requested incense to throw on the
fire; when someone had proffered it, he threw it on,
and gazing towards the south—even the south, too,
had to do with the show [1]—he said: " Spirits of my
mother and my father, receive me with favour."
With that he leaped into the fire; he was not visible,
however, but was encompassed by the flames, which
had risen to a great height.

Once more I see you laughing, Cronius, my

the south, the region of the Manes. See *Atharvaveda* 18, 3,
13; 4, 40, 2. So the monthly offerings (*çrāddhas*) to the
Manes are performed in such a way that they *end in the
south* (Manu's Laws, 3,214). The invoking of the δαίμονες
is in accord with Hindu thought; *e.g.* the liturge in Hiraṇ-
yakeçin's Gṛhya-sūtra, 2, 10⁶ (see F. Max Müller's *Sacred
Books of the East*, XXX, p. 226), after inviting the Manes,
sprinkles water towards the south, saying : ' Divine waters,
send us Agni.' The νεκράγγελοι and νερτεροδρόμοι in 41 may
be an echo of Yama's messengers that has reached Lucian.
See *Atharvaveda* 18, 2, 27 and H. C. Warren's *Buddhism in
Translations*, pp. 225–262."

καταστροφὴν τοῦ δράματος. ἐγὼ δὲ τοὺς μητρῴους
μὲν δαίμονας ἐπιβοώμενον μὰ τὸν Δί' οὐ σφόδρα
ᾐτιώμην· ὅτε δὲ καὶ τοὺς πατρῴους ἐπεκαλέσατο,
ἀναμνησθεὶς τῶν περὶ τοῦ φόνου εἰρημένων οὐδὲ
κατέχειν ἠδυνάμην τὸν γέλωτα. οἱ Κυνικοὶ δὲ
περιστάντες τὴν πυρὰν οὐκ ἐδάκρυον μέν, σιωπῇ
δὲ ἐνεδείκνυντο λύπην τινὰ εἰς τὸ πῦρ ὁρῶντες,
ἄχρι δὴ ἀποπνιγεὶς ἐπ' αὐτοῖς, "Ἀπίωμεν,"
φημί, " ὦ μάταιοι· οὐ γὰρ ἡδὺ τὸ θέαμα ὠπτημένον
γέροντα ὁρᾶν κνίσης ἀναπιμπλαμένους πονηρᾶς.
ἢ περιμένετε ἔστ' ἂν γραφεύς τις ἐπελθὼν ἀπει-
κάσῃ ὑμᾶς οἵους τοὺς ἐν τῷ δεσμωτηρίῳ ἑταίρους
τῷ Σωκράτει παραγράφουσιν; " ἐκεῖνοι μὲν οὖν
ἠγανάκτουν καὶ ἐλοιδοροῦντό μοι, ἔνιοι δὲ καὶ
ἐπὶ τὰς βακτηρίας ᾖξαν. εἶτα, ἐπειδὴ ἠπείλησα
ξυναρπάσας τινὰς ἐμβαλεῖν εἰς τὸ πῦρ, ὡς ἂν
ἕποιντο τῷ διδασκάλῳ, ἐπαύσαντο καὶ εἰρήνην
ἦγον.

38 Ἐγὼ δὲ ἐπανιὼν ποικίλα, ὦ[1] ἑταῖρε, πρὸς
ἐμαυτὸν ἐνενόουν, τὸ φιλόδοξον οἷόν τί ἐστιν
ἀναλογιζόμενος, ὡς μόνος οὗτος ὁ ἔρως ἄφυκτος
καὶ τοῖς πάνυ θαυμαστοῖς εἶναι δοκοῦσιν, οὐχ
ὅπως ἐκείνῳ τἀνδρὶ καὶ τἆλλα ἐμπλήκτως καὶ
ἀπονενοημένως βεβιωκότι καὶ οὐκ ἀναξίως τοῦ
39 πυρός. εἶτα ἐνετύγχανον[2] πολλοῖς ἀπιοῦσιν ὡς
θεάσαιντο καὶ αὐτοί· ᾤοντο γὰρ ἔτι καταλή-
ψεσθαι ζῶντα αὐτόν. καὶ γὰρ καὶ τόδε τῇ προτε-
ραίᾳ διεδέδοτο ὡς πρὸς ἀνίσχοντα τὸν ἥλιον
ἀσπασάμενος, ὥσπερ ἀμέλει καὶ τοὺς Βραχμᾶνάς
φασι ποιεῖν, ἐπιβήσεται[3] τῆς πυρᾶς. ἀπέστρεφον

---

[1] ποικίλα ὦ , Fritzsche: ποικίλως ΓΧΜF.

urbane friend, at the *dénouement* of the play. For my own part, when he called upon the guardian spirits of his mother, I did not criticise him very strongly, but when he invoked those of his father as well, I recalled the tales that had been told about his murder, and I could not control my laughter. The Cynics stood about the pyre, not weeping, to be sure, but silently evincing a certain amount of grief as they gazed into the fire, until my gorge rose at them, and I said : " Let us go away, you simpletons. It is not an agreeable spectacle to look at an old man who has been roasted, getting our nostrils filled with a villainous reek. Or are you waiting for a painter to come and picture you as the companions of Socrates in prison are portrayed beside him ? " They were indignant and reviled me, and several even took to their sticks. Then, when I threatened to gather up a few of them and throw them into the fire, so that they might follow their master, they checked themselves and kept the peace.

As I returned, I was thinking busily, my friend, reflecting what a strange thing love of glory is; how this passion alone is unescapable even by those who are considered wholly admirable, let alone that man who in other respects had led a life that was insane and reckless, and not undeserving of the fire. Then I encountered many people coming out to see the show themselves, for they expected to find him still alive. You see, on the day before it had been given out that he would greet the rising sun, as, in fact, they say the Brahmans do, before mounting the pyre.

---

[2] ἐνετύγχανον XMF : ἐτύγχανον Γ.
[3] ἐπιβήσεται ΓX : ἐπιβήσεσθαι M.

δ' οὖν τοὺς πολλοὺς αὐτῶν λέγων ἤδη τετελέσθαι
τὸ ἔργον, οἷς μὴ καὶ τοῦτ' αὐτὸ[1] περισπούδαστον
ἦν, κἂν αὐτὸν ἰδεῖν τὸν τόπον καί τι λείψανον
καταλαμβάνειν τοῦ πυρός.

Ἔνθα δή, ὦ ἑταῖρε, μυρία πράγματα εἶχον
ἅπασι διηγούμενος καὶ ἀνακρίνουσιν καὶ ἀκριβῶς
ἐκπυνθανομένοις. εἰ μὲν οὖν ἴδοιμί τινα χαρίεντα,
ψιλὰ ἂν ὥσπερ σοὶ τὰ πραχθέντα διηγούμην,
πρὸς δὲ τοὺς βλᾶκας καὶ πρὸς τὴν ἀκρόασιν
κεχηνότας ἐτραγῴδουν τι παρ' ἐμαυτοῦ, ὡς
ἐπειδὴ ἀνήφθη μὲν ἡ πυρά, ἐνέβαλεν δὲ φέρων
ἑαυτὸν ὁ Πρωτεύς, σεισμοῦ πρότερον μεγάλου
γενομένου σὺν μυκηθμῷ τῆς γῆς, γὺψ ἀναπτά-
μενος ἐκ μέσης τῆς φλογὸς οἴχοιτο ἐς τὸν οὐρανὸν
ἀνθρωπιστὶ[2] μεγάλῃ τῇ φωνῇ λέγων

" ἔλιπον γᾶν, βαίνω δ' ἐς Ὄλυμπον."

ἐκεῖνοι μὲν οὖν ἐτεθήπεσαν καὶ προσεκύνουν ὑπο-
φρίττοντες καὶ ἀνέκρινόν με πότερον πρὸς ἕω ἢ
πρὸς δυσμὰς ἐνεχθείη ὁ γύψ· ἐγὼ δὲ τὸ ἐπελθὸν
ἀπεκρινάμην αὐτοῖς.

40   Ἀπελθὼν δὲ ἐς τὴν πανήγυριν ἐπέστην τινὶ
πολιῷ ἀνδρὶ καὶ νὴ τὸν Δί' ἀξιοπίστῳ τὸ πρόσωπον
ἐπὶ τῷ πώγωνι καὶ τῇ λοιπῇ σεμνότητι, τά τε
ἄλλα διηγουμένῳ περὶ τοῦ Πρωτέως καὶ ὡς
μετὰ τὸ καυθῆναι θεάσαιτο αὐτὸν ἐν λευκῇ ἐσθῆτι
μικρὸν ἔμπροσθεν, καὶ νῦν ἀπολίποι περιπατοῦντα
φαιδρὸν ἐν τῇ ἑπταφώνῳ στοᾷ κοτίνῳ τε ἐστεμμέ-

---

[1] τοῦτ' αὐτὸ X[2] : ταὐτὸ ΓΧ[1]MF.
[2] ἀνθρωπιστὶ Harmon : ἀνθρωπίνῃ MSS.

---

[1] At the death of Plato and of Augustus it was an eagle;
in the case of Polycarp, a dove.

THE PASSING OF PEREGRINUS

Well, I turned back most of them by saying the deed had been done already, those to whom it was not in itself highly desirable to see the actual spot, anyhow, and gather up some relic of the fire.

In that business, I assure you, my friend, I had no end of trouble, telling the story to all while they asked questions and sought exact information. Whenever I noticed a man of taste, I would tell him the facts without embellishment, as I have to you; but for the benefit of the dullards, agog to listen, I would thicken the plot a bit on my own account, saying that when the pyre was kindled and Proteus flung himself bodily in, a great earthquake first took place, accompanied by a bellowing of the ground, and then a vulture, flying up out of the midst of the flames, went off to Heaven,[1] saying, in human speech, with a loud voice :

" I am through with the earth; to Olympus I fare."

They were wonder-struck and blessed themselves with a shudder, and asked me whether the vulture sped eastwards or westwards; I made them whatever reply occurred to me.

On my return to the festival, I came upon a grey-haired man whose face, I assure you, inspired confidence in addition to his beard and his general air of consequence, telling all about Proteus, and how, since his cremation, he had beheld him in white raiment a little while ago, and had just now left him walking about cheerfully in the Portico of the Seven Voices,[2] wearing a garland of wild olive. Then on

[2] This was a portico on the east side of the Altis which had a sevenfold echo (Pausan., V, 21, 17; Pliny, XXXVI, 100).

THE WORKS OF LUCIAN

νον. εἶτ᾽ ἐπὶ πᾶσι προσέθηκε τὸν γῦπα, διομνύ-
μενος ἦ μὴν αὐτὸς ἑωρακέναι ἀναπτάμενον ἐκ
τῆς πυρᾶς, ὃν ἐγὼ μικρὸν ἔμπροσθεν ἀφῆκα
πέτεσθαι καταγελῶντα τῶν ἀνοήτων καὶ βλακικῶν
τὸν τρόπον.

41   Ἐννόει τὸ λοιπὸν οἷα εἰκὸς ἐπ᾽ αὐτῷ γενή-
σεσθαι, ποίας μὲν οὐ μελίττας ἐπιστήσεσθαι [1]
ἐπὶ τὸν τόπον, τίνας δὲ τέττιγας οὐκ ἐπάσεσθαι,[2]
τίνας δὲ κορώνας οὐκ ἐπιπτήσεσθαι καθάπερ
ἐπὶ τὸν Ἡσιόδου τάφον, καὶ τὰ τοιαῦτα. εἰκόνας
μὲν γὰρ παρά τε Ἠλείων αὐτῶν παρά τε τῶν
ἄλλων Ἑλλήνων, οἷς καὶ ἐπεσταλκέναι ἔλεγεν,[3]
αὐτίκα μάλα οἶδα πολλὰς ἀναστησομένας. φασὶ
δὲ πάσαις σχεδὸν ταῖς ἐνδόξοις πόλεσιν ἐπιστολὰς
διαπέμψαι αὐτόν, διαθήκας τινὰς καὶ παραινέσεις
καὶ νόμους· καί τινας ἐπὶ τούτῳ πρεσβευτὰς
τῶν ἑταίρων ἐχειροτόνησεν, νεκραγγέλους καὶ
νερτεροδρόμους προσαγορεύσας.

42   Τοῦτο τέλος τοῦ κακοδαίμονος Πρωτέως ἐγένετο, ἀνδρός, ὡς βραχεῖ λόγῳ περιλαβεῖν, πρὸς
ἀλήθειαν μὲν οὐδεπώποτε ἀποβλέψαντος, ἐπὶ δόξῃ
δὲ καὶ τῷ παρὰ τῶν πολλῶν ἐπαίνῳ ἄπαντα
εἰπόντος ἀεὶ καὶ πράξαντος, ὡς καὶ εἰς πῦρ

[1] ἐπιστήσεσθαι MF : ἐπιστήσασθαι ΓΧ.
[2] ἐπάσεσθαι Wyttenbach : ἐπάγεσθαι ΓΧΜ.
[3] ἔλεγον du Soul, ἐλέγετο Fritzsche ; but ἔλεγεν is right.
Proteus presumably said it in his speech. Cf. ἐχειροτόνησεν

46

THE PASSING OF PEREGRINUS

top of it all he put the vulture, swearing that he himself had seen it flying up out of the pyre, when I myself had just previously let it fly to ridicule fools and dullards.

Imagine what is likely to happen in his honour hereafter, how many bees will not settle on the place, what cicadas will not sing upon it, what crows will not fly to it, as they did to the tomb of Hesiod,[1] and so forth! As to statues, I know that many will be set up right soon by the Eleans themselves and also by the other Greeks, to whom he said he had sent letters. The story is that he despatched missives to almost all the famous cities—testamentary dispositions, so to speak, and exhortations and prescriptions—and he appointed a number of ambassadors for this purpose from among his comrades, styling them " messengers from the dead " and " underworld couriers." [2]

So ended that poor wretch Proteus, a man who (to put it briefly) never fixed his gaze on the verities, but always did and said everything with a view to glory and the praise of the multitude, even to the

[1] See Pausanias (IX, 38, 3): when Orchomenus was afflicted by a plague, the Delphic priestess told its people that their only salvation was to bring there from Naupactus the bones of Hesiod, and that a crow would show them the tomb. Her words were borne out by the event.

[2] In the letters of Ignatius he recommends to the Church of Smyrna the election of a special messenger, styled " ambassador of God " (θεοπρεσβευτής : ad Smyrn., 11) or " courier of God " (θεοδρόμος : ad Polyc., 7), to be sent to Syria. The verbal coincidence is notable (cf. Lightfoot), and seems to indicate a knowledge of these letters, but on the part of Peregrinus, not Lucian.

... προσαγορεύσας below. What he then said was later expanded by others (φασί).

ἀλέσθαι, ὅτε μηδὲ ἀπολαύειν τῶν ἐπαίνων ἔμελλεν
ἀναίσθητος αὐτῶν γενόμενος.

43 Ἔν ἔτι σοι προσδιηγησάμενος παύσομαι, ὡς
ἔχῃς ἐπὶ πολὺ γελᾶν. ἐκεῖνα μὲν γὰρ πάλαι
οἶσθα, εὐθὺς ἀκούσας μου ὅτε ἥκων ἀπὸ Συρίας
διηγούμην [1] ὡς ἀπὸ Τρωάδος συμπλεύσαιμι αὐτῷ
καὶ τήν τε ἄλλην τὴν ἐν τῷ πλῷ τρυφὴν καὶ τὸ
μειράκιον τὸ ὡραῖον ὃ ἔπεισε κυνίζειν ὡς ἔχοι τινὰ
καὶ αὐτὸς Ἀλκιβιάδην, καὶ ὡς ἐπεὶ ταραχθείημεν [2] τῆς νυκτὸς ἐν μέσῳ τῷ Αἰγαίῳ [3] γνόφου
καταβάντος καὶ κῦμα παμμέγεθες ἐγείραντος
ἐκώκυε μετὰ τῶν γυναικῶν ὁ θαυμαστὸς καὶ
44 θανάτου κρείττων εἶναι δοκῶν. ἀλλὰ μικρὸν πρὸ
τῆς τελευτῆς, πρὸ ἐννέα σχεδόν που ἡμερῶν,
πλεῖον, οἶμαι, τοῦ ἱκανοῦ ἐμφαγὼν ἤμεσέν τε
τῆς νυκτὸς καὶ ἑάλω πυρετῷ μάλα σφοδρῷ.
ταῦτα δέ μοι Ἀλέξανδρος ὁ ἰατρὸς διηγήσατο μετα-
κληθεὶς ὡς ἐπισκοπήσειεν αὐτόν. ἔφη οὖν κατα-
λαβεῖν αὐτὸν χαμαὶ κυλιόμενον καὶ τὸν φλογμὸν
οὐ φέροντα καὶ ψυχρὸν αἰτοῦντα πάνυ ἐρωτικῶς,
ἑαυτὸν δὲ μὴ δοῦναι. καίτοι εἰπεῖν ἔφη πρὸς
αὐτὸν ὡς εἰ πάντως θανάτου δέοιτο, ἥκειν αὐτὸν
ἐπὶ τὰς θύρας αὐτόματον, ὥστε καλῶς ἔχειν
ἕπεσθαι μηδὲν τοῦ πυρὸς δεόμενον· τὸν δ᾽ αὖ
φάναι, " Ἀλλ᾽ οὐχ ὁμοίως ἔνδοξος ὁ τρόπος
γένοιτ᾽ ἄν, πᾶσιν κοινὸς ὤν."

[1] διηγούμην Γ: διηγουμένου MF. Levi cites X (his P1) both
for the same reading as Γ, and for ἦκον . . . διηγουμένου.
[2] ἐπεὶ ταραχθείημεν Meiser: ἐπιταραχθείημεν ΓΧ: ἐπιταραχ-
θείη μὲν MF.
[3] Αἰγαίῳ M²: ἀγῶνι M¹ΓΓΧ. The conjecture, if it is
one, is right. Things are always happening in " mid-Aegean "
with Lucian (Dial. Mar. 8, 2; 10, 1). Mras rightly sets

extent of leaping into fire, when he was sure not to enjoy the praise because he could not hear it.

I shall add one thing more to my story before I stop, in order that you may be able to have a good laugh. For of course you have long known that other tale of mine, as you heard it from me at once, when on my return from Syria I recounted how I sailed from the Troad in his company, and about his self-indulgence on the voyage, and the handsome boy whom he had persuaded to turn Cynic that he too might have an Alcibiades, and how, when we were disturbed during the night in mid-Aegean by a tempest that descended and raised an enormous sea, this wondrous person who was thought to be superior to death fell to wailing along with the women! Well, a short time before his end, about nine days, it may be, having eaten more than enough, I suppose, he was sick during the night and was taken with a very violent fever. This was told me by Alexander the physician, who had been called in to see him. He said that he found him rolling on the ground, unable to stand the burning, pleading very passionately for a drink of cold water, but that he would not give it to him. Moreover, he told him, he said, that Death, if he absolutely wanted him, had come to his door spontaneously, so that it would be well to go along, without asking any favour from the fire; and Proteus replied: " But that way would not be so notable, being common to all men."

---

aside Levi's interpretation of ἀγῶνι as meaning *lutta d'amore*, but his own defence of it as meaning "discrimen" does not properly reckon with the context. The archetype had a peculiar pointed ω, frequently confused with αι and νι, and these with it.

45 Ταῦτα μὲν ὁ Ἀλέξανδρος. ἐγὼ δὲ οὐδ' αὐτὸς
πρὸ πολλῶν ἡμερῶν εἶδον αὐτὸν ἐγκεχρισμένον,
ὡς ἀποδακρύσειε τῷ δριμεῖ φαρμάκῳ. ὁρᾷς;
οὐ πάνυ τοὺς ἀμβλυωποῦντας ὁ Αἰακὸς παραδέ-
χεται. ὅμοιον ὡς εἴ τις ἐπὶ σταυρὸν ἀναβή-
σεσθαι μέλλων τὸ ἐν τῷ δακτύλῳ πρόσπταισμα
θεραπεύοι. τί σοι δοκεῖ ὁ Δημόκριτος, εἰ ταῦτα
εἶδε; κατ' ἀξίαν γελάσαι ἂν ἐπὶ τῷ ἀνδρί; καίτοι
πόθεν εἶχεν ἐκεῖνος τοσοῦτον γέλωτα; σὺ δ'
οὖν, ὦ φιλότης, γέλα καὶ αὐτός, καὶ μάλιστα
ὁπόταν τῶν ἄλλων ἀκούῃς θαυμαζόντων αὐτόν.

THE PASSING OF PEREGRINUS

That is Alexander's story. And I myself not many days previously saw him smeared with ointment in order that the sharp salve might relieve his vision by making him shed tears. Do you get the idea? Aeacus is reluctant to receive people with weak eyes! It is as if a man about to go up to the cross should nurse the bruise on his finger. What do you think Democritus would have done, had he seen this? Would not he have laughed at the man as roundly as he deserved? And yet, where could he have got that much laughter? Well, my friend, you may have your laugh also, particularly when you hear the rest of them admiring him.

THE RUNAWAYS

A comic dialogue in three scenes attacking sham philosophers : Peregrinus, the rabble of low fellows masquerading as Cynics, and one of them whom he dubs " Cantharus " (Scarabee), describing him as settled at Philippopolis in Thrace in the company of two other runaway slaves and the errant wife of a former host of his.

This is assuredly an outgrowth of the hot dispute about the character and motives of Peregrinus which broke out even before he leaped into the flames and for months afterwards must have raged wherever Greek was spoken. Lucian, deeply involved in it from the first, finds the Cynic advocates of their new saint so obnoxious that he wishes to make a direct attack on them. He wants to bring in Peregrinus, but must do it with care, not only to avoid cutting into the field of his *Peregrinus* (by now either out or certainly in preparation), but above all to prevent Cantharus and his fellows from escaping the direct issue. His solution is clever. We gather that the death of their holy man, far from being regarded in Heaven as the proper Heraclean ending of a Heraclean life, is a stench in the nostrils of Zeus, who knows no more than Apollo what it is all about. Nobody so much as calls Proteus a philosopher, and Philosophy was not even there when it happened. He is clearly linked with the false philosophers of whom she complains ; but only by innuendo, and indignation finds nothing solid to lay hold of.

The dialogue is constructed with unusual attention to the dramatic effects of suspense and surprise. Philosophy's vigorous flailing of the Cynic pack is delayed with obvious purpose, and the devastating onslaught on Cantharus is masked to the last possible moment. In handling the search for him, however, Lucian's technique is not quite perfect, since he lets us think at first that it has no definite objective. Also, towards the end the lines themselves do not always make it clear who speaks them—a matter in which Lucian is generally very resourceful (A. R. Bellinger, *Yale Classical Studies*, I [1928], pp. 3–40). Either he was hasty or he had not yet attained his later facility.

The dialogue was written late in 165 or early in A.D. 166, almost certainly in Philippopolis.

ΔΡΑΠΕΤΑΙ

ΑΠΟΛΛΩΝ

1 Ἀληθῆ ταῦτά φασιν, πάτερ, ὡς ἐμβάλοι τις
φέρων αὐτὸν εἰς τὸ πῦρ κατέναντι Ὀλυμπίων, ἤδη
πρεσβύτης ἄνθρωπος, οὐκ ἀγεννὴς θαυματοποιὸς
τὰ τοιαῦτα; ἡ Σελήνη γὰρ ἡμῖν διηγεῖτο, αὐτὴ
ἑωρακέναι καιόμενον λέγουσα.

ΖΕΥΣ

Καὶ πάνυ ἀληθῆ, ὦ Ἄπολλον· ὡς μή ποτε
γενέσθαι ὤφελεν.

ΑΠΟΛΛΩΝ

Οὕτω χρηστὸς ὁ γέρων ἦν καὶ ἀνάξιος ἐν πυρὶ
ἀπολωλέναι;

ΖΕΥΣ

Καὶ τοῦτο μὲν ἴσως· ἀλλ᾽ ἐγὼ πολλὴν τὴν
ἀηδίαν μέμνημαι ἀνασχόμενος τότε ὑπὸ κνίσης
πονηρᾶς, οἵαν εἰκὸς ἀποφέρεσθαι ὀπτωμένων
ἀνθρωπείων σωμάτων. εἰ γοῦν μὴ εἰς τὴν Ἀρα-
βίαν ὡς εἶχον εὐθὺς ἀπιὼν ᾠχόμην, ἀπολώλειν

---

[1] The Olympic games were timed to come at the full of the
moon, and the cremation took place at moon-rise (*Peregr.*, 36).

[2] By dividing Apollo's question and emphasising the negative
in the second part, the translation seeks to reproduce the
ambiguity of Zeus's reply, which in the Greek is sufficiently

THE RUNAWAYS

APOLLO

Is the report true, father, that someone threw himself bodily into the fire, in the very face of the Olympic festivities, quite an elderly man, not a bad hand at such hocus-pocus? Selene told me, saying that she herself had seen him burning.[1]

ZEUS

Yes, quite true, Apollo. If only it had never happened!

APOLLO

Was the old man so good? Was he not worthy of a death by fire?

ZEUS

Yes, that he was, very likely.[2] But my point is that I remember having had to put up with a great deal of annoyance at the time on account of a horrid stench such as you might expect to arise from roasting human bodies. In fact, if I had not at once gone straight to Araby, I should have come to a sad end,

subtle to have misled more than one scholar into the notion that Zeus (and therefore Lucian) is praising Peregrinus. Nothing could be farther from his (or Lucian's) real thought, that the fellow deserved death. The ambiguity is of course deliberate, to foil and annoy "Scarabee" and his sort; cf. below, § 7.

ἄν, εὖ ἴσθι, ἀτοπίᾳ τοῦ καπνοῦ· καὶ ὅμως ἐν
τοσαύτῃ εὐωδίᾳ καὶ ἀφθονίᾳ τῶν ἀρωμάτων
καὶ ἐν λιβανωτῷ παμπόλλῳ μόλις αἱ ῥῖνες ἐπιλα-
θέσθαι μοι καὶ ἀπομαθεῖν ἤθελον τὴν κηλῖδα
ἐκείνην τῆς ὀσμῆς, ἀλλὰ καὶ νῦν ὀλίγου δέω
ναυτιᾶν ὑπομνησθεὶς αὐτῆς.

ΑΠΟΛΛΩΝ

2 Τί δὲ βουλόμενος, ὦ Ζεῦ, τοιαῦτα εἴργασται
ἑαυτόν; ἢ τί τὸ ἀγαθόν, ἀπανθρακωθῆναι ἐμπεσόντα εἰς τὴν πυράν;

ΖΕΥΣ

Τοῦτο μὲν οὐκ ἄν, ὦ παῖ, φθάνοις καὶ Ἐμ-
πεδοκλεῖ πρὸ αὐτοῦ ἐγκαλῶν, ὃς ἐς τοὺς κρατῆρας ἤλατο καὶ αὐτὸς ἐν Σικελίᾳ.

ΑΠΟΛΛΩΝ

Μελαγχολίαν τινὰ δεινὴν λέγεις. ἀτὰρ οὗτός
γε τίνα ποτὲ ἄρα τὴν αἰτίαν ἔσχε τῆς ἐπιθυμίας;

ΖΕΥΣ

Αὐτοῦ σοι λόγον ἐρῶ ὃν ἔλεξε πρὸς τὴν πανήγυριν, ἀπολογούμενος πρὸς αὐτοὺς ὑπὲρ τῆς
3 τελευτῆς. ἔφη γάρ, εἴ γε μέμνημαι—ἀλλὰ
τίς αὕτη σπουδῇ πρόσεισι τεταραγμένη καὶ δα-
κρύουσα, πάνυ ἀδικουμένῃ ἐοικυῖα; μᾶλλον δὲ
Φιλοσοφία ἐστίν, καὶ τοὔνομά γε τοὐμὸν ἐπιβοᾶται
σχετλιάζουσα. τί, ὦ θύγατερ, δακρύεις; ἢ τί ἀπολιποῦσα τὸν βίον ἐλήλυθας; ἆρα μὴ οἱ ἰδιῶται
αὖθις ἐπιβεβουλεύκασί σοι ὡς τὸ πρόσθεν, ὅτε

you may depend on it, from the awfulness of the
reek. Even as it was, amid all that fragrance and
abundance of sweet scents, with frankincense in
profusion, my nostrils hardly consented to forget and
unlearn the taint of that odour; why, even now I
almost retch at the memory of it!

APOLLO

What was his idea, Zeus, in doing that to himself,
or what was the good of his getting incinerated by
jumping into the blazing pyre?

ZEUS

Well, that criticism, my boy, you had better
address first to Empedocles, who himself sprung into
that crater in Sicily.

APOLLO

A terrible case of melancholia, that! But this
man—what reason in the world did he have for
wanting to do it?

ZEUS

I will repeat for you a speech of his own, which he
delivered to the assembled pilgrims, defending himself before them for putting an end to himself. He
said, if my memory serves me—But who is this
woman coming up in haste, excited and tearful, like
someone suffering great wrongs? Stay, it is Philosophy, and she is calling upon me by name, in bitter-
ness of spirit. Why the tears, my daughter? Why
have you left the world and come here? Surely it
cannot be that the common sort have once again
combined against you as before, when they put

τὸν Σωκράτην ἀπέκτειναν ὑπὸ Ἀνύτου κατηγορη-
θέντα, εἶτα φεύγεις διὰ τοῦτο αὐτούς;

ΦΙΛΟΣΟΦΙΑ

Οὐδὲν τοιοῦτον, ὦ πάτερ, ἀλλ' ἐκεῖνοι μέν, ὁ
πολὺς λεώς, ἐπῄνουν καὶ διὰ τιμῆς ἦγον, αἰδούμενοι καὶ θαυμάζοντές με καὶ μονονουχὶ προσκυ-
νοῦντες, εἰ καὶ μὴ σφόδρα ξυνίεσαν ὧν λέγοιμι.
οἱ δέ—πῶς ἂν εἴποιμι;—οἱ ξυνήθεις καὶ φίλοι
φάσκοντες εἶναι καὶ τοὔνομα τοὐμὸν ὑποδυόμενοι,
ἐκεῖνοί με τὰ δεινότατα εἰργάσαντο.

ΖΕΥΣ

4   Οἱ φιλόσοφοι ἐπιβουλήν τινα ἐπιβεβουλεύκασί
σοι;

ΦΙΛΟΣΟΦΙΑ

Οὐδαμῶς, ὦ πάτερ, οἵ γε ξυνηδίκηνταί μοι
καὶ αὐτοί.

ΖΕΥΣ

Πρὸς τίνων οὖν ἠδίκησαι, εἰ μήτε τοὺς ἰδιώτας
μήτε τοὺς φιλοσόφους αἰτιᾷ ;

ΦΙΛΟΣΟΦΙΑ

Εἰσίν τινες, ὦ Ζεῦ, ἐν μεταιχμίῳ τῶν τε πολλῶν
καὶ τῶν φιλοσοφούντων, τὸ μὲν σχῆμα καὶ βλέμμα
καὶ βάδισμα ἡμῖν ὅμοιοι καὶ κατὰ τὰ αὐτὰ ἐσταλ-
μένοι· ἀξιοῦσι γοῦν ὑπ' ἐμοὶ τάττεσθαι καὶ
τοὔνομα τὸ ἡμέτερον ἐπιγράφονται, μαθηταὶ καὶ
ὁμιληταὶ καὶ θιασῶται ἡμῶν εἶναι λέγοντες·

Socrates to death through a charge brought by
Anytus, and that you are fleeing from them for that
reason?

PHILOSOPHY

Nothing of the sort, father. On the contrary,
they—the multitude—spoke well of me and held me
in honour, respecting, admiring, and all but worshipping me, even if they did not much understand what
I said. But the others—how shall I style them?—
those who say they are my familiars and friends and
creep under the cloak of my name, they are the
people who have done me the direst possible injuries.

ZEUS

Have the philosophers made a plot against you?

PHILOSOPHY

By no means, father. Why, they themselves have
been wronged in common with me!

ZEUS

At whose hands, then, have you been wronged,
if you have no fault to find either with the common
sort or with the philosophers?

PHILOSOPHY

There are some, Zeus, who occupy a middle ground
between the multitude and the philosophers. In
deportment, glance, and gait they are like us, and
similarly dressed; as a matter of fact, they want to
be enlisted under my command and they enroll themselves under my name, saying that they are my
pupils, disciples, and devotees. Nevertheless, their

THE WORKS OF LUCIAN

ὁ βίος δὲ παμμίαρος αὐτῶν, ἀμαθίας καὶ θράσους
καὶ ἀσελγείας ἀνάπλεως, ὕβρις οὐ μικρὰ καθ᾽
ἡμῶν. ὑπὸ τούτων, ὦ πάτερ, ἠδικημένη πέ-
φευγα.

ΖΕΥΣ

5   Δεινὰ ταῦτα, ὦ θύγατερ. ἀλλὰ τί μάλιστα
ἠδικήκασί σε;

ΦΙΛΟΣΟΦΙΑ

Σκόπει, ὦ πάτερ, εἰ μικρά. σὺ γὰρ κατιδὼν
τὸν βίον ἀδικίας καὶ παρανομίας μεστὸν ἅτε
ἀμαθίᾳ καὶ ὕβρει ξυνόντα καὶ ταραττόμενον ὑπ᾽
αὐτῶν, κατελεήσας τὸ ἀνθρώπειον ὑπὸ τῇ ἀγνοίᾳ
ἐλαυνόμενον ἐμὲ κατέπεμψας, ἐντειλάμενος ἐπιμε-
ληθῆναι ὡς παύσαιντο μὲν ἀδικοῦντες ἀλλήλους
καὶ βιαζόμενοι καὶ ὅμοια τοῖς θηρίοις βιοῦντες,
ἀναβλέψαντες δὲ πρὸς τὴν ἀλήθειαν εἰρηνικώτερον
ξυμπολιτεύοιντο. ἔφης γοῦν πρός με καταπέμπων,
" Ἃ μὲν πράττουσιν οἱ ἄνθρωποι καὶ ὡς διάκεινται
ὑπὸ τῆς ἀμαθίας, ὦ θύγατερ, καὶ αὐτὴ ὁρᾷς·
ἐγὼ δέ (ἐλεῶ γὰρ αὐτούς) σέ, ἣν μόνην ἰάσασθαι
ἂν τὰ γιγνόμενα οἶμαι, προκρίνας ἐξ ἁπάντων
ἡμῶν πέμπω ἰασομένην."

ΖΕΥΣ

6   Οἶδα πολλὰ καὶ ταῦτα[1] εἰπὼν τότε. σὺ δὲ
τὰ μετὰ ταῦτα ἤδη λέγε, ὅπως μὲν ὑπεδέξαντό σε
καταπταμένην τὸ πρῶτον, ἅτινα δὲ νῦν ὑπ᾽
αὐτῶν πέπονθας.

---

[1] The expression is unusual, and possibly wrong. Various
conjectures are πολλὰ καὶ τοιαῦτα, πολλὰ τοιαῦτα, and (Capps)
ἄλλα πολλὰ καὶ ταῦτα. Perhaps πολλὰ κατ᾽ αὐτά (i.e. τὰ
γιγνόμενα)?

abominable way of living, full of ignorance, impudence, and wantonness, is no trifling outrage against me. It is they, father, who have inflicted the wrongs that have made me flee.

ZEUS

This is a sad state of affairs, daughter. But in just what way have they wronged you?

PHILOSOPHY

See for yourself, father, whether the wrongs are trifling. When you observed that the life of man was full of wrongdoing and transgression because stupidity and high-handedness were ingrained in it, and disturbed it, you pitied humanity, harried as it was by ignorance, and therefore sent me down, enjoining me to see to it that they should stop wronging each other, doing violence, and living like beasts; that they should instead fix their eyes on the verities and manage their society more peaceably. Anyhow, you said to me in sending me down: "What men do and how they are affected by stupidity, daughter, you see for yourself. I pity them, and so, as I think that you alone might be able to cure what is going on, I have selected you from among us all and send you to effect the cure."

ZEUS

I know I said a great deal at the time, including all this. But go on and tell me what followed, how they received you when you flew down for the first time and what has befallen you now at their hands.

THE WORKS OF LUCIAN

Ἧιξα μέν, ὦ πάτερ, οὐκ ἐπὶ τοὺς Ἕλληνας
εὐθύς, ἀλλ᾽ ὅπερ ἐδόκει μοι χαλεπώτερον τοῦ
ἔργου εἶναι, τὸ βαρβάρους παιδεύειν καὶ διδάσκειν,
τοῦτο πρῶτον ἠξίουν ἐργάσασθαι· τὸ Ἑλληνικὸν
δὲ εἴων ὡς ῥᾷστα ὑποβαλέσθαι οἷόν τε[1] καὶ τάχιστα,
ὥς γε ᾤμην, ἐνδεξόμενον τὸν χαλινὸν καὶ ὑπαχθη-
σόμενον τῷ ζυγῷ. ὁρμήσασα δὲ εἰς Ἰνδοὺς τὸ
πρῶτον, ἔθνος μέγιστον τῶν ἐν τῷ βίῳ, οὐ χαλεπῶς
ἔπεισα καταβάντας ἀπὸ τῶν ἐλεφάντων ἐμοὶ
συνεῖναι, ὥστε καὶ γένος ὅλον, οἱ Βραχμᾶνες,
τοῖς Νεχραίοις καὶ Ὀξυδράκαις ὅμορον, οὗτοι
πάντες ὑπ᾽ ἐμοὶ τάττονται καὶ βιοῦσίν τε[2] κατὰ
τὰ ἡμῖν δοκοῦντα, τιμώμενοι πρὸς τῶν περιοίκων
ἁπάντων, καὶ ἀποθνήσκουσι παράδοξόν τινα τοῦ
θανάτου τρόπον.

7 Τοὺς γυμνοσοφιστὰς λέγεις. ἀκούω γοῦν τά
τε ἄλλα περὶ αὐτῶν καὶ ὅτι ἐπὶ πυρὰν μεγίστην
ἀναβάντες ἀνέχονται καιόμενοι, οὐδὲν τοῦ σχήματος ἢ τῆς καθέδρας ἐντρέποντες.[3] ἀλλ᾽ οὐ
μέγα τοῦτο· ἔναγχος γοῦν καὶ Ὀλυμπίασιν
τὸ ὅμοιον ἐγὼ εἶδον γενόμενον, εἰκὸς δὲ καὶ σὲ
παρεῖναι καιομένου τότε τοῦ γέροντος.

---

[1] οἷόν τε after ὑποβαλέσθαι Mras : after χαλινὸν MSS.
[2] τε Fritzsche : γε MSS.
[3] ἐκτρέποντες N, edd. ; but cf. *Peregr.*, 25.

THE RUNAWAYS

PHILOSOPHY

When I sped off, father, I did not head for the
Greeks straightway, but as it seemed to me the more
difficult part of my task to educate and instruct the
foreigners, I decided to do that first; the Greek world
I let be, as possible to subject very easily and likely
(I thought so, anyhow) to take the bridle and submit
to the harness very soon. Making for the Indians
to begin with, the most numerous population in the
world, I had no difficulty about persuading them to
come down off their elephants and associate with
me. Consequently, a whole tribe, the Brahmans,
who border upon the Nechraei and the Oxydracae,[1]
are all enlisted under my command and not only live
in accordance with my tenets, honoured by all their
neighbours, but die a marvellous kind of death.

ZEUS

You mean the gymnosophists.[2] Anyhow, I am
told, among other things about them, that they
ascend a very lofty pyre and endure cremation without any change in their outward appearance or their
sitting position.[3] But that is nothing much. Just
now, for example, at Olympia I saw the same sort of
thing done, and very likely you too were there at the
time when the old man was burned.

[1] The Nechraei are not mentioned elsewhere, unless, as
Fritzsche suggests, they are the Nereae of Pliny (*Nat. Hist.*,
VI, 76). The Oxydracae made themselves famous by their
resolute opposition to the invasion of Alexander; they lived
in the Punjab.
[2] A generic name given by the Greeks to the holy men
of India who lived naked.
[3] Apparently a correction of *Peregrinus*, where (p. 30) the
position is spoken of as "lying."

THE WORKS OF LUCIAN

Οὐδὲ ἀνῆλθον, ὦ πάτερ, εἰς 'Ολυμπίαν δέει
τῶν καταράτων ἐκείνων οὓς ἔφην, ὅτι πολλοὺς
αὐτῶν ἑώρων ἀπιόντας, ὡς λοιδορήσαιντο τοῖς
ξυνεληλυθόσι καὶ βοῆς τὸν ὀπισθόδομον ἐμπλήσω-
σιν ὑλακτοῦντες, ὥστε οὐδὲ εἶδον ἐκεῖνον ὅπως
ἀπέθανεν.

8   Μετὰ δ' οὖν[1] τοὺς Βραχμᾶνας εἰς Αἰθιοπίαν εὐθύς, εἶτα εἰς Αἴγυπτον κατέβην, καὶ
ξυγγενομένη τοῖς ἱερεῦσιν καὶ προφήταις αὐτῶν καὶ τὰ θεῖα παιδεύσασα ἐς Βαβυλῶνα
ἀπῆρα Χαλδαίους καὶ μάγους μυήσουσα, εἶτα
εἰς Σκυθίαν ἐκεῖθεν, εἶτα εἰς Θράκην, ἔνθα μοι
Εὔμολπός τε καὶ 'Ορφεὺς συνεγενέσθην, οὓς καὶ
προαποστείλασα ἐς τὴν 'Ελλάδα, τὸν μὲν ὡς
τελέσειεν αὐτούς, τὸν Εὔμολπον—ἐμεμαθήκει γὰρ
τὰ θεῖα παρ' ἡμῶν ἅπαντα—τὸν δὲ ὡς ἐπάδων
προσβιβάζοι τῇ μουσικῇ, κατὰ πόδας εὐθὺς εἱπόμην.

9   Καὶ τὸ μὲν πρῶτον εὐθὺς ἐλθοῦσαν οὔτε πάνυ
ἠσπάσαντο οἱ 'Έλληνες οὔτε ὅλως ἀπέκλεισαν·
κατ' ὀλίγον δὲ προσομιλοῦσα ἑπτὰ ἐκ τῶν ἁπάντων
ἑταίρους καὶ μαθητὰς προσηγαγόμην, καὶ ἄλλον
ἐξ Σάμου καὶ ἄλλον ἐξ 'Εφέσου καὶ 'Αβδηρόθεν
ἄλλον, ὀλίγους παντάπασιν.

10 Μεθ' οὓς τὸ σοφιστῶν φῦλον οὐκ οἶδ' ὅπως
μοι παρενεφύετο, οὔτε ζηλοῦν τἀμὰ ἐς βάθος

---

[1] δ' οὖν Jacobitz: γοῦν MSS.

---

[1] The word is chosen because specially appropriate to Cynic "dogs."

[2] The seven were the Seven Sages, who as listed by Plato in the *Protagoras* (343 A) were Thales of Miletus, Pittacus of

THE RUNAWAYS

PHILOSOPHY

I did not even go to Olympia, father, for fear of
those detestable fellows whom I spoke of, since I
saw many of them taking their way there in order to
upbraid the assembled pilgrims and fill the back room
of the temple with the noise of their howling.[1]
Consequently, I did not see how he died.

But to resume—after the Brahmans I went direct
to Ethiopia, and then down to Egypt; and after
associating with their priests and prophets and
instructing them in religion, I departed for Babylon,
to initiate Chaldeans and Magi; then from there to
Scythia, and then to Thrace, where I conversed with
Eumolpus and Orpheus, whom I sent in advance to
Greece, one of them, Eumolpus, to give them the
mysteries, as he had learned all about religion from
me, and the other to win them over by the witchery
of his music. Then I followed at once on their
heels.

Just at first, on my arrival, the Greeks neither
welcomed me very warmly nor shut the door in my
face outright. But gradually, as I associated with
them, I attached to myself seven companions and
pupils from among them all; then another from
Samos, another from Ephesus, and one more from
Abdera—only a few in all.[2]

After them, the Sophist tribe somehow or other
fastened themselves to my skirts. They were
neither profoundly interested in my teaching nor

Mytilene, Bias of Priene, Solon of Athens, Cleobulus of Lindos,
Myson of Chenae, and Chilon of Sparta; but Periander of
Corinth was often included instead of Myson. The three
whom Philosophy acquired later were Pythagoras of Samos,
Heraclitus of Ephesus, and Democritus of Abdera.

65

οὔτε κομιδῇ ἀπᾷδον, ἀλλ' οἷον τὸ Ἱπποκενταύρων
γένος, σύνθετόν τι καὶ μικτόν[1] ἐν μέσῳ ἀλα-
ζονείας καὶ φιλοσοφίας πλαζόμενον, οὔτε τῇ
ἀγνοίᾳ τέλεον προσεχόμενον οὔτε ἡμᾶς ἀτενέσι
τοῖς ὀφθαλμοῖς καθορᾶν δυνάμενον, ἀλλ' οἷον
λημῶντες ὑπὸ τοῦ ἀμβλυώττειν ἀσαφές τι καὶ
ἀμυδρὸν ἡμῶν εἴδωλον ἢ σκιὰν ἐνίοτε ἰδόντες
ἄν· οἱ δὲ ᾤοντο ἀκριβῶς πάντα κατανενοηκέναι.
ὅθεν παρ' αὐτοῖς ἡ ἀχρεῖος ἐκείνη καὶ περιττὴ
σοφία καί, ὡς αὐτοὶ ᾤοντο, ἀπρόσμαχος ἀνεφλέ-
γετο, αἱ κομψαὶ καὶ ἄποροι καὶ ἄτοποι ἀποκρίσεις
καὶ δυσέξοδοι καὶ λαβυρινθώδεις ἐρωτήσεις.
11 εἶτα κωλυόμενοι καὶ ἐλεγχόμενοι πρὸς τῶν ἑταίρων
τῶν ἐμῶν ἠγανάκτουν καὶ συνίσταντο ἐπ' αὐτούς,
καὶ τέλος δικαστηρίοις ὑπῆγον καὶ παρεδίδοσαν
πιομένους τοῦ κωνείου. ἐχρῆν μὲν οὖν ἴσως τότε
φυγεῖν εὐθὺς καὶ μηκέτι ἀνέχεσθαι τὴν συνου-
σίαν αὐτῶν· νῦν δὲ Ἀντισθένης με καὶ Διογένης
καὶ μετὰ μικρὸν Κράτης καὶ Μένιππος οὗτος
ἔπεισαν ὀλίγον ὅσον ἐπιμετρῆσαι τῆς μονῆς,
ὡς μήποτε ὤφελον· οὐ γὰρ ἂν τοσαῦτα ἐπεπόνθειν
ὕστερον.

ΖΕΥΣ

12   Οὐδέπω μοι λέγεις, ὦ Φιλοσοφία, τίνα ἠδίκησαι,
ἀλλὰ ἀγανακτεῖς μόνον.

---

[1] μικτόλ N : μικρὸν ΓΒ.

altogether at variance, but like the Hippocentaur
breed, something composite and mixed, astray in the
interspace between quackery and philosophy, neither
completely addicted to ignorance nor yet able to keep
me envisioned with an intent gaze; being purblind,
as it were, through their dim-sightedness they merely
glimpsed at times an indistinct, dim presentment or
shadow of me, yet thought they had discerned everything with accuracy.   So there flared up among them
that useless and superfluous " wisdom " of theirs,
in their own opinion invincible—those clever, baffling,
absurd replies and perplexing, mazy queries.   Then,
on being checked and shown up by my comrades,
they were indignant and combined against them, at
length bringing them before courts and handing
them over to drink the hemlock.   I ought perhaps
at that time to have fled incontinently, no longer
putting up with their company; but Antisthenes
and Diogenes, and presently Crates and Menippus,
you know,[1] persuaded me to mete them out an
additional modicum of delay.   O that I had not done
so! for I should not have undergone such sufferings
later.

ZEUS

You have not yet told me what wrongs have been
done you, Philosophy; you merely vent your
indignation.

[1] "This" Menippus, not because Lucian thinks of him as
attending Philosophy in her return to Heaven, or still less
because he is carelessly adapting something by Menippus in
which that was the case (Helm), but simply because when
Lucian wrote these words Menippus enjoyed among the
reading public a high degree of popularity, to which by this
time Lucian himself had contributed significantly.

ΦΙΛΟΣΟΦΙΑ

Καὶ μὴν ἄκουε, ὦ Ζεῦ, ἡλίκα ἐστίν. μιαρὸν
γάρ τι φῦλον ἀνθρώπων καὶ ὡς τὸ πολὺ δουλικὸν
καὶ θητικόν, οὐ ξυγγενόμενον ἡμῖν ἐκ παίδων
ὑπ᾽ ἀσχολίας· ἐδούλευεν γὰρ ἢ ἐθήτευεν ἢ ἄλλας
τινὰς τέχνας οἵας εἰκὸς τοὺς τοιούτους ἐμάνθανεν,
σκυτεύειν ἢ τεκταίνειν ἢ περὶ πλυνοὺς ἔχειν
ἢ ἔρια ξαίνειν, ὡς εὐεργὰ εἴη ταῖς γυναιξὶν καὶ
εὐμήρυτα καὶ κατάγοιτο εὐμαρῶς ὁπότε ἢ κρόκην
ἐκεῖναι στρέφοιεν ἢ μίτον κλώθοιεν. τοιαῦτα
τοίνυν ἐν παισὶ [1] μελετῶντες οὐδὲ ὄνομα τὸ
ἡμέτερον ᾔδεσαν. ἐπεὶ δὲ εἰς ἄνδρας τελεῖν
ἤρξαντο καὶ κατεῖδον τὴν αἰδῶ, ὅση παρὰ τῶν
πολλῶν ἐστιν τοῖς ἑταίροις τοῖς ἐμοῖς, καὶ ὡς
ἀνέχονται οἱ ἄνθρωποι τὴν παρρησίαν αὐτῶν καὶ
χαίρουσιν θεραπευόμενοι καὶ συμβουλεύουσι πεί-
θονται καὶ ἐπιτιμώντων ὑποπτήσσουσι, ταῦτα
πάντα τυραννίδα οὐ μικρὰν ἡγοῦντο εἶναι.

13   Τὸ μὲν δὴ μανθάνειν ὅσα τῇ τοιαύτῃ προαιρέσει
πρόσφορα μακρὸν ἦν, μᾶλλον δὲ κομιδῇ ἀδύνατον,
αἱ τέχναι δὲ γλίσχραι, καὶ σὺν πόνῳ καὶ μόγις
ἱκανὰ παρέχειν ἐδύναντο. ἐνίοις δὲ καὶ ἡ δουλεία
βαρὺ καὶ (ὥσπερ οὖν ἐστιν) ἀφόρητον ἐφαίνετο.
ἔδοξε δὴ σκοπουμένοις τὴν ὑστάτην ἄγκυραν,
ἣν ἱερὰν οἱ ναυτιλλόμενοί φασιν, καθιέναι, καὶ
ἐπὶ τὴν βελτίστην ἀπόνοιαν ὁρμήσαντες, ἔτι τε
καὶ τόλμαν καὶ ἀμαθίαν καὶ ἀναισχυντίαν προσ-
παρακαλέσαντες, αἵπερ αὐτοῖς μάλιστα συναγωνίζονται, καὶ λοιδορίας καινὰς [2] ἐκμελετήσαντες,

---

[1] παῖσι N: πᾶσι ΓΜΗΧΒΟ.
[2] καινὰς Γ: κενὰς N: τινὰς ΒΟ.   Cf. *Icarom.*, 30.

THE RUNAWAYS

But do listen, Zeus, and hear how great they are. There is an abominable class of men, for the most part slaves and hirelings, who had nothing to do with me in childhood for lack of leisure, since they were performing the work of slaves or hirelings or learning such trades as you would expect their like to learn—cobbling, building, busying themselves with fuller's tubs, or carding wool to make it easy for the women to work, easy to wind, and easy to draw off when they twist a yarn or spin a thread. Well, while they were following such occupations in youth, they did not even know my name. But when they began to be reckoned as adults and noticed how much respect my companions have from the multitude and how men tolerate their plain-speaking, delight in their ministrations, hearken to their advice, and cower under their censure, they considered all this to be a suzerainty of no mean order.

Now to learn all that is requisite for such a calling would have been a long task, say rather an impossible one. Their trades, however, were petty, laborious, and barely able to supply them with just enough. To some, moreover, servitude seemed grievous and (as indeed it is) intolerable. It seemed best to them, therefore, as they reflected upon the matter, to let go their last anchor, which men that sail the seas call the " sacred " one;[1] so, resorting to good old Desperation, inviting the support, too, of Hardihood, Stupidity, and Shamelessness, who are their principal partisans, and committing to memory novel terms of abuse, in order to have them at hand and at their

---

[1] Nowadays known as the " sheet " anchor.

ὡς πρόχειροι εἶεν καὶ ἀνὰ στόμα, ταύτας μόνας
ξυμβολὰς ἔχοντες—ὁρᾷς ὁποῖα πρὸς φιλοσοφίαν
ἐφόδια;—σχηματίζουσιν καὶ μετακοσμοῦσιν αὑτοὺς εὖ μάλα εἰκότως καὶ πρὸς ἐμέ, οἷόν τι ἀμέλει
ὁ Αἴσωπός φησι ποιῆσαι τὸν ἐν τῇ Κύμῃ ὄνον,
ὃς λεοντὴν περιβαλόμενος καὶ τραχὺ ὀγκώμενος
ἠξίου λέων καὶ αὐτὸς εἶναι· καί πού τινες καὶ
ἦσαν ἴσως οἱ πιστεύοντες αὐτῷ.

14 Τὰ δ᾽ ἡμέτερα πάνυ ῥᾷστα, ὡς οἶσθα, καὶ ἐς
μίμησιν πρόχειρα—τὰ προφανῆ λέγω—καὶ οὐ
πολλῆς τῆς πραγματείας δεῖ τριβώνιον περιβαλέ-
σθαι καὶ πήραν ἐξαρτήσασθαι καὶ ξύλον ἐν τῇ
χειρὶ ἔχειν καὶ βοᾶν, μᾶλλον δὲ ὀγκᾶσθαι ἢ
ὑλακτεῖν, καὶ λοιδορεῖσθαι ἅπασιν· τὴν ἀσφάλειαν
γὰρ αὐτοῖς τοῦ μηδὲν ἐπὶ τούτῳ παθεῖν ἡ πρὸς τὸ
σχῆμα αἰδὼς παρέξειν ἔμελλεν. ἡ ἐλευθερία δὲ
πρόχειρος ἄκοντος τοῦ δεσπότου, κἂν εἰ βούλοιτο
ἀπάγειν, παταχθησομένου τῷ ξύλῳ. καὶ τὰ ἄλ-
φιτα οὐκέτ᾽ ὀλίγα οὐδὲ ὡς πρὸ τοῦ μᾶζα ψιλή,
τὸ δὲ ὄψον οὐ[1] τάριχος ἢ θύμον, ἀλλὰ κρέα
παντοδαπὰ καὶ οἶνος οἷος ἥδιστος, καὶ χρυσίον
παρ᾽ ὅτου ἂν ἐθέλωσι· δασμολογοῦσι γὰρ ἐπιφοι-
τῶντες ἤ, ὡς αὐτοί φασιν, ἀποκείρουσιν τὰ πρόβατα, δώσειν τε πολλοὺς οἴονται[2] ἢ αἰδοῖ τοῦ
σχήματος ἢ δέει τοῦ μὴ ἀκοῦσαι κακῶς.

15 Καὶ γὰρ αὖ κἀκεῖνο ἑώρων, οἶμαι, ὡς ἐξ ἴσου
καταστήσονται τοῖς ὀρθῶς φιλοσοφοῦσιν, οὐδέ
τις ὁ δικάσων καὶ διακρινῶν τὰ τοιαῦτα ἔσται,
ἢν μόνον τὰ ἔξω ᾖ ὅμοια. ἀρχὴν γὰρ οὐδὲ τὸν

---

[1] οὐ NΓ[1], edd.: ἢ Γ[2]BA.
[2] οἷόν τε ΓΜ.

tongue's end, with these as their only countersigns (you perceive what a rare equipment it is for philosophy), they very plausibly transform themselves in looks and apparel to counterfeit my very self, doing, I vow, the same sort of thing that Aesop says the jackass in Cyme did, who put on a lion skin and began to bray harshly, claiming to be a lion himself; and no doubt there were actually some who believed him!

What characterises us is very easily attainable, as you know, and open to imitation—I mean what meets the eye. It does not require much ceremony to don a short cloak, sling on a wallet, carry a staff in one's hand, and shout—say rather, bray, or howl, and slang everyone. Assurance of not suffering for it was bound to be afforded them by the usual respect for the cloth. Freedom is in prospect, against the will of their master, who, even if he should care to assert possession by force, would get beaten with the staff. Bread, too, is no longer scanty or, as before, limited to bannocks of barley; and what goes with it is not salt fish or thyme but meat of all sorts and wine of the sweetest, and money from whomsoever they will; for they collect tribute, going from house to house, or, as they themselves express it, they " shear the sheep "; and they expect many to give, either out of respect for their cloth or for fear of their abusive language.

Moreover, they discerned, I assume, the further advantage that they would be on an equal footing with true philosophers, and that there would be nobody who could pass judgment and draw distinctions in such matters, if only the externals were similar. For, to begin with, they do not even

ἔλεγχον δέχονται, ἢν ἔρηταί τις οὑτωσὶ κοσμίως
καὶ κατὰ βραχύ, ἀλλ᾽ εὐθὺς βοῶσιν καὶ ἐπὶ τὴν
ἀκρόπολιν τὴν ἑαυτῶν ἀναφεύγουσι, τὴν λοιδορίαν,
καὶ πρόχειρον τὸ ξύλον. καὶ ἢν μὲν τὰ ἔργα
ζητῇς, οἱ λόγοι πολλοί, ἢν δὲ ἀπὸ τῶν λόγων κρίνειν
ἐθέλῃς, τὸν βίον ἀξιοῦσι σκοπεῖν.

16   Τοιγαροῦν ἐμπέπλησται πᾶσα πόλις τῆς τοιαύτης
ῥᾳδιουργίας, καὶ μάλιστα τῶν Διογένη καὶ Ἀντι-
σθένη καὶ Κράτητα ἐπιγραφομένων καὶ ὑπὸ τῷ
κυνὶ ταττομένων, οἳ τὸ μὲν χρήσιμον ὁπόσον
ἔνεστι τῇ φύσει τῶν κυνῶν, οἷον τὸ φυλακτικὸν
ἢ οἰκουρικὸν ἢ φιλοδέσποτον ἢ μνημονικόν,
οὐδαμῶς ἐζηλώκασιν, ὑλακὴν δὲ καὶ λιχνείαν
καὶ ἁρπαγὴν καὶ ἀφροδίσια συχνὰ καὶ κολακείαν
καὶ τὸ σαίνειν τὸν διδόντα καὶ περὶ τραπέζας
ἔχειν, ταῦτα ἀκριβῶς ἐκπεπονήκασιν.

17   Ὄψει τοίνυν μετὰ μικρὸν οἷα ἔσται. οἱ γὰρ
ἐκ τῶν ἐργαστηρίων ἅπαντες ἀναπηδήσαντες ἐρή-
μους τὰς τέχνας ἐάσουσιν ὅταν ὁρῶσι σφᾶς μέν,
πονοῦντας καὶ κάμνοντας ἕωθεν ἐς ἑσπέραν ἐπικε-
κυφότας τοῖς ἔργοις, μόγις ἀποζῶντας ἐκ τῆς
τοιαύτης μισθαρνίας, ἀργοὺς δὲ καὶ γόητας ἀνθρώπους ἐν ἅπασιν ἀφθόνοις βιοῦντας, αἰτοῦντας
μὲν τυραννικῶς, λαμβάνοντας δὲ προχείρως, ἀγαν-
ακτοῦντας δέ, εἰ μὴ λάβοιεν, οὐκ ἐπαινοῦντας δέ,
οὐδ᾽ εἰ λάβοιεν. ταῦτα ὁ ἐπὶ Κρόνου βίος δοκεῖ
αὐτοῖς καὶ ἀτεχνῶς τὸ μέλι αὐτὸ ἐς τὰ στόματα
ἐσρεῖν ἐκ τοῦ οὐρανοῦ.

18   Καὶ ἧττον ἂν δεινὸν τὸ πρᾶγμα ἦν, εἰ τοιοῦτοι
ὄντες μηδὲν εἰς ἡμᾶς ἄλλο ἐξύβριζον· οἱ δέ, μάλα

THE RUNAWAYS

tolerate investigation if you question them ever so
temperately and concisely; at once they begin
shouting and take refuge in their peculiar citadel,
abusiveness and a ready staff. Also, if you ask about
their works, their words are copious, and if you wish
to judge them by their words, they want you to
consider their lives.

Consequently, every city is filled with such up-
starts, particularly with those who enter the names
of Diogenes, Antisthenes, and Crates as their patrons
and enlist in the army of the dog. Those fellows have
not in any way imitated the good that there is in the
nature of dogs, as, for instance, guarding property,
keeping at home, loving their masters, or remember-
ing kindnesses, but their barking, gluttony, thievish-
ness, excessive interest in females, truckling, fawning
upon people who give them things, and hanging
about tables—all this they have copied with painful
accuracy.

You shall see what will happen presently. All the
men in the workshops will spring to their feet and
leave their trades deserted when they see that by
toiling and moiling from morning till night, doubled
over their tasks, they merely eke out a bare existence
from such wage-earning, while idle frauds live in
unlimited plenty, asking for things in a lordly way,
getting them without effort, acting indignant if they
do not, and bestowing no praise even if they do. It
seems to them that this is 'life in the age of Cronus,'
and really that sheer honey is distilling into their
mouths from the sky!

The thing would not be so dreadful if they offended
against us only by being what they are. But
although outwardly and in public they appear very

73

σεμνοὶ καὶ σκυθρωποὶ τὰ ἔξω καὶ τὰ δημόσια
φαινόμενοι, ἢν παιδὸς ὡραίου ἢ γυναικὸς λάβωνται
καλῆς ἢ ἐλπίσωσιν,[1] σιωπᾶν ἄξιον οἷα ποιοῦσιν.
ἔνιοι δὲ καὶ ξένων τῶν σφετέρων γυναῖκας ἀπάγουσι μοιχεύσοντες κατὰ τὸν Ἰλιέα ἐκεῖνον νεανίσκον, ὡς φιλοσοφοῖεν δὴ καὶ αὐται· εἶτα κοινὰς
αὐτὰς ἅπασι τοῖς ξυνοῦσι προθέμενοι Πλάτωνός
τι δόγμα οἴονται ποιεῖν, οὐκ εἰδότες ὅπως ὁ
ἱερὸς ἐκεῖνος ἠξίου κοινὰς ἡγεῖσθαι τὰς γυναῖκας.

19 ἃ μὲν γὰρ ἐν τοῖς συμποσίοις δρῶσιν καὶ ἃ μεθύ-
σκονται, μακρὸν ἂν εἴη λέγειν. καὶ ταῦτα ποιοῦσι
πῶς οἴει κατηγοροῦντες αὐτοὶ μέθης καὶ μοιχείας
καὶ λαγνείας καὶ φιλαργυρίας· οὐδὲν γοῦν οὕτως
εὕροις ἂν[2] ἄλλο ἄλλῳ ἐναντίον ὡς τοὺς λόγους
αὐτῶν καὶ τὰ ἔργα. οἷον κολακείαν μισεῖν φασιν,
κολακείας ἕνεκα τὸν Γναθωνίδην ἢ τὸν Στρου-
θίαν ὑπερβαλέσθαι δυνάμενοι. ἀληθεύειν τοὺς ἄλλους προτρέποντες, οὐκ ἂν οὐδὲ κινῆσαι τὴν
γλῶτταν μὴ μετὰ τοῦ καὶ ψεύσασθαι δύναιντο.
ἡδονὴ πᾶσιν ἐχθρὸν τῷ λόγῳ καὶ ὁ Ἐπίκουρος
πολέμιος, ἔργῳ δὲ διὰ ταύτην ἅπαντα πράττουσιν.
τὸ δ' ὀξύχολον καὶ μικραίτιον καὶ πρὸς ὀργὴν
ῥάδιον ὑπὲρ τὰ βρεφύλλια τὰ νεογνά· γέλωτα
γοῦν οὐ μικρὸν παρέχουσι τοῖς θεωμένοις, ὁπόταν
ὑπὸ τῆς τυχούσης αἰτίας ἐπιζέσῃ μὲν αὐτοῖς ἡ

---

[1] Fritzsche reads καὶ λήσειν ἐλπίσωσιν. But Lucian is
thinking of incidents like that in his *Symp.*, 15 (I, p. 426).
[2] ἂν Bélin; not in MSS.

---

[1] There is here an allusion to "Scarabee"; see below,
§ 30.
[2] Paris.   [3] Plato, *Republ.*, V, 459 E.

THE RUNAWAYS

reverend and stern, if they get a handsome boy
or a pretty woman in their clutches or hope to, it is
best to veil their conduct in silence. Some even
carry off the wives of their hosts,[1] to seduce them after
the pattern of that young Trojan,[2] pretending that
the women are going to become philosophers; then
they tender them, as common property, to all their
associates and think they are carrying out a tenet of
Plato's,[3] when they do not know on what terms that
holy man thought it right for women to be so
regarded. What they do at drinking-parties, how
intoxicated they become, would make a long story.
And while they do all this, you cannot imagine how
they berate drunkenness and adultery and lewdness
and covetousness. Indeed you could not find any
two things so opposed to each other as their words
and their deeds. For instance, they claim to hate
toadying, when as far as that goes they are able to
outdo Gnathonides or Struthias;[4] and although
they exhort everyone else to tell the truth, they
themselves cannot so much as move their tongues
except in a lie. To all of them pleasure is nominally
an odious thing and Epicurus a foeman; but in
practice they do everything for the sake of it. In
irascibility, pettishness, and proneness to anger they
are beyond young children; indeed, they give no little
amusement to onlookers when their blood boils up in

[4] Gluttonous parasites of the New Comedy. Struthias,
whose name is evidently connected with the greediness of the
sparrow, figures in the *Toady (Colax)* of Menander. The
play in which Gnathonides appeared is unknown, but Gnatho
("Jowl") is mentioned by Plutarch to exemplify a typical
parasite (*Symp.*, VII, 6, 2), and in utilising part of the *Toady*
for his *Eunuchus* Terence changed the name of the chief rôle
from Struthias to Gnatho.

75

χολή, πελιδνοὶ δὲ τὴν χροιὰν βλέπωνται, ἰταμόν
τι καὶ παράφορον δεδορκότες, καὶ ἀφροῦ, μᾶλλον
δὲ ἰοῦ, μεστὸν αὐτοῖς ᾖ τὸ στόμα.

20 Μὴ σύ γε κεῖθι τύχοις, ὅτε ὁ μιαρὸς ἐκεῖνος
ἐκχεῖται βόρβορος, "Χρυσίον μὲν ἢ ἀργύριον,
Ἡράκλεις, οὐδὲ κεκτῆσθαι ἀξιῶ·[1] ὀβολὸς ἱκανός,
ὡς θέρμους πριαίμην· ποτὸν γὰρ ἢ κρήνη ἢ ποταμὸς παρέξει." καὶ μετ' ὀλίγον αἰτοῦσιν οὐκ
ὀβολοὺς οὐδὲ δραχμὰς ὀλίγας, ἀλλὰ πλούτους
ὅλους, ὥστε τίς ἔμπορος τοσοῦτον ἀπὸ τοῦ φόρτου
ἐμπολήσειεν ἂν ὅσον τούτοις φιλοσοφία ἐς χρη-
ματισμὸν συντελεῖ; εἶτ' ἐπειδὰν ἱκανῶς συλλέ-
ξωνται καὶ ἐπισιτίσωνται, ἀπορρίψαντες ἐκεῖνο τὸ
δύστηνον τριβώνιον ἀγροὺς ἐνίοτε καὶ ἐσθῆτας τῶν
μαλθακῶν ἐπρίαντο καὶ παῖδας κομήτας καὶ
συνοικίας ὅλας, μακρὰ χαίρειν φράσαντες τῇ
πήρᾳ τῇ Κράτητος καὶ τῷ τρίβωνι τῷ Ἀντισθέ-
νους καὶ τῷ πίθῳ τῷ Διογένους.

21 Οἱ ἰδιῶται δὲ ταῦτα ὁρῶντες καταπτύουσιν
ἤδη φιλοσοφίας καὶ ἅπαντας εἶναι τοιούτους
οἴονται κἀμὲ τῆς διδασκαλίας αἰτιῶνται, ὥστε
πολλοῦ ἤδη χρόνου ἀδύνατόν μοι γεγένηται κἂν
ἕνα τινὰ προσαγαγέσθαι αὐτῶν, ἀλλὰ τὸ τῆς
Πηνελόπης ἐκεῖνο πάσχω· ὁπόσον γὰρ δὴ ἐγὼ
ἐξυφήνω, τοῦτο ἐν ἀκαρεῖ αὖθις ἀναλύεται. ἡ
Ἀμαθία δὲ καὶ ἡ Ἀδικία ἐπιγελῶσιν, ὁρῶσαι
ἀνεξέργαστον ἡμῖν τὸ ἔργον καὶ ἀνήνυτον τὸν πόνον.

---

[1] ἀξιῶ N : ἀξιῶν ΓΜΗΧΒΟ.

them for some trivial reason, so that they look livid in colour, with a reckless, insane stare, and foam (or rather, venom) fills their mouths.

And " may you never chance to be there "[1] when that vile filth of theirs is exuded! " As to gold or silver, Heracles! I do not want even to own it. An obol is enough, so that I can buy lupines, for a spring or a stream will supply me with drink." Then after a little they demand, not obols nor a few drachmas, but whole fortunes. What shipman could make as much from his cargoes as philosophy contributes to these fellows in the way of gain? And then, when they have levied tribute and stocked themselves up to their heart's content, throwing off that ill-conditioned philosopher's cloak, they buy farms every now and then, and luxurious clothing, and long-haired pages, and whole apartment-houses, bidding a long farewell to the wallet of Crates, the mantle of Antisthenes, and the jar of Diogenes.

The unschooled, seeing all this, now spit scornfully at philosophy, thinking that all of us are like this and blaming me for my teachings, so that for a long time now it has been impossible for me to win over a single one of them. I am in the same fix as Penelope,[2] for truly all that I weave is instantly unravelled again; and Stupidity and Wrongdoing laugh in my face to see that I cannot bring my work to completion and my toil to an end.

[1] The words are those of Circe to Odysseus, alluding to Charybdis (*Odyssey*, XII, 106).
[2] The story of Penelope's web is told several times in the *Odyssey* ; II, 93–110; XIX, 138–156; XXIV, 129–146.

ΖΕΥΣ

22 Οἷα, ὦ θεοί, πέπονθεν ἡμῖν ἡ Φιλοσοφία πρὸς
τῶν καταράτων ἐκείνων. ὥστε ὥρα σκοπεῖν
ὅ τι καὶ πρακτέον ἢ ὅπως αὐτοὺς μετελευστέον.
ὁ μὲν γὰρ κεραυνὸς ἀπάγει μιᾷ πληγῇ καὶ ὁ
θάνατος ταχύς.

ΑΠΟΛΛΩΝ

Ἐγώ σοι,[1] ὦ πάτερ, ὑποθήσομαι· μισῶ γὰρ
καὶ αὐτὸς ἤδη τοὺς ἀλαζόνας ἀμούσους ὄντας,
ὑπὲρ τῶν Μουσῶν ἀγανακτῶν. κεραυνοῦ μὲν
γὰρ ἢ τῆς σῆς δεξιᾶς οὐδαμῶς ἐκεῖνοι ἄξιοι,
τὸν Ἑρμῆν δὲ αὐτοκράτορα, εἰ δοκεῖ, τῆς κολάσεως κατάπεμψον ἐπ' αὐτούς, ὃς ἅτε δὴ περὶ
λόγους ἔχων καὶ αὐτὸς τάχιστα εἴσεται τούς τε
ὀρθῶς φιλοσοφοῦντας καὶ τοὺς μή. εἶτα τοὺς μὲν
ἐπαινέσεται, ὡς τὸ εἰκός, οἱ δὲ κολασθήσονται
ὅπως ἂν ἐκείνῳ παρὰ τὸν καιρὸν δοκῇ.

ΖΕΥΣ

23 Εὖ λέγεις, ὦ Ἄπολλον. ἀλλὰ καὶ σύ, ὦ
Ἡράκλεις, ἅμα καὶ τὴν Φιλοσοφίαν αὐτὴν ἔχοντες
ἄπιτε ὡς τάχιστα εἰς τὸν βίον. τρισκαιδέκατον
γοῦν ἆθλον οἴου τοῦτον οὐ σμικρὸν ἐκτελέσειν,
ἢν ἐκκόψῃς μιαρὰ οὕτω καὶ ἀναίσχυντα θηρία.

ΗΡΑΚΛΗΣ

Καὶ μὴν ἄμεινον ἦν, ὦ πάτερ, τὴν κόπρον
ἐκκαθᾶραι αὖθις τὴν Αὐγέου ἢ τούτοις συμπλέ-
κεσθαι. ἀπίωμεν δ' ὅμως.

---

[1] σοι Fritzsche: τοι MSS.

THE RUNAWAYS

ZEUS

Ye gods! what treatment our dear Philosophy has had from those scoundrels! It is high time, then, to see what is to be done and how they are to be punished. Well, the thunderbolt despatches at a single blow, and the death is a swift one.

APOLLO

I will offer you a suggestion, father, for I myself have come to detest the knaves; the Muses mean nothing to them, so I am indignant on behalf of the Nine. Those fellows are by no means worthy of a thunderbolt or of that right hand of yours. Send Hermes down to get after them, if you think best, with unlimited powers in the matter of their punishment. As he himself is interested in argumentation, he will very soon know those who are genuine students of philosophy and those who are not. Then he will commend the former, naturally, and the latter will be punished as he sees fit in the circumstances.

ZEUS

A good idea, Apollo. But you go too, Heracles; take along Philosophy herself and all be off, as quickly as you can, to the world. Bear in mind that you will be doing a thirteenth labour of no mean order if you exterminate such pestilential, shameless beasts.

HERACLES

On my word, father, I should have preferred to clean out the muck of Augeas once more, rather than to get involved with these creatures. Let us be off, however.

ΦΙΛΟΣΟΦΙΑ

Ἄκουσα μέν, ἀκολουθητέον δὲ κατὰ τὰ δό-
ξαντα τῷ πατρί.

ΕΡΜΗΣ

24 Κατίωμεν, ὡς κἂν ὀλίγους αὐτῶν ἐπιτρίψωμεν
σήμερον. ποίαν δὲ χρὴ τραπέσθαι, ὦ Φιλοσοφία; σὺ γὰρ οἶσθα ὅπου εἰσίν. ἢ πρόδηλον
ὅτι ἐν τῇ Ἑλλάδι;

ΦΙΛΟΣΟΦΙΑ

Οὐδαμῶς, ἢ πάνυ ὀλίγοι, ὅσοι ὀρθῶς φιλοσοφοῦσιν, ὦ Ἑρμῆ. οὗτοι δὲ οὐδὲν Ἀττικῆς
πενίας δέονται, ἀλλ᾽ ἔνθα πολὺς χρυσὸς ἢ ἄργυρος
ὀρύττεται, ἐκεῖ που ζητητέοι εἰσὶν ἡμῖν.

ΕΡΜΗΣ

Οὐκοῦν εὐθὺ τῆς Θρᾴκης ἀπιτέον.

ΗΡΑΚΛΗΣ

Εὖ λέγεις, καὶ ἡγήσομαί γε ὑμῖν τῆς ὁδοῦ.
οἶδα γὰρ τὰ Θρᾳκῶν ἅπαντα, συχνάκις ἐπελθών.
καί μοι τήνδε ἤδη τραπώμεθα.

ΕΡΜΗΣ

Ποίαν λέγεις;

ΗΡΑΚΛΗΣ

25 Ὁρᾶτε, ὦ Ἑρμῆ καὶ Φιλοσοφία, δύο μὲν
ὄρη μέγιστα καὶ κάλλιστα ὀρῶν ἁπάντων (Αἷμός
ἐστιν τὸ μεῖζον, ἡ καταντικρὺ δὲ Ῥοδόπη)
πεδίον δὲ ὑποπεπταμένον πάμφορον, ἀπὸ τῶν
προπόδων ἑκατέρων εὐθὺς ἀρξάμενον, καί τινας

THE RUNAWAYS

PHILOSOPHY

I do not want to go with you, but I must, in accordance with father's orders.

HERMES

Let us be going down, so that we may exterminate at least a few of them to-day. What direction should we take, Philosophy? You know where they are. In Greece, no doubt?

PHILOSOPHY

Not by any means, or only a few, those who are genuine students of philosophy, Hermes. These others have no use for Attic poverty; we must look for them in some quarter where much gold or silver is mined.

HERMES

Then we must make straight for Thrace.

HERACLES

Quite right, and indeed I will show you the way, as I know the whole of Thrace from repeated visits. So, if you please, let us now take this direction.

HERMES

What direction do you mean?

HERACLES

Do you see two ranges, Hermes and Philosophy, the highest and most beautiful of all mountains (the higher is Haemus, the one opposite is Rhodope), and a plain of great fertility outspread beneath them, beginning at the very foothills of each? Also,

λόφους τρεῖς πάνυ καλοὺς ἀνεστηκότας, οὐκ
ἀμόρφους τὴν τραχύτητα, οἷον ἀκροπόλεις πολλὰς
τῆς ὑποκειμένης πόλεως. καὶ ἡ πόλις γὰρ ἤδη
φαίνεται.

ΕΡΜΗΣ

Νὴ Δί᾽, ὦ Ἡράκλεις, μεγίστη καὶ καλλίστη
ἁπασῶν· πόρρωθεν γοῦν ἀπολάμπει τὸ κάλλος.
καί τις καὶ ποταμὸς μέγιστος παραμείβεται,
πάνυ ἐν χρῷ ψαύων αὐτῆς.

ΗΡΑΚΛΗΣ

Ἕβρος μὲν οὗτος, ἡ δὲ πόλις ἔργον Φιλίππου
ἐκείνου. καὶ ἡμεῖς ἤδη πρόσγειοι καὶ ὑπονέ-
φελοι·[1] ὥστε ἐπιβαίνωμεν ἀγαθῇ τύχῃ.

ΕΡΜΗΣ

26   Οὕτω γινέσθω. τί δ᾽ οὖν χρὴ ποιεῖν, ἢ πῶς[2]
τὰ θηρία ἐξιχνευτέον;

ΗΡΑΚΛΗΣ

Τοῦτο μὲν σὸν ἤδη ἔργον, ὦ Ἑρμῆ· κῆρυξ
γὰρ εἶ, ὥστε οὐκ ἂν φθάνοις κηρύττων.

ΕΡΜΗΣ

Οὐδὲν τοῦτο χαλεπόν, ἀλλὰ τά γε ὀνόματα
οὐκ ἐπίσταμαι αὐτῶν. σὺ οὖν, Φιλοσοφία, λέγε
οὕστινας ὀνομαστέον, καὶ τὰ σημεῖα προσέτι.

ΦΙΛΟΣΟΦΙΑ

Οὐδὲ αὐτὴ μὲν οἶδα τὸ σαφὲς οἵτινες ὀνομά-
ζονται διὰ τὸ μὴ ξυγγεγενῆσθαί ποτε αὐτοῖς·
ἀπὸ δ᾽ οὖν τῆς ἐπιθυμίας ἣν ἔχουσι περὶ τὰ κτή-

---

[1] ὑπονέφελοι edd.: ἐπινέφελοι MSS.
[2] ἢ πῶς Bekker: ὅπως MSS.

three very beautiful eminences standing up, not so rough as to be shapeless? They look like multiple citadels belonging to the city beneath them. For the city, too, is now in sight.

HERMES

Yes, by Zeus, Heracles, the greatest and loveliest of all cities! In fact, its beauty is radiant from afar. And also, a very large river flows past it, coming quite close to it.

HERACLES

That is the Hebrus, and the city was built by the famous Philip.[1] We are now close to earth and the clouds are above us, so let us make a landing, with the blessing of Heaven.

HERMES

Very well. But what is to be done now? How are we to track the beasts out?

HERACLES

That is up to you, Hermes; you are a crier, so be quick and do your office.

HERMES

Nothing hard about that, but I do not know their names. Tell me, Philosophy, what I am to call them, and their marks of identification as well.

PHILOSOPHY

I myself do not know for certain what they are called, because of my not having had anything to do with them ever. But to judge from the craving for

---

[1] Philippopolis.

ματα, οὐκ ἂν ἁμάρτοις προσκαλῶν Κτήσωνας ἢ
Κτησίππους ἢ Κτησικλέας ἢ Εὐκτήμονας ἢ Πολυ-
κτήτους.

ΕΡΜΗΣ

27 Εὖ λέγεις. ἀλλὰ τίνες οὗτοί εἰσιν ἢ τί περι-
σκοποῦσιν καὶ αὐτοί; μᾶλλον δὲ καὶ προσίασιν καί
τι καὶ ἐρέσθαι θέλουσιν.

ΑΝΗΡ

Ἆρ' ἂν ἔχοιτε ἡμῖν, ὦ ἄνδρες, εἰπεῖν, ἢ σύ,
ὦ βέλτιστε, εἴ τινας τρεῖς γόητας ἅμα εἴδετε καί
τινα γυναῖκα ἐν χρῷ κεκαρμένην εἰς τὸ Λακωνι-
κόν, ἀρρενωπὴν καὶ κομιδῇ ἀνδρικήν;

ΦΙΛΟΣΟΦΙΑ

Παπαῖ, τὰ ἡμέτερα οὗτοι ζητοῦσιν.

ΑΝΗΡ

Πῶς τὰ ὑμέτερα; δραπέται γὰρ ἐκεῖνοι ἅπαντες. ἡμεῖς δὲ τὴν γυναῖκα μάλιστα μέτιμεν
ἠνδραποδισμένην πρὸς αὐτῶν.

ΕΡΜΗΣ

Εἴσεσθε δὴ[1] καθ' ὅ τι καὶ ζητοῦμεν αὐτούς.
τὸ νῦν δὲ ἅμα κηρύττωμεν.
    Εἴ τις εἶδεν[2] ἀνδράποδον Παφλαγονικὸν τῶν
ἀπὸ Σινώπης βαρβάρων, ὄνομα τοιοῦτον οἷον ἀπὸ
κτημάτων, ὕπωχρον, ἐν χρῷ κουρίαν, ἐν γενείῳ
βαθεῖ, πήραν ἐξημμένον καὶ τριβώνιον ἀμπεχό-

---

[1] δὴ Gesner: δὲ MSS.
[2] εἶδεν Fritzsche: not in MSS.

riches which they have, you will not make any mistake if you call them Richman or Richmews or Richrenown or Goodrich or Richards.

HERMES

Right you are.—But who are these people and why are they too looking about them? However, they are coming up and want to ask a question.

HUSBAND

Could you tell us, gentlemen, or you, kind lady, whether you have seen three rogues together, and a woman with her hair closely clipped in the Spartan style, boyish-looking and quite masculine?

PHILOSOPHY

Aha! They are looking for our quarry!

HUSBAND

How yours? Those fellows are all fugitive slaves, and for my part I am particularly in search of the woman, whom they have kidnapped.

HERMES

You will soon find out why we are in search of them. But at present let us make a joint proclamation.

" If anyone has seen a Paphlagonian slave, one of those barbarians from Sinope, with a name of the kind that has 'rich' in it, sallow, close-cropped,[1] wearing a long beard, with a wallet slung from his shoulder and a short cloak about him, quick-

[1] As a Cynic, the man should wear his hair long; but we are informed that he has Stoic leanings (§ 31).

THE WORKS OF LUCIAN

μενον, ὀργίλον, ἄμουσον, τραχύφωνον, λοίδορον,
μηνύειν ἐπὶ ῥητῷ αὐτόν.

ΔΕΣΠΟΤΗΣ Α

28 Ἀνόμοιον, ὦ[1] οὗτος, ὃ κηρύττεις· ὡς ἐκείνῳ
γε ὄνομα ἦν παρ᾽ ἐμοὶ Κάνθαρος, καὶ ἐκόμα δὲ
καὶ τὸ γένειον ἐτίλλετο καὶ τέχνην τὴν ἐμὴν
ἠπίστατο· ἀπέκειρεν γὰρ ἐν τῷ γναφείῳ καθή-
μενος ὁπόσον περιττὸν τοῖς ἱματίοις τῶν κροκύδων
ἐπανθεῖ.

ΦΙΛΟΣΟΦΙΑ

Ἐκεῖνος αὐτός ἐστιν, ὁ οἰκέτης ὁ σός, ἀλλὰ
νῦν φιλοσόφῳ ἔοικεν ἀκριβῶς ἑαυτὸν ἐπιγνάψας.[2]

ΔΕΣΠΟΤΗΣ Α

Ὢ τῆς τόλμης, ὁ Κάνθαρος φιλοσοφεῖ, φησίν, ἡμῶν δὲ οὐδεὶς λόγος.[3]

ΔΕΣΠΟΤΗΣ Β

Ἀμέλει ἅπαντας ἀνευρήσομεν· ξυνίησιν γάρ,
ὥς φησιν, αὕτη.

ΕΡΜΗΣ

29 Τίς δ᾽ οὗτος ἄλλος ὁ προσιών ἐστιν, ὦ Ἡράκλεις,
ὁ καλός, ὁ τὴν κιθάραν;

ΗΡΑΚΛΗΣ

Ὀρφεύς ἐστιν, σύμπλους ἐπὶ τῆς Ἀργοῦς ἐμός,
ἥδιστος κελευστῶν ἁπάντων· πρὸς γοῦν τὴν
ᾠδὴν αὐτοῦ ἥκιστα ἐκάμνομεν ἐρέττοντες. χαῖρε,

[1] αὐτόν. ‖ ἀνόμοιον, ὦ Harmon : αὐτονόμῳ. ‖ νοῶ MSS.
[2] ἐπιγνάψας Γ²Χ²ΗΒΑ : ἐπιγράψας ΓΧ¹Ν.
[3] In Γ the double point (:) indicating a change of speaker
follows φησίν, not λογος.

86

tempered, uneducated, harsh-voiced, and abusive,
let him give information for the stipulated reward."

FIRST SLAVE-OWNER

Your proclamation does not tally, man! His name
when I had him was Scarabee; furthermore, he
wore his hair long, kept his chin hairless, and knew my
trade. It was his business to sit in my fuller's shop
and shear off the excessive nap that makes cloaks
fuzzy.

PHILOSOPHY

That is the very man, your slave; but now he
looks like a philosopher, for he has given himself a
thorough dry-cleaning.

FIRST SLAVE-OWNER (to Second and Third)

The impudence of him! Scarabee is setting up
for a philosopher, she says, and we do not enter into
his speculations at all!

SECOND SLAVE-OWNER

Never mind, we shall find them all, for this woman
knows them, by what she says.

HERMES

Who is this other person coming up, Heracles,
the handsome man with the lyre?

HERACLES

It is Orpheus, my shipmate on the Argo, the
most tuneful of all chanteymen. Indeed, as we
rowed to his singing, we hardly grew tired at all.

87

ὦ ἄριστε καὶ μουσικώτατε Ὀρφεῦ· οὐκ ἐπιλέ-
λησαι γάρ που Ἡρακλέους.

ΟΡΦΕΥΣ

Νὴ καὶ ὑμεῖς γε, ὦ Φιλοσοφία καὶ Ἡράκλεις καὶ
Ἑρμῆ. ἀλλὰ καιρὸς ἀποδιδόναι τὰ μήνυτρα,
ὡς ἔγωγε πάνυ σαφῶς ὃν ζητεῖτε οἶδα.

ΕΡΜΗΣ

Οὐκοῦν δεῖξον, ὦ παῖ Καλλιόπης, ἔνθα ἐστίν·
χρυσίου γὰρ οὐδέν, οἶμαι, δέῃ σοφὸς ὤν.

ΟΡΦΕΥΣ

Εὖ φής. ἐγὼ δὲ τὴν μὲν οἰκίαν δείξαιμ' ἂν
ὑμῖν ἔνθα οἰκεῖ, αὐτὸν δὲ οὐκ ἄν, ὡς μὴ κακῶς
ἀκούοιμι πρὸς αὐτοῦ· μιαρὸς γὰρ εἰς ὑπερβολὴν
καὶ μόνον τοῦτο ἐκμεμελέτηκεν.

ΕΡΜΗΣ

Δεῖξον μόνον.

ΟΡΦΕΥΣ

Αὕτη πλησίον. ἐγὼ δὲ ἄπειμι ὑμῖν ἐκποδών,
ὡς μηδ' ἴδοιμι αὐτόν.

ΦΙΛΟΣΟΦΙΑ

30 Ἐπίσχες. οὐ γυναικός ἐστι φωνὴ ῥαψωδούσης
τι τῶν Ὁμήρου;

ΕΡΜΗΣ

Νὴ Δία· ἀλλ' ἀκούσωμεν ὅ τι καὶ λέγει.

THE RUNAWAYS

Good-day to you, Orpheus, best of men and first of musicians. Surely you have not forgotten Heracles.

ORPHEUS

A very good-day to you also, Philosophy, Heracles, and Hermes. But the time has come to pay your reward, since I am very well acquainted with the man for whom you are looking.

HERMES

Then show us where he is, son of Calliope, for you have no need of gold, I take it, being a wise man.

ORPHEUS

You are right. I will show you the house where he lives, but not the man himself, so as not to be slanged by him. He is excessively foul-mouthed; that is the only thing he has thoroughly mastered.

HERMES

Only show us.

ORPHEUS

Here it is, close by. I am going away from your neighbourhood, so that I may not even see him.

PHILOSOPHY

Hold! Is not that the voice of a woman, reciting something of Homer's?

HERMES

Yes, surely; but let us hear what she is saying.

ΓΥΝΗ [1]

Ἐχθρὸς γάρ μοι κεῖνος ὁμῶς Ἀΐδαο πύλησιν,
ὃς χρυσὸν φιλέει μὲν ἐνὶ φρεσίν, ἄλλο δὲ εἴπῃ.

ΕΡΜΗΣ

Οὐκοῦν τὸν Κάνθαρόν σοι μισητέον.

ΓΥΝΗ

Ξεινοδόκον [2] κακὰ ῥέξεν, ὅ κεν φιλότητα
παράσχῃ.

ΑΝΗΡ

Περὶ ἐμοῦ τοῦτο τὸ ἔπος, οὗ τὴν γυναῖκα
ᾤχετο ἀπάγων διότι αὐτὸν ὑπεδεξάμην.

ΓΥΝΗ

Οἰνοβαρές, κυνὸς ὄμματ' ἔχων, κραδίην δ'
        ἐλάφοιο,
οὔτε ποτ' ἐν πολέμῳ ἐναρίθμιος οὔτ' ἐνὶ βουλῇ,
Θερσῖτ' ἀκριτόμυθε, κακῶν πανάριστε κολοιῶν
μάψ, ἀτὰρ οὐ κατὰ κόσμον, ἐριζέμεναι βασι-
        λεῦσιν.

ΔΕΣΠΟΤΗΣ Α

Εἰκότως τῷ καταράτῳ [3] τὰ ἔπη.

---

[1] δραπετίς (N) edd. prior to Bekker.
[2] μισητέον: ξεινοδόκον Γ, thus giving (by the double point)
ξεινοδόκον . . . παράσχῃ to the Wife. Other MSS. and all
previous editions give these words to Hermes, reading μισητέον ὃς ξεινοδόκον.
[3] τῷ καταράτῳ Harmon: τοῦ καταράτου MSS.

THE RUNAWAYS

WOMAN

Hateful to me that man, no less than the portals of
  Hades,
Who in his heart loves gold, and yet maintains that
  he does not.[1]

HERMES

Then you must needs hate Scarabee!

WOMAN

Ever his host he abuseth, if anyone showeth him
  kindness.[2]

HUSBAND

That verse refers to me, for he went off with my
wife because I took him in.

WOMAN

Heavy with wine, dog-eyed, with the timid heart of
  a roe-deer,
Never of any account in the fray or in giving of
  counsel,
Loose-mouthed fool, Thersites, of evil jackdaws the
  foremost
Idle strife with kings to promote in no spirit of
  order![3]

FIRST SLAVE-OWNER

The verses just fit the scoundrel!

[1] *Iliad*, IX, 312 (= *Odyssey*, XIV, 156) and 313, which reads
ὅς χ' ἕτερον μὲν κεύθῃ ἐνὶ φρεσίν, ἄλλο δὲ εἴπῃ.
[2] *Iliad*, III, 354, with a slight change, ῥέξεν for ῥέξαι.
[3] *Iliad*, I, 225; II, 202, 246 (the close is Lucian's: Homer
has λιγύς περ ἐὼν ἀγορητής), and 214.

ΓΥΝΗ

Πρόσθε κύων, ὄπιθεν δὲ λέων, μέσση δὲ
χίμαιρα
δεινὸν ἀποπνείουσα τρίτου κυνὸς ἀγριον [1] ὁρμήν.

ΑΝΗΡ

31 Οἴμοι, γύναι, ὅσα πέπονθας ὑπὸ κυνῶν τοσούτων.
φασὶ δ' αὐτὴν καὶ κυεῖν ἀπ' αὐτῶν.

ΕΡΜΗΣ

Θάρρει, Κέρβερόν τινα τέξεταί σοι ἢ Γηρυόνην, ὡς ἔχοι ὁ Ἡρακλῆς οὗτος αὖθις πόνον. ἀλλὰ
καὶ προΐασιν, ὥστε οὐδὲν δεῖ κόπτειν τὴν θύραν.

ΔΕΣΠΟΤΗΣ Α

Ἔχω σε, ὦ Κάνθαρε. νῦν σιωπᾷς; φέρ'
ἴδωμεν ἅτινά σοι ἡ πήρα ἔχει, θέρμους ἴσως ἢ
ἄρτου τρύφος.[2] οὐ μὰ Δί', ἀλλὰ ζώνην χρυσίου.

ΗΡΑΚΛΗΣ

Μὴ θαυμάσῃς· Κυνικὸς γὰρ ἔφασκεν εἶναι τὸ
πρόσθεν ἐπὶ τῆς Ἑλλάδος, ἐνταῦθα δὲ Χρυσίπ-
πειος ἀκριβῶς ἐστιν.[3] τοιγαροῦν Κλεάνθην οὐκ

---

[1] ἀγριον Fritzsche : ἀγρίου MSS.
[2] Γ has double points after ἔχει and τρύφος, but the fact
that μὴ θαυμάσῃς is addressed to one person favours running
the speech on rather than (e.g.) giving θέρμους . . . τρύφος
to ΔΕΣΠΟΤΗΣ Β.
[3] Double point in Γ.

THE RUNAWAYS

WOMAN

Dog in the fore-parts, aye, and a lion behind; in the
middle a she-goat,
Shedding the terrible reek of the third dog's furious
onslaught![1]

HUSBAND

Dear me, wife! how outrageously you have been
treated by all those dogs! It is even said that they
have lined her.

HERMES

No fear, you will soon have her bringing into the
world a Cerberus or a Geryon, to make more work
for Heracles here.[2]—But they are coming out, so
there is no need to knock at the door.

FIRST SLAVE-OWNER

I've got you, Scarabee! Now you have nothing
to say, have you? Come, let us see what your wallet
has in it, lupines, no doubt, or a crust of bread. No,
by Zeus! A purse of gold!

HERACLES

Don't be surprised! Formerly, in Greece, he
claimed to be a Cynic, but here he reveals himself
in his true colours as a Chrysippean. Therefore you

---

[1] *Iliad*, VI, 181 and 182 with liberal alterations. The
original is: Πρόσθε λέων, ὄπιθεν δὲ δράκων, μέσση δὲ χίμαιρα
δεινὸν ἀποπνείουσα πυρὸς μένος αἰθομένοιο.

[2] The progeny of three Cynics is expected to have three
heads, like the dog Cerberus, whom Heracles, as his eleventh
labour, brought up from Hades, or three bodies, like Geryon,
whose cattle Heracles lifted as his tenth labour.

εἰς μακρὰν αὐτὸν ὄψει· κρεμήσεται γὰρ ἀπὸ τοῦ
πώγωνος οὕτω μιαρὸς ὤν.

ΔΕΣΠΟΤΗΣ Β

32   Σὺ δέ, ὦ κακέ, οὐ Ληκυθίων οὑμὸς δραπέτης
τυγχάνεις[1]; οὐ μὲν οὖν ἄλλος. ὦ τοῦ γέλωτος.
εἶτα τί οὐκ ἂν γένοιτο; καὶ Ληκυθίων φιλοσοφεῖ.

ΕΡΜΗΣ

Ὁ τρίτος δὲ οὗτος ἀδέσποτος ὑμῖν ἐστιν;

ΔΕΣΠΟΤΗΣ Γ

Οὐδαμῶς, ἀλλ᾽ ὁ δεσπότης ἐγὼ ἑκὼν ἀφίημι
αὐτὸν ἀπολωλέναι.

ΕΡΜΗΣ

Ὅτι τί;

ΔΕΣΡΟΤΗΣ Γ

Ὅτι δεινῶς τῶν ὑποσάθρων ἐστίν. τὸ δ᾽
ὄνομα Μυρόπνουν αὐτὸν ἐκαλοῦμεν.

ΕΡΜΗΣ

Ἡράκλεις ἀλεξίκακε, ἀκούεις; ἔπειτα πήρα
καὶ βάκτρον.—καὶ αὐτὸς ἀπόλαβε τὴν γυναῖκα σύ.

---

[1] τυγχάνεις Γ¹: τυγχάνεις ὤν Γ², cett., edd. Cf. Plato,
Gorg., 502 B and *Rep.* 369 B, cited by Goodwin, *G.M.T.*,
§ 902, and references in F. Karsten, *de Ellipseos Usu Luc.*
(1889), p. 36, including from Lucian *Eun.*, 2, *Abd.*, 15, *Vit.
Auct.*, 19; cf. also below, *Eun.*, 8.

shall soon see him a Cleanthes, for he is going to be
hung up by the beard because he is such a villain.[1]

SECOND SLAVE-OWNER

And you, scoundrel! are you not Pomander, who
ran away from me? Nobody else! O how you
make me laugh! After that, what cannot happen?
Even Pomander a philosopher!

HERMES

This third fellow—has he no master among you?

THIRD SLAVE-OWNER

Yes, I am his master, but even so, I gladly consign
him to perdition!

HERMES

Why?

THIRD SLAVE-OWNER

Because he is a fearful sort of rotter. The name
we used to call him was Stinkadore.

HERMES

Heracles, deliver us! do you hear that? And
then wallet and staff! Here, you! (to HUSBAND)
Take away your wife, yourself!

---

[1] Lucian is playing on names here. When Scarabee was
a Cynic, he had gone to the " dogs." Now, as a devotee of
gold, he can only be styled a Chrysippean; ergo a Stoic.
It may be that Lucian is japing at something in the history
of Cleanthes with his talk about beards and hanging, but
there is no evidence except a late scholium on *Longaevi*, 19,
which says that Cleanthes died of starvation or strangulation.
Anyhow, hanging Scarabee up by the beard will certainly
make a " Famous Posy " of him.

THE WORKS OF LUCIAN

ΑΝΗΡ

Μηδαμῶς. οὐκ ἂν ἀπολάβοιμι βιβλίον μοι
τῶν παλαιῶν κυοῦσαν.

ΕΡΜΗΣ

Πῶς βιβλίον;

ΑΝΗΡ

Ἔστιν τι, ὦ ἀγαθέ, Τρικάρανος βιβλίον.

ΕΡΜΗΣ

Οὐδὲν ἄτοπον, ἐπεὶ καὶ Τριφάλης.[1]

ΦΙΛΟΣΟΦΙΑ

33 Σόν, ὦ Ἑρμῆ, δικάζειν τὸ μετὰ τοῦτο.

ΕΡΜΗΣ

Οὕτω μοι δοκεῖ, ταύτην μέν, ἵνα μηδὲν τέρας
μηδὲ πολυκέφαλον τέκῃ, οἴχεσθαι παρὰ τὸν
ἄνδρα ὀπίσω ἐς τὴν Ἑλλάδα, τὼ δύο δὲ τούτω
δραπετίσκω παραδοθέντε τοῖν δεσπόταιν μανθάνειν ἃ πρὸ τοῦ, τὸν μὲν ἀποπλύνειν τὰς ῥυπώσας
τῶν ὀθονῶν, τὸν Ληκυθίωνα, τὸν Μυρόπνουν δὲ
αὖθις ἀκεῖσθαι τῶν ἱματίων τὰ διερρωγότα,
μαλάχῃ γε πρότερον μαστιγωθέντε.[2] ἔπειτα καὶ

---

[1] MSS. add ὁ (not in N) τῶν κωμικῶν εἷς, which I excise as
a patent gloss, and a mistaken one.
[2] μαστιγωθέντε De Jong: μαστιγωθέντα MSS.

---

[1] The book called *Three-Headed* was an attack on Athens,
Sparta, and Thebes, attributed to Theopompus (cf. below, p.
409) but probably written by Anaximenes.
[2] The *Triphales* of Aristophanes, supposed to have been a
scurrilous satire on Alcibiades.

THE RUNAWAYS

HUSBAND

Never in the world! I don't care to take her away with an old book under her apron.

HERMES

Book? What do you mean?

HUSBAND

My dear fellow, there is a book called Tricipitine.[1]

HERMES

Nothing surprising in that, as there is one called Triphallic.[2]

PHILOSOPHY

It is for you, Hermes, to give judgement now.

HERMES

This is my decision. As for the woman, to insure against her bringing into the world anything portentous or many-headed, she shall go back to Greece to live with her husband. This pair of runaway slaves shall be turned over to their masters and continue to learn their former trades; Pomander to wash dirty linen, Stinkadore once again to mend torn cloaks; but first they shall both be beaten with mallows.[3] Finally, this fellow (to SCARABEE)

[3] This meant a good caning, for the mallow that is meant is the kind that according to Theophrastus "grows tall and becomes tree-like" and "becomes as great as a spear, and men accordingly use it as a walking-stick" (Lavatera arborea; see Sir A. Hort's Theophrastus, *Enquiry into Plants* (L.C.L.), Vol. I, p. 25, and Vol. II, p. 463). But probably its prescription by Lucian in this and other similar cases is due in part at least to the implication of "softness" in the name.

τοῦτον παραδοθῆναι τοῖς πιττωταῖς, ὡς ἀπόλοιτο
παρατιλλόμενος τὰ πρῶτα, ῥυπώσῃ προσέτι καὶ
γυναικείᾳ τῇ πίττῃ, εἶτα ἐς τὸν Αἶμον ἀναχθέντα
γυμνὸν ἐπὶ τῆς χιόνος μένειν συμπεποδισμένον
τὼ πόδε.

ΚΑΝΘΑΡΟΣ

Φεῦ τῶν κακῶν, ὀτοτοῖ, παππαπαιάξ.

ΔΕΣΠΟΤΗΣ Α

Τί τοῦτο παρεντίθης τῶν τραγικῶν σου[4] δια-
λόγων; ἀλλ᾽ ἀκολούθει παρὰ τοὺς πιττωτὰς
ἤδη, ἀποδυσάμενός γε πρότερον τὴν λεοντῆν,
ὡς γνωσθῇς ὄνος ὤν.

---

[4] σου Γ: σὺ other MSS. σου is right; the "dialogues" of
Cantharus are his "diatribes."

shall be turned over to the pitch-plasterers, so that he may be murdered by having his hair pulled out, and with filthy, nasty pitch, besides; then he shall be taken to the summit of Haemus and left standing there naked in the snow with his feet tied together.

SCARABEE

Ah, woe is me! Oh, oh! Alackaday!

FIRST SLAVE-OWNER

Why are you lugging in that quotation out of those melodramatic discourses of yours? Come along with me to the pitch-plasterers now; but first strip off that lion skin, that you may be known for the ass that you are.

TOXARIS, OR FRIENDSHIP

A conversation between Toxaris, a Scythian, and Mnesippus, a Greek, on the subject of friendship. Toxaris explains that the memory of Orestes and Pylades is honoured in Scythia despite the havoc they wrought there because the Scythians regard them as models of loyal friendship, which they hold in the highest esteem. The Greeks, he thinks, are better nowadays at praising than at practising it. To settle the question of superiority, Mnesippus tells five stories of Greek loyalty, and Toxaris five of Scythian : all are declared on oath to be authentic and recent happenings. The outcome, however, can only be a draw because no umpire has been appointed, and the two swear friendship with each other.

The stories, then, are the thing, and the dialogue is just a framing-tale in which to display them. Its time is present. Toxaris, therefore, has nothing but the name in common with the Toxaris whom Lucian in his *Scythian* (Vol. VI) represents to have come to Athens before Anacharsis and to have received worship there after death as the Hero-Physician. Yet this Toxaris too has visited Athens and lived long among the Greeks. The dialogue takes place somewhere in Hellas, but the scene is not definitely fixed. The manner of the allusion to Athens in § 21 seems to exclude that city. The diction of the piece suggests a relatively early date. It may have been written about A.D. 163 in Asia.

The oaths of Toxaris and Mnesippus attest Lucian's mastery of the stock devices of a story-teller rather than the authenticity of his tales. Most of his stories, both Scythian and Greek, are probable enough to be founded on fact. Several are notably romantic, and were probably either made up by Lucian or borrowed from current romances, in which the hero usually had a friend as well as a sweetheart (cf. A. Calderini, *Caritone di Afrodisia*, pp. 104–106). In the matter of Scythia his dependence on literary sources has been indicated by Rostovtzeff (*Skythien und der Bosporus*, pp. 96–99), who has pointed out that his background is realistic and plausible in its general effect, but inaccurate in historical and geographic details, and argues that he drew extensively upon Greek novels with a Scythian plot.

ΤΟΞΑΡΙΣ Η ΦΙΛΙΑ

ΜΝΗΣΙΠΠΟΣ

1 Τί φῄς, ὦ Τόξαρι ; θύετε Ὀρέστῃ καὶ Πυλάδῃ ὑμεῖς οἱ Σκύθαι καὶ θεοὺς εἶναι πεπιστεύκατε αὐτούς ;

ΤΟΞΑΡΙΣ

Θύομεν, ὦ Μνήσιππε, θύομεν, οὐ μὴν θεούς γε οἰόμενοι εἶναι, ἀλλὰ ἄνδρας ἀγαθούς.

ΜΝΗΣΙΠΠΟΣ

Νόμος δὲ ὑμῖν καὶ ἀνδράσιν ἀγαθοῖς ἀποθανοῦσι θύειν ὥσπερ θεοῖς ;

ΤΟΞΑΡΙΣ

Οὐ μόνον, ἀλλὰ καὶ ἑορταῖς καὶ πανηγύρεσιν τιμῶμεν αὐτούς.

ΜΝΗΣΙΠΠΟΣ

Τί θηρώμενοι παρ' αὐτῶν ; οὐ γὰρ δὴ ἐπ' εὐμενείᾳ θύετε αὐτοῖς, νεκροῖς γε οὖσιν.

TOXARIS, OR FRIENDSHIP

MNESIPPUS

What about it, Toxaris? Do you Scythians sacrifice to Orestes and Pylades, and have you come to believe that they are gods?

TOXARIS

We sacrifice, Mnesippus, we sacrifice; not, however, because we think them gods, but good men.[1]

MNESIPPUS

Is it your custom to sacrifice to good men when they are dead, as if they were gods?

TOXARIS

Not only that, but we honour them with festivals and pilgrimages.

MNESIPPUS

What do you crave from them? For surely it is not to gain their grace that you sacrifice to them, in view of the fact that they are dead.

[1] The existence of a cult of Orestes and Pylades in Scythia is not otherwise attested, and is credible only in a limited sense, as a local development of Greek hero-worship; see below, on the Oresteum, § 6.

ΤΟΞΑΡΙΣ

Οὐ χεῖρον μὲν ἴσως, εἰ καὶ οἱ νεκροὶ ἡμῖν
εὐμενεῖς εἶεν· οὐ μὴν ἀλλὰ πρὸς [1] τοὺς ζῶντας
ἄμεινον οἰόμεθα πράξειν μεμνημένοι τῶν ἀρίστων,
καὶ τιμῶμεν ἀποθανόντας, ἡγούμεθα γὰρ οὕτως
ἂν ἡμῖν πολλοὺς ὁμοίους αὐτοῖς ἐθελῆσαι γενέσθαι.

ΜΝΗΣΙΠΠΟΣ

2 Ἀλλὰ ταῦτα μὲν ὀρθῶς γιγνώσκετε. Ὀρέστην
δὲ καὶ Πυλάδην τίνος μάλιστα θαυμάσαντες
ἰσοθέους ἐποιήσασθε, καὶ ταῦτα ἐπήλυδας ὑμῖν
ὄντας καὶ τὸ μέγιστον πολεμίους ; οἵ γε, ἐπεὶ
σφᾶς ναυαγίᾳ περιπεσόντας οἱ τότε Σκύθαι συλλαβόντες ἀπῆγον ὡς τῇ Ἀρτέμιδι καταθύσοντες,
ἐπιθέμενοι τοῖς δεσμοφύλαξι καὶ τῆς φρουρᾶς
ἐπικρατήσαντες τόν τε βασιλέα κτείνουσι καὶ
τὴν ἱέρειαν παραλαβόντες, ἀλλὰ καὶ τὴν Ἄρτεμιν αὐτὴν ἀποσυλήσαντες ᾤχοντο ἀποπλέοντες,
καταγελάσαντες τοῦ κοινοῦ τῶν Σκυθῶν. ὥστε
εἰ διὰ ταῦτα τιμᾶτε τοὺς ἄνδρας, οὐκ ἂν φθάνοιτε

_____
[1] ἀλλὰ καὶ πρὸς N.

_____

[1] Both here and below in § 6 Lucian omits as self-understood
the point that Orestes discovers the priestess to be his sister
Iphigenia, previously thought to have perished at Aulis
under the sacrificial knife.

[2] In the point that this version of the story makes the Greeks
escape by overpowering the Scythians and killing Thoas,
their king, it differs significantly both from Euripides in the
Iphigenia among the Taurians and from Sophocles in the
Chryses, in which Thoas was killed, to be sure, but only after
they had somehow got away and he had overtaken them at
"Sminthe," whose ruler, Chryses, turning out to be the son
of Agamemnon and Chryseis, and so the half-brother of
Orestes and Iphigenia, aids them to kill their pursuer.
Elsewhere in extant ancient literature the Lucianic version

TOXARIS, OR FRIENDSHIP

TOXARIS

Well, we should be none the worse off, perhaps, if even the dead should be gracious to us. However, we think it will be better for the living if we do not forget men of high achievement, and we honour them after death because we consider that in this way we can get many to wish to become like them.

MNESIPPUS

In that matter, to be sure, your judgement is sound. But as regards Orestes and Pylades, on just what ground did you so admire them, that you have put them on a parity with the gods, and that too when they were trespassers upon your soil and— what is most significant—enemies? Why, when the Scythians of that day seized them after their shipwreck and dragged them off intending to sacrifice them to Artemis, they set upon the keepers of their prison, overpowered the watch, and not only slew the king but carried off the priestess,[1] nay even kidnapped Artemis herself, and then went sailing away, after having made a mock of the Scythian commonwealth.[2] So if that is why you honour those

is found only in Servius and in accounts derived from him (Serv. *in Aen.*, II, 216; cf. [Hyginus], 261, and *Mythogr. Vat.*, II, 202). It may have been the accepted version of the cult of Diana at Aricia (Preller, Robert), but cannot be of Latin origin. It is surely the early version, effaced in the literary tradition by the influence of Euripides, but perpetuated (as early myths often were) in art through a painting by some famous Hellenistic master, later reflected not only in Graeco-Roman sarcophagus-reliefs but in the murals of some Graeco-Scythian Oresteum (§ 6). Lucian's knowledge of it may safely be ascribed to an allusion to those murals in the literary source from which he derives the curious mixture of fact and fiction in § 6.

πολλοὺς ὁμοίους αὐτοῖς ἐξεργασάμενοι. καὶ τοὐν-
τεῦθεν αὐτοὶ ἤδη πρὸς τὰ παλαιὰ σκοπεῖτε, εἰ
καλῶς ἔχει ὑμῖν πολλοὺς ἐς τὴν Σκυθίαν Ὀρέστας
καὶ Πυλάδας καταίρειν. ἐμοὶ μὲν γὰρ δοκεῖτε
τάχιστα ἂν οὕτως ἀσεβεῖς αὐτοὶ καὶ ἄθεοι γενέσθαι,
τῶν περιλοίπων θεῶν τὸν αὐτὸν τρόπον ὑμῖν
ἐκ τῆς χώρας ἀποξενωθέντων. εἶτ᾽, οἶμαι, ἀντὶ
τῶν θεῶν ἁπάντων τοὺς ἐπ᾽ ἐξαγωγῇ αὐτῶν
ἥκοντας ἄνδρας ἐκθειάσετε καὶ ἱεροσύλοις ὑμῶν
οὖσιν[1] θύσετε ὡς θεοῖς.

3 Εἰ γὰρ μὴ ἀντὶ τούτων Ὀρέστην καὶ Πυλάδην
τιμᾶτε, ἀλλ᾽ εἰπέ, τί ἄλλο,[2] ὦ Τόξαρι, ἀγαθὸν
ὑμᾶς εἰργάσαντο ἀνθ᾽ ὅτου, πάλαι οὐ θεοὺς εἶναι
δικαιώσαντες αὐτούς, νῦν τὸ ἔμπαλιν θύσαντες
αὐτοῖς θεοὺς νενομίκατε, καὶ ἱερείοις ὀλίγου δεῖν
τότε γενομένοις ἱερεῖα νῦν προσάγετε ; γελοῖα
γὰρ ἂν ταῦτα δόξειε καὶ ὑπεναντία τοῖς πάλαι.

ΤΟΞΑΡΙΣ

Καὶ ταῦτα μέν, ὦ Μνήσιππε, γενναῖα τῶν
ἀνδρῶν ἐκείνων ἃ κατέλεξας. τὸ γὰρ δύο ὄντας
οὕτω μέγα τόλμημα τολμῆσαι καὶ τοσοῦτον
ἀπὸ τῆς αὐτῶν ἀπάραντας ἐκπλεῦσαι ἐς τὸν
Πόντον ἀπείρατον ἔτι τοῖς Ἕλλησιν ὄντα πλὴν
μόνων τῶν ἐπὶ τῆς Ἀργοῦς ἐς τὴν Κολχίδα
στρατευσάντων, μὴ καταπλαγέντας μήτε τοὺς
μύθους τοὺς ἐπ᾽ αὐτῷ[3] μήτε τὴν προσηγορίαν κατα-
δείσαντας ὅτι ἄξενος ἐκαλεῖτο, οἷα, οἶμαι, ἀγρίων

---

[1] οὖσιν ΓΝΒ : not in M(C)A.
[2] εἰπέ, τί ἄλλο Schmieder : εἴπερ τι ἄλλο MSS.
[3] ἐπ᾽ αὐτῷ Seager : ἐν αὐτῷ MSS.

heroes, you will very soon produce many like them! Draw the conclusion for yourselves in the light of what happened of old whether it is desirable for you that many an Orestes and Pylades should descend upon Scythia. To me it seems that very soon, under those conditions, you would become irreligious yourselves, yes, godless, after the remainder of your gods had been similarly shipped out of the country to foreign parts. And then, I suppose, in place of the whole company of gods, you will deify the men who came to obtain them for export and will sacrifice to the robbers of your temples as gods!

If that is not why you honour Orestes and Pylades, do tell me, Toxaris, what other benefit have they done you to bring it about that although formerly you deemed them anything but gods, now, on the contrary, you have made them pass for gods by sacrificing to them, and you now bring victims to men who at that time very nearly became victims? This conduct, you know, might be thought ridiculous and inconsistent with that of former times.

TOXARIS

As a matter of fact, Mnesippus, even these actions that you have described evince nobility in those men. That two should dare so bold a deed; that they should sail so far from their own country as to cruise out into the Pontus (still unexplored by any of the Greeks except the force that fared upon the Argo to Colchis) undismayed either by the fables regarding it or by its name through any terror inspired by the fact that it was called "Inhospitable" (I suppose because savage peoples dwelt

ἐθνῶν περιοικούντων, καὶ ἐπειδὴ ἑάλωσαν, οὕτως
ἀνδρείως χρήσασθαι τῷ πράγματι καὶ μὴ ἀγαπῆ-
σαι εἰ διαφεύξονται [1] μόνον, ἀλλὰ τιμωρησαμένους
τὸν βασιλέα τῆς ὕβρεως καὶ τὴν Ἄρτεμιν ἀναλα-
βόντας ἀποπλεῦσαι, πῶς ταῦτα οὐ θαυμαστὰ καὶ
θείας τινὸς τιμῆς ἄξια παρὰ πάντων ὁπόσοι
ἀρετὴν ἐπαινοῦσιν ; ἀτὰρ οὐ ταῦτα ἡμεῖς Ὀρέστῃ
καὶ Πυλάδῃ ἐνιδόντες ἥρωσιν αὐτοῖς χρώμεθα.

ΜΝΗΣΙΠΠΟΣ

4   Λέγοις ἂν ἤδη ὅ τι τὸ σεμνὸν καὶ θεῖον ἄλλο
ἐξειργάσαντο· ἐπεὶ ὅσον ἐπὶ τῷ πλῷ [2] καὶ τῇ
ἀποδημίᾳ πολλοὺς ἄν σοι θειοτέρους ἐκείνων
ἀποδείξαιμι, τοὺς ἐμπόρους, καὶ μάλιστα τοὺς
Φοίνικας αὐτῶν, οὐκ εἰς τὸν Πόντον οὐδὲ ἄχρι
τῆς Μαιώτιδος καὶ τοῦ Βοσπόρου μόνον ἐσπλέοντας,
ἀλλὰ πανταχοῦ τῆς Ἑλληνικῆς καὶ βαρβαρικῆς
θαλάττης ναυτιλλομένους· ἅπασαν γὰρ οὗτοι ἀκτὴν
καὶ πάντα αἰγιαλόν, ὡς εἰπεῖν, διερευνησάμενοι
καθ᾽ ἕκαστον ἔτος ὀψὲ τοῦ μετοπώρου εἰς τὴν
αὑτῶν ἐπανίασιν. οὓς κατὰ τὸν αὐτὸν λόγον
θεοὺς νόμιζε, καὶ ταῦτα καπήλους καὶ ταριχοπώλας,
εἰ τύχοι, τοὺς πολλοὺς αὐτῶν ὄντας.

ΤΟΞΑΡΙΣ

5   Ἄκουε δή, ὦ θαυμάσιε, καὶ σκόπει καθ᾽ ὅσον
ἡμεῖς οἱ βάρβαροι εὐγνωμονέστερον ὑμῶν περὶ
τῶν ἀγαθῶν ἀνδρῶν κρίνομεν, εἴ γε ἐν Ἄργει μὲν
καὶ Μυκήναις οὐδὲ τάφον ἔνδοξον ἔστιν ἰδεῖν

---

[1] διαφεύξονται M, edd.: διαφυλάξονται other MSS.
[2] ἐπὶ τῷ πλῷ Fritzsche; ἐν τῷ πλῷ MSS.

all about it);[1] that after their capture they faced
the situation so courageously, and were not content
simply to make their escape but punished the king
for his insolence and took Artemis with them when
they sailed away—why is not all this admirable and
worthy of divine honour in some sort from all who
praise manhood? Yet that is not what we see in
Orestes and Pylades, to treat them as heroes.

MNESIPPUS

Please go on and say what else they did that
is imposing and godlike; since as far as concerns their
voyage and their foreign travel I could point you
many who are more godlike than they—the merchant
traders, and particularly the Phoenicians among
them, who not only sail into the Pontus or as far as
Lake Maeotis and the Cimmerian Bosporus,[2] but
cruise everywhere in Greek and foreign waters; for
these fellows comb every single shore and every strand,
you may say, each year before returning late in the
autumn to their own country. On the same principle,
you should account them gods, even though most of
them are pedlars and, it may be, fishmongers!

TOXARIS

Listen then, you amazing fellow, and learn how
much more generously than you Greeks we barbarians judge good men. In Argos and Mycenae
there is not even a respectable tomb of Orestes or

---

[1] According to Apollodorus (Strabo, VII, 298–299) the
Pontus was at first called *Axeinos* (" Inhospitable ") because
of its storminess and the ferocity of the tribes that surrounded
it; later, after the Ionian settlements on its coast, it was
called *Euxeinos* (" Hospitable "). Pindar knows both names
(*Pyth.*, IV, 203; *Nem.* IV, 49).

[2] The Sea of Azov and the Straits of Kertsch.

THE WORKS OF LUCIAN

Ὀρέστου ἢ Πυλάδου, παρ' ἡμῖν δὲ καὶ νεὼς
ἀποδέδεικται αὐτοῖς ἅμα ἀμφοτέροις, ὥσπερ εἰκὸς
ἦν, ἑταίροις γε οὖσι, καὶ θυσίαι προσάγονται καὶ
ἡ ἄλλη τιμὴ ἅπασα, κωλύει τε οὐδὲν ὅτι ξένοι
ἦσαν ἀλλὰ μὴ Σκύθαι ἀγαθοὺς κεκρίσθαι καὶ
ὑπὸ Σκυθῶν τῶν ἀρίστων θεραπεύεσθαι.¹ οὐ
γὰρ ἐξετάζομεν ὅθεν οἱ καλοὶ καὶ ἀγαθοί εἰσιν,
οὐδὲ φθονοῦμεν εἰ μὴ φίλοι ὄντες ἀγαθὰ εἰργάσαντο, ἐπαινοῦντες δὲ ἃ ἔπραξαν, οἰκείους αὐτοὺς
ἀπὸ τῶν ἔργων ποιούμεθα.

"Ὁ δὲ δὴ μάλιστα καταπλαγέντες τῶν ἀνδρῶν
ἐκείνων ἐπαινοῦμεν τοῦτό ἐστιν, ὅτι ἡμῖν ἔδοξαν
φίλοι οὗτοι δὴ ἄριστοι ἁπάντων γεγενῆσθαι καὶ
τοῖς ἄλλοις νομοθέται καταστῆναι ὡς χρὴ τοῖς
6 φίλοις ἁπάσης τύχης κοινωνεῖν.² καὶ ἅ γε μετ'
ἀλλήλων ἢ ὑπὲρ ἀλλήλων ἔπαθον ἀναγράψαντες οἱ
πρόγονοι ἡμῶν ἐπὶ στήλης χαλκῆς ἀνέθεσαν εἰς
τὸ Ὀρέστειον, καὶ νόμον ἐποιήσαντο πρῶτον

¹ καὶ ὑπὸ Σκυθῶν τῶν ἀρίστων θεραπεύεσθαι inserted here by
Geist; after ἁπάσης τύχης κοινωνεῖν (end of § 5) in MSS.
² See n. 1.

---

[1] Nothing could be more natural than for some Graeco-
Scythian city in South Russia (Crimea?) to have had an
Oresteum like this, with a set of murals commemorating the
exploits of Orestes and Pylades. Indeed, the existence of the
paintings is practically guaranteed by two considerations:
they represent a version of the story of Orestes among
the Taurians that is not known to us prior to Lucian except
in art; and that version, involving as it does his killing of the
king, is not likely to have been preferred to the Euripidean
by Lucian for his present purpose, if the paintings were imaginary. Here there seems to be a core of fact which Lucian
can have derived only from some previous writer; and we may
perhaps also safely believe that the deified heroes obtained
sufficient prestige among the native part of the population of

Pylades to be seen, but among us a temple has been assigned them, to both together, as was reasonable since they were comrades, and sacrifices are offered them, and all sorts of honours besides. The fact that they were not Scythians but foreigners is no hindrance to their having been accounted good men and their being cherished by the foremost Scythians; for we do not enquire what country proper men come from, nor do we bear a grudge if men who are not friendly have done noble deeds; we commend what they have accomplished and count them our own in virtue of their achievements.

What especially impressed us in these men and gains our commendation is this: it seemed to us that as friends they, surely, had proved themselves the best in the world, and had established precedents for everyone else in regard to the way in which friends should share all their fortunes. All that they went through in each other's company or for each other's sake our ancestors inscribed on a tablet of bronze which they set up in the Oresteum; [1] and they made it the law that the first study and lesson for

the city and its environs to gain them a Scythian name (Korakoi: § 7 end). Compare the Herodotean tale (IV, 103) of the worship of Iphigenia among the Taurians. This kernel of fact, however, has been enveloped in a hull of fiction by transporting the sanctuary to a mythical Scythian capital without a name and making it the focus of a great national cult of friendship—a happy conceit in view of the custom of swearing " blood-brotherhood " (§ 37), but sheer fiction none the less. It is perhaps possible that Lucian drew the fact from some Hellenistic historian and supplied the fiction himself; but it is more likely that he found both already combined in his source, and connected with one or more of the tales of Scythian friendship that he puts into the mouth of Toxaris (cf. especially p. 173, n. 2).

τοῦτο μάθημα καὶ παίδευμα τοῖς παισὶ τοῖς
σφετέροις εἶναι τὴν στήλην ταύτην καὶ τὰ ἐπ'
αὐτῆς γεγραμμένα διαμνημονεῦσαι. θᾶττον γοῦν
τοὔνομ' ἂν [1] ἕκαστος αὐτῶν ἐπιλάθοιτο τοῦ πατρὸς
ἢ τὰς Ὀρέστου καὶ Πυλάδου πράξεις ἀγνοήσειεν.

Ἀλλὰ καὶ ἐν τῷ περιβόλῳ τοῦ νεὼ τὰ αὐτὰ
ὁπόσα ἡ στήλη δηλοῖ γραφαῖς ὑπὸ τῶν παλαιῶν
εἰκασμένα δείκνυται, πλέων Ὀρέστης ἅμα τῷ φίλῳ,
εἶτα ἐν τοῖς κρημνοῖς διαφθαρείσης αὐτῷ [2] τῆς
νεὼς συνειλημμένος καὶ πρὸς τὴν θυσίαν παρεσκευασμένος, καὶ ἡ Ἰφιγένεια ἤδη κατάρχεται
αὐτῶν. καταντικρὺ δὲ ἐπὶ τοῦ ἑτέρου τοίχου
ἤδη ἐκδεδυκὼς τὰ δεσμὰ γέγραπται καὶ φονεύων
τὸν Θόαντα καὶ πολλοὺς ἄλλους τῶν Σκυθῶν,
καὶ τέλος ἀποπλέοντες, ἔχοντες τὴν Ἰφιγένειαν καὶ
τὴν θεόν. οἱ Σκύθαι δὲ ἄλλως ἐπιλαμβάνονται
τοῦ σκάφους ἤδη πλέοντος, ἐκκρεμαννύμενοι τῶν
πηδαλίων καὶ ἐπαναβαίνειν πειρώμενοι· εἶτ' οὐδὲν
ἀνύσαντες οἱ μὲν αὐτῶν τραυματίαι, οἱ δὲ καὶ
δέει τούτου, ἀπονήχονται πρὸς τὴν γῆν. ἔνθα δὴ
καὶ μάλιστα ἴδοι τις ἂν ὁπόσην ὑπὲρ ἀλλήλων
εὔνοιαν ἐπεδείκνυντο, ἐν τῇ πρὸς τοὺς Σκύθας
συμπλοκῇ. πεποίηκεν γὰρ ὁ γραφεὺς ἑκάτερον
ἀμελοῦντα μὲν τῶν καθ' ἑαυτὸν πολεμίων, ἀμυνόμενον δὲ τοὺς ἐπιφερομένους θατέρῳ καὶ πρὸ
ἐκείνου ἀπαντᾶν πειρώμενον τοῖς τοξεύμασιν καὶ
παρ' οὐδὲν τιθέμενον εἰ ἀποθανεῖται σώσας τὸν
φίλον καὶ τὴν ἐπ' ἐκεῖνον φερομένην πληγὴν
προαρπάσας τῷ ἑαυτοῦ σώματι.

7   Τὴν δὴ τοσαύτην εὔνοιαν αὐτῶν καὶ τὴν ἐν τοῖς
δεινοῖς κοινωνίαν καὶ τὸ πιστὸν καὶ φιλέταιρον

───────────────
[1] τοὔνομ' ἂν Stallbaum : τοὔνομα MSS.

their children should be this tablet and the memoris
ing of all that had been written upon it. In point
of fact, every one of them would sooner forget the
name of his own father than fail to know the achievements of Orestes and Pylades.

But in the temple close, too, the very same matters
that are set forth on the tablet are to be seen represented in paintings by the ancients; Orestes voyag-
ing with his friend, and then, after his ship had been
destroyed on the rocks, his arrest and preparation
for the sacrifice; Iphigenia is already consecrating
them. Opposite this, on the other wall, he is
depicted as just out of his fetters, slaying Thoas
and many more of the Scythians. Finally, they are
sailing off, with Iphigenia and the goddess; the
Scythians meanwhile are vainly laying hold of the
ship, which is already under way, hanging to the
rudders and trying to get aboard; then, unable to
accomplish anything, they swim back to land, some
of them because they are wounded, others for fear
of that. It is just there that one may see how much
good-will they displayed in each other's interest;
I mean, in the engagement with the Scythians.
For the artist has portrayed each of them paying
no heed to the foemen opposite himself, but encoun-
tering those who are assailing the other, trying to meet
their missiles in his stead, and counting it nothing
to die if he saves his friend and intercepts with his
own body the stroke that is being directed at the
other.

That great good-will of theirs, that common front
amid those perils, that faithfulness and comradely

---

[2] αὐτῶν NB.

καὶ τὸ ἀληθὲς καὶ βέβαιον τοῦ πρὸς ἀλλήλους
ἔρωτος, οὐκ ἀνθρώπινα ταῦτα ᾠήθημεν εἶναι,
ἀλλά τινος γνώμης βελτίονος ἢ κατὰ τοὺς πολλοὺς
τούτους ἀνθρώπους, οἳ μέχρι μὲν κατ' οὖρον
ὁ πλοῦς εἴη τοῖς φίλοις,[1] ἀγανακτοῦσιν εἰ μὴ ἐπ'
ἴσης κοινωνήσουσιν τῶν ἡδέων, εἰ δέ τι καὶ μικρὸν[2]
ἀντιπνεύσειεν[3] αὐτοῖς, οἴχονται μόνους τοῖς κιν-
δύνοις ἀπολιπόντες. καὶ γὰρ οὖν καὶ τόδε ὅπως
εἰδῆς, οὐδὲν Σκύθαι φιλίας μεῖζον οἴονται εἶναι,
οὐδὲ ἔστιν ἐφ' ὅτῳ ἄν τις Σκύθης μᾶλλον σεμνύ-
ναιτο ἢ ἐπὶ τῷ συμπονῆσαι φίλῳ ἀνδρὶ καὶ κοινωνῆ-
σαι τῶν δεινῶν, ὥσπερ οὐδὲν ὄνειδος μεῖζον παρ'
ἡμῖν τοῦ προδότην φιλίας γεγενῆσθαι δοκεῖν.
διὰ ταῦτα Ὀρέστην καὶ Πυλάδην τιμῶμεν, ἀρί-
στους γενομένους τὰ Σκυθῶν ἀγαθὰ καὶ ἐν φιλίᾳ
διενεγκόντας, ὃ πρῶτον ἡμεῖς ἁπάντων θαυμάζομεν, καὶ τοὔνομα ἐπὶ τούτοις αὐτῶν ἐθέμεθα
Κοράκους[4] καλεῖσθαι· τοῦτο δέ ἐστιν ἐν τῇ ἡμετέρᾳ
φωνῇ ὥσπερ ἂν εἴ τις λέγοι " φίλιοι δαίμονες."

ΜΝΗΣΙΠΠΟΣ

8   Ὦ Τόξαρι, οὐ μόνον ἄρα τοξεύειν ἀγαθοὶ ἦσαν
Σκύθαι καὶ τὰ πολεμικὰ τῶν ἄλλων ἀμείνους,
ἀλλὰ καὶ ῥῆσιν εἰπεῖν ἁπάντων πιθανώτατοι.
ἐμοὶ γοῦν τέως ἄλλως γιγνώσκοντι ἤδη καὶ
αὐτῷ δίκαια ποιεῖν δοκεῖτε οὕτως Ὀρέστην καὶ
Πυλάδην ἐκθειάσαντες. ἐλελήθεις δέ με, ὦ γενναῖε, καὶ γραφεὺς ἀγαθὸς ὤν. πάνυ γοῦν ἐναργῶς

---

[1] Previous editions throw τοῖς φίλοις with what follows,
by setting the comma before it.
[2] Text NB: other MSS. repeat τι after μικρόν.

love, that genuineness and solidity of their affection
for one another were not, we thought, of this world,
but marked a spirit too noble for these men about
us of the common sort, who, as long as the course of
their friends is with the wind, take it ill if they do
not give them an equal share in all their delights,
but if even a slight breath sets against them, they
bear away, entirely abandoning them to their perils.
For I would have you know this also—Scythians
think that there is nothing greater than friendship,
and there is not anything upon which a Scythian
will pride himself more than on aiding a friend and
sharing his dangers, just as there is no greater disgrace among us than to bear the name of having
played false to friendship. That is why we honour
Orestes and Pylades, because they practised best
what Scythians hold good, and excelled in friendship, an achievement which we admire before all
things else; in token whereof we have given them
the name of Korakoi to go by, which in our language
is as much as to say " guiding spirits of friendship."

MNESIPPUS

Toxaris, it has turned out that Scythians are not
only good archers and better than all others in warfare, but the most convincing of all peoples at making
speeches. Anyhow, I, who formerly had a different
opinion, now myself think you do right in thus deifying
Orestes and Pylades. And I had failed, my accomplished friend, to grasp the fact that you are also a
good painter. Very animated indeed was the sketch

---

[3] ἀντιπνεύσειεν N : ἀντιπνεύσει A ἀντιπνεύσῃ BM and Γ², in
an erasure; Γ¹ must have written -ει.

[4] Κονάχους C²A² (ν over ρ, χ over κ).

ἐπέδειξας ἡμῖν τὰς ἐν τῷ Ὀρεστείῳ εἰκόνας καὶ
τὴν μάχην τῶν ἀνδρῶν καὶ τὰ ὑπὲρ ἀλλήλων
τραύματα. πλὴν ἀλλ᾽ οὐκ ᾠήθην ἂν οὕτω ποτὲ
περισπούδαστον εἶναι φιλίαν ἐν Σκύθαις· ἅτε γὰρ
ἀξένους[1] καὶ ἀγρίους ὄντας αὐτοὺς ἔχθρᾳ μὲν ἀεὶ
συνεῖναι καὶ ὀργῇ καὶ θυμῷ, φιλίαν δὲ μηδὲ πρὸς
τοὺς οἰκειοτάτους ἐπαναιρεῖσθαι, τεκμαιρόμενος
τοῖς τε ἄλλοις ἃ περὶ αὐτῶν ἀκούομεν καὶ ὅτι
κατεσθίουσι τοὺς πατέρας ἀποθανόντας.

ΤΟΞΑΡΙΣ

9   Εἰ μὲν καὶ τὰ ἄλλα ἡμεῖς τῶν Ἑλλήνων καὶ
δικαιότεροι τὰ πρὸς τοὺς γονέας καὶ ὁσιώτεροί
ἐσμεν, οὐκ ἂν ἐν τῷ παρόντι φιλοτιμηθείην πρὸς
σέ. ὅτι δὲ οἱ φίλοι οἱ[2] Σκύθαι πολὺ πιστότεροι τῶν
Ἑλλήνων φίλων εἰσὶν καὶ ὅτι πλείων φιλίας λόγος
παρ᾽ ἡμῖν ἢ παρ᾽ ὑμῖν, ῥᾴδιον ἐπιδεῖξαι· καὶ
πρὸς θεῶν τῶν Ἑλλήνων μὴ πρὸς ἀχθηδόνα μου
ἀκούσῃς ἣν εἴπω τι ὧν κατανενόηκα πολὺν ἤδη
χρόνον ὑμῖν συγγινόμενος.

Ὑμεῖς γάρ μοι δοκεῖτε τοὺς μὲν περὶ φιλίας
λόγους ἄμεινον ἄλλων ἂν εἰπεῖν δύνασθαι, τἄργα
δὲ αὐτῆς οὐ μόνον οὐ κατ᾽ ἀξίαν τῶν λόγων
ἐκμελετᾶν, ἀλλ᾽ ἀπόχρη ὑμῖν ἐπαινέσαι τε αὐτὴν
καὶ δεῖξαι ἡλίκον ἀγαθόν ἐστιν· ἐν δὲ ταῖς χρείαις
προδόντες τοὺς λόγους δραπετεύετε οὐκ οἶδ᾽ ὅπως
ἐκ μέσων τῶν ἔργων. καὶ ὁπόταν ὑμῖν οἱ τραγῳ-
δοὶ τὰς τοιαύτας φιλίας ἐπὶ τὴν σκηνὴν ἀναβιβά-

---

[1] ἀξένους du Soul: ξένους MSS.
[2] οἱ Bekker: not in MSS.

that you drew for us of the pictures in the Oresteum, of the fighting of your heroes, and the wounds that each bore for the other. However, I should not have expected friendship to be so highly cherished among the Scythians, for as they are inhospitable and uncivilised I thought that they always were well acquainted with hatred, anger, and bad humour but did not enter into friendship even with their closest kin, judging by all that we hear about them, and especially the report that they eat their dead fathers![1]

TOXARIS

Whether we are in general not only more just than the Greeks towards our parents but more reverential is a question which I would rather not debate with you at present. But that Scythian friends are far more faithful than Greek friends and that friendship matters more with us than with you is easily demonstrated; and in the name of your Gods of Greece, do not listen to me with displeasure if I mention one of the observations which I have made after having lived with your people for a long time now.

It seems to me that you Greeks can indeed say all that is to be said about friendship better than others, but not only fail to practise its works in a manner that befits your words,—no, you are content to have praised it and shown what a very good thing it is, but in its times of need you play traitor to your words about it and beat a hasty retreat, somehow or other, out of the press of deeds. And whenever your tragedians put friendships of this kind on

---

[1] Alluded to also in *Funerals*, 21 (IV, p. 126). Cf. Herodotus, IV, 26 (of the Issedones), and I, 216 (of the Massagetae).

σαντες δεικνύωσιν ἐπαινεῖτε καὶ ἐπικροτεῖτε καὶ
κινδυνεύουσιν αὐτοῖς ὑπὲρ ἀλλήλων οἱ πολλοὶ
καὶ ἐπιδακρύετε, αὐτοὶ δὲ οὐδὲν ἄξιον ἐπαίνου
ὑπὲρ τῶν φίλων παρέχεσθαι τολμᾶτε, ἀλλ' ἤν
του φίλος δεηθεὶς τύχῃ, αὐτίκα μάλα ὥσπερ τὰ
ὀνείρατα οἴχονται ὑμῖν ἐκποδὼν ἀποπτάμεναι αἱ
πολλαὶ ἐκεῖναι τραγῳδίαι, τοῖς κενοῖς τούτοις καὶ
κωφοῖς προσωπείοις ἐοικότας ὑμᾶς ἀπολιποῦσαι,
ἃ διηρμένα¹ τὸ στόμα καὶ παμμέγεθες κεχηνότα
οὐδὲ τὸ σμικρότατον φθέγγεται. ἡμεῖς δὲ ἔμ-
παλιν· ὅσῳ γὰρ δὴ λειπόμεθα ἐν τοῖς περὶ φιλίας
λόγοις, τοσοῦτον ἐν τοῖς ἔργοις αὐτῆς πλεονεκτοῦ-
μεν.

10   Εἰ δ' οὖν² δοκεῖ, οὕτω νῦν ποιῶμεν. τοὺς μὲν
παλαιοὺς φίλους ἀτρεμεῖν ἐάσωμεν, εἴ τινας ἢ
ἡμεῖς ἢ ὑμεῖς τῶν πάλαι καταριθμεῖν ἔχομεν,
ἐπεὶ κατά γε τοῦτο πλεονεκτοῖτε ἄν, πολλοὺς καὶ
ἀξιοπίστους μάρτυρας τοὺς ποιητὰς παρεχόμενοι
τὴν Ἀχιλλέως καὶ Πατρόκλου φιλίαν καὶ τὴν
Θησέως καὶ Πειρίθου καὶ τῶν ἄλλων ἑταιρείαν
ἐν καλλίστοις ἔπεσι καὶ μέτροις ῥαψῳδοῦντας·
ὀλίγους δέ τινας προχειρισάμενοι τῶν καθ' ἡμᾶς
αὐτοὺς καὶ τὰ ἔργα αὐτῶν διηγησάμενοι, ἐγὼ
μὲν τὰ Σκυθικά, σὺ δὲ τὰ Ἑλληνικά, ὁπότερος³
ἂν ἐν τούτοις κρατῇ καὶ ἀμείνους παράσχηται
τοὺς φίλους, αὐτός τε νενικηκὼς ἔσται καὶ τὴν
αὑτοῦ ἀνακηρύξει, κάλλιστον ἀγῶνα καὶ σεμνό-
τατον ἀγωνισάμενος. ὡς ἔγωγε πολὺ ἥδιον ἂν

¹ διηρμένα Coraës: διηρημένα MSS.
² δ' οὖν Dindorf : γοῦν MSS.
³ Ἑλληνικά, καὶ ὁπότερος MSS. Bekker's excision of καί

the stage and exhibit them to you, you bestow praise and applause, yes, even tears upon them, most of you, when they face danger for each other's sake; yet you yourselves dare not come out with any praiseworthy deed for the sake of your friends. On the contrary, if a friend happens to stand in need of anything, those many tragic histories take wing and vanish from your path on the instant, like dreams, and leave you looking like those empty, silent masks which, for all their open mouths, widely agape, do not utter even the slightest sound. We are your opposites; for we have as much the better of you in practising friendship as we fall short of you in talking about it.

If you like, then, let us do this; let us leave the friends of former times to rest in peace, whomsoever, I mean, of the ancients either we or you are able to enumerate; for there, to be sure, you would outdo us by citing many trustworthy witnesses, your poets, who have rehearsed in the most beautiful of epic lines and lyric verses the friendship of Achilles and Patroclus and the comradeship of Theseus, Peirithous, and all the rest. Instead, let us take up just a few of our own contemporaries and recount their deeds, I for the Scythian side, you for the Greek; then whichever of us wins in this by bringing out better examples of friendship shall not only be adjudged victor himself but shall be allowed to name his country in the proclamation, inasmuch as he will have taken part in a right glorious and noble contest. For my own part, I think I would

---

gives the sentence a proper conclusion. To read διηγησώμεθα above (B²N) necessitates excising καὶ before τὰ ἔργα.

μοι δοκῶ μονομαχῶν ἡττηθεὶς ἀποτμηθῆναι τὴν
δεξιάν, ὅπερ ἥττης[1] Σκυθικῆς ἐπιτίμιόν ἐστιν, ἢ
χείρων ἄλλου κατὰ φιλίαν κεκρίσθαι, καὶ ταῦτα
Ἕλληνος, Σκύθης αὐτὸς ὤν.

ΜΝΗΣΙΠΠΟΣ

11 Ἔστιν μέν, ὦ Τόξαρι, οὐ φαῦλον τὸ ἔργον
ἀνδρὶ οἵῳ σοὶ πολεμιστῇ μονομαχῆσαι, πάνυ
εὐστόχους καὶ τεθηγμένους παρεσκευασμένῳ τοὺς
λόγους. οὐ μὴν ἀγεννῶς γε οὕτως καταπροδοὺς
ἐν βραχεῖ τὸ Ἑλληνικὸν ἅπαν ὑποχωρήσομαί σοι·
καὶ γὰρ ἂν εἴη πάνδεινον ὑπὸ δυοῖν μὲν ἐκείνοιν
ἡττηθῆναι τοσούτους τῶν Σκυθῶν ὁπόσους οἵ
τε μῦθοι δηλοῦσι καὶ αἱ ὑμέτεραι παλαιαὶ γραφαί,
ἃς μικρῷ πρόσθεν εὖ μάλα ἐξετραγῴδησας, Ἕλληνας δὲ πάντας, τοσαῦτα ἔθνη καὶ τοσαύτας
πόλεις, ἐρήμην ὑπὸ σοῦ ἁλῶναι. εἰ γὰρ τοῦτο
γένοιτο, οὐ τὴν δεξιὰν ὥσπερ ὑμεῖς ἀλλὰ τὴν
γλῶτταν ἀποτμηθῆναι καλόν. πότερον δὲ ὡρί-
σθαι χρὴ τὸν ἀριθμὸν ἡμῖν τῶν φιλικῶν τούτων
πράξεων, ἢ ὁπόσῳ ἄν τις πλείους ἔχῃ λέγειν,
τοσούτῳ εὐπορώτερος ἂν δόξειεν πρὸς τὴν νίκην;

ΤΟΞΑΡΙΣ

Οὐδαμῶς, ἀλλ᾽ ὡρίσθω μὴ ἐν τῷ πλήθει αὐτῶν
τὸ κράτος, ἀλλ᾽ εἰ ἀμείνους καὶ τομώτεραι φαίνοιντο
αἱ σαὶ τῶν ἐμῶν ἴσαι τὸν ἀριθμὸν οὖσαι, καιριώ-
τερα δῆλον ὅτι ἐργάσονταί μοι τραύματα[2] καὶ
θᾶττον ἐνδώσω πρὸς τὰς πληγάς.

---

[1] ἥττης Bekker : τῆς MSS.
[2] τὰ τραύματα N.

much rather be defeated in single combat and have my right hand cut off, which is the penalty for defeat in Scythia, than to be pronounced inferior to anyone else in the matter of friendship, and above all to a Greek, when I am myself a Scythian.

MNESIPPUS

It is no mean undertaking, Toxaris, to engage in single combat with a man-at-arms like yourself, equipped with very accurate and well-sharpened shafts of speech. Nevertheless, I shall not so ignobly betray of a sudden the whole Greek cause as to yield you the field. It would be shocking if, when they two defeated as many Scythians as are indicated by the stories and by those ancient paintings in your country which you described with such histrionic expressiveness a little while ago, all the Greeks, including so many peoples and so many cities, should lose by default to you alone. If that should take place, it would be fitting for me to be docked, not of my right hand, as your people are, but of my tongue. But ought we to set ourselves a limit to the number of these exploits of friendship, or should we hold that the more of them a man can tell, the better off he is as regards the victory?

TOXARIS

By no means; let us prescribe that the victory does not in this case reside with the greater numbers. No, if yours turn out to be better and more telling than mine, though equal in number, they will obviously inflict more serious wounds upon me and I shall succumb to your blows more quickly.

ΜΝΗΣΙΠΠΟΣ

Εὖ λέγεις, καὶ ὡρίσθωσαν ὁπόσαι ἱκαναί. πέντε
ἔμοιγε δοκοῦσιν ἑκατέρῳ.[1]

ΤΟΞΑΡΙΣ

Κἀμοὶ δοκεῖ. πρότερος δὲ λέγε, ἀλλ' ἐπομοσάμενος ἦ μὴν ἀληθῆ ἐρεῖν· ἄλλως γὰρ ἀναπλάττειν[2] τὰ τοιαῦτα οὐ πάνυ χαλεπὸν καὶ ὁ
ἔλεγχος ἀφανής. εἰ δὲ ὀμόσειας, οὐχ ὅσιον
ἀπιστεῖν.

ΜΝΗΣΙΠΠΟΣ

Ὁμούμεθα, εἴ τι καὶ ὅρκου δεῖν νομίζεις. τίς
δέ σοι τῶν ἡμετέρων θεῶν ἄρ' ἱκανός ; ὁ Φίλιος ;

ΤΟΞΑΡΙΣ

Καὶ μάλα· ἐγὼ δὲ τὸν ἐπιχώριον ὀμοῦμαί σοι
ἐν τῷ ἐμαυτοῦ λόγῳ.

ΜΝΗΣΙΠΠΟΣ

12 Ἴστω τοίνυν ὁ Ζεὺς ὁ Φίλιος, ἦ μὴν ὁπόσα ἂν
λέγω πρὸς σὲ ἢ αὐτὸς εἰδὼς ἢ παρ' ἄλλων ὁπόσον
οἷόν τε ἦν δι' ἀκριβείας ἐκπυνθανόμενος ἐρεῖν,
μηδὲν παρ' ἐμαυτοῦ ἐπιτραγῳδῶν. καὶ πρώτην
γέ σοι τὴν Ἀγαθοκλέους καὶ Δεινίου φιλίαν
διηγήσομαι, ἀοίδιμον ἐν τοῖς Ἴωσι γενομένην.

Ἀγαθοκλῆς γὰρ οὗτος ὁ Σάμιος οὐ πρὸ πολλοῦ
ἐγένετο, ἄριστος μὲν πρὸς φιλίαν, ὡς ἔδειξεν, τὰ
ἄλλα δὲ οὐδὲν ἀμείνων Σαμίων τῶν πολλῶν οὔτε
ἐς τὸ γένος οὔτε ἐς τὴν ἄλλην περιουσίαν. Δεινίᾳ

[1] ἑκατέρῳ N : ἑκατέρως ΓΜΒC.
[2] ἀναπλάττειν Harmon : ἂν πράττειν MSS. (ἂν omitted in A),
πλάττειν edd.

TOXARIS, OR FRIENDSHIP

MNESIPPUS

You are right, so let us settle how many will do. Five, I should think, for each.

TOXARIS

I think so too; and you may speak first, after taking oath that you will assuredly tell the truth. Merely to make up such tales is not at all hard, and there is no obvious means of disproof. But if you should take your oath, it would not be right to disbelieve you.

MNESIPPUS

We shall do so, if you really think an oath is at all essential. But which of our gods will satisfy you? Zeus Philios?

TOXARIS

Yes indeed; and I will take the oath of my own country for you when I myself speak.

MNESIPPUS

Well then, as Zeus Philios is my witness, I solemnly swear that whatever I shall tell you I will say either from my own knowledge or from information obtained of others with all the accuracy that was possible, without contributing any dramaturgy on my own part. And the first friendship of which I shall give you an account is that of Agathocles and Deinias, which has become far-famed among the Ionians.

Agathocles of Samos, to whom I refer, lived not long ago, and was peerless in friendship, as he proved, but otherwise not at all superior to the general run of Samians either in family or in means.

δὲ τῷ Λύσωνος [1] Ἐφεσίῳ φίλος ἐκ παίδων ἦν. ὁ δὲ Δεινίας ἐπλούτει ἄρα εἰς ὑπερβολήν, καὶ ὥσπερ εἰκὸς νεόπλουτον ὄντα, πολλοὺς καὶ ἄλλους εἶχε περὶ ἑαυτόν, ἱκανοὺς μὲν συμπιεῖν καὶ πρὸς ἡδονὴν συνεῖναι, φιλίας δὲ πλεῖστον ὅσον ἀποδέοντας.

Τέως μὲν οὖν ἐν τούτοις καὶ ὁ Ἀγαθοκλῆς ἐξητάζετο, καὶ συνῆν καὶ συνέπινεν αὐτοῖς οὐ πάνυ χαίρων τῇ τοιαύτῃ διατριβῇ, καὶ ὁ Δεινίας οὐδὲν αὐτὸν ἐντιμότερον εἶχεν τῶν κολάκων. τελευταῖον δὲ καὶ προσέκρουε τὰ πολλὰ ἐπιτιμῶν, καὶ φορτικὸς ἐδόκει ὑπομιμνήσκων ἀεὶ τῶν προγόνων καὶ φυλάττειν παραγγέλλων ἃ μετὰ πολλῶν καμάτων ὁ πατὴρ αὐτῷ κτησάμενος κατέλιπεν, ὥστε διὰ ταῦτα οὐδὲ ἐπὶ τοὺς κώμους ἀπῆγεν ἔτι αὐτόν, ἀλλὰ μόνος μετ' ἐκείνων ἐκώμαζε, λανθάνειν πειρώμενος τὸν Ἀγαθοκλέα.

13 Καὶ δή ποτε ὑπὸ τῶν κολάκων ἐκείνων ὁ ἄθλιος ἀναπείθεται ὡς ἐρῴη αὐτοῦ Χαρίκλεια Δημώνακτος γυνή, ἀνδρὸς ἐπιφανοῦς καὶ πρώτου Ἐφεσίων τὰ πολιτικά· καὶ γραμματεῖά τε εἰσεφοίτα παρὰ τῆς γυναικὸς αὐτῷ καὶ στέφανοι ἡμιμάραντοι καὶ μῆλά τινα ἀποδεδηγμένα καὶ ἄλλα ὁπόσα αἱ μαστροποὶ ἐπὶ τοῖς νέοις μηχανῶνται,[2] κατὰ μικρὸν αὐτοῖς ἐπιτεχνώμεναι τοὺς ἔρωτας καὶ ἀναφλέγουσαι τὸ πρῶτον ἐρᾶσθαι νομίζοντας (ἐπαγωγότατον γὰρ τοῦτό γε, καὶ μάλιστα τοῖς καλοῖς εἶναι οἰομένοις), ἄχρι ἂν λάθωσιν εἰς τὰ δίκτυα ἐμπεσόντες.

Ἡ Χαρίκλεια δὲ ἦν ἀστεῖόν μέν τι γύναιον,

---

[1] Λύσωνος Α: Λυσίωνος ΓΝΒ. In § 15 all but Ν read Λύσωνος.
[2] τοῖς νέοις ἐπιμηχάνωνται (C)Α. But cf. ἐπὶ τούτῳ μεμηχανῆσθαι, Dial. Mer., 4, 2.

He and Deinias, the son of Lyson, of Ephesus, were friends from their boyhood. But Deinias turned out to be enormously rich; and as was natural in one whose wealth was new, he had many others about him who were well enough as boon companions and agreeable associates, but as far as could be from friends.

Well, for a time Agathocles was put to the test among them, associating with them and drinking with them, though he took little pleasure in that kind of pastime; and Deinias held him in no higher esteem than his toadies. But at length Agathocles began to give offence by rebuking him frequently, and came to be considered a nuisance by reminding him always of his ancestors and admonishing him to keep what his father had acquired with much labour and left to him. Consequently Deinias no longer even took him along when he caroused about the town, but used to go alone with those others, trying to escape the eye of Agathocles.

In course of time those flatterers persuaded the poor fellow that Charicleia was in love with him. She was the wife of Demonax, a distinguished man, foremost among the Ephesians in public affairs. Notes from the woman kept coming into his house; also, half-faded wreaths, apples with a piece bitten out, and every other contrivance with which go-betweens lay siege to young men, gradually working up their love-affairs for them and inflaming them at the start with the thought that they are adored (for this is extremely seductive, especially to those who think themselves handsome), until they fall unawares into the net.

Charicleia was a dainty piece of femininity, but

ἑταιρικὸν δὲ ἐκτόπως καὶ τοῦ προστυχόντος ἀεί,
καὶ εἰ πάνυ ἐπ' ὀλίγῳ ἐθελήσειέ τις· καὶ εἰ προσίδοι
τις μόνον, εὐθὺς ἐπένευε, καὶ δέος οὐδὲν ἦν μή πη [1]
ἀντείποι Χαρίκλεια. δεινὴ δὲ καὶ τὰ ἄλλα, καὶ [2]
τεχνῖτις παρ' ἥντινα βούλει τῶν ἑταιρῶν ἐπισπά-
σασθαι ἐραστὴν καὶ ἀμφίβολον ἔτι ὄντα ὅλον
ὑποποιήσασθαι καὶ ἐνεχόμενον ἤδη ἐπιτεῖναι καὶ
προσεκκαῦσαι ἄρτι μὲν ὀργῇ, ἄρτι δὲ κολακείᾳ,
καὶ μετὰ μικρὸν ὑπεροψίᾳ καὶ τῷ πρὸς ἕτερον
ἀποκλίνειν δοκεῖν, καὶ ὅλη συνεκεκρότητο ἀπαντα-
χόθεν ἡ γυνὴ καὶ πολλὰ μηχανήματα παρεσκεύαστο
κατὰ τῶν ἐραστῶν.

14   Ταύτην οὖν τότε οἱ Δεινίου κόλακες παρα-
λαμβάνουσιν ἐπὶ τὸ μειράκιον, καὶ τὰ πολλὰ
ὑπεκωμῴδουν, συνωθοῦντες αὐτὸν εἰς τὸν ἔρωτα
τῆς Χαρικλείας. ἡ δὲ πολλοὺς ἤδη νέους ἐκτραχη-
λίσασα καὶ μυρίους ἔρωτας ὑποκριναμένη καὶ
οἴκους πολυταλάντους ἀνατρέψασα, ποικίλον τι
καὶ πολυγύμναστον κακόν, παραλαβοῦσα εἰς τὰς
χεῖρας ἁπλοϊκὸν καὶ ἄπειρον τῶν τοιούτων μηχανη-
μάτων νεανίσκον οὐκ ἀνῆκεν ἐκ τῶν ὀνύχων,
ἀλλὰ περιέχουσα πανταχόθεν καὶ διαπείρασα,
ὅτε ἤδη παντάπασιν ἐκράτει, αὐτή τε ἀπώλετο
ὑπὸ τῆς ἄγρας καὶ τῷ κακοδαίμονι Δεινίᾳ μυρίων
κακῶν αἰτία ἐγένετο.

Τὸ μὲν γὰρ πρῶτον εὐθὺς ἐκεῖνα ἐπ' αὐτὸν καθίει
τὰ γραμμάτεια, συνεχῶς [3] πεμπομένη τὴν ἄβραν,
ὡς ἐδάκρυσε καὶ ἐπηγρύπνησε καὶ τέλος ὡς

---

[1] μή πη Γ¹B² : μή ποι Γ² (οι in erasure) B¹N ; μή τι C, edd.
Cf. *Lexiph.*, 11.
[2] καὶ ΓΝB : not in A.

outrageously meretricious, giving herself to anyone
who happened to meet her, even if he should want
her at very little cost; if you but looked at her, she
nodded at once, and there was no fear that Charicleia
might perhaps be reluctant. She was clever too, in
every way, and an artist comparable with any
courtesan you please at alluring a lover, bringing
him into complete subjection when he was still of
two minds, and when at last he was in her toils
working him up and fanning his flame, now by anger,
now by flattery, soon by scorn and by pretending to
have an inclination for someone else. She was every
bit of her thoroughly sophisticated, that woman, and
plentifully armed with siege-engines to train upon
her lovers.

This, then, was the ally whom Deinias' toadies
at that time enlisted against the boy, and they constantly played up to her lead, unitedly thrusting
him into the affair with Charicleia. And she, who
already had given many young fellows a bad fall,
who, times without number, had played at being in
love, who had ruined vast estates, versatile and
thoroughly practised mischief-maker that she was—
once she got into her clutches a simple youngster who
had no experience of such enginery, she would not
let him out of her talons but encompassed him all
round about and pierced him through and through,
until, when at last she had him wholly in her power,
she not only lost her own life through her quarry
but caused poor Deinias misfortunes without end.

From the very first she kept baiting him with
those notes, sending her maid continually, making
out that she had cried, that she had lain awake,

---

[3] συνεχῶς N: καὶ συνεχῶς Γ, vulg.

THE WORKS OF LUCIAN

ἀπάγξει ἑαυτὴν ἡ ἀθλία ὑπὸ τοῦ ἔρωτος, ἕως δὴ
ὁ μακάριος ἐπείσθη καλὸς εἶναι καὶ ταῖς Ἐφεσίων
γυναιξὶ περιπόθητος, καί που συνηνέχθη πολλὰ
15 ἱκετευθείς. τὸ ἐντεῦθεν ἤδη ῥᾷον, ὡς τὸ εἰκός,
ἁλώσεσθαι ἔμελλεν ὑπὸ γυναικὸς καλῆς καὶ πρὸς
ἡδονήν τε ὁμιλῆσαι ἐπισταμένης καὶ ἐν καιρῷ
δακρῦσαι καὶ μεταξὺ τῶν λόγων ἐλεεινῶς ὑποστενά-
ξαι καὶ ἀπιόντος ἤδη λαβέσθαι καὶ εἰσελθόντι
προσδραμεῖν καὶ καλλωπίζεσθαι ὡς ἂν μάλιστα
ἀρέσειε, καί που καὶ ᾆσαι καὶ κιθαρίσαι.

Οἷς ἅπασι κατὰ τοῦ Δεινίου ἐκέχρητο· καὶ
ἐπεὶ ᾔσθετο πονηρῶς ἔχοντα καὶ διάβροχον ἤδη
τῷ ἔρωτι καὶ τακερὸν γεγενημένον, ἄλλο ἐπὶ τούτοις ἐπενόει καὶ τὸν ἄθλιον ἀπώλλυε· κύειν τε
γὰρ ἐξ αὐτοῦ σκήπτεται —ἱκανὸν δὲ καὶ τοῦτο
βλᾶκα ἐραστὴν προσεκπυρῶσαι—καὶ οὐκέτι ἐφοίτα
πρὸς αὐτόν, φυλάττεσθαι ὑπὸ τἀνδρὸς λέγουσα
πεπυσμένου τὸν ἔρωτα.

Ὁ δ᾽ οὐκέτι οἷός τε ἦν φέρειν τὸ πρᾶγμα,
οὐδὲ ἠνείχετο μὴ ὁρῶν αὐτήν, ἀλλὰ ἐδάκρυε καὶ
τοὺς κόλακας εἰσέπεμπεν καὶ τοὔνομα τῆς Χαρικλείας ἐπεβοᾶτο καὶ τὴν εἰκόνα περιβαλὼν αὐτῆς—ἐπεποίητο δὲ λίθου λευκοῦ—ἐκώκυε, καὶ
τέλος καταβαλὼν ἑαυτὸν εἰς τοὔδαφος ἐκυλίνδετο
καὶ λύττα ἦν ἀκριβὴς τὸ πρᾶγμα. τὰ μὲν γὰρ
δῶρα οὐ κατὰ μῆλα καὶ στεφάνους ἀντεδίδοτο
αὐτῇ, ἀλλὰ συνοικίαι ὅλαι καὶ ἀγροὶ καὶ θερά-
παιναι καὶ ἐσθῆτες εὐανθεῖς καὶ χρυσὸν ὁπόσον
ἐθελήσειε.[1]

---

[1] ἐθελήσειε A : ἐθελήσει ΓΝΒΜ.

and at last that she would hang herself for love, poor girl, until the blessed simpleton became convinced that he was handsome and adored by the women of Ephesus, and of course made a rendezvous after many entreaties. After that, naturally, it was bound to be an easy matter for him to be captured by a beautiful woman, who knew how to please him with her company, to weep on occasion, to sigh piteously in the midst of her conversation, to lay hold of him when he was at last going away, to run up to him when he came in, to adorn herself in the way that would best please him, and of course to sing and to strum the lyre.

All this she had brought into play against Deinias; and then, when she discerned that he was in a bad way, having by that time become thoroughly permeated with love and pliable, she employed another artifice to complete the poor boy's undoing. She pretended to be with child by him (this too is an effective way to fire a sluggish lover); moreover, she discontinued her visits to him, saying that she was kept in by her husband, who had found out about their affair.

Deinias was now unable to bear the situation and could not endure not seeing her. He wept, he sent his toadies, he called upon the name of Charicleia, he embraced her statue (having had one of marble made for him), he wailed; at last he flung himself on the ground and rolled about, and his condition was absolute insanity. Naturally, the gifts which he exchanged for hers were not on a par with apples and wreaths, but whole apartment-houses, farms, and serving-women, gay clothing, and all the gold that she wanted.

129

Καὶ τί γάρ ; ἐν βραχεῖ ὁ Λύσωνος οἶκος,
ὀνομαστότατος τῶν ἐν Ἰωνίᾳ γενόμενος, ἐξήντλητο
16 ἤδη καὶ ἐξεκεκένωτο. εἶτα, ὡς ἤδη αὖς ἦν,
ἀπολιποῦσα αὐτὸν ἄλλον τινὰ Κρῆτα νεανίσκον
τῶν ὑποχρύσων ἐθήρα καὶ μετέβαινεν ἐπ᾽ ἐκεῖνον
καὶ ἤρα ἤδη αὐτοῦ, κἀκεῖνος ἐπίστευεν.

Ἀμελούμενος οὖν ὁ Δεινίας οὐχ ὑπὸ τῆς Χαρικλείας μόνον ἀλλὰ καὶ ὑπὸ τῶν κολάκων (κἀκεῖνοι
γὰρ ἐπὶ τὸν Κρῆτα ἤδη τὸν ἐρώμενον μετελη-
λύθεσαν) ἔρχεται παρὰ τὸν Ἀγαθοκλέα καὶ
πάλαι εἰδότα ὡς ἔχοι πονηρῶς τὰ πράγματα
αὐτῷ, καὶ αἰδούμενος τὸ πρῶτον ὅμως διηγεῖτο
πάντα—τὸν ἔρωτα, τὴν ἀπορίαν, τὴν ὑπεροψίαν
τῆς γυναικός, τὸν ἀντεραστὴν τὸν Κρῆτα, καὶ
τέλος ὡς οὐ βιώσεται μὴ οὐχὶ συνὼν τῇ Χαρικλείᾳ. ὁ δὲ ἄκαιρον εἶναι νομίσας ἐν τούτῳ ἀπομνη-
μονεύειν τῷ Δεινίᾳ διότι οὐ προσίετο μόνον
αὐτὸν τῶν φίλων ἀλλὰ τοὺς κόλακας αὐτοῦ προετί-
μα τότε, ἣν μόνον εἶχεν πατρῴαν οἰκίαν ἐν Σάμῳ
ἀπεμπολήσας ἧκεν αὐτῷ τὴν τιμὴν κομίζων, τρία
τάλαντα.

Λαβὼν δὲ ὁ Δεινίας οὐκ ἀφανὴς εὐθὺς ἦν τῇ
Χαρικλείᾳ καλός ποθεν αὖθις γεγενημένος, καὶ
αὖθις ἡ ἄβρα καὶ τὰ γραμματεῖα, καὶ μέμψις
ὅτι μὴ πολλοῦ χρόνου ἀφίκετο, καὶ οἱ κόλακες
συνέθεον ἐπικαλαμησόμενοι, ὁρῶντες ἐδώδιμον
17 ἔτι ὄντα τὸν Δεινίαν. ὡς δὲ ὑπέσχετο ἥξειν παρ᾽
αὐτὴν καὶ ἧκε περὶ πρῶτον ὕπνον καὶ ἔνδον ἦν, ὁ
Δημῶναξ, ὁ τῆς Χαρικλείας ἀνήρ, εἴτε ἄλλως
αἰσθόμενος εἴτε καὶ ἀπὸ συνθήματος [1] τῆς γυναικός

---

[1] συνθήματος B: συνθέματος Γ: συνθήκης N.

TOXARIS, OR FRIENDSHIP

Why make a long story of it? In a trice the estate of Lyson, which had been the most famous in Ionia, was completely pumped out and exhausted. And then, when at last he was drained dry, she left him, pursued another gilded youth from Crete, and went over to him; now she loved him, and he put faith in it.

Neglected not only by Charicleia but by the toadies, for they too had now gone over to the Cretan whom she loved, Deinias sought out Agathocles, who had long known that things were going badly with him. Though overcome with shame at first, nevertheless he told the whole story—his passion, his desperate straits, the woman's disregard, the Cretan rival—and in conclusion said that he would not remain alive if he could not have Charicleia. Agathocles thought it unseasonable at that moment to remind Deinias that he used never to be glad to see him, and him only, of all his friends, but used always to give preference to his toadies in those days. So he sold all that he had, the house that he had inherited in Samos, and came back bringing him the price, three talents.

When Deinias received this, it was at once patent to Charicleia that in some way he had once more become handsome. Again the maid, and the notes, and reproof because he had not come for a long while; and the toadies came running up to dangle a line for him, seeing that Deinias was still good for a meal. But when he had promised to come to her, had actually come, in the early hours of the night, and was inside the house, Demonax, the husband of Charicleia, whether through accidental detection of him or through arrangement with his wife—both

(ἄμφω γὰρ λέγεται) ἐπαναστὰς ὥσπερ ἐκ λόχου
τήν τε αὔλειον ἀποκλείειν ἐκέλευεν καὶ συλλαμβάνειν τὸν Δεινίαν, πῦρ καὶ μάστιγας ἀπειλῶν καὶ
ξίφος ὡς ἐπὶ μοιχὸν σπασάμενος.

Ὁ δὲ συνιδὼν οὗ κακῶν ἦν, μοχλόν τινα πλησίον
κείμενον ἁρπάσας αὐτόν τε ἀποκτείνει τὸν Δημώ-
νακτα, πατάξας εἰς τὸν κρόταφον, καὶ τὴν Χαρί-
κλειαν, οὐ μιᾷ πληγῇ ταύτην, ἀλλὰ καὶ τῷ μοχλῷ
πολλάκις καὶ τῷ ξίφει τοῦ Δημώνακτος ὕστερον.
οἱ δ' οἰκέται τέως μὲν ἑστήκεσαν ἄφωνοι, τῷ παρα-
δόξῳ τοῦ πράγματος ἐκπεπληγμένοι, εἶτα πειρώμενοι συλλαμβάνειν, ὡς καὶ αὐτοῖς ἐπῄει
μετὰ τοῦ ξίφους, ἐκεῖνοι μὲν ἔφευγον, ὁ Δεινίας δὲ
ὑπεξέρχεται [1] τηλικοῦτον ἔργον εἰργασμένος.

Καὶ τὸ μέχρι τῆς ἕω παρὰ τῷ Ἀγαθοκλεῖ
διέτριβεν, ἀναλογιζόμενοι τὰ πεπραγμένα καὶ περὶ
τῶν μελλόντων ὅ τι ἀποβήσεται σκοποῦντες·
ἕωθεν δὲ οἱ στρατηγοὶ παρῆσαν—ἤδη γὰρ τὸ πρᾶγμα
διεβεβόητο—καὶ συλλαβόντες τὸν Δεινίαν, οὐδ'
αὐτὸν ἔξαρνον ὄντα μὴ οὐχὶ πεφονευκέναι, ἀπάγουσι παρὰ τὸν ἁρμοστὴν ὃς ἥρμοζε τὴν Ἀσίαν
τότε. ὁ δὲ βασιλεῖ τῷ μεγάλῳ ἀναπέμπει αὐτόν·
καὶ μετ' οὐ πολὺ κατεπέμφθη ὁ Δεινίας εἰς Γύαρον
νῆσον τῶν Κυκλάδων, ἐν ταύτῃ φεύγειν εἰς ἀεὶ
τεταγμένος ὑπὸ βασιλέως.

18   Ὁ δὲ Ἀγαθοκλῆς καὶ τἆλλα μὲν συνῆν καὶ
συναπῆρεν εἰς τὴν Ἰταλίαν καὶ συνεισῆλθεν εἰς τὸ
δικαστήριον μόνος τῶν φίλων καὶ πρὸς οὐδὲν
ἐνεδέησεν. ἐπεὶ δὲ ἤδη ἔφευγεν ὁ Δεινίας, οὐδὲ
τότε ἀπελείφθη τοῦ ἑταίρου, καταδικάσας δὲ
αὐτὸς αὑτοῦ διέτριβεν ἐν Γυάρῳ καὶ συνέφευγεν

---

[1] ὑπεξέρχεται NB: ὑπέρχεται ΓC, ἐξέρχεται M.

stories are told—springing out upon him as if from
ambush, gave orders to lock the outer door and to
seize Deinias, threatening him with burning and
scourging and coming at him with drawn sword,
as an adulterer.

Perceiving what a calamitous situation he was in,
Deinias seized a bar that lay near and killed not
only Demonax himself, striking him on the temple,
but also Charicleia, not with one blow in her case, but
by striking her first with the bar again and again
and afterwards with the sword of Demonax. The
servants stood speechless in the meantime, dazed
by the suddenness of the thing; then they tried to
seize him, but when he made at them too with the
sword, they fled, and Deinias made good his escape
in spite of his monstrous deed.

The time that remained until dawn he spent with
Agathocles in going over all that had happened and
considering what would come of it in future. At
dawn the magistrates appeared, for by then the
thing had been noised abroad; they arrested
Deinias, who himself did not deny that he had
committed the murders, and brought him before the
governor who then administered Asia. He sent
him to the Emperor, and before long Deinias was
committed to the island of Gyaros, one of the
Cyclades, condemned by the Emperor to live there
in perpetual exile.

Agathocles alone of all his friends kept with him,
sailed with him to Italy, went to the trial with him,
and failed him in nothing. Moreover, when at
length Deinias went into exile, he did not desert his
comrade even then, but of his own accord sentenced
himself to live in Gyaros and share his exile; and

αὐτῷ, καὶ ἐπειδὴ παντάπασιν ἠπόρουν τῶν ἀναγκαίων, παραδοὺς ἑαυτὸν τοῖς πορφυρεῦσι συγκατε-
δύετο καὶ τὸ γινόμενον ἐκ τούτου ἀποφέρων
ἔτρεφε τὸν Δεινίαν· καὶ νοσήσαντά τε ἐπὶ μήκιστον
ἐθεράπευσε καὶ ἀποθανόντος οὐκέτι ἐπανελθεῖν
εἰς τὴν ἑαυτοῦ ἠθέλησεν, ἀλλ᾽ αὐτοῦ ἐν τῇ νήσῳ
ἔμεινεν αἰσχυνόμενος καὶ τεθνεῶτα ἀπολιπεῖν τὸν
φίλον.

Τοῦτό σοι ἔργον φίλου Ἕλληνος οὐ πρὸ πολλοῦ
γενόμενον· ἔτη γὰρ οὐκ οἶδα εἰ πέντε ἤδη διελή-
λυθεν ἀφ᾽ οὗ Ἀγαθοκλῆς ἐν Γυάρῳ ἀπέθανεν.

ΤΟΞΑΡΙΣ

Καὶ εἴθε γε, ὦ Μνήσιππε, ἀνώμοτος ὢν ταῦτα
ἔλεγες, ἵνα καὶ ἀπιστεῖν ἂν ἐδυνάμην αὐτοῖς·
οὕτω Σκυθικόν τινα φίλον τὸν Ἀγαθοκλέα τοῦτον
διηγήσω. πλὴν οὐ [1] δέδια μή τινα καὶ ἄλλον
ὅμοιον εἴπῃς αὐτῷ.

ΜΝΗΣΙΠΠΟΣ

19 Ἄκουε τοίνυν καὶ ἄλλον, ὦ Τόξαρι, Εὐθύδικον
τὸν Χαλκιδέα. διηγεῖτο δέ μοι περὶ αὐτοῦ Σιμύλος
ὁ ναύκληρος ὁ Μεγαρικός, ἐπομοσάμενος ἦ μὴν
αὐτὸς ἑωρακέναι τὸ ἔργον. πλεῖν μὲν γὰρ ἔφη
ἐξ Ἰταλίας Ἀθήναζε περὶ δύσιν Πλειάδος συλλο-
γιμαίους τινὰς ἀνθρώπους κομίζων, ἐν δὲ τούτοις
εἶναι τὸν Εὐθύδικον καὶ μετ᾽ αὐτοῦ Δάμωνα,
Χαλκιδέα καὶ τοῦτον, ἑταῖρον αὐτοῦ· ἡλικιώτας
δὲ εἶναι, τὸν μὲν Εὐθύδικον ἐρρωμένον καὶ καρτερόν,
τὸν δὲ Δάμωνα ὕπωχρον καὶ ἀσθενικόν, ἄρτι ἐκ
νόσου μακρᾶς, ὡς ἐδόκει, ἀνιστάμενον.

---

[1] οὐ Bekker : οὖν B. Not in other MSS.

when they were completely in want of necessities, he joined the purple-fishers, dived with them, brought home what he earned by this, and so supported Deinias. Besides, when the latter fell ill, he took care of him for a very long time, and when he died, did not care to return again to his own country, but remained there in the island, ashamed to desert his friend even after his death.

There you have the deed of a Greek friend which took place not long ago; I hardly think five years have passed since Agathocles died in Gyaros.

TOXARIS

I do wish, Mnesippus, you had told this story without taking an oath, so that I might have been able to disbelieve it, for this Agathocles whom you have described is very much of a Scythian friend. However, I have no fear that you will be able to name any other like him.

MNESIPPUS

Listen then, Toxaris, to the tale of another, Euthydicus of Chalcis. It was repeated to me by Simylus, the sea-captain of Megara, who took his solemn oath that he himself had seen the deed. He said that he was making a voyage from Italy to Athens at about the season of the setting of the Pleiades, carrying a miscellaneous collection of passengers, among whom was Euthydicus, and with him Damon, also of Chalcis, his comrade. They were of the same age, but Euthydicus was vigorous and strong, while Damon was pale and sickly, just convalescing, it seemed, from a prolonged illness.

Ἄχρι μὲν οὖν Σικελίας εὐτυχῶς διαπλεῦσαι
ἔφη ὁ Σιμύλος σφᾶς· ἐπεὶ δὲ τὸν πορθμὸν διαπερά-
σαντες ἐν αὐτῷ ἤδη τῷ Ἰονίῳ ἔπλεον, χειμῶνα
μέγιστον ἐπιπεσεῖν αὐτοῖς. καὶ τὰ μὲν πολλὰ
τί ἄν τις λέγοι, τρικυμίας τινὰς καὶ στροβίλους καὶ
χαλάζας καὶ ἄλλα ὅσα χειμῶνος κακά; ἐπεὶ δὲ
ἤδη σφᾶς κατὰ τὴν Ζάκυνθον εἶναι ἀπὸ ψιλῆς
τῆς κεραίας πλέοντας, ἔτι καὶ σπείρας τινὰς
ἐπισυρομένους, ὡς τὸ ῥόθιον ἐπιδέχεσθαι τῆς
ὁρμῆς, περὶ μέσας νύκτας οἷον ἐν τοσούτῳ σάλῳ
ναυτιάσαντα τὸν Δάμωνα ἐμεῖν ἐκκεκυφότα[1]
ἐς τὴν θάλασσαν· εἶτα, οἶμαι, τῆς νεὼς βιαιότερον
ἐς ὃ ἐκεκύφει μέρος ἐπικλιθείσης καὶ τοῦ κύματος
συναπώσαντος, ἐκπεσεῖν αὐτὸν ἐπὶ τὴν κεφαλὴν ἐς
τὸ πέλαγος, οὐδὲ γυμνὸν τὸν ἄθλιον,[2] ὡς ἂν καὶ
ῥᾷον δύνασθαι νεῖν. εὐθὺς οὖν βοᾶν πνιγόμενον
καὶ μόγις ἑαυτὸν ὑπερέχοντα τοῦ κλύδωνος.

20 Τὸν δὲ Εὐθύδικον, ὡς ἤκουσε—τυχεῖν δὲ γυμνὸν
ἐν τῇ εὐνῇ ὄντα—ῥῖψαι ἑαυτὸν εἰς τὴν θάλασσαν καὶ
καταλαβόντα τὸν Δάμωνα ἤδη ἀπαγορεύοντα—
φαίνεσθαι γὰρ ἐπὶ πολὺ ταῦτα τῆς σελήνης κατα-
λαμπούσης—συμπαρανήχεσθαι καὶ συγκουφίζειν.
σφᾶς δὲ ἐπιθυμεῖν μὲν αὐτοῖς βοηθεῖν καὶ ἐλεεῖν
τὴν συμφορὰν τῶν ἀνδρῶν, μὴ δύνασθαι δέ,
μεγάλῳ τῷ πνεύματι ἐλαυνομένους. πλὴν ἐκεῖνά γε
ποιῆσαι, φελλούς τε γὰρ πολλοὺς ἀφεῖναι αὐτοῖς
καὶ τῶν κοντῶν τινας, ὡς ἐπὶ τούτων ἀπονή-
ξαιντο, εἴ τινι αὐτῶν περιτύχοιεν, καὶ τέλος καὶ
τὴν ἀποβάθραν αὐτὴν οὐ μικρὰν οὖσαν.

---

[1] ἐκκεκυφότα Harmon: ἐξ ἐγκεκυφότα Γ, ἐγκεκυφότα other
MSS.
[2] τὸν ἄθλιον: only N has the article.

TOXARIS, OR FRIENDSHIP

As far as Sicily they had made a fortunate passage, said Simylus; but when they had run through the straits and in due time were sailing in the Adriatic itself, a great tempest fell upon them. Why repeat the many details of his story—huge seas, cyclones, hail, and all the other evils of a storm? But when they were at last abreast of Zacynthos,[1] sailing with the yard bare, and also dragging hawsers in their wake to check the fury of their driving, towards midnight Damon became seasick, as was natural in weather so rough, and began to vomit, leaning outboard. Then, I suppose because the ship was hove down with greater force towards the side over which he was leaning and the high sea contributed a send, he fell overboard head-first; and the poor fellow was not even without his clothes, so as to have been able to swim more easily. So he began at once to call for help, choking and barely able to keep himself above the water.

When Euthydicus, who happened to be undressed and in his bunk, heard him, he flung himself into the sea, got to Damon, who was already giving out (all this was visible at a long distance because the moon was shining) and helped him by swimming beside him and bearing him up. The rest of them, he said, wanted to aid the men and deplored their misfortune, but could not do it because the wind that drove them was too strong; however, they did at least something, for they threw them a number of pieces of cork and some spars, on which they might swim if they chanced upon any of them, and finally even the gang plank, which was not small.

[1] Zante.

THE WORKS OF LUCIAN

Ἐννόησον τοίνυν πρὸς θεῶν ἥντινα ἄν τις
ἄλλην ἐπίδειξιν ἐπιδείξαιτο εὐνοίας βεβαιοτέραν
πρὸς ἄνδρα φίλον ἐν νυκτὶ ἐκπεσόντα ἐς πέλαγος
οὕτως ἠγριωμένον ἢ κοινωνήσας τοῦ θανάτου;
καί μοι ἐπ᾽ ὀφθαλμῶν λαβὲ τὴν ἐπανάστασιν τῶν
κυμάτων, τὸν ἦχον τοῦ ὕδατος ἐπικλωμένου,
τὸν ἀφρὸν περιζέοντα, τὴν νύκτα καὶ τὴν ἀπόγνωσιν·
εἶτα ἀποπνιγόμενον ἐκεῖνον καὶ μόγις ἀνακύπτοντα
καὶ τὰς χεῖρας ὀρέγοντα τῷ ἑταίρῳ, τὸν δὲ
ἐπιπηδῶντα εὐθὺς καὶ συννέοντα καὶ δεδιότα μὴ
προαπόληται[1] αὐτοῦ ὁ Δάμων. οὕτω γὰρ ἂν μάθοις
ὡς οὐκ ἀγεννῆ σοι καὶ τοῦτον φίλον τὸν Εὐθύδικον
διηγησάμην.

ΤΟΞΑΡΙΣ

21 Πότερον δὲ ἀπώλοντο, ὦ Μνήσιππε, οἱ ἄνδρες,
ἤ τις αὐτοῖς ἐκ παραλόγου σωτηρία ἐγένετο;
ὡς ἔγωγε οὐ μετρίως δέδοικα ὑπὲρ αὐτῶν.

ΜΝΗΣΙΠΠΟΣ

Θάρρει, ὦ Τόξαρι, ἐσώθησαν, καὶ ἔτι καὶ
νῦν εἰσιν Ἀθήνησιν ἄμφω φιλοσοφοῦντες. ὁ μὲν
γὰρ Σιμύλος ταῦτα μόνα εἶχε λέγειν ἅ ποτε εἶδε
τῆς νυκτός, τὸν μὲν[2] ἐκπίπτοντα, τὸν δὲ ἐπιπηδῶντα,
καὶ νηχομένους ἐς ὅσον ἐν νυκτὶ καθορᾶν ἐδύνατο.
τὰ δὲ ἀπὸ τούτου οἱ ἀμφὶ τὸν Εὐθύδικον αὐτοὶ
διηγοῦνται. τὸ μὲν γὰρ πρῶτον φελλοῖς τισι
περιπεσόντας ἀνέχειν ἐπὶ τούτων ἑαυτοὺς καὶ
ἀπονήχεσθαι πονηρῶς, ὕστερον δὲ τὴν ἀποβάθραν ἰδόντας ἤδη πρὸς ἕω προσνήξασθαί τε αὐτῇ
καὶ τὸ λοιπὸν ἐπιβάντας εὐμαρῶς προσενεχθῆναι
τῇ Ζακύνθῳ.

[1] προαπόληται vulg.: προαπολεῖται ΓΝΒ.

138

Think now, in the name of the gods! what firmer proof of affection could a man display towards a friend who had fallen overboard at night into a sea so wild, than that of sharing his death? I beg you, envisage the tumult of the seas, the roar of the breaking water, the boiling spume, the night, the despair; then one man strangling, barely keeping up his head, holding his arms out to his friend, and the other leaping after him at once, swimming with him, fearing that Damon would perish first. In that way you can appreciate that in the case of Euthydicus too it is no common friend whom I have described.

TOXARIS

Did the men lose their lives, Mnesippus, or were they unaccountably saved, somehow? I am very concerned about them.

MNESIPPUS

Never fear, Toxaris; they were saved and are now at Athens, both of them, studying philosophy. Simylus, to be sure, could only tell this tale about what he had once seen in the night—the one falling overboard, the other leaping after him, and both swimming as long as he could distinguish them in the darkness. But the sequel was told by Euthydicus himself. In the beginning they came upon some corks on which they supported themselves and kept afloat uncomfortably, but afterwards, seeing the gang plank at last, towards daybreak, they swam to it and then, after climbing upon it, easily drifted to Zacynthos.

---

[2] τὸν μὲν N: not in ΓΒ(C)A.

22 Μετὰ δὲ τούτους οὐ φαύλους ὄντας, ὡς ἔγωγ'
ἂν εἴποιμι, ἄκουσον ἤδη τρίτον ἄλλον οὐδέν τι
χείρονα αὐτῶν.

Εὐδαμίδας Κορίνθιος Ἀρεταίῳ τῷ Κορινθίῳ καὶ
Χαριξένῳ [1] τῷ Σικυωνίῳ φίλοις ἐκέχρητο εὐπόροις
οὖσι πενέστατος αὐτὸς ὤν· ἐπεὶ δὲ ἀπέθνῃσκε,
διαθήκας ἀπέλιπε τοῖς μὲν ἄλλοις ἴσως γελοίους,[2]
σοὶ δὲ οὐκ οἶδα εἰ τοιαῦται δόξουσιν ἀνδρὶ ἀγαθῷ
καὶ φιλίαν τιμῶντι καὶ περὶ τῶν ἐν αὐτῇ πρωτείων
ἁμιλλωμένῳ· ἐγέγραπτο γὰρ ἐν αὐταῖς, " Ἀπο-
λείπω Ἀρεταίῳ μὲν τὴν μητέρα μου τρέφειν καὶ
γηροκομεῖν, Χαριξένῳ δὲ τὴν θυγατέρα μου
ἐκδοῦναι μετὰ προικὸς ὁπόσην ἂν πλείστην ἐπι-
δοῦναι παρ' αὐτοῦ δύνηται "—ἦν δὲ αὐτῷ καὶ
μήτηρ πρεσβῦτις καὶ θυγάτριον ὡραῖον ἤδη γάμου—
" ἢν δέ τι ἅτερος αὐτῶν ἐν τοσούτῳ πάθῃ, τὴν
ἐκείνου μερίδα," φησίν, " ἐχέτω ὁ ἕτερος."
τούτων ἀναγνωσθεισῶν τῶν διαθηκῶν οἱ τὴν
πενίαν μὲν εἰδότες τοῦ Εὐδαμίδα, τὴν φιλίαν δὲ
ἢ πρὸς τοὺς ἄνδρας ἦν αὐτῷ ἀγνοοῦντες ἐν παιδιᾷ
τὸ πρᾶγμα ἐποιοῦντο καὶ οὐδεὶς ὅστις οὐ γελῶν
ἀπηλλάττετο, " Οἷον Ἀρεταῖος καὶ Χαρίξενος οἱ
εὐδαίμονες κλῆρον διαδέξονται," λέγοντες, " εἴπερ
ἀποτίσουσιν Εὐδαμίδα καὶ ζῶντες αὐτοὶ κληρονομή-
σονται ὑπὸ τοῦ νεκροῦ."

23 Οἱ κληρονόμοι δὲ οἷς ταῦτα κατελέλειπτο,
ὡς ἤκουσαν, ἧκον εὐθὺς διαιτῶντες τὰ ἐκ τῶν
διαθηκῶν. ὁ μὲν οὖν Χαρίξενος πέντε μόνας
ἡμέρας ἐπιβιοὺς ἀπέθανεν, ὁ δὲ Ἀρεταῖος ἄριστος
κληρονόμων γενόμενος τήν τε αὐτοῦ καὶ τὴν

---

[1] Χαριξένῳ BN: Χαριξείνῳ Γ(C)Α. Similarly just below;
but Χαρίξενος without variants further on, and in § 23.

After these friends, who were by no means despicable, I should say, let me tell you now of a third who was not a bit inferior to them.

Eudamidas of Corinth had formed friendships with Aretaeus of Corinth and Charixenus of Sicyon, who were both rich, while he was extremely poor. When he died, he left a will which very likely appeared ridiculous to everyone else, but I hardly think it will seem so to you, since you are a good man, a worshipper of friendship, and a competitor for the first prize in it. It was set down in the will: " I leave to Aretaeus my mother to support and cherish in her old age, and to Charixenus my daughter to bestow in marriage with the largest dowry that he can give her out of his own means " (besides an aged mother he had also a daughter, already marriageable); " and if anything should befall either of these men in the meantime, his interest is to go to the other." When this will was read, all who knew of the poverty of Eudamidas but were unaware of the friendship which he had with the men considered the thing a joke, and every one of them went away laughing. " What a fine fortune Aretaeus and Charixenus, the lucky fellows, are coming into," said they, " if they must pay out money to Eudamidas and have the dead man inherit from them while they themselves are still alive! "

The heirs to whom these legacies had been left, on hearing of it, came at once to administer the will. Charixenus, to be sure, outlived his friend only five days; but Aretaeus proved himself the best of legatees. Assuming both his own interest and the

---

² γελοίους ΓΝΒ : γελοίας CA.

ἐκείνου μερίδα παραλαβὼν τρέφει τε τοῦ Εὐδαμίδα
τὴν μητέρα καὶ τὴν θυγατέρα οὐ πρὸ πολλοῦ
ἐκδέδωκεν, ἀπὸ ταλάντων πέντε ὧν εἶχεν δύο μὲν
τῇ ἑαυτοῦ θυγατρί, δύο δὲ τῇ τοῦ φίλου ἐπιδούς,
καὶ τὸν γάμον γε αὐταῖν ἐπὶ μιᾶς ἡμέρας ἠξίωσε
γενέσθαι.

Τί σοι δοκεῖ, ὦ Τόξαρι, ὁ Ἀρεταῖος οὗτος;
ἆρα φαῦλον παράδειγμα φιλίας παρεσχῆσθαι τοιαῦτα
κληρονομήσας καὶ μὴ προδοὺς τὰς διαθήκας τοῦ
φίλου; ἢ τίθεμεν καὶ τοῦτον ἐν ταῖς τελείαις
ψήφοις μίαν τῶν πέντε εἶναι;

ΤΟΞΑΡΙΣ

Καὶ οὗτος μὲν καλός·[1] ἐγὼ δὲ τὸν Εὐδαμίδαν
πολὺ μᾶλλον ἐθαύμασα τοῦ θάρσους ὃ εἶχεν ἐπὶ
τοῖς φίλοις. ἐδήλου γὰρ ὡς καὶ αὐτὸς ἂν τὰ
ὅμοια ἔπραξεν ἐπ' αὐτοῖς, εἰ μὴ καὶ ἐν διαθήκαις
ταῦτα ἐνεγέγραπτο, ἀλλὰ πρὸ τῶν ἄλλων ἧκεν
ἂν ἄγραφος κληρονόμος τῶν τοιούτων.

ΜΝΗΣΙΠΠΟΣ

24 Εὖ λέγεις. τέταρτον δέ σοι διηγήσομαι Ζηνόθεμιν τὸν Χαρμόλεω[2] Μασσαλίηθεν.

Ἐδείχθη δέ μοι ἐν Ἰταλίᾳ πρεσβεύοντι ὑπὲρ
τῆς πατρίδος, καλὸς ἀνὴρ καὶ μέγας καὶ πλούσιος,
ὡς ἐδόκει· παρεκάθητο δὲ αὐτῷ γυνὴ ἐπὶ ζεύγους
ὁδοιπορούντι τά τε ἄλλα εἰδεχθὴς καὶ ξηρὰ τὸ
ἥμισυ τὸ δεξιὸν καὶ τὸν ὀφθαλμὸν ἐκκεκομμένη,
παλλώβητόν τι καὶ ἀπρόσιτον μορμολυκεῖον. εἶτα
ἐπεὶ ἐθαύμασα εἰ καλὸς οὗτος καὶ ὡραῖος ὢν
ἀνέχεται παροχουμένην τοιαύτην αὐτῷ γυναῖκα,

---

[1] καλῶς ΓΒ.
[2] Χαρμόλεω Β: Χαρμόλεων Ν, Χαρμολέου Γ(C)Α.

TOXARIS, OR FRIENDSHIP

other's, he supported Eudamidas' mother and also not long ago portioned his daughter off, giving, out of five talents that he had, dowries of two talents to his own daughter and two to his friend's; moreover, he thought fit that they should both be married on the same day.

What is your opinion, Toxaris, of this man Aretaeus? Has he set a bad example of friendship in accepting such legacies and not playing false to his his friend's last will? Or shall we put him down among those definitely elected as one of the five?

TOXARIS

Yes, he too is noble; but to me Eudamidas is far more wonderful for the confidence he had in his friends. He made it plain that he himself would have done likewise for them; indeed, he would not have hung back if it had not been set down in a will, but would have presented himself before all the rest as an heir to such bequests by intestate succession.

MNESIPPUS

You are quite right.—As the fourth I shall tell you of Zenothemis, son of Charmolaus, of Massilia.

He was pointed out to me in Italy when I was there as an ambassador of my country, a handsome, tall man, and a wealthy one, it seemed. His wife sat beside him as he passed through the street on a chariot; not only was she repulsive in general, but her right side was shrivelled and the eye wanting— a hideously disfigured, unapproachable nightmare. Then, when I expressed my surprise that he, a handsome and attractive man, could endure to have such a woman riding at his side, the person who

ὁ δείξας αὐτὸν διηγεῖτό μοι τὴν ἀνάγκην τοῦ
γάμου ἀκριβῶς εἰδὼς ἕκαστα· Μασσαλιώτης δὲ
καὶ αὐτὸς ἦν.

"Μενεκράτει γάρ," ἔφη, "τῷ πατρὶ τῆς δυσμόρφου
ταύτης φίλος ἦν ὁ Ζηνόθεμις, πλουτοῦντι καὶ
τιμωμένῳ ὁμότιμος ὤν. χρόνῳ δὲ ὁ Μενεκράτης
ἀφῃρέθη τὴν οὐσίαν ἐκ καταδίκης, ὅτεπερ καὶ
ἄτιμος ἐγένετο ὑπὸ τῶν ἑξακοσίων ὡς ἀποφηνάμενος
γνώμην παράνομον. οὕτω δὲ οἱ Μασσαλιῶται
κολάζομεν," ἔφη, "εἴ τις παράνομα γράψειεν.
ἐλυπεῖτο οὖν ὁ Μενεκράτης καὶ ἐπὶ τῇ καταδίκῃ,
ἐπεὶ ἐκ πλουσίου πένης καὶ ἐξ ἐνδόξου ἄδοξος ἐν
ὀλίγῳ ἐγένετο· μάλιστα δὲ αὐτὸν ἠνία θυγάτηρ
αὕτη, ἐπίγαμος ἤδη καὶ [1] ὀκτωκαιδεκαέτις οὖσα,
ἣν οὐδὲ μετὰ πάσης τῆς οὐσίας τοῦ πατρὸς ἦν
πρὸ τῆς καταδίκης ἐκέκτητο ἠξίωσεν ἄν τις τῶν
γε εὐγενῶν[2] καὶ πενήτων ῥᾳδίως παραλαβεῖν,
οὕτως κακοδαίμονα οὖσαν τὴν ὄψιν. ἐλέγετο δὲ
καὶ καταπίπτειν πρὸς τὴν σελήνην αὐξανομένην.

25 "'Ως δὲ ταῦτα πρὸς τὸν Ζηνόθεμιν ἀπωδύρετο,
'Θάρρει,' ἔφη, 'ὦ Μενέκρατες, οὔτε γὰρ ἀπορή-
σεις τῶν ἀναγκαίων καὶ ἡ θυγάτηρ σου ἄξιον τοῦ
γένους τινὰ εὑρήσει νυμφίον.' καὶ ταῦτα ἅμα
διεξιὼν λαβόμενος αὐτοῦ τῆς δεξιᾶς ἦγεν εἰς τὴν
οἰκίαν καὶ τήν τε οὐσίαν πολλὴν οὖσαν ἐνείματο
πρὸς αὐτὸν καὶ δεῖπνον παρασκευασθῆναι κελεύσας
εἱστία τοὺς φίλους καὶ τὸν Μενεκράτη, ὡς δή
τινα τῶν ἑταίρων πεπεικὼς ὑποστῆναι τῆς κόρης
τὸν γάμον. ἐπεὶ δὲ ἐδεδείπνητο αὐτοῖς καὶ

---

[1] καὶ ΓΒ. It is needed, for she was marriageable at
an earlier age than eighteen.

[2] εὐγενῶν Γ : ἀγενῶν Β, vulg. (ἀγεννῶν Ν).

had pointed him out told me what had made the marriage obligatory. He was accurately informed about it all, for he too was a Massaliote.

" Menecrates," he said, " the father of the misshapen woman yonder, had a friend, Zenothemis, who, like himself, was wealthy and distinguished. In course of time Menecrates had his property confiscated by judicial sentence, when he was disfranchised by the Six Hundred for presenting an unconstitutional measure. That," said he, " is the punishment we Massaliotes inflict whenever anyone proposes an unconstitutional enactment. Menecrates was distressed, of course, by the condemnation itself, since in a moment he had become poor instead of rich and dishonoured instead of honoured; but most of all he was worried about this daughter, who was then marriageable, and eighteen; but even with all the wealth which her father had possessed before his condemnation, no well-born man, though poor, would readily have agreed to accept her, so unfortunate was she in her appearance. It was said, too, that she had attacks of the falling sickness when the moon was waxing.

" When he was lamenting these misfortunes to Zenothemis, the latter said: ' Never fear, Menecrates; you shall not lack what you need, and your daughter will find a husband worthy of her lineage.' As he spoke, he grasped him by the hand, took him home, and shared his great wealth with him. Also, he ordered a dinner prepared and invited his friends, including Menecrates, to a wedding-feast, pretending to have persuaded one of his comrades to promise to marry the girl. When their dinner was over and

ἔσπεισαν τοῖς θεοῖς, ἐνταῦθα δὴ μεστὴν αὐτῷ τὴν φιάλην προτείνας, ' Δέδεξο,' εἶπεν, ' ὦ Μενέκρατες, παρὰ τοῦ γαμβροῦ φιλοτησίαν· ἄξομαι γὰρ ἐγὼ τήμερον τὴν σὴν θυγατέρα Κυδιμάχην· τὴν προῖκα δὲ πάλαι εἴληφα, τάλαντα πέντε καὶ εἴκοσι.' τοῦ δέ, ' "Απαγε,' λέγοντος, ' μὴ σύ γε, ὦ Ζηνόθεμι· μὴ οὕτω μανείην ὡς περιδεῖν σε νέον καὶ καλὸν ὄντα κόρῃ αἰσχρᾷ καὶ λελωβημένῃ συγκαταζευγνύμενον,' ὁ δέ, ταῦτα διεξιόντος, ἀράμενος τὴν νύμφην ἀπῄει εἰς τὸν θάλαμον καὶ μετ' ὀλίγον προῆλθεν διακορήσας αὐτήν.

"Καὶ τὸ ἀπ' ἐκείνου σύνεστιν ὑπεραγαπῶν καὶ
26 πάντῃ ὡς ὁρᾷς περιαγόμενος αὐτήν. καὶ οὐχ ὅπως αἰσχύνεται τῷ γάμῳ, ἀλλὰ καὶ σεμνυνομένῳ ἔοικεν, ἐπιδεικνύμενος ὡς καταφρονεῖ μὲν τῶν ἐν τῷ σώματι καλῶν ἢ αἰσχρῶν καὶ πλούτου καὶ δόξης, ἀφορᾷ δὲ ἐς τὸν φίλον καὶ τὸν Μενεκράτη, οὐδὲ οἴεται χείρω πρὸς φιλίαν ὑπὸ τῆς ψήφου τῶν ἑξακοσίων γεγονέναι.

" Πλὴν ἤδη γε τούτων οὕτως αὐτὸν ἠμείψατο ἡ τύχη. παιδίον γὰρ πάγκαλον ἐκ τῆς αἰσχίστης αὐτῷ ταύτης ἐγένετο, καὶ πρώην γε, ἐπεὶ ἀράμενος αὐτὸ εἰσεκόμισεν ὁ πατὴρ εἰς τὸ βουλευτήριον θαλλῷ ἐστεμμένον καὶ μέλανα ἀμπεχόμενον, ὡς ἐλεεινότερον φανείη ὑπὲρ τοῦ πάππου, τὸ μὲν βρέφος ἀνεγέλασε πρὸς τοὺς βουλευτὰς καὶ συνεκρότει τὼ χεῖρε, ἡ βουλὴ δὲ ἐπικλασθεῖσα πρὸς αὐτὸ ἀφίησι τῷ Μενεκράτει τὴν καταδίκην

they had poured the libation to the gods, at that moment Zenothemis held out to him his cup, full of wine, and said: 'Accept, Menecrates, the loving-cup from your son-in-law, for I shall this day wed your daughter Cydimache; her dowry I received long ago, amounting to twenty-five talents.' The other said: 'No, no, Zenothemis, do not! May I never be so mad as to suffer you, who are young and handsome, to make a match with an ugly, disfigured girl!' But while he was saying this, Zenothemis picked up the girl bodily and went into his chamber, from which he returned presently, after having made her his wife.

" From that time on he has lived with her, cherishing her beyond measure and taking her about with him everywhere, as you see. Not only is he unashamed of his marriage, but indeed seems to be proud of it, offering it as proof that he thinks little of physical beauty or ugliness and of wealth and glory, but has high regard for his friend, for Menecrates, and does not believe that the latter's worth, as regards friendship, was lessened by the vote of the Six Hundred.

Already, however, Fortune has requited him for this conduct. He has had a beautiful boy by this ugly woman; and besides, only recently, when the father took the child in his arms and brought him into the Senate-house wreathed with leaves of olive and dressed in black, in order that he might excite greater pity on behalf of his grandfather, the baby burst into laughter before the senators and clapped his two hands, whereupon the senate, softened by him, set the condemnation aside in favour of Menecrates, so that he is now in full possession of his rights

καὶ ἤδη ἐπίτιμός ἐστι, τηλικούτῳ συνηγόρῳ χρησάμενος πρὸς τὸ συνέδριον."

Τοιαῦτα ὁ Μασσαλιώτης ἔλεγεν τὸν Ζηνόθεμιν
εἰργάσθαι ὑπὲρ τοῦ φίλου, ὡς ὁρᾷς, οὐ μικρὰ οὐδὲ
ὑπὸ πολλῶν ἂν Σκυθῶν γενόμενα, οἵ γε κἂν τὰς
παλλακὰς ἀκριβῶς τὰς καλλίστας ἐκλέγεσθαι
λέγονται.

27 Λοιπὸς ἡμῖν ὁ πέμπτος, καί μοι δοκῶ οὐκ
ἄλλον ἐρεῖν Δημητρίου τοῦ Σουνιέως ἐπιλαθόμενος.

Συνεκπλεύσας γὰρ ἐς τὴν Αἴγυπτον ὁ Δημήτριος
'Αντιφίλῳ τῷ 'Αλωπεκῆθεν, ἑταίρῳ ἐκ παίδων
ὄντι καὶ συνεφήβῳ, συνῆν καὶ συνεπαιδεύετο,
αὐτὸς μὲν τὴν ἄσκησιν τὴν Κυνικὴν ἀσκούμενος
ὑπὸ τῷ 'Ροδίῳ ἐκείνῳ σοφιστῇ, ὁ δὲ 'Αντίφιλος
ἰατρικὴν ἄρα ἐμελέτα. καὶ δή ποτε ὁ μὲν Δημήτριος ἔτυχεν ἐς τὴν Αἴγυπτον[1] ἀποδημῶν κατὰ
θέαν τῶν πυραμίδων καὶ τοῦ Μέμνονος· ἤκουε γὰρ
ταύτας ὑψηλὰς οὔσας μὴ παρέχεσθαι σκιάν, τὸν δὲ
Μέμνονα βοᾶν πρὸς ἀνατέλλοντα τὸν ἥλιον. τούτων ἐπιθυμήσας Δημήτριος, θέας μὲν τῶν πυραμίδων, ἀκροάσεως δὲ τοῦ Μέμνονος, ἀναπεπλεύκει
κατὰ τὸν Νεῖλον ἕκτον ἤδη μῆνα, ὀκνήσαντα πρὸς
τὴν ὁδὸν καὶ τὸ θάλπος ἀπολιπὼν τὸν 'Αντίφιλον.

28 'Ο δὲ ἐν τοσούτῳ συμφορᾷ ἐχρήσατο μάλα
γενναίου τινὸς φίλου δεομένῃ. οἰκέτης γὰρ αὐτοῦ,
Σύρος καὶ τοὔνομα καὶ τὴν πατρίδα, ἱεροσύλοις τισὶ
κοινωνήσας συνεισῆλθέν τε αὐτοῖς εἰς τὸ 'Ανουβίδειον

---

[1] There is no need to supply ἄνω (Hartman). The back-
country (χώρα), Egypt, was a thing apart from Alexandria. In
the report of a trial held at Alexandria occurs the statement:
"Her brother is in Egypt, but will come soon" (Hunt,
Select Papyri (L.C.L.), II, No. 263, l. 27; cf. l. 32).

and privileges through employing so tiny an advocate
to present his case to the members in session."

Such are the deeds which, according to the
Massaliote, Zenothemis performed for his friend ;
as you see, they are not trivial, or likely to have
been done by many Scythians, who even in the
matter of concubines are said to be careful to select
the most beautiful.

We have the fifth remaining, and I do not purpose
to forget Demetrius of Sunium and tell of anyone
else.

Demetrius sailed to Egypt with Antiphilus of
Alopece, his friend from boyhood and comrade in their
military training. There they lived and studied
together ; he himself followed the Cynic school of
philosophy under that sophist from Rhodes,[1] while
Antiphilus for his part studied medicine. Well, one
time Demetrius happened to have gone into Egypt
to see the pyramids and the statue of Memnon, for
he had heard that the pyramids, though high, cast
no shadow, and that Memnon utters a cry to the
rising sun. Eager, therefore, to see the pyramids
and to hear Memnon, Demetrius had cruised off up the
Nile six months before, leaving behind him Antiphilus,
who feared the journey and the heat.

In the meantime the latter met with a calamity
which required a very staunch friend. His slave,
Syrus by name and Syrian by nationality, joined
certain temple-robbers, and entered the temple of

[1] It has been suggested that this may have been Agathobulus (cf. p. 19, n. 3), but with little to go on except that
Agathobulus must have been teaching Cynicism in Alexandria
at about the time which this tale presupposes for the Rhodian
sophist. It is hardly safe to assume that he cannot have
had any rivals.

καὶ ἀποσυλήσαντες τὸν θεὸν χρυσᾶς τε φιάλας
δύο καὶ κηρύκιον, χρυσοῦν καὶ τοῦτο, καὶ
κυνοκεφάλους ἀργυροῦς καὶ ἄλλα τοιαῦτα, κατέ-
θεντο πάντα παρὰ τῷ Σύρῳ· εἶτ' ἐμπεσόντες—
ἑάλωσαν γάρ τι ἀπεμπολῶντες—ἅπαντα εὐθὺς
ἔλεγον στρεβλούμενοι ἐπὶ τοῦ τροχοῦ, καὶ ἀγό-
μενοι ἧκον ἐπὶ τὴν οἰκίαν τοῦ Ἀντιφίλου, καὶ τὰ
φώρια ἐξέφερον ὑπὸ κλίνῃ τινὶ ἐν σκοτεινῷ κείμενα.
ὅ τε οὖν Σύρος ἐδέδετο εὐθὺς καὶ ὁ δεσπότης
αὐτοῦ Ἀντίφιλος, οὗτος μὲν καὶ μεταξὺ ἀκροώ-
μενος τοῦ διδασκάλου ἀνασπασθείς.[1] ἐβοήθει δὲ
οὐδείς, ἀλλὰ καὶ οἱ τέως ἑταῖροι ἀπεστρέφοντο ὡς
τὸ Ἀνουβίδειον σεσυληκότα καὶ ἀσέβημα αὐτῶν
ἡγοῦντο εἶναι εἰ συνέπιόν ποτε ἢ συνειστιάθησαν
αὐτῷ. καὶ οἱ λοιποὶ δὲ τῶν οἰκετῶν, δύο ὄντες,
ἅπαντα ἐκ τῆς οἰκίας συσκευασάμενοι ᾤχοντο
φεύγοντες.

29   Ἐδέδετο οὖν ὁ ἄθλιος Ἀντίφιλος πολὺν ἤδη
χρόνον, ἁπάντων ὅσοι ἦσαν κακοῦργοι ἐν τῷ
δεσμωτηρίῳ μιαρώτατος εἶναι δοκῶν, καὶ ὁ
ἐπὶ τῶν δεσμῶν Αἰγύπτιος, δεισιδαίμων ἄνθρωπος,
ᾤετο χαριεῖσθαι καὶ τιμωρήσειν τῷ θεῷ βαρὺς
τῷ Ἀντιφίλῳ ἐφεστώς. εἰ δ' ἀπολογοῖτό ποτε,
λέγων ὡς οὐδὲν τοιοῦτον εἴργασται, ἀναίσχυντος
ἐδόκει καὶ πολὺ πλέον ἐπὶ τούτῳ ἐμισεῖτο. ὑπενό-
σει τοιγαροῦν ἤδη καὶ πονηρῶς εἶχεν οἷον εἰκὸς
χαμαὶ καθεύδοντα καὶ τῆς νυκτὸς οὐδὲ ἀποτείνειν
τὰ σκέλη δυνάμενον ἐν τῷ ξύλῳ κατακεκλειμένα·
τῆς μὲν γὰρ ἡμέρας ὁ κλοιὸς ἤρκει καὶ ἡ ἑτέρα
χεὶρ πεπεδημένη, εἰς δὲ τὴν νύκτα ἔδει ὅλον κατα-

---

[1] Cf. Tyrann., 5: ἐκεῖνος ὁ τοὺς ἐφήβους ἀνασπῶν.

Anubis with them. They robbed the god of two golden libation-bowls, a caduceus, also of gold, some dog-headed figures of silver, and other such matters, all of which they left in trust with Syrus. Then, after their imprisonment (for they were taken when they tried to sell something), they at once told everything when they were broken on the wheel, came under escort to the house of Antiphilus, and fetched out the stolen goods, which were lying under a bed in a dark corner. Consequently Syrus was confined at once, and with him his master, Antiphilus, who was actually seized while he listened to a lecture by his teacher. Nobody came to his assistance; on the contrary, even his erstwhile friends turned their backs upon him on the ground that he had robbed the Anubideum and considered it an act of impiety on their own part if they had ever drunk or eaten with him. Moreover, the two remaining servants bundled up everything in the house and made off.

Poor Antiphilus therefore remained in confinement for a long time, regarded as the most villainous of all the malefactors that there were in the prison, and the Egyptian keeper, a superstitious fellow, thought to gratify and avenge his god by exercising his authority over Antiphilus with a heavy hand. Whenever he defended himself, saying that he had not done anything of the sort, he was thought brazen-faced, and was detested much more for it. Consequently, he sickened at length and was ill, as might be expected in view of the fact that he slept on the ground and at night could not even stretch out his legs, which were confined in the stocks. By day, to be sure, the collar was sufficient, together with manacles upon one hand; but for the night he had to be fully secured by his

THE WORKS OF LUCIAN

δεδέσθαι. καὶ μὴν καὶ τοῦ οἰκήματος ἡ δυσοσμία καὶ τὸ πνῖγος, ἐν ταὐτῷ πολλῶν δεδεμένων καὶ ἐστενοχωρημένων[1] καὶ μόλις ἀναπνεόντων, καὶ τοῦ σιδήρου ὁ ψόφος καὶ ὕπνος ὀλίγος—ταῦτα πάντα χαλεπὰ ἦν καὶ ἀφόρητα οἵῳ ἀνδρὶ ἐκείνων ἀήθει καὶ ἀμελετήτῳ πρὸς οὕτω σκληρὰν τὴν δίαιταν.

30 Ἀπαγορεύοντος δὲ αὐτοῦ καὶ μηδὲ σῖτον αἱρεῖσθαι θέλοντος, ἀφικνεῖταί ποτε καὶ ὁ Δημήτριος, οὐδὲν εἰδὼς τῶν ἤδη γεγενημένων. καὶ ἐπειδὴ ἔμαθεν, ὡς εἶχεν εὐθὺς ἐπὶ τὸ δεσμωτήριον δρομαῖος ἐλθών, τότε μὲν οὐκ εἰσεδέχθη, ἑσπέρα γὰρ ἦν, καὶ ὁ δεσμοφύλαξ πάλαι κεκλεικὼς τὴν θύραν ἐκάθευδε, φρουρεῖν τοῖς οἰκέταις παρακελευσάμενος· ἕωθεν δὲ εἰσέρχεται πολλὰ ἱκετεύσας. καὶ παρελθὼν ἐπὶ πολὺ μὲν ἐζήτει τὸν Ἀντίφιλον ἄδηλον ὑπὸ τῶν κακῶν γεγενημένον, καὶ περιὼν ἀνεσκοπεῖτο καθ᾽ ἕκαστον τῶν δεδεμένων, ὥσπερ εἰώθασιν οἱ τοὺς οἰκείους νεκρούς, ἤδη ἑώλων ὄντων, ἀναζητοῦντες ἐν ταῖς παρατάξεσιν. καὶ εἴ γε μὴ τοὔνομα ἐβόησεν, Ἀντίφιλον Δεινομένους, κἂν ἐπὶ πολὺ ἠγνόησεν ἂν ὅστις ἦν, τοσοῦτον ἤλλακτο ὑπὸ τῶν δεινῶν. ὡς δὲ τὴν φωνὴν αἰσθόμενος ἀνεβόησεν καὶ προσιόντος διαστείλας τὴν κόμην καὶ ἀπάγων τοῦ προσώπου αὐχμηρὰν καὶ συμπεπιλημένην ἔδειξεν αὐτὸν ὅστις ἦν, ἄμφω μὲν αὐτίκα πίπτουσιν ἰλιγγιάσαντες ἐπὶ τῇ ἀπροσδοκήτῳ θέᾳ.

Χρόνῳ δὲ ἀναλαβὼν αὐτόν τε καὶ τὸν Ἀντίφιλον ὁ Δημήτριος καὶ σαφῶς ἕκαστα ὡς εἶχεν ἐκπυθόμενος παρ᾽ αὐτοῦ θαρρεῖν τε παρακελεύεται καὶ διελὼν τὸ τριβώνιον τὸ μὲν ἥμισυ αὐτὸς

---

[1] στενοχωρουμένων MCA.

bonds. Moreover, the stench of the room and its stifling air (since many were confined in the same place, cramped for room, and scarcely able to draw breath), the clash of iron, the scanty sleep—all these conditions were difficult and intolerable for such a man, unwonted to them and unschooled to a life so rigorous.

He was giving up the struggle and refusing even to take food when Demetrius came back, knowing nothing of what had happened until then. As soon as he found out, he set off, just as he was, straight for the prison at a run. At that time, however, he was not admitted, for it was evening and the keeper had long ago locked the door and gone to sleep, after directing his servants to keep watch; but in the morning he obtained admission by vehement entreaty. After entering he made a long search for Antiphilus, who had become unrecognisable through his miseries. He went about examining each of the prisoners just as people do who seek out their own dead among the altered bodies on battle-fields. Indeed, had he not called his name aloud, "Antiphilus, son of Deinomenes," he would not for a long time have known which was he, so greatly had he been changed by his dire straits. But Antiphilus, hearing his voice, cried out; and, as Demetrius approached, he parted his long hair, all unkempt and matted, drew it away from his face, and so disclosed his identity. At once both fell in a faint at the unexpected sight.

After a time Demetrius brought both himself and Antiphilus to their senses, and ascertained from him definitely how everything stood. Then he bade him have no fear, and tearing his short cloak in two, put

ἀναβάλλεται, τὸ λοιπὸν δὲ ἐκείνῳ δίδωσιν, ἃ
εἶχε πιναρὰ καὶ ἐκτετρυχωμένα ῥάκη περισπά-
31 σας. καὶ τὸ ἀπὸ τούτου πάντα τρόπον συνῆν
ἐπιμελούμενος αὐτοῦ καὶ θεραπεύων· παραδοὺς
γὰρ ἑαυτὸν τοῖς ἐν τῷ λιμένι ἐμπόροις ἕωθεν εἰς
μέσην ἡμέραν οὐκ ὀλίγον ἀπέφερεν ἀχθοφορῶν.
εἶτ' ἐπανελθὼν ἂν ἐκ τοῦ ἔργου, μέρος μὲν τοῦ
μισθοῦ τῷ δεσμοφύλακι καταβαλὼν τιθασὸν αὐτῷ
καὶ εἰρηνικὸν ἀπειργάζετο αὐτόν, τὸ λοιπὸν δὲ
εἰς τὴν τοῦ φίλου θεραπείαν ἱκανῶς αὐτῷ διήρκει.
καὶ τὰς μὲν ἡμέρας συνῆν τῷ Ἀντιφίλῳ παρα-
μυθούμενος, ἐπεὶ δὲ νὺξ καταλάβοι, ὀλίγον πρὸ
τῆς θύρας τοῦ δεσμωτηρίου στιβάδιόν τι ποιησά-
μενος καὶ φύλλα ὑποβαλόμενος ἀνεπαύετο.

Χρόνον μὲν οὖν τινα οὕτω διῆγον, εἰσιὼν μὲν
ὁ Δημήτριος ἀκωλύτως, ῥᾷον δὲ φέρων τὴν
32 συμφορὰν ὁ Ἀντίφιλος. ὕστερον δὲ ἀποθανόντος
ἐν τῷ δεσμωτηρίῳ λῃστοῦ τινος ὑπὸ φαρμάκων,
ὡς ἐδόκει, φυλακή τε ἀκριβὴς ἐγένετο καὶ οὐκέτι
παρῄει εἰς τὸ οἴκημα οὐδὲ εἷς τῶν δεομένων.[1]
ἐφ' οἷς ἀπορῶν καὶ ἀνιώμενος, οὐκ ἔχων ἄλλως
παρεῖναι τῷ ἑταίρῳ, προσαγγέλλει ἑαυτὸν ἐλθὼν
πρὸς τὸν ἁρμοστήν, ὡς εἴη κεκοινωνηκὼς τῆς
ἐπὶ τὸν Ἄνουβιν ἐπιβουλῆς.

Ὡς δὲ τοῦτο εἶπεν, ἀπήγετο εὐθὺς ἐς τὸ δεσμωτήριον, καὶ ἀχθεὶς παρὰ τὸν Ἀντίφιλον τοῦτο
γοῦν μόλις, πολλὰ ἱκετεύσας τὸν δεσμοφύλακα,
ἐξειργάσατο παρ' αὐτοῦ, πλησίον τῷ Ἀντιφίλῳ καὶ ὑπὸ τῷ αὐτῷ κλοιῷ δεδέσθαι. ἔνθα δὴ
καὶ μάλιστα ἔδειξε τὴν εὔνοιαν ἣν εἶχε πρὸς
αὐτόν, ἀμελῶν μὲν τῶν καθ' ἑαυτὸν δεινῶν

---

[1] δεομένων G. Hermann: λεγομένων C: λελυμένων ΓΜΝΒ.

on one of the halves himself and gave the remainder to Antiphilus, after stripping from him the filthy, worn-out rags that he was wearing. From that time forth, too, he shared his life in every way, attending and cherishing him; for by hiring himself out to the shipmen in the harbour from early morning until noon, he earned a good deal of money as a stevedore. Then, on returning from his work, he would give part of his pay to the keeper, thus rendering him tractable and peaceful, and the rest sufficed well enough for the maintenance of his friend. Each afternoon he remained with Antiphilus, keeping him in heart; and when night overtook him, he slept just in front of the prison door, where he had made a place to lie and had put down some leaves.

For some time they carried on in this way, Demetrius coming in without hindrance and Antiphilus bearing his misfortune more lightly. But later, after a certain brigand had died in the prison (by poison, it was thought) a close guard was instituted, and not one of those who sought admission could enter the gaol any longer. Perplexed and distressed over this situation, as he had no other way to be with his comrade, he went to the governor and incriminated himself, alleging that he had been an accomplice in the attempt upon Anubis.

When he had made that statement, he was haled straight to prison, and on being brought in with Antiphilus, he managed with difficulty, by dint of urgent entreaties addressed to the warden, to obtain from him one concession, at least—that of being confined near Antiphilus and in the same set of irons. Then indeed, more than any other time, he displayed the affection which he had for him, neglecting his own

(καίτοι ἐνόσησε καὶ αὐτός), ἐπιμελούμενος δὲ
ὅπως ἐκεῖνος μάλιστα καθευδήσει καὶ ἧττον
ἀνιάσεται· ὥστε ῥᾷον ἔφερον μετ' ἀλλήλων κακο-
παθοῦντες.

33 Χρόνῳ δὲ καὶ τοιόνδε τι προσπεσὸν ἔπαυσεν
ἐπὶ πλέον αὐτοὺς δυστυχοῦντας. εἷς γὰρ τῶν
δεδεμένων, οὐκ οἶδ' ὅθεν ῥίνης εὐπορήσας καὶ
συνωμότας πολλοὺς τῶν δεσμωτῶν προσλαβών,
ἀποπρίει τε τὴν ἅλυσιν ᾗ ἐδέδεντο ἑξῆς, τῶν
κλοιῶν εἰς αὐτὴν διειρομένων, καὶ ἀπολύει ἅπαντας·
οἱ δὲ ἀποκτείναντες εὐμαρῶς ὀλίγους ὄντας τοὺς
φύλακας ἐκπηδῶσιν ἀθρόοι. ἐκεῖνοι μὲν οὖν τὸ
παραυτίκα ἔνθα ἐδύναντο ἕκαστος διασπαρέντες
ὕστερον συνελήφθησαν οἱ πολλοί· ὁ Δημήτριος
δὲ καὶ ὁ Ἀντίφιλος κατὰ χώραν ἔμειναν, καὶ τοῦ
Σύρου λαβόμενοι ἤδη ἀπιόντος. ἐπεὶ δὲ ἡμέρα
ἐγένετο, μαθὼν ὁ τὴν Αἴγυπτον ἐπιτετραμμένος
τὸ συμβεβηκὸς ἐπ' ἐκείνους μὲν ἔπεμψεν τοὺς
διωξομένους, μεταστειλάμενος δὲ τοὺς ἀμφὶ τὸν
Δημήτριον ἀπέλυσε τῶν δεσμῶν, ἐπαινέσας ὅτι
μόνοι οὐκ ἀπέδρασαν.

Ἀλλ' οὐκ ἐκεῖνοί γε ἠγάπησαν οὕτως ἀφιέ-
μενοι, ἐβόα δὲ ὁ Δημήτριος καὶ δεινὰ ἐποίει,
ἀδικεῖσθαι σφᾶς οὐ μικρὰ εἰ δόξουσι κακοῦργοι
ὄντες ἐλέῳ ἢ ἐπαίνῳ τοῦ μὴ ἀποδρᾶναι ἀφεῖσθαι·
καὶ τέλος ἠνάγκασαν τὸν δικαστὴν ἀκριβῶς τὸ
πρᾶγμα ἐξετάσαι. ὁ δὲ ἐπεὶ ἔμαθεν οὐδὲν ἀδι-
κοῦντας, ἐπαινέσας αὐτούς, τὸν Δημήτριον δὲ
καὶ πάνυ θαυμάσας, ἀφίησι παραμυθησάμενος

adversities (though he himself had fallen ill) but taking care that Antiphilus should sleep as well as possible and should suffer less distress. So they bore their discomforts more easily by sharing them with each other.

In time an accident occurred which relieved them from further misfortune. One of the men in irons, having somehow obtained possession of a file and enlisted many of the prisoners in a plot, cut the chain to which they were all attached in a row, with their fetters strung upon it, and so set them all free; whereupon they easily killed the guards, who were few, and escaped together. Well, those others scattered at once, going wherever each one of them could, and afterwards were arrested, most of them. Demetrius and Antiphilus, however, remained where they were, and seized Syrus just as he was about to go. When daylight came, as soon as the prefect of Egypt learned what had happened, he sent men to hunt down the others, but summoned Demetrius and his friend and freed them from imprisonment, praising them because they alone did not run away.

They were not the men, however, to be content with being released in that way. Demetrius cried out and made a great stir, saying that grave injustice was being done them, since it would be thought that they were criminals, and were being released by way of mercy or commendation because they had not run away; and at length they forced the magistrate to undertake an accurate investigation of the affair. When he discovered that they were not guilty, he commended them, expressing very great admiration for Demetrius, and in dismissing them condoled with them over the punishment which they had undergone

ἐπὶ τῇ κολάσει ἦν ἠνέσχοντο ἀδίκως δεθέντες,
καὶ ἑκάτερον δωρησάμενος παρ' αὐτοῦ, δραχμαῖς
μὲν μυρίαις τὸν Ἀντίφιλον, δὶς τοσαύταις δὲ τὸν
Δημήτριον.

34 Ὁ μὲν οὖν Ἀντίφιλος ἔτι καὶ νῦν ἐν Αἰγύπτῳ
ἐστίν, ὁ δὲ Δημήτριος καὶ τὰς αὐτοῦ δισμυρίας
ἐκείνῳ καταλιπὼν ᾤχετο ἀπιὼν εἰς τὴν Ἰνδικὴν
παρὰ τοὺς Βραχμᾶνας, τοσοῦτον εἰπὼν πρὸς τὸν
Ἀντίφιλον, ὡς συγγνωστὸς ἂν εἰκότως νομίζοιτο ἤδη ἀπολιπὼν αὐτόν· οὔτε γὰρ αὐτὸς
δεῖσθαι τῶν χρημάτων, ἔστ' ἂν αὐτὸς ᾖ ὅπερ
ἐστίν, ἀρκεῖσθαι ὀλίγοις δυνάμενος, οὔτε ἐκείνῳ
ἔτι δεῖν φίλου, εὐμαρῶν αὐτῷ τῶν πραγμάτων
γεγενημένων.

Τοιοῦτοι, ὦ Τόξαρι, οἱ Ἕλληνες φίλοι. εἰ δὲ
μὴ προδιεβεβλήκεις ἡμᾶς ὡς ἐπὶ ῥήμασι μέγα
φρονοῦντας, καὶ αὐτοὺς ἄν σοι τοὺς λόγους διεξῆλ-
θον, πολλοὺς καὶ ἀγαθοὺς ὄντας, οὓς ὁ Δημήτριος
εἶπεν ἐν τῷ δικαστηρίῳ, ὑπὲρ αὐτοῦ μὲν οὐδὲν
ἀπολογούμενος, ὑπὲρ τοῦ Ἀντιφίλου δέ, καὶ
δακρύων προσέτι καὶ ἱκετεύων καὶ τὸ πᾶν ἐφ'
ἑαυτὸν ἀναδεχόμενος, ἄχρι μαστιγούμενος ὁ Σύρος
ἀμφοτέρους ἀφίησιν αὐτούς.

35 Ἐγὼ μὲν οὖν τούτους ὀλίγους ἀπὸ πλειόνων,
οὓς πρώτους ἡ μνήμη ὑπέβαλε, διηγησάμην σοι
ἀγαθοὺς καὶ βεβαίους φίλους. καὶ τὸ λοιπὸν
ἤδη καταβὰς ἀπὸ τοῦ λόγου σοὶ τὴν ῥήτραν
παραδίδωμι· σὺ δὲ ὅπως μὴ χείρους ἐρεῖς τοὺς
Σκύθας, ἀλλὰ πολλῷ τούτων ἀμείνους, αὐτῷ σοὶ
μελήσει, εἴ τι καὶ τῆς δεξιᾶς πεφρόντικας, ὡς
μὴ ἀποτμηθείης αὐτήν. ἀλλὰ χρὴ ἄνδρα ἀγαθὸν
εἶναι· ἐπεὶ καὶ γελοῖα ἂν πάθοις Ὀρέστην μὲν καὶ

through their unjust imprisonment and presented each of them with a gift out of his own pocket, Antiphilus with ten thousand drachmas and Demetrius with twice as much.

Antiphilus is still in Egypt, but Demetrius left his own twenty thousand to his friend and went away to India, to join the Brahmans, merely saying to Antiphilus that he might fairly be held excusable for leaving him now; for he himself would not want the money as long as he remained what he was, able to content himself with little, and Antiphilus would not need a friend any longer, since his circumstances had become easy.

That, Toxaris, is what Greek friends are like. If you had not previously calumniated us as priding ourselves greatly upon words, I should have repeated for you the very speech, a long one and a good one, that Demetrius made in the court-room, not defending himself at all but only Antiphilus; weeping, moreover, and imploring, and taking the whole thing upon himself until Syrus under the lash exonerated both of them.

I have told you these few instances out of a greater number (the first that my memory supplied), of friends that were good and true; and now, dismounting from my steed, I yield the word henceforth to you. How you are to make out that your Scythians are not worse, but much better than these men, will be your own look-out, if you are at all concerned about your right hand, for fear of having it cut off. But you must show yourself a man of prowess, for you would put yourself in a laughable position if, after your very expert laudation of Orestes and

Πυλάδην πάνυ σοφιστικῶς ἐπαινέσας, ὑπὲρ δὲ
τῆς Σκυθίας φαῦλος ῥήτωρ φαινόμενος.[1]

ΤΟΞΑΡΙΣ

Εὖ γε, ὦ Μνήσιππε, ὅτι καὶ παροτρύνεις με
πρὸς τὸν λόγον, ὥσπερ οὐ πάνυ σοι μέλον εἰ
ἀποτμηθείης τὴν γλῶτταν κρατηθεὶς ἐν τοῖς λόγοις.
πλὴν ἄρξομαί γε ἤδη, μηδὲν ὥσπερ σὺ καλλιλο-
γησάμενος· οὐ γὰρ Σκυθικὸν τοῦτο, καὶ μάλιστα
ἐπειδὰν τὰ ἔργα ὑπερφθέγγηται τοὺς λόγους.
προσδοκήσῃς δὲ μηδὲν τοιοῦτο παρ᾽ ἡμῶν οἷα σὺ
διεξελήλυθας, ἐπαινῶν εἴ τις ἄπροικον ἔγημεν
αἰσχρὰν γυναῖκα ἢ εἴ τις ἀργύριον ἐπέδωκε
γαμουμένῃ φίλου ἀνδρὸς θυγατρὶ δύο τάλαντα,
ἢ[2] καὶ νὴ Δί᾽ εἴ τις παρέσχεν ἑαυτὸν δεδησόμενον
ἐπὶ προδήλῳ τῷ μικρὸν ὕστερον λυθήσεσθαι·
πάνυ γὰρ εὐτελῆ ταῦτα καὶ μεγαλουργὸν ἐν αὐτοῖς
36 ἢ ἀνδρεῖον ἔνι οὐδέν. ἐγὼ δέ σοι διηγήσομαι
φόνους πολλοὺς καὶ πολέμους καὶ θανάτους ὑπὲρ
τῶν φίλων, ἵν᾽ εἰδῇς ὡς παιδιὰ τὰ ὑμέτερά ἐστιν
παρὰ τὰ Σκυθικὰ ἐξετάζεσθαι.

Καίτοι οὐδὲ ἀλόγως αὐτὸ πεπόνθατε, ἀλλὰ
εἰκότως τὰ μικρὰ ταῦτα ἐπαινεῖτε· οὐδὲ γὰρ
οὐδέ εἰσιν ὑμῖν ἀφορμαὶ ὑπερμεγέθεις πρὸς ἐπίδειξιν φιλίας ἐν εἰρήνῃ βαθείᾳ βιοῦσιν, ὥσπερ
οὐδ᾽ ἂν[3] ἐν γαλήνῃ μάθοις εἰ ἀγαθὸς ὁ κυβερνήτης
ἐστί· χειμῶνος γὰρ δεήσει σοὶ πρὸς τὴν διάγνωσιν.
παρ᾽ ἡμῖν δὲ συνεχεῖς οἱ πόλεμοι, καὶ ἢ ἐπελαύ-
νομεν ἄλλοις ἢ ὑποχωροῦμεν ἐπιόντας ἢ συμπε-

---

[1] φαινόμενος ΓΒ: γενόμενος NCA.
[2] ἢ Lehmann: not in MSS.
[3] ἂν Geist: not in MSS.

TOXARIS, OR FRIENDSHIP

Pylades, you should reveal yourself a poor spokesman on behalf of Scythia.

Well done, Mnesippus! You are giving me encouragement for my speech, as if it did not matter at all to you whether you get the worst of it in our dispute and have your tongue docked. However, I shall begin at once, without any display of fine words such as you have made; for that is not a Scythian habit, especially when the deeds speak louder than the words. And do not expect from us anything like what you told of when you commended a man if he married an ugly wife without a dowry, or if he gave money to the amount of two talents to the daughter of a friend on her marriage, or even, by Zeus, if he allowed himself to be imprisoned when it was obvious that he would soon be released; for those are very paltry matters, and there is nothing of greatness or bravery in them. I shall tell you of many deeds of blood and battles and deaths for the sake of friends, that you may know the achievements of your people to be child's play in comparison with those of the Scythians.

Yet it is not unaccountable that this is so with you Greeks, but natural for you to praise these trivial matters; for you lack, you entirely lack momentous occasions for the display of friendship, living as you do in profound peace. Just so in calm weather a man cannot tell whether his sailing-master is good; he will need a storm to determine that. With us, however, wars are continuous, and we are always either invading the territory of others, or withdrawing before invaders, or meeting in battle over

161

σόντες ὑπὲρ νομῆς ἢ λείας μαχόμεθα, ἔνθα μάλιστα
δεῖ φίλων ἀγαθῶν· καὶ διὰ τοῦτο ὡς βεβαιότατα
συντιθέμεθα τὰς φιλίας, μόνον τοῦτο ὅπλον ἄμαχον
καὶ δυσπολέμητον εἶναι νομίζοντες.

37 Πρότερον δέ σοι εἰπεῖν βούλομαι ὃν τρόπον
ποιούμεθα τοὺς φίλους, οὐκ ἐκ τῶν πότων, ὥσπερ
ὑμεῖς, οὐδὲ εἰ συνέφηβός τις ἢ γείτων ἦν, ἀλλ'
ἐπειδάν τινα ἴδωμεν ἀγαθὸν ἄνδρα καὶ μεγάλα
ἐργάσασθαι δυνάμενον, ἐπὶ τοῦτον ἅπαντες σπεύ-
δομεν, καὶ ὅπερ ὑμεῖς ἐν τοῖς γάμοις, τοῦτο ἡμεῖς
ἐπὶ τῶν φίλων ποιεῖν ἀξιοῦμεν, ἐπὶ πολὺ μνηστευό-
μενοι καὶ πάντα ὁμοῦ πράττοντες ὡς μὴ διαμαρτά-
νοιμεν τῆς φιλίας μηδὲ ἀπόβλητοι δόξωμεν εἶναι.
κἀπειδὰν προκριθείς τις ἤδη φίλος ᾖ, συνθῆκαι
τὸ ἀπὸ τούτου καὶ ὅρκος ὁ μέγιστος, ἦ μὴν καὶ
βιώσεσθαι μετ' ἀλλήλων καὶ ἀποθανεῖσθαι, ἢν
δέῃ, ὑπὲρ τοῦ ἑτέρου τὸν ἕτερον· καὶ οὕτω ποιοῦ-
μεν. ἀφ' οὗ γὰρ ἂν[1] ἐντεμόντες ἅπαξ τοὺς
δακτύλους ἐνσταλάξωμεν τὸ αἷμα εἰς κύλικα καὶ
τὰ ξίφη ἄκρα βάψαντες ἅμα ἀμφότεροι ἐπι-
σχόμενοι πίωμεν, οὐκ ἔστιν ὅ τι τὸ μετὰ τοῦτο
ἡμᾶς διαλύσειεν ἄν. ἐφεῖται δὲ τὸ μέγιστον
ἄχρι τριῶν ἐς τὰς συνθήκας εἰσιέναι· ὡς ὅστις
ἂν πολύφιλος ᾖ, ὅμοιος ἡμῖν δοκεῖ ταῖς κοιναῖς
ταύταις καὶ μοιχευομέναις γυναιξί, καὶ οἰόμεθα
οὐκέθ' ὁμοίως ἰσχυρὰν αὐτοῦ τὴν φιλίαν εἶναι,
πρὸς πολλὰς εὐνοίας διαιρεθεῖσαν.

38 Ἄρξομαι δὲ ἀπὸ τῶν Δανδάμιδος πρώην γενο-

---

[1] ἂν Struve: not in MSS.

---

[1] Cf. Herodotus, IV, 70, who, however, makes no reference
to the point that both drink from the same cup at the same

pasturage or stolen cattle, where need for good friends is greatest; and for that reason we cement our friendships as strongly as we can, thinking this to be the only irresistible and unconquerable weapon of war.

First of all, I wish to tell you how we make our friends. Not through boon-companionship, as you do, nor because a man has been a comrade of ours in military training or a neighbour. No, when we see a brave man, capable of great achievements, we all make after him, and we think fit to behave in forming friendships as you do in seeking brides, paying them protracted court and doing everything in their company to the end that we may not fall short of attaining their friendship or be thought to deserve rejection. And when a man has been singled out and is at last a friend, there ensue formal compacts and the most solemn of oaths that we will not only live with one another but die, if need be, for each other; and we do just that. For, once we have cut our fingers, let the blood drip into a cup, dipped our sword-points into it, and then, both at once, have set it to our lips and drunk, there is nothing thereafter that can dissolve the bond between us.[1] We are permitted at most to enter into three such compacts, since a man of many friends resembles, we think, promiscuous women with their lovers, and we consider that his friendship is no longer of the same strength when it has been split up into a multitude of loyalties.

I shall begin with the affair of Dandamis, which

time, which is proved by a gold plaque from the tomb of Kul-Oba near Kertch (often reproduced; e.g., Minns, *Scythians and Greeks*, p. 203), where a drinking horn is used.

μένων. ὁ γὰρ Δάνδαμις ἐν τῇ πρὸς Σαυρομάτας
συμπλοκῇ, ἀπαχθέντος αἰχμαλώτου Ἀμιζώκου τοῦ
φίλου αὐτοῦ—μᾶλλον δὲ πρότερον ὀμοῦμαί σοι τὸν
ἡμέτερον ὅρκον, ἐπεὶ καὶ τοῦτο ἐν ἀρχῇ διωμολο-
γησάμην· οὐ μὰ γὰρ τὸν Ἄνεμον καὶ τὸν Ἀκινάκην, οὐδὲν πρὸς σέ, ὦ Μνήσιππε, ψεῦδος ἐρῶ περὶ
τῶν φίλων τῶν Σκυθῶν.[1]

ΜΝΗΣΙΠΠΟΣ

Ἐγὼ μὲν οὐ πάνυ σου ὀμνύντος ἐδεόμην· σὺ
δὲ ὅμως εὖ ποιῶν οὐδένα θεῶν [2] ἐπωμόσω.

ΤΟΞΑΡΙΣ

Τί σὺ λέγεις ; οὔ σοι δοκοῦσιν ὁ Ἄνεμος καὶ
ὁ Ἀκινάκης θεοὶ εἶναι ; οὕτως ἄρα ἠγνόησας ὅτι
ἀνθρώποις μεῖζον οὐδέν ἐστιν ζωῆς τε καὶ θανάτου ;
ὁπόταν τοίνυν τὸν Ἄνεμον καὶ τὸν Ἀκινάκην
ὀμνύωμεν, ταῦτα ὀμνύομεν ὡς τὸν μὲν ἄνεμον
ζωῆς αἴτιον ὄντα, τὸν ἀκινάκην δὲ ὅτι ἀποθνήσκειν
ποιεῖ.

ΜΝΗΣΙΠΠΟΣ

Καὶ μὴν εἰ διά γε τοῦτο, καὶ ἄλλους ἂν ἔχοιτε
πολλοὺς θεοὺς οἷος ὁ Ἀκινάκης ἐστί, τὸν Ὀιστὸν
καὶ τὴν Λόγχην καὶ Κώνειον δὲ καὶ Βρόχον καὶ τὰ
τοιαῦτα· ποικίλος γὰρ οὗτος ὁ θεὸς ὁ θάνατος καὶ
ἀπείρους τὰς ἐφ᾽ ἑαυτὸν παρέχεται ἀγούσας
ὁδούς.

ΤΟΞΑΡΙΣ

Ὁρᾷς τοῦτο ὡς ἐριστικὸν ποιεῖς καὶ δικανικόν,
ὑποκρούων μεταξὺ καὶ διαφθείρων μου τὸν λόγον ;
ἐγὼ δὲ ἡσυχίαν ἦγον σοῦ λέγοντος.

---

[1] σκυθῶν ΓΝΒΜ : σκυθικῶν (C)A vulg. Cf. § 9, οἱ φίλοι
οἱ Σκύθαι.
[2] τῶν θεῶν C.

happened recently. In our engagement with the Sauromatae, when Amizoces had been taken prisoner, his friend Dandamis—but stay! first let me take my oath for you in our way, since that also was part of the agreement that I made with you in the beginning. I swear by Wind and Glaive that I shall tell you no falsehood, Mnesippus, about Scythian friends.

MNESIPPUS

I scarcely felt the need of your swearing, but you did well to avoid taking oath by any god!

TOXARIS

What is that you say? Do you not think Wind and Glaive are gods? Were you really so unaware that there is nothing more important to mankind than life and death? Well then, when we swear by Wind and Glaive, we do so because the wind is the source of life, and the glaive the cause of death.[1]

MNESIPPUS

Well, really, if that is the reason, you could have many other such gods as Glaive is—Arrow, Spear, Poison, Halter, and the like; for this god Death takes many shapes and puts at our disposal an infinite number of roads that lead to him.

TOXARIS

Don't you see how it smacks of sophists bickering and lawyers in court for you to act this way, interrupting and spoiling my story? I kept still while you were talking.

[1] Herodotus alludes to Scythian sword-worship (IV, 62), but says nothing of their worshipping the wind, which Rostovtzeff takes to be an invention of Lucian's.

THE WORKS OF LUCIAN

ΜΝΗΣΙΠΠΟΣ

'Αλλ' οὐκ αὖθίς γε, ὦ Τόξαρι, ποιήσω τοῦτο,
πάνυ γὰρ ὀρθῶς ἐπετίμησας· ὥστε θαρρῶν τό γε
ἐπὶ τούτῳ λέγε, ὡς μηδὲ παρόντος ἐμοῦ τοῖς
λόγοις, οὕτω σιωπήσομαί σοι.

ΤΟΞΑΡΙΣ

39 Τετάρτη μὲν ἦν ἡμέρα τῆς φιλίας Δανδάμιδι καὶ
'Αμιζώκῃ, ἀφ' οὗ τὸ ἀλλήλων αἷμα συνεπεπώ-
κεσαν· ἧκον δὲ ἡμῖν ἐπὶ τὴν χώραν Σαυρομάται
μυρίοις μὲν ἱππεῦσιν, οἱ πεζοὶ δὲ τρὶς τοσοῦτοι
ἐπεληλυθέναι ἐλέγοντο. οἷα δὲ οὐ προϊδομένοις
τὴν ἔφοδον αὐτῶν ἐπιπεσόντες[1] ἅπαντας μὲν
τρέπουσι, πολλοὺς δὲ τῶν μαχίμων κτείνουσι,
τοὺς δὲ καὶ ζῶντας ἀπάγουσι, πλὴν εἴ τις ἔφθη
διανηξάμενος εἰς τὸ πέραν τοῦ ποταμοῦ, ἔνθα
ἡμῖν τὸ ἥμισυ τοῦ στρατοπέδου καὶ μέρος τῶν
ἁμαξῶν ἦν· οὕτω γὰρ ἐσκηνώσαμεν τότε, οὐκ
οἶδα ὅ τι δόξαν τοῖς ἀρχιπλάνοις ἡμῶν, ἐπ'
ἀμφοτέρας τὰς ὄχθας τοῦ Τανάϊδος.

Εὐθὺς οὖν ἥ τε λεία περιηλαύνετο καὶ τὰ αἰχμά-
λωτα συνείχετο καὶ τὰς σκηνὰς διήρπαζον καὶ
τὰς ἁμάξας κατελαμβάνοντο, αὐτάνδρους τὰς
πλείστας ἁλισκομένας, καὶ ἐν ὀφθαλμοῖς ἡμῶν
ὑβρίζοντες τὰς παλλακίδας καὶ τὰς γυναῖκας·
40 ἡμεῖς δὲ ἠνιώμεθα τῷ πράγματι. ὁ δὲ 'Αμιζώκης
ἀγόμενος—ἑαλώκει γάρ—ἐβόα τὸν φίλον ὀνομαστί,
κακῶς δεδεμένος, καὶ ὑπεμίμνησκεν τῆς κύλικος

---

[1] ἐπεισπεσόντες C.

166

TOXARIS, OR FRIENDSHIP

MNESIPPUS

I won't do it again, anyhow, Toxaris, for you were quite right in your reproof. Therefore, you may proceed confidently, as if I were not even here while you are talking, so silent shall I be for you.

TOXARIS

The friendship of Dandamis and Amizoces was three days old, counting from the time when they drank each other's blood, when the Sauromatae descended upon our country with ten thousand horse; and the foot came over the border, it was said, in thrice that number. As our people had not foreseen their attack, they not only routed us completely when they fell upon us, but slew many of the fighting men and took the rest prisoners, except one or another who succeeded in swimming over to the other side of the river, where we had half our encampment and part of the wagons; for that was the way in which we had pitched our tents at the time, since for some reason unknown to me it had seemed good to the leaders of our horde—on both banks of the Tanais.[1]

At once they began to round up the cattle, secure the prisoners, plunder the tents, and seize the wagons, taking most of them with all their occupants and offering violence to our concubines and wives before our very eyes; and we were distressed over the situation. But as Amizoces was being dragged away—for he had been taken—he called upon his friend by name because of his disgraceful captivity

---

[1] This dates the tale's origin at a time when the Scythians and the Sauromatae, or Sarmatians, faced each other on opposite sides of the Don, as Rostovtzeff has pointed out.

THE WORKS OF LUCIAN

καὶ τοῦ αἵματος. ὧν ἀκούσας ὁ Δάνδαμις οὐδὲν
ἔτι μελλήσας ἁπάντων ὁρώντων διανήχεται εἰς
τοὺς πολεμίους· καὶ οἱ μὲν Σαυρομάται διηρ-
μένοι τοὺς ἄκοντας ὥρμησαν ἐπ' αὐτὸν ὡς κατα-
κεντήσοντες, ὁ δὲ ἐβόα τὸ " Ζίριν." [1] τοῦτο δὲ ἦν
τις εἴπῃ, οὐκέτι φονεύεται ὑπ' αὐτῶν, ἀλλὰ
δέχονται αὐτὸν ὡς ἐπὶ λύτροις ἥκοντα.

Καὶ δὴ ἀναχθεὶς πρὸς τὸν ἄρχοντα αὐτῶν
ἀπῄτει τὸν φίλον, ὁ δὲ λύτρα ᾔτει· μὴ γὰρ προήσεσθαι, εἰ μὴ μεγάλα ὑπὲρ αὐτοῦ λάβοι. [2] ὁ
Δάνδαμις δέ, " Ἃ μὲν εἶχον," φησίν, " ἅπαντα
διήρπασται ὑφ' ὑμῶν, εἰ δέ τι δύναμαι γυμνὸς
ὑποτελέσαι, ἕτοιμος ὑποστῆναι ὑμῖν, καὶ πρόσ-
ταττε ὅ τι ἂν θέλῃς. εἰ βούλει δέ, ἐμὲ ἀντὶ
τούτου λαβὼν [3] κατάχρησαι πρὸς ὅ τι σοι φίλον."
ὁ δὲ Σαυρομάτης, " Οὐδέν," ἔφη, " δεῖ ὅλον
κατέχεσθαί σε, καὶ ταῦτα Ζίριν ἥκοντα, σὺ δὲ
ὧν ἔχεις μέρος καταβαλὼν ἄγου τὸν φίλον."
ἤρετο ὁ Δάνδαμις ὅ τι καὶ βούλεται λαβεῖν·
ὁ δὲ τοὺς ὀφθαλμοὺς ᾔτησεν. ὁ δὲ αὐτίκα παρέσχεν ἐκκόπτειν αὐτούς· κἀπειδὴ ἐξεκέκοπτο καὶ
ἤδη τὰ λύτρα εἶχον οἱ Σαυρομάται, παραλαβὼν
τὸν Ἀμιζώκην ἐπανῄει ἐπερειδόμενος αὐτῷ, καὶ
ἅμα διανηξάμενοι ἀπεσώθησαν πρὸς ἡμᾶς.

41   Τοῦτο γενόμενον παρεμυθήσατο ἅπαντας Σκύθας
καὶ οὐκέτι ἡττᾶσθαι ἐνόμιζον, ὁρῶντες ὅτι τὸ

[1] τὸ Ζίριν Schmieder; τὸ ζηρίν C; τὸν ζίριν Γ; τὸν ζῖριν N;
τὸν ζίρην B. Below (Ζίριν ἥκοντα) the same variations in
spelling occur. The corruption of τὸ to τὸν arose from knowing, or guessing (from the context below), that *Zirin* was a
masculine noun.
[2] λάβοι N: λάβῃ ΓBC.   [3] λαβὼν NB: not in ΓΜ(C)A.

and reminded him of the cup and the blood. When Dandamis heard that, without an instant's hesitation, under the eyes of everyone he swam over to the enemy. The Sauromatae rushed at him with brandished javelins, intending to spear him to death, but he called out "Zirin." If anyone says that, he is not killed by them, but is received as coming to offer ransom.[1]

On being brought up to the leader, he demanded his friend back, but the man asked for ransom; he would not let him go, he said, unless he got a great deal for him. Dandamis replied: "All that I had has been carried off by your people; but if in any way I can make payment as I stand, I am ready to proffer it to you. Lay on me whatever command you will; if you like, take me in his place and use me as you please." The Sauromatian answered: "There is no need for you to put yourself completely in our power, especially when you come as Zirin; pay part of what you possess, and take away your friend." Dandamis asked what he would have; whereupon the other demanded his eyes, and at once he allowed them to be put out. When that had been done and the Sauromatae had their ransom, taking Amizoces, he set off for home leaning upon him, and by swimming across together they got back to us in safety.

This occurrence heartened all the Scythians, and they no longer thought themselves beaten, seeing

[1] It is clear from the use of the word *Zirin* below that it does not mean "ransom" or "ransomer," and cannot be connected with late Persian *Zer*, "gold," as Vasmer suggests (*Iranier in Südrussland*, p. 39). It must denote something like "brother," "friend," "envoy."

μέγιστον ἡμῖν τῶν ἀγαθῶν οὐκ ἀπήγαγον οἱ
πολέμιοι, ἀλλ' ἔτι[1] ἦν παρ' ἡμῖν ἡ ἀγαθὴ γνώμη
καὶ ἡ πρὸς τοὺς φίλους πίστις. καὶ τοὺς Σαυρομάτας δὲ τὸ αὐτὸ οὐ μετρίως ἐφόβησε, λογι-
ζομένους πρὸς οἵους ἄνδρας ἐκ παρασκευῆς μαχοῦν-
ται, εἰ καὶ ἐν τῷ ἀπροσδοκήτῳ τότε ὑπερέσχον·
ὥστε νυκτὸς ἐπιγενομένης ἀπολιπόντες τὰ πλεῖστα
τῶν βοσκημάτων καὶ τὰς ἁμάξας ἐμπρήσαντες
ᾤχοντο φεύγοντες. ὁ μέντοι Ἀμιζώκης οὐκέτι
ἠνέσχετο βλέπειν αὐτὸς ἐπὶ τυφλῷ τῷ Δανδάμιδι, ἀλλὰ τυφλώσας καὶ αὐτὸς ἑαυτὸν ἀμφότεροι κάθηνται ὑπὸ τοῦ κοινοῦ τῶν Σκυθῶν δημοσίᾳ
μετὰ πάσης τιμῆς τρεφόμενοι.

42   Τί τοιοῦτον, ὦ Μνήσιππε, ὑμεῖς ἔχοιτε ἂν
εἰπεῖν, εἰ καὶ ἄλλους σοι δέκα δοίη τις ἐπὶ τοῖς
πέντε καταριθμήσασθαι, ἀνωμότους, εἰ βούλει,
ὡς καὶ πολλὰ ἐπιψεύδοιο αὐτοῖς ; καίτοι ἐγὼ
μέν σοι γυμνὸν τὸ ἔργον διηγησάμην· εἰ δὲ σύ
τινα τοιοῦτον ἔλεγες, εὖ οἶδα, ὁπόσα ἂν κομψὰ
ἐγκατέμιξας τῷ λόγῳ, οἷα ἱκέτευεν ὁ Δάνδαμις
καὶ ὡς ἐτυφλοῦτο καὶ ἃ εἶπεν καὶ ὡς ἐπανῆκεν
καὶ ὡς ὑπεδέξαντο αὐτὸν ἐπευφημοῦντες οἱ
Σκύθαι καὶ ἄλλα ὁποῖα ὑμεῖς μηχανᾶσθαι εἰώθατε
πρὸς τὴν ἀκρόασιν.

43   Ἄκουε δ' οὖν[2] καὶ ἄλλον ἰσότιμον, Βελίτταν,
Ἀμιζώκου τούτου ἀνεψιόν, ὃς ἐπεὶ κατασπασθέντα
ἐκ τοῦ ἵππου ὑπὸ λέοντος εἶδε Βάσθην τὸν φίλον
(ἅμα δὲ ἔτυχον θηρῶντες) καὶ ἤδη ὁ λέων περι-
πλακεὶς αὐτῷ ἐνεπεφύκει τῷ λαιμῷ καὶ τοῖς

---

[1] ἔτι Paetzolt : ὅτι MSS.
[2] δ' οὖν Jacobitz : γοῦν MSS.

that the greatest of all our treasures had not been carried off by the enemy, but we still had among us staunch resolution and loyalty to friends. Furthermore, the Sauromatae were daunted more than a little by that same thing, when they considered what manner of men they were about to face in pitched battle, even though in the surprise attack for the moment they had obtained the upper hand. So when night had fallen, abandoning most of the flocks and herds and firing the wagons, they vanished in flight. Amizoces, however, could not bear to have his own sight when Dandamis was blind, but put out his eyes with his own hands; and now both of them sit idle, maintained with every show of honour at public expense by the Scythian folk.

What similar deed, Mnesippus, could you mention, even if you were allowed to enumerate ten more instances over and above your five, unsupported by oath, if you liked, so that you might adorn them with plenty of fiction? Then too, I have told you the naked facts; but if you were describing anyone like that, I know very well how many embellishments you would intersperse in the story, telling how Dandamis pleaded, how he was blinded, what he said, how he returned, how he was received with laudation by the Scythians, and other matters such as you Greeks are in the habit of manufacturing to gratify your hearers.

But let me tell you about another man equally honoured, Belitta, cousin of that same Amizoces. He saw that his friend Basthes had been dragged off his horse by a lion (it chanced that they were hunting together), and already the lion, lying upon him, had fastened upon his throat and was tearing him

ὄνυξιν ἐσπάρασσε, καταπηδήσας καὶ αὐτὸς ἐπι-
πίπτει κατόπιν τῷ θηρίῳ καὶ περιέσπα, πρὸς
ἑαυτὸν παροξύνων καὶ μετάγων καὶ διὰ τῶν
ὀδόντων μεταξὺ διείρων τοὺς δακτύλους καὶ τὸν
Βάσθην, ὡς οἷόν τε ἦν, ὑπεξελεῖν πειρώμενος τοῦ
δήγματος, ἄχρι δὴ ὁ λέων ἀφεὶς ἐκεῖνον ἡμιθνῆτα
ἤδη ἐπὶ τὸν Βελίτταν ἀπεστράφη καὶ συμπλακεὶς
ἀπέκτεινε κἀκεῖνον· ὁ δὲ ἀποθνήσκων τὸ γοῦν
τοσοῦτον ἔφθη πατάξας τῷ ἀκινάκῃ τὸν λέοντα
εἰς τὸ στέρνον ὥστε ἅμα πάντες ἀπέθανον, καὶ
ἡμεῖς ἐθάψαμεν αὐτοὺς δύο τάφους ἀναχώσαντες
πλησίον, ἕνα μὲν τῶν φίλων, ἕνα δὲ καταντικρὺ
τοῦ λέοντος.

44 Τρίτην δέ σοι διηγήσομαι, ὦ Μνήσιππε, τὴν
Μακέντου[1] φιλίαν καὶ Λογχάτου καὶ Ἀρσακόμα.
ὁ γὰρ Ἀρσακόμας οὗτος ἠράσθη Μαζαίας τῆς
Λευκάνορος, τοῦ βασιλεύσαντος ἐν Βοσπόρῳ,
ὁπότε ἐπρέσβευεν ὑπὲρ τοῦ δασμοῦ ὃν οἱ Βοσπορανοὶ ἀεὶ φέροντες ἡμῖν τότε ἤδη τρίτον μῆνα
ὑπερήμεροι ἐγεγένηντο. ἐν τῷ δείπνῳ οὖν ἰδὼν
τὴν Μαζαίαν μεγάλην καὶ καλὴν παρθένον ἤρα
καὶ πονηρῶς εἶχε.[2] τὰ μὲν οὖν περὶ τῶν φόρων

---

[1] Μακέτου N, and so in N throughout.

[2] K. G. P. Schwartz proposed setting this sentence after
the one that here, as in the MSS., follows it. That would
indeed improve greatly the sequence of thought, but is highly
unsatisfactory from the palaeographical standpoint. The
disturbance is probably a consequence of the abridgement
to which Lucian subjected the story.

with his claws. Springing to the ground, he attacked
the animal from behind and tried to draw him away,
provoking him, diverting his attention, inserting
his fingers between his teeth, and endeavouring in
every possible way to extract Basthes from the grip
of his jaws, until at last the lion left Basthes half-
dead and turning upon Belitta, seized and killed him.
In dying, however, he at least succeeded in stabbing
the lion in the breast with his sword, so that they all
died together, and in burying them we made two
barrows in close proximity, one for the friends and
one facing it for the lion.[1]

The third friendship of which I shall tell you,
Mnesippus, is that of Macentes, Lonchates, and
Arsacomas. This Arsacomas fell in love with
Mazaea, the daughter of Leucanor, who had become
king in Bosporus,[2] when he was there on a mission
regarding the tribute which is regularly paid us by
the people of Bosporus but at that time was more
than two months overdue. Well, at the banquet
he caught sight of Mazaea, a tall and beautiful
girl, instantly fell in love with her and was hard hit.
The matter of the contributions had been settled

[1] This tale, with its lion (in South Russia, about A.D. 150!)
and the poetic justice of the animal's entombment, distinctly
suggests a literary source, perhaps an epigram.

[2] History knows no king of Bosporus named Leucanor,
nor any Eubiotus, set down below as his illegitimate brother
and successor (§ 51). In a fragment of a Greek romance,
however, of which the plot is laid in Scythia (*Papiri della
Società Italiana*, VIII, 981) there is a character, evidently a
ruler, named Eubiotus, and Rostovtzeff points to this as
evidence that Lucian's tale, itself a miniature romance, is
drawn from some historical novel (*Skythien und der Bosporus*,
p. 98). I have noted in it several passages which seem to be
abridgements of a more detailed story.

διεπέπρακτο ἤδη, καὶ ἐχρημάτιζεν αὐτῷ ὁ βασιλεὺς
καὶ εἱστία, ἤδη αὐτὸν ἀποπέμπων. ἔθος δέ ἐστιν
ἐν Βοσπόρῳ τοὺς μνηστῆρας ἐπὶ τῷ δείπνῳ αἰτεῖν
τὰς κόρας καὶ λέγειν οἵτινες ὄντες ἀξιοῦσι κατα-
δεχθῆναι ἐπὶ τὸν γάμον, καὶ δὴ καὶ τότε ἔτυχον
ἐν τῷ δείπνῳ πολλοὶ μνηστῆρες παρόντες, βασιλεῖς
καὶ βασιλέων παῖδες· καὶ [1] Τιγραπάτης ἦν ὁ Λαζῶν
δυνάστης καὶ Ἀδύρμαχος ὁ Μαχλυηνῆς ἄρχων
καὶ ἄλλοι πολλοί. δεῖ δὲ τῶν μνηστήρων ἕκαστον,
προσαγγείλαντα ἑαυτὸν διότι μνηστευσόμενος ἥκει,
δειπνεῖν ἐν τοῖς ἄλλοις κατακείμενον ἐφ' ἡσυχίας·
ἐπὰν δὲ παύσωνται δειπνοῦντες, αἰτήσαντα φιάλην
ἐπισπεῖσαι κατὰ τῆς τραπέζης καὶ μνηστεύεσθαι τὴν
παῖδα πολλὰ ἐπαινοῦντα ἑαυτόν, ὡς τις ἢ γένους
ἢ πλούτου ἢ δυνάμεως ἔχει. [2]

45   Πολλῶν οὖν κατὰ τόνδε τὸν νόμον σπεισάντων
καὶ αἰτησάντων καὶ βασιλείας καὶ πλούτους
καταριθμησαμένων τελευταῖος ὁ Ἀρσακόμας αἰτή-
σας τὴν φιάλην οὐκ ἔσπεισεν, οὐ γὰρ ἔθος ἡμῖν
ἐκχεῖν τὸν οἶνον, ἀλλὰ ὕβρις εἶναι δοκεῖ τοῦτο εἰς
τὸν θεόν· πιὼν δὲ ἀμυστί, "Δός μοι," εἶπεν,
"ὦ βασιλεῦ, τὴν θυγατέρα σου Μαζαίαν γυναῖκα
ἔχειν πολὺ ἐπιτηδειοτέρῳ τούτων ὄντι ὁπόσα γε
ἐπὶ τῷ πλούτῳ καὶ τοῖς κτήμασι." τοῦ δὲ Λευκάνορος θαυμάσαντος—ἠπίστατο γὰρ πένητα τὸν
Ἀρσακόμαν καὶ Σκυθῶν τῶν πολλῶν—καὶ ἐρομένου,
"Πόσα δὲ βοσκήματα ἢ πόσας ἁμάξας ἔχεις, ὦ
Ἀρσακόμα ; ταῦτα γὰρ ὑμεῖς πλουτεῖτε," "Ἀλλ'
οὐχ ἁμάξας," ἔφη, "ἔχω οὐδὲ ἀγέλας, ἀλλ' εἰσί μοι
δύο φίλοι καλοὶ καὶ ἀγαθοὶ οἷοι οὐκ ἄλλῳ Σκυθῶν."

----

[1] ὧν καὶ Hartman ; perhaps right.
[2] ὥς τις . . . ἔχει C : ὅστις . . . ἔχοι ΓΝΒ.

already, and the king was giving him audience and entertaining him in connection with his dismissal. It is customary, however, in Bosporus for suitors to bespeak brides at dinner and tell who they are that they should think themselves worthy of acceptance, and at this time it chanced that many of them were at the banquet, kings and the sons of kings; Tigrapates the dynast of the Lazi was there, and Adyrmachus, the ruler of Machlyene, and many others. Each of the suitors, after announcing that he has come to propose, must then take dinner, lying in his place among the others, in silence; but when they have finished dinner, he must call for a goblet of wine, pour a drink-offering upon the table, and sue for the girl's hand, commending himself freely according to his standing in family or wealth or power.

Many, therefore, in accordance with this usage had poured their libation, made their request, and enumerated their kingdoms and treasures. Then, last of all, Arsacomas asked for the cup. He did not make libation, for it is not our custom to pour out our wine; on the contrary, we hold that to be an offence to the god. Instead, he drank it out at a single draught, and said: " O King, give me your daughter Mazaea for my wife, since I am a much better match than these men, at least in point of wealth and property." Leucanor was surprised, for he knew that Arsacomas was poor and just an ordinary Scythian, and he asked: " How many cattle and how many wagons have you, Arsacomas, since they constitute the wealth of your people?" "Why," said he, " I own no wagons or herds, but I have two noble friends, such as no other Scythian has."

Τότε μὲν οὖν ἐγελάσθη ἐπὶ τούτοις καὶ παρώφθη καὶ μεθύειν ἔδοξεν, ἕωθεν δὲ προκριθεὶς τῶν ἄλλων Ἀδύρμαχος ἔμελλεν ἀπάξειν τὴν νύμφην

46 παρὰ τὴν Μαιῶτιν ἐς τοὺς Μάχλυας.[1] ὁ δὲ Ἀρσακόμας ἐπανελθὼν οἴκαδε μηνύει τοῖς φίλοις ὡς ἀτιμασθείη ὑπὸ τοῦ βασιλέως καὶ γελασθείη ἐν τῷ συμποσίῳ, πένης εἶναι δόξας. " Καίτοι," ἔφη, " ἐγὼ διηγησάμην αὐτῷ τὸν πλοῦτον ὁπόσος ἐστίν μοι, ὑμᾶς, ὦ Λογχάτα καὶ Μακέντα, καὶ τὴν εὔνοιαν τὴν ὑμετέραν, πολὺ ἀμείνω καὶ βεβαιοτέραν τῆς Βοσπορανῶν δυνάμεως. ἀλλ' ἐμοῦ ταῦτα διεξιόντος ἡμᾶς μὲν ἐχλεύαζεν καὶ κατεφρόνει, Ἀδυρμάχῳ δὲ τῷ Μάχλυϊ παρέδωκεν ἀπάγειν τὴν νύμφην, ὅτι χρυσᾶς τε[2] φιάλας ἐλέγετο ἔχειν δέκα καὶ ἁμάξας τετρακλίνους ὀγδοήκοντα καὶ πρόβατα καὶ βοῦς πολλούς. οὕτως ἄρα προετίμησεν ἀνδρῶν ἀγαθῶν βοσκήματα πολλὰ καὶ ἐκπώματα περίεργα καὶ ἁμάξας βαρείας.

" Ἐγὼ δέ, ὦ φίλοι, δι' ἀμφότερα ἀνιῶμαι· καὶ γὰρ ἐρῶ τῆς Μαζαίας, καὶ ἡ ὕβρις ἐν τοσούτοις ἀνθρώποις οὐ μετρίως μου καθίκετο. οἶμαι δὲ καὶ ὑμᾶς ἐπ' ἴσης ἠδικῆσθαι· τὸ γὰρ τρίτον μετῆν ἑκάστῳ ἡμῶν[3] τῆς ἀτιμίας, εἴ γε οὕτω βιοῦμεν ὡς ἀφ' οὗ συνεληλύθαμεν εἷς ἄνθρωπος ὄντες καὶ τὰ αὐτὰ ἀνιώμενοι καὶ τὰ αὐτὰ χαίροντες."

" Οὐ μόνον," ἐπεῖπεν ὁ Λογχάτης, " ἀλλὰ ἕκαστος ἡμῶν ὅλος ὕβρισται, ὁπότε σὺ τοιαῦτα ἔπαθες."

47 " Πῶς οὖν," ὁ Μακέντης ἔφη, " χρησόμεθα τοῖς παροῦσι ; " " Διελώμεθα," ἔφη ὁ Λογχάτης,

---

[1] Text ΓΝΒΓΜ[1]; cf. § 52 fin. The reading ἐς τὴν Μαιῶτιν παρὰ τοὺς Μαχλύας bases only on Μ[2].
[2] τε Fritzsche: γε MSS.

Well, at the time they laughed at him on account
of this remark and ignored him, thinking that he
was drunk; Adyrmachus was preferred, and in the
morning was to take away his bride along Lake
Maeotis to the Machlyans. But Arsacomas returned
home and informed his friends how he had been dishonoured by the king and laughed at in the banquet
because he was considered poor. " And yet," said
he, " I told him what riches I possess in you two,
Lonchates and Macentes, and that your devotion
was better and more lasting than sovereignty over
the people of Bosporus. But in spite of my saying
this, he ridiculed and contemned us, and gave the
maiden to Adyrmachus the Machlyan to take away,
because he was said to own ten golden goblets,
eighty four-bunk wagons, and many sheep and
cattle. So far above brave men did he value great
flocks and herds, artistic drinking-cups, and heavy
wagons.

" Now for my part, my friends, I am doubly distressed, for not only do I love Mazaea but this
insult in the presence of so many men has affected
me deeply. And I think that you also have been
equally injured, for a third of the disgrace belonged
to each of us, since we live in the understanding
that from the time when we came together we have
been but as one man, distressed by the same things,
pleased by the same things." " Not only that,"
Lonchates added, " but each of us is completely
disgraced in your suffering such treatment."

" How, then, shall we handle the situation? "
said Macentes. " Let us divide the task between

---

3 ἡμῶν NB: ὑμῶν ΓΑ.

" τὸ ἔργον· καὶ ἐγὼ μὲν ὑπισχνοῦμαι Ἀρσακόμα
τὴν κεφαλὴν κομιεῖν τὴν[1] Λευκάνορος, σὲ δὲ
χρὴ τὴν νύμφην ἐπανάγειν αὐτῷ." "Οὕτω[2] γινέσθω," ἔφη· "σὺ δέ, ὦ Ἀρσακόμα, ἐν τοσούτῳ
—εἰκὸς γὰρ καὶ στρατιᾶς καὶ πολέμου τὸ μετὰ
τοῦτο δεήσειν—ἡμᾶς αὐτοῦ περιμένων συνάγειρε
καὶ παρασκεύαζε ὅπλα καὶ ἵππους καὶ τὴν ἄλλην
δύναμιν ὡς πλείστην. ῥᾷστα δ' ἂν πολλοὺς προσ-
αγάγοις αὐτός τε ἀγαθὸς ὢν καὶ ἡμῖν οὐκ ὀλίγων
ὄντων οἰκείων, μάλιστα δὲ εἰ καθέζοιο ἐπὶ τῆς
βύρσης τοῦ βοός." ἔδοξε ταῦτα, καὶ ὁ μὲν ἐχώρει
ὡς εἶχεν εὐθὺς ἐπὶ τοῦ Βοσπόρου, ὁ Λογχάτης,
ὁ Μακέντης δὲ ἐπὶ τοὺς Μάχλυας, ἱππότης ἑκάτερος,
ὁ δὲ Ἀρσακόμας οἴκοι μένων τοῖς τε ἡλικιώταις
διελέγετο καὶ ὥπλιζε δύναμιν παρὰ τῶν οἰκείων,
τέλος δὲ καὶ ἐπὶ τῆς βύρσης ἐκαθέζετο.

48 Τὸ δὲ ἔθος ἡμῖν τὸ περὶ τὴν βύρσαν οὕτως
ἔχει· ἐπειδὰν ἀδικηθείς τις πρὸς ἑτέρου, ἀμύνασθαι
βουλόμενος, ἴδῃ καθ' ἑαυτὸν οὐκ ἀξιόμαχος ὤν,
βοῦν ἱερεύσας τὰ μὲν κρέα κατακόψας ἥψησεν,
αὐτὸς δὲ ἐκπετάσας χαμαὶ τὴν βύρσαν κάθηται ἐπ'
αὐτῆς, εἰς τοὐπίσω παραγαγὼν[3] τὼ χεῖρε ὥσπερ
οἱ ἐκ τῶν ἀγκώνων δεδεμένοι. καὶ τοῦτό ἐστιν
ἡμῖν ἡ μεγίστη ἱκετηρία. παρακειμένων δὲ τῶν
κρεῶν τοῦ βοὸς προσιόντες οἱ οἰκεῖοι καὶ τῶν
ἄλλων ὁ βουλόμενος μοῖραν ἕκαστος λαβὼν ἐπιβὰς
τῇ βύρσῃ τὸν δεξιὸν πόδα ὑπισχνεῖται κατὰ
δύναμιν, ὁ μὲν πέντε ἱππέας παρέξειν ἀσίτους καὶ
ἀμίσθους, ὁ δὲ δέκα, ὁ δὲ πλείους, ὁ δὲ ὁπλίτας

---

[1] τὴν ΓΝΒ: τοῦ (C)A.
[2] οὕτω ΝΒ: not in ΓΜ(C)A.

us," Lonchates replied; " I engage to bring Arsacomas the head of Leucanor, and you must fetch
his bride home to him." " Very well," said the
other; " and in the meantime, Arsacomas, as it is
likely that we shall presently need to take the field
and go to war, you, awaiting us here, should collect
and make ready arms, horses, and a very large force.
You might very easily enlist many, since you yourself are brave and we have plenty of relatives, and
it would be especially easy if you should sit on the
ox-hide." Those plans were approved, and Lonchates, just as he was, made straight for Bosporus,
while Macentes headed for the Machlyans, both of
them mounted. Arsacomas, remaining at home,
held conferences with his comrades and armed a
force recruited from his relatives; then at last he
sat upon the hide.

Our custom in the matter of the hide is as follows.
When a man who has been wronged by another wishes
to avenge himself but sees that by himself he is not
strong enough, he sacrifices a bull, cuts up and cooks
the meat, spreads the hide out on the ground, and
sits on it, with his hands held behind his back like a
man bound by the elbows. That is our strongest
appeal for aid. The meat of the bull is served up,
and as the man's kinsmen and all else who wish
approach, each takes a portion of it, and then, setting his right foot upon the hide, makes a pledge
according to his ability, one that he will furnish five
horsemen to serve without rations or pay, another
ten, another still more, another foot-soldiers, heavy-

---

[3] παραγαγὼν NB, Suidas: παράγων ΓΑ. Cf. *Nav.*, 30.

ἢ[1] πεζοὺς ὁπόσους ἂν δύνηται, ὁ δὲ μόνον ἑαυτόν,
ὁ πενέστατος. ἀθροίζεται οὖν[2] ἐπὶ τῆς βύρσης
πολὺ πλῆθος ἐνίοτε, καὶ τὸ τοιοῦτο σύνταγμα
βεβαιότατόν τέ ἐστι συμμεῖναι καὶ ἀπρόσμαχον
τοῖς ἐχθροῖς ἅτε καὶ ἔνορκον ὄν· τὸ γὰρ ἐπιβῆναι
τῆς βύρσης ὅρκος ἐστίν.

Ὁ μὲν οὖν Ἀρσακόμας ἐν τούτοις ἦν, καὶ
ἠθροίσθησαν αὐτῷ ἱππεῖς μὲν ἀμφὶ τοὺς πεντακισ-
χιλίους, ὁπλῖται δὲ καὶ πεζοὶ συναμφότεροι δισμύ-
49 ριοι. ὁ δὲ Λογχάτης ἀγνοούμενος παρελθὼν ἐς τὸν
Βόσπορον προσέρχεται τῷ βασιλεῖ διοικουμένῳ
τι τῆς ἀρχῆς καὶ φησὶν ἥκειν μὲν ἀπὸ τοῦ κοινοῦ
τῶν Σκυθῶν, ἰδίᾳ δὲ αὐτῷ μεγάλα πράγματα
κομίζων. τοῦ δὲ λέγειν κελεύσαντος, “ Οἱ μὲν
Σκύθαι,” φησίν, “ τὰ κοινὰ ταῦτα καὶ τὰ καθ᾽
ἡμέραν ἀξιοῦσιν, μὴ ὑπερβαίνειν τοὺς νομέας
ὑμῶν ἐς τὸ πεδίον ἀλλὰ μέχρι τοῦ τράχωνος
νέμειν· τοὺς δὲ λῃστὰς οὓς αἰτιᾶσθε ὡς κατατρέ-
χοντας ὑμῶν τὴν χώραν οὐ φασὶν ἀπὸ κοινῆς
γνώμης ἐκπέμπεσθαι, ἀλλὰ ἰδίᾳ ἕκαστον ἐπὶ τῷ
κέρδει κλωπεύειν· εἰ δέ τις ἁλίσκοιτο αὐτῶν,[3]
σὲ κύριον εἶναι κολάζειν. ταῦτα μὲν ἐκείνοι
50 ἐπεστάλκασιν, ἐγὼ δὲ μηνύω[4] σοι μεγάλην ἔφοδον
ἐσομένην ἐφ᾽ ὑμᾶς ὑπ᾽ Ἀρσακόμα τοῦ Μαριάντα,

---

[1] ἢ du Soul: not in MSS.
[2] οὖν Jacobitz: γοῦν MSS.
[3] αὐτὸν B: i.e., αὐτὸν σὲ, and so Bekker and Dindorf.
[4] μηνύσω NA.

---

[1] Lucian is our only authority for this curious custom;
the allusions to it in Suidas and the *paroemiographi* (Gaisford,
Bodl. 355, Coisl. 207; Leutsch, Append. II, 80, Apostol.

armed or light-armed, as many as he can, and another simply himself, if he is very poor. So a very large force is sometimes raised on the hide, and such an army is especially dependable as regards holding together and very hard for the enemy to conquer, since it is under oath; for setting foot on the hide is an oath.[1]

Arsacomas, then, was thus engaged; and he raised some five thousand horse and twenty thousand foot, heavy-armed and light-armed together. Lonchates in the meantime entered Bosporus unrecognised, approached the king while he was attending to a matter of government, and said that he came with a message from the Scythian commonwealth, but also in his private capacity brought him important news. When he was bidden to speak, he said: "The Scythians make one of their ordinary, every-day requests, that your herdsmen shall not encroach upon the plain but shall graze only as far as the stony ground; and they say that the cattle-lifters whom you charge with overrunning your country are not sent out by order of the state but steal for profit, each on his own account; if any one of them should be captured, you have full authority to punish him. That is their message. But on my own part, I give you notice that a great attack upon you is about to be made by Arsacomas, the son of

VII, 75) are mere quotations from Lucian, and Gilbert Cognatus' mysterious reference to "Zenodotus" and "the ox of the Homolotti" derives (by way of Erasmus, *Adagia*: "Bos Homolottorum") from Zenobius, II, 83: βοῦς ὁ Μολοτ-τῶν! That the Molossian custom of cutting up (but not eating) an ox in connection with making treaties has nothing to do with the Scythian usage is clear from the more detailed explanation of it in Coisl. 57 (Gaisford, p. 126).

ὃς ἐπρέσβευε πρώην παρὰ σὲ καί, οἶμαι, διότι αἰτή-
σας τὴν θυγατέρα οὐκ ἔτυχε παρὰ σοῦ, ἀγανακτεῖ
καὶ ἐπὶ τῆς βύρσης ἑβδόμην ἡμέραν ἤδη κάθηται
καὶ συνῆκται στρατὸς οὐκ ὀλίγος αὐτῷ."

" "Ἤκουσα," ἔφη ὁ Λευκάνωρ, " καὶ αὐτὸς
ἀθροίζεσθαι δύναμιν ἀπὸ βύρσης, ὅτι δ᾽ ἐφ᾽ ἡμᾶς
συνίσταται καὶ ὅτι Ἀρσακόμας ὁ ἐλαύνων ἐστὶν
ἠγνόουν." " Ἀλλ᾽ ἐπὶ σέ," ἔφη ὁ Λογχάτης, " ἡ
παρασκευή. ἐμοὶ δὲ ἐχθρὸς ὁ Ἀρσακόμας ἐστί,
καὶ ἄχθεται διότι προτιμῶμαι αὐτοῦ ὑπὸ τῶν
γεραιτέρων καὶ ἀμείνων τὰ πάντα δοκῶ εἶναι·
εἰ δέ μοι ὑπόσχοιο τὴν ἑτέραν σου θυγατέρα
Βαρκέτιν, οὐδὲ[1] τὰ ἄλλα ἀναξίω ὑμῶν ὄντι, οὐκ εἰς
μακρὰν σοι ἥξω τὴν κεφαλὴν αὐτοῦ κομίζων."
" Ὑπισχνοῦμαι," ἔφη ὁ βασιλεύς, μάλα περιδεὴς
γενόμενος· ἔγνω γὰρ τὴν αἰτίαν τῆς ὀργῆς τῆς
Ἀρσακόμα τὴν ἐπὶ τῷ γάμῳ, καὶ ἄλλως ὑπέπτησσεν
ἀεὶ τοὺς Σκύθας.

Ὁ δὲ Λογχάτης, " Ὄμοσον," εἶπεν, " ἦ μὴν
φυλάξειν τὰς συνθήκας, μηδὲ ἀπαρνήσεσθαι τότε
ἤδη, τούτων γενομένων."[2] καὶ ἐπεὶ ἀνατεί-
νας εἰς τὸν οὐρανὸν ἤθελεν ὀμνύειν, " Μὴ σύ γε
ἐνταῦθα," εἶπεν, " μὴ καί τις ὑπίδηται τῶν ὁρώντων
ἐφ᾽ ὅτῳ ὀρκωμοτοῦμεν, ἀλλὰ εἰς τὸ ἱερὸν τοῦ
Ἄρεως τουτὶ εἰσελθόντες, ἐπικλεισάμενοι τὰς
θύρας ὀμνύωμεν, ἀκουσάτω δὲ μηδείς· εἰ γάρ τι

[1] οὐδὲ Fritzsche : οὔτε MSS.
[2] Punctuation Bekker's and mine : ἀπαρνήσεσθαι. τότε ἤδη
τούτων γενομένων καὶ ἐπεὶ vulg. Bekker set the full stop
after γενομένων ; I have added the comma after ἤδη.

Mariantes, who came to you recently on a mission, and—no doubt because he asked you for your daughter and did not obtain his request from you—is incensed; he has been sitting on the hide for six days now,[1] and has collected a great host."

" I myself," said Leucanor, " had heard that a force was being raised on the hide, but did not know that it is being formed against us or that Arsacomas is the organiser of it." " Why," said Lonchates, " the preparations are directed at you in person. But Arsacomas is no friend of mine, bearing a grudge against me because I am held in higher regard by our dignitaries and considered in all respects a better man. If you will promise me your other daughter, Barcetis, since even on other grounds I am not unworthy of alliance with you, before long I will come and bring you his head." " I promise," said the king, who had become thoroughly alarmed because he recognised the just ground for the anger of Arsacomas in connection with his proposal of marriage; and besides, he stood in perpetual dread of the Scythians.

Lonchates replied: " Swear that you will keep the agreement, and will not go back on your word then, when the thing is done." When the king lifted his hands toward Heaven and was in purpose to swear, the other said: " Not here, for fear that some onlooker may suspect the reason of our oath. No, let us enter the sanctuary of Ares yonder and lock the doors before we swear; and let nobody hear us!

[1] It should not be inferred that it has taken Lonchates all this time to reach the city and its king. As the king has heard of the Scythian mustering before Lonchates sees him, it is evident that there was some delay, whether accidental or deliberate.

THE WORKS OF LUCIAN

τούτων πύθοιτο Ἀρσακόμας, δέδια μὴ προθύσηται
με τοῦ πολέμου, χεῖρα οὐ μικρὰν ἤδη περιβεβλη-
μένος." "Εἰσίωμεν," ἔφη ὁ βασιλεύς, "ὑμεῖς δὲ
ἀπόστητε ὅτι πορρωτάτω· μηδεὶς δὲ παρέστω
ἐς τὸν νεὼν ὄντινα μὴ ἐγὼ καλέσω."

Ἐπεὶ δὲ οἱ μὲν εἰσῆλθον, οἱ δορυφόροι δὲ
ἀπέστησαν, σπασάμενος τὸν ἀκινάκην, ἐπισχὼν
τῇ ἑτέρᾳ τὸ στόμα ὡς μὴ βοήσειε, παίει παρὰ τὸν
μαστόν, εἶτα ἀποτεμὼν τὴν κεφαλὴν ὑπὸ τῇ χλαμύδι
ἔχων ἐξήει, μεταξὺ διαλεγόμενος δῆθεν αὐτῷ
καὶ διὰ ταχέων ἥξειν λέγων, ὡς δὴ ἐπί τι πεμφθεὶς
ὑπ' ἐκείνου. καὶ οὕτως ἐπὶ τὸν τόπον ἀφικόμενος
ἔνθα καταδεδεμένον καταλελοίπει τὸν ἵππον, ἀναβὰς ἀφιππάσατο εἰς τὴν Σκυθίαν. δίωξις δὲ οὐκ
ἐγένετο αὐτοῦ, ἐπὶ πολὺ ἀγνοησάντων τὸ γεγονὸς
τῶν Βοσπορανῶν, καὶ ὅτε ἔγνωσαν, ὑπὲρ τῆς
βασιλείας στασιαζόντων.

51   Ταῦτα μὲν ὁ Λογχάτης ἔπραξεν καὶ τὴν ὑπόσχεσιν ἀπεπλήρωσεν τῷ Ἀρσακόμᾳ παραδοὺς τὴν
κεφαλὴν τοῦ Λευκάνορος. ὁ Μακέντης δὲ καθ'
ὁδὸν ἀκούσας τὰ ἐν Βοσπόρῳ γενόμενα ἧκεν
εἰς τοὺς Μάχλυας καὶ πρῶτος ἀγγείλας αὐτοῖς τὸν
φόνον τοῦ βασιλέως, "Ἡ πόλις δέ," ἔφη, "ὦ
Ἀδύρμαχε, σὲ γαμβρὸν ὄντα ἐπὶ τὴν βασιλείαν
καλεῖ· ὥστε σὺ μὲν προελάσας παραλάμβανε τὴν

¹ In the story as it came to Lucian, Lonchates and Macentes, before parting, must have arranged that the latter
was to wait at some point (perhaps where their routes di-
verged) until the former should return with the news of his
success. It would have been fatal to the plot against the
king to have Adyrmachus bring to the city a false report of the
king's death before Lonchates was able to strike. Besides, a

184

If Arsacomas should get any knowledge of this, I am afraid that he may initiate the war by making a victim of me, as he is already surrounded by a large band." "Let us enter," responded the king. " Gentlemen, withdraw as far as possible, and let no one present himself in the temple who is not summoned by me."

When they had entered and the guardsmen had withdrawn, Lonchates drew his sword, clapped one hand over the king's mouth, that he might not cry out, and stabbed him in the breast. Then he cut off his head and carried it out with him under his cloak, keeping up, as he did so, a pretended conversation with him and saying that he would return speedily, as if he had been sent by the king to fetch something. Getting in this way to the place where he had left his horse tied, he mounted and rode off to Scythia. There was no pursuit of him, since the Bosporans remained long in ignorance of what had happened, and when they did find out about it, they fell to squabbling over the throne.

That, then, is what Lonchates did, and so fulfilled his promise to Arsacomas by giving him the head of Leucanor. As for Macentes, while on his way he had heard what had happened in Bosporus, and when he reached the Machlyans was the first to report to them the tidings of the king's death,[1] adding: " And the city, Adyrmachus, calls you to the throne, as his son-in-law; so you yourself must ride on ahead and take over the government, appear-

---

week or more (p. 183 and note) has elapsed before Macentes reaches the Machlyans, yet he returns in less than forty-eight hours, riding night and day, to be sure, but with the horse carrying double and therefore obliged to rest frequently.

ἀρχήν, τεταραγμένοις τοῖς πράγμασιν ἐπιφανείς,
ἡ κόρη δέ σοι κατόπιν ἐπὶ τῶν ἁμαξῶν ἐπέσθω·
ῥᾷον γὰρ οὕτω προσάξεις Βοσπορανῶν τοὺς πολλούς,
ἰδόντας τὴν Λευκάνορος θυγατέρα. ἐγὼ δὲ Ἀλανός
τέ εἰμι καὶ τῇ παιδὶ ταύτῃ συγγενὴς μητρόθεν·
παρ' ἡμῶν γὰρ οὖσαν τὴν Μάστειραν ἠγάγετο ὁ
Λευκάνωρ. καὶ νῦν σοι ἥκω παρὰ τῶν Μαστείρας
ἀδελφῶν τῶν ἐν Ἀλανίᾳ παρακελευομένων ὅτι
τάχιστα ἐλαύνειν ἐπὶ τὸν Βόσπορον καὶ μὴ περι-
ιδεῖν ἐς[1] Εὐβίοτον περιελθοῦσαν τὴν ἀρχήν,
ὃς ἀδελφὸς ὢν νόθος Λευκάνορος Σκύθαις μὲν
ἀεὶ φίλος ἐστίν, Ἀλανοῖς δὲ ἀπέχθεται."

Ταῦτα δὲ ἔλεγεν ὁ Μακέντης ὁμόσκευος καὶ
ὁμόγλωττος τοῖς Ἀλανοῖς ὤν· κοινὰ γὰρ ταῦτα
Ἀλανοῖς καὶ Σκύθαις, πλὴν ὅτι οὐ πάνυ κομῶσιν
οἱ Ἀλανοὶ ὥσπερ οἱ Σκύθαι. ἀλλὰ ὁ Μακέντης
καὶ τοῦτο εἴκαστο αὐτοῖς καὶ ἀποκεκάρκει τῆς
κόμης ὁπόσον εἰκὸς ἦν ἔλαττον κομᾶν τὸν Ἀλανὸν
τοῦ Σκύθου· ὥστε ἐπιστεύετο διὰ ταῦτα καὶ
ἐδόκει[2] Μαστείρας καὶ Μαζαίας συγγενὴς εἶναι.

52 "Καὶ νῦν," ἔφη, "ὦ Ἀδύρμαχε, ἐλαύνειν
τε[3] ἕτοιμος ἅμα σοι ἐπὶ τὸν Βόσπορον, ἢν ἐθέλῃς,
μένειν τε, εἰ δέοι, καὶ τὴν παῖδα ἄγειν." "Τοῦτο,"
ἔφη, "καὶ μᾶλλον," ὁ Ἀδύρμαχος, "ἐθελήσαιμ'
ἄν, ἀφ' αἵματος ὄντα σε Μαζαίαν ἄγειν. ἢν μὲν
γὰρ ἅμα ἡμῖν ἴῃς ἐπὶ Βόσπορον, ἱππεῖ ἑνὶ πλείους

___

[1] ὡς A : for ἐς cf. Herodotus III, 140.
[2] καὶ ἐδόκει not in A.
[3] τε N (Bekker): not in other MSS:

___

[1] Abridgement seems to enter here; for the fact that
Eubiotus is the illegitimate brother of Leucanor does not in

ing suddenly in the midst of things while they are
unsettled; but the girl must follow you in your wagon-
train, for in that way it will be easier for you to win
over the common people in Bosporus, after they have
seen the daughter of Leucanor. For myself, I am
an Alan, and also related to the girl through her
mother, since Masteira, whom Leucanor married,
was of our people; and I come to you now on the
part of Masteira's brothers in the country of the
Alans, who urge you to ride with all speed to Bosporus
and not to let the government go over to Eubiotus,
who being the illegitimate brother of Leucanor, is
always friendly to the Scythians and detests the
Alans." [1]

Macentes was able to say this because he wore the
same dress and spoke the same tongue as the Alans.
These characteristics are common to Alans and
Scythians, except that the Alans do not wear their
hair very long, as the Scythians do. Macentes, however, had made himself resemble them in this also,
and had docked his hair by as much as an Alan's
would probably be shorter than a Scythian's.
Therefore he was believed, and was thought to be a
relative of Masteira and Mazaea.

" Now then, Adyrmachus," said he, " I am ready
to ride with you to Bosporus, if you wish, or to remain,
if necessary, and conduct the girl." " That," said
Adyrmachus, " is what I should like better—that
as you are of her blood, you should conduct Mazaea.
For if you go with us to Bosporus, we should gain

itself adequately account for his attitude toward the Scythians
and the Alans. Was his mother a Scythian, or perhaps a
Sarmatian ? At this time he is living among the Sarmatians
(§ 54).

ἂν γενοίμεθα· εἰ δέ μοι τὴν γυναῖκα ἄγοις, ἀντὶ
πολλῶν ἂν γένοιο."

Ταῦτα ἐγίνετο καὶ ὁ μὲν ἀπήλαυνε παραδοὺς τῷ
Μακέντῃ ἄγειν τὴν Μαζαίαν παρθένον ἔτι οὖσαν.
ὁ δὲ ἡμέρας μὲν ἐπὶ τῆς ἁμάξης ἦγεν αὐτήν,
ἐπεὶ δὲ νὺξ κατέλαβεν, ἀναθέμενος ἐπὶ τὸν ἵππον—
ἐτεθεραπεύκει δὲ ἕνα σφίσιν ἄλλον ἱππέα ἕπεσθαι—
ἀναπηδήσας καὶ αὐτὸς οὐκέτι παρὰ τὴν Μαιῶτιν
ἤλαυνεν, ἀλλ᾽ ἀποτραπόμενος εἰς τὴν μεσόγειαν ἐν
δεξιᾷ λαβὼν τὰ Μιτραίων ὄρη, διαναπαύων μεταξὺ
τὴν παῖδα, τριταῖος ἐτέλεσεν ἐκ Μαχλύων ἐς
Σκύθας. καὶ ὁ μὲν ἵππος αὐτῷ, ἐπειδὴ ἐπαύσατο
53 τοῦ δρόμου, μικρὸν ἐπιστὰς ἀποθνήσκει, ὁ δὲ
Μακέντης ἐγχειρίσας τὴν Μαζαίαν τῷ Ἀρσακόμᾳ,
" Δέδεξο," εἶπεν, " καὶ παρ᾽ ἐμοῦ τὴν ὑπόσχεσιν."

Τοῦ δὲ πρὸς τὸ ἀνέλπιστον τοῦ θεάματος κατα-
πλαγέντος καὶ χάριν ὁμολογοῦντος, " Παῦε,"
ἔφη ὁ Μακέντης, " ἄλλον με ποιῶν σεαυτοῦ·
τὸ γὰρ χάριν ἐμοὶ ὁμολογεῖν ἐφ᾽ οἷς ἔπραξα
τούτοις τοιόνδε ἐστὶν ὥσπερ ἂν εἰ [1] ἡ ἀριστερά
μου χάριν εἰδείη τῇ δεξιᾷ διότι τρωθεῖσάν ποτε
αὐτὴν ἐθεράπευσε καὶ φιλοφρόνως ἐπεμελήθη
καμνούσης. γελοῖα τοίνυν καὶ ἡμεῖς ἂν ποιοῖμεν
εἰ πάλαι ἀναμιχθέντες καὶ ὡς οἷόν τε ἦν εἰς ἕνα
συνελθόντες ἔτι μέγα νομίζοιμεν εἶναι εἰ τὸ μέρος
ἡμῶν ἔπραξέ τι χρηστὸν ὑπὲρ ὅλου τοῦ σώματος·

---

[1] εἰ Guyet: not in MSS.

---

[1] Macentes comes alone; this single horseman is therefore
presumably a Machlyan, and hostile. What, then, becomes
of him? Only implications enlighten us. For some reason
Macentes does not do the obvious thing—kill him at night

but a single horseman; but if you should conduct my wife, you would be as good as many."

That was put into effect, and he rode off, leaving it to Macentes to conduct Mazaea, who was still a maid. And he did indeed escort her upon her wagon during the day; but when night overtook them, he set her upon his horse—he had seen to it that only one other horseman should attend them [1]— himself leaped to his seat, and instead of continuing to ride along the shore of Lake Maeotis, turned off into the interior, taking on his right the mountains of the Mitraeans. Stopping only at intervals to allow the girl to rest, on the third day he succeeded in reaching Scythia from Machlyene; his horse, on ceasing to run, stood still for a moment and fell dead, while Macentes, delivering Mazaea to Arsacomas, said: "Accept from me also the fulfilment of my promise!"

Arsacomas was amazed at the unexpectedness of that sight, and tried to express his gratitude, but Macentes said: "Stop making me a different person from yourself! To express gratitude to me for what I have done in this is just as if my left hand should be grateful to my right for ministering to it when it had been wounded and taking care of it fondly while it was weak. So with us—it would be ridiculous if, after having fused ourselves together long ago and united, as far as we could, into a single person, we should continue to think it a great thing if this or that part of us has done something useful in behalf of the whole body; for it

and take his horse. Either he eludes them, or they elude him; and instead of following them, he posts ahead to over-take Adyrmachus with the news (§ 54).

THE WORKS OF LUCIAN

ὑπὲρ αὐτοῦ γὰρ ἔπραττεν, μέρος ὂν τοῦ ὅλου εὖ
πάσχοντος."

Οὕτως μὲν ὁ Μακέντης ἔφη τῷ Ἀρσακόμᾳ
54 χάριν ὁμολογήσαντι. ὁ δὲ Ἀδύρμαχος ὡς ἤκουσε
τὴν ἐπιβουλήν, εἰς μὲν τὸν Βόσπορον οὐκέτι
ἦλθεν—ἤδη γὰρ Εὐβίοτος ἦρχεν, ἐπικληθεὶς ἐκ
Σαυροματῶν, παρ' οἷς διέτριβεν—εἰς δὲ τὴν
αὑτοῦ ἐπανελθὼν καὶ στρατιὰν πολλὴν συναγαγὼν
διὰ τῆς ὀρεινῆς εἰσέβαλεν εἰς τὴν Σκυθίαν· καὶ
ὁ Εὐβίοτος οὐ μετὰ πολὺ καὶ οὗτος εἰσέπεσεν
ἄγων πανδημεὶ μὲν τοὺς Ἕλληνας, Ἀλανοὺς δὲ
καὶ Σαυρομάτας ἐπικλήτους ἑκατέρους δισμυ-
ρίους. ἀναμίξαντες δὲ τὰ στρατεύματα ὁ
Εὐβίοτος καὶ ὁ Ἀδύρμαχος, ἐννέα μυριάδες
ἅπαντες ἐγένοντο καὶ τούτων τὸ τρίτον ἱπποτο-
ξόται.

Ἡμεῖς δὲ—καὶ γὰρ αὐτὸς μετέσχον τῆς ἐξόδου
αὐτοῖς, ἐπιδοὺς ἐν τῇ βύρσῃ τότε ἱππέας αὐτοτε-
λεῖς ἑκατόν—οὐ πολλῷ ἔλαττον τῶν τρισμυρίων
σὺν τοῖς ἱππεῦσιν ἀθροισθέντες ὑπεμένομεν τὴν
ἔφοδον· ἐστρατήγει δὲ ὁ Ἀρσακόμας. καὶ ἐπειδὴ
προσιόντας εἴδομεν αὐτούς, ἀντεπήγομεν, προεπ-
αφέντες τὸ ἱππικόν. γενομένης δὲ ἐπὶ πολὺ μάχης
καρτερᾶς ἐνεδίδου ἤδη τὰ ἡμέτερα καὶ παρερρή-
γνυτο ἡ φάλαγξ, καὶ τέλος εἰς δύο διεκόπη τὸ
Σκυθικὸν ἅπαν, καὶ τὸ μὲν ὑπέφυγεν, οὐ πάνυ
σαφῶς ἡττημένον, ἀλλ' ἀναχώρησις ἐδόκει ἡ
φυγή· οὐδὲ γὰρ οἱ Ἀλανοὶ ἐτόλμων ἐπὶ πολὺ
διώκειν. τὸ δὲ ἥμισυ, ὅπερ καὶ ἔλαττον, περι-
σχόντες οἱ Ἀλανοὶ καὶ Μάχλυες ἔκοπτον πανταχόθεν ἀφθόνως ἀφιέντες τῶν ὀϊστῶν καὶ ἀκοντίων,

was working in its own behalf as a part of the whole organism to which the good was being done."

This, then, was the reply of Macentes to Arsacomas when he expressed his gratitude. But when Adyrmachus heard of the stratagem, instead of going on to Bosporus, inasmuch as Eubiotus had been summoned from the Sauromatae, with whom he was living, and was already on the throne, he returned to his own country, and after assembling a great army, advanced through the hill-country into Scythia. Eubiotus, too, presently made an incursion with his Greeks in full force and allied levies of Alans and Sauromatae numbering twenty thousand from each. After Eubiotus and Adyrmachus had combined their armies, they amounted in all to ninety thousand, a third of them mounted archers.

For our part (and I say *our*, because I myself took part in their expedition, having offered on the hide at that time a hundred self-supporting horsemen) we had raised not much less than thirty thousand, including the horsemen, and were awaiting their onset; our commander was Arsacomas. When we saw them coming on, we marched forward to meet them, sending our horsemen out in advance. After a long and hard-fought battle, our side in time began to give ground, the phalanx began to break, and at last the entire Scythian force was cut in two. One part began to withdraw, but it was not at all certain that they were beaten; indeed, their flight was considered a retreat, for even the Alans did not venture to pursue them any distance. The other, smaller part was surrounded by the Alans and Machlyans, who were hammering it from all sides, loosing arrows and javelins without stint; so that

THE WORKS OF LUCIAN

ὥστε πάνυ ἐπονοῦντο ἡμῶν οἱ περιεσχημένοι,
καὶ ἤδη προΐεντο οἱ πολλοὶ τὰ ὅπλα.

55 Ἐν τούτοις δὲ καὶ ὁ Λογχάτης καὶ ὁ Μακέντης
ἔτυχον ὄντες καὶ ἐτέτρωντο ἤδη προκινδυνεύοντες,
ὁ μὲν στυρακίῳ εἰς[1] τὸν μηρόν, ὁ Λογχάτης, ὁ
Μακέντης δὲ πελέκει εἰς τὴν κεφαλὴν καὶ κοντῷ
εἰς τὸν ὦμον. ὅπερ αἰσθόμενος ὁ Ἀρσακόμας,
ἐν ἡμῖν τοῖς ἄλλοις ὤν, δεινὸν ἡγησάμενος εἰ
ἄπεισι καταλιπὼν τοὺς φίλους, προσβαλὼν τοὺς
μύωπας τῷ ἵππῳ ἐμβοήσας ἤλαυνε διὰ τῶν
πολεμίων κοπίδα διηρμένος, ὥστε τοὺς Μάχλυας
μηδὲ ὑποστῆναι τὸ ῥόθιον τοῦ θυμοῦ, ἀλλὰ διαιρε-
θέντες ἔδωκαν αὐτῷ διεξελθεῖν.

Ὁ δὲ ἀνακτησάμενος τοὺς φίλους καὶ τοὺς
ἄλλους ἅπαντας παρακαλέσας ὥρμησεν ἐπὶ τὸν
Ἀδύρμαχον καὶ πατάξας τῇ κοπίδι παρὰ τὸν αὐχένα
μέχρι τῆς ζώνης διέτεμεν. πεσόντος δὲ ἐκείνου
διελύθη τὸ Μαχλυϊκὸν ἅπαν, καὶ τὸ Ἀλανικὸν οὐ
μετὰ πολύ, καὶ οἱ Ἕλληνες ἐπὶ τούτοις· ὥστε
ἐκρατοῦμεν ἐξ ὑπαρχῆς ἡμεῖς καὶ ἐπεξήλθομεν ἂν
ἐπὶ πολὺ κτείνοντες, εἰ μὴ νὺξ τὸ ἔργον ἀφείλετο.

Εἰς δὲ τὴν ἐπιοῦσαν ἱκέται παρὰ τῶν πολεμίων
ἥκοντες ἐδέοντο φιλίαν ποιεῖσθαι, Βοσπορανοὶ
μὲν ὑποτελέσειν διπλάσιον τὸν δασμὸν ὑπισχνού-
μενοι, Μάχλυες δὲ ὁμήρους δώσειν ἔφασαν, οἱ
Ἀλανοὶ δὲ ἀντὶ τῆς ἐφόδου ἐκείνης Σινδιανοὺς
ἡμῖν χειρώσασθαι ὑπέστησαν ἐκ πολλοῦ διεστῶτας.
ἐπὶ τούτοις ἐπείσθημεν, δόξαν πολὺ πρότερον

those of us who had been surrounded were suffering severely, and the rank and file were already throwing away their arms.

Lonchates and Macentes happened to be in this part, and had already received wounds from fighting in the front ranks, Lonchates in the thigh with the spike of a spear-butt, Macentes on the head with an axe and on the shoulder with a javelin. When Arsacomas, who was with us others, perceived that, thinking it would be dreadful if he should go away and abandon his friends, he put spurs to his horse, gave a great shout, and charged among the enemy with uplifted battle-axe, so that the Machlyans could not even face the fury of his wrath but separated and allowed him to go through.

He encouraged his friends and rallied all the others, then rushed at Adyrmachus, struck him at the base of the neck with his axe, and clove him to the belt. Upon his fall they gave way—the whole Machlyan force first, the Alans not long afterwards, and the Greeks next. So we had the upper hand once more, and might have pursued them for a long distance, killing them, if night had not ended the business.

On the next day men came to us as suppliants from the enemy and asked us to make friends; the Bosporans promised to pay us twice as much tribute, the Machlyans said that they would give hostages, and the Alans to make up for that attack undertook to help us by subduing the Sindians, who had revolted some time previously. On those terms we assented, but only after the approval of Arsacomas

---

[1] στυρακίῳ εἰς Fritzsche: πυρακτωθεὶς MSS.

Ἀρσακόμᾳ καὶ Λογχάτῃ, καὶ ἐγένετο εἰρήνη
ἐκείνων πρυτανευόντων ἕκαστα.

Τοιαῦτα, ὦ Μνήσιππε, τολμῶσιν ποιεῖν Σκύθαι
ὑπὲρ τῶν φίλων.

ΜΝΗΣΙΠΠΟΣ

56 Πάνυ τραγικά, ὦ Τόξαρι, καὶ μύθοις ὅμοια·
καὶ ἵλεως μὲν ὁ Ἀκινάκης καὶ ὁ Ἄνεμος εἶεν,
οὓς ὤμοσας· εἰ δ᾽ οὖν¹ τις ἀπιστοίη αὐτοῖς, οὐ
πάνυ μεμπτὸς εἶναι δόξειεν ἄν.

ΤΟΞΑΡΙΣ

Ἀλλ᾽ ὅρα, ὦ γενναῖε, μὴ φθόνος ὑμῶν ἡ ἀπι-
στία ᾖ. πλὴν οὐκ ἐμὲ ἀποτρέψεις ἀπιστῶν καὶ
ἄλλα τοιαῦτα εἰπεῖν ἃ οἶδα ὑπὸ Σκυθῶν γενόμενα.

ΜΝΗΣΙΠΠΟΣ

Μὴ μακρὰ μόνον, ὦ ἄριστε, μηδὲ οὕτως ἀφέτοις
χρώμενος τοῖς λόγοις· ὡς νῦν γε, ἄνω καὶ κάτω
τὴν Σκυθίαν καὶ τὴν Μαχλυανὴν² διαθέων καὶ
εἰς τὸν Βόσπορον ἀπιών, εἶτ᾽ ἐπανιών, πάνυ μου
κατεχρήσω τῇ σιωπῇ.

ΤΟΞΑΡΙΣ

Πειστέον καὶ ταῦτά σοι νομοθετοῦντι καὶ διὰ
βραχέων λεκτέον, μὴ καὶ κάμῃς ἡμῖν τῇ ἀκοῇ
57 συμπερινοστῶν. μᾶλλον δὲ ἄκουσον ἐμοὶ αὐτῷ
οἷα φίλος, Σισίννης τοὔνομα, ὑπηρέτησεν.

---

¹ δ᾽ οὖν Fritzsche : γοῦν MSS.
² Cf. Μαχλυηνή in § 34.

---

¹ Macentes would seem to have died of his wounds, though
Lucian does not say so. It may be noted, too, that although

and Lonchates had been given; [1] and when the treaty of peace was made, they negotiated the details.

Such are the deeds, Mnesippus, that Scythians dare to do for their friends.

MNESIPPUS

They are very dramatic, Toxaris, and quite like fables. May Glaive and Wind, by whom you swore, be good to me, but really, if one were to disbelieve them, one would not seem very open to criticism.

TOXARIS

But see to it, my gallant adversary, that your disbelief is not jealousy! Nevertheless, I am not the man to let your disbelieving me deter me from telling you other such deeds that I know to have been done by Scythians.

MNESIPPUS

Only don't let them be too protracted, my excellent friend, and don't use such an unembarrassed flow of speech; for as it is, by running hither and thither through Scythia and Machlyene, and by going off to Bosporus and then coming back again, you have taken very liberal advantage of my silence.

TOXARIS

In this too I must obey your dictates; I must speak briefly so that I shall not have you getting completely tired out by following me all about with your attention. No, rather let me tell you how I myself was assisted by a friend named Sisinnes.

the Sauromatians contributed 20,000 men to the invading force, we hear nothing of their part either in the battle or in the settlement.

THE WORKS OF LUCIAN

Ὅτε γὰρ Ἀθήναζε ἀπῄειν οἴκοθεν ἐπιθυμίᾳ
παιδείας τῆς Ἑλληνικῆς, κατέπλευσα ἐς Ἄμαστριν
τὴν Ποντικήν· ἐν προσβολῇ δέ ἐστιν τοῖς ἀπὸ
Σκυθίας προσπλέουσιν,[1] οὐ πολὺ τῆς Καράμβεως
ἀπέχουσα, ἡ πόλις. εἵπετο δὲ ὁ Σισίννης ἑταῖρος
ἐκ παιδὸς ὤν. ἡμεῖς μὲν οὖν καταγωγήν τινα ἐπὶ
τῷ λιμένι σκεψάμενοι κἀκ τοῦ πλοίου ἐς αὐτὴν
μετασκευασάμενοι ἠγοράζομεν, οὐδὲν πονηρὸν
ὑφορώμενοι· ἐν τοσούτῳ δὲ κλῶπές τινες ἀνασπά-
σαντες τὸ κλεῖστρον ἐκφέρουσιν ἅπαντα, ὡς μηδὲ
τὰ ἐς ἐκείνην τὴν ἡμέραν διαρκέσοντα καταλιπεῖν.

Ἐπανελθόντες οὖν οἴκαδε καὶ τὸ γεγονὸς
μαθόντες, δικάζεσθαι μὲν τοῖς γείτοσι πολλοῖς
οὖσιν ἢ τῷ ξένῳ οὐκ ἐδοκιμάζομεν, δεδιότες μὴ
συκοφάνται δόξωμεν τοῖς πολλοῖς λέγοντες ὡς
ὑφείλετο ἡμῶν τις δαρεικοὺς τετρακοσίους καὶ
ἐσθῆτα πολλὴν καὶ δάπιδάς τινας καὶ τὰ ἄλλα
58 ὁπόσα εἴχομεν· ἐσκοπούμεθα δὲ περὶ τῶν παρόντων ὅ τι πράξομεν, ἄποροι παντάπασιν ἐν τῇ
ἀλλοδαπῇ γενόμενοι. κἀμοὶ μὲν ἐδόκει ὡς εἶχον
αὐτοῦ παραβύσαντα ἐς τὴν πλευρὰν τὸν ἀκινάκην
ἀπελθεῖν τοῦ βίου πρὶν ἀγεννές τι ὑποστῆναι
λιμῷ ἢ δίψει πιεσθέντα, ὁ δὲ Σισίννης παρεμυθεῖτο
καὶ ἱκέτευεν μηδὲν τοιοῦτο ποιεῖν· αὐτὸς γὰρ
ἐπινοήσειν ὅθεν ἕξομεν ἱκανῶς τὰς τροφάς.

Καὶ τότε μὲν ξύλα ἐκ τοῦ λιμένος παρεκό-
μισεν καὶ ἧκεν ἡμῖν ἀπὸ τοῦ μισθοῦ ἐπισιτισάμενος·
ἕωθεν δὲ περιιὼν κατὰ τὴν ἀγορὰν εἶδε προπομπὴν[2]
τινα, ὡς ἔφη, γενναίων καὶ καλῶν νεανίσκων.

[1] πλέουσιν A.
[2] προπομπήν Γ: πομπήν N cett. Note ὡς ἔφη.

196

TOXARIS, OR FRIENDSHIP

When I was going away from home to Athens by reason of my desire for Greek culture, I put in at Amastris, on the Black Sea; the city is a port of call for those sailing this way from Scythia, not far distant from Carambis. I was accompanied by Sisinnes, who had been my companion from childhood. After looking out a lodging near the port and transferring our effects to it from the vessel, we went shopping, without suspecting any mischief. In the meantime thieves pried the door open and carried off everything, so as not to leave even enough to suffice for that day.

When we returned home and found out what had happened, we did not think it best to proceed against the neighbours, who were numerous, or against our host, fearing that we should be accounted blackmailers in public opinion if we said that someone had robbed us of four hundred darics, a great deal of clothing, some rugs, and all the other things that we had. So we discussed the situation to see what we should do, now that we had become absolutely penniless in a strange country. My own thought was to plunge my sword into my side forthwith, and make my exit from life before enduring any unseemly experience under the pressure of hunger or thirst, but Sisinnes encouraged me and begged me not to do anything of that sort, for he himself would discover a means of our having enough to live on.

That day, therefore, he carried lumber in from the port and came back with supplies for us which he had procured with his wages. But the next morning, while going about in the market-place he saw a sort of procession, as he put it, of high-spirited,

μονομαχεῖν δὲ οὗτοι ἐπὶ μισθῷ ἀνδρολογηθέντες
εἰς τρίτην ἡμέραν διαγωνιεῖσθαι ἔμελλον. καὶ
δὴ τὸ πᾶν ὡς εἶχεν ἀμφ' αὑτοὺς πυθόμενος,
ἐλθὼν ὡς ἐμέ, " Μηκέτι, ὦ Τόξαρι," ἔφη, " σαυτὸν
πένητα λέγε, εἰς γὰρ τρίτην ἡμέραν πλούσιόν σε
ἀποφανῶ."

59 Ταῦτα εἶπε, καὶ πονηρῶς τὸ μεταξὺ ἀποζή-
σαντες, ἐνστάσης ἤδη τῆς θέας ἐθεώμεθα καὶ
αὐτοί· παραλαβὼν γάρ με ὡς ἐπὶ τερπνόν τι καὶ
παράδοξον θέαμα τῶν Ἑλληνικῶν ἄγει εἰς τὸ
θέατρον. καὶ καθίσαντες ἑωρῶμεν τὸ μὲν πρῶτον
θηρία κατακοντιζόμενα καὶ ὑπὸ κυνῶν διωκόμενα
καὶ ἐπ' ἀνθρώπους δεδεμένους ἀφιέμενα, κακούργους τινάς, ὡς εἰκάζομεν. ἐπεὶ δὲ εἰσῆλθον οἱ
μονομάχοι καί τινα παραγαγὼν ὁ κῆρυξ εὐμεγέθη
νεανίσκον εἶπεν, ὅστις ἂν ἐθέλῃ τούτῳ μονομαχῆσαι, ἥκειν εἰς τὸ μέσον δραχμὰς ληψόμενον
μυρίας μισθὸν τῆς μάχης, ἐνταῦθα ἐξανίσταται ὁ
Σισίννης καὶ καταπηδήσας ὑπέστη μαχεῖσθαι καὶ
τὰ ὅπλα ᾔτει, καὶ τὸν μισθὸν λαβών, τὰς μυρίας
ἐμοὶ φέρων ἐνεχείρισε, καὶ " Εἰ μὲν κρατήσαιμι,
ὦ Τόξαρι," εἶπεν, " ἅμα ἄπιμεν ἔχοντες τὰ
ἀρκοῦντα, ἢν δὲ πέσω, θάψας με ὑποχώρει ὀπίσω
ἐς Σκύθας."

60 Ἐγὼ μὲν ἐπὶ τούτοις ἐκώκυον, ὁ δὲ λαβὼν τὰ
ὅπλα τὰ μὲν ἄλλα περιεδήσατο, τὸ κράνος δὲ
οὐκ ἐπέθηκεν,[1] ἀλλ' ἀπὸ γυμνῆς τῆς κεφαλῆς
καταστὰς ἐμάχετο. καὶ τὸ μὲν πρῶτον τιτρώ-
σκεται αὐτός, καμπύλῳ τῷ ξίφει ὑποτμηθεὶς
τὴν ἰγνύαν, ὥστε αἷμα ἔρρει πολύ· ἐγὼ δὲ προετε-
θνήκειν ἤδη τῷ δέει. θρασύτερον δὲ ἐπιφερό-

[1] οὐκ ἐπέθηκεν K. F. Hermann: οὐ κατέθηκεν MSS.

handsome young men. These had been enrolled to fight duels for hire and were to settle their combats on the next day but one. Well, he found out all about them, and then came to me, saying: " Toxaris, you need not call yourself a poor man any longer; on the day after to-morrow I shall make you rich."

Those were his words; accordingly, we eked out a wretched existence during the interval, and when at length the spectacle began we were there looking on, for taking me with him on the pretext of going to see a Greek show that would be enjoyable and novel, he had brought me to the theatre. We took our seats, and first we saw wild beasts brought down with javelins, hunted with dogs, and loosed upon men in chains—criminals, we conjectured. Then the gladiators entered, and the herald, bringing in a tall youth, said that whoever wanted to fight with that man should come forward, and would receive ten thousand drachmas in payment for the encounter. Thereupon Sisinnes arose, and, leaping down, undertook to fight and requested arms. On receiving his pay, the ten thousand drachmas, he promptly put it in my hands, saying: " If I win, Toxaris, we shall go away together, with all that we need; but if I fall, bury me and go back to Scythia."

While I was lamenting over this, he was given his armour and fastened it on, except that he did not put on the helmet but took position bareheaded and fought that way. He himself received the first wound, an under-cut in the back of the thigh, dealt with a curved sword, so that blood flowed copiously. For my part, I was already as good as dead in my fright. But he waited until his opponent rushed

THE WORKS OF LUCIAN

μενον τηρήσας τὸν ἀντίπαλον παίει εἰς τὸ στέρνον
καὶ διήλασεν, ὥστε αὐτίκα ἐπεπτώκει πρὸ τοῖν
ποδοῖν αὐτοῦ. ὁ δὲ κάμνων καὶ αὐτὸς ἀπὸ τοῦ
τραύματος ἐπεκάθιζε τῷ νεκρῷ, καὶ μικροῦ δεῖν
ἀφῆκεν αὐτὸν ἡ ψυχή, ἀλλ' ἐγὼ προσδραμὼν
ἀνέστησα καὶ παρεμυθησάμην. ἐπεὶ δὲ ἀφεῖτο
ἤδη νενικηκώς, ἀράμενος αὐτὸν ἐκόμισα εἰς τὴν
οἰκίαν· καὶ ἐπὶ πολὺ θεραπευθεὶς ἐπέζησε μὲν
καὶ ἔστι μέχρι νῦν ἐν Σκύθαις, γήμας τὴν ἐμὴν
ἀδελφήν· χωλὸς δέ ἐστιν ὅμως ἀπὸ τοῦ τραύματος.

Τοῦτο, ὦ Μνήσιππε, οὐκ ἐν Μάχλυσιν οὐδὲ
ἐν Ἀλανίᾳ ἐγένετο, ὡς ἀμάρτυρον εἶναι καὶ
ἀπιστεῖσθαι δύνασθαι, ἀλλὰ πολλοὶ πάρεισιν Ἀμα-
στριανῶν μεμνημένοι τὴν μάχην[1] τοῦ Σισίννου.

61 Πέμπτον ἔτι σοι τὸ Ἀβαύχα ἔργον διηγησάμενος παύσομαι. ἧκέν ποτε οὗτος ὁ Ἀβαύχας εἰς
τὴν Βορυσθενιτῶν πόλιν ἐπαγόμενος καὶ γυναῖκα,
ἧς ἥρα μάλιστα, καὶ παιδία δύο· τὸ μὲν ἐπιμαστί-
διον ἄρρεν, τὸ δὲ ἕτερον, ἡ κόρη, ἑπτέτις ἦν.
συναπεδήμει δὲ καὶ ἑταῖρος αὐτοῦ, Γυνδάνης,
οὗτος μὲν καὶ νοσῶν ἀπὸ τραύματος ὃ ἐτέτρωτο
κατὰ τὴν ὁδὸν ὑπὸ λῃστῶν ἐπιπεσόντων σφίσι·
διαμαχόμενος γὰρ πρὸς αὐτοὺς ἐλαύνεται εἰς τὸν
μηρόν, ὥστε οὐδὲ ἑστάναι ἐδύνατο ὑπὸ τῆς ὀδύνης.
νύκτωρ δὲ καθευδόντων—ἔτυχον δὲ ἐν ὑπερῴῳ
τινὶ οἰκοῦντες—πυρκαϊὰ μεγάλη ἐξανίσταται καὶ
πάντα περιεκλείετο καὶ περιεῖχεν ἡ φλὸξ ἀπαντα-
χόθεν τὴν οἰκίαν. ἐνταῦθα δὴ ἀνεγρόμενος ὁ
Ἀβαύχας καταλιπὼν τὰ παιδία κλαυθμυριζόμενα

[1] τὴν μάχην ΓΝΒ: τῆς μάχης ΜΑ.

200

upon him too confidently; then he stabbed him in the breast and ran him through, so that on the instant he fell at his feet. Himself labouring under his wound, he sat down upon the body and his life almost left him, but I, running up, revived and inspirited him. When at length he was dismissed as victor, I picked him up and carried him to our lodgings. After long treatment he survived and still lives in Scythia, with my sister as his wife; he is lame, however, from his wound.

That, Mnesippus, did not happen either in Machlyene or among the Alans, so as to be unattested and possible to disbelieve; there are many Amastrians here who remember the fight of Sisinnes.

As the fifth, I shall tell you the deed of Abauchas, and then I shall stop. Once upon a time this man Abauchas came to the city of the Borysthenites,[1] bringing his wife, of whom he was exceptionally fond, and two children, one of whom, a boy, was a child in arms, while the other, a girl, was seven years old. There came with him also a companion of his, Gyndanes, who was ill of a wound which he had received on the way from robbers who had attacked them. In fighting with them he had got a thrust in the thigh, so that he could not even stand for the pain of it. During the night, as they slept— they chanced to be living in an upper story—a great fire broke out, every avenue of escape was being cut off, and the flames were encompassing the house on all sides. At that juncture Abauchas woke up; abandoning his crying children, shaking off his wife

[1] Olbia.

καὶ τὴν γυναῖκα ἐκκρεμαννυμένην [1] ἀποσεισάμενος
καὶ σώζειν αὐτὴν παρακελευσάμενος, ἀράμενος
τὸν ἑταῖρον κατῆλθεν καὶ ἔφθη διεκπαίσας καθ'
ὃ μηδέπω τελέως ἀπεκέκαυτο ὑπὸ τοῦ πυρός.
ἡ γυνὴ δὲ φέρουσα τὸ βρέφος εἵπετο, ἀκολου-
θεῖν κελεύσασα καὶ τὴν κόρην. ἡ δὲ ἡμίφλεκτος
ἀφεῖσα τὸ παιδίον ἐκ τῆς ἀγκάλης μόλις διεπήδησε
τὴν φλόγα, καὶ ἡ παῖς σὺν αὐτῇ, παρὰ μικρὸν
ἐλθοῦσα κἀκείνη ἀποθανεῖν. καὶ ἐπεὶ ὠνείδισέν
τις ὕστερον τὸν Ἀβαύχαν διότι προδοὺς τὰ τέκνα
καὶ τὴν γυναῖκα ὁ δὲ Γυνδάνην ἐξεκόμισεν,
" Ἀλλὰ παῖδας μέν," ἔφη, " καὶ αὖθις ποιήσασθαί
μοι ῥᾴδιον, καὶ ἄδηλον εἰ ἀγαθοὶ ἔσονται οὗτοι·
φίλον δὲ οὐκ ἂν εὕροιμι ἄλλον ἐν πολλῷ χρόνῳ
τοιοῦτον οἷος Γυνδάνης ἐστίν, πεῖράν μοι πολλὴν
τῆς εὐνοίας παρεσχημένος."

62 Εἴρηκα, ὦ Μνήσιππε, ἀπὸ πολλῶν πέντε τούτους προχειρισάμενος. ἤδη δὲ καιρὸς ἂν [2] εἴη
κεκρίσθαι ὁπότερον ἡμῶν ἢ τὴν γλῶτταν ἢ τὴν
δεξιὰν ἀποτετμῆσθαι δέοι. τίς οὖν ὁ δικάσων
ἐστίν;

ΜΝΗΣΙΠΠΟΣ

Οὐδὲ εἷς· οὐ γὰρ ἐκαθίσαμέν τινα δικαστὴν
τοῦ λόγου. ἀλλ' οἶσθα ὃ δράσωμεν ; [3] ἐπειδὴ
νῦν ἄσκοπα τετοξεύκαμεν, αὖθις ἑλόμενοι διαιτητὴν
ἄλλους ἐπ' ἐκείνῳ εἴπωμεν φίλους, εἶτα ὃς ἂν

---

[1] ἐκκρεμαννυμένην ed. Flor., ἐκκρεμανυμένην ΓΒ: ἐκκρεμα-
μένην Ν, vulg.
[2] ἂν Geist: not in MSS.
[3] δράσωμεν Γ: δράσομεν other MSS.

---

[1] The reasoning of Abauchas on this point is suspiciously
like that ascribed to Seleucus Nicator by Lucian in the

as she hung upon him and urging her to save herself, he carried his comrade down and managed to burst through at a place which the fire had not yet completely burned away. His wife, carrying the baby, followed, telling the girl too to come along. Half-burned, she let the child fall from her arms and barely leaped through the flames, and with her the little girl, who also came very near losing her life. When someone afterwards rebuked Abauchas for abandoning his wife and children but bringing out Gyndanes, he said: "Why, I can easily have other children, and it was uncertain whether these would be good for anything, but I could not in a long time find another friend like Gyndanes, who has given me abundant proof of his devotion." [1]

I have finished, Mnesippus, the story of these five, whom I have selected out of many. And now it is perhaps time to decide which of us is to have either his tongue or his right hand cut off, as the case may be. Who, then, will be our judge?

MNESIPPUS

No one at all; for we did not appoint any judge of the debate. But do you know what we ought to do? Since this time we have shot into the void, let us some other day choose an umpire and in his presence tell of other friends; then, whichever of us

---

Goddess of Syria (18 : Vol. IV, p. 364), to Antigone by Sophocles (*Antig.* 905–912), and to the wife of Intaphernes by Herodotus (III, 119). We cannot, however, be entirely certain in the case of Abauchas that it derives from the Herodotean story. There are parallels from India (in the Ramayana and in the Jatakas: *Hermes*, XXVIII, 465) and from Persia: *ibid.*, XXIX, 155); cf. also, for modern Syria, A. Goodrich-Freer, *Arabs in Tent and Town*, p. 25.

ἥττων γένηται, ἀποτετμήσεται τότε, ἢ ἐγὼ τὴν
γλῶτταν ἢ σὺ τὴν δεξιάν. ἢ τοῦτο μὲν ἄγροικον,
ἐπεὶ δὲ καὶ σὺ φιλίαν ἐπαινεῖν ἔδοξας, ἐγὼ δὲ
οὐδὲν ἄλλο ἡγοῦμαι ἀνθρώποις εἶναι τούτου κτῆμα
ἄμεινον ἢ κάλλιον, τί οὐχὶ [1] καὶ ἡμεῖς συνθέμενοι
πρὸς ἡμᾶς αὐτοὺς φίλοι τε αὐτόθεν εἶναι καὶ εἰσαεὶ
ἔσεσθαι ἀγαπῶμεν ἄμφω νικήσαντες, τὰ μέγιστα
ἆθλα προσλαβόντες, ἀντὶ μιᾶς γλώττης καὶ μιᾶς
δεξιᾶς δύο ἑκάτερος ἐπικτησάμενοι καὶ προσέτι
γε καὶ ὀφθαλμοὺς τέτταρας καὶ πόδας τέτταρας
καὶ ὅλως διπλᾶ πάντα; τοιοῦτόν τι γάρ ἐστι
συνελθόντες δύο ἢ τρεῖς φίλοι, ὁποῖον τὸν
Γηρυόνην οἱ γραφεῖς ἐνδείκνυνται, ἄνθρωπον ἑξά-
χειρα καὶ τρικέφαλον· ἐμοὶ γὰρ δοκεῖν,[2] τρεῖς
ἐκεῖνοι ἦσαν ἅμα πράττοντες πάντα, ὥσπερ ἐστὶ
δίκαιον φίλους γε ὄντας.

ΤΟΞΑΡΙΣ

63 Εὖ λέγεις· καὶ οὕτω ποιῶμεν.

ΜΝΗΣΙΠΠΟΣ

Ἀλλὰ μήτε αἵματος, ὦ Τόξαρι, μήτε ἀκινάκου
δεώμεθα τὴν φιλίαν ἡμῖν βεβαιώσοντος· ὁ γὰρ
λόγος ὁ παρὼν καὶ τὸ τῶν ὁμοίων ὀρέγεσθαι πολὺ
πιστότερα τῆς κύλικος ἐκείνης ἣν πίνετε, ἐπεὶ τά
γε τοιαῦτα οὐκ ἀνάγκης ἀλλὰ γνώμης δεῖσθαί μοι
δοκεῖ.

gets beaten shall at that time have his tongue cut off if it be I, or his right hand if it be you. Or, if that is crude, inasmuch as you have resolved to extol friendship and I myself think that men have no other possession better or nobler than this, why should not we ourselves make an agreement with each other to be friends from this instant and remain so for ever, content that both have won and thereby have obtained magnificent prizes, since instead of a single tongue or a single right hand each of us will get two, and what is more, two pairs of eyes and of feet; in a word, everything multiplied by two? For the union of two or three friends is like the pictures of Geryon that artists exhibit—a man with six hands and three heads. Indeed, to my mind Geryon was three persons acting together in all things, as is right if they are really friends.

TOXARIS

Good! let us do so.

MNESIPPUS

But let us not feel the need of blood, Toxaris, or any sword to confirm our friendship. This conversation of ours just now and the similarity of our ideals are far more dependable sureties than that cup which your people drink, since achievements like these require resolution rather than compulsion, it seems to me.

---

[1] Text N: κάλλιον εἶναί τι· οὐχὶ ΓΒΑ.
[2] δοκεῖν Hartman: δοκεῖ MSS.

ΤΟΞΑΡΙΣ

Ἐπαινῶ ταῦτα, καὶ ἤδη ὦμεν φίλοι καὶ ξένοι, ἐμοὶ μὲν σὺ ἐνταῦθα ἐπὶ τῆς Ἑλλάδος, ἐγὼ δὲ σοὶ εἴ ποτε ἐς τὴν Σκυθίαν ἀφίκοιο.

ΜΝΗΣΙΠΠΟΣ

Καὶ μήν, εὖ ἴσθι, οὐκ ἂν ὀκνήσαιμι καὶ ἔτι πορρωτέρω ἐλθεῖν, εἰ μέλλω τοιούτοις φίλοις ἐντεύξεσθαι οἷος σύ, ὦ Τόξαρι, διεφάνης ἡμῖν ἀπὸ τῶν λόγων.

TOXARIS, OR FRIENDSHIP

TOXARIS

I approve all this; so let us now be friends and each the other's host, you mine here in Hellas and I yours if ever you should come to Scythia.

MNESIPPUS

Truly you may be very sure that I shall not hesitate to go even farther if I am to meet such friends as you, Toxaris, have clearly shown me that you are, by what you have said.

THE DANCE

An encomiastic treatise, set in a frame of dialogue. The Cynic Crato, who has no manner of use for pantomimic dancing or those who go to see it, is converted by Lycinus.

In that form of dancing, a dramatic plot was enacted by a masked and costumed dancer, supported by an actor (p. 271, n. 3). The dancer's lines were spoken for him by someone else. There was also a chorus, and, for accompaniment, the flute and the syrinx, with various instruments of percussion, including the "iron shoe" (p. 285, n. 2). The name pantomime, denoting properly the dancer, not the dance, and coined in Italy, according to Lucian (§ 67), is eschewed by Lucian and the other Atticists, who speak simply of " dancers." Inscriptions show a cumbrous official designation voicing a claim to affinity with tragedy (τραγικῆς ἐνρύθμου κινήσεως ὑποκριτής, see L. Robert, *Hermes*, LXV [1930], 106–122). The art was sometimes called " tragic " dancing (Athen., I, 20), but not by Lucian, who, moreover, does not let himself in for the error that it was invented by Bathyllus and Pylades (Athen., *l.c.*; Zosimus, I, 6), but represents only that it began to attain perfection under Augustus.

Vastly popular, it invited notice from rhetoricians as well as philosophers. Aristides issued an invective against it, now lost, but in good part recoverable from quotations in the reply of Libanius (cf. Mesk, *Wiener Studien*, XXX [1908], 59–74). Lucian knew the book of Aristides, then quite new, but elected not to reply to it directly. His dialogue was probably written, as D. S. Robertson has indicated, at Antioch in 162–165 A.D., when the Emperor Verus was there, in compliment to him because of his interest in dancers (*Essays and Studies presented to William Ridgeway*, p. 180; cf. L. Robert, cited above). The treatment is on traditional lines, especially in respect of its emphasis upon gods, heroes, and nations who have practised or patronized the art, and poets and philosophers who have sanctioned it; compare, for instance, *The Parasite*, and *Astrology*. It is not meant to be taken too seriously, in this part above all.

209

ΠΕΡΙ ΟΡΧΗΣΕΩΣ

ΛΥΚΙΝΟΣ

1 Ἐπεὶ τοίνυν, ὦ Κράτων, δεινήν τινα ταύτην
κατηγορίαν ἐκ πολλοῦ, οἶμαι, παρεσκευασμένος
κατηγόρηκας ὀρχήσεών [1] τε καὶ αὐτῆς ὀρχηστικῆς,
καὶ προσέτι ἡμῶν γε τῶν χαιρόντων τῇ τοιαύτῃ
θέᾳ ὡς ἐπὶ φαύλῳ καὶ γυναικείῳ πράγματι μεγάλην σπουδὴν ποιουμένων, ἄκουσον ὅσον τοῦ
ὀρθοῦ διημάρτηκας καὶ ὡς λέληθας σεαυτὸν τοῦ
μεγίστου τῶν ἐν τῷ βίῳ ἀγαθῶν κατηγορῶν.
καὶ συγγνώμη σοι εἰ ἐξ ἀρχῆς βίῳ αὐχμηρῷ
συζῶν καὶ μόνον τὸ σκληρὸν ἀγαθὸν ἡγούμενος
ὑπ᾽ ἀπειρίας αὐτῶν κατηγορίας ἄξια εἶναι νενό-
μικας.

ΚΡΑΤΩΝ

2 Ἀνὴρ δὲ τίς ὢν ὅλως,[2] καὶ ταῦτα παιδείᾳ
σύντροφος καὶ φιλοσοφίᾳ τὰ μέτρια ὡμιληκώς,
ἀφέμενος, ὦ Λυκῖνε, τοῦ περὶ τὰ βελτίω σπουδάζειν
καὶ τοῖς παλαιοῖς συνεῖναι κάθηται καταυλού-
μενος, θηλυδρίαν ἄνθρωπον ὁρῶν ἐσθῆσι μαλακαῖς
καὶ ᾄσμασιν ἀκολάστοις ἐναβρυνόμενον καὶ μιμού-
μενον ἐρωτικὰ γύναια, τῶν πάλαι τὰς μαχλοτάτας,
Φαίδρας καὶ Παρθενόπας καὶ Ῥοδόπας τινάς,

---

[1] ὀρχήσεως Α.

THE DANCE

WELL, Crato, this is a truly forceful indictment that you have brought, after long preparation, I take it, against dances and the dancer's art itself, and besides against us who like to see that sort of show, accusing us of displaying great interest in something unworthy and effeminate; but now let me tell you how far you have missed the mark and how blind you have been to the fact that you were indicting the greatest of all the good things in life. For that I can excuse you if, having been wedded to a rude creed from the first and considering only what is hard to be good, through unacquaintance with it all you have thought that it deserved indicting.

CRATO

Who that is a man at all, a life-long friend of letters, moreover, and moderately conversant with philosophy, abandons his interest, Lycinus, in all that is better and his association with the ancients to sit enthralled by the flute, watching a girlish fellow play the wanton with dainty clothing and bawdy songs and imitate love-sick minxes, the most erotic of all antiquity, such as Phaedra and Parthenope and

---

² ὅλως Γ² (interlinear, abbreviated) Vat. 87: ὦ λῶστε Γ¹ vulg. (ὦ omitted in N). Cf. καὶ οὐδεὶς ὅλως εἶδε, *Gallus*, 29.

καὶ ταῦτα πάντα ὑπὸ κρούμασιν καὶ τερετίσμασι
καὶ ποδῶν κτύπῳ, καταγέλαστα ὡς ἀληθῶς
πράγματα καὶ ἥκιστα ἐλευθέρῳ ἀνδρὶ καὶ οἵῳ σοὶ
πρέποντα ; ὥστε ἔγωγε πυθόμενος ὡς ἐπὶ τοιαύτῃ
θέᾳ σχολάζοις, οὐκ ᾐδέσθην μόνον ὑπὲρ σοῦ
ἀλλὰ καὶ ἠνιάθην εἰ Πλάτωνος καὶ Χρυσίππου καὶ
Ἀριστοτέλους ἐκλαθόμενος κάθησαι τὸ ὅμοιον
πεπονθὼς τοῖς τὰ ὦτα πτερῷ κνωμένοις, καὶ
ταῦτα μυρίων ἄλλων ὄντων ἀκουσμάτων καὶ
θεαμάτων σπουδαίων, εἰ τούτων τις δέοιτο, τῶν
κυκλίων[1] αὐλητῶν καὶ τῶν κιθάρᾳ τὰ ἔννομα
προσᾳδόντων, καὶ μάλιστα τῆς σεμνῆς τραγῳδίας καὶ τῆς φαιδροτάτης κωμῳδίας, ἅπερ καὶ
ἐναγώνια εἶναι ἠξίωται.

3 Πολλῆς οὖν, ὦ γενναῖε, τῆς ἀπολογίας σοι
δεήσει πρὸς τοὺς πεπαιδευμένους, εἰ βούλει μὴ
παντάπασιν ἐκκεκρίσθαι καὶ τῆς τῶν σπουδαίων
ἀγέλης ἐξεληλάσθαι. καίτοι τό γε ἄμεινον ἐκεῖνό
ἐστιν, οἶμαι, ἀρνήσει τὸ πᾶν ἰάσασθαι καὶ μηδὲ τὴν
ἀρχὴν ὁμολογεῖν τι τοιοῦτον παρανενομηκέναι σοι.
πρὸς δ' οὖν τοὐπιὸν ὅρα ὅπως μὴ λάθῃς ἡμῖν
ἐξ ἀνδρὸς τοῦ πάλαι Λυδή τις ἢ Βάκχη γενόμενος,
ὅπερ οὐ σὸν ἂν ἔγκλημα εἴη μόνον, ἀλλὰ καὶ

---

[1] κυκλίων N : κυκλι ων Γ (*i.e.*, space left and accent omitted
because of variant reading in original) : κυκλικῶν (ECA)
vulg. Cp. § 26 αὐλητὰς κυκλίους.

---

[1] Parthenope, the beloved of Metiochus the Phrygian, was
the heroine of a lost romance; on the extant fragment,
see *New Chapters in the Hist. of Greek Lit.*, III, 238–240.
Rhodope is probably the Thracian mentioned below in § 51,
who married Haemus, her brother; they insolently likened
themselves to Zeus and Hera, and were turned into the
mountains known by their names.

Rhodope,[1] every bit of this, moreover, accompanied by strumming and tootling and tapping of feet ? [2] —a ridiculous business in all truth, which does not in the least become a freeborn gentleman of your sort. So for my part, when I learned that you give your time to such spectacles, I was not only ashamed on your account but sorely distressed that you should sit there oblivious of Plato and Chrysippus and Aristotle, getting treated like people who have themselves tickled in the ear with a feather, and that too when there are countless other things to hear and see that are worth while, if one wants them—flute-players who accompany cyclic choruses, singers of conventional compositions for the lyre,[3] and in especial, grand tragedy and comedy, the gayest of the gay ; all these have even been held worthy to figure in competitions.

You will need, therefore, to do a great deal of pleading in your own defence, my fine fellow, when you confront the enlightened, if you wish to avoid being eliminated absolutely and expelled from the fold of the serious-minded. And yet the better course for you, I suppose, is to mend the whole matter by pleading not guilty and not admitting at all that you have committed any such misdemeanour. Anyhow, keep an eye to the future and see to it that you do not surprise us by changing from the man that you were of old to a Lyde or a Bacche. That would be a reproach not only to you but to us, unless, follow-

[2] See p. 285, n. 2, below.

[3] The reference is to the citharoedi, soloists who played their own accompaniment on the lyre; of their songs, called nomes, the *Persians* of Timotheus is the only surviving specimen.

THE WORKS OF LUCIAN

ἡμῶν, εἰ μή σε κατὰ τὸν Ὀδυσσέα τοῦ λωτοῦ
ἀποσπάσαντες ἐπὶ τὰς συνήθεις διατριβὰς ἐπανά-
ξομεν πρὶν λάθῃς τελέως ὑπὸ τῶν ἐν τῷ θεάτρῳ
Σειρήνων κατεσχημένος. καίτοι ἐκεῖναι μὲν τοῖς
ὠσὶν μόνοις ἐπεβούλευον καὶ διὰ τοῦτο κηροῦ
ἐδέησεν πρὸς τὸν παράπλουν αὐτῶν· σὺ δὲ καὶ
δι᾽ ὀφθαλμῶν ἔοικας ὅλος δεδουλῶσθαι.

ΛΥΚΙΝΟΣ

4   Παπαῖ, ὦ Κράτων, ὡς κάρχαρόν τινα ἔλυσας
ἐφ᾽ ἡμᾶς τὸν σαυτοῦ κύνα. πλὴν τό γε παράδειγμα,
τὴν τῶν Λωτοφάγων καὶ Σειρήνων εἰκόνα, πάνυ
ἀνομοιοτάτην μοι δοκεῖς εἰρηκέναι ὧν πέπονθα, παρ᾽
ὅσον τοῖς μὲν τοῦ λωτοῦ γευσαμένοις καὶ τῶν
Σειρήνων ἀκούσασιν ὄλεθρος ἦν τῆς τε ἐδωδῆς
καὶ τῆς ἀκροάσεως τοὐπιτίμιον, ἐμοὶ δὲ πρὸς τῷ
τὴν ἡδονὴν παρὰ πολὺ ἡδίω πεφυκέναι[1] καὶ τὸ
τέλος ἀγαθὸν ἀποβέβηκεν· οὐ γὰρ εἰς λήθην τῶν
οἴκοι οὐδ᾽ εἰς ἀγνωσίαν τῶν κατ᾽ ἐμαυτὸν περιί-
σταμαι, ἀλλ᾽ εἰ χρὴ μηδὲν ὀκνήσαντα εἰπεῖν,
μακρῷ πινυτώτερος καὶ τῶν ἐν τῷ βίῳ διορατι-
κώτερος ἐκ τοῦ θεάτρου σοι ἐπανελήλυθα. μᾶλλον
δέ, τὸ τοῦ Ὁμήρου αὐτὸ εἰπεῖν καλόν, ὅτι ὁ τοῦτο
ἰδὼν τὸ θέαμα "τερψάμενος νεῖται καὶ πλείονα
εἰδώς."

ΚΡΑΤΩΝ

Ἡράκλεις, ὦ Λυκῖνε, οἷα πέπονθας, ὃς οὐδ᾽
αἰσχύνῃ ἐπ᾽ αὐτοῖς, ἀλλὰ καὶ σεμνυνομένῳ ἔοικας.
τὸ γοῦν δεινότατον τοῦτό ἐστιν, ὅτι μηδὲ ἰάσεώς
τινα ἡμῖν ὑποφαίνεις ἐλπίδα, ἐπαινεῖν τολμῶν τὰ
οὕτως αἰσχρὰ καὶ κατάπτυστα.

[1] πεφηνέναι ΓΝΕ².

THE DANCE

ing the example of Odysseus, we can pull you away from your lotus and fetch you back to your wonted pursuits before you unwittingly fall quite under the spell of these Sirens in the theatre. But those other Sirens assailed only the ears, so that wax alone was needed for sailing past them; you, however, seem to have been subjugated from top to toe, through the eyes as well as the ears.

LYCINUS

Heavens, Crato, what sharp teeth there are in this dog of yours that you have let loose on us! But as for your parallel, the simile of the Lotus-Eaters and the Sirens, it seems to me quite unlike what I have been through, since in the case of those who tasted the lotus and heard the Sirens, death was the penalty for their eating and listening, while in my case not only is the pleasure more exquisite by a great deal but the outcome is happy; I am not altered into forgetfulness of things at home or ignorance of my own concerns, but—if I may speak my mind without any hesitancy—I have come back to you from the theatre with far more wisdom and more insight into life. Or rather, I may well put it just as Homer does: he who has seen this spectacle " Goes on his way diverted and knowing more than aforetime." [1]

CRATO

Heracles, Lycinus! How deeply you have been affected! You are not even ashamed of it all but actually seem proud. In fact, that is the worst part of it: you do not show us any hope of a cure when you dare to praise what is so shameful and abominable.

[1] *Odyssey*, XII, 188.

ΛΥΚΙΝΟΣ

5 Εἰπέ μοι, ὦ Κράτων, ταυτὶ δὲ περὶ ὀρχήσεως
καὶ τῶν ἐν τῷ θεάτρῳ γινομένων ἰδὼν πολλάκις
αὐτὸς ἐπιτιμᾷς, ἢ ἀπείρατος ὢν τοῦ θεάματος
ὅμως αἰσχρὸν αὐτὸ καὶ κατάπτυστον, ὡς φής,
νομίζεις ; εἰ μὲν γὰρ εἶδες, ἐξ ἴσου ἡμῖν καὶ σὺ
γεγένησαι· εἰ δὲ μή, ὅρα μὴ ἄλογος ἡ ἐπιτίμησις
εἶναί σου δόξῃ καὶ θρασεῖα, κατηγοροῦντος ὧν
ἀγνοεῖς.

ΚΡΑΤΩΝ

Ἔτι γὰρ τοῦτό μοι τὸ λοιπὸν[1] ἦν, ἐν βαθεῖ
τούτῳ τῷ πώγωνι καὶ πολιᾷ τῇ κόμῃ καθῆσθαι
μέσον ἐν τοῖς γυναίοις καὶ τοῖς μεμηνόσιν ἐκείνοις
θεαταῖς, κροτοῦντά τε προσέτι καὶ ἐπαίνους
ἀπρεπεστάτους ἐπιβοῶντα ὀλέθρῳ τινὶ ἀνθρώπῳ
ἐς οὐδὲν δέον κατακλωμένῳ.

ΛΥΚΙΝΟΣ

Συγγνωστά σου ταῦτα, ὦ Κράτων. εἰ δέ μοι
πεισθείης ποτὲ καὶ ὅσον πείρας ἕνεκα παράσχοις
σεαυτὸν ἀναπετάσας τοὺς ὀφθαλμούς, εὖ οἶδα ὡς
οὐκ ἀνάσχοιο ἂν μὴ οὐχὶ πρὸ τῶν ἄλλων θέαν ἐν
ἐπιτηδείῳ καταλαμβάνων ὅθεν καὶ ὄψει ἀκριβῶς
καὶ ἀκούσῃ ἅπαντα.

ΚΡΑΤΩΝ

Μὴ ὥρας[2] ἄρα ἱκοίμην, εἴ τι τοιοῦτον ἀνασχοί-
μην ποτέ, ἔστ' ἂν δασύς τε εἴην τὰ σκέλη καὶ τὸ

---

[1] μοι λοιπὸν C; but cf. *Pseudol.*, 13 πάνυ γοῦν τοῦτ' ἐστὶ τὸ
λοιπόν.
[2] ὥρας Γ: ὥραισιν cett. (but E by the second hand, in an
erasure): ὥρασιν Jacobitz. The same variations occur elsewhere: *Dial. Deor.*, 6, 5 ὥρας Γ; ὥραισιν cett.; *Dial. Mer.*,

THE DANCE

LYCINUS

Tell me, Crato, do you pass this censure upon
dancing and what goes on in the theatre after having
seen it often yourself, or is it that without being
acquainted with the spectacle, you nevertheless
account it shameful and abominable, as you put it?
If you have seen it, you have put yourself on the same
footing with us; if not, take care that your censure
does not seem unreasonable and overbold when you
denounce things of which you know nothing.

CRATO

Why, is that what was still in store for me—with
beard so long and hair so grey, to sit in the midst of
a parcel of hussies and a frantic audience like that,
clapping my hands, moreover, and shouting very
unbecoming words of praise to a noxious fellow who
doubles himself up for no useful purpose?

LYCINUS

This talk is excusable in your case, Crato. But if
you would only take my word for it and just for the
experiment's sake submit, with your eyes wide open,
I know very well that you could not endure not to
get ahead of everyone else in taking up an advantage-
ously placed seat from which you could see well and
hear everything.

CRATO

May I never reach ripeness of years if I ever
endure anything of the kind, as long as my legs
are hairy and my beard unplucked! At present I

10, 3 ὥρας FZ, ὥραισιν PN. Cf. Menander, *Peric.*, 131, and
Phasma, 43 (references for which I am very grateful to
Edward Capps).

γένειον ἀπαράτιλτος· ὡς νῦν γε καὶ σὲ ἤδη ἐλεῶ
τελέως ἡμῖν ἐκβεβακχευμένον.

ΛΥΚΙΝΟΣ

6 Βούλει οὖν ἀφέμενος, ὦ ἑταῖρε, τῶν βλασφημιῶν τούτων ἀκοῦσαί μού τι περὶ ὀρχήσεως
λέγοντος καὶ τῶν ἐν αὐτῇ καλῶν, καὶ ὡς οὐ
τερπνὴ μόνον ἀλλὰ καὶ ὠφέλιμός ἐστιν τοῖς θεωμένοις, καὶ ὅσα παιδεύει καὶ ὅσα διδάσκει, καὶ
ὡς ῥυθμίζει τῶν ὁρώντων τὰς ψυχάς, καλλίστοις
θεάμασιν ἐγγυμνάζουσα καὶ ἀρίστοις ἀκούσμασιν
ἐνδιατρίβουσα καὶ κοινόν τι ψυχῆς καὶ σώματος
κάλλος ἐπιδεικνυμένη ; τὸ γὰρ καὶ μετὰ μουσικῆς
καὶ ῥυθμοῦ ταῦτα πάντα ποιεῖν οὐ ψόγος ἂν αὐτῆς
ἀλλ᾽ ἔπαινος μᾶλλον εἴη.

ΚΡΑΤΩΝ

Ἐμοὶ μὲν οὐ πάνυ σχολὴ μεμηνότος ἀνθρώπου
ἀκροᾶσθαι τὴν νόσον τὴν αὑτοῦ ἐπαινοῦντος·
σὺ δὲ εἰ βούλει λῆρόν τινα κατασκεδάσαι μου,
ἕτοιμος φιλικὴν ταύτην λειτουργίαν ὑποστῆναι
καὶ παρασχεῖν τὰ ὦτα, καὶ ἄνευ κηροῦ παρακούειν
τῶν φαύλων δυνάμενος. ὥστε ἤδη σιωπήσομαί
σοι, καὶ λέγε ὁπόσα ἐθέλεις ὡς μηδὲ ἀκούοντός
τινος.

ΛΥΚΙΝΟΣ

7 Εὖ γε, ὦ Κράτων, καὶ τούτου ἐδεόμην μάλιστα·
εἴσῃ γὰρ μετ᾽ ὀλίγον[1] εἰ λῆρός εἶναί σοι δόξει
τὰ λεχθησόμενα. καὶ πρῶτόν γε ἐκεῖνο πάνυ
ἠγνοηκέναι μοι δοκεῖς, ὡς οὐ νεώτερον τὸ τῆς
ὀρχήσεως ἐπιτήδευμα τοῦτό ἐστιν οὐδὲ χθὲς καὶ
πρῴην ἀρξάμενον, οἷον κατὰ τοὺς προπάτορας

---

[1] μετ᾽ ὀλίγον Fritzsche : κατ᾽ ὀλίγον MSS.

quite pity *you*; to the dismay of the rest of us, you have become absolutely infatuated!

LYCINUS

Then are you willing to leave off your abuse, my friend, and hear me say something about dancing and about its good points, showing that it brings not only pleasure but benefit to those who see it; how much culture and instruction it gives; how it imports harmony into the souls of its beholders, exercising them in what is fair to see, entertaining them with what is good to hear, and displaying to them joint beauty of soul and body? That it does all this with the aid of music and rhythm would not be reason to blame, but rather to praise it.

CRATO

I have little leisure to hear a madman praise his own ailment, but if you want to flood me with nonsense, I am ready to submit to it as a friendly service and lend you my ears, for even without wax I can avoid hearing rubbish. So now I will hold my peace for you, and you may say all that you wish as if nobody at all were listening.

LYCINUS

Good, Crato; that is what I wanted most. You will very soon find out whether what I am going to say will strike you as nonsense. First of all, you appear to me to be quite unaware that this practice of dancing is not novel, and did not begin yesterday or the day before, in the days of our grandfathers, for instance, or in those of their grandfathers. No,

ἡμῶν ἢ τοὺς ἐκείνων, ἀλλ' οἵ γε τἀληθέστατα
ὀρχήσεως πέρι γενεαλογοῦντες ἅμα τῇ πρώτῃ
γενέσει τῶν ὅλων φαῖεν ἄν σοι καὶ ὄρχησιν ἀναφῦναι,
τῷ ἀρχαίῳ ἐκείνῳ Ἔρωτι συναναφανεῖσαν. ἡ
γοῦν χορεία τῶν ἀστέρων καὶ ἡ πρὸς τοὺς ἀπλανεῖς
τῶν πλανήτων συμπλοκὴ καὶ εὔρυθμος αὐτῶν
κοινωνία καὶ εὔτακτος ἁρμονία τῆς πρωτογόνου
ὀρχήσεως δείγματά ἐστιν. κατ' ὀλίγον δὲ αὐξανο-
μένη καὶ τῆς πρὸς τὸ βέλτιον ἀεὶ προσθήκης
τυγχάνουσα, νῦν ἔοικεν ἐς τὸ ἀκρότατον ἀποτετε-
λέσθαι καὶ γεγενῆσθαι ποικίλον τι καὶ παναρ-
μόνιον καὶ πολύμουσον ἀγαθόν.

8 Πρῶτον δέ φασιν Ῥέαν ἡσθεῖσαν τῇ τέχνῃ ἐν
Φρυγίᾳ μὲν τοὺς Κορύβαντας, ἐν Κρήτῃ δὲ τοὺς
Κουρῆτας ὀρχεῖσθαι κελεῦσαι, καὶ οὐ τὰ μέτρια
ὤνατο τῆς τέχνης αὐτῶν, οἵ γε περιορχούμενοι
διεσώσαντο αὐτῇ τὸν Δία, ὥστε καὶ σῶστρα εἰκότως
ἂν ὁ Ζεὺς ὀφείλειν ὁμολογοίη αὐτοῖς, ἐκφυγὼν διὰ
τὴν ἐκείνων ὄρχησιν τοὺς πατρῴους ὀδόντας.
ἐνόπλιος δὲ αὐτῶν ἡ ὄρχησις ἦν, τὰ ξίφη μεταξὺ
κροτούντων πρὸς τὰς ἀσπίδας καὶ πηδώντων ἔνθεόν
τι καὶ πολεμικόν.

---

[1] That is to say, the Hesiodean, cosmogonic Eros, elder
brother of the Titans, not Aphrodite's puny boy.

[2] The Corybantes, mentioned frequently by Lucian, are
to him male supernatural beings (*Timon*, 41), alien denizens
of Olympus like Pan, Attis, and Sabazius (*Icarom.*, 27;
cf. *Parl. of the Gods*, 9), whom Rhea attached to herself
because they too were crazy; in her orgies, one cuts his arm
with a sword, another runs about madly, another blows the
Phrygian horn, another sounds some instrument of percussion
(*Dial. Deor.*, 12, 1; cf. *Tragodopod.*, 38). He does not ascribe
to them any regular dance, or confuse them with the Curetes,
as others often did.

THE DANCE

those historians of dancing who are the most veracious can tell you that Dance came into being contemporaneously with the primal origin of the universe, making her appearance together with Love—the love that is age-old.[1] In fact, the concord of the heavenly spheres, the interlacing of the errant planets with the fixed stars, their rhythmic agreement and timed harmony, are proofs that Dance was primordial. Little by little she has grown in stature and has obtained from time to time added embellishments, until now she would seem to have reached the very height of perfection and to have become a highly diversified, wholly harmonious, richly musical boon to mankind.

In the beginning, they say, Rhea, charmed with the art, ordered dances to be performed not only in Phrygia by the Corybantes[2] but in Crete by the Curetes, from whose skill she derived uncommon benefit, since they saved Zeus for her by dancing about him; Zeus, therefore, might well admit that he owes them a thank-offering, since it was through their dancing that he escaped his father's teeth. They danced under arms, clashing their swords upon their shields as they did so and leaping in a frantic, warlike manner.[3]

[3] This is Lucian's only mention of the Curetes. His account of their dance agrees with representations in ancient art (cf. Kekulé-von Rohden, *Archit. röm. Tonreliefs,* Pl. 25) as well as with the description of Lucretius (II, 629–639), who had seen it performed by mimic Curetes in the train of the Great Mother. Lucian's use of the past tense (ἦν) suggests not only that his knowledge of them came from books but that he thought the dance obsolete. That, however, can hardly have been the case, for we have now a cletic hymn invoking (Zeus) Kouros, discovered at Palaecastro in Crete, which probably belongs to the cult with which the Curetes

THE WORKS OF LUCIAN

Μετὰ δέ, Κρητῶν οἱ κράτιστοι ἐνεργῶς ἐπιτη-
δεύσαντες αὐτὸ ἄριστοι ὀρχησταὶ ἐγένοντο, οὐχ
οἱ ἰδιῶται μόνον, ἀλλὰ καὶ οἱ βασιλικώτεροι καὶ
πρωτεύειν ἀξιοῦντες. ὁ γοῦν Ὅμηρος τὸν
Μηριόνην, οὐκ αἰσχύναι βουλόμενος ἀλλὰ κοσμῆσαι,
ὀρχηστὴν προσεῖπεν, καὶ οὕτως ἄρα ἐπίσημος ἦν
καὶ γνώριμος ἅπασιν ἐπὶ τῇ ὀρχηστικῇ ὥστε οὐχ
οἱ Ἕλληνες μόνον ταῦτα ἠπίσταντο περὶ αὐτοῦ
ἀλλὰ καὶ οἱ Τρῶες αὐτοί, καίτοι πολέμιοι ὄντες·
ἑώρων γάρ, οἶμαι, καὶ τὴν ἐν τῷ πολεμεῖν αὐτοῦ
κουφότητα καὶ εὐρυθμίαν, ἣν ἐξ ὀρχήσεως ἐκέκτητο.
φησὶν δὲ τὰ ἔπη ὧδέ πως·

Μηριόνη, τάχα κέν σε καὶ ὀρχηστήν περ ἐόντα
ἔγχος ἐμὸν κατέπαυσε.

καὶ ὅμως οὐ κατέπαυσεν αὐτόν· ἅτε γὰρ ἠσκημένος ἐν τῇ ὀρχηστικῇ, ῥᾳδίως, οἶμαι, διεδίδρασκεν
τὰς ἐπ᾽ αὐτὸν ἀφέσεις τῶν ἀκοντίων.

9   Πολλοὺς δὲ καὶ ἄλλους τῶν ἡρώων εἰπεῖν
ἔχων τοῖς αὐτοῖς ἐγγεγυμνασμένους καὶ τέχνην
τὸ πρᾶγμα πεποιημένους, ἱκανὸν ἡγοῦμαι τὸν
Νεοπτόλεμον, Ἀχιλλέως μὲν παῖδα ὄντα, πάνυ δὲ
διαπρέψαντα ἐν τῇ ὀρχηστικῇ καὶ εἶδος τὸ κάλλιστον αὐτῇ προστεθεικότα, Πυρρίχιον ἀπ᾽ αὐτοῦ
κεκλημένον· καὶ ὁ Ἀχιλλεύς, ταῦτα ὑπὲρ τοῦ
παιδὸς πυνθανόμενος, μᾶλλον ἔχαιρεν, οἶμαι,
ἢ ἐπὶ τῷ κάλλει καὶ τῇ ἄλλῃ ἀλκῇ αὐτοῦ. τοιγαροῦν τὴν Ἴλιον, τέως ἀνάλωτον οὖσαν, ἡ

THE DANCE

Thereafter, all the doughtiest of the Cretans practised it energetically and became excellent dancers, not only the common sort but the men of princely blood who claimed leadership. For example, Homer calls Meriones a dancer, not desiring to discredit but to distinguish him; and he was so conspicuous and universally known for his dancing that not only the Greeks but the very Trojans, though enemies, were aware of this about him. They saw, I suppose, his lightness and grace in battle, which he got from the dance. The verses go something like this:

" Meriones, in a trice that spear of mine would
     have stopped you,
   Good as you are at the dance." [1]

Nevertheless, it did not stop him, for as he was well versed in dancing, it was easy for him, I suppose, to avoid the javelins they launched at him.

Although I could mention many others among the heroes who were similarly trained and made an art of the thing, I consider Neoptolemus sufficient. Though the son of Achilles, he made a great name for himself in dancing and contributed to it the variety which is most beautiful, called Pyrrhic after him; and upon hearing this about his son, Achilles was more pleased, I am sure, than over his beauty and all his prowess. So, though till then Troy had been

---

were connected, and is a late Imperial copy of an early Hellenistic text (Diehl, *Anth. Lyr. Graeca*, II, p. 279). Their dancing saved Zeus from being discovered and swallowed by his father Cronus because the clashing of their weapons drowned his infantine wailing.

[1] *Iliad*, XVI, 617–618.

THE WORKS OF LUCIAN

ἐκείνου ὀρχηστικὴ καθεῖλεν καὶ εἰς ἔδαφος
κατέρριψεν.

10   Λακεδαιμόνιοι μέν, ἄριστοι Ἑλλήνων εἶναι δο-
κοῦντες, παρὰ Πολυδεύκους καὶ Κάστορος καρυατί-
ζειν μαθόντες (ὀρχήσεως δὲ καὶ τοῦτο εἶδος,
ἐν Καρύαις τῆς Λακωνικῆς διδασκόμενον) ἅπαντα
μετὰ Μουσῶν ποιοῦσιν, ἄχρι τοῦ πολεμεῖν πρὸς
αὐλὸν καὶ ῥυθμὸν καὶ εὔτακτον ἔμβασιν τοῦ ποδός·
καὶ τὸ πρῶτον σύνθημα Λακεδαιμονίοις πρὸς τὴν
μάχην ὁ αὐλὸς ἐνδίδωσιν. τοιγαροῦν καὶ ἐκράτουν
ἁπάντων, μουσικῆς αὐτοῖς καὶ εὐρυθμίας ἡγου-
μένης.

Ἴδοις δ' ἂν νῦν ἔτι καὶ τοὺς ἐφήβους αὐτῶν οὐ
μεῖον ὀρχεῖσθαι ἢ ὁπλομαχεῖν μανθάνοντας· ὅταν
γὰρ ἀκροχειρισάμενοι καὶ παίσαντες καὶ παι-
σθέντες ἐν τῷ μέρει παύσωνται, εἰς ὄρχησιν αὐτοῖς
ἡ ἀγωνία τελευτᾷ, καὶ αὐλητὴς μὲν ἐν τῷ μέσῳ
κάθηται ἐπαυλῶν καὶ κτυπῶν τῷ ποδί, οἱ δὲ κατὰ
στοῖχον ἀλλήλοις ἑπόμενοι σχήματα παντοῖα ἐπιδείκνυνται πρὸς ῥυθμὸν ἐμβαίνοντες, ἄρτι μὲν

---

[1] Since Neoptolemus was also called Pyrrhus, it was
inevitable that the invention of the Pyrrhic dance should be
ascribed to him. According to Archilochus (Fr. 190 Bergk),
he originated it when he danced for joy over killing Eurypylus.
That Achilles was more pleased to hear of this than when
Odysseus told him of his son's beauty and bravery (*Odyssey*,
XI, 505–540) is known to us only from Lucian, as also the real
reason for the fall of Troy. Lucian's persiflage derives especial
point from the fact that by this time the Pyrrhic had become
anything but a war-dance. Athenaeus does not hesitate
to call it Dionysiac (XIV, 631A) and compare it with the
cordax.

[2] This statement is decidedly unorthodox. Others say
that the Spartans derived their war-dances from Castor and

impregnable, his skill in dancing took it and tumbled it to the ground.[1]

The Spartans, who are considered the bravest of the Greeks, learned from Pollux and Castor to do the Caryatic, which is another variety of dance exhibited at Caryae in Lacedaemon,[2] and they do everything with the aid of the Muses, to the extent of going into battle to the accompaniment of flute and rhythm and well-timed step in marching; indeed, the first signal for battle is given to the Spartans by the flute. That is how they managed to conquer everybody, with music and rhythm to lead them.

Even now you may see their young men studying dancing quite as much as fighting under arms. When they have stopped sparring and exchanging blow for blow with each other, their contest ends in dancing, and a flute-player sits in the middle, playing them a tune and marking time with his foot, while they, following one another in line, perform figures of all sorts in rhythmic step, now those of

Pollux, and that Castor gave them a fine martial tune, the *Kastoreion*. It remained for Lucian to ask us to imagine the horse-tamer and his pugilistic twin, with basket-like contrivances on their heads, facing each other demurely and executing on tip-toe the graceful figures of the dance performed in honour of Artemis by the maidens of Caryae—the famous Caryatides! What these figures looked like is well known to us from ancient reliefs (cf. G. H. Chase, *Loeb Collection of Arretine Pottery*, Pl. III, No. 53, and the Albani relief in F. Weege, *Der Tanz in der Antike*, Fig. 52). Sculptural representations of the Caryatides in their statuesque poses, functioning as architectural supports, were so frequent that the name was extended to other similar figures just as it is now when it is applied to the Attic "Maidens" of the Erechtheum porch.

πολεμικά, μετ᾽ ὀλίγον δὲ χορευτικά, ἃ Διονύσῳ
11 καὶ ᾽Αφροδίτῃ φίλα. τοιγαροῦν καὶ τὸ ᾆσμα
ὃ μεταξὺ ὀρχούμενοι ᾄδουσιν ᾽Αφροδίτης ἐπί-
κλησίς ἐστιν καὶ ᾽Ερώτων, ὡς συγκωμάζοιεν
αὐτοῖς καὶ συνορχοῖντο. καὶ θάτερον δὲ τῶν
ᾀσμάτων—δύο γὰρ ᾄδεται—διδασκαλίαν ἔχει ὡς
χρὴ ὀρχεῖσθαι. "Πόρρω" γάρ, φασίν, "ὦ
παῖδες, πόδα μετάβατε καὶ κωμάξατε¹ βέλτιον,"
τουτέστιν ἄμεινον ὀρχήσασθε.

῞Ομοια δὲ καὶ οἱ τὸν ὅρμον καλούμενον ὀρχού-
12 μενοι ποιοῦσιν. ὁ δὲ ὅρμος ὄρχησίς ἐστιν κοινὴ
ἐφήβων τε καὶ παρθένων, παρ᾽ ἕνα χορευόντων
καὶ ὡς ἀληθῶς ὅρμῳ ἐοικότων· καὶ ἡγεῖται μὲν
ὁ ἔφηβος τὰ νεανικὰ ὀρχούμενος καὶ ὅσοις ὕστερον
ἐν πολέμῳ χρήσεται, ἡ παρθένος δὲ ἕπεται κοσμίως
τὸ θῆλυ χορεύειν διδάσκουσα, ὡς εἶναι τὸν ὅρμον
ἐκ σωφροσύνης καὶ ἀνδρείας πλεκόμενον. καὶ αἱ
γυμνοπαιδίαι² δὲ αὐτοῖς ὁμοίως ὄρχησίς ἐστιν.

13 ῝Α δὲ ῞Ομηρος ὑπὲρ ᾽Αριάδνης ἐν τῇ ἀσπίδι
πεποίηκεν καὶ τοῦ χοροῦ ὃν αὐτῇ Δαίδαλος
ἤσκησεν ὡς ἀνεγνωκότι σοι παρίημι, καὶ τοὺς
ὀρχηστὰς δὲ τοὺς δύο οὓς ἐκεῖ ὁ ποιητὴς κυβιστη-
τῆρας καλεῖ, ἡγουμένους τοῦ χοροῦ, καὶ πάλιν ἃ ἐν
τῇ αὐτῇ ἀσπίδι λέγει· "Κοῦροι δ᾽ ὀρχηστῆρες
ἐδίνεον,"³ ὥς τι κάλλιστον τοῦτο τοῦ ῾Ηφαίστου
ἐμποιήσαντος τῇ ἀσπίδι. τοὺς μὲν γὰρ Φαίακας

¹ κωμάξατε Γ² : κωμάσατε Γ¹ vulg.
² γυμνοπαιδίαι Meursius : γυμνοποδίαι MSS.
³ ἐδίνεον N (du Soul) : ἐδίνευον cett.

---

¹ We have no knowledge of these two songs from any other
sources. Lucian's quotation from the second is given among
the Carmina Popularia by Bergk (17) and Diehl (22).

war and presently those of the choral dance, that
are dear to Dionysus and Aphrodite. That is why
the song which they sing while dancing is an invo-
cation of Aphrodite and of the Loves, that they may
join their revel and their dances. The second of the
songs, moreover—for two are sung—even contains
instruction how to dance : " Set your foot before you,
lads," it says, " and frolic yet more featly," [1] that is,
dance better.

The same sort of thing is done by those who dance
what is called the String of Beads. That is a dance
of boys and girls together who move in a row and
truly resemble a string of beads. The boy precedes,
doing the steps and postures of young manhood,
and those which later he will use in war, while the
maiden follows, showing how to do the women's
dance with propriety ; hence the string is beaded
with modesty and with manliness. In like manner
their Bareskin Plays are dancing.[2]

Taking it that you have read what Homer has to
say about Ariadne in " The Shield," and about the
chorus that Daedalus fashioned for her,[3] I pass it
by ; as also the two dancers whom the poet there
calls tumblers, who lead the chorus, and again what
he says in that same " Shield " : " Youthful dancers
were circling "; which was worked into the shield
by Hephaestus as something especially beautiful.[4]
And that the Phaeacians should delight in dancing

[2] Very little is known about the Spartan " Bareskin Plays "
except that they included processional choruses of naked youths
which competed with each other in dancing and singing,
in a place called the Chorus, near the agora.
[3] *Iliad*, XVIII, 593.
[4] *Iliad*, XVIII, 605–606.

καὶ πάνυ εἰκὸς ἦν ὀρχήσει χαίρειν, ἁβρούς τε
ὄντας καὶ ἐν πάσῃ εὐδαιμονίᾳ διατρίβοντας. ὁ
γοῦν Ὅμηρος τοῦτο αὐτῶν μάλιστα θαυμάζοντα
πεποίηκε τὸν Ὀδυσσέα καὶ τὰς μαρμαρυγὰς τῶν
ποδῶν θεώμενον.

14 Ἐν μέν γε Θεσσαλίᾳ τοσοῦτον ἐπέδωκεν τῆς
ὀρχηστικῆς ἡ ἄσκησις, ὥστε τοὺς προστάτας καὶ
προαγωνιστὰς αὐτῶν προορχηστῆρας ἐκάλουν·
καὶ δηλοῦσι τοῦτο αἱ τῶν ἀνδριάντων ἐπιγραφαὶ
οὓς τοῖς ἀριστεύουσιν ἀνίστασαν· " Προὔκρινεν "
γάρ, φασίν,[1] " προορχηστῆρα ἁ πόλις." καὶ αὖθις,
" Εἰλατίωνι τὰν εἰκόνα ὁ δᾶμος εὖ ὀρχησαμένῳ
τὰν μάχαν."

15 Ἐῶ λέγειν, ὅτι τελετὴν οὐδεμίαν ἀρχαίαν
ἔστιν εὑρεῖν ἄνευ ὀρχήσεως, Ὀρφέως δηλαδὴ καὶ
Μουσαίου καὶ τῶν τότε ἀρίστων ὀρχηστῶν κατα-
στησαμένων αὐτάς, ὥς τι κάλλιστον καὶ τοῦτο
νομοθετησάντων, σὺν ῥυθμῷ καὶ ὀρχήσει μυεῖσθαι.
ὅτι δ' οὕτως ἔχει, τὰ μὲν ὄργια σιωπᾶν ἄξιον τῶν
ἀμυήτων ἔνεκα, ἐκεῖνο δὲ πάντες ἀκούουσιν,
ὅτι τοὺς ἐξαγορεύοντας τὰ μυστήρια ἐξορχεῖσθαι
λέγουσιν οἱ πολλοί.

16 Ἐν Δήλῳ δέ γε οὐδὲ αἱ θυσίαι ἄνευ ὀρχήσεως
ἀλλὰ σὺν ταύτῃ καὶ μετὰ μουσικῆς ἐγίγνοντο.
παίδων χοροὶ συνελθόντες ὑπ' αὐλῷ καὶ κιθάρᾳ οἱ
μὲν ἐχόρευον, ὑπωρχοῦντο δὲ οἱ ἄριστοι προκρι-

---

[1] φησί C, edd.

---

[1] *Odyssey*, VIII, 256–258.
[2] No such inscriptions are known to us, and I fear there is

was very natural, since they were people of refinement and they lived in utter bliss. In fact, Homer has represented Odysseus as admiring this in them above all else and watching " the twinkling of their feet." [1]

In Thessaly the cultivation of dancing made such progress that they used to call their front-rank men and champions " fore-dancers." This is demonstrated by the inscriptions upon the statues which they dedicated in honour of those who showed prowess in battle. " The citie," they say, " hath esteemed him fore-dancer; " and again, " To Eilation the folk hath sett up thys ymage for that he danced the bataille well." [2]

I forbear to say that not a single ancient mystery-cult can be found that is without dancing, since they were established, of course, by Orpheus and Musaeus, the best dancers of that time, who included it in their prescriptions as something exceptionally beautiful to be initiated with rhythm and dancing. To prove that this is so, although it behoves me to observe silence about the rites on account of the uninitiate, nevertheless there is one thing that everybody has heard; namely, that those who let out the mysteries in conversation are commonly said to " dance them out."

At Delos, indeed, even the sacrifices were not without dancing, but were performed with that and with music. Choirs of boys came together, and while they moved and sang to the accompaniment of flute and lyre, those who had been selected from among them as the best performed an interpre-

little likelihood that the soil of Thessaly will ever confirm the testimony of Lycinus.

θέντες ἐξ αὐτῶν. τὰ γοῦν τοῖς χοροῖς γραφόμενα
τούτοις ᾄσματα ὑπορχήματα ἐκαλεῖτο καὶ ἐμπέ-
πλησto τῶν τοιούτων ἡ λύρα.

17 Καὶ τί σοι τοὺς Ἕλληνας λέγω, ὅπου καὶ
Ἰνδοὶ ἐπειδὰν ἕωθεν ἀναστάντες προσεύχωνται
τὸν Ἥλιον, οὐχ ὥσπερ ἡμεῖς τὴν χεῖρα κύσαντες
ἡγούμεθα ἐντελῆ ἡμῶν εἶναι τὴν εὐχήν, ἀλλ᾽
ἐκεῖνοι πρὸς τὴν ἀνατολὴν στάντες ὀρχήσει τὸν
Ἥλιον ἀσπάζονται, σχηματίζοντες ἑαυτοὺς σιωπῇ
καὶ μιμούμενοι τὴν χορείαν τοῦ θεοῦ· καὶ τοῦτ᾽
ἐστιν Ἰνδῶν καὶ εὐχὴ καὶ χοροὶ καὶ θυσία. διὸ καὶ
τούτοις ἱλεοῦνται τὸν θεὸν δίς, καὶ ἀρχομένης καὶ
δυομένης τῆς ἡμέρας.

18 Αἰθίοπες δέ γε καὶ πολεμοῦντες σὺν ὀρχήσει
αὐτὸ δρῶσιν, καὶ οὐκ ἂν ἀφείη τὸ βέλος Αἰθίοψ
ἀνὴρ ἀφελὼν τῆς κεφαλῆς—ταύτῃ γὰρ ἀντὶ φαρέτρας
χρῶνται περιδέοντες αὐτῇ ἀκτινηδὸν τὰ βέλη—εἰ
μὴ πρότερον ὀρχήσαιτο καὶ τῷ σχήματι ἀπειλήσειε
καὶ προεκφοβήσειε τῇ ὀρχήσει τὸν πολέμιον.

19 Ἄξιον δέ, ἐπεὶ τὴν Ἰνδικὴν καὶ τὴν Αἰθιοπίαν
διεξεληλύθαμεν, καὶ ἐς τὴν γείτονα αὐτῶν Αἴγυπτον
καταβῆναι τῷ λόγῳ. δοκεῖ γάρ μοι ὁ παλαιὸς
μῦθος καὶ Πρωτέα τὸν Αἰγύπτιον οὐκ ἄλλο τι
ἢ ὀρχηστήν τινα γενέσθαι λέγειν, μιμητικὸν

---

[1] That the " hyporchematic " style of dancing was inter-
pretative, which in Lucian's description of it is only implicit,
is expressly stated by Athenaeus (I, 15 D). In previously
referring to it as " dance accompanying song " (τὴν πρὸς ᾠδὴν
ὄρχησις), he seems to agree with Lucian in the point that its
performers do not themselves sing. Elsewhere in his work
(XIV, 631 C) he gives a definition (from Aristocles) that is
diametrically opposed : " when the chorus dances singing."
But this is connected with a highly theoretical classification

tative dance. Indeed, the songs that were written
for these choirs were called Hyporchemes (interpre-
tative dances), and lyric poetry is full of them.[1]

Yet why do I talk to you of the Greeks? Even
the Indians, when they get up in the morning and
pray to the sun, instead of doing as we do, who think
that when we have kissed our hand the prayer is
complete, face the sunrise and welcome the God
of Day with dancing, posturing in silence and imitating the dance of the god; and that, to the Indians,
is prayer and dance and sacrifice all in one. So
they propitiate their god with those rites twice each
day, when it begins and when it declines.

The Ethiopians, moreover, even in waging war,
do it dancing, and an Ethiopian may not let fly the
shaft that he has taken from his head (for they use
the head in place of a quiver, binding the shafts
about it like rays) unless he has first danced, menacing
the enemy by his attitude and terrifying him in
advance by his prancing.[2]

Since we have spoken of India and of Ethiopia,
it will repay us to make an imaginary descent into
Egypt, their neighbour. For it seems to me that the
ancient myth about Proteus the Egyptian means
nothing else than that he was a dancer, an imitative

of dances under six heads, three of which are dramatic
(tragic, comic, satyric) and three lyric (pyrrhic, gymnopaedic,
hyporchematic). As we know that gymnopaedic choruses
"danced singing," it seems pretty clear that the definition of
"hyporchematic" has been incorrectly transmitted in the
text.

[2] Heliodorus in the *Aethiopica* (IX, 19) goes into greater
detail. Cf. also H. P. L'Orange, *Symbolae Osloenses* XII
(1934), 105–113, who calls attention to representations
of Roman auxiliaries with arrows bound to their heads in
the frieze of the Arch of Constantine.

ἄνθρωπον καὶ πρὸς πάντα σχηματίζεσθαι καὶ
μεταβάλλεσθαι δυνάμενον, ὡς καὶ ὕδατος ὑγρότητα
μιμεῖσθαι καὶ πυρὸς ὀξύτητα ἐν τῇ τῆς κινήσεως
σφοδρότητι καὶ λέοντος ἀγριότητα καὶ παρδάλεως
θυμὸν καὶ δένδρου δόνημα, καὶ ὅλως ὅ τι καὶ
θελήσειεν. ὁ δὲ μῦθος παραλαβὼν πρὸς τὸ
παραδοξότερον τὴν φύσιν αὐτοῦ διηγήσατο, ὡς
γιγνομένου ταῦτα ἅπερ ἐμιμεῖτο. ὅπερ δὴ καὶ
τοῖς νῦν ὀρχουμένοις πρόσεστιν, ἴδοις τ᾽ ἂν
οὖν αὐτοὺς πρὸς τὸν καιρὸν¹ ὠκέως διαλλατ-
τομένους καὶ αὐτὸν μιμουμένους τὸν Πρωτέα.
εἰκάζειν δὲ χρὴ καὶ τὴν Ἔμπουσαν τὴν ἐς μυρίας
μορφὰς μεταβαλλομένην τοιαύτην τινὰ ἄνθρωπον
ὑπὸ τοῦ μύθου παραδεδόσθαι.

20 Ἐπὶ τούτοις δίκαιον μηδὲ τῆς Ῥωμαίων
ὀρχήσεως ἀμνημονεῖν, ἣν οἱ εὐγενέστατοι αὐτῶν
τῷ πολεμικωτάτῳ τῶν θεῶν Ἄρει, οἱ Σάλιοι
καλούμενοι (ἱερωσύνης δὲ τοῦτο ὄνομα), ὀρχοῦνται,
21 σεμνοτάτην τε ἅμα καὶ ἱερωτάτην. Βιθυνὸς δὲ
μῦθος, καὶ οὗτος οὐ πάνυ τῶν Ἰταλιωτικῶν ἀλλότριος, φησὶν² τὸν Πρίαπον δαίμονα πολεμιστήν,
τῶν Τιτάνων οἶμαι ἕνα ἢ τῶν Ἰδαίων Δακτύλων
τοῦτο ἔργον πεποιημένον, τὰ ἐνόπλια παιδεύειν,
παραλαβόντα παρὰ τῆς Ἥρας τὸν Ἄρη, παῖδα
μὲν ἔτι, σκληρὸν δὲ καὶ πέρα τοῦ μετρίου ἀνδρικόν,
μὴ πρότερον ὁπλομαχεῖν διδάξαι πρὶν τέλειον
ὀρχηστὴν ἀπειργάσατο. καὶ ἐπὶ τούτῳ καὶ
μισθὸς αὐτῷ παρὰ τῆς Ἥρας ἐγένετο, δεκάτην

---

¹ τὸν καιρὸν Urban: τὸν αὐτὸν καιρὸν MSS.
² φησὶν Harmon: οἱ (ὃς) MSS. The relative, a gloss, has
displaced the verb, which itself, when abbreviated, often
makes trouble; cf. p. 238, n. 1, below.

fellow, able to shape himself and change himself into anything, so that he could imitate even the liquidity of water and the sharpness of fire in the liveliness of his movement; yes, the fierceness of a lion, the rage of a leopard, the quivering of a tree, and in a word whatever he wished. Mythology, however, on taking it over, described his nature in terms more paradoxical, as if he became what he imitated. Now just that thing is characteristic of the dancers to-day, who certainly may be seen changing swiftly at the cue and imitating Proteus himself. And we must suppose that in Empusa, who changes into countless forms, some such person has been handed down by mythology.[1]

Next in order, it is proper that we should not forget that Roman dance which the best-born among them, called Salii (which is the name of a priesthood), perform in honour of Ares, the most bellicose of the gods—a dance which is at once very majestic and very sacred. And a Bithynian story, not very divergent, moreover, from those current in Italy, says that Priapus, a warlike deity, one of the Titans, I suppose, or one of the Idaean Dactyls who made a business of giving lessons in fencing, had Ares put into his charge by Hera while Ares was still a boy, though hard-muscled and immoderately virile; and that he did not teach him to handle weapons until he had made him a perfect dancer. Indeed, for this he even got a pension from Hera, to receive

[1] Empusa, one of Hecate's associates, used to frighten people by appearing suddenly out of dark places in one horrid form or another; she seems to have been particularly given to manifesting herself with legs like those of an ass.

ἀεὶ τῶν ἐκ πολέμου περιγιγνομένων τῷ Ἄρει
παρ' αὐτοῦ λαμβάνειν.

22 Τὰ μὲν γὰρ Διονυσιακὰ καὶ Βακχικὰ οἶμαί σε
μὴ περιμένειν ἐμοῦ ἀκοῦσαι, ὅτι ὄρχησις ἐκεῖνα
πάντα ἦν. τριῶν γοῦν οὐσῶν τῶν γενικωτάτων
ὀρχήσεων, κόρδακος καὶ σικιννίδος καὶ ἐμμελείας,
οἱ Διονύσου θεράποντες οἱ Σάτυροι ταύτας ἐφευ-
ρόντες ἀφ' αὐτῶν ἑκάστην ὠνόμασαν, καὶ ταύτῃ τῇ
τέχνῃ χρώμενος ὁ Διόνυσος, φασίν,[1] Τυρρηνοὺς καὶ
Ἰνδοὺς καὶ Λυδοὺς ἐχειρώσατο καὶ φῦλον οὕτω
μάχιμον τοῖς αὐτοῦ[2] θιάσοις κατωρχήσατο.

23 Ὥστε, ὦ θαυμάσιε, ὅρα μὴ ἀνόσιον ᾖ κατηγορεῖν ἐπιτηδεύματος θείου τε ἅμα καὶ μυστικοῦ
καὶ τοσούτοις θεοῖς ἐσπουδασμένου καὶ ἐπὶ
τιμῇ αὐτῶν δρωμένου καὶ τοσαύτην τέρψιν ἅμα
καὶ παιδείαν[3] ὠφέλιμον παρεχομένου.

Θαυμάζω δέ σου κἀκεῖνο, εἰδὼς Ὁμήρου
καὶ Ἡσιόδου μάλιστα ἐραστὴν ὄντα σε (αὖθις
γὰρ ἐπὶ τοὺς ποιητὰς ἐπάνειμι), πῶς ἀντιφθέγ-
γεσθαι ἐκείνοις τολμᾷς πρὸ τῶν πάντων ὄρχησιν
ἐπαινοῦσιν. ὁ μὲν γὰρ Ὅμηρος τὰ ἥδιστα καὶ
κάλλιστα καταλέγων, ὕπνον καὶ φιλότητα καὶ
μολπὴν καὶ ὄρχησιν, μόνην ταύτην ἀμύμονα
ὠνόμασεν, προσμαρτυρήσας νὴ Δία καὶ τὸ ἡδὺ
τῇ μολπῇ, ἅπερ ἀμφότερα τῇ ὀρχηστικῇ πρόσεστιν,
καὶ ᾠδὴ γλυκερὰ καὶ ὀρχησμὸς[4] ἀμύμων, ὃν

---

[1] φασίν Harmon: ὃς ΓΩΦϹ: not in EN.
[2] αὐτοῦ Madvig: αὐτοῦ Φ Vat. 87: αὐτοῖς ΓΝ (ΕΩϹ).
[3] παιδιὰν ΝΕ².   [4] ὀρχηθμὸς A.

---

[1] This Bithynian myth of Priapus is not recorded elsewhere,
but as it is known that Priapus was held in high honour there,
it may well be that he was associated with Ares and that
armed dances played a part in the cult.

THE DANCE

from Ares in perpetuity a tenth of all that accrued to him in war.[1]

As to the Dionysiac and Bacchic rites, I expect you are not waiting for me to tell you that every bit of them was dancing. In fact, their most typical dances, which are three in number, the Cordax, the Sicinnis, and the Emmeleia, were invented by the attendants of Dionysus, the Satyrs, who named them all after themselves,[2] and it was by the exercise of this art, they say, that Dionysus subdued the Tyrrhenians, the Indians, and the Lydians, dancing into subjection with his bands of revellers a multitude so warlike.

Therefore, you amazing fellow, take care that it isn't impious to denounce a practice at once divine and mystic, cultivated by so many gods, performed in their honour, and affording at once amusement and profitable instruction in such degree!

Another thing surprises me in you, since I know that you are a great lover of Homer and Hesiod—I am going back, you see, to the poets once more—how you dare contradict them when they praise dancing above all things else. When Homer enumerated all that is sweetest and best—sleep, love, song, and dance [3]—it was this alone that he called "blameless," and what is more, he ascribes sweetness to song; but both these things pertain to the dancer's art, both dulcet song and blameless

---

[2] The drama belonged to Dionysus, and each form of it had its typical dance, that of tragedy being the Emmeleia, that of comedy the Cordax, and that of the satyr-play the Sicinnis (Ath., I, 20 E; cf. below, § 26). That they were named from satyrs seems to be Lucian's own idea, though the Sicinnis was sometimes said to owe its name to its Cretan or barbarian inventor.

[3] *Iliad*, XIII, 636 ff.

235

σὺ νῦν μωμᾶσθαι ἐπινοεῖς. καὶ πάλιν ἐν ἑτέρῳ
μέρει τῆς ποιήσεως·

    "Αλλῳ μὲν γὰρ ἔδωκε θεὸς πολεμήϊα ἔργα,
    ἄλλῳ δ' ὀρχηστύν τε καὶ ἱμερόεσσαν ἀοιδήν.

ἱμερόεσσα γὰρ ὡς ἀληθῶς ἡ μετ' ὀρχήσεως ᾠδὴ
καὶ δῶρον θεῶν τοῦτο κάλλιστον. καὶ ἔοικεν εἰς
δύο διῃρηκὼς ὁ "Ομηρος τὰ πάντα πράγματα,
πόλεμον καὶ εἰρήνην, τοῖς τοῦ πολέμου μόνα ταῦτα
24 ὡς κάλλιστα ἀντιτεθεικέναι. ὁ δὲ Ἡσίοδος, οὐ
παρ' ἄλλου ἀκούσας ἀλλ' ἰδὼν αὐτὸς ἔωθεν εὐθὺς
ὀρχουμένας τὰς Μούσας, ἐν ἀρχῇ τῶν ἐπῶν τοῦτο
περὶ αὐτῶν τὸ μέγιστον ἐγκώμιον διηγεῖται,
ὅτι " περὶ κρήνην ἰοειδέα πόσσ' ἁπαλοῖσιν ὀρχεῦν-
ται," τοῦ πατρὸς τὸν βωμὸν περιχορεύουσαι.

    Ἀλλὰ σὺ μέν, ὦ γενναῖε, μονονουχὶ θεομαχῶν
25 ὑβρίζεις εἰς τὴν ὀρχηστικήν· ὁ Σωκράτης δέ,
σοφώτατος ἀνήρ, εἴ γε πιστευτέον τοῦτο περὶ
αὐτοῦ λέγοντι τῷ Πυθίῳ, οὐ μόνον ἐπήνει τὴν
ὀρχηστικὴν ἀλλὰ καὶ ἐκμαθεῖν αὐτὴν ἠξίου,
μέγιστον νέμων[1] εὐρυθμίᾳ καὶ εὐμουσίᾳ καὶ κινή-
σει ἐμμελεῖ καὶ εὐσχημοσύνῃ τοῦ κινουμένου·
καὶ οὐκ ᾐδεῖτο γέρων ἀνὴρ ἕν τῶν σπουδαιοτάτων
μαθημάτων καὶ τοῦτο ἡγούμενος εἶναι. καὶ ἔμελ-
λέν γε ἐκεῖνος περὶ ὀρχηστικὴν οὐ μετρίως σπουδά-
σεσθαι, ὅς γε καὶ τὰ μικρὰ οὐκ ὤκνει μανθάνειν,
ἀλλὰ καὶ εἰς τὰ διδασκαλεῖα τῶν αὐλητρίδων
ἐφοίτα καὶ παρ' ἑταίρας γυναικὸς οὐκ ἀπηξίου

          [1] ἀπονέμων C.

---

    [1] *Iliad*, XIII, 730, 731. But after ὀρχηστύν Lucian sub-
stitutes for ἑτέρῳ κίθαριν καὶ ἀοιδήν the close of *Odyssey*,
I, 421.

dancing—which you now take it into your head to
blame! And again, in another part of his poetry: [1]

> One man getteth from God the gift of achievement
>   in warfare,
> One, the art of the dance, and song that stirreth
>   the heart-strings.

Singing combined with dancing does in truth stir the
heart-strings, and it is the choicest gift of the gods.
Also, it appears that in classifying all activities
under two heads, war and peace, Homer has set
off against those of war these, and these only, as
peerless. As for Hesiod, who was not told by
someone else about the dancing of the Muses but
saw it himself at break of day, he begins his poem [2]
by saying about them as the highest possible praise
that they " dance with delicate footfall about the
violet waters," circling round the altar of their sire.

In spite of this, my high-spirited friend, you
insult dancing almost to the point of quarrelling
with the gods; and yet Socrates (the wisest of
men, if we may believe Apollo, who said so) not
only commended it but wanted to learn it, attributing
the greatest value to observance of rhythm and
music, to harmonious movement and to gracefulness
of limb; and he was not ashamed, aged as he was,
to consider it one of the most important subjects
of study. [3] He would, of course, be uncommonly
enthusiastic over dancing, since he did not hesitate
to study even what was trivial, and not only used to
attend the schools of the flute-girls, but did not

[2] The *Theogony*.
[3] In the *Symposium* of Xenophon (II, 15–16) Socrates
commends dancing as an exercise, and expresses a desire to
learn figures that he has just seen. Cf. Diog. Laert., II, 5, 15.

σπουδαῖόν τι ἀκούειν, τῆς Ἀσπασίας. καίτοι
ἐκεῖνος ἄρτι ἀρχομένην ἑώρα τότε τὴν τέχνην καὶ
οὐδέπω εἰς τοσοῦτον κάλλος διηρθρωμένην. εἰ
δὲ τοὺς νῦν ἐπὶ μέγιστον αὐτὴν προαγαγόντας
ἐθεᾶτο, εὖ οἶδα, πάντων ἂν ἐκεῖνός γε ἀφέμενος
μόνῳ τῷ θεάματι τούτῳ τὸν νοῦν ἂν προσεῖχεν καὶ
τοὺς παῖδας οὐκ ἂν ἄλλο τι πρὸ αὐτοῦ ἐδιδάξατο.

26   Δοκεῖς δέ μοι, ὅταν κωμῳδίαν καὶ τραγῳδίαν
ἐπαινῇς, ἐπιλελῆσθαι ὅτι καὶ ἐν ἑκατέρᾳ ἐκείνων
ὀρχήσεως ἴδιόν τι εἶδός ἐστιν, οἷον τραγικὴ [1]
μὲν ἡ ἐμμέλεια, κωμῳδικὴ δὲ ὁ κόρδαξ, ἐνίοτε δὲ
καὶ τρίτης, [2] σικιννίδος, προσλαμβανομένης. ἐπεὶ
δὲ ἐν ἀρχῇ καὶ προετίμησας τῆς ὀρχήσεως τὴν
τραγῳδίαν καὶ κωμῳδίαν καὶ αὐλητὰς κυκλίους
καὶ κιθαρῳδίαν, ἐναγώνια ταῦτα καὶ διὰ τοῦτο
σεμνὰ προσειπών, φέρε νῦν ἀντεξετάσωμεν τῇ
ὀρχήσει ἕκαστον αὐτῶν. καίτοι τὸν μὲν αὐλόν,
εἰ δοκεῖ, καὶ τὴν κιθάραν παρῶμεν· μέρη γὰρ τῆς
τοῦ ὀρχηστοῦ ὑπηρεσίας καὶ ταῦτα.

27   Τὴν τραγῳδίαν δέ γε ἀπὸ τοῦ σχήματος πρώτου
καταμάθωμεν οἷα ἐστίν, ὡς εἰδεχθὲς ἅμα καὶ
φοβερὸν θέαμα εἰς μῆκος ἄρρυθμον ἠσκημένος
ἄνθρωπος, ἐμβάταις ὑψηλοῖς ἐποχούμενος, πρόσωπον ὑπὲρ κεφαλῆς ἀνατεινόμενον ἐπικείμενος
καὶ στόμα κεχηνὸς πάμμεγα ὡς καταπιόμενος
τοὺς θεατάς. ἐῶ λέγειν προστερνίδια καὶ προ-

---

[1] τραγικὴ, and κωμῳδικὴ ΦC: τραγικῇ, and κωμῳδικῇ ΓΕΝ.
[2] τρίτης C: τρίτη ΓΕΦΝ.

disdain to listen to serious discourse from Aspasia, a courtesan.[1] Yet the art was just beginning when he saw it then, and had not yet been elaborated to such a high degree of beauty. If he could see those who now have advanced it to the utmost, that man, I am sure, dropping everything else, would have given his attention to this spectacle alone; and he would not have had his young friends learn anything else in preference to it.

Again, it seems to me that when you praise comedy and tragedy, you have forgotten that in each of them there is a special form of dance; that is to say, the tragic is the Emmeleia and the comic the Cordax, though sometimes a third form, the Sicinnis, is included also.[2] But since at the outset you gave greater honour to tragedy and comedy and cyclic flute-players and singing with the lyre than to the dance, calling these competitive and therefore grand—come, let us now compare each one of them with the dance. And yet, suppose we omit the flute, if you do not mind, and the lyre, since they are parts of the dancer's paraphernalia.

As far as tragedy is concerned, let us form our first opinion of its character from its outward semblance. What a repulsive and at the same time frightful spectacle is a man tricked out to disproportionate stature, mounted upon high clogs, wearing a mask that reaches up above his head, with a mouth that is set in a vast yawn as if he meant to swallow up the spectators! I forbear to speak of pads for

[1] See Plato, *Menexenus*, 235 E and 249 C; Xen., *Oecon.*, III, 14.
[2] The Sicinnis, though regarded as the characteristic dance of the satyr-play, was sometimes presented in comedy.

γαστρίδια, προσθετὴν καὶ ἐπιτεχνητὴν παχύτητα
προσποιούμενος, ὡς μὴ τοῦ μήκους ἡ ἀρρυθμία
ἐν λεπτῷ μᾶλλον ἐλέγχοιτο· εἶτ᾽ ἔνδοθεν αὐτὸς
κεκραγώς, ἑαυτὸν ἀνακλῶν καὶ κατακλῶν, ἐνίοτε
καὶ περιᾴδων τὰ ἰαμβεῖα καί, τὸ δὴ αἴσχιστον,
μελῳδῶν τὰς συμφοράς, καὶ μόνης τῆς φωνῆς
ὑπεύθυνον παρέχων ἑαυτόν· τὰ γὰρ ἄλλα τοῖς
ποιηταῖς ἐμέλησεν πρὸ πολλοῦ ποτε γενομένοις.
καὶ μέχρι μὲν Ἀνδρομάχη τις ἢ Ἑκάβη ἐστίν,
φορητὸς ἡ ᾠδή· ὅταν δὲ Ἡρακλῆς αὐτὸς εἰσελθὼν
μονῳδῇ, ἐπιλαθόμενος αὐτοῦ καὶ μήτε τὴν λεοντῆν
αἰδεσθεὶς μήτε τὸ ῥόπαλον ὃ περίκειται, σολοικίαν
εὖ φρονῶν εἰκότως φαίη ἄν τις τὸ πρᾶγμα.
28 καὶ γὰρ αὖ ὅπερ ἐνεκάλεις τῇ ὀρχηστικῇ, τὸ
ἄνδρας ὄντας μιμεῖσθαι γυναῖκας, κοινὸν τοῦτο
καὶ τῆς τραγῳδίας καὶ τῆς κωμῳδίας ἔγκλημα
ἂν εἴη· πλείους γοῦν ἐν αὐταῖς τῶν ἀνδρῶν αἱ
29 γυναῖκες. ἡ κωμῳδία δὲ καὶ τῶν προσώπων αὐτῶν
τὸ καταγέλαστον μέρος τοῦ τερπνοῦ αὐτῇ νενόμικεν,
οἷα Δάων καὶ Τιβείων καὶ μαγείρων πρόσωπα.

Τὸ δὲ τοῦ ὀρχηστοῦ σχῆμα ὡς μὲν κόσμιον καὶ
εὐπρεπὲς οὐκ ἐμὲ χρὴ λέγειν, δῆλα γὰρ τοῖς μὴ
τυφλοῖς ταῦτα· τὸ δὲ πρόσωπον αὐτὸ ὡς κάλλιστον καὶ τῷ ὑποκειμένῳ δράματι ἐοικός, οὐ
κεχηνὸς δὲ ὡς ἐκεῖνα ἀλλὰ συμμεμυκός· ἔχει γὰρ
30 πολλοὺς τοὺς ὑπὲρ αὐτοῦ βοῶντας. πάλαι μὲν
γὰρ αὐτοὶ[1] καὶ ᾖδον καὶ ὠρχοῦντο· εἶτ᾽ ἐπειδὴ

---

[1] οἱ αὐτοὶ N (Seager, Struve): but Fritzsche was right in
objecting. Cf. infra, ἄλλους αὐτοῖς ὑπᾴδειν.

---

[1] I.e., it is in art what a solecism is in grammar.
[2] Names of slaves in comedy.

the breast and pads for the paunch, wherewith he
puts on an adscititious, counterfeit corpulence, so that
the disproportion in height may not betray itself
the more conspicuously in a slender figure. Then
too, inside all this, you have the man himself bawling
out, bending forward and backward, sometimes
actually singing his lines, and (what is surely the
height of unseemliness) melodising his calamities,
holding himself answerable for nothing but his voice,
as everything else has been attended to by the poets,
who lived at some time in the distant past. To be
sure, as long as he is an Andromache or a Hecuba,
his singing can be tolerated; but when he enters
as Heracles in person and warbles a ditty, forgetting
himself and taking no shame either for the lion-skin
that he is wearing or for the club, a man in his right
mind may properly term the thing a solecism.[1]
And by the way, the charge you were bringing
against the dance, that men imitate women, would
be a common charge against both tragedy and
comedy. Indeed, in them the female parts out-
number the male! Moreover, comedy accounts the
ridiculousness of the masks themselves as part of
what is pleasing in her; for example, the masks of
Davuses and Tibiuses,[2] and of cooks.

On the other hand, that the appearance of the
dancer is seemly and becoming needs no assertion
on my part, for it is patent to all who are not blind.
His mask itself is most beautiful, and suited to the
drama that forms the theme; its mouth is not wide
open, as with tragedy and comedy, but closed, for
he has many people who do the shouting in his
stead. In the past, to be sure, they themselves
both danced and sang; but afterwards, since the

κινουμένων τὸ ᾆσμα τὴν ᾠδὴν ἐπετάραττεν,
ἄμεινον ἔδοξεν ἄλλους αὐτοῖς ὑπᾴδειν.

31 Αἱ δὲ ὑποθέσεις κοιναὶ ἀμφοτέροις, καὶ οὐδέν
τι διακεκριμέναι τῶν τραγικῶν αἱ ὀρχηστικαί,
πλὴν ὅτι ποικιλώτεραι αὗται καὶ πολυμαθέστεραι
καὶ μυρίας μεταβολὰς ἔχουσαι.

32 Εἰ δὲ μὴ ἐναγώνιος ἡ ὄρχησις, ἐκείνην εἶναί
φημι αἰτίαν, τὸ δόξαι τοῖς ἀγωνοθέταις μεῖζον
καὶ σεμνότερον τὸ πρᾶγμα ἢ ὥστε εἰς ἐξέτασιν
καλεῖσθαι. ἐῶ λέγειν ὅτι πόλις ἐν Ἰταλίᾳ, τοῦ
Χαλκιδικοῦ γένους ἡ ἀρίστη, καὶ τοῦτο ὥσπερ τι
κόσμημα τῷ παρ᾽ αὐτοῖς ἀγῶνι προστέθεικεν.[1]

33 Ἐθέλω δέ σοι ἐνταῦθα ἤδη ἀπολογήσασθαι
ὑπὲρ τῶν παραλελειμμένων τῷ λόγῳ παμπόλλων
ὄντων, ὡς μὴ δόξαν ἀγνοίας ἢ ἀμαθίας παράσχωμαι.
οὐ γάρ με λέληθεν ὅτι πολλοὶ πρὸ ἡμῶν περὶ
ὀρχήσεως συγγεγραφότες τὴν πλείστην διατριβὴν
τῆς γραφῆς ἐποιήσαντο πάντα τῆς ὀρχήσεως τὰ
εἴδη ἐπεξιόντες καὶ ὀνόματα αὐτῶν καταλέγοντες
καὶ οἷα ἑκάστη καὶ ὑφ᾽ ὅτου εὑρέθη, πολυμαθίας
ταύτῃ ἐπίδειξιν ἡγούμενοι παρέξειν. ἐγὼ δὲ
μάλιστα μὲν τὴν περὶ ταῦτα φιλοτιμίαν ἀπειρό-
καλόν τε καὶ ὀψιμαθῆ καὶ ἐμαυτῷ ἄκαιρον οἴομαι

34 εἶναι καὶ διὰ τοῦτο παρίημι· ἔπειτα δὲ κἀκεῖνό
σε ἀξιῶ ἐννοεῖν καὶ μεμνῆσθαι, ὅτι μοι νῦν οὐ
πᾶσαν ὄρχησιν πρόκειται γενεαλογεῖν, οὐδὲ τοῦτον
τὸν σκοπὸν ὑπεστησάμην τῷ λόγῳ, ὀρχήσεων

---

[1] The allusion is to Naples and to the important games
instituted there by Augustus in 2 A.D., on which see R. M.
Geer, "The Greek Games at Naples," *Transactions of the*

panting that came of their movement disturbed their singing, it seemed better that others should accompany them with song.

The themes of tragedy and the dance are common to both, and there is no difference between those of the one and those of the other, except that the themes of the dance are more varied and more unhackneyed, and they contain countless vicissitudes.

If the dance does not feature in contests, I maintain that it is because the governors of the games thought the thing too important and too grand to be called into competition. I forbear to mention that a city in Italy, the fairest that belongs to the Chalcidian race, has added it, by way of embellishment, to the games that are held there.[1]

At this point I should like to defend the numerous omissions in my account, that I may not create an impression that I lack sense or learning. I am not unaware that many before our time who have written about the dance have made it the chief matter of their essays to enumerate all its forms and list their names, telling what each is like and by whom it was discovered, thinking to make a display of wide learning thereby. But for my own part, first and foremost, I think that to be zealous about these things is tasteless, pedantic, and as far as I am concerned, out of place, and for that reason I pass them over. Besides, I want you to understand and remember that the topic which I have proposed for myself at present is not to give the history of every form of the dance, and I have not taken it upon myself as the aim of my discussion to enumerate

American Philological Association, LXVI (1935), especially n. 19 in regard to the inclusion of pantomimic contests.

THE WORKS OF LUCIAN

ὀνόματα καταριθμήσασθαι, πλὴν ὅσων ἐν ἀρχῇ
ὀλίγων ἐπεμνήσθην τὰς γενικωτέρας αὐτῶν προ-
χειρισάμενος· ἀλλὰ τό γε ἐν τῷ παρόντι μοι
κεφάλαιον τοῦ λόγου τοῦτό ἐστιν, τὴν νῦν ὄρχησιν
καθεστῶσαν ἐπαινέσαι καὶ δεῖξαι ὅσα ἐν αὐτῇ
τερπνὰ καὶ χρήσιμα περιλαβοῦσα ἔχει, οὐ πάλαι
ἀρξαμένη ἐς τοσοῦτο κάλλος ἐπιδιδόναι, ἀλλὰ κατὰ
τὸν Σεβαστὸν μάλιστα.

Αἱ μὲν γὰρ πρῶται ἐκεῖναι ὥσπερ τινὲς ῥίζαι
καὶ θεμέλιοι[1] τῆς ὀρχήσεως ἦσαν, τὸ δὲ ἄνθος
αὐτῆς καὶ τὸν τελεώτατον καρπόν, ὅσπερ[2] νῦν
μάλιστα ἐς τὸ ἀκρότατον ἀποτετέλεσται, τοῦτον[3]
οὖν ὁ ἡμέτερος λόγος διεξέρχεται, παρεὶς τὸ
θερμαυστρίζειν καὶ γέρανον ὀρχεῖσθαι καὶ τὰ
ἄλλα ὡς μηδὲν τῇ νῦν ταύτῃ ἔτι προσήκοντα.
οὐδὲ γὰρ ἐκεῖνο τὸ Φρύγιον τῆς ὀρχήσεως εἶδος,
τὸ παροίνιον καὶ συμποτικόν, μετὰ μέθης γιγνό-
μενον ἀγροίκων πολλάκις πρὸς αὔλημα γυναικεῖον
ὀρχουμένων σφοδρὰ καὶ καματηρὰ[4] πηδήματα,
καὶ νῦν ἔτι ταῖς ἀγροικίαις ἐπιπολάζοντα,[5] ὑπ'
ἀγνοίας παρέλιπον, ἀλλ' ὅτι μηδὲν ταῦτα τῇ νῦν
ὀρχήσει κοινωνεῖ. καὶ γὰρ ὁ Πλάτων ἐν τοῖς
Νόμοις τὰ μέν τινα εἴδη ἐπαινεῖ ταύτης, τὰ δὲ
πάνυ ἀπαξιοῖ, διαιρῶν αὐτὰ ἔς τε τὸ τερπνὸν καὶ

---

[1] θεμέλια C, contrary to Lucianic usage.
[2] ὅσπερ ΕΦΩ Ν²: ὥσπερ ΓΝ¹: ὅπερ (C)Α.
[3] τοῦτον οὖν Γ¹: τοῦτο νῦν Γ², other MSS.
[4] σφόδρα καὶ καματηρὰ ΕΝ: καὶ omitted in other MSS. Cf.
Hist. Conscr. 43.

names of dances, except for the few that I mentioned
at the outset, in touching upon the more characteristic of them. No, at present anyhow, the chief
object of my discussion is to praise the dance as
it now exists and to show how much that is pleasurable and profitable it comprises in its embrace,
although it did not begin to attain such a height of
beauty in days of old, but in the time of Augustus,
approximately.[1]

Those early forms were roots, so to speak, or
initial stages, of the dance; but the flowering of
it and the consummate fruition, which precisely
at this moment has been brought to the highest
point of perfection—that is what our discussion
treats of, omitting the Tongs and the Crane-dance [2]
and so forth as no longer having anything to do with
the dancing of to-day. And as to that "Phrygian"
form of the dance, the one that accompanied wine and
revelry, performed amidst drunkenness, generally
by peasants who executed, to the music of flutes
played by women, violent and trying gambols still
prevalent in the country districts, that too I have
not omitted out of ignorance but because those
gambols have nothing to do with our present dance.
As you know, Plato in the Laws praises certain
forms of the dance, but strongly condemns certain
others, dividing them with reference to what is

---

[1] See Athenaeus I, 20 D, where Bathyllus and Pylades are
given as its inventors, on the authority of Aristonicus.

[2] The Tongs seems to have involved the performance of
entrechats (Eustathius on *Odyss.*, VIII, p. 1161). The Crane-
dance was said to have been first danced about the altar
at Delos by Theseus and his companions, imitating the escape
from the Labyrinth (Pollux, IV, 101).

---

[5] ἐπιπολάζον Madvig, but cf. ταῦτα, below.

τὸ χρήσιμον καὶ ἀπελαύνων αὐτῶν τὰ ἀσχημονέ-
στερα, προτιμῶν δὲ καὶ θαυμάζων θάτερα.

35 Καὶ περὶ μὲν αὐτῆς ὀρχήσεως τοσαῦτα· τὸ
γὰρ πάντα ἐπεξιόντα μηκύνειν τὸν λόγον ἀπειρόκαλον. ἃ δὲ τὸν ὀρχηστὴν αὐτὸν ἔχειν χρὴ καὶ
ὅπως δεῖ ἠσκῆσθαι καὶ ἃ μεμαθηκέναι καὶ οἷς
κρατύνειν τὸ ἔργον, ἤδη σοι δίειμι, ὡς μάθῃς
οὐ τῶν ῥᾳδίων καὶ τῶν εὐμεταχειρίστων οὖσαν
τὴν τέχνην, ἀλλὰ πάσης παιδεύσεως ἐς τὸ ἀκρότατον ἀφικνουμένην, οὐ μουσικῆς μόνον ἀλλὰ καὶ
ῥυθμικῆς καὶ μετρικῆς, καὶ τῆς σῆς φιλοσοφίας
μάλιστα, τῆς τε φυσικῆς καὶ τῆς ἠθικῆς· τὴν γὰρ
διαλεκτικὴν αὐτῆς περιεργίαν ἄκαιρον αὐτῇ νενόμικεν. οὐ μὴν οὐδὲ ῥητορικῆς ἀφέστηκεν, ἀλλὰ
καὶ ταύτης μετέχει, καθ' ὅσον ἤθους τε καὶ
πάθους ἐπιδεικτική ἐστιν, ὧν καὶ οἱ ῥήτορες
γλίχονται. οὐκ ἀπήλλακται δὲ καὶ γραφικῆς καὶ
πλαστικῆς, ἀλλὰ καὶ τὴν ἐν ταύταις εὐρυθμίαν
μάλιστα μιμουμένη φαίνεται, ὡς μηδὲν ἀμείνω
μήτε Φειδίαν αὐτῆς μήτε Ἀπελλῆν εἶναι δοκεῖν.

36 Πρὸ πάντων δὲ Μνημοσύνην καὶ τὴν θυγατέρα
αὐτῆς Πολύμνιαν ἵλεως ἔχειν αὐτῇ πρόκειται, καὶ
μεμνῆσθαι πειρᾶται ἁπάντων. κατὰ γάρ τοι τὸν
Ὁμηρικὸν Κάλχαντα τὸν ὀρχηστὴν εἰδέναι χρὴ
" τά τ' ἐόντα τά τ' ἐσσόμενα πρό τ' ἐόντα,"
ὡς μηδὲν αὐτὸν διαλανθάνειν,[1] ἀλλ' εἶναι πρόχειρον
τὴν μνήμην αὐτῶν. καὶ τὸ μὲν κεφάλαιον τῆς
ὑποσχέσεως,[2] μιμητική τίς ἐστιν ἐπιστήμη καὶ
δεικτικὴ καὶ τῶν ἐννοηθέντων ἐξαγορευτικὴ καὶ

[1] διαλαθεῖν C, but cf. § 76.
[2] τῆς ὑποσχέσεως ΓΕΦ: τῆς ὑποθέσεως (ΩC) vulg. N omits.
Cf. *Pisc.*, 31.

pleasurable and profitable and rejecting the more
unseemly sorts, but valuing and admiring the rest.[1]

About the dance itself, let this suffice; for it would
be tasteless to prolong my discussion by taking up
everything. What qualifications the dancer on his
part ought to have, how he should have been trained,
what he should have studied, and by what means
he should strengthen his work, I shall now set forth
for you, to show you that Dance is not one of the
facile arts that can be plied without pains, but
reaches to the very summit of all culture, not only
in music but in rhythm and metre, and especially
in your own favourite, philosophy, both physics and
ethics. To be sure, Dance accounts philosophy's
inordinate interest in dialectics inappropriate to
herself. From rhetoric, however, she has not held
aloof, but has her part in that too, inasmuch as
she is given to depicting character and emotion,
of which the orators also are fond. And she has not
kept away from painting and sculpture, but manifestly copies above all else the rhythm that is in
them, so that neither Phidias nor Apelles seems at
all superior to her.

Before all else, however, it behoves her to enjoy
the favour of Mnemosyne and her daughter Polymnia,
and she endeavours to remember everything. Like
Calchas in Homer, the dancer must know "what is,
and what shall be, and was of old," [2] so thoroughly
that nothing will escape him, but his memory of it
all will be prompt. To be sure, it professes in the
main to be a science of imitation and portrayal, of
revealing what is in the mind and making intelligible

---

[1] *Laws*, VII, 814 E–816 C.
[2] *Iliad*, I, 70.

τῶν ἀφανῶν σαφηνιστική, καὶ ὅπερ ὁ Θουκυδίδης
περὶ τοῦ Περικλέους ἔφη ἐπαινῶν τὸν ἄνδρα,
τοῦτο καὶ τὸ τοῦ ὀρχηστοῦ ἀκρότατον ἂν ἐγκώμιον
εἴη, γνῶναί τε τὰ δέοντα καὶ ἑρμηνεῦσαι αὐτά·
ἑρμηνείαν δὲ νῦν τὴν σαφήνειαν τῶν σχημάτων
λέγω. ἡ δὲ πᾶσα τῷ ἔργῳ χορηγία ἡ παλαιὰ
ἱστορία ἐστίν, ὡς προεῖπον, καὶ ἡ πρόχειρος
37 αὐτῆς μνήμη τε καὶ μετ᾿ εὐπρεπείας ἐπίδειξις·
ἀπὸ γὰρ χάους εὐθὺς καὶ τῆς πρώτης τοῦ κόσμου
γενέσεως ἀρξάμενον χρὴ αὐτὸν ἅπαντα εἰδέναι ἄχρι τῶν κατὰ τὴν Κλεοπάτραν τὴν Αἰγυπτίαν.

Τούτῳ γὰρ τῷ διαστήματι περιωρίσθω ἡμῖν ἡ
τοῦ ὀρχηστοῦ πολυμαθία καὶ τὰ διὰ μέσου μάλιστα ἴστω, Οὐρανοῦ τομήν, Ἀφροδίτης γονάς,
Τιτάνων μάχην, Διὸς γένεσιν, Ῥέας ἀπάτην,
λίθου ὑποβολήν, Κρόνου δεσμά, τὸν τῶν τριῶν
38 ἀδελφῶν κλῆρον. εἶτα ἑξῆς Γιγάντων ἐπανάστασιν, πυρὸς κλοπήν, ἀνθρώπων πλάσιν, Προ-
μηθέως κόλασιν, Ἔρωτος ἰσχὺν ἑκατέρου,[1] καὶ
μετὰ ταῦτα Δήλου πλάνην καὶ Λητοῦς ὠδῖνας καὶ

---

[1] ἀμφοτέρου C.

---

[1] Thucydides, II, 60.

[2] The compendium of mythology that follows is notable
not only for its brevity but for its arrangement on geographical
lines, which is unique, and I think was adopted by Lucian
as an aid to memory, since the passage was clearly composed
off-hand and very little retouched. He must have thought
of it not only as displaying his own command of mythology
and knowledge of what Pindar calls "the short road" in
story-telling, but as a help to dancers, libretto-writers, and
audiences, and incidentally of interest to the latter as a memory-
test (cf. *True Story*, I; *The Dead Come to Life*, 6; *Mistaken
Critic*, 6). This is certainly the way in which most of its

THE DANCE

what is obscure. What Thucydides said of Pericles in praising the man would also be the highest possible commendation of a dancer, " to know what is meet and express it; " [1] and by expressing I mean the intelligibility of his postures. But his whole accoutrement for the work is ancient story, as I have said, and the prompt recollection and graceful presentation of it. Beginning with Chaos and the primal origin of the world, he must know everything down to the story of Cleopatra the Egyptian.[2]

Let this be the range we prescribe for the dancer's learning, and let him know thoroughly all that lies within it : the castration of Uranus, the begetting of Aphrodite, the battle of the Titans, the birth of Zeus, the stratagem of Rhea, the substitution of the stone, the fetters of Cronus, the casting of lots among the three brothers.[3] Then, in order, the revolt of the Giants, the theft of fire, the fashioning of man,[4] the punishment of Prometheus, the power of the two Erotes; [5] and after that, the errancy of Delos, the

readers will want to use it now. Those who, perhaps from interest in it as a dancer's repertory, wish to study it and find the notes given here and the further hints in the Index insufficient to their purpose should make use of Sir J. G. Frazer's Apollodorus (L.C.L.), which will make it all plain sailing.

[3] Zeus, Poseidon, and Hades, for their respective dominions.

[4] The allusion is not to the making of Pandora, but to the legend of the moulding of man out of earth and water by Prometheus, with the help of Athena, who supplied the breath of life : see Lucian's *Prometheus*, 1, and 11–17; *A Literary Prometheus*, 4; and Frazer on Apollodorus I, 7, 1, to whose references add Callimachus, Fr. 87 and Fr. 133 Schn. (Mair [L.C.L.], pp. 292, 310). It took place at Iconium in Lycaonia; cf. Stephanus of Byzantium, s.v. Ἰκόνιον.

[5] The ancient cosmogonic Eros of § 7, and the son of Aphrodite.

THE WORKS OF LUCIAN

Πύθωνος ἀναίρεσιν καὶ Τιτυοῦ ἐπιβουλὴν καὶ τὸ μέσον τῆς γῆς εὑρισκόμενον πτήσει τῶν ἀετῶν.

39 Δευκαλίωνα ἐπὶ τούτοις, καὶ τὴν μεγάλην ἐπ' ἐκείνου τοῦ βίου ναυαγίαν, καὶ λάρνακα μίαν λείψανον τοῦ ἀνθρωπίνου¹ γένους φυλάττουσαν, καὶ ἐκ λίθων ἀνθρώπους πάλιν. εἶτα Ἰάκχου σπαραγμὸν καὶ Ἥρας δόλον καὶ Σεμέλης κατάφλεξιν καὶ Διονύσου ἀμφοτέρας τὰς γονάς, καὶ ὅσα περὶ Ἀθηνᾶς καὶ ὅσα περὶ Ἡφαίστου καὶ Ἐριχθονίου, καὶ τὴν ἔριν τὴν περὶ τῆς Ἀττικῆς, καὶ Ἁλιρρόθιον καὶ τὴν πρώτην ἐν Ἀρείῳ πάγῳ κρίσιν, καὶ ὅλως τὴν Ἀττικὴν πᾶσαν μυθολο-

40 γίαν· ἐξαιρέτως δὲ τὴν Δήμητρος πλάνην καὶ Κόρης εὕρεσιν καὶ Κελεοῦ ξενίαν καὶ Τριπτολέμου γεωργίαν καὶ Ἰκαρίου ἀμπελουργίαν καὶ τὴν Ἠριγόνης συμφοράν, καὶ ὅσα περὶ Βορέου καὶ ὅσα περὶ Ὠρειθυίας καὶ Θησέως καὶ Αἰγέως. ἔτι δὲ τὴν Μηδείας ὑποδοχὴν καὶ αὖθις ἐς Πέρσας φυγὴν καὶ τὰς Ἐρεχθέως θυγατέρας καὶ τὰς Πανδίονος, ἅ τε ἐν Θρᾴκῃ ἔπαθον καὶ ἔπραξαν. εἶτα ὁ Ἀκάμας καὶ ἡ Φυλλὶς καὶ ἡ προτέρα δὲ τῆς Ἑλένης ἁρπαγὴ καὶ ἡ στρατεία τῶν Διοσκούρων

---

¹ ἀνθρωπείου C.

---

[1] Two eagles let fly by Zeus, one from the east, the other from the west, met at Delphi; the Navel-stone (Omphalos) marked the spot, the centre of the earth, and had two eagles of gold set up by it (Pindar, *Pyth.*, IV, 6, with the scholia; Frazer, Pausanias, Vol. V, pp. 314–315).

[2] Dionysus Zagreus (Sabazius), son of Persephone, was dismembered by the Titans, boiled in a cauldron, and eaten; Zeus swallowed his heart. He was reborn as Iacchus.

travail of Leto, the killing of Pytho, the plot of
Tityus, and the discovery of earths' central point
by the flight of the eagles.[1]

Next comes Deucalion, with the great shipwreck
of life in his time, and the single ark conserving a
remnant of the human race, and men created afresh
from stones. Then the dismemberment of Iacchus,[2]
the trick of Hera,[3] the burning of Semele, the double
birth of Dionysus, the story of Athena and the story
of Hephaestus and Erichthonius, the rivalry for
Attica, Halirrhothius and the first trial on the
Areopagus, and in a word, Attic mythology complete;
but particularly the wandering of Demeter, the
finding of Core, the visit to Celeus, the husbandry
of Triptolemus; the vine-planting of Icarius, and
the sad fate of Erigone; the story of Boreas, of
Oreithyia, of Theseus and Aegeus. Also, the
reception of Medea and her later flight to Persia,
the daughters of Erechtheus, and the daughters of
Pandion, with what they suffered and did in Thrace.
Then Acamas, Phyllis,[4] the first rape of Helen, the
campaign of the Dioscuri against the city, the fate

[3] Inducing Semele to beg Zeus to come to her in all his
majesty.
[4] The Thracian princess Phyllis hanged herself because her
lover, one of the sons of Theseus, did not return to her. As
the story is usually told, the lover was Demophon (Apoll.,
Epit., vi, 16–17; Ovid, *Heroides*, ii). Another version,
however, gave that part to Acamas (Aeschines, II, 31),
and that is probably Lucian's intention here. But it is also
possible that he expects us to supply from memory the name
of Demophon in connection with that of Phyllis, and to associate with that of Acamas his affair with Laodice, daughter of
Priam, who came to him self-invited (Lycophron, *Alex.*, 496),
and later, at the fall of Troy, gave him Munitus, the son she
had borne him, and was herself swallowed up by the earth.

ἐπὶ τὴν πόλιν καὶ τὸ Ἱππολύτου πάθος καὶ Ἡρα-
κλειδῶν κάθοδος· Ἀττικὰ γὰρ καὶ ταῦτα εἰκότως
ἂν νομίζοιτο.

Ταῦτα μὲν τὰ Ἀθηναίων ὀλίγα πάνυ δείγματος
ἕνεκα ἐκ πολλῶν τῶν παραλελειμμένων διῆλθον.
41 ἑξῆς δὲ τὰ Μέγαρα καὶ Νῖσος καὶ Σκύλλα καὶ
πορφυροῦς πλόκαμος καὶ Μίνωος πόρος καὶ περὶ
τὴν εὐεργέτιν ἀχαριστία. οἷς ἑξῆς ὁ Κιθαιρὼν
καὶ τὰ Θηβαίων καὶ Λαβδακιδῶν πάθη καὶ Κάδμου
ἐπιδημία καὶ βοὸς ὄκλασις καὶ ὄφεως ὀδόντες καὶ
Σπαρτῶν ἀνάδοσις καὶ αὖθις τοῦ Κάδμου εἰς
δράκοντα μεταβολὴ καὶ πρὸς λύραν τείχισις καὶ
μανία τοῦ τειχοποιοῦ καὶ τῆς γυναικὸς αὐτοῦ
τῆς Νιόβης ἡ μεγαλαυχία καὶ ἡ ἐπὶ τῷ πένθει
σιγὴ καὶ τὰ Πενθέως καὶ Ἀκταίωνος καὶ τὰ
Οἰδίποδος καὶ Ἡρακλῆς σὺν τοῖς ἄθλοις αὐτοῦ
ἅπασιν καὶ ἡ τῶν παίδων σφαγή.
42 Εἶθ᾽ ἡ Κόρινθος πλέα καὶ αὕτη μύθων, τὴν
Γλαύκην καὶ τὸν Κρέοντα ἔχουσα, καὶ πρὸ αὐτῶν τὸν Βελλεροφόντην καὶ τὴν Σθενέβοιαν καὶ
Ἡλίου μάχην καὶ Ποσειδῶνος, καὶ μετὰ ταῦτα
τὴν Ἀθάμαντος μανίαν καὶ τῶν Νεφέλης παίδων
ἐπὶ τοῦ κριοῦ τὴν διαέριον φυγήν, . . . Ἰνοῦς [1]
καὶ Μελικέρτου ὑποδοχήν.

[1] καὶ τὴν Ἰνοῦς Bekker, but more than that has been lost.
No lacuna in MSS.

---

[1] Minos tied her to the stern of his ship and dragged her
in its wake. In representing this as an "expedient," Lucian

of Hippolytus, and the return of the Heracleidae;
for all this may properly be considered Attic.

These Athenian tales that I have run over are
a very few by way of example out of the many that
have been omitted. And next comes Megara, with
Nisus and Scylla, the purple lock, the expedient of
Minos, and his ingratitude towards his benefactress.[1]
To these succeed Cithaeron, with all that befell the
Thebans and the house of Labdacus; the advent
of Cadmus, the heifer's taking ground, the serpent's
teeth, and the emergence of the Sown Men; further,
the transformation of Cadmus into a serpent, the
rising of the walls to the music of the lyre, the
madness of the wall-builder,[2] the boastfulness of his
wife Niobe, and her grief-stricken silence, the story
of Pentheus and of Actaeon, the story of Oedipus,
Heracles with all his labours, and the murder of his
children.

Then comes Corinth, also full of myths, since she
has Glauce and Creon, and before them Bellerophon
and Stheneboea, and the quarrel between Helius
and Poseidon;[3] afterwards, the madness of Athamas,
the flight of the children of Nephele through the
air on the back of the ram, and the reception of Ino
and Melicertes.[4]

seems to be thinking of it as Minos' way of carrying out a
previous bargain with Scylla to " take her with him," or the
like. So Tarpeia bargained with the Sabines for what they
had on their arms, expecting their bracelets; but they crushed
her with their shields.

[2] Amphion, who went mad of grief over the slaying of his
and Niobe's children by Apollo and Artemis.

[3] For the possession of Corinth; Briareus, as mediator,
awarded the Isthmus to Poseidon, Acro-Corinth to Helius.

[4] In Corinth, as the sea-divinities Palaemon and Leucothea.

43 Ἐπὶ τούτοις τὰ Πελοπιδῶν καὶ Μυκῆναι καὶ
τὰ ἐν αὐταῖς καὶ πρὸ αὐτῶν, Ἴναχος καὶ Ἰὼ καὶ
ὁ φρουρὸς αὐτῆς Ἄργος καὶ Ἀτρεὺς καὶ Θυέστης
καὶ Ἀερόπη, καὶ τὸ χρυσοῦν ἀρνίον καὶ Πελο-
πείας¹ γάμος καὶ Ἀγαμέμνονος σφαγὴ καὶ Κλυ-
ταιμήστρας² τιμωρία· καὶ ἔτι πρὸ τούτων ἡ τῶν
ἑπτὰ λοχαγῶν στρατεία καὶ ἡ τῶν φυγάδων
γαμβρῶν τοῦ Ἀδράστου ὑποδοχὴ καὶ ὁ ἐπ᾽
αὐτοῖς χρησμὸς καὶ ἡ τῶν πεσόντων ἀταφία καὶ
Ἀντιγόνης διὰ ταῦτα καὶ Μενοικέως ἀπώλεια.

44 καὶ τὰ ἐν Νεμέᾳ δέ, ἡ Ὑψιπύλη καὶ Ἀρχέμορος,
ἀναγκαιότατα τῷ ὀρχηστῇ μνημονεύματα. καὶ
πρὸ αὐτῶν εἴσεται τὴν Δανάης παρθένευσιν καὶ
Περσέως γένεσιν καὶ τὸν ἐπὶ τὰς Γοργόνας ἆθλον
αὐτῷ προῃρημένον, ᾧ οἰκεία καὶ ἡ Αἰθιοπικὴ
διήγησις, Κασσιέπεια καὶ Ἀνδρομέδα καὶ Κηφεύς,
οὓς καὶ ἄστροις ἐγκατέλεξεν ἡ τῶν μετὰ ταῦτα
πίστις. κἀκεῖνα δὲ τὰ ἀρχαῖα τὰ Αἰγύπτου καὶ
Δαναοῦ εἴσεται καὶ τὴν ἐπιθαλάμιον ἐπιβουλήν.

45 Οὐκ ὀλίγα δὲ καὶ ἡ Λακεδαίμων τοιαῦτα παρέχεται, τὸν Ὑάκινθον καὶ τὸν τοῦ Ἀπόλλωνος ἀντεραστὴν Ζέφυρον καὶ τὴν ὑπὸ τῷ δίσκῳ τοῦ μειρακίου
σφαγὴν καὶ τὸ ἐκ τοῦ αἵματος ἄνθος καὶ τὴν ἐν

---

¹ Πελοπίας MSS.
² So (Κλυτεμήστρας) Γ : other MSS. -μν-.

---

¹ Daughter of Thyestes, and by him mother of Aegisthus
(Hyginus 87 and 88; cf. Frazer, Apollodorus, II, p. 168, n. 1).
She is mentioned as a pantomimic rôle by Juvenal, VII, 92 :
praefectos Pelopea facit, Philomela tribunos.
² One of Adrastus' daughters was to wed a boar, the other
a lion. Tydeus had a boar for his shield-device, Polynices
a lion.

THE DANCE

Next is the story of the descendants of Pelops, with Mycenae and what happened there, and previously—Inachus, Io, and her warder Argus; Atreus, Thyestes, Aerope, and the golden lamb; the defloration of Pelopeia;[1] the slaying of Agamemnon, and the punishment of Clytemestra. Even before that, the expedition of the Seven Captains, with Adrastus' reception of the exiles who became his sons-in-law, and the oracle about them,[2] the refusal to bury the fallen, and the death of Antigone and Menoeceus on that account. Also what happened on Nemean soil, the story of Hypsipyle and Archemorus, is very essential for the dancer to remember.[3] And from an earlier time he will know the enforced virginity of Danae, the birth of Perseus, and the quest of the Gorgons which he assumed. Related to this is the Ethiopian tale of Cassiopea, Andromeda, and Cepheus, who have been placed in the roll of constellations by the faith of men of after time. And he will also know that ancient tale of Aegyptus and Danaus, and the bride-night plot.

Sparta, too, affords not a few stories of this sort :[4] Hyacinthus, and Apollo's rival, Zephyrus; the lad's slaying with the discus, the flower that came from the blood, and the word of woe (AI) that is written

[3] Just why it should be so essential is not very obvious. The infant Archemorus was killed by a dragon when his nurse Hypsipyle left him at a spring in order to point out the way to Thebes to the army of the seven chieftains. But Lucian's remark may have been called forth by the thought of Hypsipyle's earlier history as queen of Lemnos—her killing her husband and saving her father, and her love for Jason.

[4] One wonders whether Lucian's omission of the story of Leda is careless or intentional.

αὐτῷ αἰάζουσαν ἐπιγραφήν, καὶ τὴν Τυνδάρεω
ἀνάστασιν καὶ τὴν Διὸς ἐπὶ τούτῳ κατ' Ἀσκληπιοῦ ὀργήν· ἔτι δὲ καὶ τὸν Πάριδος ξενισμὸν
καὶ τὴν Ἑλένης ἁρπαγὴν μετὰ τὴν ἐπὶ τῷ μήλῳ
46 κρίσιν. νομιστέον γὰρ τῇ Σπαρτιατικῇ ἱστορίᾳ
καὶ τὴν Ἰλιακὴν συνῆφθαι, πολλὴν οὖσαν καὶ
πολυπρόσωπον· καθ' ἕκαστον γοῦν τῶν ἐκεῖ
πεσόντων δρᾶμα τῇ σκηνῇ πρόκειται· καὶ μεμνῆσθαι δὲ[1] τούτων δεῖ μάλιστα,[2] ἀπὸ τῆς ἁρπαγῆς
εὐθὺς ἄχρι τῶν ἐν τοῖς νόστοις γεγενημένων καὶ
τῆς Αἰνείου πλάνης καὶ Διδοῦς ἔρωτος.

Ὧν οὐκ ἀλλότρια καὶ τὰ περὶ τὸν Ὀρέστην
δράματα καὶ τὰ ἐν Σκυθίᾳ τῷ ἥρωι τετολμη-
μένα. οὐκ ἀπῳδὰ δὲ καὶ τὰ πρὸ τούτων, ἀλλὰ
τοῖς Ἰλιακοῖς συγγενῆ, Ἀχιλλέως ἐν Σκύρῳ
παρθένευσις καὶ Ὀδυσσέως μανία καὶ Φιλοκτή-
του ἐρημία, καὶ ὅλως ἡ πᾶσα Ὀδύσσειος πλάνη
καὶ Κίρκη καὶ Τηλέγονος καὶ ἡ Αἰόλου τῶν ἀνέμων δυναστεία καὶ τὰ ἄλλα μέχρι τῆς τῶν μνηστήρων τιμωρίας· καὶ πρὸ τούτων ἡ κατὰ Παλαμή-
δους ἐπιβουλὴ καὶ ἡ Ναυπλίου ὀργὴ καὶ ἡ Αἴαντος
μανία καὶ ἡ θατέρου ἐν ταῖς πέτραις ἀπώλεια.

---

[1] δὲ ΓΕΦΩΑ: δέον N, δεῖ vulg.
[2] δεῖ μάλιστα Harmon: ἀεὶ μάλιστα MSS. Many editors
punctuate ἀεί, μάλιστα, but μάλιστα cannot be taken with
what follows.

---

[1] The tale is told by Lucian in *Dialogues of the Gods*, 16
(14), and there too the scene is laid in Sparta; cf. Apoll.,
III, 10, 3. It figured also among the tales of Northern
Greece (Apoll., I, 3, 3).

[2] Dido's story essentially as it was told in the Greek of
Tinaeus may still be read in the Latin of Justin (XVIII, 4–6);
but Aeneas played no part in it. His introduction into it

on it.[1] Also the resurrection of Tyndareus, and
Zeus's anger at Asclepius over it. Further, the
entertainment of Paris and the rape of Helen, after
his judgement in the matter of the apple. For we
must recognise that there is a connecting bond
between Spartan story and that of Troy, which is
copious and full of parts to play; in fact, for each
person who fell there, a drama offers itself to the
theatre. These themes must be kept in mind above
all others, from the time of the rape straight through
to what happened in the " Home-farings," with
the wandering of Aeneas and the love of Dido.[2]

The dramas that centre upon Orestes, including
that hero's adventures in Scythia, are not alien to
all this; and what went before is not incongruous,
either, but akin to the story of Troy—the virgin
life of Achilles in Scyros, the madness of Odysseus,
the marooning of Philoctetes, and, in general,
the whole wandering of Odysseus, including Circe,
Telegonus,[3] Aeolus' sway over the winds, and all
the rest of it, to the punishment of the suitors.
Also, preceding this, the plot against Palamedes, and
the wrath of Nauplius, the madness of Ajax, and the
death of the other Ajax among the rocks.

cannot be traced further back than Naevius. It probably
came to Lucian by way of Vergil, from whom, however, it
is hardly likely that he derived it at first hand.

[3] Telegonus, the son of Circe and Odysseus, does not appear
in the *Odyssey*, but was the hero of a late sequel to it, the
Telegony. Its content is reflected in an abstract by Proclus
(Evelyn White, *Hesiod*, etc. [L.C.L.], p. 530) and in Apoll.,
Epit., VII, 34–37. In stating that its author represented
Telegonus as Odysseus' son by Calypso, Eustathius is mani-
festly in error, for the part played by Circe in the conclusion
of the story makes it certain that Circe was his mother.

257

THE WORKS OF LUCIAN

47 Ἔχει πολλὰς καὶ Ἦλις ἀφορμὰς τοῖς ὀρχεῖσθαι
πειρωμένοις, τὸν Οἰνόμαον, τὸν Μυρτίλον, τὸν
Κρόνον, τὸν Δία, τοὺς πρώτους τῶν Ὀλυμπίων
48 ἀγωνιστάς. πολλὴ δὲ καὶ ἡ κατ᾽ Ἀρκαδίαν
μυθολογία, Δάφνης φυγή, Καλλιστοῦς θηρίωσις,
Κενταύρων παροινία, Πανὸς γοναί, Ἀλφειοῦ
ἔρως καὶ ὕφαλος ἀποδημία.

49 Ἀλλὰ κἂν εἰς τὴν Κρήτην ἀφίκῃ τῷ λόγῳ,
πάμπολλα κἀκεῖθεν ἡ ὄρχησις ἐρανίζεται, τὴν
Εὐρώπην, τὴν Πασιφάην, τοὺς ταύρους ἀμφοτέρους, τὸν λαβύρινθον, τὴν Ἀριάδνην, τὴν Φαίδραν,
τὸν Ἀνδρόγεων, τὸν Δαίδαλον, τὸν Ἴκαρον, τὸν
Γλαῦκον, τὴν Πολυΐδου μαντικήν, τὸν Τάλω, τὸν
50 χαλκοῦν τῆς Κρήτης περίπολον. κἂν εἰς Αἰτωλίαν
μετέλθῃς, κἀκεῖ πολλὰ ἡ ὄρχησις καταλαμβάνει,
τὴν Ἀλθαίαν, τὸν Μελέαγρον, τὴν Ἀταλάντην, τὸν
δαλόν, καὶ ποταμοῦ καὶ Ἡρακλέους πάλην καὶ
Σειρήνων γένεσιν καὶ Ἐχινάδων ἀνάδοσιν καὶ μετὰ
τὴν μανίαν Ἀλκμαίωνος οἴκησιν· εἶτα Νέσσον καὶ
Δηϊανείρας ζηλοτυπίαν, ἐφ᾽ ᾗ τὴν ἐν Οἴτῃ πυράν.

51 Ἔχει καὶ Θράκη πολλὰ τῷ ὀρχησομένῳ ἀναγ-
καῖα, τὸν Ὀρφέα, τὸν ἐκείνου σπαραγμὸν καὶ
τὴν λάλον αὐτοῦ κεφαλὴν τὴν ἐπιπλέουσαν τῇ

---

[1] Probably the wrestling match between Cronus and Zeus,
by which Zeus won possession of Olympia, is meant here rather
than the games in which the gods competed under the presi-
dency of Zeus (Paus., V, 7, 10), or the wrestling match between
Zeus and Heracles (Lyc., 39–43), or the games held by Heracles,
in which the competitors were his contemporaries (Pindar,
Ol., X, 60–75).

[2] The Minotaur, and the bull that fathered him.

[3] Clearly Lucian has in mind the legend that made them
daughters of Earth (Eur., Hel., 168), engendered of the blood

THE DANCE

Elis too has many subjects for those who essay the dance—Oenomaus and Myrtilus, Cronus and Zeus, and the first contestants in the Olympic games ;[1] and the Arcadian mythology also is copious—the flight of Daphne, the transformation of Callisto into a wild beast, the drunken riot of the Centaurs, the birth of Pan, the love of Alpheus, and his journey into foreign parts beneath the sea.

Indeed, even if you go to Crete in fancy, the dance garners very many contributions from there—Europe, Pasiphae, both the bulls,[2] the labyrinth, Ariadne, Phaedra, Androgeos, Daedalus and Icarus, Glaucus and the soothsaying skill of Polyidus, and Talus, the bronze roundsman of Crete. Or if you cross over to Aetolia, there too the dance finds a great deal—Althea, Meleager, Atalanta, the brand, the wrestling-match between Heracles and the river (Achelous), the birth of the Sirens,[3] the emergence of the Echinades,[4] and the settlement of Alcmaeon there after his madness; then Nessus, and the jealousy of Deianeira, and, consequent upon it, the pyre in Oeta.

Thrace also has much that is essential to one who intends to dance—Orpheus, his dismemberment and his talking head that voyaged on the lyre;[5]

that dropped from the wound of Achelous, inflicted by Heracles through breaking off one of his horns (Libanius, *Progymn.*, 4).

[4] Five of the Echinades were nymphs, turned into islands for their failure to invite Achelous to a sacrifice. A sixth, Perimele, was a maiden who was thrown into the sea by her father because she had given herself to Achelous; in answer to Achelous' prayer, Poseidon changed her into an island. So, at all events, says Ovid (*Met.*, VIII, 577–610).

[5] The story of the head of Orpheus is told by Lucian in *The Ignorant Book-Collector*, 11–12 (Vol. III, pp. 188 ff.).

THE WORKS OF LUCIAN

λύρᾳ, καὶ τὸν Αἷμον καὶ τὴν Ῥοδόπην, καὶ τὴν
52 Λυκούργου κόλασιν. καὶ Θεσσαλία δὲ ἔτι ¹ πλείω
παρέχεται, τὸν Πελίαν, τὸν Ἰάσονα, τὴν Ἄλκηστιν,
τὸν τῶν πεντήκοντα νέων στόλον, τὴν Ἀργώ,
53 τὴν λάλον αὐτῆς τρόπιν, τὰ ἐν Λήμνῳ, τὸν Αἰήτην,
τὸν Μηδείας ὄνειρον, τὸν Ἀψύρτου σπαραγμὸν καὶ
τὰ ἐν τῷ παράπλῳ γενόμενα, καὶ μετὰ ταῦτα τὸν
Πρωτεσίλαον καὶ τὴν Λαοδάμειαν.
54 Κἂν εἰς τὴν Ἀσίαν πάλιν διαβῇς, πολλὰ κἀκεῖ
δράματα· ἡ γὰρ Σάμος εὐθὺς καὶ τὸ Πολυκράτους
πάθος καὶ τῆς θυγατρὸς αὐτοῦ μέχρι Περσῶν
πλάνη, καὶ τὰ ἔτι ἀρχαιότερα, ἡ τοῦ Ταντάλου
φλυαρία καὶ ἡ παρ' αὐτῷ θεῶν ἑστίασις καὶ ἡ
Πέλοπος κρεουργία καὶ ὁ ἐλεφάντινος ὦμος
αὐτοῦ.
55 Καὶ ἐν Ἰταλίᾳ δὲ ὁ Ἠριδανὸς καὶ Φαέθων καὶ
αἴγειροι ἀδελφαὶ θρηνοῦσαι καὶ ἤλεκτρον δακρύου-
56 σαι. εἴσεται δὲ ὁ τοιοῦτος καὶ τὰς Ἑσπερίδας καὶ
τὸν φρουρὸν τῆς χρυσῆς ὀπώρας δράκοντα καὶ
τὸν Ἄτλαντος μόχθον καὶ τὸν Γηρυόνην καὶ τὴν
57 ἐξ Ἐρυθείας ἔλασιν τῶν βοῶν. οὐκ ἀγνοήσει

¹ ἔτι vulg.: ἐπὶ ΓΕΦΝΩΑ.

¹ Apollonius of Rhodes (III, 616–682) describes at some
length a dream of Medea's, shortly after the arrival of Jason,
to the effect that he came to win her, that she helped him
with the oxen; that she was chosen to arbitrate the strife
that arose, and decided in Jason's favour; whereupon her
parents clamoured, and she awoke. Since this dream is
not traditional, its inclusion in Lucian's list is perhaps to be
explained by assuming that he knew of its actual use as a
pantomimic theme.

THE DANCE

Haemus and Rhodope; the punishment of Lycurgus; and Thessaly affords still more—Pelias, Jason, Alcestis, the expedition of the fifty youths, the Argo and her talking keel, the incidents at Lemnos, Aeëtes, the dream of Medea,[1] the dismemberment of Apsyrtus, the happenings of the cruise, and after that, Protesilaus and Laodameia.

If you cross the sea again to Asia, there are many dramas there—Samos, at the outset, with the fate of Polycrates and his daughter's wanderings, extending to Persia,[2] and the stories that are still older—the loquaciousness of Tantalus, the feast of the gods at his house, the butchering of Pelops, and his shoulder of ivory.

In Italy, moreover, we have the Eridanus, and Phaethon, and the poplars that are his sisters, mourning and weeping amber. And a man of the sort I have in mind will know about the Hesperides, too, and the dragon that guards the golden fruit, and the toil of Atlas, and about Geryon, and the lifting of his cattle from Erytheia. And

[2] This allusion is puzzling. Nothing about the daughter of Polycrates is known to us except that she foretold her father's death through a dream (Herod., III, 124). Since Herodotus tells also how Syloson, the brother of Polycrates, went to Egypt as an exile, earned the gratitude of Darius, who was serving there as a guardsman, by giving him a cloak which Darius coveted and sought to buy, and later, after the death of Polycrates, visited Susa and obtained from Darius his restoration to Samos and establishment as ruler of the island, it has been thought that Lucian has been guilty of confusing the brother with the daughter. But Lucian was a little too well acquainted with Herodotus (and the world with the story of Syloson's cloak) to make this quite credible. A gap in the text here is easily possible, but it may also be that Hellenistic imagination gave the daughter a romantic history which dancers had selected for portrayal.

δὲ καὶ τὰς μυθικὰς μεταμορφώσεις ἁπάσας,
ὅσοι¹ εἰς δένδρα ἢ θηρία ἢ ὄρνεα ἠλλάγησαν καὶ
ὅσαι ἐκ γυναικῶν ἄνδρες ἐγένοντο, τὸν Καινέα
λέγω καὶ τὸν Τειρεσίαν καὶ τοὺς τοιούτους.

58 Καὶ ἐν Φοινίκῃ δὲ Μύρραν καὶ τὸ Ἀσσύριον
ἐκεῖνο πένθος μεριζόμενον, καὶ ταῦτα εἴσεται,
καὶ τὰ νεώτερα δὲ ὅσα μετὰ τὴν Μακεδόνων ἀρχὴν
ἐτολμήθη ὑπό τε Ἀντιπάτρου καὶ παρὰ Σε-
59 λεύκῳ² ἐπὶ τῷ Στρατονίκης ἔρωτι. τὰ γὰρ
Αἰγυπτίων, μυστικώτερα ὄντα, εἴσεται μέν, συμ-
βολικώτερον δὲ ἐπιδείξεται· τὸν Ἔπαφον λέγω καὶ
τὸν Ὄσιριν καὶ τὰς τῶν θεῶν εἰς τὰ ζῷα μεταβολάς.

Πρὸ πάντων δὲ τὰ περὶ τοὺς ἔρωτας αὐτῶν καὶ
αὐτοῦ τοῦ Διὸς καὶ εἰς ὅσα ἑαυτὸν μετεσκεύασεν
60 εἴσεται, καὶ³ τὴν ἐν Ἅιδου ἅπασαν τραγῳδίαν καὶ
τὰς κολάσεις καὶ τὰς ἐφ᾽ ἑκάστῃ αἰτίας καὶ τὴν
Πειρίθου καὶ Θησέως ἄχρι τοῦ Ἅιδου ἑταιρείαν.
61 συνελόντι δὲ εἰπεῖν, οὐδὲν τῶν ὑπὸ τοῦ Ὁμήρου καὶ
Ἡσιόδου καὶ τῶν ἀρίστων ποιητῶν καὶ μάλιστα
τῆς τραγῳδίας λεγομένων ἀγνοήσει.

¹ ὅσοι Bekker: ὅσαι MSS.
² Σελεύκῳ Harmon : Σελεύκου MSS.
³ μετεσκεύασεν εἴσεται, καὶ Harmon: μετεσκεύασεν. εἴσεται
δὲ καὶ MSS.

---

¹ Caeneus and Tiresias are coupled also in *Gallus*, 19.
On Caeneus, a woman who at her own request was changed by
Poseidon into a man, see especially Sir J. G. Frazer's note on
Apoll., *Epit.*, I, 22.
² Mother of Adonis, called Smyrna by Apollodorus (III,
14, 4); cf. Ovid, *Met.*, X, 298–518.
³ The words πένθος μεριζόμενον, which I have translated
"dissevered woe," seem to me to be certainly sound, and to
reflect the identification of Adonis with Osiris then current,
the piecemeal recovery of his dismembered body (with, no

THE DANCE

he will not fail to know all the fabulous transformations, the people who have been changed into trees or beasts or birds, and the women who have turned into men; Caeneus, I mean, and Tiresias, and their like.[1]

In Phoenicia he will know about Myrrha [2] and that Syrian tale of dissevered woe,[3] as well as the more recent happenings that followed the establishment of Macedonian rule, the bold deeds of Antipater as well as those at the court of Seleucus over the affections of Stratonice.[4] Since Egyptian tales are somewhat mystic, he will know them, but will present them more symbolically; I mean Epaphus and Osiris and the transfigurations of the gods into their bestial forms.

Before all else, however, he will know the stories of their loves, including the loves of Zeus himself, and all the forms into which he changed himself, and also the whole show in the realm of Hades, with the punishments and the reasons for each, and how the comradeship of Peirithous and Theseus brought them even to Hades. To sum it up, he will not be ignorant of anything that is told by Homer and Hesiod and the best poets, and above all by tragedy.

doubt, renewed mourning over every part), and in particular, the coming of the head to Byblus; see Lucian's *Dea Syria*, 7 (IV, p. 344). The phrase is very similar to the λακιστὸν μόρον ("piecemeal doom") which Lucian quotes (from a lost tragedy) in the *Piscator* 2 (III, p. 3), and may have been suggested by it. On "Assyrian" for Syrian, see the Index.

[4] The allusion to Antipater is inexplicable, unless it is to the son of Cassander, who murdered his mother (Justin., XVI, 1, 1). The story of Antiochus' love for Stratonice, the wife of his father, Seleucus Nicator, its detection by a physician, and the father's resignation of wife and kingdom to his son is a favourite with Lucian, and is told in *Dea Syria*, 17–18 (IV, pp. 360 ff.).

THE WORKS OF LUCIAN

Ταῦτα πάνυ ὀλίγα ἐκ πολλῶν, μᾶλλον δὲ ἀπείρων τὸ πλῆθος, ἐξελὼν τὰ κεφαλαιωδέστερα κατέλεξα, τὰ ἄλλα τοῖς τε ποιηταῖς ᾄδειν ἀφεὶς καὶ τοῖς ὀρχησταῖς αὐτοῖς δεικνύναι καὶ σοὶ προσεξευρίσκειν καθ' ὁμοιότητα τῶν προειρημένων, ἅπερ ἅπαντα πρόχειρα καὶ πρὸς τὸν καιρὸν ἕκαστον τῷ ὀρχηστῇ προπεπορισμένα καὶ προτεταμιευμένα κεῖσθαι ἀναγκαῖον.

62 Ἐπεὶ δὲ μιμητικός ἐστι καὶ κινήμασι τὰ ᾀδόμενα δείξειν ὑπισχνεῖται, ἀναγκαῖον αὐτῷ, ὅπερ καὶ τοῖς ῥήτορσι, σαφήνειαν ἀσκεῖν, ὡς ἕκαστον τῶν δεικνυμένων ὑπ' αὐτοῦ δηλοῦσθαι μηδενὸς ἐξηγητοῦ δεόμενον, ἀλλ' ὅπερ ἔφη ὁ Πυθικὸς χρησμός, δεῖ τὸν θεώμενον ὄρχησιν καὶ κωφοῦ συνιέναι καὶ μὴ λαλέοντος τοῦ ὀρχηστοῦ ἀκούειν.

63 Ὃ δὴ καὶ Δημήτριον τὸν Κυνικὸν παθεῖν λέγουσιν. ἐπεὶ γὰρ καὶ αὐτὸς ὅμοιά σοι κατηγόρει τῆς ὀρχηστικῆς, λέγων τοῦ αὐλοῦ καὶ τῶν συρίγγων καὶ τῶν κτύπων πάρεργόν τι τὸν ὀρχηστὴν εἶναι, μηδὲν αὐτὸν πρὸς τὸ δρᾶμα συντελοῦντα, κινούμενον δὲ ἄλογον ἄλλως κίνησιν καὶ μάταιον, οὐδενὸς αὐτῇ νοῦ προσόντος, τῶν δὲ ἀνθρώπων τοῖς περὶ τὸ πρᾶγμα γοητευομένων,[1] ἐσθῆτι σηρικῇ καὶ προσωπείῳ εὐπρεπεῖ, αὐλῷ τε καὶ τερετίσμασι καὶ τῇ τῶν ᾀδόντων εὐφωνίᾳ, οἷς κοσμεῖσθαι μηδὲν ὂν τὸ τοῦ ὀρχηστοῦ πρᾶγμα, ὁ τότε κατὰ τὸν Νέρωνα εὐδοκιμῶν ὀρχηστής, οὐκ

[1] γοητευομένων Φ² vulg.: γοητευομένοις ΓΕΦ¹ΩΝΑ.

---

[1] That given to Croesus, Herod., I, 47; there was, of course, no reference to dancing in it. The maid of Pytho vaunted her knowledge of the number of the sands and the measure of the

THE DANCE

These are a very few themes that I have selected out of many, or rather out of an infinite number, and set down as the more important, leaving the rest for the poets to sing of, for the dancers themselves to present, and for you to add, finding them by their likeness to those already mentioned, all of which must lie ready, provided and stored by the dancer in advance to meet every occasion.

Since he is imitative and undertakes to present by means of movements all that is being sung, it is essential for him, as for the orators, to cultivate clearness, so that everything which he presents will be intelligible, requiring no interpreter. No, in the words of the Delphic oracle,[1] whosoever beholds dancing must be able " to understand the mute and hear the silent " dancer.

That is just what happened, they say, in the case of Demetrius the Cynic. He too was denouncing the dance just as you do, saying that the dancer was a mere adjunct to the flute and the pipes and the stamping, himself contributing nothing to the presentation but making absolutely meaningless, idle movements with no sense in them at all; but that people were duped by the accessories of the business—the silk vestments, the beautiful mask, the flute and its quavers, and the sweet voices of the singers, by all of which the dancer's business, itself amounting to nothing at all, was embellished. Thereupon the dancer at that time, under Nero,

sea and her ability to understand the mute and hear the silent, before demonstrating her power by replying to the test-question " What is Croesus now doing " with the answer that she could smell turtle and lamb boiling in a bronze pot with a lid of bronze. That response, we are told, hit the mark.

THE WORKS OF LUCIAN

ἀσύνετος, ὥς φασιν, ἀλλ' εἰ καί τις ἄλλος ἔν τε
ἱστορίας μνήμη καὶ κινήσεως κάλλει διενεγκών,
ἐδεήθη τοῦ Δημητρίου εὐγνωμονεστάτην, οἶμαι,
τὴν δέησιν, ἰδεῖν ὀρχούμενον, ἔπειτα κατηγορεῖν
αὐτοῦ· καὶ ὑπέσχετό γε ἄνευ αὐλοῦ καὶ ἀσμάτων
ἐπιδείξεσθαι αὐτῷ. καὶ οὕτως ἐποίησεν· ἡσυχίαν
γὰρ τοῖς τε κτυποῦσι καὶ τοῖς αὐλοῦσι καὶ αὐτῷ
παραγγείλας τῷ χορῷ, αὐτὸς ἐφ' ἑαυτοῦ ὠρχήσατο
τὴν Ἀφροδίτης καὶ Ἄρεος μοιχείαν, Ἥλιον
μηνύοντα καὶ Ἥφαιστον ἐπιβουλεύοντα καὶ τοῖς
δεσμοῖς ἀμφοτέρους, τήν τε Ἀφροδίτην καὶ τὸν
Ἄρη, σαγηνεύοντα, καὶ τοὺς ἐφεστῶτας θεοὺς
ἕκαστον αὐτῶν, καὶ αἰδουμένην μὲν τὴν Ἀφροδίτην,
ὑποδεδοικότα[1] δὲ καὶ ἱκετεύοντα τὸν Ἄρη, καὶ
ὅσα τῇ ἱστορίᾳ ταύτῃ πρόσεστιν, ὥστε τὸν
Δημήτριον ὑπερησθέντα τοῖς γιγνομένοις τοῦτον
ἔπαινον ἀποδοῦναι τὸν μέγιστον τῷ ὀρχηστῇ·
ἀνέκραγε γὰρ καὶ μεγάλῃ τῇ φωνῇ ἀνεφθέγξατο,
" Ἀκούω, ἄνθρωπε, ἃ ποιεῖς· οὐχ ὁρῶ μόνον,
ἀλλά μοι δοκεῖς ταῖς χερσὶν αὐταῖς λαλεῖν."

64 Ἐπεὶ δὲ κατὰ τὸν Νέρωνά ἐσμεν τῷ λόγῳ,
βούλομαι καὶ βαρβάρου ἀνδρὸς τὸ ἐπὶ τοῦ αὐτοῦ
ὀρχηστοῦ γενόμενον εἰπεῖν, ὅπερ μέγιστος ἔπαινος
ὀρχηστικῆς γένοιτ' ἄν. τῶν γὰρ ἐκ τοῦ Πόντου
βαρβάρων βασιλικός τις ἄνθρωπος κατά τι χρέος
ἥκων ὡς τὸν Νέρωνα ἐθεᾶτο μετὰ τῶν ἄλλων
τὸν ὀρχηστὴν ἐκεῖνον οὕτω σαφῶς ὀρχούμενον
ὡς καίτοι μὴ ἐπακούοντα τῶν ἀδομένων—ἡμίελλην
γάρ τις ὢν ἐτύγχανεν—συνεῖναι ἁπάντων. καὶ

[1] ὑποδεδυκότα Γ[1]Ε.

in high repute, who was no fool, they say, and
excelled, if ever a man did, in remembrance of
legends and beauty of movement,[1] made a request
of Demetrius that was very reasonable, I think—to
see him dancing and then accuse him; he promised,
indeed, to perform for him without flute or songs.
That is what he did; enjoining silence upon the
stampers and flute-players and upon the chorus
itself, quite unsupported, he danced the amours of
Aphrodite and Ares, Helius tattling, Hephaestus
laying his plot and trapping both of them with his
entangling bonds, the gods who came in on them,
portrayed individually, Aphrodite ashamed, Ares
seeking cover and begging for mercy, and everything
that belongs to this story,[2] in such wise that Demetrius
was delighted beyond measure with what was taking
place and paid the highest possible tribute to the
dancer; he raised his voice and shouted at the top
of his lungs: " I hear the story that you are acting,
man, I do not just see it; you seem to me to be
talking with your very hands! "

Since we are under Nero in fancy, I wish to tell
the remark of a barbarian concerning the same
dancer, which may be considered a very great tribute
to his art. One of the barbarians from Pontus, a
man of royal blood, came to Nero on some business
or other, and among other entertainments saw that
dancer perform so vividly that although he could
not follow what was being sung—he was but half
Hellenised, as it happened—he understood every-

[1] Probably the first of the several famous dancers who took
Paris as their stage name, of whom the emperor, some said,
was so jealous that he put him to death (Suetonius, *Nero*, 54).

[2] Homer, *Odyssey*, VIII, 266-320; cf. Lucian, *Deor. Dial.*,
21 (17).

δὴ ἀπιὼν ἤδη ἐς τὴν οἰκείαν,[1] τοῦ Νέρωνος
δεξιουμένου καὶ ὅ τι βούλοιτο αἰτεῖν κελεύοντος
καὶ δώσειν ὑπισχνουμένου, " Τὸν ὀρχηστήν,"
ἔφη, " δοὺς τὰ μέγιστα εὐφρανεῖς." τοῦ δὲ Νέρωνος ἐρομένου, " Τί ἄν σοι χρήσιμος γένοιτο ἐκεῖ ; "
" Προσοίκους," ἔφη, " βαρβάρους ἔχω, οὐχ ὁμο-
γλώττους, καὶ ἑρμηνέων οὐ ῥᾴδιον εὑπορεῖν πρὸς
αὐτούς. ἢν οὖν τινος δέωμαι, διανεύων οὗτος
ἕκαστά μοι ἑρμηνεύσει." τοσοῦτον ἄρα καθίκετο
αὐτοῦ ἡ μίμησις τῆς ὀρχήσεως ἐπίσημός τε καὶ
σαφὴς φανεῖσα.

65 Ἡ δὲ πλείστη διατριβὴ καὶ ὁ σκοπὸς τῆς ὀρχηστικῆς ἡ ὑπόκρισίς ἐστιν, ὡς ἔφην, κατὰ τὰ αὐτὰ
καὶ τοῖς ῥήτορσιν ἐπιτηδευομένη, καὶ μάλιστα τοῖς
τὰς καλουμένας ταύτας μελέτας διεξιοῦσιν· οὐδὲν
γοῦν καὶ ἐν ἐκείνοις μᾶλλον ἐπαινοῦμεν ἢ τὸ[2]
ἐοικέναι τοῖς ὑποκειμένοις προσώποις καὶ μὴ ἀπῳδὰ
εἶναι τὰ λεγόμενα τῶν εἰσαγομένων ἀριστέων ἢ
τυραννοκτόνων ἢ πενήτων ἢ γεωργῶν, ἀλλ' ἐν
ἑκάστῳ τούτων τὸ ἴδιον καὶ τὸ ἐξαίρετον δείκνυσθαι.

66 Ἐθέλω γοῦν σοι καὶ ἄλλου βαρβάρου ῥῆσιν ἐπὶ
τούτοις εἰπεῖν. ἰδὼν γὰρ πέντε πρόσωπα τῷ
ὀρχηστῇ παρεσκευασμένα—τοσούτων γὰρ μερῶν
τὸ δρᾶμα ἦν—ἐζήτει, ἕνα ὁρῶν τὸν ὀρχηστήν,
τίνες οἱ ὀρχησόμενοι καὶ ὑποκρινούμενοι τὰ λοιπὰ
προσωπεῖα εἶεν· ἐπεὶ δὲ ἔμαθεν ὅτι αὐτὸς[3]
ὑποκρινεῖται καὶ ὑπορχήσεται τὰ πάντα, " Ἐλελήθεις," ἔφη, " ὦ βέλτιστε, σῶμα μὲν τοῦτο ἕν,
πολλὰς δὲ τὰς ψυχὰς ἔχων."

---

[1] οἰκίαν MSS, corrected by Jacobitz.
[2] Text Madvig: οἶδε(ν) γοῦν καὶ ἐν ἐκείνοις μᾶλλον ἐπαινου-
μένη τὸ (τῷ) MSS.

thing. So when it came to be time for him to go back to his own country, Nero, in saying good-bye, urged him to ask for anything that he wanted, and promised to give it him. "If you give me the dancer," said he, "you will please me mightily!" When Nero asked, "What good would he be to you there?", he replied, "I have barbarian neighbours who do not speak the same language, and it is not easy to keep supplied with interpreters for them. If I am in want of one, therefore, this man will interpret everything for me by signs." So deeply had he been impressed by that disclosure of the distinctness and lucidity of the mimicry of the dance.

The chief occupation and the aim of dancing, as I have said, is impersonating, which is cultivated in the same way by the rhetoricians, particularly those who recite these pieces that they call " exercises "; for in their case also there is nothing which we commend more highly than their accommodating themselves to the rôles which they assume, so that what they say is not inappropriate to the princes or tyrant-slayers or poor people or farmers whom they introduce, but in each of these what is individual and distinctive is presented.

In that connection I should like to tell you something that was said by another barbarian. Noticing that the dancer had five masks ready—the drama had that number of acts—since he saw but the one dancer, he enquired who were to dance and act the other rôles, and when he learned that the dancer himself was to act and dance them all, he said; " I did not realise, my friend, that though you have only this one body, you have many souls."

---

³ ὁ αὐτὸς N, edd.

67 Ταῦτα μὲν ὁ βάρβαρος. οὐκ ἀπεικότως δὲ καὶ
οἱ Ἰταλιῶται τὸν ὀρχηστὴν παντόμιμον καλοῦσιν,
ἀπὸ τοῦ δρωμένου σχεδόν. καλὴ γὰρ ἡ ποιητικὴ
παραίνεσις ἐκείνη, τό, " ὦ παῖ, ποντίου θηρὸς
πετραίου νόον ἔχων [1] πάσαις πολίεσσιν ὁμίλει,"
καὶ τῷ ὀρχηστῇ ἀναγκαία· καὶ δεῖ προσφύντα τοῖς
πράγμασιν συνοικειοῦν [2] ἑαυτὸν ἑκάστῳ τῶν δρωμένων.

Τὸ δὲ ὅλον ἤθη καὶ πάθη δείξειν καὶ ὑποκρινεῖ-
σθαι ἡ ὄρχησις ἐπαγγέλλεται, νῦν μὲν ἐρῶντα,
νῦν δὲ ὀργιζόμενόν τινα εἰσάγουσα, καὶ ἄλλον
μεμηνότα καὶ ἄλλον λελυπημένον, καὶ ἅπαντα
ταῦτα μεμετρημένως. τὸ γοῦν παραδοξότατον,
τῆς αὐτῆς ἡμέρας ἄρτι μὲν Ἀθάμας μεμηνώς,
ἄρτι δὲ Ἰνὼ φοβουμένη δείκνυται, καὶ ἄλλοτε
Ἀτρεὺς ὁ αὐτός, καὶ μετὰ μικρὸν Θυέστης, εἶτα
Αἴγισθος ἢ Ἀερόπη· καὶ πάντα ταῦτα εἷς ἄνθρω-
πός ἐστιν.

68 Τὰ μὲν οὖν ἄλλα θεάματα καὶ ἀκούσματα
ἑνὸς ἑκάστου ἔργου τὴν ἐπίδειξιν ἔχει· ἢ γὰρ
αὐλός ἐστιν ἢ κιθάρα ἢ διὰ φωνῆς μελῳδία ἢ
τραγικὴ δραματουργία ἢ κωμικὴ γελωτοποιία·
ὁ δὲ ὀρχηστὴς τὰ πάντα ἔχει συλλαβών, καὶ
ἔνεστιν ποικίλην καὶ παμμιγῆ τὴν παρασκευὴν
αὐτοῦ ἰδεῖν, αὐλόν, σύριγγα, ποδῶν κτύπον,
κυμβάλου ψόφον, ὑποκριτοῦ εὐφωνίαν, ᾀδόντων
ὁμοφωνίαν.

---

[1] ἔχων ΓΦΝΕΑ : ἴσχων vulg. The quotation is inexact, and
less complete than in *Athen.*, XII, 513 c: ὦ τέκνον, ποντίου
θηρὸς πετραίου χρωτὶ μάλιστα νόον, προσφέρων πάσαις πολίεσσιν
ὁμίλει.

[2] συνοικειοῦν vulg. : συνοικεῖν MSS.

THE DANCE

Well, that is the way the barbarian viewed it. And the Greeks of Italy quite appropriately call the dancer a pantomime, precisely in consequence of what he does.[1] That poetical precept,[2] " My son, in your converse with all cities keep the way of the sea-creature that haunts the rocks," is excellent, and for the dancer essential ; he must cleave close to his matters and conform himself to each detail of his plots.

In general, the dancer undertakes to present and enact characters and emotions, introducing now a lover and now an angry person, one man afflicted with madness, another with grief, and all this within fixed bounds. Indeed, the most surprising part of it is that within the selfsame day at one moment we are shown Athamas in a frenzy, at another Ino in terror ; presently the same person is Atreus, and after a little, Thyestes ; then Aegisthus, or Aerope ; yet they all are but a single man.

Moreover, the other performances that appeal to eye and ear contain, each of them, the display of a single activity ; there is either flute or lyre or vocal music or tragedy's mummery or comedy's buffoonery. The dancer, however, has everything at once, and that equipment of his, we may see, is varied and comprehensive—the flute, the pipes, the tapping of feet, the clash of cymbals, the melodious voice of the actor,[3] the concord of the singers.

[1] The name signifies one who mimics everything.

[2] Pindar, Fr. 43 (173) Schroeder ; the reference is to the cuttle, which was supposed to take protective colouring to match its background. Cf. Theognis, 215–218.

[3] The actor (there seems to have been but one) supported the dancer by assuming secondary rôles like the " Odysseus" mentioned below (p. 285). Cf. also p. 394, n. 1, and p. 402, n. 1.

69 Ἔτι δὲ τὰ μὲν ἄλλα θατέρου τῶν ἐν τῷ ἀνθρώπῳ
ἔργα ἐστίν, τὰ μὲν ψυχῆς, τὰ δὲ σώματος· ἐν δὲ
τῇ ὀρχήσει ἀμφότερα συμμέμικται. καὶ γὰρ
διανοίας ἐπίδειξιν τὰ γιγνόμενα ἔχει καὶ σωματικῆς
ἀσκήσεως ἐνέργειαν, τὸ δὲ μέγιστον ἡ σοφία
τῶν δρωμένων καὶ τὸ [1] μηδὲν ἔξω λόγου. Λε-
σβῶναξ γοῦν ὁ Μυτιληναῖος, ἀνὴρ καλὸς καὶ
ἀγαθός, χειρισόφους τοὺς ὀρχηστὰς ἀπεκάλει καὶ
ᾔει ἐπὶ τὴν θέαν αὐτῶν ὡς βελτίων ἀναστρέψων
ἀπὸ τοῦ θεάτρου. Τιμοκράτης δὲ ὁ διδάσκαλος
αὐτοῦ ἰδών ποτε ἅπαξ, οὐκ ἐξεπίτηδες ἐπιστάς,
ὀρχηστὴν τὰ αὐτοῦ ποιοῦντα, " Οἵου με," ἔφη
" θεάματος ἡ πρὸς φιλοσοφίαν αἰδὼς ἀπεστέρηκεν."

70 Εἰ δ' ἔστιν ἀληθῆ ἃ περὶ ψυχῆς ὁ Πλάτων λέγει,
τὰ τρία μέρη αὐτῆς καλῶς ὁ ὀρχηστὴς δείκνυσιν,
τὸ θυμικὸν ὅταν ὀργιζόμενον ἐπιδείκνυται, τὸ
ἐπιθυμητικὸν ὅταν ἐρῶντας ὑποκρίνηται, τὸ λογι-
στικὸν ὅταν ἕκαστα τῶν παθῶν χαλιναγωγῇ·
τοῦτο μέν γε ἐν ἅπαντι μέρει τῆς ὀρχήσεως καθάπερ ἡ ἁφὴ ἐν ταῖς αἰσθήσεσιν παρέσπαρται.[2]
κάλλους δὲ προνοῶν καὶ τῆς ἐν τοῖς ὀρχήμασιν
εὐμορφίας, τί ἄλλο ἢ τὸ τοῦ Ἀριστοτέλους
ἐπαληθεύει, τὸ κάλλος ἐπαινοῦντος καὶ μέρος
τρίτον ἡγουμένου τἀγαθοῦ καὶ τοῦτο εἶναι;
ἤκουσα δέ τινος καὶ περιττότερόν τι νεανιευομένου

---

[1] τὸ N only.   [2] κατέσπαρται A.

---

[1] Because of their extensive use of gestures. For the word
see also *Rhet. Praec.*, 17 (Vol. IV, p. 157), where it is recom-
mended by the sophist, and *Lexiph.*, 14 (p. 312 of this volume),
where it is used by Lexiphanes.
[2] *Republic*, IV, 436–441.

Then, too, all the rest are activities of one or the other of the two elements in man, some of them activities of the soul, some of the body; but in dancing both are combined. For there is display of mind in the performance as well as expression of bodily development, and the most important part of it is the wisdom that controls the action, and the fact that nothing is irrational. Indeed, Lesbonax of Mytilene, a man of excellent parts, called dancers "handiwise," [1] and used to go to see them with the expectation of returning from the theatre a better man. Timocrates, too, his teacher, one day, for the sole and only time, came in by chance, saw a dancer ply his trade and said: "What a treat for the eyes my reverence for philosophy has deprived me of!'

If what Plato [2] says about the soul is true, the three parts of it are excellently set forth by the dancer —the orgillous part when he exhibits a man in a rage, the covetous part when he enacts lovers, and the reasoning part when he bridles and governs each of the different passions; this last, to be sure, is disseminated through every portion of the dance just as touch is disseminated through the other senses. [3] And in planning for beauty and for symmetry in the figures of the dance, what else does he do but confirm the words of Aristotle, who praised beauty and considered it to be one of the three parts of the chief good? [4] Moreover, I have heard a man express an excessively venturesome opinion

---

[3] Touch was considered not only a separate faculty, but an element in the activity of the other four senses, each of which was regarded as based in some sort upon physical contact; for the method of explanation see Lucretius, IV, 324–721.

[4] Aristotle, *Eth. Nicom.*, I, 8.

THE WORKS OF LUCIAN

ὑπὲρ τῆς τῶν ὀρχηστικῶν προσωπείων σιωπῆς,
ὅτι καὶ αὕτη Πυθαγορικόν τι δόγμα αἰνίττεται.

71 Ἔτι δὲ τῶν ἄλλων ἐπιτηδευμάτων τῶν μὲν τὸ
τερπνόν, τῶν δὲ τὸ χρήσιμον ὑπισχνουμένων,
μόνη ὄρχησις ἄμφω ἔχει, καὶ πολύ γε τὸ χρήσιμον
ὠφελιμώτερον ὅσῳ μετὰ τοῦ τερπνοῦ γίγνεται.
πόσῳ γὰρ τοῦτο ὁρᾶν ἥδιον ἢ πυκτεύοντας νεανί-
σκους καὶ αἵματι ῥεομένους, καὶ παλαίοντας
ἄλλους ἐν κόνει, οὓς ἡ ὄρχησις πολλάκις ἀσφαλέστερον ἅμα καὶ εὐμορφότερον καὶ τερπνότερον
ἐπιδείκνυται. τὴν μὲν οὖν γε σύντονον κίνησιν
τῆς ὀρχηστικῆς καὶ στροφὰς αὐτῆς καὶ περιαγωγὰς
καὶ πηδήματα καὶ ὑπτιασμοὺς τοῖς μὲν ἄλλοις
τερπνὰ εἶναι συμβέβηκεν ὁρῶσιν, τοῖς δὲ ἐνερ-
γοῦσιν αὐτοῖς ὑγιεινότατα· γυμνασίων γὰρ τὸ
κάλλιστόν τε ἅμα καὶ εὐρυθμότατον τοῦτο φαίην
ἂν ἔγωγε εἶναι, μαλάττον μὲν τὸ σῶμα καὶ κάμπτον
καὶ κουφίζον καὶ εὐχερὲς εἶναι πρὸς μεταβολὴν
διδάσκον, ἰσχύν τε οὐ μικρὰν περιποιοῦν τοῖς
σώμασιν.

72 Πῶς οὖν οὐ παναρμόνιόν τι χρῆμα ὄρχησις,
θήγουσα μὲν τὴν ψυχήν, ἀσκοῦσα δὲ καὶ τὸ σῶμα,
τέρπουσα δὲ τοὺς ὁρῶντας, διδάσκουσα δὲ πολλὰ
τῶν πάλαι ὑπ' αὐλοῖς καὶ κυμβάλοις καὶ μελῶν
εὐρυθμίᾳ καὶ κηλήσει διά τε ὀφθαλμῶν καὶ ἀκοῆς ;
εἴτ' οὖν[1] φωνῆς εὐμοιρίαν ζητεῖς, ποῦ ἂν ἀλλαχόθι
εὕροις, ἢ ποῖον πολυφωνότερον ἄκουσμα ἢ ἐμμελέ-
στερον ; εἴτε αὐλοῦ καὶ σύριγγος τὸ λιγυρώτερον,

[1] εἴτ' οὖν Fritzsche: εἰ γοῦν MSS.

274

about the silence of the characters in the dance, to the effect that it was symbolic of a Pythagorean tenet.[1]

Again, some of the other pursuits promise to give pleasure and others profit, but only the dance has both; and indeed the profit in it is far more beneficial for being associated with pleasure. How much more delightful it is to see than young men boxing, astream with blood, and other young men wrestling in the dust! Why, the dance often presents them in a way that is less risky and at the same time more beautiful and pleasurable. As to the energetic movement of the dance, its twists and turns and leaps and back-flung poses, they are really not only pleasurable to the spectators, but highly healthful for the performers themselves. I should call it the most excellent and best balanced of gymnastic exercises, since besides making the body soft, supple and light, and teaching it to be adroit in shifting, it also contributes no little strength.

Then why is not dancing a thing of utter harmony, putting a fine edge upon the soul, disciplining the body, delighting the beholders and teaching them much that happened of old, to the accompaniment of flute and cymbals and cadenced song and magic that works its spell through eye and ear alike? If it is felicity of the human voice that you seek, where else can you find it or what can you hear that is more richly vocal or more melodious? If it is the high-pitched music of the flute or of the syrinx,

[1] Cf. Athenaeus, I, 20 D, speaking of the dancer Memphis: " He discloses what the Pythagorean philosophy is, revealing everything to us in silence more clearly than those who profess themselves teachers of the art of speech."

ἅλις καὶ τούτων ἐν ὀρχήσει ἀπολαῦσαί σοι πάρεστιν.
ἐῶ λέγειν ὡς ἀμείνων τὸ ἦθος ὁμιλῶν τῇ τοιαύτῃ
θέᾳ γενήσῃ, ὅταν ὁρᾷς[1] τὸ θέατρον μισοῦν μὲν τὰ
κακῶς γιγνόμενα, ἐπιδακρῦον δὲ τοῖς ἀδικουμένοις,
καὶ ὅλως τὰ ἤθη τῶν ὁρώντων παιδαγωγοῦν.

73 ὃ δέ ἐστι μάλιστα ἐπὶ τῶν ὀρχηστῶν ἐπαινέσαι, τοῦτο ἤδη ἐρῶ· τὸ γὰρ ἰσχύν τε ἅμα καὶ
ὑγρότητα τῶν μελῶν ἐπιτηδεύειν ὁμοίως παράδοξον εἶναί μοι δοκεῖ ὡς εἴ τις ἐν τῷ αὐτῷ καὶ
Ἡρακλέους τὸ καρτερὸν καὶ Ἀφροδίτης τὸ ἁβρὸν
δεικνύοι.

74 Ἐθέλω δὲ ἤδη καὶ ὑποδεῖξαί σοι τῷ λόγῳ ὁποῖον
χρὴ εἶναι τὸν ἄριστον ὀρχηστὴν ἔν τε ψυχῇ καὶ
σώματι. καίτοι τῆς μὲν ψυχῆς προεῖπον τὰ πλεῖ-
στα· μνημονικόν τε γὰρ εἶναι[2] καὶ εὐφυᾶ καὶ
συνετὸν καὶ ὀξὺν ἐπινοῆσαι καὶ καιροῦ μάλιστα
ἐστοχάσθαι φημὶ δεῖν αὐτόν, ἔτι δὲ κριτικόν τε
ποιημάτων καὶ ᾀσμάτων καὶ μελῶν τῶν ἀρίστων
διαγνωστικὸν καὶ τῶν κακῶς πεποιημένων ἐλεγ-

75 κτικόν. τὸ δὲ σῶμα κατὰ τὸν Πολυκλείτου
κανόνα ἤδη ἐπιδείξειν μοι δοκῶ· μήτε γὰρ
ὑψηλὸς ἄγαν ἔστω καὶ πέρα τοῦ μετρίου ἐπιμήκης
μήτε ταπεινὸς καὶ νανώδης τὴν φύσιν, ἀλλ'
ἔμμετρος ἀκριβῶς, οὔτε πολύσαρκος, ἀπίθανον
γάρ, οὔτε λεπτὸς ἐς ὑπερβολήν· σκελετῶδες τοῦτο
καὶ νεκρικόν.

76 Ἐθέλω γοῦν σοι καὶ δήμου τινὸς οὐ φαύλου τὰ
τοιαῦτα ἐπισημαίνεσθαι βοὰς εἰπεῖν· οἱ γὰρ
Ἀντιοχεῖς, εὐφυεστάτη πόλις καὶ ὄρχησιν μάλιστα
πρεσβεύουσα, οὕτως ἐπιτηρεῖ τῶν λεγομένων καὶ
τῶν γιγνομένων ἕκαστα, ὡς μηδένα μηδὲν αὐτῶν

---

[1] ὁρᾷς μὲν τὸ ΓΝΕΑ.   [2] εἶναι Harmon : not in MSS.

in the dance you may enjoy that also to the full. I
forbear to mention that you will become better in
character through familiarity with such a spectacle,
when you see the assembly detesting misdeeds, weeping over victims of injustice, and in general schooling the characters of the individual spectators. But
let me tell you in conclusion what is particularly to
be commended in our dancers: that they cultivate
equally both strength and suppleness of limb seems
to me as amazing as if the might of Heracles and
the daintiness of Aphrodite were to be manifested
in the same person.

I wish now to depict for you in words what a good
dancer should be like in mind and in body. To be
sure, I have already mentioned most of his mental
qualities. I hold, you know, that he should be
retentive of memory, gifted, intelligent, keenly
inventive, and above all successful in doing the
right thing at the right time; besides, he should be
able to judge poetry, to select the best songs and
melodies, and to reject worthless compositions.
What I propose to unveil now is his body, which will
conform to the canon of Polyclitus. It must be
neither very tall and inordinately lanky, nor short
and dwarfish in build, but exactly the right measure,
without being either fat, which would be fatal to
any illusion, or excessively thin; for that would
suggest skeletons and corpses.

To illustrate, I should like to tell you about the
cat-calls of a certain populace that is not slow to
mark such points. The people of Antioch, a very
talented city which especially honours the dance,
keep such an eye upon everything that is done and
said that nothing ever escapes a man of them. When

διαλανθάνειν. μικροῦ μὲν γὰρ ὀρχηστοῦ εἰσελ-
θόντος καὶ τὸν Ἕκτορα ὀρχουμένου μιᾷ φωνῇ
πάντες ἀνεβόησαν, " ˟Ω[1] Ἀστυάναξ, Ἕκτωρ δὲ
ποῦ ; " ἄλλοτε δέ ποτε μηκίστου τινὸς ὑπὲρ τὸ
μέτριον ὀρχεῖσθαι τὸν Καπανέα ἐπιχειροῦντος καὶ
προσβάλλειν τοῖς Θηβαίων τείχεσιν, " Ὑπέρβηθι,"
ἔφησαν, " τὸ τεῖχος, οὐδέν σοι δεῖ κλίμακος."
καὶ ἐπὶ τοῦ παχέος δὲ καὶ πιμελοῦς ὀρχηστοῦ
πηδᾶν μεγάλα πειρωμένου, " Δεόμεθα," ἔφασαν,
" φεῖσαι[2] τῆς θυμέλης." τὸ δὲ ἐναντίον τῷ πάνυ
λεπτῷ ἐπεβόησαν, " Καλῶς ἔχε," ὡς νοσοῦντι.
τούτων οὐ τοῦ γελοίου ἕνεκα ἐπεμνήσθην,[3] ἀλλ᾽
ὡς ἴδῃς ὅτι καὶ δῆμοι ὅλοι μεγάλην σπουδὴν
ἐποιήσαντο ἐπὶ τῇ ὀρχηστικῇ, ὡς ῥυθμίζειν τὰ
καλὰ καὶ τὰ αἰσχρὰ αὐτῆς δύνασθαι.

77 Εὐκίνητος δὲ τὸ μετὰ τοῦτο πάντως ἔστω καὶ
τὸ σῶμα λελυμένος τε ἅμα καὶ συμπεπηγώς,
ὡς λυγίζεσθαί τε ὅπη καιρὸς καὶ συνεστάναι
78 καρτερῶς, εἰ τούτου δέοι. ὅτι δὲ οὐκ ἀπήλλακται
ὄρχησις καὶ τῆς ἐναγωνίου χειρονομίας ἀλλὰ μετέχει
καὶ τῶν Ἑρμοῦ καὶ Πολυδεύκους καὶ Ἡρακλέους
ἐν ἀθλήσει καλῶν ἴδοις ἂν ἑκάστῃ τῶν μιμήσεων
ἐπισχών.

Ἡροδότῳ μὲν οὖν τὰ δι᾽ ὀμμάτων φαινόμενα
πιστότερα εἶναι τῶν ὤτων δοκεῖ· ὀρχήσει δὲ καὶ
τὰ ὤτων καὶ ὀφθαλμῶν πρόσεστιν. οὕτω δὲ
79 θέλγει ὄρχησις ὥστε ἂν ἐρῶν τις εἰς τὸ θέατρον
παρέλθοι, ἐσωφρονίσθη ἰδὼν ὅσα ἔρωτος κακὰ
τέλη· καὶ λύπῃ ἐχόμενος ἐξέρχεται τοῦ θεάτρου

---

[1] ὦ Harmon: ὡς MSS. σὺ Fritzsche, ὅδ᾽ Bekker.
[2] φεῖσαι ΓΩ: φεῖσθαι Ε, πεφεῖσθαι ΝΑ.
[3] ὑπεμνήσθην ΓΕ.

a diminutive dancer made his entrance and began
to play Hector, they all cried out in a single voice,
" Ho there, Astyanax! where is Hector?" On
another occasion, when a man who was extremely tall
undertook to dance Capaneus and assault the walls
of Thebes, " Step over the wall," they said, " you
have no need of a ladder!" And in the case of the
plump and heavy dancer who tried to make great
leaps, they said, " We beg you, spare the stage!"
On the other hand, to one who was very thin they
called out: " Good health to you," as if he were ill.
It is not for the joke's sake that I have mentioned
these comments, but to let you see that entire
peoples have taken a great interest in the art of
dancing, so that they could regulate its good and
bad points.

In the next place, the dancer must by all means
be agile and at once loose-jointed and well-knit, so
as to bend like a withe as occasion arises and to be
stubbornly firm if that should be requisite. That
dancing does not differ widely from the use of the
hands which figures in the public games—that it has
something in common with the noble sport of Hermes
and Pollux and Heracles, you may note by observing
each of its mimic portrayals.

Herodotus says that what is apprehended through
the eyes is more trustworthy than hearing;[1] but
dancing possesses what appeals to ear and eye alike.
Its spell, too, is so potent that if a lover enters the
theatre, he is restored to his right mind by seeing all
the evil consequences of love; and one who is in the
clutch of grief leaves the theatre in brighter mood,

---

[1] Herodotus, I, 8.

φαιδρότερος ὥσπερ τι φάρμακον ληθεδανὸν καὶ
κατὰ τὸν ποιητὴν νηπενθές τε καὶ ἄχολον πιών.
σημεῖον δὲ τῆς πρὸς τὰ γιγνόμενα οἰκειότητος
καὶ τοῦ γνωρίζειν ἕκαστον τῶν ὁρώντων τὰ δεικνύ-
μενα τὸ καὶ δακρύειν πολλάκις τοὺς θεατάς,
ὁπόταν τι οἰκτρὸν καὶ ἐλεεινὸν φαίνηται. ἡ μέν
γε Βακχικὴ ὄρχησις ἐν Ἰωνίᾳ μάλιστα καὶ ἐν
Πόντῳ σπουδαζομένη, καίτοι σατυρικὴ οὖσα,
οὕτω κεχείρωται τοὺς ἀνθρώπους τοὺς ἐκεῖ
ὥστε κατὰ τὸν τεταγμένον ἕκαστοι καιρόν, ἁπάντων
ἐπιλαθόμενοι τῶν ἄλλων, κάθηνται δι᾽ ἡμέρας
τιτᾶνας καὶ κορύβαντας καὶ σατύρους καὶ βου-
κόλους ὁρῶντες. καὶ ὀρχοῦνταί γε ταῦτα οἱ
εὐγενέστατοι καὶ πρωτεύοντες ἐν ἑκάστῃ τῶν
πόλεων, οὐχ ὅπως αἰδούμενοι ἀλλὰ καὶ μέγα φρο-
νοῦντες ἐπὶ τῷ πράγματι μᾶλλον ἤπερ[1] ἐπ᾽
εὐγενείαις καὶ λειτουργίαις καὶ ἀξιώμασι προγονι-
κοῖς.

80 Ἐπεὶ δὲ τὰς ἀρετὰς ἔφην τὰς ὀρχηστικάς,
ἄκουε καὶ τὰς κακίας αὐτῶν. τὰς μὲν οὖν ἐν
σώματι ἤδη ἔδειξα, τὰς δὲ τῆς διανοίας οὕτως
ἐπιτηρεῖν, οἶμαι, δύναιο ἄν. πολλοὶ γὰρ αὐτῶν
ὑπ᾽ ἀμαθίας—ἀμήχανον γὰρ ἅπαντας εἶναι σοφούς—
καὶ σολοικίας δεινὰς ἐν τῇ ὀρχήσει ἐπιδείκνυνται,
οἱ μὲν ἄλογα κινούμενοι καὶ μηδέν, ὥς φασι,
πρὸς τὴν χορδήν, ἕτερα μὲν γὰρ ὁ πούς, ἕτερα
δ᾽ ὁ ῥυθμὸς λέγει· οἱ δὲ εὔρυθμα μέν, τὰ πράγματα
δὲ μετάχρονα ἢ πρόχρονα, οἷον ἐγώ ποτε ἰδὼν
μέμνημαι. τὰς γὰρ Διὸς γονὰς ὀρχούμενός τις
καὶ τὴν τοῦ Κρόνου τεκνοφαγίαν παρωρχεῖτο

---

[1] μᾶλλον ἤπερ Fritzsche : μᾶλλόν περ ἢ MSS.

as if he had taken some potion that brings forgetfulness and, in the words of the poet, " surcease from
sorrow and anger." [1]   An indication that each of
those who see it follows closely what is going on and
understands what is being presented lies in the fact
that the spectators often weep when anything sad
and pitiful reveals itself.   And certainly the Bacchic
dance that is especially cultivated in Ionia and in
Pontus, although it is a satyr-show, nevertheless
has so enthralled the people of those countries that
when the appointed time comes round they each and
all forget everything else and sit the whole day
looking at titans, corybantes, satyrs, and rustics.
Indeed, these parts in the dance are performed by
the men of the best birth and first rank in every one
of their cities, not only without shame but with
greater pride in the thing than in family trees and
public services and ancestral distinctions.

Now that I have spoken of the strong points of
dancers, let me tell you also of their defects.   Those
of the body, to be sure, I have already set forth;
those of the mind I think you will be able to note
with this explanation.   Many of them, through
ignorance—for it is impossible that they should all
be clever—exhibit dreadful solecisms, so to speak,
in their dancing.   Some of them make senseless
movements that have nothing to do with the harp-
string, as the saying goes; for the foot says one
thing and the music another.   Others suit their
movements to the music, but bring in their themes
too late or too soon, as in a case which I remember to
have seen one time.   A dancer who was presenting
the birth of Zeus, with Cronus eating his children,

[1] *Odyssey*, IV, 221.

τὰς Θυέστου συμφοράς, τῷ ὁμοίῳ παρηγμένος.
καὶ ἄλλος τὴν Σεμέλην ὑποκρινόμενος βαλλομένην
τῷ κεραυνῷ τὴν Γλαύκην αὐτῇ εἴκαζε μεταγενε-
στέραν οὖσαν. ἀλλ' οὐκ ἀπό γε τῶν τοιούτων
ὀρχηστῶν ὀρχήσεως αὐτῆς, οἶμαι, καταγνωστέον
οὐδὲ τὸ ἔργον αὐτὸ μισητέον, ἀλλὰ τοὺς μέν,
ὥσπερ εἰσίν, ἀμαθεῖς νομιστέον, ἐπαινετέον δὲ
τοὺς ἐννόμως καὶ κατὰ ῥυθμὸν τῆς τέχνης ἱκανῶς
ἕκαστα δρῶντας.

81   Ὅλως δὲ τὸν ὀρχηστὴν δεῖ πανταχόθεν ἀπηκρι-
βῶσθαι, ὡς εἶναι τὸ πᾶν εὔρυθμον, εὔμορφον,
σύμμετρον, αὐτὸ αὑτῷ ἐοικός, ἀσυκοφάντητον,
ἀνεπίληπτον, μηδαμῶς ἐλλιπές, ἐκ τῶν ἀρίστων
κεκραμένον, τὰς ἐνθυμήσεις ὀξύν, τὴν παιδείαν
βαθύν, τὰς ἐννοίας ἀνθρώπινον μάλιστα. ὁ γοῦν
ἔπαινος αὐτῷ τότ' ἂν γίγνοιτο ἐντελὴς παρὰ τῶν
θεατῶν ὅταν ἕκαστος τῶν ὁρώντων γνωρίζῃ τὰ
αὑτοῦ, μᾶλλον δὲ ὥσπερ ἐν κατόπτρῳ τῷ ὀρχηστῇ[1]
ἑαυτὸν βλέπῃ καὶ ἃ πάσχειν αὐτὸς καὶ ἃ ποιεῖν
εἴωθεν· τότε γὰρ οὐδὲ κατέχειν ἑαυτοὺς οἱ
ἄνθρωποι ὑφ' ἡδονῆς δύνανται, ἀλλ' ἀθρόοι πρὸς
τὸν ἔπαινον ἐκχέονται, τὰς τῆς ἑαυτοῦ ψυχῆς
ἕκαστος εἰκόνας ὁρῶντες καὶ αὑτοὺς γνωρίζοντες.
ἀτεχνῶς γὰρ τὸ Δελφικὸν ἐκεῖνο τὸ Γνῶθι σεαυτὸν
ἐκ τῆς θέας αὐτοῖς περιγίγνεται, καὶ ἀπέρχονται
ἀπὸ τοῦ θεάτρου ἅ τε χρὴ αἱρεῖσθαι καὶ ἃ φεύγειν
μεμαθηκότες καὶ ἃ πρότερον ἠγνόουν διδαχθέντες.

---

[1] Text E²: ὥσπερ ἐν κατόπτρῳ ὀρχηστῇ E¹ΓΑ : ὥσπερ κατόπτρῳ τῷ ὀρχηστῇ N.

went off into presenting the misfortunes of Thyestes because the similarity led him astray. And another, trying to enact Semele stricken by the thunderbolt, assimilated her to Glauce, who was of a later generation.[1] But we should not condemn the dance itself, I take it, or find fault with the activity itself on account of such dancers; we should consider them ignorant, as indeed they are, and should praise those who do everything satisfactorily, in accordance with the regulations and the rhythm of the art.[2]

In general, the dancer should be perfect in every point, so as to be wholly rhythmical, graceful, symmetrical, consistent, unexceptionable, impeccable, not wanting in any way, blent of the highest qualities, keen in his ideas, profound in his culture, and above all, human in his sentiments. In fact, the praise that he gets from the spectators will be consummate when each of those who behold him recognises his own traits, or rather sees in the dancer as in a mirror his very self, with his customary feelings and actions. Then people cannot contain themselves for pleasure, and with one accord they burst into applause, each seeing the reflection of his own soul and recognising himself. Really, that Delphic monition " Know thyself " realises itself in them from the spectacle, and when they go away from the theatre they have learned what they should choose and what avoid, and have been taught what they did not know before.

[1] The reason for confusing the two parts lay in the fact that both were burned to death, since Glauce perished by the poisoned robe which Medea sent her.

[2] Compare *Astrology* 2, where the same argument (borrowed from Plato's *Gorgias*, 456 D–457 E) is employed in defence of astrology.

82 Γίνεται δέ, ὥσπερ ἐν λόγοις, οὕτω δὲ καὶ ἐν
ὀρχήσει ἡ πρὸς τῶν πολλῶν λεγομένη κακοζηλία
ὑπερβαινόντων τὸ μέτρον τῆς μιμήσεως καὶ πέρα
τοῦ δέοντος ἐπιτεινόντων, καὶ εἰ μέγα τι δεῖξαι δέοι,
ὑπερμέγεθες ἐπιδεικνυμένων, καὶ εἰ ἁπαλόν, καθ᾽
ὑπερβολὴν θηλυνομένων, καὶ τὰ ἀνδρώδη ἄχρι τοῦ
ἀγρίου καὶ θηριώδους προαγόντων.

83 Οἷον ἐγώ ποτε μέμνημαι ἰδὼν ποιοῦντα ὀρχηστὴν
εὐδοκιμοῦντα πρότερον, συνετὸν μὲν τὰ ἄλλα καὶ
θαυμάζεσθαι ὡς ἀληθῶς ἄξιον, οὐκ οἶδα δὲ ἥτινι
τύχῃ εἰς ἀσχήμονα ὑπόκρισιν δι᾽ ὑπερβολὴν
μιμήσεως ἐξοκείλαντα. ὀρχούμενος γὰρ τὸν
Αἴαντα μετὰ τὴν ἧτταν εὐθὺς μαινόμενον, εἰς
τοσοῦτον ὑπερεξέπεσεν ὥστε οὐχ ὑποκρίνασθαι
μανίαν ἀλλὰ μαίνεσθαι αὐτὸς εἰκότως ἄν τινι
ἔδοξεν. ἑνὸς γὰρ τῶν τῷ σιδηρῷ ὑποδήματι
κτυπούντων τὴν ἐσθῆτα κατέρρηξεν, ἑνὸς δὲ τῶν
ὑπαυλούντων τὸν αὐλὸν ἁρπάσας τοῦ Ὀδυσσέως
πλησίον ἑστῶτος καὶ ἐπὶ τῇ νίκῃ μέγα φρονοῦντος
διεῖλε τὴν κεφαλὴν κατενεγκών, καὶ εἴ γε μὴ ὁ
πῖλος ἀντέσχεν καὶ τὸ πολὺ τῆς πληγῆς ἀπε-
δέξατο, ἀπωλώλει ἂν ὁ κακοδαίμων Ὀδυσσεύς,
ὀρχηστῇ παραπαίοντι περιπεσών. ἀλλὰ τό γε
θέατρον ἅπαν συνεμεμήνει τῷ Αἴαντι καὶ ἐπήδων
καὶ ἐβόων καὶ τὰς ἐσθῆτας ἀνερρίπτουν, οἱ μὲν

---

[1] Compare with this story that told of Pylades by Macrobius
(*Sat.*, II, 7, 16): cum in Hercule furente prodisset et non
nullis incessum histrioni convenientem non servare videretur,
deposita persona ridentes increpuit *μωροί, μαινόμενον
ὀρχοῦμαι.* hac fabula et sagittas iecit in populum.

THE DANCE

As in literature, so too in dancing what is generally called " bad taste " comes in when they exceed the due limit of mimicry and put forth greater effort than they should; if something large requires to be shown, they represent it as enormous; if something dainty, they make it extravagantly effeminate, and they carry masculinity to the point of savagery and bestiality.

Something of that sort, I remember, I once saw done by a dancer who until then had been in high esteem, as he was intelligent in every way and truly worth admiring; but by some ill-luck, I know not what, he wrecked his fortunes upon an ugly bit of acting through exaggerated mimicry.[1] In presenting Ajax going mad immediately after his defeat, he so overleaped himself that it might well have been thought that instead of feigning madness he was himself insane; for he tore the clothes of one of the men that beat time with the iron shoe,[2] and snatching a flute from one of the accompanists, with a vigorous blow he cracked the crown of Odysseus, who was standing near and exulting in his victory; indeed, if his watch-cap had not offered resistance and borne the brunt of the blow, poor Odysseus would have lost his life through falling in the way of a crazy dancer. The pit, however, all went mad with Ajax, leaping and shouting and flinging up their garments;

[2] A shoe with heavy sole, originally of wood, but by Lucian's time of iron (cf. Libanius, *pro saltatoribus*, 97), called in Greek κρούπεζα, in Latin *scrupeda* or *scabellum*, was worn by the flute-player or (as here) by a person specially assigned, the *scabellarius*, to mark the time for the dancer and the singers. An illustration of a flute-player wearing the *scabellum*, from a mosaic in the Vatican, will be found in Daremberg et Saglio, *Dict. des Ant.*, s.v. *scabellum* (Fig. 6142).

285

THE WORKS OF LUCIAN

συρφετώδεις καὶ αὐτὸ τοῦτο ἰδιῶται τοῦ μὲν
εὐσχήμονος οὐκ ἐστοχασμένοι οὐδὲ τὸ χεῖρον
ἢ τὸ κρεῖττον ὁρῶντες, ἄκραν δὲ μίμησιν τοῦ
πάθους τὰ τοιαῦτα οἰόμενοι εἶναι· οἱ ἀστειό-
τεροι δὲ συνιέντες μὲν καὶ αἰδούμενοι ἐπὶ τοῖς
γινομένοις, οὐκ ἐλέγχοντες δὲ σιωπῇ τὸ πρᾶγμα,
τοῖς δὲ ἐπαίνοις καὶ αὐτοὶ τὴν ἄνοιαν τῆς ὀρχήσεως
ἐπικαλύπτοντες, καὶ ἀκριβῶς ὁρῶντες ὅτι οὐκ
Αἴαντος ἀλλὰ ὀρχηστοῦ μανίας τὰ γιγνόμενα
ἦν. οὐ γὰρ ἀρκεσθεὶς τούτοις ὁ γενναῖος ἄλλο [1]
μακρῷ τούτου γελοιότερον ἔπραξε· καταβὰς
γὰρ εἰς τὸ μέσον ἐν τῇ βουλῇ δύο ὑπατικῶν μέσος
ἐκαθέζετο, πάνυ δεδιότων μὴ καὶ αὐτῶν τινα
ὥσπερ κριὸν μαστιγώσῃ λαβών.

Καὶ τὸ πρᾶγμα οἱ μὲν ἐθαύμαζον, οἱ δὲ ἐγέλων, οἱ
δὲ ὑπώπτευον μὴ ἄρα ἐκ τῆς ἄγαν μιμήσεως
εἰς τὴν τοῦ πάθους ἀλήθειαν ὑπηνέχθη. καὶ
84 αὐτὸν μέντοι φασὶν ἀνανήψαντα οὕτως μετανοῆσαι
ἐφ᾽ οἷς ἐποίησεν ὥστε καὶ νοσῆσαι ὑπὸ λύπης,
ὡς ἀληθῶς ἐπὶ μανίᾳ κατεγνωσμένον. καὶ ἐδήλωσέ
γε τοῦτο σαφῶς αὐτός· αἰτούντων γὰρ αὖθις
τῶν στασιωτῶν [2] αὐτοῦ τὸν Αἴαντα ὀρχήσασθαι
αὐτοῖς, παραιτησάμενος, "Τὸν ὑποκριτήν," ἔφη [3]
πρὸς τὸ θέατρον, "ἱκανόν ἐστιν ἅπαξ μανῆναι."
μάλιστα δὲ αὐτὸν ἠνίασεν ὁ ἀνταγωνιστὴς καὶ
ἀντίτεχνος· τοῦ γὰρ ὁμοίου Αἴαντος αὐτῷ γρα-
φέντος οὕτω κοσμίως καὶ σωφρόνως τὴν μανίαν

---

[1] ἄλλο Jacobitz: ἀλλὰ MSS. (ἄλλα . . . γελοιότερα N).
[2] συστασιωτῶν E²N.
[3] παραιτησάμενος, "Τὸν ὑποκριτήν," ἔφη Harmon: παρα-
στησάμενος τὸν ὑποκριτὴν ἔφη MSS.

THE DANCE

for the riff-raff, the absolutely unenlightened, took
no thought for propriety and could not perceive
what was good or what was bad, but thought that
sort of thing consummate mimicry of the ailment,
while the politer sort understood, to be sure, and were
ashamed of what was going on, but instead of censur-
ing the thing by silence, they themselves applauded
to cover the absurdity of the dancing, although
they perceived clearly that what went on came from
the madness of the actor, not that of Ajax.   For, not
content with all this, our hero did something else that
was far more laughable.   Coming down among the
public, he seated himself among the senators,
between two ex-consuls, who were very much afraid
that he would seize one of them and drub him, taking
him for a wether!

The thing caused some to marvel, some to laugh,
and some to suspect that perhaps in consequence of
his overdone mimicry he had fallen into the real
ailment.   Moreover, the man himself, they say,
once he had returned to his sober senses, was so
sorry for what he had done that he really became
ill through distress and in all truth was given up
for mad.   Indeed, he himself showed his repentance
clearly, for when his supporters asked him to dance
Ajax for them once more, begging to be excused,
he said to the audience, " For an actor, it is enough
to have gone mad once! " [1]   What irked him most
was that his antagonist and rival, when cast for Ajax
in the same rôle, enacted his madness so discreetly

[1] The point is that only a philosopher like Chrysippus
may go mad more than once.   Lucian delights in alluding
to the story that Chrysippus took the hellebore treatment
three times (*True Story*, II, 18; *Philosophies for Sale*, 23).

THE WORKS OF LUCIAN

ὑπεκρίνατο ὡς ἐπαινεθῆναι, μείνας ἐντὸς τῶν
τῆς ὀρχήσεως ὅρων καὶ μὴ παροινήσας εἰς τὴν
ὑπόκρισιν.

85 Ταῦτά σοι, ὦ φιλότης, ὀλίγα ἐκ παμπόλλων
παρέδειξα ὀρχήσεως ἔργα καὶ ἐπιτηδεύματα,
ὡς μὴ πάνυ ἄχθοιό μοι ἐρωτικῶς θεωμένῳ αὐτά.
εἰ δὲ βουληθείης κοινωνῆσαί μοι τῆς θέας, εὖ
οἶδα ἐγὼ πάνυ ἁλωσόμενόν σε καὶ ὀρχηστομανή-
σοντά γε προσέτι. ὥστε οὐδὲν δεήσομαι τὸ τῆς
Κίρκης ἐκεῖνο πρὸς σὲ εἰπεῖν, τό

> θαυμά μ' ἔχει ὡς οὔτι πιὼν τάδε φάρμακ'
> ἐθέλχθης,

θελχθήσῃ γάρ, καὶ μὰ Δί' οὐκ ὄνου κεφαλὴν ἢ
συὸς καρδίαν ἕξεις, ἀλλ' ὁ μὲν νόος σοι ἐμπεδώ-
τερος ἔσται, σὺ δὲ ὑφ' ἡδονῆς οὐδὲ ὀλίγον τοῦ
κυκεῶνος ἄλλῳ μεταδώσεις πιεῖν. ὅπερ γὰρ ὁ
Ὅμηρος περὶ τῆς Ἑρμοῦ ῥάβδου τῆς χρυσῆς λέγει,
ὅτι καὶ " ἀνδρῶν ὄμματα θέλγει " δι' αὐτῆς

> ὧν ἐθέλει, τοὺς δ' αὖτε καὶ ὑπνώοντας ἐγείρει,

τοῦτο ἀτεχνῶς ὄρχησις ποιεῖ καὶ τὰ ὄμματα
θέλγουσα καὶ ἐγρηγορέναι ποιοῦσα καὶ ἐπεγείρουσα
τὴν διάνοιαν πρὸς ἕκαστα τῶν δρωμένων.

ΚΡΑΤΩΝ

Καὶ μὴν ἤδη ἐγώ, ὦ Λυκῖνε, πείθομαί τέ σοι
καὶ ἀναπεπταμένα ἔχω καὶ τὰ ὦτα καὶ τὰ ὄμματα.
καὶ μέμνησό γε, ὦ φιλότης, ἐπειδὰν εἰς τὸ θέατρον
ἴῃς, κἀμοί[1] παρὰ σαυτῷ θέαν καταλαμβάνειν,
ὡς μὴ μόνος ἐκεῖθεν σοφώτερος ἡμῖν ἐπανίοις.

---

[1] κἀμοί N : καί μοι ΓΕΑ.

288

and sanely as to win praise, since he kept within the bounds of the dance and did not debauch the histrionic art.

These, my friend, are but a few out of manifold achievements and activities of the dance, and I have given you a glimpse of them in order that you may not be highly displeased with me for viewing them with ardent eyes. If you should care to join me in looking on, I know very well that you will be wholly enthralled and will even catch the dancer-craze. So I shall not need to say to you what Circe said:

" Wonder holds me to see that you drained this
    draught unenchanted." [1]

For you will be enchanted, and by Zeus it will not be any donkey's head or pig's heart that you will have, but your mind will be more firmly established and you will be so enraptured that you will not give even a tiny bit of the brew to anyone else to drink. Homer says, you know, of the golden wand of Hermes that he " charmeth the eyes of men " with it,

" Whomsoever he wishes, and others he wakes
    that are sleeping." [2]

Really, dancing does just that: it charms the eyes and makes them wide awake, and it rouses the mind to respond to every detail of its performances.

CRATO

Upon my word, Lycinus, I have come to the point of believing you and am all agog, ear and eye alike. Do remember, my friend, when you go to the theatre, to reserve me a seat at your side, in order that you may not be the only one to come back to us wiser!

[1] *Odyssey*, X, 326.   [2] *Ibid.*, V, 47 f.

LEXIPHANES

LEXIPHANES ("Word-flaunter"), whose enthusiasm for Attic diction is equalled by his want of ideas, of schooling, and of taste, has his jacket soundly dusted by his friend Lycinus. The piece is sufficiently similar to the *Professor of Public Speaking* to have given rise to the idea that it is aimed at the same man, and that Lexiphanes is Pollux, the lexicographer (cf. IV, p. 133). To the argument of E. E. Seiler against this view (which was not that of Ranke), two points may be added, which seem to settle the matter. The "namesake of the sons of Zeus and Leda " cannot be Lexiphanes because "fifteen, or anyhow not more than twenty, Attic words" with which to besprinkle his speeches suffice him (IV, p. 155), whereas Lexiphanes revels in rarities and glories in the obscurity of his style. Moreover, Lexiphanes is so thoroughly addicted to this jargon of his that he uses it even in conversation. How, then (unless we assume that Lucian's castigation reformed him), can he ever have written in a style as normal as that of the *Onomasticon*?

Curiously enough, the cult of rare words is not conspicuous in the Greek prose of the time, but in the Latin, with Fronto as its most ardent devotee. The Atticists so tempered zeal with discretion that nothing comparable to the extravagances of Lexiphanes is to be found outside of the pages of Athenaeus (III, 97 c : Gulick, I, p. 419), where Cynulcus takes Ulpian to task for just this sort of thing, adverts upon Pompeianus of Philadelphia as a bird of the same feather, and implies a wider circle by alluding to "the Ulpianean sophists." This is certainly the group to which our man belonged (cf. c. 14). The time is right—just right if Ulpian was the father of the famous jurist; and these people not only use the selfsame jargon (see the notes for the parallels), but employ it even in conversation. Seiler's contention that Lexiphanes is Pompeianus is highly probable but not wholly certain because it is impossible to fix the extent to which the vocabulary of the "Ulpianeans" was common stock.

A conspicuous feature of Lucian's parody of Lexiphanes is the use of words no longer generally employed in the old sense but in a new and very different one, so that double meanings result. Adequate translation therefore is often quite impossible, for the lack of an equivalent expression.

ΛΕΞΙΦΑΝΗΣ

ΛΥΚΙΝΟΣ

1 Λεξιφάνης ὁ καλὸς μετὰ βιβλίου ;

ΛΕΞΙΦΑΝΗΣ

Νὴ Δί', ὦ Λυκῖνε, γράμμα ἐστὶν τητινόν τι
τῶν ἐμῶν κομιδῇ νεοχμόν.

ΛΥΚΙΝΟΣ

Ἤδη γάρ τι καὶ περὶ αὐχμῶν ἡμῖν γράφεις ;

ΛΕΞΙΦΑΝΗΣ

Οὐ δῆτα, οὐδὲ αὐχμὸν εἶπον, ἀλλὰ ὥρα σοι
τὸ ἀρτιγραφὲς οὕτω καλεῖν. σὺ δὲ κυψελόβυστα
ἔοικας ἔχειν τὰ ὦτα.

ΛΥΚΙΝΟΣ

Σύγγνωθι, ὦ ἑταῖρε· πολὺ γὰρ τοῦ αὐχμοῦ τὸ
νεοχμὸν μετέχει. ἀλλ' εἰπέ μοι, τίς ὁ νοῦς τῷ
συγγράμματι ;

ΛΕΞΙΦΑΝΗΣ

Ἀντισυμποσιάζω τῷ Ἀρίστωνος ἐν αὐτῷ.

---

¹ With τητινόν cf. τῆτες, ascribed to Pompeianus of
Philadelphia in Athenaeus, III, 98 B.

LEXIPHANES

LYCINUS

Lexiphanes, the glass of fashion, with a book?

LEXIPHANES

Yes, Lycinus; 'tis one of my own productions of this very season,[1] quite recent.

LYCINUS

Why, are you now writing us something indecent? [2]

LEXIPHANES

No, forsooth, and I did not say indecent. Come, it is full time you learned to apply that word of mine to things newly indited. It would seem that your ears are stopped with wax.

LYCINUS

Excuse me, my friend. Between indecent and recent there is a great deal in common. But tell me, what is the theme of your work?

LEXIPHANES

I am counter-banqueting the son of Aristo in it.

---

[2] Lucian pretends to confuse νεοχμός (recent, novel) with αὐχμός (drought)—an equivoque quite impossible, I think, to reproduce exactly in English.

THE WORKS OF LUCIAN

ΛΥΚΙΝΟΣ

Πολλοὶ μὲν οἱ Ἀρίστωνες· σὺ δὲ ὅσον ἀπὸ τοῦ συμποσίου τὸν Πλάτωνά μοι ἔδοξας λέγειν.

ΛΕΞΙΦΑΝΗΣ

Ὀρθῶς ἀνέγνως. τὸ δὲ λεγόμενον ὡς ἄλλῳ παντὶ ἀνόητον ἂν ἦν.

ΛΥΚΙΝΟΣ

Οὐκοῦν ὀλίγα μοι αὐτοῦ ἀνάγνωθι τοῦ βιβλίου, ὅπως μὴ παντάπασιν ἀπολειποίμην τῆς ἑστιάσεως· νέκταρος γάρ τινος ἔοικας οἰνοχοήσειν ἡμῖν ἀπ' αὐτοῦ.

ΛΕΞΙΦΑΝΗΣ

Τὸν μὲν εἴρωνα πεδοῖ κατάβαλε· σὺ δὲ εὔπορα ποιήσας τὰ ὦτα ἤδη ἄκουε. ἀπέστω δὲ ἡ ἐπιβύστρα ἡ Κυψελίς.

ΛΥΚΙΝΟΣ

Λέγε θαρρῶν, ὡς ἔμοιγε οὔτε Κύψελός τις οὔτε Περίανδρος ἐν τοῖς ὠσὶν κάθηται.

ΛΕΞΙΦΑΝΗΣ

Σκόπει δὴ μεταξύ, ὅπως διαπεραίνομαι, ὦ Λυκῖνε, τὸν λόγον, εἰ εὔαρχός τέ[1] ἐστι καὶ πολλὴν τὴν εὐλογίαν ἐπιδεικνύμενος καὶ εὔλεξις, ἔτι δὲ εὐώνυμος.

[1] τε Jacobitz : γε MSS.

---

[1] Lycinus is quoting a famous mixed metaphor in Homer (*Iliad*, I, 598 and IV, 3, with the scholia) and implies that he expects Lexiphanes to regale him similarly.

LEXIPHANES

LYCINUS

There are many " Aristos," but to judge from your "banquet" I suppose you mean Plato.

LEXIPHANES

You rede me right, but what I said would have been caviare to the general.

LYCINUS

Well then, you must read me a few passages from the book, so that I shan't miss the feast entirely. I dare say you will properly " wine us with nectar " out of it.[1]

LEXIPHANES

Suppress Master Irony, then, and make your ears permeable before you give them to me. Avaunt with the obturations of Dame Cypselis![2]

LYCINUS

Say your say confidently, for no Cypselus nor any Periander[3] has taken up lodgings in *my* ears.

LEXIPHANES

Consider withal how I carry myself in the book —whether it has a good entrance, a rich display of good discourse and composure,[4] and good store of egregious words.

---

[2] The name Cypselis (Waxy) is coined from *cypselê* (ear-wax).

[3] Periander comes in because he too was a Cypselid.

[4] For εὔλεξις cf. *A Professor of Public Speaking*, 17 (IV, p. 157).

ΛΥΚΙΝΟΣ

Ἔοικε τοιοῦτος εἶναι σός γε ὤν. ἀλλ' ἄρξαι ποτέ.

ΛΕΞΙΦΑΝΗΣ

2   " Εἶτα δειπνήσομεν," ἦ δ' ὃς ὁ Καλλικλῆς, " εἶτα τὸ δειλινὸν περιδινησόμεθα ἐν Λυκείῳ, νῦν δὲ ἤδη καιρός ἐστιν χρίεσθαι τὸ ἡλιοκαὲς καὶ πρὸς τὴν εἴλην θέρεσθαι καὶ λουσαμένους ἀρτοσιτεῖν· καὶ ἤδη γε ἀπιτητέα. σὺ δέ, ὦ παῖ, στλεγγίδα μοι καὶ βύρσαν καὶ φωσώνια καὶ ῥύμματα ναυστολεῖν ἐς τὸ βαλανεῖον καὶ τοὐπίλουτρον κομίζειν· ἔχεις δὲ χαμᾶζε παρὰ τὴν ἐγγυοθήκην δύ' ὀβολώ. σὺ δὲ τί καὶ πράξεις, ὦ Λεξίφανες, ἥξεις ἢ ἐλινύσεις ἔτι αὐτόθι ; "

" Κἀγώ," ἦν δὲ ἐγώ, " τρίπαλαι λουτιῶ· οὐκ εὐπόρως τε γὰρ ἔχω καὶ τὰ ἀμφὶ τὴν τράμιν μαλακίζομαι ἐπ' ἀστράβης ὀχηθείς. ὁ γὰρ ἀστραβηλάτης ἐπέσπερχεν καίτοι ἀσκωλιάζων αὐτός.[1] ἀλλὰ καὶ ἐν αὐτῷ οὐκ ἀκμὴς ἦν τῷ ἀγρῷ· κατέλαβον γὰρ τοὺς ἐργάτας λιγυρίζοντας τὴν θερινὴν ᾠδήν, τοὺς δὲ τάφον τῷ ἐμῷ πατρὶ κατασκευάζοντας. συντυμβωρυχήσας οὖν αὐτοῖς καὶ τοῖς ἀναχοῦσιν τὰ ἄνδηρα καὶ αὐτὸς ὀλίγα συγχειροπονήσας ἐκείνους μὲν διαφῆκα τοῦ τε κρύους ἕνεκα καὶ ὅτι καύματα ἦν· οἶσθα δὲ ὡς ἐν κρύει σφοδρῷ γίνεται τὰ καύματα. ἐγὼ δὲ περιελθὼν τὰ ἀρώματα σκόροδά τε εὗρον ἐν αὐτοῖς πεφυκότα καὶ γηπαττάλους τινὰς ἀνορύξας καὶ τῶν σκανδίκων καὶ βρακάνων λαχανευσάμενος, ἔτι δὲ κάχρυς πριάμενος—οὔπω δὲ οἱ λειμῶνες ἀνθοσμίαι ἦσαν,

---

[1] Literally, " dancing on wine-skins."

LEXIPHANES

LYCINUS

It is sure to have that, being yours.   But do begin now.

LEXIPHANES

(*reads*)

" Then we shall dine," quoth Callicles, " and then, at eventide, fetch a turn in the Lyceum; but now it is high season to endue ourselves with sunburn and tepify ourselves in the calid ambient, and after laving, to break bread.   We must away forthwith. My lad, convoy me my strigil, scrip, diapers, and purgaments to the bath-house, and fetch the where-withal.   'Tis on the floor, mark you, alongside the coffer, a brace of obols.   And you, Lexiphanes, whatever shall you do?   Shall you come, or tarry yet a while hereabouts ? "

" I too," said I, " am yearning to ablute these ages past, for I am ill-conditioned, susceptible behind from riding pillion on a mule.   The muleteer kept me going, though he himself was jigging it hot-foot.[1] But even in the country I was not unassiduous, for I found the yokels caroling the harvest-home; some of them, too, were preparing a grave for my father.   After I had assisted them in the engraving and for a brief space shared the handiwork of the dikers, I dispersed them on account of the cold and because they were getting burned (in severe cold, you know, burning ensues).[2]   For myself, I got about the simples, found prickmadam growing among them, exhumed sundry radishes, garnered chervils and potherbs, and bought groats.   But the meads were not yet redolent enough for travelling by shank's

---

[2] Cf. Athen., 98 B, καύματα, meaning "frosts" (Pompeianus).

THE WORKS OF LUCIAN

ὡς αὐτοποδητὶ βαδίζειν—ἀνατεθεὶς ἐπὶ τὴν ἀστρά-
βην ἐδάρην τὸν ὄρρον· καὶ νῦν βαδίζω τε ὀδυνηρῶς
καὶ ἰδίῳ θαμὰ καὶ μαλακιῶ τὸ σῶμα καὶ δέομαι
διανεῦσαι ἐν τῷ ὕδατι ἐπὶ πλεῖστον· χαίρω δὲ
3 μετὰ κάματον ἀπολούμενος. ἀποθρέξομαι οὖν καὶ
αὐτὸς ὡς [1] τὸν παῖδα, ὃν εἰκὸς ἢ παρὰ τῇ λεκι-
θοπώλιδι ἢ παρὰ τῷ γρυμαιοπώλῃ με περιμένειν·
καίτοι προηγόρευτο αὐτῷ ἐπὶ τὰ γέλγη [2] ἀπαντᾶν.

’Αλλ’ εἰς καιρὸν οὑτοσὶ αὐτὸς ἐμπολήσας γε,
ὡς ὁρῶ, πυριάτην τέ τινα καὶ ἐγκρυφίας καὶ
γήτεια καὶ φύκας [3] καὶ οἶβον τουτονὶ καὶ λωγάνιον
καὶ τοῦ βοὸς τὸ πολύπτυχον ἔγκατον καὶ φώκτας.
Εὖ γε, ὦ ’Αττικίων, ὅτι μοι ἄβατον ἐποίησας τὸ
πολὺ τῆς ὁδοῦ.” “ ’Εγὼ δέ,” ἦ δ’ ὅς, “ σίλλος,
ὦ δέσποτα, γεγένημαι σὲ περιορῶν. σὺ δὲ ποῦ
χθὲς ἐδείπνεις; μῶν παρὰ ’Ονομακρίτῳ; ” “ Οὔ,
μὰ Δί’,” ἦν δ’ ἐγώ, “ ἀλλ’ ἀγρόνδε [4] ᾠχόμην ψύττα
κατατείνας· οἶσθα δὲ ὡς φίλαγρός εἰμι. ὑμεῖς δὲ
ἴσως ᾤεσθέ με λαταγεῖν κοττάβους. ἀλλ’ εἰσιῶν
ταῦτά τε καὶ τὰ ἄλλα ἡδύνειν καὶ τὴν κάρδοπον
4 σμῆν, ὡς θριδακίνας μάττοιτε ἡμῖν. ἐγὼ δὲ
ξηραλοιφήσω ἀπελθών.”

“ Καὶ ἡμεῖς,” ἦ δ’ ὅς ὁ Φιλῖνος, “ ἐγώ τε καὶ
’Ονόμαρχος καὶ ‘Ελλάνικος οὑτοσὶ ἐψόμεθα· καὶ
γὰρ ὁ γνώμων σκιάζει μέσην τὴν πόλον, καὶ

---

[1] ὡς Gesner: not in MSS.
[2] γέλγη Meursius: σέλγη MSS.
[3] φύκας is right: cf. Aristotle, *Hist. An.*, 6, 13, ὁ φύκης.
[4] ἀγρόνδε N: ἀγρόν γε ΓΕΑ.

---

[1] The form διανεῦσαι may be referred either to νέω (swim
back and forth) or to νεύω (beckon back and forth, exchange
" becks and nods ").

298

mare; so I mounted the pillion and had my rump
excoriated. Now I walk excruciatingly, I perspire
amain, my flesh is very weak, and I want to play
about[1] in the water no end. I delight in the
prospect of dissolution after toil.[2] Therefore I shall
betake myself incontinently to my urchin, who
belike attends me at the pease-porridge woman's or
the frippery, although he was forewarned to turn
up at the comfit-shop.

"In the nick of time, however, here he is himself,
and I see he has chaffered beestings-pudden, ash-
cake, chibbals, hakot, nape of beef—mark you!—
dewlap, manyplies, and lamb's fries. Good, Atticion! You have made most of my journey invious."
"For my part," quoth he, "I have got squinny,
master, keeping an eye out for you. Where were you
dining yesterday? With Onomacritus, prithee?"
"Nay, gadzooks," quoth I: "I made off to the
countryside, helter-skelter. You know how I adore
rusticating. The rest of you no doubt supposed
that I was playing toss-pot. But go you in and
relish all of this; also cleanse the kneading-trough,
that you may work us up some lettuce-loaf. I
myself shall be off and bestow upon myself an
inunction sans immersion."[3]

"We," quoth Philinos, "I and Onomarchus and
Hellanicus here, shall have after you, for the style
shadows the middle of the bowl,[4] and it is to be

[2] The Attic contraction of ἀπολουόμενος to ἀπολούμενος
produces identity of form with the future of ἀπόλλυμαι.
Cf. Athen., 97 E (Ulpian); 98 A (Pompeianus).
[3] Not a "dry-rub," but a "rub-down" without a previous
bath.
[4] Of the sundial.

THE WORKS OF LUCIAN

δέος μὴ ἐν λουτρίῳ ἀπολουσώμεθα κατόπιν τῶν
Καριμάντων¹ μετὰ τοῦ σύρφακος βύζην ὠστιζό-
μενοι." καὶ ὁ Ἑλλάνικος ἔφη, " Ἐγὼ δὲ καὶ
δυσωπῶ· καὶ γὰρ τὰ κόρα μοι ἐπιτεθόλωσθον καὶ
σκαρδαμύττω θαμὰ καὶ ἀρτίδακρύς εἰμι καὶ τὰ
ὄμματά μοι φαρμακᾷ καὶ δέομαι Ἀσκληπιάδου
τινὸς ὀφθαλμοσόφου, ὃς ταράξας καὶ ἐγχέας μοι
φάρμακον ἀπερυθριᾶσαί τε ποιήσει τοὺς ὀφθαλμοὺς
καὶ μηκέτι τι λημαλέους εἶναι μηδὲ διερὸν βλέπειν."

5   Τοιαῦτα ἄττα διεξιόντες ἅπαντες οἱ παρόντες
ἀπῄειμεν· κἀπειδήπερ ἥκομεν εἰς τὸ γυμνάσιον
ἀπησθημένοι ἤδη, ὁ μέν τις ἀκροχειριασμῷ, ὁ δὲ
τραχηλισμῷ καὶ ὀρθοπάλῃ ἐχρῆτο, ὁ δὲ λίπα
χρισάμενος ἐλυγίζετο, ὁ δὲ ἀντέβαλλε τῷ κωρύκῳ,
ὁ δὲ μολυβδαίνας χερμαδίους δράγδην² ἔχων
ἐχειροβόλει. εἶτα συντριβέντες καὶ ἀλλήλους κατα-
νωτισάμενοι καὶ ἐμπαίξαντες τῷ γυμνασίῳ ἐγὼ
μὲν καὶ Φιλῖνος ἐν τῇ θερμῇ πυέλῳ καταιονηθέντες
ἐξῄειμεν· οἱ λοιποὶ δὲ τὸ ψυχροβαφὲς κάρα δελφινί-
σαντες παρένεον ὑποβρύχιοι θαυμασίως.

Ἀναστρέψαντες δὲ αὖθις ἄλλος ἄλλοσε ἄλλα ἐδρῶ-
μεν. ἐγὼ μὲν ὑποδησάμενος ἐξυόμην τὴν κεφαλὴν
τῇ ὀδοντωτῇ ξύστρᾳ· καὶ γὰρ οὐ κηπίον, ἀλλὰ
σκάφιον ἐκεκάρμην, ὡς ἂν οὐ πρὸ πολλοῦ τὸν

¹ Γαριμάντων Meineke (Hesych., Et. Magn.). But the word
is very likely from Μαρικᾶς (Herodian in Et. Magn.), meaning
κίναιδος (Hesych. *s.v.* μαρικᾶν), or, perhaps more accurately,
παιδικά; for the declension Μαρικᾶς, Μαρικᾶντος cf. Herodian,
II, 636, 26 Lentz. Hence Γαριμᾶς (or Γαρίμας) is apparently
a degradation of Καριμᾶς. The Γαράμαντες in Libya have
nothing to do with this; cf. Lucian, *Dips.* 2.

² δράγδην Harmon: ἀράγδην MSS.

LEXIPHANES

feared that we may lave in the leavings of the
bargashes, along with the scum, in a jostle." Then
said Hellanicus: " I look askew, for my dollies are
obfuscate, I nictitate full oft, and I am lachrymose;
mine eyes want drugging, I require some scion of
Aesculapius, sage in ophthalmotherapy, who will
compound and decant a specific for me, and so
effect that my ruddy optics may be decoloured
and no longer be rheumatic or have a humorous
cast."

Discoursing in this wise, all those of us present
were gone. When we came to the gymnasium, we
despoiled ourselves. One exercised himself at
wrestling with shoulder-holds, another with neck-
holds, standing; one sleeked himself with unguent
and essayed eluding grasps; one countered the
wind-bag,[1] one, grasping leaden sows, whipped his
arms about. Then, once we were dressed down [2]
and had backed each other, and used the gymnasium
for our sport, Philinus and I imbathed ourselves in
the hot pool and emerged, while the rest, beducking
their sconces in the cold plunge, swam about
subaquaneous in wondrous guise.

Upon reversion, we imbused ourselves with this,
that or t'other. I myself indued my boots, dressed
my scalp with a tined card,[3] for I had got shorn
with the " bowl " cut, not the " bush "; for not long

---

[1] He exercised with the "punching-bag."
[2] To Lexiphanes, συντριβέντες is an allusion to the "rub-
down" previous mentioned; but others would infer from it
that somebody had cracked their crowns for them. Cf.
Athen., 98 A (Pompeianus).
[3] The regular word for comb (κτείς or κτένιον) was not
elegant enough for Lexiphanes.

THE WORKS OF LUCIAN

κόννον καὶ τὴν κορυφαίαν ἀποκεκομηκώς· ἄλλος
ἐθερμοτράγει, ὁ δὲ ἤμει τὸν νῆστιν, ὁ δὲ ἀραιὰς
ποιῶν τὰς ῥαφανῖδας ἐμυστιλᾶτο τοῦ ἰχθυηροῦ
ζωμοῦ, ἄλλος ἤσθιεν φαυλίας, ὁ δὲ ἐρρόφει τῶν
κριθῶν.

6 Κἀπειδὴ καιρὸς ἦν, ἐπ' ἀγκῶνος ἐδειπνοῦμεν·
ἔκειντο δὲ καὶ ὀκλαδίαι καὶ ἀσκάνται. τὸ μὲν
δὴ δεῖπνον ἦν ἀπὸ συμφορῶν. παρεσκεύαστο δὲ
πολλὰ καὶ ποικίλα, δίχηλα ὕεια [1] καὶ σχελίδες καὶ
ἠτριαία καὶ τοκάδος ὑὸς τὸ ἐμβρυοδόχον ἔντερον
καὶ λοβὸς ἐκ ταγήνου καὶ μυττωτὸς καὶ ἀβυρτάκη
καὶ τοιαῦταί τινες καρυκεῖαι καὶ θρυμματίδες καὶ
θρῖα καὶ μελιτοῦτται·[2] τῶν δὲ ὑποβρυχίων τὰ
σελάχια πολλὰ καὶ ὅσα ὀστράκινα τὸ δέρμα καὶ
τεμάχη Ποντικὰ τῶν ἐκ σαργάνης καὶ κωπαΐ-
δες καὶ ὄρνις σύντροφος καὶ ἀλεκτρυὼν ἤδη ἀπῳδὸς
καὶ ἰχθὺς ἦν παράσιτος· καὶ οἶν δὲ ὅλον ἱπνοκαῇ
εἴχομεν καὶ βοὸς λειπογνώμονος κωλήν. ἄρτοι
μέντοι ἦσαν σιφαῖοι, οὐ φαῦλοι, καὶ ἄλλοι νουμήνιοι,
ὑπερήμεροι τῆς ἑορτῆς, καὶ λάχανα τά τε ὑπόγεια
καὶ τὰ ὑπερφυῆ· οἶνος δὲ ἦν οὐ γέρων, ἀλλὰ τῶν
ἀπὸ βύρσης, ἤδη μὲν ἀγλευκής, ἄπεπτος δὲ
ἔτι.

7 Ποτήρια δὲ ἔκειτο παντοῖα ἐπὶ τῆς δελφῖδος [3]

---

[1] Text edd.: πολλαὶ καὶ ποικίλαι (καὶ) δίχηλαι ὕειαι MSS.
[2] μελιτοῦτται Jacobitz: μελιτοῦται MSS. (μελιτοῦται E²).
[3] δελφῖδος (suggested by Coraës) Γ²: δελφῖδος Γ¹: δελφινίδος
E (in erasure) N, vulg.

ago my chaps and crown had been displumed.[1]
Someone else was gobbling lupines, another was
evomiting his jejunity, another was diminishing
radishes and sopping up a mess of fishy pottage,
another was eating flummery,[2] and yet another en-
gorging barley brose.

When the time was ripe, we dined on our elbows.
Both faldstools and truckles were at hand. The
dinner was picked up;[3] many different viands had
been made ready, pig's trotters, spareribs, tripe, the
caul of a sow that had littered, panned pluck, spoon-
meat of cheese and honey, shallot-pickle and other
such condiments, crumpets, stuffed fig-leaves, sweets.
Of submarine victuals, too, there were many sorts of
selacian, all the ostraceans, cuts of Pontic tunny in
hanapers, Copaic lassies,[4] vernacular fowl, muted
chanticleers, and an odd fish—the parasite. Yes,
and we had a whole sheep barbecued, and the
hind-quarter of an edentulous ox. Besides, there
was bread from Siphae, not bad, and novilunar buns,
too late for the fair, as well as vegetables, both
underground and over grown. And there was wine,
not vetust, but out of a leathern bottle, dry by
now but still crude.

Drinking-cups of all kinds stood on the dresser,

---

[1] Apparently the " bush " cut required a good head of
hair, but did not need to be combed. Both styles had been
for centuries out of fashion in Lexiphanes' day.

[2] In the Greek the food is different (queen olives), but the
name carries a similar suggestion of rubbish.

[3] The phrase ἀπὸ συμφορῶν to Lexiphanes meant " off
contributions " (of the individual guests), but to anyone else in
his day it meant " off catastrophes."

[4] Copaic eels.

THE WORKS OF LUCIAN

τραπέζης, ὁ κρυψιμέτωπος καὶ τρυήλης [1] Μεντορουρ-
γῆς εὐλαβῆ ἔχων τὴν κέρκον καὶ βομβυλιὸς καὶ
δειροκύπελλον καὶ γηγενῆ πολλὰ οἷα Θηρικλῆς
ὦπτα, εὐρυχαδῆ τε καὶ ἄλλα εὔστομα, τὰ μὲν
Φωκαῆθεν, τὰ δὲ Κνιδόθεν, πάντα μέντοι ἀνεμοφόρητα καὶ ὑμενόστρακα. κυμβία δὲ ἦν καὶ
φιαλίδες καὶ ποτήρια γραμματικά, ὥστε μεστὸν
ἦν τὸ κυλικεῖον.

8   Ὁ μέντοι ἱπνολέβης ὑπερπαφλάζων ἐς κεφαλὴν
ἡμῖν ἐπέτρεπε τοὺς ἄνθρακας. ἐπίνομεν δὲ ἀμυστὶ
καὶ ἤδη ἀκροθώρακες ἦμεν· εἶτ' ἐχριόμεθα βακχά-
ριδι καὶ εἰσεκύκλησέ τις ἡμῖν τὴν ποδοκτύπην καὶ
τριγωνίστριαν· μετὰ δὲ ὁ μέν τις ἐπὶ τὴν κατήλιφα
ἀναρριχησάμενος . . . [2] ἐπιφόρημα ἐξήτει, ὁ δὲ
ληκίνδα ἔπαιζεν, ἄλλος ἐρρικνοῦτο σὺν γέλωτι τὴν
ὀσφῦν.

9   Καὶ ἐν ταὐτῷ λελουμένοι εἰσεκώμασαν ἡμῖν
αὐτεπάγγελτοι Μεγαλώνυμός τε ὁ δικοδίφης καὶ
Χαιρέας ὁ χρυσοτέκτων ὁ κατὰ νώτου ποικίλος καὶ
ὁ ὠτοκάταξις Εὔδημος. κἀγὼ ἠρόμην αὐτούς, τί

---

[1] τρυηλὶς Fritzsche (Hesychius): but this necessitates
changing ἔχων to ἔχουσα. τρυήλης Ω vulg., τρυήλεις ΓΕ,
τρυήλης Ν, τρυηλὴς Α.
[2] Lacuna in MSS: 12 letters long in Γ, 5–6 in E.

---

[1] This is said to be the only reference to Mentor in extant
Greek literature. The scholia allude to him as a maker of
glassware, but various allusions in Latin writers from Cicero
to Juvenal and Martial (especially Pliny, *Nat. Hist.*, XXXIII,
147) make it clear that he was a silversmith whose productions
were highly esteemed as antiques in Cicero's time. When and
where he lived is not indicated.
[2] Thericles seems to have been a Corinthian potter, contemporary with Aristophanes (Athen., XI, 470). His name
became attached to certain shapes, and even to imitations

your brow-hider, your Mentor-made[1] dipper with a convenient tail-piece, your gurgler, your long-necker, many " earth-borns " like what Thericles[2] used to bake, vessels both ventricose and patulous, some from Phocaeawards, other some from Cnidos way, all airy trifles,[3] hymen-thin. There were also boats, chalices, and lettered mugs,[4] so that the cupboard was full.

The calefactor,[5] however, slopped over on our heads and delivered us a consignment of coals. But we drank bottoms up and soon were well fortified. Then we endued ourselves with baccharis, and someone trundled in the girl that treads the mazy and juggles balls; after which, one of us, scrambling up to the cockloft, went looking for something to top off with,[6] whilst another fell to thrumming and another laughingly wriggled his hips.

Meantime, after lavation, came rollicking in to us, self-invited, Megalonymus the pettifogger, Chaereas the goldworker, he with the back of many colours, and Eudemus the broken-ear.[7] I asked

of these shapes in metal, made at Athens and Rhodes (Athen. XI, 469 B). Cicero (*in Verrem*, II, 4, 38) speaks of certain cups that are called Thericleian, made by the hand of Mentor with supreme craftsmanship.

[3] By ἀνεμοφόρητα Lexiphanes means " light enough to blow away," but might be taken to mean " wind-blown." Cf. ἀφόρητα, p. 307, n. 5.

[4] Cups with an inscription; Athenaeus, XI, 466 c (Gulick V, 56).

[5] According to Athen., III, 98 c, the name ἱπνολέβης was used by the " Ulpianean Sophists " for the apparatus for heating water which the Romans called a μιλιάριον.

[6] The word ἐπιφόρημα means at once *coverlet* and (in Ionic) *dessert*.

[7] Chaereas' back bore the stripes of the lash; Eudemus was a pugilist with " cauliflower " ears.

παθόντες ὀψὲ ἥκοιεν. ὁ μὲν οὖν Χαιρέας, " Ἐγώ,"
ἦ δ' ὅς, " λῆρόν τινα ἐκρότουν καὶ ἐλλόβια καὶ
πέδας τῇ θυγατρὶ τῇ ἐμῇ καὶ διὰ τοῦτο ὑμῖν ἐπιδεί-
πνιος ἀφῖγμαι." " Ἐγὼ δέ," ἦ δ' ὃς ὁ Μεγαλώνυμος, " περὶ ἄλλα εἶχον· ἦν μὲν γὰρ ἄδικος ἡ
ἡμέρα, ὡς ἴστε, καὶ ἄλογος· ὡς ἂν οὖν ἐχεγλωτ-
τίας οὔσης οὔτε ῥησιμετρεῖν εἶχον οὔτε ἡμερολεγδὸν
προσυδρονομεῖσθαι·[1] πυθόμενος δὲ ὅτι ὁ στρατηγὸς ὀπτός ἐστιν, λαβὼν ἄχρηστα ἱμάτια εὐήτρια
καὶ ἀφόρητα ὑποδήματα ἐξέφρησα ἐμαυτόν.

10 " Εἶτ' εὐθὺς ἐντυγχάνω δᾳδούχῳ τε καὶ ἱερο-
φάντῃ καὶ τοῖς ἄλλοις ἀρρητοποιοῖς Δεινίαν σύρουσιν
ἄγδην ἐπὶ τὴν ἀρχήν, ἔγκλημα ἐπάγοντας ὅτι
ὠνόμαζεν αὐτούς, καὶ ταῦτα εὖ εἰδὼς ὅτι ἐξ οὗπερ
ὠσιώθησαν, ἀνώνυμοί τέ εἰσι καὶ οὐκέτι ὀνομαστοὶ
ὡς ἂν ἱερώνυμοι ἤδη γεγενημένοι."

" Οὐκ οἶδα," ἦν δ' ἐγώ, " ὃν λέγεις τὸν Δεινίαν·
αἰκάλλει[2] δ' οὖν με τοὔνομα." " Ἔστιν," ἦ δ'

---

[1] προσυδρονομεῖσθαι Harmon, from πρὸς ὑδωρονομεῖσθαι Γ:
ὡς ὑδρονομεῖσθαι other MSS.
[2] αἰκάλλει Bekker: ἐκάλει MSS.

---

[1] For ἄδικος ("unjust") as applied to a day in the sense
that court was not held on it, cf. Athen. 98 B (Pompeianus).
[2] Both the verbs of the original (rendered " palaver "
and " solicit ") refer to pleading in court and carry allusions
to the custom of timing pleas by the water-clock. One of
them (ῥησιμετρεῖν) is ridiculed in the *Mistaken Critic*, 24 (p.
400).

LEXIPHANES

them what possessed them to come late. Quoth
Chaereas : " I was forging trumpery for my daughter,
balls and chains, and that is why I have come in
on top of your dinner." " For my part," quoth
Megalonymus, " I was about other matters. The
day was incapable of justice,[1] as ye wit, and incom-
petent for pleading ; wherefore, as there was a truce
of the tongue, I was unable either to palaver or, as
is my diurnal habit, to solicit.[2] Learning that the
magistrate was being grilled in public,[3] I took an
unvalued [4] cloak, of sheer tissue, and priceless [5] boots,
and emitted myself.

Forthwith I hit upon the Torch-bearer and the
Hierophant, with the other participants in un-
utterable rites,[6] haling Deinias neck and crop to
the office, bringing the charge that he had named
them, albeit he knew right well that from the time
when they were hallowed they were nameless
and thenceforth ineffable, as being now all Hierony-
muses."[7]

" I do not know," said I, " the Deinias that you
mention, but the name intrigues me."[8] " A clove-

---

[3] Lexiphanes would be understood to mean " roasted,"
but what he really meant was " visible." Cf. Athen., 98 A
(Pompeianus).

[4] For ἄχρηστα, usually "useless," in the sense "unused,"
cf. Athen., 98 A (Pompeianus), 97 E (Ulpian).

[5] In the Greek, ἀφόρητα ("unbearable") in the sense
" unworn," cf. Athen., 98 A (Pompeianus).

[6] Those of the Eleusinian Mysteries.

[7] The adjective " of hallowed name " was itself used as a
name. Unintentionally, Lexiphanes suggests that they have
changed their names.

[8] No doubt because the name *deinias* was given to a variety
of drinking pot (Athenaeus, XI, 467 D–E).

ὅς, " ἐν τοῖς σκιραφείοις ἐγκαψικήδαλος [1] ἄνθρωπος
τῶν αὐτοληκύθων καὶ τῶν αὐτοκαβδάλων, ἀεὶ
κουριῶν, ἐνδρομίδας ὑποδούμενος ἢ βαυκίδας,
ἀμφιμάσχαλον ἔχων." " Τί οὖν," ἦν δ' ἐγώ,
" ἔδωκεν ἀμηγέπη δίκην ἢ λὰξ πατήσας ᾤχετο ; "
" Καὶ μὴν ἐκεῖνός γε," ἦ δ' ὅς, " ὁ τέως σαυλούμενος,[2] ἤδη ἔμπεδός ἐστιν· ὁ γὰρ στρατηγὸς
καίτοι ἀτιμαγελοῦντι καρπόδεσμά τε αὐτῷ περι-
θεὶς καὶ περιδέραιον ἐν ποδοκάκαις καὶ ποδο-
στράβαις ἐποίησεν εἶναι. ὥστε ἔνδεσμος ὢν
ὑπέβδυλλέν τε ὁ κακοδαίμων ὑπὸ τοῦ δέους καὶ
πορδαλέος ἦν καὶ χρήματα ἀντίψυχα διδόναι
ἤθελεν."

11   " Ἐμὲ δέ," ἦ δ' ὃς ὁ Εὔδημος, " ὑπὸ τὸ
ἀκροκνεφὲς μετεστείλατο Δαμασίας ὁ πάλαι μὲν
ἀθλητὴς καὶ πολυνίκης, νῦν δὲ ἤδη ὑπὸ γήρως
ἔξαθλος ὤν· οἶσθα τὸν χαλκοῦν τὸν [3] ἑστῶτα ἐν
τῇ ἀγορᾷ. καὶ τὰ μὲν πιττῶν τὰ δὲ εὔων διετέλεσεν,[4] ἐξοικιεῖν γὰρ ἔμελλε τήμερον εἰς ἀνδρὸς
τὴν θυγατέρα καὶ ἤδη ἐκάλλυνεν αὐτήν. εἶτα
Τερμέριόν [5] τι κακὸν ἐμπεσὸν διέκοψε τὴν ἑορτήν·
ὁ γὰρ υἱὸς αὐτοῦ ὁ Δίων, οὐκ οἶδ' ἐφ' ὅτῳ λυπηθείς,
μᾶλλον δὲ θεοσεχθρίᾳ σχεθείς, ἀπῆγξεν ἑαυτόν,
καὶ εὖ ἴστε, ἀπωλώλει ἄν, εἰ μὴ ἐγὼ ἐπιστὰς ἀπηγ-
χόνισά τε αὐτὸν καὶ παρέλυσα τῆς ἐμβροχῆς, ἐπὶ

[1] ἐγκαψικήδαλος ΕΝ : ἐγκαμψικήδαλος Γ, ἐγκαμψικίδαλος Ω,
ἐγκαψικίδαλος edd.   The second part of the word (ἅπαξ λεγόμενον) is clearly from κήδαλον, not κίδαλον.
[2] σαυλούμενος Seiler ; αὐλούμενος MSS.
[3] τὸν is excised by Headlam and Herwerden, but to do that,
I think, is to retouch Lucian's picture of Lexiphanes.
[4] διετέλεσεν Seiler : διετέλεσα MSS.
[5] Τερμέριόν Ν (Cobet) : μερμέριόν ΓΕΑ.

LEXIPHANES

engulfing haunter of gaming-houses," quoth he;
" one of those bezonians, those joculators, a curli-
locks, wearing lace boots or pantoffles, with manches
to his shirt."¹ " Well," said I, " did he in some
wise pay the piper; or did he take himself off after
setting his heel upon them?" " Verily," said he,
" that fellow, the whilom swaggerer, is now en-
sconced; for, notwithstanding his reluctation, the
magistrate decked him out with wristlets and a
necklace and lodged him in the bilboes and the stocks.
Wherefore, being impounded, the sorry wretch
fusted for fear, and trumped, and was fain to give
weregelt."²

" I," quoth Eudemus, " was summoned as it grew
crepuscular by Damasias the quondam athlete and
champion, now out of the lists for eld—the brazen
image, you know, in the square.³ He was hard at it
a-plucking and a-singeing, for he intended to marry
off his daughter to-day and was busking her. Then
a Termerian⁴ misadventure befell that cut short the
gala day. Distraught over I know not what, or more
likely overtaken by divine detestation, his son Dion
hung himself, and, depend upon it, he would have
been undone if I had not been there to slip the
noose and relieve him of his coil. Squatting on my

¹ The word here used for boots (ἐνδρομίδας) had another
meaning—a kind of woman's cloak.
² In my opinion χρήματα ἀντίψυχα is misused here, for it
means " blood-money," or weregelt, rather than " ransom."
³ Out of compliment to him as a champion, his statue was
set up in the square.
⁴ What a " Termerian misfortune " was, the ancients
themselves do not seem to have known, except that it was a
great one, and that " Termerian " was derived from a name—
according to Suidas, that of a tyrant's keep in Caria, used as
a prison.

πολύ τε ὀκλὰξ παρακαθήμενος ἐπένυσσον[1] τὸν
ἄνθρωπον, βαυκαλῶν καὶ διακωδωνίζων, μή πη
ἔτι συνεχὴς εἴη τὴν φάρυγγα. τὸ δὲ μάλιστα
ὀνῆσαν ἐκεῖνο ἦν, ὅτι ἀμφοτέραις κατασχὼν
αὐτοῦ τὰ ἄκρα διεπίεσα."

12 " Μῶν ἐκεῖνον," ἦν δ' ἐγώ, " φὴς Δίωνα τὸν
καταπύγονα καὶ λακκοσχέαν, τὸν μύρτωνα καὶ
σχινοτρώκταν νεανίσκον, ἀναφλῶντα καὶ βλιμά-
ζοντα, ἤν τινα πεώδη καὶ πόσθωνα αἴσθηται ;
μίνθων[2] ἐκεῖνός γε καὶ λαικαλέος." " Ἀλλά τοί
γε τὴν θεόν," ἦ δ' ὃς ὁ Εὔδημος, " θαυμάσας—
Ἄρτεμις γάρ ἐστιν αὐτοῖς ἐν μέσῃ τῇ αὐλῇ, Σκο-
πάδειον ἔργον—ταύτῃ προσπεσόντες ὅ τε Δαμασίας
καὶ ἡ γυνὴ αὐτοῦ, πρεσβῦτις ἤδη καὶ τὴν κεφαλὴν
πολιὰς ἀκριβῶς, ἱκέτευον ἐλεῆσαι σφᾶς· ἡ δὲ
αὐτίκα ἐπένευσεν, καὶ σῶς ἦν, καὶ νῦν Θεόδωρον,
μᾶλλον δὲ περιφανῶς Ἀρτεμίδωρον ἔχουσι τὸν
νεανίσκον. ἀνέθεσαν οὖν αὐτῇ τά τε ἄλλα καὶ
βέλη καὶ τόξα, ὅτι χαίρει τούτοις· τοξότις γὰρ καὶ
ἑκηβόλος καὶ τηλέμαχος ἡ Ἄρτεμις."

13 " Πίνωμεν οὖν," ἦ δ' ὃς ὁ Μεγαλώνυμος, " καὶ
γὰρ καὶ λάγυνον τουτονὶ παρηβηκότος ἥκω ὑμῖν
κομίζων καὶ τυροῦ τροφαλίδας[3] καὶ ἐλαίας
χαμαιπετεῖς—φυλάττω δ' αὐτὰς ὑπὸ σφραγῖσιν
θριπηδέστοις—καὶ ἄλλας ἐλαίας νευστὰς καὶ πήλινα

---

[1] ἐπένυσσον N : ἐπίνυσσον ΓΕ : ἐπινύσσων Ω.
[2] μίνθων Bekker, Mras : μιν ἐών ΓΝΕ : βινέων Ω(?). Mras
compares Philod., de Vitiis, p. 37 Jensen.
[3] τροφαλίδας Seiler : τρυφαλίδας MSS.

---

[1] Eudemus means to convey the idea that he undid the
noose and attempted to relieve the man, but his language
is so open to misunderstanding that it suggests quite the

LEXIPHANES

hunkers beside him for a long time, I jobbed him,
titillating and sounding him lest perchance his
windpipe still hang together. But what helped
most was that I confined his extremes with both
hands and applied pressure." [1]

" Prithee," quoth I, " dost mean that notable
Dion, the slack-pursed libertine, the toothpick-
chewing aesthete, who strouts and gropes if ever he
sees anyone that is well hung? He is a scapegrace
and a rutter." " Well," said Eudemus, " Damasias
in amaze invoked the goddess—they have an Artemis
in the middle of the hall, a Scopadean masterpiece
—and he and his wife, who is now elderly and quite
lyart-polled,[2] flung themselves upon her and besought
her to pity them. She at once inclined her head,
and he was well; so that now they have a Theodore [3]
or rather, manifestly an Artemidore [4] in the young
man. So they have made offerings of all sorts
to her, including bows and arrows, since she takes
pleasure in these; for Artemis is a good bowyer,
she is a Far-darter, a very Telemachus." [5]

" Let us be drinking, then," quoth Megalonymus,
" for I am come bringing you this senile flagon,
green cheese, windfallen olives—I keep them under
wormscriven seals [6]—and other olives, soused, and

opposite—that his aim was rather to undo the unhappy
subject of his ministrations.
[2] With a punning allusion to Athena *Polias*.
[3] " Gift-of-God."   [4] " Gift-of-Artemis."
[5] As an " archeress " (but *toxotis* was also an arrow-window)
Artemis was not only, like her brother, a Far-darter, but a
Far-fighter (Telemachus).
[6] Since in worm-eaten wood the " galleries " are never
identical in pattern, sections of it were very suitable for use as
seals; but in the day of Lexiphanes only an antiquarian is
likely to have possessed one.

ταυτὶ ποτήρια, ὀξυόστρακα, εὐπυνδάκωτα, ὡς
ἐξ αὐτῶν πίνοιμεν, καὶ πλακοῦντα ἐξ ἐντέρων κρω-
βυλώδη τὴν πλοκήν. σὺ δ᾽, ὦ παῖ, πλέον μοι τοῦ
ὕδατος ἔγχει, ὡς μὴ καραιβαρεῖν ἀρξαίμην κἄτά
σοι τὸν παιδοβοσκὸν καλῶ ἐπὶ σέ· ἴστε γὰρ ὡς
ὀδυνῶμαι καὶ διέμπιλον ἔχω τὴν κεφαλήν. μετὰ
14 δὲ τὸν ποτὸν συνυθλήσομεν οἷα [1] καὶ ἅττ᾽ ἐώθαμεν·
οὐ γὰρ ἄκαιρον δήπουθεν ἐν οἴνῳ φλύειν.”

“ ’Επαινῶ τοῦτο,” ἦν δ᾽ ἐγώ, “ καὶ γὰρ ὅτιπερ
ὄφελός ἐσμεν τῆς ἀττικίσεως ἄκρον.” “ Εὖ λέγεις,” ἦ δ᾽ ὃς ὁ Καλλικλῆς· “ τὸ γὰρ ἐρεσχηλεῖν
ἀλλήλους συχνάκις λάλης θηγάνη γίγνεται.” “ ’Εγὼ
δέ,” ἦ δ᾽ ὃς ὁ Εὔδημος—“ κρύος γάρ ἐστιν—ἥδιον
ἂν εὐζωροτέρῳ ὑποπυκνάζοιμι· καὶ γὰρ χειμωθνής
εἰμι, καὶ χλιανθεὶς ἥδιον ἂν [2] ἀκούοιμι τῶν χειρεσό-
φων τούτων, τοῦ τε αὐλητοῦ καὶ τῆς βαρβιτῳδοῦ.”

15 “ Τί ταῦτα ἔφησθα, ὦ Εὔδημε ; ” ἦν δ᾽ ἐγώ·
“ ἀλογίαν ἡμῖν ἐπιτάττεις ὡς ἀστόμοις οὖσι καὶ
ἀπεγλωττισμένοις ; ἐμοὶ δὲ ἡ γλῶττά τε ἤδη
λογᾷ καὶ δὴ ἀνηγόμην γε ὡς ἀρχαιολογήσων
ὑμῖν καὶ κατανίψων ἀπὸ γλώττης ἅπαντας.
ἀλλὰ σὺ τὸ ὅμοιον εἰργάσω με ὥσπερ εἴ τις ὁλκάδα
τριάρμενον ἐν οὐρίῳ πλέουσαν, ἐμπεπνευματω-
μένου τοῦ ἀκατίου, εὐφοροῦσάν τε καὶ ἀκροκυ-
ματοῦσαν, ἕκτοράς τινας ἀμφιστόμους καὶ ἰσχάδας
σιδηρᾶς ἀφεὶς καὶ ναυσιπέδας ἀναχαιτίζοι τοῦ
δρόμου τὸ ῥόθιον, φθόνῳ τῆς εὐηνεμίας.”

---

[1] συνυθλήσομεν οἷα edd.: συνυθλησόμενοι MSS. (-οι om. N).
[2] ἂν Jacobitz: not in MSS.

---

[1] Cf. Dancing, 69 (p. 272), and the note there.

these earthen cups of cockle-shell, stanchly bottomed, for us to drink out of, and a cake of chitterlings braided like a topknot. My lad, pour in more of the water for me, that I may not begin to have a head, and then call your keeper to come for you. You know that I have my pains and keep my head invested. And now that we have drunk, we shall gossip according to our wont, for in good sooth it is not inopportune to prate when we are in our cups."

"I approve this," said I, "and why not, for we are the sheer quintessence of Atticism." "Very true," quoth Callicles, "for quizzing each other incessantly is a whet to loquacity." "As to me," said Eudemus, "since it is brumal I had liefer fence myself with stiffer drink. I am starved with cold, and when I am warmed I would fain hear these handiwise [1] folk, the flute-player and the harper."

"What was that you said, Eudemus?" said I. "Do you enjoin alogy upon us as if we were inarticulate and elinguid? My tongue is already pregnant with utterance, and in sooth I set sail in the intent to archaise with you and wash you up with my tongue, one and all. But you have treated me as if a three-masted vessel were sailing before the wind with full kites, running easy and spooming over the billows, and then someone, letting go double-tongued refrainers,[2] pigs of iron,[3] and bowers, were to curb the impetuosity of her course, begrudging her the fair wind."

[2] In view of the fact that to the Greeks Hector was a "holder," Lexiphanes can cause us to imagine that hero performing new and strange feats.

[3] For ἰσχάς ("fig") used, in the sense "holder," to apply to an anchor, cf. Athen., 99 c–d, where it is attributed to Sophocles (Fr. 761 Pearson).

313

THE WORKS OF LUCIAN

" Οὐκοῦν," ἦ δ' ὅς, " σὺ μέν, εἰ βούλει, πλεῖ καὶ
νεῖ καὶ θεῖ κατὰ τοῦ κλύδωνος, ἐγὼ δὲ ἀπόγειος
πίνων ἅμα ὥσπερ ὁ τοῦ Ὁμήρου Ζεὺς ἢ ἀπὸ
φαλάκρων ἢ ἀπὸ τῆς ἀκρουρανίας ὄψομαι διαφερό-
μενόν σέ τε καὶ τὴν ναῦν πρύμνηθεν ὑπὸ[1] τοῦ
ἀνέμου κατουρουμένην."

ΛΥΚΙΝΟΣ

16 Ἅλις, ὦ Λεξίφανες, καὶ ποτοῦ καὶ ἀναγνώ-
σεως. ἐγὼ γοῦν ἤδη μεθύω σοι καὶ ναυτιῶ
καὶ ἢν μὴ τάχιστα ἐξεμέσω πάντα ταῦτα ὁπόσα
διεξελήλυθας, εὖ ἴσθι, κορυβαντιάσειν μοι δοκῶ
περιβομβούμενος ὑφ' ὧν κατεσκέδασάς μου ὀνομάτων. καίτοι τὸ μὲν πρῶτον γελᾶν ἐπῄει μοι
ἐπ' αὐτοῖς, ἐπειδὴ δὲ πολλὰ καὶ πάντα ὅμοια
ἦν, ἠλέουν σε τῆς κακοδαιμονίας ὁρῶν εἰς λαβύρινθον ἄφυκτον ἐμπεπτωκότα καὶ νοσοῦντα νόσον
τὴν μεγίστην, μᾶλλον δὲ μελαγχολῶντα.

17 Ζητῶ οὖν πρὸς ἐμαυτὸν ὁπόθεν τὰ τοσαῦτα κακὰ
συνελέξω καὶ ἐν ὁπόσῳ χρόνῳ καὶ ὅπου κατα-
κλείσας εἶχες τοσοῦτον ἐσμὸν ἀτόπων καὶ διαστρό-
φων ὀνομάτων, ὧν τὰ μὲν αὐτὸς ἐποίησας, τὰ
δὲ κατορωρυγμένα ποθὲν ἀνασπῶν κατὰ τὸ
ἰαμβεῖον[2]

ὄλοιο θνητῶν ἐκλέγων τὰς συμφοράς·

τοσοῦτον βόρβορον συνερανίσας κατήντλησάς μου
μηδέν σε δεινὸν εἰργασμένου. δοκεῖς δέ μοι
μήτε φίλον τινὰ ἢ οἰκεῖον ἢ εὔνουν ἔχειν μήτε
ἀνδρὶ ἐλευθέρῳ πώποτε καὶ παρρησίαν ἄγοντι

---

[1] ὑπὸ N : ἀπὸ other MSS. [2] Source unknown.

LEXIPHANES

" Well, then," quoth he, " you, if you like, may sail and swim and course over the main, but I from off the land, with a drink at my elbow, like Homer's Zeus, shall look upon you either from a bald cop or the pitch of heaven as you drive and the wind gives your vessel a saucy fairing from astern."

LYCINUS

Enough, Lexiphanes, both of the drinking-party and of the reading. I am already half-seas-over and squeamish, and if I do not very soon jettison all this gallimaufry of yours, depend upon it, I expect to go raving crazy with the roaring in my ears from the words with which you have showered me. At first I was inclined to laugh at it all, but when it turned out to be such a quantity and all of a sort, I pitied you for your hard luck, seeing that you had fallen into a labyrinthine maze from which there was no escaping and were afflicted with the most serious of all illnesses—I mean, were as mad as a hatter.

I have been quietly wondering from what source you have culled so much pestilential stuff, and how long it took you, and where you locked up and kept such a swarm of outlandish distorted expressions, of which you made some yourself and resurrected others from the graves in which they lay buried somewhere. As the verse puts it,

Plague take you, that you garner mortal woes,

such a mess of filthy bilge water did you get together and fling over me, when I had done you no harm at all. You seem to me not only to be destitute of friends and relatives and well-wishers but never to have fallen in with an independent man practising frank-

ἐντετυχηκέναι, ὃς τἀληθὲς εἰπὼν ἔπαυσεν ἄν σε
ὑδέρῳ μὲν ἐχόμενον καὶ ὑπὸ τοῦ πάθους διαρ-
ραγῆναι κινδυνεύοντα, σαυτῷ δὲ εὔσαρκον εἶναι
δοκοῦντα καὶ εὐρωστίαν οἰόμενον τὴν συμφορὰν
καὶ ὑπὸ μὲν τῶν ἀνοήτων ἐπαινούμενον ἀγνοούντων
ἃ πάσχεις, ὑπὸ δὲ τῶν πεπαιδευμένων εἰκότως
ἐλεούμενον.

18   Ἀλλ' εἰς καλὸν γὰρ τουτονὶ Σώπολιν ὁρῶ τὸν
ἰατρὸν προσιόντα, φέρε τούτῳ ἐγχειρίσαντές σε
καὶ διαλεχθέντες ὑπὲρ τῆς νόσου ἴασίν τινά σοι
εὑρώμεθα· συνετὸς γὰρ ἀνήρ[1] καὶ πολλοὺς ἤδη
παραλαβὼν ὥσπερ σὲ ἡμιμανεῖς καὶ κορυζῶντας
ἀπήλλαξεν ἐγχέας φάρμακον. χαῖρε, Σώπολι, καὶ
τουτονὶ Λεξιφάνην παραλαβὼν ἑταῖρον, ὡς οἶσθα,
ἡμῖν ὄντα, λήρῳ δὲ νῦν καὶ ξένῃ περὶ τὴν φωνὴν
νόσῳ ξυνόντα καὶ κινδυνεύοντα ἤδη τελέως ἀπολωλέναι σῶσον ἑνί γέ τῳ τρόπῳ.

ΛΕΞΙΦΑΝΗΣ

19   Μὴ ἐμέ, Σώπολι, ἀλλὰ τουτονὶ Λυκῖνον, ὃς
περιφανῶς μακκοᾷ καὶ ἄνδρας πεφρενωμένους
ὀλισθογνωμονεῖν οἴεται καὶ κατὰ τὸν Μνησάρχου
τὸν Σάμιον σιωπὴν καὶ γλωτταργίαν ἡμῖν ἐπι-
βάλλει. ἀλλὰ μὰ τὴν ἀναίσχυντον Ἀθηνᾶν καὶ
τὸν μέγαν θηριομάχον Ἡρακλέα οὐδ' ὅσον τοῦ
γρῦ καὶ τοῦ φνεῖ φροντιοῦμεν αὐτοῦ· ὀττεύομαι
γοῦν μηδὲ ὅλως ἐντυγχάνειν αὐτῷ. ἔοικα δὲ
καὶ ῥιναυλήσειν[2] τοιαῦτα ἐπιτιμῶντος ἀκούων.

---

[1] ἀνήρ MSS.: corr. Dindorf.
[2] ῥιναυλήσειν Gesner: ῥιναυστήσειν MSS.

ness, who by telling you the truth might have relieved you, dropsical as you are and in danger of bursting with the disease, although to yourself you appear to be in good point and you consider your calamity the pink of condition. You are praised by the fools, to be sure, who do not know what ails you; but the intelligent fittingly pity you.

But what luck! here I see Sopolis the physician drawing near. Come now, suppose we put you in his hands, have a consultation with him about your complaint, and find some cure for you. The man is clever, and often before now, taking charge of people like yourself, half crazed and full of drivel, he has relieved them with his doses of medicine. —Good-day to you, Sopolis. Do take charge of Lexiphanes here, who is my friend, as you know, and at present has on him a nonsensical, outlandish distemper affecting his speech which is likely to be the death of him outright. Do save him in one way or another.

Not me, Sopolis, but this man Lycinus, who is patently maggoty and thinks that well-furnished heads want wits, and imposes silence and a truce of the tongue upon us in the style of the son of Mnesarchus, the Samian.[1] But I protest, by bashless Athena and by mighty Heracles, slayer of ferines, I shan't bother even a flock or a doit about him! In fact I abominate meeting him at all, and I am fit to snort when I hear him pass such censure. Any-

---

[1] Pythagoras; in *Philosophies for Sale*, 3 (II, 454) Lucian alludes to the five years of silence which he imposed on his pupils.

καὶ ἤδη γε ἄπειμι παρὰ τὸν ἑταῖρον Κλεινίαν, ὅτι
πυνθάνομαι χρόνου ἤδη ἀκάθαρτον εἶναι αὐτῷ τὴν
γυναῖκα καὶ ταύτην νοσεῖν, ὅτι μὴ ῥεῖ. ὥστε
οὐκέτι οὐδ᾽ ἀναβαίνει αὐτήν, ἀλλ᾽ ἄβατος καὶ
ἀνήροτός ἐστιν.

ΣΩΠΟΛΙΣ

20   Τί δὲ νοσεῖ, ὦ Λυκῖνε, Λεξιφάνης ;

ΛΥΚΙΝΟΣ

Αὐτὰ ταῦτα, ὦ Σώπολι. οὐκ ἀκούεις οἷα
φθέγγεται ; καὶ ἡμᾶς τοὺς νῦν προσομιλοῦντας
καταλιπὼν πρὸ χιλίων ἐτῶν ἡμῖν διαλέγεται
διαστρέφων τὴν γλῶτταν καὶ ταυτὶ τὰ ἀλλόκοτα
συντιθεὶς καὶ σπουδὴν ποιούμενος ἐπ᾽ αὐτοῖς,
ὡς δή τι μέγα ὄν, εἴ τι ξενίζοι καὶ τὸ καθεστηκὸς
νόμισμα τῆς φωνῆς παρακόπτοι.

ΣΩΠΟΛΙΣ

Μὰ Δί᾽ οὐ μικράν τινα λέγεις τὴν νόσον, ὦ
Λυκῖνε. βοηθητέα γοῦν τῷ ἀνδρὶ πάσῃ μηχανῇ
καὶ—κατὰ θεὸν γὰρ τῶν χολώντων [1] τινι φάρμακον
τουτὶ κερασάμενος ἀπήειν, ὡς πιὼν ἐμέσειε—φέρε
πρῶτος αὐτὸς πίθι, ὦ Λεξίφανες, ὡς ὑγιὴς ἡμῖν
καὶ καθαρὸς γένοιο, τῆς τοιαύτης τῶν λόγων ἀτοπίας
κενωθείς. ἀλλὰ πείσθητί μοι καὶ πίθι καὶ ῥᾴων ἔσῃ.

ΛΕΞΙΦΑΝΗΣ

Οὐκ οἶδ᾽ ὃ καὶ δράσετέ με, ὦ Σώπολι, σύ τε
καὶ Λυκῖνος, πιπίσκοντες τουτουὶ τοῦ φαρμάκου.
δέδοικα γοῦν μὴ πῶμα [2] γένοιτό μοι τοῦτο τῶν
λόγων τὸ πόμα.

---

[1] χολώντων Γ (Cobet): χολωτῶν N vulg.
[2] πτῶμα N, edd.   But πῶμα is used by Lexiphanes in the
sense of "lid," πόμα as Attic for "drink."

LEXIPHANES

how, I am this moment going off to my comrade
Cleinias's because I am informed that for some time
now his wife is irregular[1] and out of sorts by reason
of wanting issue, so that he no longer even knows
her; she is unapproachable and uncultivated.

SOPOLIS

What ails him, Lycinus?

LYCINUS

Just that, Sopolis! Can't you hear how he talks?
Abandoning us, who converse with him now, he talks
to us from a thousand years ago, distorting his
language, making these preposterous combinations,
and taking himself very seriously in the matter, as
if it were a great thing for him to use an alien
idiom and debase the established currency of speech.

SOPOLIS

By Zeus, it is no trivial disorder you tell of, Lycinus.
The man must be helped by all means. As good
luck would have it, I came away with this medicine,
made up for an insane person, so that by taking it he
might throw off his bile. Come, you be the first to
take it, Lexiphanes, that we may have you cured
and cleansed, once you have rid yourself of such
impossible language. Do obey me and take it, and
you will feel better.

LEXIPHANES

I don't know what you and Lycinus mean to do
to me, Sopolis, plying me with this drench. Indeed,
I fear your draught may chill my vocabulary.

[1] As applied to a woman ἧς ἐπεσχημένα τὰ γυναικεῖα,
ἀκάθαρτος is accredited in Athen., 98, to " this word-chasing
sophist "; *i.e.* Pompeianus, according to Casaubon. Cf. 97 f.

319

ΛΥΚΙΝΟΣ

Πῖθι καὶ μὴ μέλλε, ὡς ἀνθρώπινα ἤδη φρονοίης
καὶ λέγοις.

ΛΕΞΙΦΑΝΗΣ

Ἰδοὺ πείθομαι καὶ πίομαι. φεῦ, τί τοῦτο ;
πολὺς ὁ βορβορυγμός. ἐγγαστρίμυθόν τινα ἔοικα
πεπωκέναι.

ΣΩΠΟΛΙΣ

21 Ἄρξαι δὴ ἐμεῖν. βαβαί. πρῶτον τουτὶ τὸ
μῶν, εἶτα μετ' αὐτὸ ἐξελήλυθεν τὸ κᾆτα, εἶτα ἐπ'
αὐτοῖς τὸ ἦ δ' ὅς καὶ ἀμηγέπη καὶ λῷστε καὶ
δήπουθεν καὶ συνεχὲς τὸ ἄττα. βίασαι δ' ὅμως,
καὶ κάθες εἰς τὴν φάρυγγα τοὺς δακτύλους.
οὐδέπω τὸ ἴκταρ ἐμήμεκας οὐδὲ τὸ σκορδινᾶσθαι
οὐδὲ τὸ τευτάζεσθαι οὐδὲ τὸ σκύλλεσθαι.[1] πολλὰ
ἔτι ὑποδέδυκε καὶ μεστή σοι αὐτῶν ἡ γαστήρ.
ἄμεινον δέ, εἰ καὶ κάτω διαχωρήσειεν ἂν ἔνια·
ἡ γοῦν σιληπορδία μέγαν τὸν ψόφον ἐργάσεται
συνεκπεσοῦσα μετὰ τοῦ πνεύματος.

Ἀλλ' ἤδη μὲν καθαρὸς οὑτοσὶ πλὴν εἴ τι με-
μένηκεν ὑπόλοιπον ἐν τοῖς κάτω ἐντέροις. σὺ δὲ τὸ
μετὰ τοῦτο παραλαβὼν αὐτόν, ὦ Λυκῖνε, μεταπαί-
δευε καὶ δίδασκε ἃ χρὴ λέγειν.

---

[1] σκύλλεσθαι N: σκύλεσθαι ΓΕΑ.

LEXIPHANES

LYCINUS

Drink without delay, that at last you may be human in thought and speech.

LEXIPHANES

There, I obey and drink. Oh me, what is this? The bombilation is vast! I would seem to have swallowed a familiar spirit.[1]

SOPOLIS

Begin now to lighten yourself. Aha! First, this "prithee," then after it "eftsoons" has come up; then on their heels his "quoth he" and "in some wise," and "fair sir," and "in sooth," and his incessant "sundry." Make an effort, however; put your fingers down your throat. You have not yet given up "instanter" or "pandiculation" or "divagation" or "spoliation." Many things still lurk in hiding and your inwards are full of them.[2] It would be better if some should take the opposite course. Anyhow, "vilipendency" will make a great racket when it comes tumbling out on the wings of the wind.

Well, this man is now purged, unless something has remained behind in his lower intestines. It is for you next, Lycinus, to take him on, mending his education and teaching him what to say.

[1] Cf. i Sam. (in the Septuagint, i Kings) 28, 8.
[2] Some of these words (λῶστε, ἴκταρ, σκορδινᾶσθαι, τευτάζεσθαι, σκύλλεσθαι) have not been used by Lexiphanes in this present exhibition of his powers. Compare the list in *A Professor of Public Speaking*, 16 : τὸ ἄττα καὶ κᾶτα καὶ μῶν καὶ ἀμηγέπη καὶ λῶστε.

ΛΥΚΙΝΟΣ

22 Οὕτω ποιήσομεν, ὦ Σώπολι, ἐπειδήπερ ἡμῖν
προωδοποίηται τὰ παρὰ σοῦ· καὶ πρὸς σὲ τὸ
λοιπόν, ὦ Λεξίφανες, ἡ συμβουλή. εἴπερ ἄρ'
ἐθέλεις ὡς ἀληθῶς ἐπαινεῖσθαι ἐπὶ λόγοις κἀν τοῖς
πλήθεσιν εὐδοκιμεῖν, τὰ μὲν τοιαῦτα πάντα
φεῦγε καὶ ἀποτρέπου, ἀρξάμενος δὲ ἀπὸ τῶν
ἀρίστων ποιητῶν καὶ ὑπὸ διδασκάλοις αὐτοὺς
ἀναγνοὺς μέτιθι ἐπὶ τοὺς ῥήτορας, καὶ τῇ ἐκείνων
φωνῇ συντραφεὶς ἐπὶ τὰ Θουκυδίδου καὶ Πλάτωνος
ἐν καιρῷ μέτιθι, πολλὰ καὶ τῇ καλῇ κωμῳδίᾳ καὶ
τῇ σεμνῇ τραγῳδίᾳ ἐγγεγυμνασμένος· παρὰ
γὰρ τούτων ἅπαντα τὰ κάλλιστα ἀπανθισάμενος
ἔσῃ τις ἐν λόγοις· ὡς νῦν γε ἐλελήθεις σαυτὸν τοῖς
ὑπὸ τῶν κοροπλάθων εἰς τὴν ἀγορὰν πλαττομένοις
ἐοικώς, κεχρωσμένος μὲν τῇ μίλτῳ καὶ τῷ κυανῷ,
τὸ δ' ἔνδοθεν πήλινός τε καὶ εὔθρυπτος ὤν.

23 Ἐὰν ταῦτα ποιῇς, πρὸς ὀλίγον τὸν ἐπὶ τῇ ἀπαι-
δευσίᾳ ἔλεγχον ὑπομείνας καὶ μὴ αἰδεσθεὶς μετα-
μανθάνων, θαρρῶν ὁμιλήσεις τοῖς πλήθεσι καὶ
οὐ καταγελασθήσῃ ὥσπερ νῦν οὐδὲ διὰ στόματος
ἐπὶ τῷ χείρονι τοῖς ἀρίστοις ἔσῃ, Ἕλληνα καὶ
Ἀττικὸν ἀποκαλούντων σε τὸν μηδὲ βαρβάρων [1]
ἐν τοῖς σαφεστάτοις ἀριθμεῖσθαι ἄξιον. πρὸ
πάντων δὲ ἐκεῖνο μέμνησό μοι, μὴ μιμεῖσθαι τῶν
ὀλίγον πρὸ ἡμῶν γενομένων σοφιστῶν τὰ φαυλό-
τατα μηδὲ περιεσθίειν ἐκεῖνα ὥσπερ νῦν, ἀλλὰ τὰ
μὲν τοιαῦτα καταπατεῖν, ζηλοῦν δὲ τὰ ἀρχαῖα
τῶν παραδειγμάτων. μηδέ σε θελγέτωσαν αἱ
ἀνεμῶναι τῶν λόγων, ἀλλὰ κατὰ τὸν τῶν ἀθλητῶν
νόμον ἡ στερρά σοι τροφὴ συνήθης ἔστω, μάλιστα

---

[1] βαρβάρων Gronovius: βάρβαρον MSS.

LEXIPHANES

LYCINUS

That I will, Sopolis, since you have cleared the way for me, and the advice which will follow is to your address, Lexiphanes. If you really desire to be genuinely praised for style and to have a great name among the public, avoid and shun all this sort of thing. After beginning with the best poets and reading them under tutors, pass to the orators, and when you have become familiar with their diction, go over in due time to Thucydides and Plato—but only after you have first disciplined yourself thoroughly in attractive comedy and sober tragedy. When you have garnered all that is fairest from these sources, you will be a personality in letters. Before, you had unconsciously become like the images shaped for the market by the modellers of figurines, coloured with red and blue on the surface, but clay on the inside, and very fragile.

If you do this, abiding for a time the reproach of illiteracy and feeling no shame to mend your knowledge, you will address the public confidently and will not be laughed at as you are now, or talked about in an uncomplimentary manner by our best people, who dub you "the Greek" and "the Athenian" when you do not deserve to be numbered even among the most intelligible of barbarians. Before all else, however, please remember not to imitate the most worthless productions of the Sophists who lived only a little before our own time, or to go nibbling at that stuff as you do now —tread that sort of thing underfoot and copy the ancient models only. And do not let yourself be enticed by the wind-flowers of speech, but follow the custom of the athletes and habituate yourself

δὲ Χάρισι καὶ Σαφηνείᾳ θῦε, ὧν πάμπολυ λίαν
24 νῦν ἀπελέλειψο. καὶ ὁ τῦφος δὲ καὶ ἡ μεγαλαυχία
καὶ ἡ κακοήθεια καὶ τὸ βρενθύεσθαι καὶ λαρυγ-
γίζειν ἀπέστω, καὶ τὸ διασιλλαίνειν τὰ τῶν ἄλλων
καὶ οἴεσθαι ὅτι πρῶτος ἔσῃ αὐτός, ἢν τὰ πάντων
συκοφαντῆς.

Καὶ μὴν κἀκεῖνο οὐ μικρόν, μᾶλλον δὲ τὸ μέγιστον ἁμαρτάνεις, ὅτι οὐ πρότερον τὰς διανοίας
τῶν λέξεων προπαρεσκευασμένος ἔπειτα κατακο-
σμεῖς τοῖς ῥήμασιν καὶ τοῖς ὀνόμασιν, ἀλλὰ ἤν
που ῥῆμα ἔκφυλον εὕρῃς ἢ αὐτὸς πλασάμενος
οἰηθῇς εἶναι καλόν, τούτῳ ζητεῖς διάνοιαν ἐφαρ-
μόσαι καὶ ζημίαν ἡγῇ, ἂν μὴ παραβύσῃς αὐτό
που, κἂν τῷ λεγομένῳ μηδ' ἀναγκαῖον ᾖ, οἷον
πρώην τὸν θυμάλωπα[1] οὐδὲ εἰδὼς ὅ τι σημαίνει,
ἀπέρριψας οὐδὲν ἐοικότα τῷ ὑποκειμένῳ. καὶ
οἱ μὲν ἰδιῶται πάντες ἐτεθήπεσαν ὑπὸ τοῦ ξένου
πληγέντες τὰ ὦτα, οἱ πεπαιδευμένοι δὲ ἐπ' ἀμφοτέροις, καὶ σοὶ καὶ τοῖς ἐπαινοῦσιν, ἐγέλων.
25 Τὸ δὲ πάντων καταγελαστότατον ἐκεῖνό ἐστιν,
ὅτι ὑπεράττικος εἶναι ἀξιῶν καὶ τὴν φωνὴν εἰς τὸ
ἀρχαιότατον ἀπηκριβωμένος τοιαῦτα ἔνια, μᾶλλον
δὲ τὰ πλεῖστα, ἐγκαταμιγνύεις τοῖς λόγοις ἃ
μηδὲ παῖς ἄρτι μανθάνων ἀγνοήσειεν ἄν·[2] οἷον
ἐκεῖνα πῶς οἴει κατὰ γῆς δῦναι ηὐχόμην ἀκούων
σου ἐπιδεικνυμένου, ὅτε χιτώνιον μὲν καὶ τὸ
ἀνδρεῖον ᾤου λέγεσθαι, δουλάρια δὲ καὶ τοὺς
ἄρρενας τῶν ἀκολούθων ἀπεκάλεις, ἃ τίς οὐκ
οἶδεν ὅτι χιτώνιον μὲν γυναικὸς ἐσθής, δουλάρια

[1] θυμάλωπα Guyet: οὐμάλωπα MSS.
[2] ἄν Jacobitz: not in MSS.

to solid nourishment. Above all, sacrifice to the
Graces and to Clearness; you are very remote from
them at present! As for vanity, boastfulness and
malice, blustering and bawling, away with them,
and with girding at the works of all others and
thinking that you yourself will be first if you carp
at the achievements of everyone else.

Yes, and there is also this fault which you have,
not a slight one, but rather the greatest possible :
you do not prepare your thoughts in advance of
your words and subsequently dress them out in the
parts of speech, but if you find anywhere an outlandish expression or make one up yourself and
think it pretty, you endeavour to fit the thought to
it and think yourself damaged if you cannot stuff it
in somewhere, even if it is not essential to what you
are saying. For example, the other day, without
even knowing what "scintilla" meant, you tossed it
off when it had no relation at all to the subject,
and the vulgar to a man were dazed when its
unfamiliarity struck their ears, but the well-informed
laughed, not only at you but at your admirers.

What is most ridiculous of all is that although you
want to be more than Attic and have meticulously
shaped your diction after the most antiquated
pattern, some (or rather, most) of the expressions
which you intermingle with what you say are
such that even a boy just beginning school would
not fail to know them. For instance, you can't
think how I prayed for the earth to swallow me as I
listened to the exhibition you made of yourself
when you thought that "shift" meant a man's
garment also, and used "slatterns" of male servants
when who does not know that a shift is a female

THE WORKS OF LUCIAN

δὲ τὰ θήλεα καλοῦσιν; καὶ ἄλλα πολὺ τούτων
προφανέστερα, οἷον τὸ ἵπτατο καὶ τὸ ἀπαντώμενος
καὶ τὸ καθεσθείς, οὐδὲ μετοικικὰ τῆς Ἀθηναίων
φωνῆς. ἡμεῖς οὐδὲ ποιητὰς ἐπαινοῦμεν τοὺς
κατάγλωττα¹ γράφοντας ποιήματα. τὰ δὲ σά,
ὡς πεζὰ μέτροις παραβάλλειν, καθάπερ ὁ Δωσιάδα
Βωμὸς ἂν εἴη καὶ ἡ τοῦ Λυκόφρονος Ἀλεξάνδρα,
καὶ εἴ τις ἔτι τούτων τὴν φωνὴν κακοδαιμο-
νέστερος.

Ἂν ταῦτα ζηλώσῃς καὶ μεταμάθῃς, ἄριστα
βεβουλευμένος ὑπὲρ σεαυτοῦ ἔσῃ· ἢν δὲ λάθῃς
αὖθις εἰς τὴν λιχνείαν κατολισθών, ἐμοὶ μὲν
ἀποπεπλήρωται ἡ παραίνεσις, σὺ δὲ σεαυτὸν
αἰτιάσῃ, ἄν γε καὶ ξυνῆς χείρων γενόμενος.

¹ κατάγλωττα Meineke: κατὰ γλῶτταν MSS.

---

¹ ἐπέτετο ("flew") should have been used instead of ἵπτατο;
cf. Lobeck's Phrynichus, p. 324, and Lucian, *Soloecista*, 48
(Vol. VII). But Lucian himself has the condemned form
sometimes; *e.g.*, Vol. III, p. 392, twice.
² The active, ἀπαντῶν, should have been employed, not the
middle, which is poetic according to Phrynichus (p. 288).

LEXIPHANES

garment and that only women are called slatterns?
And there were other things far more obvious than
these, like "flopped"[1] and "meeting up"[2] and
"setting,"[3] which are not even naturalised in the
Attic tongue. We do not praise even poets who
compose poems that are all full of rare words, but
your compositions, if I might compare prose to verse,
would be like the "Altar" of Dosiadas, the
"Alexandra" of Lycophron, and whatever else
is still more infelicitous in diction than those works.[4]

If you imitate the men of whom I have spoken
and if you repair your education, you will have
planned the best possible course for yourself, but if
you unwittingly slip back into your preciosity, I at
least have done my part in advising you and you
may blame yourself, if indeed you are conscious of
deterioration.

[3] Forms like καθεσθείς are called "outlandish" (ἔκφυλον) by
Phrynichus (p. 269) and in the *Soloecista*, 63; but cf. Lucian,
True Story, I, 23, περικαθεσθέντες.

[4] For the *Altar* of Dosiadas see Edmonds, *Greek Bucolic Poets*,
p. 506. Lycophron's *Alexandra* (A. W. Mair) is in one volume
with Callimachus and Aratus in the L.C.L.

THE EUNUCH

A MALICIOUSLY satirical account of a competition for one of the chairs in philosophy established at Athens, along with a chair in rhetoric, by Marcus Aurelius. The chairs in philosophy were apportioned to four sects only—Platonic, Stoic, Epicurean, and Peripatetic. That there were two chairs for each of these sects, not merely one, is clear from the statement that this vacancy is due (c. 3) to the death of one of the two Peripatetics (τῶν Περιπατητικῶν οἶμαι τὸν ἕτερον). Each chair carried a stipend of 10,000 drachmas. The first appointment in rhetoric (Theodotus) was made by the emperor himself; those in philosophy were committed to Herodes Atticus, who, however, cannot have made any nominations after the first, as the chairs were established in November, 176 A.D., and the death of Herodes can hardly be dated later than 178 A.D. It is not surprising, therefore, that Lucian speaks of selection by a jury of prominent Athenians.

It is not probable that the incident occurred before 179 A.D., and it may easily have been much later. The dialogue was undoubtedly written at the time, and at Athens. The names given to the competitors are fictitious, and nothing is known that affords any ground for conjecture as to the identity of either one.

ΕΥΝΟΥΧΟΣ

ΠΑΜΦΙΛΟΣ

1 Πόθεν, ὦ Λυκῖνε, καὶ[1] τί γελῶν ἡμῖν ἀφῖξαι ;
ἀεὶ μὲν γὰρ φαιδρὸς ὢν τυγχάνεις, τουτὶ δὲ πλέον
τοῦ συνήθους εἶναί μοι δοκεῖ, ἐφ' ὅτῳ μηδὲ κατέχειν δυνατὸς εἶ τὸν γέλωτα.

ΛΥΚΙΝΟΣ

Ἐξ ἀγορᾶς μὲν ἥκω σοι, ὦ Πάμφιλε· τοῦ
γέλωτος δὲ αὐτίκα κοινωνὸν ποιήσομαί σε, ἢν
ἀκούσῃς οἵᾳ δίκῃ δικαζομένῃ παρεγενόμην, φιλοσόφων πρὸς ἀλλήλους ἐριζόντων.

ΠΑΜΦΙΛΟΣ

Καὶ τοῦτο μὲν ὡς ἀληθῶς γελοῖον λέγεις,
τὸ φιλοσοφοῦντας δικάζεσθαι πρὸς ἀλλήλους,
δέον, εἰ καί τι μέγα εἴη, κατ' εἰρήνην ἐν σφίσι
διαλύεσθαι τὰ ἐγκλήματα.

ΛΥΚΙΝΟΣ

2 Πόθεν, ὦ μακάριε, κατ' εἰρήνην ἐκεῖνοι, οἵ γε
ξυμπεσόντες ὅλας ἁμάξας βλασφημιῶν κατεσκέδα-
σαν ἀλλήλων, κεκραγότες καὶ ὑπερδιατεινόμενοι ;

---

[1] καὶ τί Herwerden: ἢ τί MSS.

THE EUNUCH

PAMPHILUS

Where have you been, Lycinus, and what are you laughing at, I should like to know, as you come? Of course, you are always in a good humour, but this appears to me to be something out of the ordinary, as you cannot restrain your laughter over it.

LYCINUS

I have been in the Agora, I'd have you know, Pamphilus; and I shall make you share my laughter at once if you let me tell you what sort of case has been tried in my presence, between philosophers wrangling with each other.

PAMPHILUS

Well, what you have already said is laughable, in all truth, that followers of philosophy should have it out with one another at law, when they ought, even if it should be something of importance, to settle their complaints peaceably among themselves.

LYCINUS

Indeed, you blessed simpleton! Peaceably! They! Why, they came together at full tilt and flung whole cartloads of abuse upon each other, shouting and straining their lungs enough to split them!

THE WORKS OF LUCIAN

ΠΑΜΦΙΛΟΣ

Ἦ που, ὦ Λυκῖνε, περὶ τῶν λόγων διεφέροντο τὰ
συνήθη ταῦτα, ἑτερόδοξοι τυγχάνοντες;

ΛΥΚΙΝΟΣ

Οὐδαμῶς, ἀλλ᾽ ἑτεροῖόν τι τοῦτο ἦν· ὁμόδοξοι
γὰρ ἄμφω καὶ ἀπὸ τῶν αὐτῶν λόγων. δίκη δὲ
ὅμως συνειστήκει καὶ δικασταὶ ψηφοφοροῦντες
ἦσαν οἱ ἄριστοι καὶ πρεσβύτατοι καὶ σοφώτατοι
τῶν ἐν τῇ πόλει καὶ ἐφ᾽ ὧν ἄν τις ᾐδέσθη παρὰ
μέλος τι φθεγξάμενος, οὐχ ὅπως ἐς τοσαύτην
ἀναισχυντίαν τραπόμενος.

ΠΑΜΦΙΛΟΣ

Οὐκοῦν λέγοις ἂν ἤδη τὸ κεφάλαιον τῆς δίκης,
ὡς καὶ αὐτὸς εἰδείην ὅ τι σοὶ τὸ κεκινηκὸς εἴη τὸν
τοσοῦτον γέλωτα.

ΛΥΚΙΝΟΣ

3 Συντέτακται μέν, ὦ Πάμφιλε, ὡς οἶσθα, ἐκ
βασιλέως μισθοφορά τις οὐ φαύλη κατὰ γένη
τοῖς φιλοσόφοις, Στωϊκοῖς λέγω καὶ Πλατωνικοῖς
καὶ Ἐπικουρείοις, ἔτι δὲ καὶ τοῖς ἐκ τοῦ Περιπάτου,
τὰ ἴσα τούτοις ἅπασιν. ἔδει δὲ ἀποθανόντος
αὐτῶν τινος ἄλλον ἀντικαθίστασθαι δοκιμασθέντα
ψήφῳ τῶν ἀρίστων. καὶ τὰ ἆθλα οὐ βοείη τις
ἦν, κατὰ τὸν ποιητήν, οὐδὲ ἱερεῖον, ἀλλὰ μύριαι
κατὰ τὸν ἐνιαυτόν, ἐφ᾽ ὅτῳ συνεῖναι τοῖς νέοις.

ΠΑΜΦΙΛΟΣ

Οἶδα ταῦτα· καί τινά φασιν αὐτῶν ἔναγχος
ἀποθανεῖν, τῶν Περιπατητικῶν οἶμαι τὸν ἕτερον.

342

THE EUNUCH

No doubt, Lycinus, they were bickering about their doctrines, as usual, being of different sects?

LYCINUS

Not at all; this was something different, for they were of the same sect and agreed in their doctrines. Nevertheless, a trial had been arranged, and the judges, endowed with the deciding vote, were the most prominent and oldest and wisest men in the city, in whose presence one would have been ashamed even to strike a false note, let alone resorting to such shamelessness.

PAMPHILUS

Then do please tell me at once the point at issue in the trial, so that I may know what it is that has stirred up so much laughter in you.

LYCINUS

Well, Pamphilus, the Emperor has established, as you know, an allowance, not inconsiderable, for the philosophers according to sect—the Stoics, I mean, the Platonics, and the Epicureans; also those of the Walk, the same amount for each of these. It was stipulated that when one of them died another should be appointed in his stead, after being approved by vote of the first citizens. And the prize was not " a shield of hide or a victim," as the poet has it,[1] but a matter of ten thousand drachmas a year, for instructing boys.

PAMPHILUS

I know all that; and one of them died, they say, recently—one of the two Peripatetics, I think.

[1] Homer, *Iliad*, XXII, 159.

ΛΥΚΙΝΟΣ

Αὕτη, ὦ Πάμφιλε, ἡ Ἑλένη ὑπὲρ ἧς ἐμονομάχουν
πρὸς ἀλλήλους. καὶ ἄχρι γε τούτου γελοῖον
οὐδὲν πλὴν [1] ἐκεῖνο ἴσως, [2] τὸ φιλοσόφους εἶναι
φάσκοντας καὶ χρημάτων καταφρονεῖν ἔπειτα
ὑπὲρ τούτων ὡς ὑπὲρ πατρίδος κινδυνευούσης καὶ
ἱερῶν πατρῴων καὶ τάφων προγονικῶν ἀγωνί-
ζεσθαι.

ΠΑΜΦΙΛΟΣ

Καὶ μὴν καὶ τὸ δόγμα τοῦτό γέ ἐστιν τοῖς
Περιπατητικοῖς, τὸ μὴ σφόδρα καταφρονεῖν χρημάτων, ἀλλὰ τρίτον τι ἀγαθὸν καὶ τοῦτο οἴεσθαι.

ΛΥΚΙΝΟΣ

Ὀρθῶς λέγεις. φασὶ γὰρ οὖν ταῦτα, καὶ κατὰ
4 τὰ πάτρια ἐγίγνετο αὐτοῖς ὁ πόλεμος. τὰ μετὰ
ταῦτα δὲ ἤδη ἄκουε.

Πολλοὶ μὲν γὰρ καὶ ἄλλοι τὸν ἐπιτάφιον τοῦ
ἀποθανόντος ἐκείνου ἠγωνίζοντο· δύο δὲ μάλιστα
ἦσαν οἱ ἀμφήριστοι αὐτῶν, Διοκλῆς τε ὁ πρεσβύτης—οἶσθα ὃν λέγω, τὸν ἐριστικόν—καὶ Βαγώας
ὁ εὐνοῦχος εἶναι δοκῶν. τὰ μὲν οὖν τῶν λόγων
προηγώνιστο αὐτοῖς καὶ τὴν ἐμπειρίαν ἑκάτερος
τῶν δογμάτων ἐπεδέδεικτο καὶ ὅτι τοῦ [3] Ἀριστοτέλους καὶ τῶν ἐκείνῳ δοκούντων εἴχετο· καὶ
5 μὰ τὸν Δί’ οὐδέτερος αὐτῶν ἀμείνων ἦν. τὸ
δ’ οὖν τέλος τῆς δίκης ἐς τοῦτο περιέστη· ἀφέμενος γὰρ ὁ Διοκλῆς τοῦ δεικνύναι τὰ αὑτοῦ
μετέβαινεν ἐπὶ τὸν Βαγώαν καὶ διελέγχειν ἐπειρᾶτο
μάλιστα τὸν βίον αὐτοῦ· κατὰ ταῦτα δὲ καὶ ὁ
Βαγώας ἀντεξήταζε τὸν ἐκείνου βίον.

---

[1] πλὴν Harmon : ἦν MSS. ἢ Urban.

THE EUNUCH

That, Pamphilus, is the Helen for whom they were
meeting each other in single combat. And up to
this point there was nothing to laugh at except perhaps that men claiming to be philosophers and to
despise lucre should fight for it as if for imperilled
fatherland, ancestral fanes, and graves of forefathers.

PAMPHILUS

Yes, but that is the doctrine of the Peripatetics,
not to despise wealth vehemently but to think it a
third " supreme good."

LYCINUS

Right you are; they do say that, and the war
that they were waging was on traditional lines. But
listen now to the sequel.

Many competitors took part in the funeral games
of the deceased, but two of them in particular were
the most favoured to win, the aged Diocles (you
know the man I mean, the dialectician) and Bagoas,
the one who is reputed to be a eunuch. The matter
of doctrines had been thrashed out between them
already, and each had displayed his familiarity with
their tenets and his adherence to Aristotle and his
placita; and by Zeus neither of them had the better
of it. The close of the trial, however, took a new
turn; Diocles, discontinuing the advertisement of
his own merits, passed over to Bagoas and made a
great effort to show up his private life, and Bagoas
met this attack by exploring the history of Diocles
in like manner.

---

² ἐκεῖνο ἴσως Urban: ἐκείνοις ὡς MSS.
³ τοῦ Fritzsche: τῶν MSS.

ΠΑΜΦΙΛΟΣ

Εἰκότως, ὦ Λυκῖνε· καὶ τὰ πλείω γε τοῦ
λόγου περὶ τούτου μᾶλλον ἐχρῆν εἶναι αὐτοῖς· ὡς
ἔγωγε, εἰ δικάζων ἐτύγχανον, ἐπὶ τῷ τοιούτῳ τὸ
πλεῖον διατρῖψαι ἄν μοι δοκῶ, τὸν ἄμεινον βιοῦντα
μᾶλλον ἢ τὸν ἐν τοῖς λόγοις αὐτοῖς προχειρότερον
ζητῶν καὶ οἰκειότερον τῇ νίκῃ νομίζων.

ΛΥΚΙΝΟΣ

6   Εὖ λέγεις, κἀμὲ ὁμόψηφον ἐν τούτῳ ἔχεις.
ἐπεὶ δὲ ἅλις μὲν εἶχον βλασφημιῶν, ἅλις δὲ ἐλέγ-
χων, τὸ τελευταῖον ἤδη ὁ Διοκλῆς ἔφη μηδὲ τὴν
ἀρχὴν θεμιτὸν εἶναι τῷ Βαγώᾳ μεταποιεῖσθαι
φιλοσοφίας καὶ τῶν ἐπ' αὐτῇ ἀριστείων εὐνούχῳ
γε ὄντι, ἀλλὰ τοὺς τοιούτους οὐχ ὅπως τούτων
ἀποκεκλεῖσθαι ἠξίου, ἀλλὰ καὶ ἱερῶν αὐτῶν καὶ
περιρραντηρίων καὶ τῶν κοινῶν ἁπάντων συλ-
λόγων, δυσοιώνιστόν τι ἀποφαίνων καὶ δυσάντητον
θέαμα, εἴ τις ἔωθεν ἐξιὼν ἐκ τῆς οἰκίας ἴδοι
τοιοῦτόν τινα. καὶ πολὺς ἦν ὁ περὶ τούτου λόγος,
οὔτε ἄνδρα οὔτε γυναῖκα εἶναι τὸν εὐνοῦχον λέγοντος, ἀλλά τι σύνθετον καὶ μικτὸν καὶ τερατῶδες,
ἔξω τῆς ἀνθρωπείας φύσεως.

ΠΑΜΦΙΛΟΣ

Καινόν γε τὸ ἔγκλημα φής, ὦ Λυκῖνε, καὶ
ἤδη γελᾶν καὶ αὐτός, ὦ ἑταῖρε, προάγομαι τῆς
παραδόξου ταύτης κατηγορίας ἀκούων. τί δ'
οὖν ἅτερος ; ἆρα τὴν ἡσυχίαν ἤγαγεν, ἤ τι πρὸς
ταῦτα καὶ αὐτὸς ἀντειπεῖν ἐτόλμησεν ;

THE EUNUCH

Naturally, Lycinus; and the greater part, certainly, of their discussion ought rather to have centred upon that. For my own part, if I had chanced to be a judge, I should have dwelt most, I think, upon that sort of thing, trying to ascertain which led the better life rather than which was the better prepared in the tenets themselves, and deeming him more suitable to win.

LYCINUS

Well said, and you have me voting with you in this. But when they had their fill of hard words, and their fill of caustic observations, Diocles at length said in conclusion that it was not at all permissible for Bagoas to lay claim to philosophy and the rewards of merit in it, since he was a eunuch; such people ought to be excluded, he thought, not simply from all that but even from temples and holy-water bowls and all the places of public assembly, and he declared it an ill-omened, ill-met sight if on first leaving home in the morning, one should set eyes on any such person. He had a great deal to say, too, on that score, observing that a eunuch was neither man nor woman but something composite, hybrid, and monstrous, alien to human nature.

PAMPHILUS

The charge you tell of, Lycinus, is novel, anyhow, and now I too, my friend, am moved to laughter, hearing of this incredible accusation. Well, what of the other? Held his peace, did he not? Or did he venture to say something himself in reply to this?

ΛΥΚΙΝΟΣ

7 Τὰ μὲν πρῶτα ὑπ᾿ αἰδοῦς καὶ δειλίας—οἰκεῖον
γὰρ αὐτοῖς τὸ τοιοῦτον—ἐπὶ πολὺ ἐσιώπα καὶ
ἠρυθρία καὶ ἰδίων φανερὸς ἦν, τέλος δὲ λεπτόν τι
καὶ γυναικεῖον ἐμφθεγξάμενος οὐ δίκαια ποιεῖν
ἔφη τὸν Διοκλέα φιλοσοφίας ἀποκλείοντα εὐνοῦχον
ὄντα, ἧς καὶ γυναιξὶ μετεῖναι· καὶ παρήγοντο
Ἀσπασία καὶ Διοτίμα καὶ Θαργηλία συνηγορή-
σουσαι αὐτῷ, καί τις Ἀκαδημαϊκὸς εὐνοῦχος ἐκ
Πελασγῶν τελῶν,[1] ὀλίγον πρὸ ἡμῶν εὐδοκιμήσας ἐν
τοῖς Ἕλλησιν. ὁ Διοκλῆς δὲ κἀκεῖνον αὐτόν, εἰ
περιῆν[2] καὶ τῶν ὁμοίων μετεποιεῖτο, εἶρξαι[3] ἂν
οὐ καταπλαγεὶς αὐτοῦ τὴν παρὰ τοῖς πολλοῖς
δόξαν· καί τινας καὶ αὐτὸς ἀπεμνημόνευε λόγους
καὶ πρὸς ἐκεῖνον ὑπό τε Στωϊκῶν καὶ Κυνικῶν
μάλιστα εἰρημένους πρὸς τὸ γελοιότερον ἐπὶ τῷ
ἀτελεῖ τοῦ σώματος.

8 Ἐν τούτοις ἦν τοῖς δικασταῖς ἡ διατριβή· καὶ τὸ
κεφάλαιον ἤδη τοῦ σκέμματος τοῦτο ἐτύγχανεν,[4]
εἰ δοκιμαστέος εὐνοῦχος ἐπὶ φιλοσοφίαν παραγγέλλων[5] καὶ νέων προστασίαν ἐγχειρισθῆναι

---

[1] ἐκ πελασγῶν τελῶν marginal in ΓΕ: ἐκ κελτῶν ΓΕ, vulg.

[2] εἰ περιῆν Ωᵇrᶜ: εἴπερ ἦν ΩΓ cett.

[3] εἶρξαι Γ: εἶρξεν vulg. For the hiatus cf. διατρίψαι ἄν,
§ 5.

[4] ἐτύγχανεν Harmon: MSS. add εἶναι (ὃν ΩΓ by correction).
Cf. *Fugit.*, 32.

[5] παραγγέλλων Γ¹: παραγγέλλειν ΝΓᶜΕ²: παρελθών Ε¹Ω:
παρελθεῖν Ω margin, late hand.

---

[1] Thargelia of Miletus was a famous hetaera, mistress of
the Antiochus who was king of Thessaly *ca.* 520–510 B.C.
She outlived him for thirty years, and was active in the cause
of Persia at the time of Xerxes' invasion of Greece. Aeschines

THE EUNUCH

At first, through shame and cowardice—for that sort of behaviour is natural to them—he remained silent a long while and blushed and was plainly in a sweat, but finally in a weak, effeminate voice he said that Diocles was acting unjustly in trying to exclude a eunuch from philosophy, in which even women had a part; and he brought in Aspasia, Diotima, and Thargelia [1] to support him; also a certain Academic eunuch hailing from among the Pelasgians, who shortly before our time achieved a high reputation among the Greeks.[2] But if that person himself were alive and advanced similar claims, Diocles would (he said) have excluded him too, undismayed by his reputation among the common sort; and he repeated a number of humorous remarks made to the man by Stoics and Cynics regarding his physical imperfection.[3]

That was what the judges dwelt upon, and the point thenceforward at issue was whether the seal of approval should be set upon a eunuch who was proposing himself for a career in philosophy and requesting that the governance of boys be committed to him. One

the Socratic wrote about her, the sophist Hippias spoke of her as beautiful and wise, and Aspasia is said to have taken her as a pattern. Diotima is the priestess of Mantinea to whom, in Plato's *Symposium*, Socrates ascribes the discourse on love which he repeats to the company. Subsequent mention of her seems to derive from that passage, and it is possible that Plato invented her.

[2] The allusion is to Favorinus of Arles, known to us from Philostratus and especially from Aulus Gellius. Part of his treatise on exile has been recovered recently from an Egyptian papyrus and published by Medea Norsa and Vitelli.

[3] Among the Cynics was Demonax; see Lucian's *Demonax*, 12 and 13 (I, pp. 150 ff.).

ἀξιῶν, τοῦ μὲν καὶ σχῆμα καὶ σώματος εὐμοιρίαν
προσεῖναι φιλοσόφῳ δεῖν λέγοντος, καὶ τὸ μέγιστον,
πώγωνα βαθὺν ἔχειν αὐτὸν καὶ τοῖς προσιοῦσι καὶ
μανθάνειν βουλομένοις ἀξιόπιστον καὶ πρέποντα
ταῖς μυρίαις ἃς χρὴ παρὰ βασιλέως ἀποφέρεσθαι,
τὸ δὲ τοῦ εὐνούχου καὶ τῶν βακήλων χεῖρον
εἶναι· τοὺς μὲν γὰρ κἂν πεπειρᾶσθαί ποτε ἀνδρείας,
τοῦτον δὲ ἐξ ἀρχῆς εὐθὺς ἀποκεκόφθαι καὶ ἀμφί-
βολόν τι ζῷον εἶναι κατὰ ταὐτὰ ταῖς κορώναις,
αἳ μήτε περιστεραῖς μήτε κόραξιν ἐναριθμοῦν-
9   το ἄν, τοῦ δὲ οὐ σωματικὴν λέγοντος εἶναι τὴν
κρίσιν, ἀλλὰ τῆς [1] ψυχῆς καὶ τῆς γνώμης ἐξέτασιν
δεῖν γίγνεσθαι καὶ τῆς τῶν δογμάτων ἐπιστήμης.
εἶθ' ὁ Ἀριστοτέλης ἐκαλεῖτο μάρτυς τοῦ λόγου,
εἰς ὑπερβολὴν θαυμάσας Ἑρμείαν τὸν εὐνοῦχον
τὸν ἐκ τοῦ Ἀταρνέως τύραννον ἄχρι τοῦ καὶ θύειν
αὐτῷ κατὰ ταὐτὰ τοῖς θεοῖς. καί τι καὶ ἐτόλμα
προστιθέναι ὁ Βαγώας τοιοῦτον, ὡς πολὺ ἐπιτη-
δειότερος τοῖς νέοις εὐνοῦχος διδάσκαλος οὐδὲ
διαβολήν τινα πρὸς αὐτοὺς ἐνδέξασθαι δυνάμενος
οὐδὲ τὸ τοῦ Σωκράτους ἐκεῖνο ἔγκλημα παθεῖν
ἂν ὡς διαφθείρων τὰ μειράκια. ἐπεὶ δὲ καὶ εἰς
τὸ ἀγένειον μάλιστα ἐσκώφθη, χαριέντως τοῦτο,
ὡς γοῦν ᾤετο, προσέρριψεν· " Εἰ γὰρ ἀπὸ πώγωνος," ἔφη, " βαθέος κρίνεσθαι δέοι τοὺς φιλοσοφοῦντας, τὸν τράγον ἂν δικαιότερον προκριθῆναι
πάντων."
10   Ἐν τούτῳ τρίτος ἄλλος παρεστώς—τὸ δὲ
ὄνομα ἐν ἀφανεῖ κείσθω—" Καὶ μήν," ἔφη, " ὦ
ἄνδρες δικασταί, οὑτοσὶ ὁ τὰς γνάθους λεῖος καὶ

---

[1] ἀλλὰ τῆς Harmon : ἀλλ' ἀλκὴν MSS.
[2] ὁ θεμιστοκλῆς NΓ² (marginal).

said that presence and a fine physical endowment should be among the attributes of a philosopher, and that above all else he should have a long beard that would inspire confidence in those who visited him and sought to become his pupils, one that would befit the ten thousand drachmas which he was to receive from the Emperor, whereas a eunuch was in worse case than a cut priest, for the latter had at least known manhood once, but the former had been marred from the very first and was an ambiguous sort of creature like a crow, which cannot be reckoned either with doves or with ravens. The other pleaded that this was not a physical examination; that there should be an investigation of soul and mind and knowledge of doctrines. Then Aristotle was cited as a witness to support his case, since he tremendously admired the eunuch Hermias, the tyrant of Atarneus, to the point of celebrating sacrifices to him in the same way as to the gods. Moreover, Bagoas ventured to add an observation to the effect that a eunuch was a far more suitable teacher for the young, since he could not incur any blame as regards them and would not incur that charge against Socrates of leading the youngsters astray. And as he had been ridiculed especially for his beardlessness, he despatched this shaft to good effect—he thought so, anyhow: " If it is by length of beard that philosophers are to be judged, a he-goat would with greater justice be given preference to all of them ! "

At this juncture a third person who was present— his name may remain in obscurity—said:[1] " As a matter of fact, gentlemen, if this fellow, so smooth

---

[1] The anonymous speaker may safely be considered the writer himself, as in the *Peregrinus*; cf. p. 8, n. 2.

τὸ φώνημα γυναικεῖος καὶ τὰ ἄλλα εὐνούχῳ ἐοικὼς
εἰ ἀποδύσαιτο, πάνυ ἀνδρεῖος ὑμῖν φανεῖται·
εἰ δὲ μὴ ψεύδονται οἱ περὶ αὐτοῦ λέγοντες, καὶ
μοιχὸς ἑάλω ποτέ, ὡς ὁ ἄξων φησίν, ἄρθρα ἐν
ἄρθροις ἔχων. ἀλλὰ τότε μὲν ἐς τὸν εὐνοῦχον
ἀναφυγὼν καὶ τοῦτο κρησφύγετον εὑρόμενος
ἀφείθη, ἀπιστησάντων τῇ κατηγορίᾳ τῶν τότε
δικαστῶν ἀπό γε τῆς φανερᾶς ὄψεως· νῦν δὲ
κἂν παλινῳδῆσαί μοι δοκεῖ τοῦ προκειμένου
μισθοῦ ἕνεκα."

11 Τούτων δὴ λεγομένων παρὰ πάντων μὲν γέλως
ἐγίγνετο, ὡς τὸ εἰκός. Βαγώας δὲ μᾶλλον ἐταράτ-
τετο καὶ παντοῖος ἦν, ἐς μυρία τρεπόμενος[1]
χρώματα καὶ ψυχρῷ τῷ ἱδρῶτι ῥεόμενος, καὶ οὔτε
συγκατατίθεσθαι τῷ περὶ[2] τῆς μοιχείας ἐγκλήματι
καλῶς ἔχειν ᾤετο οὔτε ἀχρεῖον αὑτῷ τὴν κατηγορίαν ταύτην ἐς τὸν παρόντα ἀγῶνα ἡγεῖτο εἶναι.

ΠΑΜΦΙΛΟΣ

Γελοῖα, ὦ Λυκῖνε, ὡς ἀληθῶς ταῦτα καὶ
ἔοικεν οὐ τὴν τυχοῦσαν ὑμῖν διατριβὴν παρεσχῆσθαι. τὸ δ' οὖν τέλος τί ἐγένετο καὶ πῶς ἔγνωσαν
ὑπὲρ αὐτῶν οἱ δικασταί ;

ΛΥΚΙΝΟΣ

12 Οὐχ ὁμόψηφοι πάντες ἦσαν, ἀλλ' οἱ μὲν ἠξίουν
ἀποδύσαντας αὐτὸν ὥσπερ τοὺς ἀργυρωνήτους
ἐπισκοπεῖν εἰ δύναται[3] φιλοσοφεῖν τά γε πρὸς τῶν
ὄρχεων· οἱ δὲ ἔτι γελοιότερον μεταστειλαμένους
τινὰς τῶν ἐξ οἰκήματος γυναικῶν κελεύειν αὐτὸν
συνεῖναι καὶ ὀπυίειν, καί τινα τῶν δικαστῶν τὸν

---

[1] τρεπόμενος N (Bekker): τραπόμενος ΓΕ.
[2] περὶ not in ΩΝ.   [3] δύναται ΓΝ: δύναιτο (ΕC) vulg.

of jowl, effeminate in voice, and otherwise similar to a eunuch, should strip, you would find him very masculine. Unless those who talk about him are lying, he was once taken in adultery, *commissis membris*, as the table of the law says. At that time he secured his acquittal by resorting to the name of eunuch and finding sanctuary in it, since the judges on that occasion discredited the accusation from the very look of him. Now, however, he may recant, I suppose, for the sake of the pelf that is in view."

Upon those remarks everyone began to laugh, as was natural, while Bagoas fell into greater confusion and was beside himself, turning all colours of the rainbow and dripping with cold sweat. On the one hand, he did not think it seemly to plead guilty to the charge of adultery; yet, on the other, he thought that this accusation would not be without its usefulness for the case then in progress.

PAMPHILUS

This is truly laughable, Lycinus, and must have given you uncommon diversion. But what was the outcome, and how did the judges decide about them?

LYCINUS

They were not all of the same opinion. Some thought they ought to strip him, as is done with slaves, and determine by inspection whether he had the parts to practise philosophy. Others made the suggestion, even more ridiculous, that they should send for some women out of bawdy-houses and bid him consort with them and cohabit; and that one of the judges, the eldest and most trustworthy,

343

πρεσβύτατόν τε καὶ πιστότατον ἐφεστῶτα ὁρᾶν
εἰ φιλοσοφεῖ. μετὰ δὲ ἐπεὶ πάντας ὁ γέλως
κατεῖχε καὶ οὐδεὶς ὅστις οὐ τὴν γαστέρα ἤλγει
βρασσόμενος ὑπ' αὐτοῦ, ἔγνωσαν ἀναπόμπιμον ἐς
τὴν Ἰταλίαν ἐκπέμψαι τὴν δίκην.

13   Καὶ νῦν ἅτερος μὲν πρὸς τὴν τῶν λόγων ἐπίδειξιν, ὥς φασιν, γυμνάζεται καὶ παρασκευάζεται
καὶ κατηγορίαν συγκροτεῖ καὶ τὸ τῆς μοιχείας
ἔγκλημα ὑποκινεῖ, ἐναντιώτατον αὐτῷ καὶ οὗτος
κατὰ τοὺς φαύλους τῶν ῥητόρων τοῦτο ποιῶν καὶ
εἰς τοὺς ἄνδρας τὸν ἀντίδικον ἐκ τοῦ ἐγκλήματος
καταλέγων· τῷ Βαγώᾳ δὲ ἕτερα, ὥς φασι, μέλει
καὶ ἀνδρίζεται τὰ πολλὰ καὶ διὰ χειρὸς ἔχει τὸ
πρᾶγμα καὶ τέλος κρατήσειν ἐλπίζει ἢν ἐπιδείξῃ
ὡς οὐδὲν χείρων ἐστὶν τῶν τὰς ἵππους ἀναβαινόντων
ὄνων. αὕτη γάρ, ὦ ἑταῖρε, φιλοσοφίας ἀρίστη
κρίσις ἔοικεν εἶναι καὶ ἀπόδειξις ἀναντίλεκτος.
ὥστε καὶ τὸν υἱόν—ἔτι δέ μοι κομιδῇ νέος ἐστίν
—εὐξαίμην ἂν οὐ τὴν γνώμην οὐδὲ τὴν γλῶτταν
ἀλλὰ τὸ αἰδοῖον ἕτοιμον ἐς φιλοσοφίαν ἔχειν.

should stand by and see whether he could practise philosophy! Then, as all were overcome by laughter and every man of them had a sore belly from shaking with it, they decided to refer the case to the highest court and send it to Italy.

Now, one of the pair is training, they say, for a demonstration of his eloquence, making his preparations, and composing an accusation. Morever, he is delicately putting forward the charge of adultery again, thereby acting in direct contradiction to himself, like a bad lawyer, and enrolling his opponent among fully enfranchised males through his accusation. As to Bagoas, he, they say, has different concerns, assiduously demonstrating his powers, keeping his case in hand, and, in sum, hoping to win if he can show that he is not a bit inferior to a jack at service. This, my friend, is apparently the best criterion of devotion to wisdom, and an irrefutable demonstration. Consequently, I may well pray that my son (who is still quite young) may be suitably endowed for the practise of philosophy with other tools than brain or tongue.

ASTROLOGY

A MOCK eulogy of judicial astrology, put into the mouth of some ancient worthy who used the Ionic dialect, almost certainly Democritus, the peer of Herodotus in Ionic prose style and the author, according to Cicero (*de Divin.*, I, 42), of a treatise on extispicy. The thing is so clever that it has duped almost everyone, including myself (I, ix), into taking it in earnest and proclaiming it spurious. Its Lucianic origin, however, is apparent if one looks closely enough. Orpheus, elsewhere in Lucian given a leading part in the introduction of philosophy (p. 65) and of dancing (p. 229) into Greece, is here the promulgator of astrology—but not "unto elucidation." Odysseus in the lower world is so eager to hear what Tiresias may have to say that he "endures to see his mother's *shadow* athirst," no doubt like to die of it, even as Tantalus (*Funerals*, 8 : IV, 116). The novel assumption that different peoples of Egypt worship different signs of the Zodiac serves to explain not only the animal shapes of their gods— a topic to which Lucian mischievously keeps recurring (cf. pp. 431 f., and III, 168), but the taboo upon fish to which, with Herodotean reticence as to its reason, he alludes in the *Goddesse of Surrye*, 14 (IV, 356). The same fondness for rationalizing myths with a twinkle in his eye, which elsewhere turns not only Proteus but Empusa into pantomimic dancers (pp. 231 f.), here asserts itself with complete abandon, in an astrological sense, even to the point of including Pasiphae among the adepts. And when sheer love of story-telling seduces him into repeating a favourite tale, that of Phaethon, his style betrays him utterly (cf. *Amber*, and *Dialogues of the Gods*, 25).

It is only mock eulogy, but still, in spite of the fun in it, not quite meant as satire or parody. It is primarily a sophistical literary exercise of the same nature as the first and second *Phalaris*, in which the fun is incidental—a Lucianic "parergy." To get something of the effect, the translation is intended to carry a suggestion of Sir Thomas Browne as he appears in the *Vulgar Errors*.

ΠΕΡΙ ΤΗΣ ΑΣΤΡΟΛΟΓΙΗΣ[1]

1 Ἀμφί τε οὐρανοῦ ἀμφί τε ἀστέρων ἡ γραφή,
οὐκ αὐτῶν ἀστέρων οὐδ' αὐτοῦ πέρι οὐρανοῦ,
ἀλλὰ μαντείης καὶ ἀληθείης, ἣ δὴ ἐκ τουτέων ἐς
ἀνθρώπων βίον ἔρχεται. ὁ δέ μοι λόγος οὐκ
ὑποθημοσύνην ἔχει οὐδὲ διδασκαλίην ἐπαγγέλλεται ὅκως ταύτην τὴν μαντοσύνην διενεκτέον,
ἀλλὰ μέμφομαι ὁκόσοι σοφοὶ ἐόντες τὰ μὲν ἄλλα
ἐπασκέουσι καὶ παισὶ[2] τοῖς ἑωυτῶν ἀπηγέονται,
μούνην δὲ ἀστρολογίην οὔτε τιμέουσιν οὔτε
2 ἐπασκέουσιν. καὶ ἡ μὲν σοφίη παλαιὴ οὐδὲ νέον
ἐς ἡμέας ἀπίκετο, ἀλλ' ἔστιν ἔργον ἀρχαίων
βασιλέων θεοφιλέων. οἱ δὲ νῦν ἀμαθίῃ καὶ
ῥᾳθυμίῃ καὶ προσέτι μισοπονίῃ κείνοισί τε ἀντί-
ξοα φρονέουσι καὶ εὖτ' ἂν ἀνδράσιν ἐπικυρέωσιν
ψεύδεα μαντευομένοις,[3] ἄστρων τε κατηγορέ-
ουσιν καὶ αὐτὴν ἀστρολογίην μισέουσιν, οὐδέ μιν
οὔτε ὑγιέα οὔτε ἀληθέα νομίζουσιν, ἀλλὰ λόγον
ψευδέα καὶ ἀνεμώλιον, οὐ δικαίως, ἐμοὶ δοκέει,[4]
φρονέοντες· οὐδὲ γὰρ τέκτονος ἀϊδρίῃ τεκτοσύνης
αὐτῆς ἀδικίη οὐδὲ αὐλητέω ἀμουσίῃ μουσικῆς
ἀσοφίη, ἀλλ' οἱ μὲν ἀμαθέες τῶν τεχνῶν, ἑκάστη
δ' ἐν ἑωυτῇ σοφή.

---

[1] ἀστρολογίας MSS.
[2] παισὶ du Soul: πᾶσι MSS.

348

ASTROLOGY

This treatise concerneth heaven and the stars, yet not the stars themselves nor heaven itself, but the auspiciall verity that from them assuredly entereth into the life of man. My discourse containeth not counsell, nor proffereth instruction how to ply this auspiciall art, but my aim is to chide those learned men who cultivate and expose unto their disciples all other studies, but neither esteem nor cultivate astrology. Although the science is ancient, not come to us newly, but the creation of divinely favoured kings of antiquity, yet men of these daies, through ignorance, supinity, and mislike of labour, hold opinions repugnant unto theirs, and when they encounter men that make false prognostickes, they impeach the stars and contemne astrology itself, which they consider neither sound nor veridicall but a vain and idle fiction; wherein, as I think, they judge unjustly. For a wright's unskillfullness argueth not the wright's art in error, nor a piper's untunefullness the art of musick devoid of sense. Rather are they ignorant of their arts, and each of these in itself rationall.[1]

[1] For the argument, cf. *The Dance*, 80.

---

[3] μαντευομένοις EΩN : -όμενοι ΓΖ.
[4] δοκέειν EN.

THE WORKS OF LUCIAN

3 Πρῶτον μὲν ὦν¹ Αἰθίοπες τόνδε τὸν λόγον
ἀνθρώποισι κατεστήσαντο. αἰτίη δὲ αὐτέοισι τὰ
μὲν ἡ σοφίη τοῦ ἔθνεος—καὶ γὰρ τἆλλα τῶν ἄλλων
σοφώτεροι Αἰθίοπες—τὰ δὲ καὶ τῆς οἰκήσιος ἡ
εὐμοιρίη· αἰεὶ γὰρ σφέας εὐδίη καὶ γαληναίη
περικέαται, οὐδὲ τῶν τοῦ ἔτεος τροπέων ἀνέχονται,
ἀλλ' ἐν μιῇ ὥρῃ οἰκέουσιν. ἰδόντες ὦν πρῶτα
τὴν σεληναίην οὐκ ἐς πάμπαν ὁμοίην φαινομένην,
ἀλλὰ πολυειδέα τε γιγνομένην καὶ ἐν ἄλλοτε
ἄλλῃ μορφῇ τρεπομένην, ἐδόκεεν αὐτέοισιν τὸ
χρῆμα θωύματος καὶ ἀπορίης ἄξιον. ἔνθεν δὲ
ζητέοντες εὗρον τουτέων τὴν αἰτίην, ὅτι οὐκ ἴδιον
τῇ σεληναίῃ τὸ φέγγος, ἀλλά οἱ παρ' ἠελίου
4 ἔρχεται. εὗρον δὲ καὶ τῶν ἄλλων ἀστέρων τὴν
φορήν, τοὺς δὴ πλάνητας ἡμεῖς καλέομεν—μοῦνοι
γὰρ τῶν ἄλλων κινέονται—φύσιν τε αὐτῶν καὶ
δυναστείην καὶ ἔργα τὰ ἔκαστος ἐπιτελέουσιν.
ἐν δὲ καὶ οὐνόματα αὐτέοισιν ἐπέθεσαν, οὐκ
οὐνόματα, ὅκως ἐδόκεον, ἀλλὰ σημήια.
5 Ταῦτα μὲν ὦν Αἰθίοπες ἐν τῷ οὐρανῷ ἐπέβλεψαν,
μετὰ δὲ γείτοσιν οὖσιν Αἰγυπτίοισιν ἀτελέα τὸν
λόγον παρέδοσαν, Αἰγύπτιοι δὲ παρὰ σφέων
ἐκδεξάμενοι ἡμιεργέα τὴν μαντικὴν ἐπὶ μέζον
ἤγειραν, μέτρα τε τῆς ἐκάστου κινήσιος ἐσημή-
ναντο καὶ ἐτέων ἀριθμὸν καὶ μηνῶν καὶ ὡρέων
διετάξαντο. καὶ μηνῶν μὲν σφίσι μέτρον ἡ

¹ οὖν MSS.

---

¹ In Lucian's day current theory ascribed the origin of
astronomy to the Egyptians. We must applaud his insight
in favouring the Ethiopians, since Diodorus (III, 2, 1; doubtless on good authority) records that they were the first men,

ASTROLOGY

It was the Aethiopians that first delivered this doctrine unto men. The ground thereof was in part the wisdom of that nation, the Aethiopians being in all else wiser than all men; but in part also the benignity of their clime, since clear skyes and calm weather ever invest them, and they are not subjected to the vicissitudes of the yeere, but live in onely one season.[1] Therefore when they discerned, first of all, that the moon hath not perpetually the same appearance, but carrieth a various aspect and changeth into divers figures, they accounted the thing good reason for wonder and empuzzlement. In consequence they sought and found the cause thereof, that the lustre of the moon is not her own but cometh to her from the sun. And they determined also the course of the other stars, which we call planets or wanderers because they alone of all the stars do move; also their nature and potency, and the works that are brought to pass by each of them. Also, they ascribed names unto them, that yet were not names, as they seemed, but symboles.

All which the Aethiopians observed in the skye, and afterwards they transmitted their doctrine incompleat to the Aegyptians their neighbours. And the Aegyptians, deriving from them the auspiciall art but half consummated, advanced it; and they indicated the measure of each planet's motion, and determined the numericall extension of yeares and moneths and hours. The moneths they measured by

that they first taught people to worship the gods, that the Egyptians were their colonists, and that most of the Egyptian institutions were Ethiopian. And if, as we read in the Platonic *Epinomis* and in Macrobius (*Comm. in Cic. Somn. Scip.*, I, 21, 9), the climate of Egypt is conducive to the study of the heavens, that of Ethiopia, naturally, would be far more so.

σεληναίη καὶ ἡ ταύτης ἀναστροφὴ ἐγένετο, ἔτεος
6 δὲ ἠέλιος καὶ ἡ τοῦ ἠελίου περίφορος. οἱ δὲ καὶ
ἄλλα ἐμήσαντο πολλὸν μέζω τουτέων· ἐκ γὰρ δὴ
τοῦ παντὸς ἠέρος καὶ ἀστέρων τῶν ἄλλων ἀπλανέων
τε καὶ εὐσταθέων[1] καὶ οὐδαμὰ κινεομένων δυώ-
δεκα μοίρας ἐτάμοντο τοῖσι[2] κινεομένοισι, καὶ
οἰκία . . .[3] ζῷα ἐόντα ἕκαστον αὐτῶν ἐς ἄλλην
μορφὴν μεμιμέαται, τὰ μὲν ἐνάλια, τὰ δὲ ἀνθρώπων,
τὰ δὲ θηρῶν, τὰ δὲ πτηνῶν, τὰ δὲ κτηνέων.

7 Ἀπὸ τέω δὴ καὶ ἱερὰ τὰ Αἰγύπτια πολυειδέα
ποιέεται· οὐ γὰρ πάντες Αἰγύπτιοι ἐκ τῶν δυώ-
δεκα μοιρέων πασέων ἐμαντεύοντο, ἄλλοι δὲ
ἀλλοίῃσι μοίρῃσιν ἐχρέοντο, καὶ κριὸν μὲν σέβουσιν
ὁκόσοι ἐς κριὸν ἀπέβλεπον, ἰχθύας δὲ οὐ σιτέονται
ὁκόσοι ἰχθύας ἐπεσημήναντο, οὐδὲ τράγον κτεί-
νουσιν ὅσοι αἰγόκερων ᾔδεσαν, καὶ οἱ ἄλλοι
τὰ ἄλλα ὡς ἕκαστοι ἱλάσκονται. ναὶ μὴν καὶ
ταῦρον ἐς τιμὴν τοῦ ἠερίου ταύρου σεβίζονται,
καὶ ὁ Ἆπις αὐτοῖς χρῆμα ἱερώτατον τὴν χώρην
ἐπινέμεται καί οἱ ἐκεῖ μαντήιόν γε[4] ἀνατιθέασιν
σημήιον τῆς ἐκείνου τοῦ ταύρου μαντικῆς.

8 Οὐ μετὰ πολλὸν δὲ καὶ Λίβυες ἐπέβησαν τοῦ
λόγου· καὶ γὰρ τὸ Λιβύων μαντήιον τὸ Ἄμμωνος,
καὶ τοῦτο ἐς τὸν ἠέρα καὶ ἐς τὴν τούτου σοφίην

---

[1] εὐσταθέων: Florentine ed. (1496): εὐπαθέων MSS.
[2] ἐν τοῖσι MSS.: ἐν excised by Jacobitz.
[3] Lacuna in Γ (9 letters) Ε (12-14). Probably οἰκία =
οἴκους; *i.e.*, planetary houses, cf. οἰκοδεσποτέουσι, § 20.
Read καὶ οἰκία οὐνόμασαν, τὸ δ' εἶδος ζῷα ἐόντα.
[4] γε Ν: τε ΓΕΩΖ.

the moon and her cycle, the year by the sun and his
revolution. And they devised other inventions much
greater than these. For they divided the entire skye
and the other stars that are inerrant and fixed, and do
never move, into twelve segments for such as move:
which they styled " houses," although they resemble
living creatures, each patterned after the figure of a
different kind, whereof some are sea-monsters, some
humans, some wild beasts, some volatiles, some
juments.

For this reason, indeed, the Aegyptian deities are
portrayed in various aspects.[1] For it is not to be
supposed that all Aegyptians were wont to draw
prognosticks from all the twelve signs; but some
had one sign in use, others another. The ram is
reverenced by those who looked up unto Aries, fish
is not eaten by those who attached signality unto
Pisces, the goat is not slain by those who had knowledge of Capricorn, and the other creatures are
severally venerated by other folk. Assuredly the
bull too is adored in honour of the celestial Taurus,
and Apis, esteemed by them an object of the uttermost sanctity, depastureth their land, and they that
inhabit it vouchsafe him an oracle in token of the
auspiciality of Taurus.

Not long after, the Libyans also espoused the
science; for the Libyan oracle of Ammon was founded
in regard of the heavens and his knowledge thereof;

---

[1] In accrediting the invention of the signs of the Zodiac
to the Egyptians, our author is at one with his contemporaries
(cf. Macrobius, *loc. cit.*), but in deriving from these signs the
animal forms of the Egyptian gods, and in connecting the fish-
taboo in that country with the constellation Pisces he presents
the results of original research.

ἵδρυτο,[1] παρ᾽ ὅ[2] τὸν Ἄμμωνα καὶ οὗτοι κριοπρόσ-
9 ωπον ποιέονται. ἔγνωσαν δὲ τούτων ἕκαστα
καὶ Βαβυλώνιοι, οὗτοι μέν, λέγουσιν, καὶ πρὸ τῶν
ἄλλων, ἐμοὶ δὲ δοκέει, πολλὸν ὕστερον ἐς τούτους ὁ λόγος ἀπίκετο.

10 Ἕλληνες δὲ οὔτε παρ᾽ Αἰθιόπων οὔτε παρ᾽
Αἰγυπτίων ἀστρολογίης πέρι οὐδὲν ἤκουσαν, ἀλλὰ
σφίσιν Ὀρφεὺς ὁ Οἰάγρου καὶ Καλλιόπης πρῶτος
τάδε ἀπηγήσατο, οὐ μάλα ἐμφανέως, οὐδὲ ἐς
φάος τὸν λόγον προήνεγκεν, ἀλλ᾽ ἐς γοητείην καὶ
ἱερολογίην, οἵη διανοίῃ ἐκείνου. πηξάμενος γὰρ
λύρην ὄργιά τε ἐποιέετο καὶ τὰ ἱερὰ ἤειδεν·
ἡ δὲ λύρη ἑπτάμιτος ἐοῦσα τὴν τῶν κινεομένων
ἀστέρων ἁρμονίην συνεβάλλετο. ταῦτα Ὀρφεὺς
διζήμενος καὶ ταῦτα ἀνακινέων πάντα ἔθελγεν καὶ
πάντων ἐκράτεεν· οὐ γὰρ ἐκείνην τὴν λύρην
ἔβλεπεν οὐδέ οἱ ἄλλης ἔμελε μουσουργίης, ἀλλ᾽
αὕτη Ὀρφέος ἡ μεγάλη λύρη, Ἕλληνές τε τάδε
τιμέοντες μοίρην ἐν τῷ οὐρανῷ[3] ἀπέκριναν καὶ
ἀστέρες πολλοὶ καλέονται λύρη Ὀρφέος.

Ἦν δέ κοτε Ὀρφέα ἴδῃς ἢ λίθοισιν ἢ χροιῇ
μεμιμημένον, μέσῳ ἕζεται ἴκελος ἀείδοντι, μετὰ

---

[1] εἴρητο MSS.: ἵδρυτο K. G. P. Schwartz.
[2] παρὰ MSS.: παρ᾽ ὅ Gesner.
[3] ἐν αὐτῷ οὐρανῷ MSS.: τῷ for αὐτῷ Harmon.

---

[1] In the *Goddesse of Surrye* (2) Lucian is similarly minded
as to Babylonian claims of priority in religion; and in the
Runaways Philosophy goes successively to India, Ethiopia,
Egypt, Babylon, and Greece.

[2] It seems better established that Atlas was the first
astronomer; cf. Cicero, *Tusc. Disp.*, V, 3, 8, and Vergil, *Aen.*,
I, 740. He taught the doctrine of the sphere to Heracles,
and the fact that Heracles introduced it into Greece underlies

whence they represent Ammon with a ram's head.
And the Babylonians came to know all these things,
even before the others, as they themselves say; but
I think that the science reached them long afterward.[1]

As for the Greeks, they learned not a whit of
astrology either from the Aethiopians or from the
Aegyptians. It was Orpheus, the son of Oeagrus and
Calliope, that first declared these matters unto them,
but not at all plainly, nor did he bring the science
forth unto illucidation but unto ingannation and pious
fraude, such being the humour of the man.[2] For he
made a harp and exposed his mystick rites in poesy
and his theology in song; and the harp, that had
seven chords, discoursed the harmony of the errant
spheres. It was by investigating and ventilating
these matters that he enchanted and enthralled all
creatures; for he regarded not that harp of his nor
yet concerned himselfe with other musick, but this
was the mightie harp of Orpheus,[3] and to honour
these things, the Greeks set apart a station in the
heavens and numerous stars are denominated
Orpheus his harp.

If ever you see Orpheus pictured in mosaick stones
or in pigment, he sitteth in the centre, in the simili-

the story of the golden apples of the Hesperides—so, at all
events, says Diodorus. Orpheus, however, was no doubt a
very active person in many ways; e.g. in connection with
philosophy (*Runaways*, 8) and very likely dancing (*Dance*, 15),
and the mathematician Nicomachus of Gerasa (pp. 241, 271,
274 Jan.), Lucian's contemporary, agrees with him that the
lyre of Orpheus had seven strings to match the number of the
planets and played the harmony of the spheres.

[3] The thought is that the planets form the only musical
instrument and render the only music in which Orpheus,
as primarily an astronomer, had any real interest.

THE WORKS OF LUCIAN

χερσὶν ἔχων τὴν λύρην, ἀμφὶ δέ μιν ζῷα μυρία
ἕστηκεν, ἐν οἷς καὶ ταῦρος καὶ ἄνθρωπος καὶ λέων
καὶ τῶν ἄλλων[1] ἕκαστον. εὖτ' ἂν ἐκεῖνα ἴδῃς,
μέμνησό μοι τουτέων, κοίη ἐκείνου ἀοιδή, κοίη
δὲ καὶ ἡ λύρη, κοῖος δὲ καὶ ταῦρος ἢ ὁκοῖος λέων
'Ορφέος ἐπαΐουσιν. ἢν δὲ τὰ λέγω αἴτια γνοίης,
σὺ δὲ καὶ ἐν τῷ οὐρανῷ δέρκεο ἕκαστον τουτέων.

11 Λέγουσιν δὲ Τειρεσίην ἄνδρα Βοιώτιον, τοῦ δὴ
κλέος μαντοσύνης πέρι πολλὸν ἀείρεται, τοῦτον
τὸν Τειρεσίην ἐν Ἕλλησιν εἰπεῖν ὅτι τῶν πλανεο-
μένων ἀστέρων οἱ μὲν θήλεες οἱ δὲ ἄρρενες ἐόντες
οὐκ ἴσα ἐκτελέουσιν· τῷ καί μιν διφυέα γενέσθαι
καὶ ἀμφίβιον Τειρεσίην μυθολογέουσιν, ἄλλοτε μὲν
θῆλυν ἄλλοτε δὲ ἄρρενα.

12 'Ατρέος[2] δὲ καὶ Θυέστεω περὶ τῇ πατρωίῃ
βασιληίῃ φιλονεικεόντων ἤδη τοῖσιν Ἕλλησιν
ἀναφανδὸν ἀστρολογίης τε καὶ σοφίης τῆς οὐρανίης
μάλιστ' ἔμελεν, καὶ τὸ ξυνὸν τῶν 'Αργείων ἄρχειν
ἔγνωσαν ἑωυτῶν ὅστις τοῦ ἑτέρου σοφίην προφερέ-
στερος. ἔνθα δὴ Θυέστης μὲν τὸν κριὸν σφίσιν
τὸν ἐν τῷ οὐρανῷ σημηνάμενος ἐπέδειξεν, ἀπὸ
τέω δὴ ἄρνα χρύσεον Θυέστῃ γενέσθαι μυθολογέουσιν. 'Ατρεὺς δὲ τοῦ ἡελίου πέρι καὶ τῶν
ἀντολέων αὐτοῦ λόγον ἐποιήσατο, ὅτι οὐκ ἐς
ὁμοίην φορὴν ἡέλιός τε καὶ ὁ κόσμος κινέονται,
ἀλλ' ἐς ἀντίξοον ἀλλήλοις ἀντιδρομέουσιν, καὶ

---

[1] ἄλλων omitted in all MSS. except C.
[2] 'Ατρέως MSS.

---

[1] Here again we have "independent thought." A widely
variant explanation of the myth had previously been offered
by Cephalio (cf. J. Malalas, *Chron.*, p. 40, 1, in the Bonn
edition), according to which Tiresias was a student of

356

tude of one that sings, holding in his hands the harp,
and about him stand numberless creatures, among
which a bull, a man, a lion, and others after their
kind. When you see these, bethink you, pray, what
his song was, what his harp, and what the bull or
the lion that giveth ear to him. And if you would
know the originalls that I speak of, you may behold
each of them in the heavens.

They say, moreover, that Tiresias, a Boeotian
man, whose fame as touching prophecie is greatly
cried up, declared unto the Greeks that of the errant
stars some are masle, some female, and that they
do not engender like effects; wherefore they fable
that Tiresias himself was bisexous and amphibious,
now masle, now female.[1]

When Atreus and Thyestes contended for the
throne of their fathers, even then, it is plain, the
Greeks set great store by astrologie and celestial
lore; and the commonwealth of Argos determined
that which ever of them was more excellent than the
other in this lore should bear rule. Thereupon
Thyestes indicated and made manifest unto them the
Ram in the heavens, in consequence whereof they
fable that Thyestes had a golden lamb. But Atreus
declared the doctrine of the sun and its risings, that
the sun and the First Movable[2] do not course in the
same direction, but rowle contrariwise to one another

medicine who concerned himself with the mysteries of
parturition.
[2] The firmament, or orb, of the fixed stars. This was
thought of as revolving from East to West. The sun partici-
pated, to be sure, in its motion, but had a contrary motion of
his own, which was compared to that of an ant walking on the
rim of a moving wheel in the direction contrary to the wheel's
motion.

αἱ νῦν δύσιες δοκέουσαι, τοῦ κόσμου δύσιες ἐοῦσαι, τοῦ ἠελίου ἀντολαί εἰσιν. τάδε εἰπόντα βασιλέα μιν Ἀργεῖοι ἐποιήσαντο, καὶ μέγα κλέος ἐπὶ σοφίῃ αὐτοῦ ἐγένετο.

13 Ἐγὼ δὲ καὶ περὶ Βελλεροφόντεω τοιάδε φρονέω· πτηνὸν μέν οἱ γενέσθαι ὡς [1] ἵππον οὐ μάλα πείθομαι, δοκέω δέ μιν ταύτην τὴν σοφίην μετέποντα [2] ὑψηλά τε φρονέοντα καὶ ἄστροισιν ὁμιλέοντα ἐς οὐρανὸν οὐχὶ τῷ ἵππῳ ἀναβῆναι ἀλλὰ τῇ διανοίῃ.

14 Ἴσα δέ μοι καὶ ἐς Φρίξον τὸν Ἀθάμαντος εἰρήσθω, τὸν δὴ κριῷ χρυσέῳ δι᾽ αἰθέρος ἐλάσαι μυθέονται. ναὶ μέντοι καὶ Δαίδαλον τὸν Ἀθηναῖον· ξείνη μὲν ἡ ἱστορίη, δοκέω γε μὴν [3] οὐκ ἔξω ἀστρολογίης, ἀλλὰ οἱ αὐτὸς μάλιστα ἐχρήσατο καὶ

15 παιδὶ τῷ ἑωυτοῦ κατηγήσατο. Ἴκαρος δέ, νεότητι καὶ ἀτασθαλίῃ χρεόμενος καὶ οὐκ ἐπιεικτὰ διζήμενος ἀλλὰ ἐς πόλον [4] ἀερθεὶς τῷ νῷ, ἐξέπεσε τῆς ἀληθείης καὶ παντὸς ἀπεσφάλη τοῦ λόγου καὶ ἐς πέλαγος κατηνέχθη ἀβύσσων πρηγμάτων, τὸν Ἕλληνες ἄλλως μυθολογέουσιν καὶ κόλπον ἐπ᾽ αὐτῷ ἐν τῇδε τῇ θαλάσσῃ Ἰκάριον εἰκῆ καλέουσιν.

16 Τάχα δὲ καὶ Πασιφάη, παρὰ Δαιδάλου ἀκούσασα ταύρου τε πέρι τοῦ ἐν τοῖς ἄστροισι φαινομένου καὶ αὐτῆς ἀστρολογίης, ἐς ἔρωτα τοῦ λόγου ἀπίκετο,

---

[1] ὡς not in N.
[2] μεθέποντα MSS.
[3] μὴν G. Hermann : μιν MSS. δέ μιν?
[4] πόλον edd. : πολλὸν MSS.

---

[1] Previous authors left this topic to Lucian "incomplete." That Atreus owed his kingship to his discovery of the retrograde motion of the sun was known not only to Polybius (XXXIV,

ASTROLOGY

and that which now seemeth his setting, being a
setting of the First Movable, is a rising of the sun.
At his saying this, the men of Argos made him their
king, and great renown for learning became his.[1]

Concerning Bellerophon also I am of this opinion :
that he had a volatile as horse I do not at all believe,
but conceive that he pursued this wisdom and raised
his thoughts on high and held conversation with the
stars, and thus ascended unto heaven by means
not of his horse but of his wit.

The same may be said of Phrixus, the son of
Athamas, that is fabled to have ridden through the
ayr upon a golden ram. And certainly of Daedalus
the Athenian; although his story be strange, yet
methinks it is not without relation unto astrology, but
rather he practised it constantly himself and taught
it unto his son. But because Icarus was governed
by youth and audacity, and sought not the attainable
but let his minde carry him into the zenith, he came
short of truth and defected from reason and was
precipitated into a sea of unfathomable perplexities.
But the Greeks tell an idle myth of him and loosely
call a golfe of their sea Icarian after his name.

Doubtless Pasiphae also, hearing from Daedalus
of the Bull that appeareth amongst the constellations
and of Astrology itself, fell in love with the doctrine ;

beginning) but even to Sophocles and Euripides, according
to a commentator on Aratus (Achilleus: Maass, *Comm.
in Arat.*, p. 28). It remained for Lucian to point out that
Thyestes was an astronomer also, the discoverer of the
constellation Aries, and to add a touch of paradox to the other
doctrine with his suggestion that inasmuch as the sun's proper
motion is from West to East, he is really going upward,
and therefore rising, when he sets, and downward, or setting,
when he rises.

359

THE WORKS OF LUCIAN

ἔνθεν νομίζουσιν ὅτι Δαίδαλός μιν τῷ ταύρῳ
ἐνύμφευσεν.

17 Εἰσὶν δὲ οἳ καὶ κατὰ μέρεα τὴν ἐπιστήμην
διελόντες ἕκαστοι αὐτῶν ἄλλα ἐπενοήσαντο, οἱ
μὲν τὰ ἐς τὴν σεληναίην, οἱ δὲ τὰ ἐς Δία, οἱ δὲ
τὰ ἐς ἥλιον συναγείραντες, δρόμου τε αὐτῶν πέρι
18 καὶ¹ κινήσιος καὶ δυνάμιος. καὶ Ἐνδυμίων μὲν
19 τὰ ἐς τὴν σεληναίην συνετάξατο,² Φαέθων δὲ
τοῦ ἡλίου δρόμον ἐτεκμήρατο, οὐ μέν γε ἀτρεκέως,
ἀλλ᾽ ἀτελέα τὸν λόγον ἀπολιπὼν ἀπέθανεν. οἱ δὲ
τάδε ἀγνοέοντες Ἡελίου παῖδα Φαέθοντα δοκέουσιν
καὶ μῦθον ἐπ᾽ αὐτέῳ οὐδαμὰ πιστὸν διηγέονται.
ἐλθόντα γάρ μιν παρὰ τὸν Ἥλιον τὸν πατέρα
αἰτέειν τὸ τοῦ φωτὸς ἅρμα ἡνιοχέειν, τὸν δὲ δοῦναί
τέ οἱ καὶ ὑποθέσθαι τῆς ἱππασίης τὸν νόμον.
ὁ δὲ Φαέθων ἐπειδὴ ἀνέβη τὸ ἅρμα, ἡλικίῃ καὶ
ἀπειρίῃ ἄλλοτε μὲν πρόσγειος ἡνιόχεεν, ἄλλοτε
δὲ πολλὸν τῆς γῆς ἀπαιωρούμενος· τοὺς δὲ
ἀνθρώπους κρύος τε καὶ θάλπος οὐκ ἀνασχετὸν
διέφθειρεν. ἐπὶ τοῖσι δὴ τὸν Δία ἀγανακτέοντα
βαλεῖν πρηστῆρι Φαέθοντα μεγάλῳ. πεσόντα δέ
μιν αἱ ἀδελφαὶ περιστᾶσαι πένθος μέγα ἐποίεον,
ἔστε μετέβαλον τὰ εἴδεα, καὶ νῦν εἰσιν αἴγειροι καὶ
τὸ ἤλεκτρον ἐπ᾽ αὐτῷ δάκρυον σταλάουσιν.
οὐχ οὕτω ταῦτα ἐγένετο οὐδὲ ὅσιον αὐτοῖσι πείθεσθαι, οὐδὲ Ἥλιος παῖδα ἐποιήσατο, οὐδὲ ὁ παῖς
αὐτῷ ἀπέθανεν.

¹ καὶ Seager: not in MSS.
² διετάξατο Z(ΩC).

360

whence they derive the belief that Daedalus conjoined her in wedlock with the bull.[1]

Again, there be those who, dissecting the science into parts, have made different discoveries, some collecting the particulars of the moon, some those of Jupiter, and some those of the sun, concerning their course and motion and potency. So Endymion established the motions of the moon,[2] so Phaeton inferred the course of the sun; yet not strictly, but left the theory incompleat at his death. Ignorant of this, men believe that Phaeton was Helius his son, and they relate a story of him that is not at all credible. Going, say they, unto Helius, his father, he asked to drive the car of light; whiche he suffered him to do, and also instructed him in the manner of its governance. But when Phaeton mounted the car, because of youth and inexpertness he drove now close to earth, now at a vast remove; and men were being destroyed both by cold and by heat that passed endurance. Thereupon, Jupiter in wrath smote Phaeton with a great bolt of lightning. After his fall his sisters surrounding him made great dole until they transmuted themselves, and now they are trees of black poplar and distil amber over him in place of tears. These things were not so, and it consisteth not with piety to believe in them; Helius begat no son, and no son of his perished.

[1] The reader will not fail to note how neatly this explanation of the Pasiphae myth puts a colophon upon Lucian's masterly treatment of the flight-legends, which is entirely his own.

[2] We are indebted to Germanicus, in his commentary on Aratus, for the information that Mnaseas of Sicyon credited Endymion with the discovery of the course of the moon. Having found the key to the flight-legends, it was easy for Lucian to supply a pendant to Endymion in Phaethon.

20 Λέγουσιν δὲ καὶ ἄλλα Ἕλληνες πολλὰ μυθώδεα,
τοῖσι ἐγὼ οὐ μάλα τι πείθομαι. κῶς γὰρ δὴ
ὅσιον πιστεῦσαι παῖδα Αἰνείην τῆς Ἀφροδίτης
γενέσθαι καὶ Διὸς Μίνω καὶ Ἄρεος Ἀσκάλαφον
καὶ Αὐτόλυκον Ἑρμέω ; ἀλλ᾽ οὗτοι ἕκαστος
αὐτέων θεοφιλέες ἐγένοντο καὶ σφίσι γεινομένοισι [1]
τῷ μὲν ἡ Ἀφροδίτη, τῷ δὲ ὁ Ζεύς, τῷ δὲ ὁ Ἄρης
ἐπέβλεψαν. ὁκόσοι γὰρ δὴ ἀνθρώποισι ἐν τῇ
γενεῇ ταύτῃ [2] οἰκοδεσποτέουσι, οὗτοι ὅκως τοκέες
ἑωυτοῖσι πάντα ἰκέλους [3] ἐκτελέουσιν καὶ χρόην καὶ
μορφὴν καὶ ἔργα καὶ διανοίην, καὶ βασιλεὺς μὲν
ὁ Μίνως Διὸς ἡγεομένου, καλὸς [4] δὲ Αἰνείης Ἀφροδίτης βουλήσει ἐγένετο, κλέπτης δὲ Αὐτόλυκος,
ἡ δέ οἱ κλεπτικὴ ἐξ Ἑρμέω ἀπίκετο.

21 Οὐ μὲν ὦν οὐδὲ τὸν Κρόνον Ζεὺς ἔδησεν οὐδὲ
ἐς Τάρταρον ἔρριψεν οὐδὲ τὰ ἄλλα ἐμήσατο
ὁκόσα ἄνθρωποι νομίζουσιν, ἀλλὰ φέρεται γὰρ ὁ
Κρόνος τὴν ἔξω φορὴν πολλὸν ἀπ᾽ ἡμέων καί οἱ
νωθρή τε ἡ κίνησις καὶ οὐ ῥηιδίη τοῖσιν ἀνθρώ-
ποισιν ὁρέεσθαι. διὸ δή μιν ἑστάναι λέγουσιν
ὅκως πεπεδημένον. τὸ δὲ βάθος τὸ πολλὸν τοῦ
ἠέρος Τάρταρος καλέεται.

22 Μάλιστα δ᾽ [5] ἔκ τε Ὁμήρου τοῦ ποιητέω καὶ
τῶν Ἡσιόδου ἐπέων μάθοι ἄν τις τὰ πάλαι τοῖς
ἀστρολογέουσιν ὁμοφωνέοντα. εὖτ᾽ ἂν δὲ τὴν
σειρὴν τοῦ Διὸς ἀπηγέηται καὶ τοῦ Ἡλίου τὰς

---

[1] γεινομένοισι Harmon : γεν- MSS. Cf. *Jup. Conf.*, 1.
[2] ταύτῃ omitted in N.
[3] ἰκέλους K. G. P. Schwartz : ἴκελα MSS.
[4] καλὸς Ε²N : ἄλλος ΓΕ¹ΩΖ.   [5] δ᾽ Fritzsche : not in MSS.

---

[1] Homer, in the *Iliad*, VIII, 18–26 : Zeus, boasting of his
strength, says that if a golden chain should be let down from

But the Greeks relate many other fabulosities—
which I do not credit at all. For how doth it consist
with piety to believe that Aeneas was the son of
Venus, Minos of Jupiter, Ascalaphus of Mars, or
Autolycus of Mercury? Nay, these were each and
all divinely favoured, and at their birth one of them
was under the regard of Venus, another of Jupiter,
another of Mars. For what powers soever are in
their proper houses at the moment of birth into this
life, those powers like unto parents make men
answerable to them in all respects, in complexion,
in figure, in workes, and in humour. So Minos
became a king because Jupiter was in his ascendancy,
Aeneas fair by the will of Venus, and Autolycus a
theef, whose theevery came to him from Mercury.

Moreover, it is not true, neither, that Jupiter put
Saturn in chaines or threw him into Tartarus or otherwise mistreated him as men credit. Nay, Saturn
moveth in the extream orbe, far away from us, and
his motion is sluggish and not easy to be apprehended
ocularly by human kind, whence they say that he
holdeth still as if fettered; and the vast abyss of the
ayr is called Tartarus.

'Tis chiefly from the verses of Homer the poet and
of Hesiod that we may learn that antiquity holdeth
with the astrologers. When he describeth the chain
of Jupiter[1] and the kine of the Sun, which I con-

heaven and all the other gods and goddesses should lay hold
of it, they could not pull him down, but he could pull them up,
along with the earth and the sea, fasten the chain about the
peak of Olympus, and leave everything hanging. Socrates in
the *Theaetetus*, 153 A, says that by the golden chain Homer
means nothing else than the sun; others, according to
Eustathius (695, 9), took him to mean the orbits of the
planets.

βόας,[1] τὰ δὴ ἐγὼ ἤματα εἶναι συμβάλλομαι, καὶ τὰς πόλιας τὰς ἐν τῇ ἀσπίδι Ἥφαιστος ἐποιήσατο καὶ τὸν χορὸν καὶ τὴν ἀλωήν . . .[2] τὰ μὲν γὰρ ὁκόσα ἐς τὴν Ἀφροδίτην αὐτῷ καὶ τοῦ Ἄρεος τὴν μοιχείην λέλεκται, καὶ ταῦτα ἐμφανέα οὐκ ἄλλοθεν ἢ ἐκ τῆσδε τῆς σοφίης πεποιημένα· ἡ γὰρ δὴ ὦν Ἀφροδίτης καὶ τοῦ Ἄρεος ὁμοδρομίη τὴν Ὁμήρου ἀοιδὴν ἀπεργάζεται. ἐν ἄλλοισι δὲ ἔπεσι τὰ ἔργα ἑκάστου αὐτῶν διωρίσατο, τῇ Ἀφροδίτῃ μὲν εἰπών,

ἀλλὰ σύ γ᾽ ἱμερόεντα μετέρχεο ἔργα γάμοιο·

τὰ δὲ τοῦ πολέμου,

ταῦτα δ᾽ Ἄρηι θοῷ καὶ Ἀθήνῃ πάντα μελήσει.

23 Ἅπερ οἱ παλαιοὶ ἰδόντες μάλιστα μαντηίησιν ἐχρέοντο καὶ οὐ πάρεργον αὐτὴν ἐποιέοντο, ἀλλ᾽ οὔτε πόλιας ᾤκιζον οὔτε τείχεα περιεβάλλοντο οὔτε φόνους ἐργάζοντο οὔτε γυναῖκας ἐγάμεον, πρὶν ἂν δὴ παρὰ μάντεων ἀκοῦσαι ἕκαστα. καὶ γὰρ δὴ τὰ μαντήια αὐτέοισι οὐκ ἔξω ἀστρολογίης ἦν, ἀλλὰ παρὰ μὲν Δελφοῖς παρθένος ἔχει τὴν προφητείην σύμβολον τῆς παρθένου τῆς οὐρανίης, καὶ δράκων ὑπὸ τῷ τρίποδι φθέγγεται ὅτι καὶ ἐν τοῖσιν ἄστροισι δράκων φαίνεται, καὶ ἐν Διδύμοις δὲ μαντήιον τοῦ Ἀπόλλωνος, ἐμοὶ δοκέει, καὶ τοῦτο ἐκ τῶν ἠερίων Διδύμων ὀνομάζεται.

---

[1] βόας Barnes: βολὰς MSS.
[2] Lacuna Harmon: not indicated in MSS.

---

[1] *Odyssey*, XI, 104 ff.; XII, 260 ff.
[2] *Iliad*, XVIII, 490 (the cities); 561 (the vineyard); 590 (the chorus). Following these words there appears to be a break in the text which very probably has deprived us of

ceive to be daies,[1] and the cities that Vulcan made upon the shield, and the choir, and the vineyard [2] ... All that he hath said of Venus and of Mars his passion, is also manifestly composed from no other source than this science. Indeed, it is the conjunction of Venus and Mars that createth the poetry of Homer. And in other verses he distinguished the duties of each, saying unto Venus,

> " Nay, be it thine to control the delightsome duties
> of wedlock,"

and anent those of warfare,

> " These shall all be the care of impetuous Mars and
> Minerva." [3]

Discerning all these things, the ancients had divination in very great use and counted it no parergy, but would found no cities, invest themselves with no ramparts, slay no men, wed no women, untill they had been advised in all particulars by diviners. And certainly their oracles were not aloof from astrology, but at Delphi a virgin hath the office of prophet in token of the celestial Virgin, and a serpent giveth voice beneath the tripod because a Serpent giveth light among the stars, and at Didymi also the oracle of Apollo hath its name, methinks, from the heavenly Twins.[4]

Lucian's allegorical explanation. It is easy to see that the chorus would be the planetary song and dance (cf. *Dance*, § 7), but the astronomical significance of the cities and the vineyard is just a bit obscure.

[3] *Iliad*, V, 429, 430.

[4] Modern philology soberly rejects the happy thought that Didyma (Didymi) owes its name to the constellation Didymi (Gemini), and explains that the name is Carian, like Idyma, Sidyma, Loryma, etc. (Bürchner, in Pauly-Wissowa, *s.v.*).

THE WORKS OF LUCIAN

24   Οὕτω δὲ αὐτοῖσι χρῆμα ἱρότατον ἡ μαντοσύνη
ἐδόκεεν, ὥστε δὴ Ὀδυσσεὺς ἐπειδὴ ἔκαμεν πλανεό-
μενος, ἐθελήσας ἀτρεκὲς ἀκοῦσαι περὶ τῶν ἑωυτοῦ
πρηγμάτων, ἐς τὸν Ἀΐδην ἀπίκετο, οὐκ " ὄφρα
ἴδη νέκυας καὶ ἀτερπέα χῶρον " ἀλλ' ἐς λόγους
ἐλθεῖν Τειρεσίῃ ἐπιθυμέων. καὶ ἐπειδὴ ἐς τὸν
χῶρον ἦλθεν ἔνθα οἱ Κίρκη ἐσήμηνεν καὶ ἔσκαψεν
τὸν βόθρον καὶ τὰ μῆλα ἔσφαξεν, πολλῶν νεκρῶν
παρεόντων, ἐν τοῖσι καὶ τῆς μητρὸς τῆς ἑωυτοῦ,
τοῦ αἵματος πιεῖν ἐθελόντων οὐ πρότερον ἐπῆκεν [1]
οὐδενί, οὐδὲ αὐτῇ μητρί, πρὶν Τειρεσίην γεύσασθαι
καὶ ἐξαναγκάσαι εἰπεῖν οἱ τὸ μαντήιον· καὶ ἀνέ-
σχετο διψῶσαν ὁρέων τῆς μητρὸς τὴν σκιήν.

25   Λακεδαιμονίοισι δὲ Λυκοῦργος τὴν πολιτείην
πᾶσαν ἐκ τοῦ οὐρανοῦ διετάξατο καὶ νόμον σφίσιν
ἐποιήσατο μηδαμὰ . . . [2] μηδὲ ἐς πόλεμον προ-
χωρέειν πρὶν τὴν σεληναίην πλήρεα γενέσθαι·
οὐ γὰρ ἴσην ἐνόμιζεν [3] εἶναι τὴν δυναστείην
αὐξανομένης τῆς σεληναίης καὶ ἀφανιζομένης,
26 πάντα δὲ ὑπ' αὐτῇ διοικέεσθαι. ἀλλὰ μοῦνοι
Ἀρκάδες ταῦτα οὐκ ἐδέξαντο οὐδὲ ἐτίμησαν
ἀστρολογίην, ἀνοίῃ δὲ καὶ ἀσοφίῃ [4] λέγουσιν καὶ
τῆς σεληναίης ἔμμεναι προγενέστεροι.

27   Οἱ μὲν ὦν πρὸ ἡμῶν οὕτω κάρτα ἦσαν φιλομάντιες,
οἱ δὲ νῦν, οἱ μὲν αὐτέων ἀδύνατα εἶναι λέγουσιν
ἀνθρώποισι τέλος εὕρασθαι μαντικῆς· οὐ γὰρ
εἶναί μιν οὔτε πιστὴν οὔτε ἀληθέα, οὐδὲ τὸν Ἄρεα
ἢ τὸν Δία ἐν τῷ οὐρανῷ ἡμέων ἕνεκα κινέεσθαι,

[1] ἐπῆκεν Bekker: ἄφηκεν MSS.
[2] Lacuna in Γ (12 letters) E (9 letters). A word like ἐξελαυνέειν has fallen out.
[3] ἐνόμιζεν du Soul: ἐνόμιζον MSS.

366

ASTROLOGY

So firmly did they believe divination a thing most sacred, that when Ulysses, wearied of wandering, took a phansie to learn the truth as touching his affaires, he went off unto Hell, not " to behold dead men and a land that is joyless," [1] but because he would come to speech with Tiresias. And when he was come to the place whereunto Circe directed him, and had dug his pit and slain his sheep, although many dead that were by, and amongst them his own mother, were fain to drink of the blood, he suffered none of them, not even his very mother, until he had wet the throstle of Tiresias and constrained him to deliver the prophecy, verily enduring to behold his mother's shadow athirst.

For the Spartans, Lycurgus drew from the skye his ordering of their whole polity and made it their law never to leave their country, even to go to the wars, before the moon should be at her full, for he conceited that the potency of the moon is not the same when she waxeth and when she waneth, and that all things are subject unto her sway. The Arcadians, however, and none but they, would have naught of this and yeelded no honour unto astrologie; and in their folly they affirm that they are older than the moon.

Whereas our forbears were so mightily enamoured of divination, among this generation there be some who say that it is an impossibility for mankind to conceive a useful purpose of astrologie. It is neither credible, say they, nor truthful, and Mars and Jupiter do not move in the skye for our sake, but are nothing

---

[1] *Odyssey*, XI, 94.

[4] ἀσαφίη ΓΕΝ.

THE WORKS OF LUCIAN

ἀλλὰ τῶν μὲν ἀνθρωπηίων πρηγμάτων οὐδεμίην
ὤρην ἐκεῖνοι ποιέονται οὐδ' ἔστιν αὐτέοισιν πρὸς
τάδε κοινωνίη, κατὰ σφέας δὲ χρείῃ τῆς περιφορῆς
28 ἀναστρέφονται. ἄλλοι δὲ ἀστρολογίην ἀψευδέα
μέν, ἀνωφελέα δὲ εἶναι λέγουσιν· οὐ γὰρ ὑπὸ
μαντοσύνῃ ἀλλάσσεσθαι ὁκόσα τῇσι μοίρῃσι δοκέον-
τα ἐπέρχεται.
29 Ἐγὼ δὲ πρὸς τάδε ἄμφω ἐκεῖνα ἔχω εἰπεῖν,
ὅτι οἱ μὲν ἀστέρες ἐν τῷ οὐρανῷ τὴν σφετέρην
εἰλέονται, πάρεργον δὲ σφίσι τῆς κινήσιος τῶν κατ'
ἡμέας ἕκαστον ἐπιγίγνεται. ἢ ἐθέλεις ἵππου μὲν
θέοντος καὶ ὀρνίθων καὶ ἀνδρῶν κινεομένων [1]
λίθους ἀνασαλεύεσθαι καὶ κάρφεα δονέεσθαι ὑπὸ
τῶν ἀνέμων τοῦ δρόμου, ὑπὸ δὲ τῇ δίνῃ τῶν
ἀστέρων μηδὲν ἄλλο γίγνεσθαι ; καὶ ἐκ μὲν
ὀλίγου πυρὸς ἀπορροίη ἐς ἡμέας ἔρχεται, καὶ τὸ
πῦρ οὐ δι' ἡμέας καίει τι οὐδέ οἱ μέλει τοῦ ἡμετέρου
θάλπεος, ἀστέρων δὲ οὐδεμίην ἀπορροίην δεχό-
μεθα ; καὶ μέντοι τῇ ἀστρολογίῃ τὰ μὲν φαῦλα
ἐσθλὰ ποιῆσαι ἀδύνατά ἐστιν οὐδὲ ἀλλάξαι τι
τῶν ἀπορρεόντων πρηγμάτων, ἀλλὰ τοὺς χρεο-
μένους τάδε ὠφελέει· τὰ μὲν ἐσθλὰ εἰδότας
ἀπιξόμενα [2] πολλὸν ἀπόπροσθεν εὐφρανέει, τὰ δὲ
φαῦλα εὐμαρέως δέχονται· οὐ γάρ σφισιν ἀγνοέου-
σιν ἐπέρχεται, ἀλλ' ἐν μελέτῃ καὶ προσδοκίῃ
ῥηίδια καὶ πρηέα ἡγεῖται. τάδε ἀστρολογίης
πέρι ἐγὼν ὑπολαμβάνω.

[1] κλονεομένων ΩΖ.   [2] ἀφιξόμενα MSS.

ASTROLOGY

at all solicitous of the affairs of men, wherewith they have naught in common, but accomplish their courses independently, through a necessitude of revolving. And others affirm that astrologie, although not untruthful, is unprofitable, insomuch as divination will not alter that which draweth nigh by decree of the fates.[1]

To both these opinions I may answer that although the stars do verily absolve their own course in the skye, none the less as a parergy or incidental of their motion each event among us cometh to pass. Or will you have it that although if a horse run or birds or humans move, pebbles are flung up and strawes set astir by the wind of their motion, yet the gyration of the stars bringeth naught else to pass? And that whereas from a little fire an effluxion cometh to us, although the fire burneth not for our sake at all and is not a whit sollicitous that we be warmed, yet from the stars we receive no effluxion whatever? Furthermore, astrologie is indeed impotent to convert bad into good, or to effect mutation in any of the effluents, yet is it profitable to those that employ it, in so much as the good, when they know that it is to come, delighteth them long beforehand, while the bad they accept readily, for it cometh not upon them unawares, but in vertue of contemplation and expectance is deemed easie and light. That is my opinion in the matter of astrology.

[1] Among those who so argue is Lucian's Cyniscus in *Zeus Catechized*, 12–14 (II, 76 f).

THE MISTAKEN CRITIC

A PERSONAL attack resembling the *Professor of Rhetoric* and the *Ignorant Book-Collector*, but outdoing both of them in savagery. Its motive was not so much to show up a vicious citizen as to avenge a personal insult. In passing the man, Lucian had expressed his opinion of him loudly enough to be overheard (which was doubtless his intention). He used a word that as an epithet was obsolete, and not conspicuously sanctioned by good use. Consequently, the man laughed, and ridiculed his language, which was a fatal mistake; for Lucian, always sensitive about his diction, as witness his *On a Slip of the Tongue in Salutation* (Vol. VI), was thereby provoked to pay him back with interest.

For raw, unsparing satire like this, Lucian had plenty of precedent not only in the iambics of Archilochus and Semonides, to which, with the scazons of Hipponax, he himself alludes, and in Old Comedy, but in melic poetry (not only Timocreon of Rhodes, but Anacreon). Of its use in the orators, where it conspicuously serves ulterior purposes, Aeschines against Timarchus is the classic example. After the orators it was the Cynics, particularly the street-corner type, who kept the tradition of outspokenness alive; Lucian's *Demonax* is full of illustrations.

That the name of Lucian's victim was Timarchus is, I think, an erroneous assumption from the nickname Atimarchus that was given him at Athens (§ 27; see the note there). He had been an actor and a teacher, and was then a sophist. A Syrian by birth, he had lived in Antioch, Egypt, Italy, and Greece. The piece was written soon after the incident occurred, apparently in Ephesus, where the sophist was then living. There is nothing in its content to fix its date.

ΨΕΥΔΟΛΟΓΙΣΤΗΣ Η ΠΕΡΙ ΤΗΣ
ΑΠΟΦΡΑΔΟΣ[1]

1 Ἀλλ' ὅτι μὲν ἠγνόεις τοὔνομα τὴν ἀποφράδα
παντί που δῆλον. πῶς γὰρ ἂν ᾐτιῶ βάρβαρον
εἶναί με τὴν φωνὴν ἐπ' αὐτῷ, εἰπόντα ὑπὲρ σοῦ ὡς
ἀποφράδι ὅμοιος εἴης (τὸν γὰρ τρόπον σου νὴ
Δία μέμνημαι εἰκάσας τῇ τοιαύτῃ ἡμέρᾳ), εἰ μὴ
καὶ παντάπασιν ἀνήκοος ἦσθα τοῦ ὀνόματος ;
ἐγὼ δὲ τὴν μὲν ἀποφράδα ὅ τι καὶ βούλεται εἶναι
διδάξω σε μικρὸν ὕστερον· τὸ δὲ τοῦ Ἀρχιλόχου
ἐκεῖνο ἤδη σοι λέγω, ὅτι τέττιγα τοῦ πτεροῦ
συνείληφας, εἴπερ τινὰ ποιητὴν ἰάμβων ἀκούεις
Ἀρχίλοχον, Πάριον τὸ γένος, ἄνδρα κομιδῇ
ἐλεύθερον καὶ παρρησίᾳ συνόντα, μηδὲν ὀκνοῦντα
ὀνειδίζειν, εἰ καὶ ὅτι μάλιστα λυπήσειν ἔμελλε

---

[1] So ΓΕΜ : κατὰ τιμάρχου added in Γ (marg.) Ν. περὶ τῆς
ἀποφράδος ἢ κατὰ τιμάρχου CF. In the alternative form of
the title, κατ' Ἀτιμάρχου may be what was originally intended.
Cf. § 27, n.

[1] As Lucian explains below (12–13), an *apophras hêmera*,
or "nefandous day," like a *dies nefastus* among the Latins,
was a day of ill-omen on which no courts were held and no
business affairs transacted. But the fact that a day can be
called *apophras* does not in itself justify calling a man *apophras*,
particularly as the word is of the feminine gender; and that is

THE MISTAKEN CRITIC, OR A DISCOURSE ON THE WORD NEFANDOUS

THAT you did not know the word nefandous is surely clear to everyone. When I had said of you that you were like a nefandous day—for I well remember comparing your character to a day of that kind [1]— how could you, with reference to that word, have made the stricture that I was barbarous in my speech, unless you were wholly unacquainted with it? I shall teach you presently what nefandous means; but I say to you now what Archilochus once said: "You have caught a cicada by the wing." [2] Have you ever heard of a writer of iambic verses named Archilochus, a Parian by birth, a man absolutely independent and given to frankness, who did not hesitate at all to use insulting language, no matter how much pain he was

what Lucian obviously did (cf. § 16, and especially § 23). It might have been defended by citing the comedian Eupolis (Fr. Incert., 32 M., 309 K.): "On going out, I chanced to meet a wight nefandous (ἄνθρωπος ἀποφράς) with a fickle eye." Either Lucian did not know the passage, or perhaps he thought that to reply in that way would be too like a Lexiphanes. Anyhow, he elected to infuriate his critic and divert his public by being transparently disingenuous and mendacious, and entirely evading the real issue. What his talk of "comparing" amounts to is commented on in the note on § 16.

[2] Bergk, frg. 143.

τοὺς περιπετεῖς ἐσομένους τῇ χολῇ τῶν ἰάμβων
αὐτοῦ. ἐκεῖνος τοίνυν πρός τινος τῶν τοιούτων
ἀκούσας κακῶς τέττιγα ἔφη τὸν ἄνδρα εἰληφέναι τοῦ πτεροῦ, εἰκάζων ἑαυτὸν τῷ τέττιγι ὁ
Ἀρχίλοχος φύσει μὲν λάλῳ ὄντι καὶ ἄνευ τινὸς
ἀνάγκης, ὁπόταν δὲ καὶ τοῦ πτεροῦ ληφθῇ, γεγωνό-
τερον βοῶντι. "Καὶ σὺ δή," ἔφη, "ὦ κακό-
δαιμον ἄνθρωπε, τί βουλόμενος ποιητὴν λάλον
παροξύνεις ἐπὶ σεαυτὸν αἰτίας ζητοῦντα καὶ
ὑποθέσεις τοῖς ἰάμβοις ; "

2 Ταῦτά σοι καὶ αὐτὸς ἀπειλῶ, οὐ μὰ τὸν Δία τῷ
Ἀρχιλόχῳ εἰκάζων ἐμαυτόν—πόθεν ; πολλοῦ γε
καὶ δέω—σοὶ δὲ μυρία συνειδὼς ἰάμβων ἄξια
βεβιωμένα, πρὸς ἃ μοι δοκεῖ οὐδ' ἂν ὁ Ἀρχίλοχος
αὐτὸς διαρκέσαι, προσπαρακαλέσας καὶ τὸν Σιμω-
νίδην καὶ τὸν Ἱππώνακτα συμποιεῖν μετ' αὐτοῦ
κἂν ἕν τι τῶν προσόντων σοι κακῶν, οὕτω σύ γε
παῖδας ἀπέφηνας ἐν πάσῃ βδελυρίᾳ τὸν Ὁροδοκίδην[1] καὶ τὸν Λυκάμβην καὶ τὸν Βούπαλον,
τοὺς ἐκείνων ἰάμβους. καὶ ἔοικε θεῶν τις ἐπὶ
χεῖλος ἀγαγεῖν σοι τότε τὸν γέλων ἐπὶ τῇ ἀποφράδι
λεχθείσῃ, ὡς αὐτὸς μὲν Σκυθῶν καταφανέστερος
γένοιο κομιδῇ ἀπαίδευτος ὢν καὶ τὰ κοινὰ ταῦτα
καὶ τὰ ἐν ποσὶν ἀγνοῶν, ἀρχὴν δὲ εὔλογον παράσχοις τῶν κατὰ σοῦ λόγων ἀνδρὶ ἐλευθέρῳ καὶ

---

[1] Ὁροδοκίδην ΓΕ : Ὁροδοικίδην Ν : Ὀροδοικίδην edd.

---

[1] See G. L. Hendrickson, "Archilochus and Catullus,"
Class. Philol. (1925), 155–157. With the aid of Catullus 40,
he is able to identify the poem from which Lucian quotes with
the one from which we have the fragment addressed to

THE MISTAKEN CRITIC

going to inflict upon those who would be exposed to
the gall of his iambics? Well, when he was abused
by someone of that type, he said that the man had
caught a cicada by the wing, likening himself,
Archilochus, to the cicada, which by nature is
vociferous, even without any compulsion, but when
it is caught by the wing, cries out still more lustily.
"Unlucky man," said he, "what is your idea in
provoking against yourself a vociferous poet, in search
of motives and themes for his iambics?"[1]

In these same terms I threaten you, not likening
myself to Archilochus (how could I? I am far indeed
from that!), but aware that you have done in your
life hundreds of things which deserve iambics. Even
Archilochus himself, I think, would not have been
able to cope with them, though he invited both
Simonides[2] and Hipponax to take a hand with him
in treating just one of your bad traits, so childish in
every sort of iniquity have you made Orodocides and
Lycambes and Bupalus,[3] their butts, appear. Probably it was one of the gods who brought the smile to
your lips on that occasion at my use of the word
nefandous, in order that you might become more
notorious than a Scythian for being absolutely
uneducated and ignorant of these obvious matters of
common knowledge, and that you might afford a
reasonable excuse for attacking you to an independent

"Father Lycambes" (Bergk, 88), and to reconstruct part of
the context.

[2] Of Amorgos; his name is sometimes spelt Semonides, but
not in the MSS of Lucian.

[3] Orodocides was evidently the butt of Semonides; this
is the only reference to him, and the name is not wholly
certain (Horodoecides N). Lycambes was satirised by Archilochus, and Bupalus by Hipponax.

οἴκοθέν σε ἀκριβῶς εἰδότι καὶ μηδὲν ὑποστελου-
μένῳ¹ τὸ μὴ οὐχὶ πάντα ἐξειπεῖν, μᾶλλον δὲ κηρῦ-
ξαι, ἃ πράττεις νύκτωρ καὶ μεθ' ἡμέραν ἔτι καὶ
νῦν ἐπὶ πολλοῖς τοῖς πρὶν ἐκείνοις.

3 Καίτοι μάταιον ἴσως καὶ περιττὸν ἐν παιδείας
νόμῳ παρρησιάζεσθαι πρὸς σέ. οὔτε γὰρ ἂν αὐτός
ποτε βελτίων γένοιο πρὸς τὴν ἐπιτίμησιν, οὐ μᾶλλον
ἢ κάνθαρος μεταπεισθείη ἂν μηκέτι τοιαῦτα κυλιν-
δεῖν, ἅπαξ αὐτοῖς συνήθης γενόμενος, οὔτ' εἶναι
τινα νομίζω τὸν ἀγνοοῦντα ἔτι τὰ ὑπὸ σοῦ τολ-
μώμενα καὶ ἃ γέρων ἄνθρωπος ἐς ἑαυτὸν παρα-
νομεῖς. οὐχ οὕτως ἀσφαλὴς οὐδὲ ἀφανὴς βδελυρὸς
εἶ· οὐδὲ δεῖ τινος τοῦ ἀποδύσοντος τὴν λεοντῆν,
ὡς φανερὸς γένοιο κανθήλιος ὤν, εἰ μή τις ἄρα
ἐξ Ὑπερβορέων ἄρτι ἐς ἡμᾶς ἥκοι ἢ ἐς τοσοῦτο
Κυμαῖος εἴη ὡς μὴ ἰδὼν εὐθὺς εἰδέναι ὄνων
ἁπάντων ὑβριστότατόν σε ὄντα, μὴ περιμείνας
ὀγκωμένου προσέτι ἀκούειν. οὕτω πάλαι καὶ πρὸ
ἐμοῦ καὶ παρὰ πᾶσι καὶ πολλάκις κεκήρυκται τὰ
σά, καὶ δόξαν οὐ μικρὰν ἔχεις ἐπ' αὐτοῖς, ὑπὲρ
τὸν Ἀριφράδην, ὑπὲρ τὸν Συβαρίτην Ἡμιθέωνα,²
ὑπὲρ τὸν Χῖον ἐκεῖνον Βάσταν, τὸν ἐπὶ τοῖς ὁμοίοις
σοφόν.

Ῥητέον δὲ ὅμως, εἰ καὶ ἕωλα δόξω λέγειν,

¹ ὑποστελλομένου A.
² Μίσθωνα MSS., corrected by du Soul from adv. Ind., 23.
But N has ἡμῖν θέων there; and possibly the name was
Μίνθων, a nickname. Cf. Lex. 12.

---

¹ On the habits of the tumble-bug, or dung-beetle, see the
beginning of the *Peace* of Aristophanes.
² Cf. *Runaways*, 13.
³ Ariphrades was an Athenian whom Aristophanes pilloried
for perverted relations with women. The Sybarite Hemitheon

THE MISTAKEN CRITIC

man who knows you thoroughly from home and will not refrain from telling—I should say, heralding abroad—all that you do by night and by day even now, in addition to those many incidents of your past.

And yet it is idle, no doubt, and superfluous to deal frankly with you by way of education; for in the first place you yourself could never improve in response to my censure, any more than a tumble-bug could be persuaded not to roll those balls of his any longer, when once he has become used to them.[1] In the second place, I do not believe that anyone exists who still is ignorant of your brazen performances and of the sins that you, an old man, have committed against yourself. You are not to that extent secure or unobserved in your iniquity. There is no need of anyone to strip away your lion's skin that you may be revealed a donkey, unless perhaps someone has just come to us from the Hyperboreans, or is sufficiently Cymaean[2] not to know, as soon as he sees you, that you are the most unbridled of all asses, without waiting to hear you bray. Your doings have been noised abroad so long a time, so far ahead of me, so universally and so repeatedly; and you have no slight reputation for them, surpassing Ariphrades, surpassing the Sybarite Hemitheon, surpassing the notorious Chian, Bastas, that adept in similar matters.[3]

Nevertheless, I must speak of them, even if I shall

(or Minthon; see the critical note) is alluded to as the author of an obscene book in the *Ignorant Book-Collector*, 23 (III, 203) and perhaps also in Ovid (*Trist.*, II, 417 : qui composuit nuper Sybaritica), but the name is not given there. Bastas was a nickname applied to Democritus of Chios, a musician, by Eupolis in the *Baptae* (Fr. 81 Kock).

THE WORKS OF LUCIAN

4 ὡς μὴ αἰτίαν ἔχοιμι μόνος αὐτὰ ἀγνοεῖν. μᾶλλον
δὲ παρακλητέος ἡμῖν τῶν Μενάνδρου προλόγων
εἷς, ὁ Ἔλεγχος, φίλος Ἀληθείᾳ καὶ Παρρησίᾳ
θεός, οὐχ ὁ ἀσημότατος τῶν ἐπὶ τὴν σκηνὴν
ἀναβαινόντων, μόνοις ὑμῖν ἐχθρὸς τοῖς δεδιόσι τὴν
γλῶτταν αὐτοῦ, πάντα καὶ εἰδότος καὶ σαφῶς
διεξιόντος ὁπόσα ὑμῖν σύνοιδεν. χάριεν γοῦν τοῦτο
γένοιτ᾿ ἄν, εἰ ἐθελήσειεν ἡμῖν προεισελθὼν
οὗτος διηγήσασθαι τοῖς θεαταῖς σύμπαντα τοῦ
δράματος τὸν λόγον.

Ἄγε τοίνυν, ὦ προλόγων καὶ δαιμόνων ἄριστε
Ἔλεγχε, ὅρα ὅπως σαφῶς προδιδάξῃς τοὺς
ἀκούοντας ὡς οὐ μάτην οὐδὲ φιλαπεχθημόνως οὐδ᾿
ἀνίπτοις ποσὶ κατὰ τὴν παροιμίαν ἐπὶ τόνδε τὸν
λόγον ἀπηντήκαμεν, ἀλλὰ καὶ ἴδιόν τι ἀμυνόμενοι
καὶ τὰ κοινά, μισοῦντες τὸν ἄνθρωπον ἐπὶ τῇ βδελυρίᾳ. ταῦτα μόνα εἰπὼν καὶ σαφῶς προδιηγησά-
μενος ἵλεως ἄπιθι ἐκποδών, τὰ δὲ ἄλλα ἡμῖν κατά-
λιπε· μιμησόμεθα γάρ σε καὶ διελέγξομεν τὰ πολλά,
ὡς παρρησίας γε [1] καὶ ἀληθείας ἕνεκα μηδὲν ἂν [2]
αἰτιάσασθαί σε. μήτε δὲ ἐμὲ πρὸς αὐτοὺς ἐπαινέσῃς,
ὦ φίλτατε Ἔλεγχε, μήτε τὰ ἐκείνῳ προσόντα
προεκχέῃς αὔτως· οὐ γὰρ ἄξιον θεῷ ὄντι ἐπὶ
στόμα σοι ἐλθεῖν τοὺς περὶ τῶν οὕτω καταπτύστων
λόγους.

5 "Ὁ γὰρ σοφιστὴς οὗτος εἶναι λέγων" (ὁ
πρόλογος ἤδη φησὶν ταῦτα) "ἐς Ὀλυμπίαν ποτὲ

---

[1] γε Fritzsche : τε MSS.
[2] μηδὲν ἂν De Jong, and possibly Γ[1] : μηδένα Γ[2], cett.

---

[1] We do not know the play in which Exposure appeared as
prologue and have no other information in the matter.

seem to be telling stale news, in order that I may
not bear the blame of being the only one who does
not know about them. But no! We must call in one
of Menander's Prologues, Exposure, a god devoted
to Truth and Frankness, by no means the least notable
of the characters that appear on the stage, disliked
only by you and your sort, who fear his tongue because
he knows everything and tells in plain language all
that he knows about you.[1] It would indeed be
delightful if he should prove willing to oblige us by
coming forward and telling the spectators the entire
argument of the play.

Come then, Exposure, best of prologues and divini-
ties, take care to inform the audience plainly that we
have not resorted to this public utterance gratui-
tously, or in a quarrelsome spirit, or, as the proverb has
it, with unwashen feet,[2] but to vindicate a grievance
of our own as well as those of the public, hating the
man for his depravity. Say only this, and present a
clear exposition, and then, giving us your blessing,
take yourself off, and leave the rest to us, for we shall
copy you and expose the greater part of his career so
thoroughly that in point of truth and frankness you
can find no fault with us. But do not sing my praises
to them, Exposure dear, and do not prematurely
pour out the bald truth about these traits of his; for
it is not fitting, as you are a god, that the words which
describe matters so abominable should come upon
your lips.

" This self-styled sophist " (Prologue is now speaking) " once came to Olympia, purposing to deliver

[2] Zenobius, I, 95: " going up to the roof with unwashed
feet "; unexplained by the paroemiographers or Suidas. It
must have to do with the use of the roof as a sleeping-place.

THE WORKS OF LUCIAN

ἧκε λόγον τινὰ πρὸ πολλοῦ συγγεγραμμένον
ἐπιδειξόμενος τοῖς πανηγυρισταῖς. ἦν δὲ ὑπόθεσις
τῷ συγγράμματι ὁ Πυθαγόρας κωλυόμενος ὑπό
τινος Ἀθηναίων, οἶμαι, μετέχειν τῆς Ἐλευσῖνι
τελετῆς ὡς βάρβαρος, ὅτι ἔλεγεν αὐτὸς ὁ Πυθαγόρας πρὸ τούτου ποτὲ καὶ Εὔφορβος γεγονέναι.
ἐτύγχανεν δὲ ὁ λόγος αὐτῷ κατὰ τὸν Αἰσώπου
κολοιὸν συμφορητὸς ὢν ἐκ ποικίλων ἀλλοτρίων
πτερῶν. βουλόμενος δὴ μὴ ἕωλα δόξαι λέγειν
ἀλλ' αὐτοσχεδιάζειν τὰ ἐκ τοῦ βιβλίου, δεῖται τῶν
συνήθων τινός (ἦν δὲ ἐκ Πατρῶν ἐκεῖνος, ἀμφὶ
δίκας ἔχων τὰ πολλά) ἐπειδὰν αἰτήσῃ τινὰς ὑποθέσεις τοῖς λόγοις, τὸν Πυθαγόραν αὐτῷ προελέσθαι.
καὶ οὕτως ἀνήρ[1] ἐποίησε, καὶ συνέπεισε τὸ θέατρον
ἀκούειν τὸν ὑπὲρ τοῦ Πυθαγόρου ἐκεῖνον λόγον.[2]
6 ἦν δὴ τὸ ἐπὶ τούτῳ ὁ μὲν πάνυ ἀπίθανος ἐν τῇ
ὑποκρίσει, συνείρων οἷον εἰκὸς ἐκ πολλοῦ ἐσκεμ-
μένα καὶ μεμελετημένα, εἰ καὶ ὅτι μάλιστα ἡ
ἀναισχυντία . . .[3] οὖσα ἐπήμυνε καὶ χεῖρα ὤρεγε
καὶ συνηγωνίζετο αὐτῷ. γέλως δὲ πολὺς παρὰ
τῶν ἀκουόντων· καὶ οἱ μὲν ἐς τὸν Πατρέα ἐκεῖνον
μεταξὺ ἀποβλέποντες ὑπεδήλουν ὡς οὐ λέληθε
συμπράξας αὐτῷ τὴν ῥᾳδιουργίαν, οἱ δὲ καὶ
αὐτὰ γνωρίζοντες τὰ λεγόμενα παρ' ὅλην τὴν
ἀκρόασιν διετέλεσαν ἐν τοῦτο μόνον ἔργον ἔχοντες,
ἀλλήλων πειρώμενοι ὅπως μνήμης ἔχουσι[4] πρὸς τὸ
διαγιγνώσκειν ὅτου ἕκαστον ἦν τῶν ὀλίγον πρὸ

[1] ἀνήρ MSS., corrected by Jacobitz.
[2] Text ΓΕΝ: τῶν ὑπὲρ τοῦ Πυθαγόρου ἐκείνων λόγων MFA.
[3] Lacuna G. Hermann: not indicated in MSS. πάρουσα Headlam, θεὸς οὖσα Cobet.
[4] ἔχουσι MF: ἔχωσι ΓΕΝΑ.

380

to those who should attend the festival a speech
which he had written long before. The subject of
his composition was the exclusion of Pythagoras (by
one of the Athenians, I suppose) from participation
in the Eleusinian mysteries as a barbarian, because
Pythagoras himself was in the habit of saying that
before being Pythagoras he had once been Euphorbus.[1] In truth, his speech was after the pattern of
Aesop's jackdaw, cobbled up out of motley feathers
from others. Wanting, of course, to have it thought
that he was not repeating a stale composition but
making up offhand what really came from his book,
he requested one of his familiars (it was the one from
Patras, who has so much business in the courts) to
select Pythagoras for him when he asked for subjects
to talk about. The man did so, and prevailed upon
the audience to hear that speech about Pythagoras.
In the sequel, he was very unconvincing in his
delivery, glibly reciting (as was natural) what he had
thought out long before and learned by heart, no
matter how much his shamelessness, standing by
him, defended him, lent him a helping hand, and aided
him in the struggle. There was a great deal of
laughter from his hearers, some of whom, by looking
from time to time at that man from Patras, indicated
that they had not failed to detect his part in the
improvisation, while others, recognising the expressions themselves, throughout the performance continued to have that as their sole occupation, testing
each other to find out how good their memories were
at distinguishing which one of those sophists who
achieved fame a little before our time for their

[1] Euphorbus was one of Homer's Trojans. See Lucian's
Cock, 13, 17, and 20 (II, pp. 204–214).

ἡμῶν εὐδοκιμησάντων ἐπὶ ταῖς καλουμέναις με-
λέταις σοφιστῶν.

7   "Ἐν δὲ τούτοις ἅπασι καὶ ὁ τὸν λόγον τόνδε
συγγράψας ἦν ἐν τοῖς γελῶσι καὶ αὐτός. τί δ' οὐκ
ἔμελλε γελᾶν ἐφ' οὕτω περιφανεῖ καὶ ἀπιθάνῳ καὶ
ἀναισχύντῳ τολμήματι; καί πως (ἔστιν δὲ ἀκρατὴς
γέλωτος) ὁ μὲν τὴν φωνὴν ἐντρέψας ἐς μέλος,
ὡς ᾤετο, θρῆνόν τινα ἐπηύλει τῷ Πυθαγόρᾳ, ὁ δέ,
τοῦτο δὴ τὸ τοῦ λόγου, ὄνον κιθαρίζειν πειρώμενον
ὁρῶν ἀνεκάγχασε μάλα ἡδύ, ὁ ποιητὴς οὗτος ὁ
ἐμός· ὁ δὲ εἶδεν ἐπιστραφείς. τοῦτο ἐξεπολέ-
8 μωσεν αὐτούς, τό τε ἔναγχος ἐνθένδε.¹ ἦν μὲν ἡ
τοῦ ἔτους ἀρχή, μᾶλλον δὲ ἡ ἀπὸ τῆς μεγάλης
νουμηνίας τρίτη, ἐν ᾗ οἱ Ῥωμαῖοι κατά τι ἀρχαῖον
εὔχονταί τε αὐτοὶ ὑπὲρ ἅπαντος τοῦ ἔτους εὐχάς
τινας καὶ θύουσι, Νομᾶ² τοῦ βασιλέως καταστησα-
μένου τὰς ἱερουργίας αὐτοῖς, καὶ πεπιστεύκασιν
τοὺς θεοὺς ἐν ἐκείνῃ μάλιστα τῇ ἡμέρᾳ χρηματίζειν
τοῖς εὐχομένοις. ἐν τοιαύτῃ τοίνυν ἑορτῇ καὶ
ἱερομηνίᾳ ὁ τότε γελάσας ἐν Ὀλυμπίᾳ ἐκεῖνος
ἐπὶ τῷ ὑποβολιμαίῳ Πυθαγόρᾳ ἰδὼν προσιόντα
τὸν κατάπτυστον καὶ ἀλαζόνα, τὸν τῶν ἀλλοτρίων
λόγων ὑποκριτήν (ἐτύγχανε δὲ καὶ τὸν τρόπον
ἀκριβῶς εἰδὼς αὐτοῦ καὶ τὴν ἄλλην ἀσέλγειαν καὶ
μιαρίαν τοῦ βίου καὶ ἃ ποιεῖν ἐλέγετο καὶ ἃ
ποιῶν κατείληπτο) 'Ὥρα ἡμῖν,' ἔφη πρός τινα

---

¹ The text is that of N, interpreted by adding a comma
after αὐτούς and writing τό τε for τότε. The full stop is
set after ἔναγχος in ΓΑ(MFE) and previous editions. But
ἐνθένδε makes an awkward anacoluthon with what follows
(hence ἔνθεν δὲ ΓΑ); moreover, τότε ἔναγχος is neither idio-
matic (hence the omission of τότε in MF) nor consistent with
ποτέ (6) and τοῦ πάλαι ἐκείνου γέλωτος (8).

so-called "exercises" was the author of each expression.

"Among all these, among those who laughed, was the writer of these words. And why should not he laugh at a piece of cheek so manifest and unconvincing and shameless? So, somehow or other, being one who cannot control his laughter, when the speaker had attuned his voice to song, as he thought, and was intoning a regular dirge over Pythagoras, our author, seeing an ass trying to play the lyre, as the saying goes, burst into a very melodious cachinnation, and the other turned and saw him. That created a state of war between them, and the recent affair sprang from it. It was the beginning of the year, or rather, the second day after the New Year,[1] the day on which the Romans, by an ancient custom, make prayers in person for the entire year and hold sacrifices, following ceremonies which King Numa established for them; they are convinced that on that day beyond all others the gods give ear to those who pray. Well, on that festival and high holiday, the man who burst out laughing then in Olympia at the supposititious Pythagoras saw this contemptible cheat approaching, this presenter of the speeches of others. It happened that he knew his character, too, and all his wantonness and unclean living, both what he was said to do, and what he had been caught doing. So he said to

---

[1] New Year's Day is called in the Greek "the great New-Moon-Day." The day of the festival on which the incident occurred was January third (a.d. III non. Ian.) For the vow of the consuls on that day, two gilded bulls for the health of the Imperial family, see Henzen, *Acta Fratrum Arvalium*, pp. 100–102.

---

[2] θύουσι Νομᾶ Cobet (Νουμᾶ vulg.): θύουσιν ἅμα MSS.

τῶν ἑταίρων, ‘ ἐκτρέπεσθαι τὸ δυσάντητον τοῦτο
θέαμα, ὃς φανεὶς ἔοικε τὴν ἡδίστην ἡμέραν ἀποφράδα ἡμῖν ποιήσειν.’

“ Τοῦτ’ ἀκούσας ὁ σοφιστὴς τὴν ἀποφράδα ὡς
τι ξένον καὶ ἀλλότριον τῶν Ἑλλήνων ὄνομα
ἐγέλα εὐθὺς καὶ τὸν ἄνδρα τοῦ πάλαι ἐκείνου γέλωτος ἠμύνετο, ὡς γοῦν ᾤετο, καὶ πρὸς ἅπαντας
ἔλεγεν, ‘ Ἀποφράς, τί δὲ τοῦτό ἐστι ; καρπός τις
ἢ βοτάνη τις ἢ σκεῦος ; ἆρα τῶν ἐσθιομένων ἢ
πινομένων τί ἐστιν ἀποφράς ; ἐγὼ μὲν οὔτε ἤκουσα
πώποτε οὔτ’ ἂν συνείην ποτὲ ὅ τι καὶ λέγει.’

9 ταῦθ’ ὁ μὲν ᾤετο κατὰ τούτου διεξιέναι καὶ πολὺν
ἐπῆγε τῇ ἀποφράδι τὸν γέλων· ἐλελήθει δὲ κατ’
αὐτοῦ τὸ ὕστατον τεκμήριον ἀπαιδευσίας ἐκφέ-
ρων. ἐπὶ τούτῳ τὸν λόγον τόνδε συνέγραψεν ὁ [1]
ἐμὲ προεισπέμψας ὑμῖν, ὡς δείξειε τὸν ἀοίδιμον
σοφιστὴν τὰ κοινὰ τῶν Ἑλλήνων ἀγνοοῦντα καὶ
ὁπόσα κἂν οἱ ἐπὶ τῶν ἐργαστηρίων καὶ τῶν
καπηλείων εἰδεῖεν.”

10 Ταῦτα μὲν ὁ Ἔλεγχος, ἐγὼ δέ—ἤδη γὰρ αὐτὸς
παρείληφα τοῦ δράματος τὰ λοιπά—δίκαιος ἂν
εἴην τὰ ἐκ τοῦ Δελφικοῦ τρίποδος ἤδη λέγειν,
οἷα μέν σου τὰ ἐν τῇ πατρίδι, οἷα δὲ τὰ ἐν τῇ
Παλαιστίνῃ, οἷα δὲ τὰ ἐν Αἰγύπτῳ, οἷα δὲ τὰ
ἐν Φοινίκῃ καὶ Συρίᾳ, εἶτα ἑξῆς τὰ ἐν Ἑλλάδι
καὶ Ἰταλίᾳ, καὶ ἐπὶ πᾶσι τὰ ἐν Ἐφέσῳ νῦν, ἅπερ
κεφαλαιωδέστατα τῆς ἀπονοίας τῆς σῆς καὶ

---

[1] ὁ Guyet: not in MSS.

---

[1] “ Exposure,” however devoted to Truth and Frankness,
here indulges in prevarication so obvious that its purpose is

THE MISTAKEN CRITIC

one of his friends: 'We must give a wide berth to this ill-met sight, whose appearance is likely to make the most delightful of all days nefandous for us.'[1]

"On hearing that, the sophist at once laughed at the word nefandous as if it were strange and alien to the Greeks, and paid the man back, in his own estimation, at least, for the laughter of that former time, saying to all: 'Nefandous! What, pray, is that? A fruit, or a herb, or a utensil? Can it be something to eat or drink? For my part I have never heard the word, and should never be able to guess what it means.' He thought he was directing these remarks at our friend, and he subjected 'nefandous' to a great deal of laughter; but he had unwittingly brought against himself the uttermost proof of his want of education. Under these circumstances he who sent me in to you in advance has written this composition to demonstrate that the renowned sophist does not know expressions common to all the Greeks, which even men in the workshops and the bazaars would know."

Thus far Exposure. In my own turn (for I myself have now taken over the rest of the show), I might fittingly play the part of the Delphic tripod and tell what you did in your own country, what in Palestine, what in Egypt, what in Phoenicia and Syria; then, in due order, in Greece and Italy, and on top of it all, what you are now doing at Ephesus, which is the extremity of your recklessness and the culminating

clearly to exasperate Lucian's victim rather than to impose upon his public. To say that a man's appearance would make the day *apophras* is not saying that he was " like that kind of day," let alone calling him *apophras*. See the note on § 1, above, and that on § 16, below.

κορυφὴ καὶ κορωνὶς τοῦ τρόπου. ἐπεὶ γὰρ κατὰ
τὴν παροιμίαν Ἰλιεὺς ὢν τραγῳδοὺς ἐμισθώσω,
11 καιρὸς ἤδη σοι ἀκούειν τὰ σαυτοῦ κακά. μᾶλλον
δέ, ταῦτα μὲν μηδέπω, περὶ δὲ τῆς ἀποφράδος
πρότερον.

Εἰπὲ γάρ μοι, πρὸς πανδήμου καὶ Γενετυλλίδων
καὶ Κυβήβης,[1] πῆ σοι μεμπτὸν καὶ γέλωτος
ἄξιον τοὔνομα εἶναι ἔδοξεν ἡ ἀποφράς ; νὴ Δί᾽,
οὐ γὰρ ἦν τῶν Ἑλλήνων ἴδιον, ἀλλά ποθεν ἐπεισ-
κωμάσαν αὐτοῖς ἀπὸ τῆς πρὸς Κελτοὺς ἢ Θρᾷκας
ἢ Σκύθας ἐπιμιξίας, σὺ δὲ—ἅπαντα γὰρ οἶσθα τὰ
τῶν Ἀθηναίων—ἐξέκλεισας τοῦτο εὐθὺς καὶ ἐξε-
κήρυξας τοῦ Ἑλληνικοῦ, καὶ ὁ γέλως ἐπὶ τούτῳ,
ὅτι βαρβαρίζω καὶ ξενίζω καὶ ὑπερβαίνω τοὺς
ὅρους τοὺς Ἀττικούς.

Καὶ μὴν τί ἄλλο οὕτως Ἀθηναίοις ἐπιχώριον
ὡς τουτὶ τοὔνομα, φαῖεν ἂν οἵ γε σοῦ μᾶλλον
τὰ τοιαῦτα εἰδότες· ὥστε θᾶττον ἂν Ἐρεχθέα καὶ
τὸν Κέκροπα ξένους ἀποφήναις καὶ ἐπήλυδας τῶν
Ἀθηνῶν ἢ τὴν ἀποφράδα δείξειας οὐκ οἰκείαν καὶ
12 αὐτόχθονα τῆς Ἀττικῆς. πολλὰ μὲν γάρ ἐστιν
ἃ καὶ αὐτοὶ κατὰ ταὐτὰ τοῖς πᾶσιν ἀνθρώποις ὀνο-
μάζουσιν, ἀποφράδα δὲ μόνοι ἐκεῖνοι τὴν μιαρὰν
καὶ ἀπευκτὴν καὶ ἀπαίσιον καὶ ἄπρακτον καὶ σοὶ
ὁμοίαν ἡμέραν. ἰδού, καὶ μεμάθηκας ἤδη ὁδοῦ
πάρεργον τί βούλεται αὐτοῖς ἡ ἀποφρὰς ἡμέρα.

---

[1] κυβίβης MSS. (κυβικῆς Γ).

---

[1] If people of Troy attend tragedies, they are bound to hear about the misfortunes of the Trojans.

[2] Genetyllis was originally a goddess of childbirth. Hesychius says that she resembled Hecate, received sacrifices of dogs,

point and crowning glory of your character. Now that, in the words of the proverb,[1] you who live in Troy have paid to see tragedians, it is a fitting occasion for you to hear your own misadventures. But no! not yet. First about that 'nefandous.'

Tell me, in the name of Aphrodite Pandemus and the Genetyllides[2] and Cybebe, in what respect did you think the word nefandous objectionable and fit to be laughed at? Oh, because it did not belong to the Greeks, but had somehow thrust its way in among them from their intercourse with Celts or Thracians or Scyths; wherefore you—for you know everything that pertains to the Athenians—excluded it at once and banished it from the Greek world, and your laughter was because I committed a barbarism and used a foreign idiom and went beyond the Attic bounds!

"Come now, what else is as well established on Athenian soil as that word?" people would say who are better informed than you about such matters. It would be easier for you to prove Erechtheus and Cecrops foreigners and invaders of Attica, than to show that 'nefandous' is not at home and indigenous in Attica. There are many things which they designate in the same way as everybody else, but they, and they alone, designate as nefandous a day which is vile, abominable, inauspicious, useless, and like you. There now! I have already taught you in passing what they mean by nefandous!

and was of foreign origin. But in Attica, where she was worshipped in the temple of another similar divinity, Colias, the identities of the two were apparently so thoroughly merged that they could both be called either Genetyllides or Coliades, and both were more or less blended with Aphrodite.

THE WORKS OF LUCIAN

Ὅταν μήτε αἱ ἀρχαὶ χρηματίζωσι μήτε εἰσαγώ-
γιμοι αἱ δίκαι ὦσι μήτε τὰ ἱερὰ ἱερουργῆται μήθ᾽
ὅλως τι τῶν αἰσίων τελῆται, αὕτη ἀποφρὰς ἡμέρα.
13 ἐνομίσθη δὲ τοῦτο ἄλλοις ἐπ᾽ ἄλλαις αἰτίαις·
ἢ γὰρ ἡττηθέντες μάχαις μεγάλαις ἔπειτα ἔταξαν
ἐκείνας τὰς ἡμέρας ἐν αἷς τὰ τοιαῦτα ἐπεπόν-
θεισαν ἀπράκτους καὶ ἀκύρους τῶν ἐννόμων
πράξεων εἶναι, ἢ καὶ νὴ Δία—καίτοι ἄκαιρον
ἴσως καὶ ἔξωρόν γε ἤδη, γέροντα ἄνδρα μεταπαι-
δεύειν καὶ ἀναδιδάσκειν τὰ τοιαῦτα, μηδὲ τὰ πρὸ
τούτων εἰδότα. πάνυ γοῦν τοῦτ᾽ ἔστι τὸ λοιπόν,
κἂν ἐκμάθῃς αὐτό, πᾶν ἡμῖν εἰδὼς ἔσῃ. πόθεν,
ὦ οὗτος; τὰ μὲν γὰρ ἄλλα καὶ ἀγνοῆσαι συγγνώμη
ὁπόσα ἔξω τοῦ πολλοῦ πάτου καὶ ἄδηλα τοῖς
ἰδιώταις, τὴν ἀποφράδα δὲ οὐδὲ βουληθεὶς ἂν ἄλλως
εἴποις· ἐν γὰρ τοῦτο καὶ μόνον ἁπάντων τοὔνομα.
14 Ἔστω, φησί τις, ἀλλὰ καὶ τῶν πλαιῶν ὀνομάτων τὰ μὲν λεκτέα, τὰ δ᾽ οὔ, ὁπόσα αὐτῶν μὴ
συνήθη τοῖς πολλοῖς, ὡς μὴ ταράττοιμεν τὰς ἀκοὰς
καὶ τιτρώσκοιμεν τῶν συνόντων τὰ ὦτα. ἐγὼ δέ,
ὦ βέλτιστε, πρὸς μὲν σὲ ἴσως ταῦτα περὶ σοῦ
εἰπὼν ἥμαρτον· ἐχρῆν γὰρ ἐχρῆν ἢ κατὰ Παφλα-
γόνων ἢ Καππαδοκῶν ἢ Βακτρίων πάτρια διαλέγε-
σθαί σοι, ὡς[1] ἐκμάθῃς τὰ λεγόμενα καὶ σοὶ
ἀκούειν ᾗ[2] ἡδέα. τοῖς δ᾽ ἄλλοις Ἕλλησιν οἶμαι
καθ᾽ Ἑλλάδα γλῶτταν συνεῖναι χρή. εἶτα καὶ τῶν
Ἀττικῶν κατὰ χρόνους τινὰς πολλὰ ἐντρεψάντων

[1] ὡς du Soul: ἕως MSS.
[2] ᾗ Jacobitz: not in MSS.

388

THE MISTAKEN CRITIC

When official business is not transacted, introduction of lawsuits is not permissible, sacrifice of victims is not performed, and, in general, nothing is done that requires good omens, that day is nefandous. The custom was introduced among different peoples in different ways; either they were defeated in great battles and subsequently established that those days on which they had undergone such misfortunes should be useless and invalid for their customary transactions, or, indeed—but it is inopportune, perhaps, and by now unseasonable to try to alter an old man's education and reinstruct him in such matters when he does not know even what precedes them.[1] It can hardly be that this is all that remains, and that if you learn it, we shall have you fully informed! Nonsense, man! Not to know those other expressions which are off the beaten path and obscure to ordinary folk is pardonable; but even if you wished, you could not say nefandous in any other way, for that is everyone's sole and only word for it.

" Well and good," someone will say, " but even in the case of time-honoured words, only some of them are to be employed, and not others, which are unfamiliar to the public, that we may not disturb the wits and wound the ears of our hearers." My dear sir, perhaps as far as you are concerned I was wrong to say that to you about yourself; yes, yes, I should have followed the folk-ways of the Paphlagonians or the Cappadocians or the Bactrians in conversing with you, that you might fully understand what was being said and it might be pleasing to your ears. But Greeks, I take it, should be addressed in the Greek tongue. Moreover, although even the Athenians in

---

[1] That is, he lacks even the rudiments of an education.

389

τῆς αὐτῶν φωνῆς, τοῦτο ἐν τοῖς μάλιστα τὸ
ὄνομα διετέλεσεν οὕτως ἀεὶ καὶ πρὸς ἁπάντων
αὐτῶν λεγόμενον.

15 Εἶπον ἂν καὶ τοὺς πρὸ ἡμῶν κεχρημένους
τῷ ὀνόματι, εἰ μὴ καὶ ταύτῃ σε διαταράξειν ἔμελλον, ξένα σοι καὶ ἄγνωστα ποιητῶν καὶ ῥητόρων
καὶ συγγραφέων ὀνόματα διεξιών. μᾶλλον δὲ
οὐδ᾽ ἐγώ σοι τοὺς εἰπόντας ἐρῶ, πάντες γὰρ ἴσασιν,
ἀλλὰ σύ μοι ἕνα τῶν πάλαι δείξας οὐ κεχρημένον
τῷ ὀνόματι, χρυσοῦς, φασίν, ἐν Ὀλυμπίᾳ στάθητι.[1]
καίτοι ὅστις γέρων ὢν καὶ ἀφῆλιξ τὰ τοιαῦτα ἀγνοε.
δοκεῖ μοι καὶ ὅτι Ἀθῆναι πόλις ἐστὶν ἐν τῇ
Ἀττικῇ καὶ Κόρινθος ἐπὶ τῷ Ἰσθμῷ καὶ Σπάρτη
ἐν Πελοποννήσῳ μὴ εἰδέναι.

16 Λοιπὸν ἴσως ἐκεῖνό σοι λέγειν, ὡς τὸ μὲν ὄνομα
ᾔδεις, τὴν δὲ χρῆσιν αὐτοῦ ἄκαιρον ᾐτιάσω. φέρε
δὴ καὶ ὑπὲρ τούτου πρὸς σὲ ἀπολογήσομαι τὰ
εἰκότα, σὺ δὲ προσέχειν τὸν νοῦν, εἰ μὴ πάνυ
ὀλίγον σοι μέλει τοῦ μηδὲν εἰδέναι. οἱ πάλαι πολλὰ
τοιαῦτα πρὸ ἡμῶν ἀπέρριψαν ἐς τοὺς σοὶ ὁμοίους
ἕκαστοι τοὺς τότε—ἦσαν γὰρ καὶ τότε, ὡς τὸ
εἰκός, βδελυροί τινες ἐς τὰ ἤθη καὶ μιαροὶ καὶ
κακοήθεις τὸν τρόπον—καὶ ὁ μὲν κόθορνόν τινα
εἶπεν, εἰκάσας αὐτοῦ τὸν βίον ἀμφίβολον ὄντα τοῖς
τοιούτοις ὑποδήμασιν, ὁ δὲ λύμην,[2] ὅτι τὰς
ἐκκλησίας θορυβώδης ῥήτωρ ὢν ἐπετάραττεν, ὁ
δὲ ἑβδόμην, ὅτι ὥσπερ οἱ παῖδες ἐν ταῖς ἑβδόμαις

---

[1] στάθητι (M ?) ed. Flor.: στάχυσι(ν) ΕΓΝ: στάχυας A. Cf.
Plato, *Phaedrus*, 236 B.

course of time have made many changes in their speech, this word especially has continued to be used in this way always and by all of them.

I should have named those who have employed the word before our time, were I not certain to disturb you in this way also, by reciting names of poets and rhetoricians and historians that would be foreign to you, and beyond your ken. No, I shall not name those who have used it, for they are known to all; but do you point me out one of the ancients who has not employed the word and your statue shall be set up, as the saying goes, in gold at Olympia. Indeed, any old man, full of years, who is unacquainted with such expressions is not, I think, even aware that the city of Athens is in Attica, Corinth at the Isthmus, and Sparta in the Peloponnese.

It remains, perhaps, for you to say that you knew the word, but criticised the inappropriate use of it. Come now, on this point too I shall respond to you fittingly, and you must pay attention, unless not knowing matters very little to you. The ancients were before me in hurling many such taunts at the like of you, each at the men of their day; for in that time too there were, of course, dirty fellows, disgusting traits, and ungentle dispositions. One man called a certain person "Buskin," comparing his principles, which were adaptable, to that kind of footwear; another called a man "Rampage" because he was a turbulent orator and disturbed the assembly, and another someone else "Seventh Day" because he acted in the assemblies as children do on the

---

² λύμην Harmon: λυπάην MSS. except A, which has λυπάδην.

κἀκεῖνος ἐν ταῖς ἐκκλησίαις ἔπαιζεν καὶ διεγέλα
καὶ παιδιὰν ἐποιεῖτο τὴν σπουδὴν τοῦ δήμου.
μὴ δῶς οὖν κἀμοί, πρὸς Ἀδώνιδος, εἰκάσαι
παμπόνηρον ἄνθρωπον, ἁπάσῃ κακίᾳ σύντροφον,
ἡμέρᾳ δυσφήμῳ καὶ ἀπαισίῳ ;

17 Ἡμεῖς δὲ καὶ τοὺς χωλοὺς τῷ δεξιῷ ἐκτρεπό-
μεθα, καὶ μάλιστα εἰ ἕωθεν ἴδοιμεν αὐτούς· κἂν
εἴ τις βάκηλον ἢ εὐνοῦχον ἴδοι ἢ πίθηκον εὐθὺς
ἐξιὼν τῆς οἰκίας, ἐπὶ πόδα ἀναστρέφει καὶ ἐπανέρ-
χεται, οὐκ ἀγαθὰς μαντευόμενος τὰς ἐφημέρους
ἐκείνας [1] πράξεις ἔσεσθαι αὐτῷ ὑπὸ πονηρῷ τῷ
πρώτῳ καὶ δυσφήμῳ κληδονίσματι. ἐν ἀρχῇ δὲ
καὶ ἐν θύραις καὶ ἐπὶ τῇ πρώτῃ ἐξόδῳ καὶ ἕωθεν
τοῦ ἅπαντος ἔτους εἴ τις ἴδοι κίναιδον καὶ ἀπόρ-
ρητα ποιοῦντα καὶ πάσχοντα, ἐπίσημον ἐπὶ τούτῳ
καὶ ἀπερρωγότα καὶ μονονουχὶ τοὔνομα τῶν
ἔργων αὐτῶν ὀνομαζόμενον, ἀπατεῶνα, γόητα,
ἐπίορκον, ὄλεθρον, κύφωνα, βάραθρον, μὴ φύγῃ
μηδ᾽ εἰκάσῃ τοῦτον ἀποφράδι ἡμέρᾳ ;

18 Ἀλλ᾽ οὐχὶ σὺ τοιοῦτος ; οὐκ ἂν ἔξαρνος γένοιο,
εἰ ἐγὼ τὴν ἀνδρείαν οἶδα τὴν σήν, ὅς γε καὶ μέγα
φρονεῖν ἐπὶ τούτῳ μοι δοκεῖς, ὅτι μὴ ἀπόλλυταί

---

[1] ἐφ᾽ ἡμέρας ἐκείνης Herwerden.

[1] The nickname "Buskin" was given to Theramenes.
"Seventh Day" cannot be identified, and the other nickname
is corrupted in the Greek text.

[2] Stripped of its manifest disingenuousness (for comparison
includes both simile and metaphor, and the use of simile
would have been entirely unexceptionable), this amounts to
defending what he said as a legitimate use of metaphor,
like calling a man "Buskin." The argument would be valid
if he had called the man "Apophras hêmera!" But since
we may safely say that he addressed him or spoke about him

seventh day of the month, joking and making fun and turning the earnestness of the people into jest.[1] Will you not, then, in the name of Adonis, permit me to compare an utterly vile fellow, familiar with every form of iniquity, to a disreputable and inauspicious day?[2]

We avoid those who are lame in the right foot, especially if we should see them early in the morning; and if anyone should see a cut priest or a eunuch or a monkey immediately upon leaving the house, he returns upon his tracks and goes back, auguring that his daily business for that day will not be successful, thanks to the bad and inauspicious omen at the start. But in the beginning of the whole year, at its door, on its first going forth, in its early morning, if one should see a profligate who commits and submits to unspeakable practices, notorious for it, broken in health, and all but called by the name of his actions themselves, a cheat, a swindler, a perjurer, a pestilence, a pillory, a pit,[3] will not one shun him, will not one compare him to a nefandous day?

Well, are you not such a person? You will not deny it, if I know your boldness; indeed, it seems to me that you are actually vain over the fact that you

simply as " apophras," the examples are not parallel, despite the speciousness of " hebdomas " (" Seventh Day "), formally identical with " apophras." The one locution, however, is metaphor, because " day " is understood; in the other, that is not the case, and instead of metaphor what we have to do with is an application of the adjective grammatically incorrect and really justifiable only by pleading previous use—which might have been done by adducing Eupolis (see § 1, note).

[3] That is to say, approximately, a whipping-stock, a gallows-bird; hurling into a pit was a form of capital punishment in many cities of Greece.

σοι ἡ δόξα τῶν ἔργων, ἀλλὰ πᾶσι δῆλος εἶ καὶ
περιβόητος. εἰ δὲ καὶ ὁμόσε χωρήσειας καὶ
ἀρνήσαιο μὴ τοιοῦτος εἶναι, τίσι πιστὰ ἐρεῖς ;
τοῖς πολίταις τοῖς σοῖς (ἐκεῖθεν γὰρ ἄρχεσθαι
δίκαιον) ; ἀλλὰ ἴσασιν ἐκεῖνοι τὰς πρώτας σου
τροφάς, καὶ ὡς παραδοὺς σεαυτὸν τῷ ὀλέθρῳ
ἐκείνῳ στρατιώτῃ συμπεριεφθείρου πάντα ὑπηρε-
τῶν, ἄχρι δή σε, τὸ τοῦ λόγου τοῦτο, ῥάκος
19 πολυσχιδὲς ἐργασάμενος ἐξέωσεν. κἀκεῖνα μέμνηνται, ὡς τὸ εἰκός, ἃ πρὸς τὸ θέατρον ἐνεανιεύου,
τοῖς ὀρχησταῖς ὑποκρινόμενος καὶ συνταγματάρχης
ἀξιῶν εἶναι. οὐδεὶς γοῦν πρὸ σοῦ ἂν εἰσῆλθεν εἰς
τὸ θέατρον οὐδ' ἂν ἐμήνυσεν ὅ τι τοὔνομα τῷ δράματι, ἀλλὰ σὺ κοσμίως πάνυ, χρυσᾶς ἐμβάδας
ἔχων καὶ ἐσθῆτα τυραννικήν, προεισεπέμπου εὐ-
μένειαν αἰτήσων παρὰ τοῦ θεάτρου, στεφάνους
κομίζων καὶ κρότῳ ἀπιών, ἤδη τιμώμενος πρὸς
αὐτῶν. ἀλλὰ νῦν ῥήτωρ καὶ σοφιστής· καὶ διὰ
τοῦτο ἦν πύθωνταί ποτε τὰ τοιαῦτα ὑπὲρ σοῦ
ἐκεῖνοι, τοῦτο δὴ τὸ ἐκ τῆς τραγῳδίας, " δύο
μὲν ἡλίους ὁρᾶν " δοκοῦσι, " δισσὰς δὲ Θήβας·"
καὶ πρόχειρον ἅπασιν εὐθὺς τὸ " Ἐκεῖνος ὁ τότε,
καὶ μετ' ἐκεῖνα ; " τοιγάρτοι καὶ αὐτὸς εὖ
ποιῶν οὐκ ἐπιβαίνεις τὸ παράπαν οὐδ' ἐπιχωριάζεις
αὐτοῖς, ἀλλὰ φεύγεις ἑκὼν πατρίδα οὔτε χεῖμα
κακὴν οὔτε θέρει ἀργαλέαν, ἀλλὰ καλλίστην καὶ

---

[1] This man played parts like that of the Odysseus who,
as we are told in *The Dance*, § 83, had his head broken by the
pantomimic dancer who was enacting Ajax gone mad. Such
parts did not involve dancing (cf. ὑποκρίνων, above), but
were not silent—a point made perfectly clear by another allusion to them in § 25 of this piece. Three of the rôles in which

THE MISTAKEN CRITIC

have not lost the glory of your exploits, but are
conspicuous to all and have become notorious.   If,
however, you should offer opposition and should deny
that you are such a person, who will believe what you
say?   The people of your native city (for it is fitting
to begin there)?   No, they know about your first
source of livelihood, and how you gave yourself over
to that pestilential soldier and shared his depravity,
serving him in every way until, after reducing you
to a torn rag, as the saying goes, he thrust you out.
And of course they remember also the effrontery that
you displayed in the theatre, when you acted secondary parts for the dancers and thought you were leader
of the company.[1]   Nobody might enter the theatre
before you, or indicate the name of the play ; you were
sent in first, very properly arrayed, wearing golden
sandals and the robe of a tyrant, to beg for favour
from the audience, winning wreaths and making your
exit amid applause, for already you were held in
esteem by them.   But now you are a public speaker
and a lecturer !   So those people, if ever they hear
such a thing as that about you, believe they see two
suns, as in the tragedy,[2] and twin cities of Thebes,
and everyone is quick to say, " That man who
then—, and after that—? "   Therefore you do well
in not going there at all or living in their neighbourhood, but of your own accord remaining in exile from
your native city, though it is neither " bad in winter "
not " oppressive in summer," [3] but the fairest and

Lucian's butt appeared are named there ; Ninus, Metiochus,
and Achilles.   See the note on that passage.

[2] Euripides, *Bacchae*, 913.

[3] It was therefore unlike Ascra, the home of Hesiod,
which was both. *Works and Days*, 640.

395

μεγίστην τῶν ἐν Φοινίκῃ ἁπασῶν· τὸ γὰρ ἐλέγχε-
σθαι καὶ τοῖς εἰδόσι καὶ μεμνημένοις τῶν πάλαι
ἐκείνων συνεῖναι βρόχος ὡς ἀληθῶς ἔστι σοι.
καίτοι τί ταῦτα ληρῶ ; τίνα γὰρ ἂν αἰδεσθείης
σύ ; τί δ' ἂν αἰσχρὸν ἡγήσαιο τῶν ὑστάτων ;
πυνθάνομαι δὲ καὶ κτήματα εἶναί σοι μεγάλα παρ'
αὐτοῖς, τὸ δύστηνον ἐκεῖνο πυργίον, ὡς τὸν τοῦ
Σινωπέως πίθον τὴν Διὸς αὐλὴν εἶναι πρὸς αὐτό.

Τοὺς μὲν δὴ πολίτας οὐδαμῆ οὐδαμῶς ἂν μετα-
πείσειας μὴ οὐχὶ τῶν ἁπάντων βδελυρώτατόν σε
20 ἡγεῖσθαι, ὄνειδος κοινὸν ἁπάσῃ τῇ πόλει· τάχα δ'
ἂν τοὺς ἄλλους τοὺς ἐν τῇ Συρίᾳ προσλάβοις
ὁμοψήφους, εἰ λέγοις μηδὲν πονηρὸν μηδὲ ἐπαίτιον
βεβιῶσθαί σοι. Ἡράκλεις, ἡ μὲν Ἀντιόχεια
καὶ τοὖργον αὐτὸ εἶδεν, ὅτε τὸν Ταρσόθεν ἥκοντα
ἐκεῖνον νεανίσκον ἀπαγαγών—ἀλλὰ καὶ ἀναδέρειν
αὐτὰ αἰσχρὸν ἴσως ἐμοί. πλὴν ἀλλὰ ἴσασίν γε καὶ
μέμνηνται οἱ τότε ὑμῖν ἐπιστάντες καὶ σὲ μὲν ἐς
γόνυ συγκαθήμενον ἰδόντες, ἐκεῖνον δὲ οἶσθα ὅ τι
καὶ ποιοῦντα, εἰ μὴ παντάπασιν ἐπιλήσμων τις εἶ.

21 Ἀλλ' οἱ ἐν Αἰγύπτῳ ἴσως ἀγνοοῦσί σε,[1] οἱ μετὰ
τοὺς ἐν Συρίᾳ θαυμαστοὺς ἄθλους ἐκείνους ὑποδε-
ξάμενοι φεύγοντα ἐφ' οἷς εἶπον, ὑπὸ τῶν ἱματιο-
καπήλων διωκόμενον, παρ' ὧν ἐσθῆτας πολυτε-
λεῖς πριάμενος ἐφόδια εἶχες. ἀλλ' οὐκ ἐλάττω
σοι ἡ Ἀλεξάνδρεια σύνοιδεν, οὐδὲ μὰ Δί' ἐχρῆν
δευτέραν τῆς Ἀντιοχείας κεκρίσθαι αὐτήν, ἀλλ'
ἤ τε ἀκολασία γυμνοτέρα καὶ ἡ αἰσχρουργία σοι

[1] ἀγνοήσουσί A.

largest of all the cities in Phoenicia. To be put to the proof, to associate with those who know and remember your doings of old, is truly as bad as a halter in your sight. And yet, why do I make that silly statement? What would you consider shameful, of all that goes beyond the limit? I am told that you have a great estate there—that ill-conditioned tower, to which the jar of the man of Sinope [1] would be the great hall of Zeus!

In view of all this, you can never by any means persuade your fellow-citizens not to think you the most odious man in the world, a common disgrace to the whole city. Could you, though, perhaps win over the other inhabitants of Syria to vote for you if you said that you had done nothing bad or culpable in your life? Heracles! Antioch was an eye-witness of your misconduct with that youth from Tarsus whom you took aside—but to unveil these matters is no doubt shameful for me. However, it is known about and remembered by those who surprised the pair of you then and saw him doing—you know what, unless you are absolutely destitute of memory.

Well, perhaps people in Egypt do not know you, who received you when, after those marvellous performances of yours in Syria, you went into exile for the reasons which I have mentioned, pursued by the clothiers, from whom you had bought costly garments and in that way obtained your expense-money for the journey. But Alexandria knows you to be guilty of offences just as bad, and should not have been ranked second to Antioch. No, your wantonness there was more open and your licentiousness more insane, your

---

[1] More familiar to us as the tub of Diogenes.

ἐκεῖ ἐπιμανεστέρα καὶ τοὔνομα ἐπὶ τούτοις μεῖζον
καὶ ἐπὶ πᾶσιν ἀκάλυπτος ἡ κεφαλή.

Εἷς μόνος ἂν ἐπίστευσέ σοι ἐξάρνῳ γινομένῳ
μηδὲν τοιοῦτο εἰργάσθαι καὶ βοηθὸς ἂν κατέστη,
ὁ τελευταῖος μισθοδότης, ἀνὴρ ἐν τοῖς ἀρίστοις
Ῥωμαίων. τοὔνομα δὲ αὐτὸ δώσεις ἀποσιωπῆ-
σαί μοι, καὶ ταῦτα πρὸς πάντας εἰδότας ὃν λέγω.
ἐκεῖνος τοίνυν τὰ μὲν ἄλλα ὁπόσα ἔτλη ἐν τῇ
συνουσίᾳ τολμηθέντα ὑπὸ σοῦ, τί χρὴ λέγειν;
ἀλλ᾽ ἡνίκα σε κατέλαβε τοῦ μειρακίου τοῦ οἰνοχόου
τοῦ Οἰνοπίωνος ἐν γόνασι κείμενον, τί οἴει;
ἐπίστευσεν ἄν σοι μὴ εἶναι τοιοῦτον, αὐτὸ ὁρῶν τὸ
ἔργον; οὔκ, εἴ γε μὴ παντάπασιν τυφλὸς ἦν.
ἀλλὰ ἐδήλωσεν τὴν γνώμην αὐτίκα ἐξελάσας
τῆς οἰκίας καὶ καθάρσιόν γε, ὥς φασι, περιεν-
22 εγκὼν ἐπὶ τῇ σῇ ἐξόδῳ. Ἀχαΐα μὲν γὰρ καὶ
Ἰταλία πᾶσα ἐμπέπλησται τῶν σῶν ἔργων καὶ
τῆς ἐπ᾽ αὐτοῖς δόξης· καὶ ὄναιό γε τῆς εὐκλείας.
ὥστε πρὸς τοὺς θαυμάζοντας ἔγωγε τὰ ἐν Ἐφέσῳ
νῦν πραττόμενα ὑπὸ σοῦ ἐκεῖνο λέγω, ὅπερ
ἀληθέστατον, ὡς [1] οὐκ ἂν ἐθαύμαζον εἰ τὰ πρῶτά
σου ᾔδεισαν. καίτοι καινὸν ἐνταῦθα καὶ τὸ πρὸς
τὰς γυναῖκας προσέμαθες.

23 Οὐ περὶ πόδα οὖν τῷ τοιούτῳ, εἰπέ μοι, ἀποφράδα
ὀνομάζεσθαι; ἀλλὰ τί, πρὸς Διός, καὶ φιλῆσαι
τῷ στόματι προσέτι ἀξιώσεις ἡμᾶς ἐπ᾽ ἐκείνοις
τοῖς ἔργοις; τοῦτο γοῦν τὸ ὑβριστότατον ποιεῖς,
καὶ μάλιστα πρὸς οὓς ἥκιστα ἐχρῆν, καὶ τοὺς
ὁμιλητάς, οἷς ἱκανὰ ἦν ἐκεῖνα μόνα τὰ κακὰ τοῦ
σοῦ στόματος ἀπολαύειν, τὸ βάρβαρον τῶν ὀνομάτων, τὸ τραχὺ τῆς φωνῆς, τὸ ἄκριτον, τὸ ἄτακτον,

[1] ὡς cod. Longolii: πῶς ΓΕΝΑ.

398

reputation for these things was greater, and your head was uncloaked under all circumstances.[1]

There is only one person who would have believed you if you denied having done anything of the sort, and would have come to your assistance—your latest employer, one of the first gentlemen of Rome. The name itself you will allow me to withhold, especially in addressing people who all know whom I mean. As to all the liberties taken by you while you were with him that he tolerated, why should I speak of them? But when he found you in the company of his young cup-bearer Oenopion,—what do you think? Would he have believed you? Not unless he was completely blind. No, he made his opinion evident by driving you out of his house at once, and indeed conducting a lustration, they say, after your departure. And certainly Greece as well as Italy is completely filled with your doings, and your reputation for them, and I wish you joy of your fame! Consequently, to those who marvel at what you are now doing in Ephesus, I say (and it is true as can be) that they would not wonder if they knew your early performances. Yet you have learned something new here having to do with women.

Does it not, then, fit such a man to a hair to call him nefandous? But why in the name of Zeus should you take it upon yourself to kiss us after such performances? In so doing you behave very offensively, especially to those who ought least of all to be so treated, your pupils, for whom it would have been enough to get only those other horrid boons from your lips—barbarity of language, harshness of voice, indistinctness,

---

[1] Cf. Petronius, 7 : operui caput.

τὸ πάντη ἄμουσον, καὶ τὰ τοιαῦτα· φιλῆσαι δέ
σε ἐπὶ τούτοις μὴ γένοιτο, ὦ ἀλεξίκακε. ἀσπίδα
μᾶλλον ἢ ἔχιδναν φιλῆσαι ἄμεινον. δῆγμα ἐκεῖ
τὸ κινδύνευμα, καὶ ἄλγημα, καὶ ὁ ἰατρὸς εἰσκληθεὶς
ἐπήμυνεν· ἀπὸ δὲ τοῦ σοῦ φιλήματος καὶ τοῦ
ἰοῦ ἐκείνου τίς ἂν ἢ ἱεροῖς ἢ βωμοῖς προσέλθοι ;
τίς δ᾽ ἂν θεὸς ἐπακούσειεν ἔτι εὐχομένου ; πόσων
περιρραντηρίων, πόσων ποταμῶν δεῖ ;

24 Καὶ τοιοῦτος αὐτὸς ὢν κατεγέλας τῶν ἄλλων ἐπ᾽
ὀνόμασι καὶ ῥήμασιν, ἔργα τοιαῦτα καὶ τηλικαῦτα
ἐργαζόμενος. καίτοι ἐγὼ μὲν ἀποφράδα μὴ εἰδὼς
ᾐσχυνόμην ἂν μᾶλλον, οὐχ ὅπως εἰπὼν ἀρνηθείην
ἄν· σὲ δὲ οὐδεὶς ᾐτιάσατο ἡμῶν βρωμολόγους
λέγοντα καὶ τροπομάσθλητας καὶ ῥησιμετρεῖν
καὶ ἀθηνιῶ[1] καὶ ἀνθοκρατεῖν καὶ σφενδικίζειν καὶ
χειροβλιμᾶσθαι.[2] κακὸν κακῶς σε ὁ λόγιος Ἑρμῆς
ἐπιτρίψειεν αὐτοῖς λόγοις. ποῦ γὰρ ταῦτα τῶν
βιβλίων εὑρίσκεις ; ἐν γωνίᾳ που τάχα τῶν
ἰαλέμων τινὸς ποιητῶν κατορωρυγμένα, εὑρῶτος
καὶ ἀραχνίων μεστά, ἢ που ἐκ τῶν Φιλαινίδος Δέλ-
των, ἃς διὰ χειρὸς ἔχεις· σοῦ μέντοι καὶ τοῦ σοῦ
στόματος ἄξια.

---

[1] After ἀθηνιῶ MSS. have τὸ Ἀθηνῶν ἐπιθυμῶ, omitted in
ed. Flor., 1496.

[2] χειροβλήμασθαι MSS., corrected by Cobet.

---

[1] Except for *rhesimeter* (to speak for a measured time,
as in court), which Lucian's Lexiphanes uses (*Lex.*, 9), these
words are found only here. Their meaning is :

bromologous : stench-mouthed.
tropomasthletes : oily-mannered fellows.
athenio : to yearn for Athens.

THE MISTAKEN CRITIC

confusedness, complete tunelessness, and the like, but to kiss you—forfend it, Averter of Ill! Better kiss an asp or a viper; then the risk is a bite and a pain which the doctor cures when you call him. But from the venom of your kiss, who could approach victims or altars? What god would listen to one's prayer? How many bowls of holy water, how many rivers are required?

And you, who are of that sort, laughed at others in the matter of words and phrases, when you were doing such terrible deeds! For my part, had I not known the word nefandous, I should have been ashamed, so far am I from denying that I used it. In your own case, none of us criticised you for saying " bromologous " and " tropomasthletes " and " to rhesimeter," and " Athenio," and " anthocracy " and "sphendicise" and "cheiroblime."[1] May Hermes, Lord of Language, blot you out miserably, language and all, for the miserable wretch that you are! Where in literature do you find these treasures? Perhaps buried somewhere in the closet of some composer of dirges, full of mildew and spiders' webs, or from the Tablets of Philaenis,[2] which you keep in hand. For you, however, and for your lips they are quite good enough.

anthocracy : apparently, rule of the " flower"; i.e., the select few.

sphendicise : to sling, very likely in the sense, to throw.

cheiroblime : to handle.

[2] The Tablets of Philaenis are frequently mentioned as an ars amatoria. An epigram by Aeschrion (Anth. Pal., VII, 345) says that it was not written by the woman whose name it bore, but by the sophist Polycrates. The book is therefore of the time of Polycrates, the beginning of the fourth century B.C.

25 Ἐπεὶ δὲ τοῦ στόματος ἐμνήσθην, τί φαίης ἄν, εἴ
σε ἡ γλῶττα ἐς δικαστήριον προσκαλεσαμένη [1]—
θῶμεν γὰρ οὕτως—ἀδικήματος καὶ [2] τὸ μετριώτατον
ὕβρεως διώκοι, λέγουσα " Ἐγώ σε, ὦ ἀχάριστε,
πένητα καὶ ἄπορον παραλαβοῦσα καὶ βίου δεόμενον,
τὰ μὲν πρῶτα ἐν τοῖς θεάτροις εὐδοκιμεῖν ἐποίησα,
νῦν μὲν Νίνον, νῦν δὲ Μητίοχον, εἶτα μετὰ μικρὸν
Ἀχιλλέα τιθεῖσα· μετὰ ταῦτα δὲ παῖδας συλ-
λαβίζειν διδάσκοντα μακρῷ χρόνῳ ἔβοσκον· ἤδη
δὲ καὶ τοὺς ἀλλοτρίους τούτους λόγους ὑποκρινό-
μενον σοφιστὴν εἶναι δοκεῖν ἐποίησα καὶ τὴν
μηδὲν προσήκουσαν δόξαν περιῆψα. τί τοίνυν
τηλικοῦτο ἔχων ἐγκαλεῖν τοιαῦτά με διατίθης
καὶ ἐπιτάττεις ἐπιτάγματα αἴσχιστα καὶ ὑπουρ-
γίας καταπτύστους; οὐχ ἱκανά μοι τὰ ἐπὶ τῆς
ἡμέρας ἔργα, ψεύδεσθαι καὶ ἐπιορκεῖν καὶ τοὺς
τοσούτους ὕθλους καὶ λήρους διαντλεῖν, μᾶλλον δὲ
τὸν βόρβορον τῶν λόγων ἐκείνων ἐμεῖν, ἀλλ᾽ οὐδὲ
νυκτὸς τὴν κακοδαίμονα σχολὴν ἄγειν ἐᾷς, ἀλλὰ
μόνη σοι πάντα ποιῶ καὶ πατοῦμαι καὶ μιαίνομαι,[3] καὶ ἀντὶ γλώττης ὅσα καὶ χειρὶ χρῆσθαι
διέγνωκας καὶ ὥσπερ ἀλλοτρίαν ὑβρίζεις καὶ
ἐπικλύζεις τοσούτοις κακοῖς. λαλεῖν μοι ἔργον
ἐστὶ μόνον, τὰ δὲ τοιαῦτα ποιεῖν καὶ πάσχειν
ἄλλοις μέρεσι προστέτακται. ὡς ὤφελε κἀμέ
τις ὥσπερ τὴν τῆς Φιλομήλας ἐκτεμεῖν. μακαριώ-

---

[1] προσκαλεσαμένη Bekker : προκαλεσαμένη MSS.
[2] καὶ Fritzsche : ἢ MSS.
[3] μιαίνομαι Benedictus : μαίνομαι MSS.

---

[1] As Ninus, the legendary king of Assyria, he supported a
dancer in the rôle of Semiramis, enacting a plot presumably
based on the Greek Ninus Romance (text and translation of

THE MISTAKEN CRITIC

Now that I have mentioned lips, what would you say if your tongue, summoning you to court, let us suppose, should prosecute you on a charge of injury and at the mildest, assault, saying: " Ingrate, I took you under my protection when you were poor and hard up and destitute of support, and first of all I made you successful in the theatre, making you now Ninus, now Metiochus, and then presently Achilles [1] After that, when you taught boys to spell, I kept you for a long time; and when at length you took to delivering these speeches of yours, composed by other people, I caused you to be considered a sophist, attaching to you a reputation which had nothing at all to do with you. What charge, then, have you to bring against me, so great that you treat me in this way, imposing disgraceful tasks and abominable services? Are not my daily tasks enough, lying, committing perjury, ladling out such an amount of silliness and twaddle, or (I should say) spewing out the nastiness of those speeches? Even at night you do not allow me, unlucky that I am, to take my rest, but unaided I do everything for you, am abused, defiled, treated deliberately like a hand rather than a tongue, insulted as if I were nothing to you, over-whelmed with so many injuries. My only function is to talk; other parts have been commissioned to do such things as those. Oh if only someone had cut me out, like the tongue of Philomela. More blessed

the fragments in S. Gaselee, *Daphnis and Chloe* [L.C.L.]; cf. R. M. Rattenbury, *New Chapters in the Hist. of Greek Lit.*, III, pp. 211–223). Opposite to his Metiochus the Phrygian, the dancer played Parthenope; see *The Dance*, § 1. His Achilles was very likely that hero on Scyros, disguised as a girl, with the dancer taking the part of the king's daughter whom he beguiled, Deidameia; cf. p. 257.

τεραι γοῦν μοι αἱ γλῶτται τῶν τὰ τέκνα κατεδη-
δοκότων."

26 Πρὸς θεῶν, ἢν λέγῃ ταῦτα ἡ γλῶττα, ἰδίαν
αὐτὴ φωνὴν λαβοῦσα καὶ τὸν πώγωνα συνήγορον
ἐπικαλεσαμένη, τί ἂν ἀποκρίναιο αὐτῇ ; ἐκεῖνα
δῆλον ὅτι ἃ καὶ πρὸς τὸν Γλαῦκον ἔναγχος εἴρηταί
σοι ἐπὶ πεπραγμένῳ ἤδη τῷ ἔργῳ αἰτιώμενον,
ὡς ἐπὶ τούτῳ ἔνδοξος ἐν βραχεῖ καὶ γνώριμος
ἅπασι γεγένησαι, πόθεν ἂν οὕτω περιβόητος ἐπὶ
τοῖς λόγοις γενόμενος ; ἀγαπητὸν δὲ ὁπωσοῦν
κλεινὸν καὶ ὀνομαστὸν εἶναι. εἶτα καταριθμήσεις [1]
αὐτῇ τὰς πολλάς σου προσηγορίας, ὁπόσας κατὰ
ἔθνη προσείληφας. ὃ καὶ θαυμάζω, ὅτι τὴν μὲν
ἀποφράδα ἐδυσχέρανας ἀκούσας, ἐπ᾿ ἐκείνοις δὲ
27 τοῖς ὀνόμασιν οὐκ ἠγανάκτεις, ἐν Συρίᾳ μὲν
῾Ροδοδάφνη κληθείς, ἐφ᾿ ᾧ δέ, νὴ τὴν ᾿Αθηνᾶν,
αἰσχύνομαι διηγεῖσθαι, ὥστε τό γε ἐπ᾿ ἐμοὶ
ἀσαφὲς ἔτι ἔστω· ἐν Παλαιστίνῃ δὲ Φραγμός,
ἐς τὰς ἀκάνθας τοῦ πώγωνος, οἶμαι, ὅτι ἔνυττε
μεταξύ· ἔτι γὰρ ἔξυρες αὐτόν· ἐν Αἰγύπτῳ δὲ
Συνάγχη, πρόδηλον τοῦτο· μικροῦ γοῦν φασιν
ἀποπνιγῆναί σε ναύτῃ τινὶ τῶν τριαρμένων ἐντυ-
χόντα, ὃς ἐμπεσὼν ἀπέφραξέ σοι τὸ στόμα.
᾿Αθηναῖοι μὲν γὰρ βέλτιστοι αἰνιγματῶδες οὐδέν,
ἀλλὰ γράμματος ἑνὸς προσθήκῃ τιμήσαντές σε
᾿Ατίμαρχον ὠνόμαζον· ἔδει γὰρ κἀκείνου τι
περιττότερον προσεῖναί σοι. ἐν ᾿Ιταλίᾳ δέ, βαβαί,

---

[1] καταριθμήσεις Lehmann : καταριθμήσειν MSS.

---

[1] Timarchus is the man whom Aeschines castigated for his
vices in an extant speech. From the wording of this passage
it has been very generally inferred that the name of Lucian's
butt was Timarchus. That, however, would be a singular

in my sight are the tongues of parents who have eaten
their children!"

In Heaven's name, if your tongue should say that,
acquiring a voice of its own, and getting your beard
to join in the accusation, what response would you
make? The reply, manifestly, which you made
recently to Glaucus when he rebuked you just after a
performance, that by this means you had speedily
become famous and known to everyone, and how could
you have become so notorious by making speeches?
It was highly desirable, you said, to be renowned and
celebrated in any way whatsoever. And then you
might tell it your many nicknames, acquired in
different nations. In that connection I marvel at it
that you were distressed when you heard ' nefandous '
but were not angry over those names. In Syria you
were called Rhododaphne; the reason, by Athena,
I am ashamed to tell. So as far as lies in me, it will
still remain a mystery. In Palestine, you were
Thorn-hedge, with reference, no doubt, to the
prickling of your stubbly beard; for you still kept it
shaved. In Egypt you were called Quinsy, which is
clear. In fact, they say you were nearly throttled
when you ran afoul of a lusty sailor who closed with
you and stopped your mouth. The Athenians, excellent fellows that they are, gave you no enigmatic
name but called you Atimarchus, honouring you with
the addition of a single letter because you had to have
something that went even beyond Timarchus.[1]   And
in Italy—my word! you got that epic nickname of

coincidence, which would surely have called for especial
emphasis. All that Lucian intends to convey, I think, is that
the Athenians did not nickname the man Timarchus as they
might have done, but went a step further and styled him
Atimarchus.

ἡρωϊκὸν ἐκεῖνο ἐπεκλήθης, ὁ Κύκλωψ, ἐπειδή
ποτε καὶ πρὸς ἀρχαίαν διασκευὴν παρ' αὐτὰ τὰ
τοῦ Ὁμήρου ῥαψῳδῆσαι καὶ σὺ τὴν αἰσχρουργίαν
ἐπεθύμησας. καὶ αὐτὸς μὲν ἔκεισο μεθύων ἤδη,
κισσύβιον ἔχων ἐν τῇ χειρί, βινητιῶν Πολύφημος,
νεανίας δὲ ὑπόμισθος ὀρθὸν ἔχων τὸν μοχλὸν εὖ
μάλα ἠκονημένον ἐπὶ σὲ Ὀδυσσεύς τις ἐπῄει
ὡς ἐκκόψων τὸν ὀφθαλμόν·

κἀκείνου μὲν ἅμαρτε, παραὶ δέ οἱ ἐτράπετ' ἔγχος,
αἰχμὴ δ' ἐξεσύθη [1] παρὰ νείατον ἀνθερεῶνα.

(καὶ γὰρ οὐδὲν ἄτοπον ὑπὲρ σοῦ λέγοντα ψυχρολο-
γεῖν.) σὺ δὲ ὁ Κύκλωψ, ἀναπετάσας τὸ στόμα
καὶ ὡς ἔνι πλατύτατον κεχηνώς, ἠνείχου τυφλού-
μενος ὑπ' αὐτοῦ τὴν γνάθον, μᾶλλον δὲ ὥσπερ ἡ
Χάρυβδις αὐτοῖς ναύταις καὶ πηδαλίοις καὶ
ἱστίοις ὅλον ζητῶν καταπιεῖν τὸν Οὖτιν. καὶ
ταῦτα ἑώρων καὶ ἄλλοι παρόντες. εἶτά σοι ἐς
τὴν ὑστεραίαν μία ἦν ἀπολογία ἡ μέθη καὶ ἐς
τὸν ἄκρατον ἀνέφυγες.[2]

28   Τοιούτοις δὴ καὶ τοσούτοις ὀνόμασι πλουτῶν
αἰσχύνῃ τὴν ἀποφράδα; πρὸς θεῶν εἰπέ μοι,
τί πάσχεις ἐπειδὰν κἀκεῖνα λέγωσιν οἱ πολλοί,
λεσβιάζειν σε καὶ φοινικίζειν; ἆρα καὶ ταῦτα
ὥσπερ τὴν ἀποφράδα ἀγνοεῖς καὶ οἴει τάχα που
ἐπαινεῖσθαι πρὸς αὐτῶν; ἢ ταῦτα μὲν διὰ τὸ
σύντροφον οἶσθα, τὴν ἀποφράδα δὲ ὡς ἀγνῶτα
μόνην ἀτιμάζεις καὶ ἀποκλείεις τοῦ καταλόγου
τῶν ὀνομάτων; τοιγαροῦν οὐ μεμπτὰς ἡμῖν
τίνεις τὰς δίκας, ἀλλὰ μέχρι καὶ τῆς γυναικωνίτιδος

[1] ἐξεσύθη N : ἐξελύθη ΓΕΑ.
[2] ἀνέφυγες N : ἐνέφυγες Γ(ΕΑ).

THE MISTAKEN CRITIC

Cyclops, because once, over and above your old bag of tricks, you took a notion to do an obscene parody on Homer's poetry itself, and while you lay there, drunk already, with a bowl of ivy-wood in your hand, a lecherous Polyphemus, a young man whom you had hired came at you as Odysseus, presenting his bar, thoroughly made ready, to put out your eye;

" And that he missed; his shaft was turned aside.
   Its point drove through beside the jawbone's
      root." [1]

(Of course it is not at all out of the way, in discussing you, to be silly.)   Well, you as the Cyclops, opening your mouth and setting it agape as widely as you could, submitted to having your jaw put out by him, or rather, like Charybdis, you strove to engulf your Noman whole, along with his crew, his rudder, and his sails.   That was seen by other people present. Then the next day your only defence was drunkenness, and you sought sanctuary in the unwatered wine.

Rich as you are in these choice and numerous appellations, are you ashamed of ' nefandous ' ?   In the name of the gods, tell me how you feel when the rabble call you names derived from Lesbos and Phoenicia?   Are you as unacquainted with these as with ' nefandous,' and do you perhaps think they are praising you?   Or do you know these through old acquaintance, and is it only ' nefandous ' that you scorn as unknown and exclude from your list of names? Consequently, you are paying us a penalty which cannot be considered inadequate; no, your notoriety

---

[1] The first line of this cento from the *Iliad* is XIII, 605 combined with XI, 233; the second is V, 293.

περιβόητος εἶ. πρῴην γοῦν ἐπειδή τινα γάμον
ἐν Κυζίκῳ μνᾶσθαι ἐτόλμησας, εὖ μάλα ἐκπεπυ-
σμένη πάντα ἡ βελτίστη ἐκείνη γυνή, " Οὐκ ἂν
προσείμην," ἔφη, " ἄνδρα καὶ αὐτὸν ἀνδρὸς δεόμενον."

29   Εἶτα ἐν τοιούτοις ὄντι σοι ὀνομάτων μέλει καὶ
γελᾷς καὶ τῶν ἄλλων καταπτύεις, εἰκότως· οὐ
γὰρ ἂν ἅπαντες ὅμοιά σοι λέγειν δυναίμεθα.
πόθεν ; τίς οὕτως ἐν λόγοις μεγαλότολμος, ὡς
ἐπὶ μὲν τοὺς τρεῖς μοιχοὺς ἀντὶ ξίφους τρίαιναν
αἰτεῖν ; τὸν δὲ Θεόπομπον ἐπὶ τῷ Τρικαράνῳ
κρίνοντα φάναι τριγλώχινι λόγῳ καθῃρηκέναι
αὐτὸν τὰς προὐχούσας πόλεις ; καὶ πάλιν, ἐκ-
τριαινῶσαι αὐτὸν τὴν Ἑλλάδα καὶ εἶναι Κέρβερον
ἐν τοῖς λόγοις ; πρῴην γὰρ καὶ λύχνον ἅψας
ἐζήτεις ἀδελφόν τινα, οἶμαι, ἀπολωλότα· καὶ
ἄλλα μυρία, ὧν οὐδὲ μεμνῆσθαι ἄξιον, ἢ μόνου
ἐκείνου, ὅπερ οἱ ἀκούσαντες ἀπεμνημόνευον.
πλούσιός τις, οἶμαι, καὶ δύο πένητες ἦσαν ἐχθροί·
εἶτα μεταξὺ περὶ τοῦ πλουσίου λέγων, " Ἀπέκτεινεν," ἔφης, " θάτερον τῶν πενήτων." γελασάν-
των δέ, ὡς τὸ εἰκός, τῶν παρόντων, ἐπανορθού-
μενος δὴ σὺ καὶ ἀνατιθέμενος τὸ διημαρτημένον,
" Οὐ μὲν οὖν," ἔφης, " ἀλλὰ ἄτερον αὐτῶν
ἀπέκτεινεν." ἐῶ τὰ ἀρχαῖα, τὸ τριῶν μηνοῖν καὶ
τὸ ἀνηνεμία καὶ τὸ πέταμαι καὶ ἐκχύνειν καὶ
ὅσα ἄλλα καλὰ τοῖς σοῖς λόγοις ἐπανθεῖ.

----

[1] The quaint conceit that with a trident all three might
be despatched at a blow undoubtedly embellished a rhetorical
" exercise " like Lucian's own *Tyrannicide* or *Disowned*.

[2] On the book entitled *Tricaranus* (" Tricipitine," or " Three-
Headed ") see p. 96, n. 9.

extends even to the women's quarters. Recently, for instance, when you had the hardihood to seek a match in Cyzicus, that excellent woman, who had very thoroughly informed herself in every particular said: " I do not care to have a man who needs one."

Then, being in such case, you bother about words, do you, and laugh, and insult other people? Not without reason, for we could not all use expressions like yours. How ever could we? Who is so greatly daring in language as to ask for a trident instead of a sword to use on three adulterers, as you did?[1] Or to say of Theopompus, in passing judgement on his *Tricaranus*,[2] that he had razed the outstanding cities single-handed with a three-pronged book? And again, that he had plied a ruinous trident upon Hellas, and that he was a literary Cerberus.[3] Why, the other day you even lighted a lantern and went peering about, for some " brother," I suppose, that had got astray. And there are other examples beyond counting, which it is not worth while to mention, except for one that was heard and reported. A rich man, I gather, and two poor men were on bad terms. Then, in the middle of the story, speaking of the rich man, you said: " He killed θάτερον (meaning one of the two, instead of saying τὸν ἕτερον); and when those present laughed, as was natural, by way of correcting and undoing your slip you said: " No, not that; he killed ἄτερον "! Your old-time slips I pass over, your use of the dual in speaking of three months, of ἀνηνεμία (for νηνεμία, windlessness), of πέταμαι (for πέτομαι, I fly), of ἐκχύνειν (for ἐκχεῖν, to pour out), and all the other fine flowers that adorn your compositions.

[3] Cerberus had three heads.

30 Ἃ μὲν γὰρ ὑπὸ τῆς πενίας ἐλαυνόμενος ποιεῖς,
Ἀδράστεια φίλη, οὐκ ἄν τινι ὀνειδίσαιμι. συγ-
γνωστὰ γοῦν εἴ τις λιμῷ πιεζόμενος παρακατα-
θήκας παρ᾿ ἀνδρὸς πολίτου λαβὼν εἶτα ἐπιώρ-
κησεν ἢ μὴν μὴ παρειληφέναι, ἢ εἴ τις ἀναισχύν-
τως αἰτεῖ, μᾶλλον δὲ προσαιτεῖ καὶ λωποδυτεῖ καὶ
τελωνεῖ. οὐ δὴ λέγω ταῦτα· φθόνος γὰρ οὐδεὶς
ἐξ ἅπαντος ἀμύνεσθαι τὴν ἀπορίαν. ἐκεῖνο δὲ
οὐκέτι φορητόν, πένητά σε ὄντα ἐς μόνας τὰς
τοιαύτας ἡδονὰς ἐκχεῖν τὰ ἐκ τῆς ἀναισχυντίας
περιγιγνόμενα. πλὴν ἕν[1] γέ τι καὶ ἐπαινέσαι μοι
δώσεις, πάνυ ἀστείως ὑπὸ σοῦ πεπραγμένον,
ὁπότε τοῦ Τισίου τὴν τέχνην οἶσθα ὡς τὸ δυσκόρα-
κος ἔργον αὐτὸς ἐποίησας, ἐξαρπάσας τοῦ ἀνοήτου
ἐκείνου πρεσβύτου χρυσοῦς τριάκοντα, ὁ δὲ διὰ
τὸν Τισίαν ἀντὶ τοῦ βιβλίου πεντήκοντα καὶ ἑπτα-
κοσίας ἐξέτισε κατασοφισθείς.

31 Πολλὰ ἔτι ἔχων εἰπεῖν, τὰ μὲν ἄλλα ἑκὼν
ἀφίημί σοι, ἐκεῖνο δὲ μόνον προσλέγω, πρᾶττε μὲν
ταῦτα ὅπως σοι φίλον καὶ μὴ παύσαιο τὰ τοιαῦτα
ἐς ἑαυτὸν παροινῶν, ἐκεῖνο δὲ μηκέτι, ἄπαγε·
οὐ γὰρ ὅσιον ἐπὶ τὴν αὐτὴν ἑστίαν τοὺς ταῦτα
διατιθέντας καλεῖν καὶ φιλοτησίας προπίνειν καὶ
ὄψων τῶν αὐτῶν ἅπτεσθαι. ἀλλὰ μηδὲ ἐκεῖνο
ἔστω τὸ ἐπὶ τοῖς λόγοις, φιλήματα, καὶ ταῦτα
πρὸς τοὺς οὐ πρὸ πολλοῦ ἀποφράδα σοι ἐργασα-
μένους τὸ στόμα. κἀπειδήπερ ἅπαξ φιλικῆς παραι-

---

[1] ἕν Bekker: εἴ MSS.

---

[1] Apparently, Lucian's hero had sold to the old man as
"Tisias' Handbook" a work on rhetoric which he had himself
forged. Both Tisias and his master Corax, the founder of

THE MISTAKEN CRITIC

As to what you do under the impulsion of poverty
—by our Lady of Necessity! I cannot censure a
single act. It can be overlooked, for example, if a
man in the pinch of hunger who has received moneys
entrusted to him by a man of his own city subsequently takes a false oath that he received nothing;
or if a man shamelessly asks for gifts—begs, in fact—
and steals and plies the trade of publican. That is
not what I am talking about; for there is nothing
invidious in fending off destitution by every means.
But it goes beyond what is endurable when you, a
poor man, pour the proceeds of your shamelessness
into such indulgences only. However, you will permit me to praise one thing, anyhow, that very pretty
performance of yours when you yourself—and you
know it—composed the "Tisias' Handbook," that
work of an ill-omened crow, thus robbing that stupid
old man of thirty gold pieces; for because of Tisias'
name he paid seven hundred and fifty drachmas for
the book, gulled into it by you.[1]

I have still a great deal that I might say; but I
willingly forego the rest for you, adding only this:
do as you like in everything else and do not cease to
indulge in such maudlin behaviour at your own
expense, but not that one thing—no, no! It is not
decent to ask people who so act to the same table, to
share a cup with them, and to partake of the same
food. And let there be none of this kissing after
lectures, either, especially with those who have made
'nefandous' apply to you not long before. And inasmuch as I have already begun to give friendly advice,

rhetoric, were said to have written handbooks. This pro-
duction, purporting to be by Tisias, was really the work of
an ill-omened *Korax* (crow), thievish as such birds always are.

νέσεως ἠρξάμην, κἀκεῖνα, εἰ δοκεῖ, ἄφελε,
τὸ μύρῳ χρίεσθαι τὰς πολιὰς καὶ τὸ πιττοῦσθαι
μόνα ἐκεῖνα. εἰ μὲν γὰρ νόσος τις ἐπείγει, ἅπαν τὸ
σῶμα θεραπευτέον, εἰ δὲ μηδὲν νοσεῖς τοιοῦτο,
τί σοι βούλεται καθαρὰ καὶ λεῖα καὶ ὀλισθηρὰ
ἐργάζεσθαι ἃ μηδὲ ὁρᾶσθαι θέμις; ἐκεῖνό σοι
μόνον σοφόν, αἱ πολιαὶ καὶ τὸ μηκέτι μελαίνεσθαι,
ὡς προκάλυμμα εἶεν τῆς βδελυρίας. φείδου δὴ
αὐτῶν πρὸς Διὸς κἂν τούτῳ, καὶ μάλιστα τοῦ
πώγωνος αὐτοῦ, μηδὲ μιάνῃς ἔτι μηδὲ ὑβρίσῃς·
εἰ δὲ μή, ἐν νυκτί γε καὶ σὺν σκότῳ, τὸ δὲ μεθ᾽
ἡμέραν, ἄπαγε, κομιδῇ ἄγριον καὶ θηριῶδες.

32   Ὁρᾷς, ὡς ἄμεινον ἦν σοι ἀκίνητον τὴν Καμά-
ριναν ἐᾶν, μηδὲ καταγελᾶν τῆς ἀποφράδος, ἤ
σοι ἀποφράδα τὸν βίον ὅλον ἐργάσεται; ἢ ἔτι
προσδεῖ τινος; ὡς τό γε ἐμὸν οὔ ποτε ἐλλείψει.
οὐδέπω γοῦν οἶσθα ὡς ὅλην τὴν ἅμαξαν ἐπεσπάσω,
δέον, ὦ παιπάλημα καὶ κίναδος,[1] ὑποπτήσσειν εἴ
τις ἀνὴρ δασὺς καὶ τοῦτο δὴ τὸ ἀρχαῖον, μελάμ-
πυγος δριμὺ μόνον εἰς σὲ ἀποβλέψειεν. ἴσως
ἤδη καὶ ταῦτα γελάσῃ, τὸ παιπάλημα καὶ τὸ κίναδος,
ὥσπερ τινὰ αἰνίγματα καὶ γρίφους ἀκούσας·
ἄγνωστα γάρ σοι τῶν σῶν ἔργων τὰ ὀνόματα.

---

[1] κίναδος Guyet, here and below: κίναιδος MSS., except Γ
in the second instance.

have done, if you please, with perfuming your grey
hair, and depilating only certain parts; for if some
ailment is besetting you, your whole body should be
attended to, but if nothing of that sort ails you, what
is the point of your making parts hairless, smooth,
and sleek which should not even be seen? One
thing only is prudent in you, your grey hairs, and
that you no longer dye them, so that you can have
them to cloak your iniquity. Spare them, in Heaven's
name in this point also, and particularly your beard,
too; do not defile or mistreat it any longer. If
you must, let it be at night and in darkness; but
by day—no, no!—that is absolutely uncivilised and
beastly.

Do not you see that it would have been better for
you to " leave Camarina undisturbed," [1] and not to
laugh at the word nefandous, which is going to make
your whole life nefandous? Or is something more
still required? As far as in me lies, it shall not
remain wanting. To be sure, you are not yet aware
that you have brought down the whole cartload on
top of you, though you ought to grovel, you glozing
varlet, if a man with hair on him, a swart-breech [2]
(to use the good old phrase) were simply to look at
you sourly. Perhaps you will even laugh at that,
too—that " glozing varlet "—as if you had heard
something enigmatic and riddling; for you do not
know the words for your actions. So you now have

---

[1] The inhabitants of Camarina in Sicily, though warned by
Delphi not to disturb the lagoon, also called Camarina,
which flanked the city, drained it nevertheless. By so doing,
they weakened their defences and brought about their city's
fall.

[2] An allusion to the story of Heracles and the Cercopes;
cf. Aristophanes, *Lysistrata*, 803.

ὥστε ὥρα ἤδη καὶ ταῦτα συκοφαντεῖν, εἰ μὴ τριπλῇ
καὶ τετραπλῇ σοι ἡ ἀποφρὰς ἐκτέτικεν. αἰτιῶ
δ᾽ οὖν σεαυτὸν ἐπὶ πᾶσιν· ὡς γὰρ ὁ καλὸς Εὐρι-
πίδης λέγειν εἴωθεν, ἀχαλίνων στομάτων καὶ
ἀφροσύνης καὶ ἀνομίας τὸ τέλος δυστυχία γίγνεται.

an opportunity to libel these expressions also, in case "nefandous" has not paid you out, three or four times over. Anyhow, blame yourself for everything. As that pretty wit Euripides used to say, of curbless mouths and folly and lawlessness the end is mischance.[1]

[1] *Bacchae*, 386 ff., loosely quoted, without attention to metre; καὶ ἀφροσύνης καὶ ἀνομίας is substituted for ἀνόμου τ' ἀφροσύνας, and γίγνεται is added.

THE PARLIAMENT OF THE GODS

THIS brief comic dialogue records the proceedings of an assembly on Olympus in which steps are taken to purge the celestial roster of aliens and interlopers. It has been called a sequel to *Zeus Rants* because in that dialogue (§ 42 : II, 154) the caustic remarks of the infidel Damis about the odd gods worshipped in various parts of the world force Zeus to admit that Momus had been right in expecting all this to cause trouble one day, and to promise that he would try to set everything straight. It is to be noted, however, that in the *Parliament of the Gods* there is not only no allusion, direct or indirect, to *Zeus Rants*, but no suggestion that this purgation of the body politic has any relation to hostile criticism on earth. The connection, therefore, is not remarkably close. It is too bad that Lucian has left us no record of the subsequent proceedings before the committee on credentials. An account of the appearance of Mithras would have been particularly welcome.

ΘΕΩΝ ΕΚΚΛΗΣΙΑ

ΖΕΥΣ

1 Μηκέτι τονθορύζετε, ὦ θεοί, μηδὲ κατὰ γωνίας συστρεφόμενοι πρὸς οὓς[1] ἀλλήλοις κοινολογεῖσθε, ἀγανακτοῦντες εἰ πολλοὶ ἀνάξιοι μετέχουσιν ἡμῖν τοῦ συμποσίου, ἀλλ' ἐπείπερ ἀποδέδοται περὶ τούτων ἐκκλησία, λεγέτω ἕκαστος ἐς τὸ φανερὸν τὰ δοκοῦντά οἱ καὶ κατηγορείτω. σὺ δὲ κήρυττε, ὦ Ἑρμῆ, τὸ κήρυγμα τὸ ἐκ τοῦ νόμου.

ΕΡΜΗΣ

Ἄκουε, σίγα. τίς ἀγορεύειν βούλεται τῶν τελείων θεῶν οἷς ἔξεστιν; ἡ δὲ σκέψις περὶ τῶν μετοίκων καὶ ξένων.

ΜΩΜΟΣ

Ἐγὼ ὁ Μῶμος, ὦ Ζεῦ, εἴ μοι ἐπιτρέψειας εἰπεῖν.

ΖΕΥΣ

Τὸ κήρυγμα ἤδη ἐφίησιν· ὥστε οὐδὲν ἐμοῦ δεήσει.[2]

---

[1] πρὸς οὖς ΓΡ, cf. *Gall.* 25: πρὸς τὸ οὖς Ν.
[2] δεήσει Γ: δεήσῃ ΡΝ.

THE PARLIAMENT OF THE GODS

ZEUS

No more murmuring, Gods, or gathering in corners
and whispering in each other's ears because you take
it hard that many share our table who are not worthy.
Now that a public meeting upon this question has
been authorised, let each declare his opinion openly
and bring his charges. Hermes, make the proclamation required by law.

HERMES

Hear ye! Silence! Among the gods of full standing, entitled to speak, who desires to do so? The
question concerns resident aliens and foreigners.

MOMUS

I, Momus here, Zeus, if you would let me speak.

ZEUS

The proclamation itself gives permission, so that
you will have no need of mine.

ΜΩΜΟΣ

2 Φημὶ τοίνυν δεινὰ ποιεῖν ἐνίους ἡμῶν, οἷς οὐκ
ἀπόχρη θεοὺς[1] ἐξ ἀνθρώπων αὐτοῖς γεγενῆσθαι,
ἀλλ᾽, εἰ μὴ καὶ τοὺς ἀκολούθους καὶ θεράποντας
αὐτῶν ἰσοτίμους ἡμῖν ἀποφανοῦσιν, οὐδὲν μέγα
οὐδὲ νεανικὸν οἴονται εἰργάσθαι. ἀξιῶ δέ, ὦ
Ζεῦ, μετὰ παρρησίας μοι δοῦναι εἰπεῖν· οὐδὲ
γὰρ ἂν ἄλλως δυναίμην, ἀλλὰ πάντες με ἴσασιν ὡς
ἐλεύθερός εἰμι τὴν γλῶτταν καὶ οὐδὲν ἂν κατα-
σιωπήσαιμι τῶν οὐ καλῶς γιγνομένων· διελέγχω
γὰρ ἅπαντα καὶ λέγω τὰ δοκοῦντά μοι ἐς τὸ
φανερὸν οὔτε δεδιώς τινα οὔτε ὑπ᾽ αἰδοῦς ἐπικα-
λύπτων τὴν γνώμην· ὥστε καὶ ἐπαχθὴς δοκῶ
τοῖς πολλοῖς καὶ συκοφαντικὸς τὴν φύσιν, δημόσιός
τις κατήγορος ὑπ᾽ αὐτῶν ἐπονομαζόμενος. πλὴν
ἀλλ᾽ ἐπείπερ ἔξεστιν καὶ κεκήρυκται καὶ σύ,
ὦ Ζεῦ, δίδως μετ᾽ ἐξουσίας εἰπεῖν, οὐδὲν ὑπο-
στειλάμενος ἐρῶ.

3 Πολλοὶ γάρ, φημί, οὐκ ἀγαπῶντες ὅτι αὐτοὶ
μετέχουσι τῶν αὐτῶν ἡμῖν ξυνεδρίων καὶ εὐω-
χοῦνται ἐπ᾽ ἴσης, καὶ ταῦτα θνητοὶ ἐξ ἡμισείας
ὄντες, ἔτι καὶ τοὺς ὑπηρέτας καὶ θιασώτας τοὺς
αὐτῶν ἀνήγαγον ἐς τὸν οὐρανὸν καὶ παρενέγραψαν,
καὶ νῦν ἐπ᾽ ἴσης διανομάς τε νέμονται καὶ θυσιῶν
μετέχουσιν, οὐδὲ καταβαλόντες ἡμῖν τὸ μετοίκιον.

ΖΕΥΣ

Μηδὲν αἰνιγματῶδες,[3] ὦ Μῶμε, ἀλλὰ σαφῶς καὶ διαρρήδην λέγε, προστιθεὶς καὶ τοὔνομα,
νῦν γὰρ ἐς τὸ μέσον ἀπέρριπταί σοι ὁ λόγος,

---

[1] θεοῖς Bekker.   [2] αὐτοὺς Ν.
[3] αἰνιγματῶδες Ν : αἰνιγματωδῶς ΓΡ, cett.

THE PARLIAMENT OF THE GODS

MOMUS

Well then, I say that some of us behave shockingly; it is not enough for them that they themselves have become gods instead of men, but unless they can make their very attendants and servants as good as we are, they do not think they have done anything important or enterprising. And I beg you, Zeus, to let me speak frankly, for I could not do otherwise. Everybody knows how free of speech I am, and disinclined to hush up anything at all that is ill done. I criticize everybody and express my views openly, without either fearing anyone or concealing my opinion out of respect, so that most people think me vexatious and meddling by nature; they call me a regular public prosecutor. However, inasmuch as it is according to law, and the proclamation has been made, and you, Zeus, allow me to speak with complete liberty, I shall do so, without any reservations.

Many, I say, not content that they themselves take part in the same assemblies as we and feast with us on equal terms, and that too when they are half mortal, have lugged up into heaven their own servants and boon-companions and have fraudulently registered them, so that now they receive largesses and share in sacrifices on an equal footing without even having paid us the tax of resident aliens.

ZEUS

Let us have no riddles, Momus; speak in plain and explicit language, and supply the name, too. As it is, you have flung your statement into the midst of us

ὡς πολλοὺς εἰκάζειν καὶ ἐφαρμόζειν ἄλλοτε ἄλλον τοῖς λεγομένοις. χρὴ δὲ παρρησιαστὴν ὄντα μηδὲν ὀκνεῖν λέγειν.

ΜΩΜΟΣ

4 Εὖ γε, ὦ Ζεῦ, ὅτι καὶ παροτρύνεις με πρὸς τὴν παρρησίαν· ποιεῖς γὰρ τοῦτο βασιλικὸν ὡς ἀληθῶς καὶ μεγαλόφρον, ὥστε ἐρῶ καὶ τοὔνομα. ὁ γάρ τοι γενναιότατος οὗτος Διόνυσος ἡμιάνθρωπος ὤν, οὐδὲ Ἕλλην μητρόθεν ἀλλὰ Συροφοίνικός τινος ἐμπόρου τοῦ Κάδμου θυγατριδοῦς, ἐπείπερ ἠξιώθη τῆς ἀθανασίας, οἷος μὲν αὐτός ἐστιν οὐ λέγω, οὔτε τὴν μίτραν οὔτε τὴν μέθην οὔτε τὸ βάδισμα· πάντες γάρ, οἶμαι, ὁρᾶτε ὡς θῆλυς καὶ γυναικεῖος τὴν φύσιν, ἡμιμανής, ἀκράτου ἕωθεν ἀποπνέων· ὁ δὲ καὶ ὅλην φατρίαν[1] ἐσεποίησεν ἡμῖν καὶ τὸν χορὸν ἐπαγόμενος πάρεστι καὶ θεοὺς ἀπέφηνε τὸν Πᾶνα καὶ τὸν Σιληνὸν καὶ Σατύρους, ἀγροίκους τινὰς καὶ αἰπόλους τοὺς πολλούς, σκιρτητικοὺς ἀνθρώπους καὶ τὰς μορφὰς ἀλλοκότους· ὧν ὁ μὲν κέρατα ἔχων καὶ ὅσον ἐξ ἡμισείας ἐς τὸ κάτω αἰγὶ ἐοικὼς καὶ γένειον βαθὺ καθειμένος ὀλίγον τράγου διαφέρων ἐστίν, ὁ δὲ φαλακρὸς γέρων, σιμὸς τὴν ῥῖνα, ἐπὶ ὄνου τὰ πολλὰ ὀχούμενος, Λυδὸς οὗτος, οἱ δὲ Σάτυροι ὀξεῖς τὰ ὦτα, καὶ αὐτοὶ φαλακροί, κεράσται, οἷα τοῖς ἄρτι γεννηθεῖσιν ἐρίφοις τὰ κέρατα ὑποφύεται, Φρύγες τινὲς ὄντες· ἔχουσι δὲ καὶ οὐρὰς ἅπαντες. ὁρᾶτε οἵους ἡμῖν θεοὺς ποιεῖ ὁ γεννάδας;

[1] φατρίαν ΓΝΡ: φρατρίαν (MCA) vulg., incorrectly for Lucian. Cf. Crönert, *Mem. Gr. Hercul.*, pp. 81 and 311.

all, so that many are making guesses and applying your remarks now to one and now to another. Being an exponent of frankness, you must not stick at saying anything.

MOMUS

It is splendid, Zeus, that you actually urge me to frankness; that is a truly royal, high-souled action. Therefore I shall give the name. It is this peerless Dionysus, who is half human; in fact, on his mother's side he is not even Greek, but the grandson of a Syrophoenician trader named Cadmus. Inasmuch as he has been honoured with immortality, I say nothing of the man himself—either of his hood or of his drunkenness or of his gait; for you all, I think, see that he is womanish and unmanly in his character, half crazy, with strong drink on his breath from the beginning of the day. But he has foisted upon us a whole clan; he presents himself at the head of his rout, and has made gods out of Pan and Silenus and the Satyrs, regular farm-hands and goat-herds, most of them—capering fellows with queer shapes. One of them has horns and looks like a goat from the waist down, and wears a long beard, so that he is not much different from a goat. Another is a bald-pated gaffer with a flat nose who usually rides on a donkey. He is a Lydian. The Satyrs are prick-eared, and they too are bald, with horns like those that bud on new-born kids; they are Phrygians, and they all have tails. D'ye see what sort of gods he is making for us, the bounder?

423

THE WORKS OF LUCIAN

5 Εἶτα θαυμάζομεν εἰ καταφρονοῦσιν ἡμῶν οἱ
ἄνθρωποι ὁρῶντες οὕτω γελοίους θεοὺς καὶ
τεραστίους; ἐῶ γὰρ λέγειν ὅτι καὶ δύο γυναῖκας
ἀνήγαγεν, τὴν μὲν ἐρωμένην οὖσαν αὐτοῦ, τὴν
Ἀριάδνην, ἧς καὶ τὸν στέφανον ἐγκατέλεξε τῷ
τῶν ἄστρων χορῷ, τὴν δὲ Ἰκαρίου τοῦ γεωργοῦ
θυγατέρα. καὶ ὁ πάντων γελοιότατον, ὦ θεοί,
καὶ τὸν κύνα τῆς Ἠριγόνης, καὶ τοῦτον ἀνήγαγεν,
ὡς μὴ ἀνιῷτο ἡ παῖς εἰ μὴ ἕξει ἐν τῷ οὐρανῷ
τὸ ξύνηθες ἐκεῖνο καὶ ὅπερ ἠγάπα κυνίδιον.
ταῦτα οὐχ ὕβρις ὑμῖν δοκεῖ καὶ παροινία καὶ
γέλως ; ἀκούσατε δ᾽ οὖν καὶ ἄλλους.

ΖΕΥΣ

6 Μηδέν, ὦ Μῶμε, εἴπῃς μήτε περὶ Ἀσκληπιοῦ
μήτε περὶ Ἡρακλέους· ὁρῶ γὰρ οἷ φέρῃ τῷ λόγῳ.
οὗτοι γάρ, ὁ μὲν αὐτῶν ἰᾶται καὶ ἀνίστησιν ἐκ τῶν
νόσων καὶ ἔστιν " πολλῶν ἀντάξιος ἄλλων," ὁ δὲ
Ἡρακλῆς υἱὸς ὢν ἐμὸς οὐκ ὀλίγων πόνων ἐπρίατο
τὴν ἀθανασίαν· ὥστε μὴ κατηγόρει αὐτῶν.

ΜΩΜΟΣ

Σιωπήσομαι, ὦ Ζεῦ, διὰ σέ, πολλὰ εἰπεῖν
ἔχων. καίτοι εἰ μηδὲν ἄλλο, ἔτι τὰ σημεῖα
ἔχουσι τοῦ πυρός. εἰ δὲ ἐξῆν καὶ πρὸς αὐτόν σε
τῇ παρρησίᾳ χρῆσθαι, πολλὰ ἂν εἶχον εἰπεῖν.

---

¹ Erigone; her dog Maera guided her to the spot where
Icarius lay buried. He had been slain by drunken shepherds
to whom he had given wine that Dionysus had taught him how
to make. After her suicide Erigone became *Virgo*, and
Maera, it would seem from Lucian's κυνίδιον, *Procyon* (*Canis*

THE PARLIAMENT OF THE GODS

And then we wonder that men despise us when they see such laughable and portentous deities! I omit to mention that he has also brought up two women, one his sweetheart Ariadne, whose very head-band he has admitted into the starry choir, and the other the daughter of Icarius the farmer![1] And what is most ridiculous of all, Gods, even Erigone's dog—that too he has brought up, so that the little maid shall not be distressed if she cannot have in heaven her pet, darling doggie! Does not all this look to you like insolence, impudence, and mockery? But let me tell you about others.

ZEUS

Say nothing, Momus, about either Asclepius or Heracles, for I see where you are heading in your speech. As far as they are concerned, one of them is a doctor who cures people of their illnesses and is "as good as a host in himself,"[2] whilst Heracles, though my own son, purchased his immortality at the cost of many labours; so do not denounce them.

MOMUS

I shall hold my tongue, Zeus, for your sake, although I have plenty to say. Indeed, if there were nothing else, they still carry the marks of fire![3] And if it were permissible to employ free speech about yourself, I should have plenty to say.

Minor). No doubt it is Momus' indignation about the dog that accounts for his failure to mention Icarius' introduction into the heavens as *Bootes*.

[2] *Iliad*, XI, 514, alluding to Machaon.

[3] Heracles cremated himself, and Asclepius was struck by lightning. Cf. p. 6, n. 1.

ΖΕΤΣ

Καὶ μὴν πρὸς ἐμὲ ἔξεστιν μάλιστα. μῶν δ'
οὖν κᾀμὲ ξενίας διώκεις;

ΜΩΜΟΣ

Ἐν Κρήτῃ μὲν οὐ μόνον τοῦτο ἀκοῦσαι ἔστιν,
ἀλλὰ καὶ ἄλλο τι περὶ σοῦ λέγουσιν καὶ τάφον
ἐπιδεικνύουσιν· ἐγὼ δὲ οὔτε ἐκείνοις πείθομαι οὔτε
Ἀχαιῶν Αἰγιεῦσιν ὑποβολιμαῖόν σε εἶναι φά-
7 σκουσιν. ἃ δὲ μάλιστα ἐλεγχθῆναι δεῖν ἡγοῦμαι,
ταῦτα ἐρῶ.

Τὴν γάρ τοι ἀρχὴν τῶν τοιούτων παρανομη-
μάτων καὶ τὴν αἰτίαν τοῦ νοθευθῆναι ἡμῶν τὸ
ξυνέδριον σύ, ὦ Ζεῦ, παρέσχες θνηταῖς ἐπιμι-
γνύμενος καὶ κατιὼν παρ' αὐτὰς ἐν ἄλλοτε ἄλλῳ
σχήματι, ὥστε ἡμᾶς δεδιέναι μή σε καταθύσῃ
τις ξυλλαβών, ὁπόταν ταῦρος ᾖς, ἢ τῶν χρυ-
σοχόων τις κατεργάσηται χρυσὸν ὄντα, καὶ
ἀντὶ Διὸς ἢ ὅρμος ἢ ψέλιον ἢ ἐλλόβιον ἡμῖν γένῃ.
πλὴν ἀλλὰ ἐμπέπληκάς γε τὸν οὐρανὸν τῶν
ἡμιθέων τούτων· οὐ γὰρ ἂν ἄλλως εἴποιμι. καὶ
τὸ πρᾶγμα γελοιότατόν ἐστιν, ὁπόταν τις ἄφνω
ἀκούσῃ ὅτι ὁ Ἡρακλῆς μὲν θεὸς ἀπεδείχθη, ὁ
δὲ Εὐρυσθεύς, ὃς ἐπέταττεν αὐτῷ, τέθνηκεν,
καὶ πλησίον Ἡρακλέους νεὼς οἰκέτου ὄντος καὶ
Εὐρυσθέως τάφος τοῦ δεσπότου αὐτοῦ, καὶ πάλιν
ἐν Θήβαις Διόνυσος μὲν θεός, οἱ δ' ἀνεψιοὶ αὐτοῦ

---

[1] Zeus was not only born in Crete, but buried there, in
more than one place. His critics in Lucian several times
refer to this fact (*Timon*, 4; *Zeus Rants*, 45). Lucian very

THE PARLIAMENT OF THE GODS

ZEUS

I assure you, about me it is quite permissible.
But you are not prosecuting *me* as an alien, are you?

MOMUS

Well, in Crete not only that may be heard, but
they tell another story about you and show people
a tomb. However, I put no faith either in them or
in the Achaeans of Aegium, who assert that you are a
changeling.[1] But I do intend to speak of one thing
that in my opinion ought by all means to be censured.

It was you, Zeus, who began these illegalities and
caused the corruption of our body politic by cohabit-
ing with mortal women and going down to visit them,
now in one form, now in another. It has gone so far
that we are afraid that someone may make a victim
of you if he catches you when you are a bull, or that
some goldsmith may work you up when you are gold,
and instead of Zeus we may have you turning up as a
necklace or a bracelet or an earring. However that
may be, you have filled heaven with these—demi-
gods! I do not care to put it otherwise. And it is a
very ridiculous state of things when one suddenly
hears that Heracles has been appointed a god, but
Eurystheus, who used to order him about, is dead;
and that the temple of Heracles, who was a slave,
and the tomb of Eurystheus, his master, stand side
by side; and again, that in Thebes Dionysus is a

likely means the place that was pointed out to R. Pashley in
1834 as the tomb of Zeus, on Mt. Juktas; see A. J. Cook's
Zeus, I, 157–163. The Achaean version of the birth of Zeus
which made him out a changeling is not mentioned elsewhere,
but plenty of places gave him other fathers than Cronus, which
amounts to the same thing.

THE WORKS OF LUCIAN

ὁ Πενθεὺς καὶ ὁ Ἀκταίων καὶ ὁ Λέαρχος ἀνθρώπων ἁπάντων κακοδαιμονέστατοι.

8 Ἀφ' οὗ δὲ ἅπαξ σύ, ὦ Ζεῦ, ἀνέῳξας τοῖς
τοιούτοις τὰς θύρας καὶ ἐπὶ τὰς θνητὰς ἐτράπου,
ἅπαντες μεμίμηνταί σε, καὶ οὐχ οἱ ἄρρενες μόνον,
ἀλλ', ὅπερ αἴσχιστον, καὶ αἱ θήλειαι θεοί.[1] τίς γὰρ
οὐκ οἶδεν τὸν Ἀγχίσην καὶ τὸν Τιθωνὸν καὶ τὸν
Ἐνδυμίωνα καὶ τὸν Ἰασίωνα[2] καὶ τοὺς ἄλλους;
ὥστε ταῦτα μὲν ἐάσειν μοι δοκῶ· μακρὸν γὰρ
ἂν τὸ διελέγχειν γένοιτο.

ΖΕΥΣ

Μηδὲν περὶ τοῦ Γανυμήδους, ὦ Μῶμε, εἴπῃς·
χαλεπανῶ γὰρ εἰ λυπήσεις τὸ μειράκιον ὀνειδίσας
ἐς τὸ γένος.

ΜΩΜΟΣ

Οὐκοῦν μηδὲ περὶ τοῦ ἀετοῦ εἴπω, ὅτι καὶ
οὗτος ἐν τῷ οὐρανῷ ἐστιν, ἐπὶ τοῦ βασιλείου
σκήπτρου καθεζόμενος καὶ μονονουχὶ ἐπὶ κεφαλήν
9 σοι νεοττεύων, θεὸς εἶναι δοκῶν ; ἢ καὶ τοῦτον
τοῦ Γανυμήδους ἕνεκα ἐάσομεν;
Ἀλλ' ὁ Ἄττης γε, ὦ Ζεῦ, καὶ ὁ Κορύβας καὶ
ὁ Σαβάζιος, πόθεν ἡμῖν ἐπεισεκυκλήθησαν οὗτοι,

---

[1] θήλειαι θεοί Mras : θήλειαι θεαί NH, θεαί ΓΡ vulg.
[2] Ἰασίωνα Guyet : Ἰάσονα, Ἰάσωνα MSS.

---

[1] All three were own cousins of Dionysus, being sons of
other daughters of Cadmus; Pentheus of Agave, Actaeon of
Autonoe, and Learchus of Ino. Learchus was killed by his
father Athamas.

[2] In *Icaromenippus*, 27 (II, 312) a similar list of " alien
gods of doubtful status " is given, in which, besides Pan,
Attis, and Sabazius, we find the Corybantes. For Lucian's
conception of them, see the note on *The Dance*, 8 (p. 220, n. 2).
Here only one Corybas is remarked in the sacred precincts.

god, but his cousins Pentheus, Actaeon, and Learchus were of all mankind the most ill-fated.[1]

From the moment that you, Zeus, once opened our doors to such as they and turned your attention to mortal women, everyone else has copied you, and not the male sex alone but—what is most unseemly— even the goddesses. Who does not know about Anchises, Tithonus, Endymion, Iasion, and the rest of them? So I think I shall omit those incidents, for it would take too long if I were to pass censure on them.

ZEUS

Say nothing about Ganymede, Momus, for I shall be angry if you vex the little lad by disparaging his birth.

MOMUS

Then am I not to speak of the eagle, either, and say that he too is in heaven, where he sits upon your royal sceptre and all but nests on your head, passing for a god? Or must I omit him also, for the sake of Ganymede?

But Attis at all events, Zeus, and Corybas [2] and Sabazius [3]—how did they get trundled in upon us?

Does Lucian think of him as that one who was slain by the others (Clem. Alex., *Protr.*, II, 19), and so as the central figure of the cult?

[3] Sabazius was the centre of a wide-spread and important mystery-religion, which merged with that of Dionysus (Zagreus). He is frequently represented sitting in the palm of a great hand opened in a gesture like that of benediction (thumb and first two fingers extended), see Cook's *Zeus*, I, 390, Fig. 296. Multitudes of attributes always surround him, and the bull, the ram, and the snake figured in his cult. On initiation, a snake was passed through the clothing of the initiate, and " snake through the bosom " is said to have been the pass-word (Clem. Alex., *Protr.*, III, 15, 1).

ἢ ὁ Μίθρης ἐκεῖνος, ὁ Μῆδος, ὁ τὸν κάνδυν καὶ
τὴν τιάραν, οὐδὲ ἑλληνίζων τῇ φωνῇ, ὥστε οὐδ'
ἢν προπίῃ τις ξυνίῃσι ; τοιγαροῦν οἱ Σκύθαι
ταῦτα ὁρῶντες, οἱ Γέται αὐτῶν,[1] μακρὰ ἡμῖν
χαίρειν εἰπόντες αὐτοὶ ἀπαθανατίζουσι καὶ θεοὺς
χειροτονοῦσιν οὓς ἂν ἐθελήσωσι, τὸν αὐτὸν τρόπον ὅνπερ καὶ Ζάμολξις δοῦλος ὢν παρενεγράφη
οὐκ οἶδ' ὅπως διαλαθών.

10   Καίτοι πάντα ταῦτα, ὦ θεοί, μέτρια. σὺ δέ,
ὦ κυνοπρόσωπε καὶ σινδόσιν ἐσταλμένε Αἰγύπτιε,
τίς εἶ, ὦ βέλτιστε, ἢ πῶς ἀξιοῖς θεὸς εἶναι ὑλακτῶν ;
τί δὲ βουλόμενος καὶ ὁ ποικίλος οὗτος ταῦρος ὁ
Μεμφίτης προσκυνεῖται καὶ χρᾷ καὶ προφήτας
ἔχει ; αἰσχύνομαι γὰρ[2] ἴβιδας καὶ πιθήκους
εἰπεῖν καὶ τράγους καὶ ἄλλα πολλῷ γελοιότερα
οὐκ οἶδ' ὅπως ἐξ Αἰγύπτου παραβυσθέντα ἐς
τὸν οὐρανόν, ἃ ὑμεῖς, ὦ θεοί, πῶς ἀνέχεσθε ὁρῶντες
ἐπ' ἴσης ἢ καὶ μᾶλλον ὑμῶν προσκυνούμενα ;
ἢ σύ, ὦ Ζεῦ, πῶς φέρεις ἐπειδὰν κριοῦ κέρατα
φύσωσί σοι ;

---

[1] ὁρῶντες οἱ Γέται αὐτῶν ΓΝ, ὁρῶντες καὶ οἱ Γέται αὐτῶν Ρ.
[2] γὰρ ΡΓ² : δὲ Ν, and no doubt Γ¹.

---

[1] Lucian recognises that the Getae were not Scythians but
Thracians in *Icaromenippus*, 16, and that Zamolxis belongs
to the Thracians in *True Story*, II, 17, and *Zeus Rants*, 44.
On the other hand, the god is styled Scythian in *The Scythian*,
1 and 4, and in the passage before us, though he is ascribed to

Or Mithras yonder, the Mede, with his caftan and his cap, who does not even speak Greek, so that he cannot even understand if one drinks his health? The result is that the Scythians—the Getae among them—seeing all this have told us to go hang, and now confer immortality on their own account and elect as gods whomsoever they will, in the selfsame way that Zamolxis, a slave, obtained fraudulent admission to the roster, getting by with it somehow or other.[1]

All that, however, is as nothing, Gods.—You there, you dog-faced, linen-vested Egyptian, who are you, my fine fellow, and how do you make out that you are a god, with that bark of yours?[2] And with what idea does this spotted bull of Memphis[3] receive homage and give oracles and have prophets? I take shame to mention ibises and monkeys and billy-goats and other creatures far more ludicrous that somehow or other have been smuggled out of Egypt into heaven. How can you endure it, Gods, to see them worshipped as much as you, or even more? And you, Zeus, how can you put up with it when they grow ram's horns upon you?[4]

the Getae, they are represented as Scythian. Perhaps these two pieces are earlier than the others, and earlier than *Toxaris*, where Zamolxis is not mentioned. Zamolxis obtained his "fraudulent registration" by hiding in a cave and not appearing for four years, according to Herodotus (IV, 95). Strabo (VII, 5), who says that he was counsellor to the king, who connived at the fraud, adds that he was followed by a continuous succession of such gods; and to these Lucian must be alluding when he speaks of their electing gods.

[2] Anubis.
[3] Apis.
[4] Zeus Ammon.

ΖΕΥΣ

11 Αἰσχρὰ ὡς ἀληθῶς ταῦτα φῂς τὰ περὶ τῶν
Αἰγυπτίων· ὅμως δ᾽ οὖν, ὦ Μῶμε, τὰ πολλὰ αὐτῶν αἰνίγματά ἐστιν, καὶ οὐ πάνυ χρὴ καταγελᾶν ἀμύητον ὄντα.

ΜΩΜΟΣ

Πάνυ γοῦν μυστηρίων, ὦ Ζεῦ, δεῖ ἡμῖν, ὡς
εἰδέναι θεοὺς μὲν τοὺς θεούς, κυνοκεφάλους δὲ
τοὺς κυνοκεφάλους.

ΖΕΥΣ

Ἔα, φημί, τὰ περὶ Αἰγυπτίων· ἄλλοτε γὰρ περὶ
τούτων ἐπισκεψόμεθα ἐπὶ σχολῆς. σὺ δὲ τοὺς
ἄλλους λέγε.

ΜΩΜΟΣ

12 Τὸν Τροφώνιον, ὦ Ζεῦ, καὶ ὃ μάλιστά με
ἀποπνίγει, τὸν Ἀμφίλοχον, ὃς ἐναγοῦς ἀνθρώπου
καὶ μητρολῴου [1] υἱὸς ὢν μαντεύεται ὁ γενναῖος ἐν
Κιλικίᾳ, ψευδόμενος τὰ πολλὰ καὶ γοητεύων τοῖν
δυοῖν ὀβολοῖν ἕνεκα. τοιγαροῦν οὐκέτι σύ, ὦ
Ἄπολλον, εὐδοκιμεῖς, ἀλλὰ ἤδη πᾶς λίθος καὶ
πᾶς βωμὸς χρησμῳδεῖ, ὃς ἂν ἐλαίῳ περιχυθῇ καὶ
στεφάνους ἔχῃ καὶ γόητος ἀνδρὸς εὐπορήσῃ,
οἷοι πολλοί εἰσιν. ἤδη καὶ ὁ Πολυδάμαντος
τοῦ ἀθλητοῦ ἀνδριὰς ἰᾶται τοὺς πυρέττοντας ἐν

---

[1] μητραλοίου N, edd.

THE PARLIAMENT OF THE GODS

ZEUS

All these points that you mention about the Egyptians are in truth unseemly. Nevertheless, Momus,
most of them are matters of symbolism and one who
is not an adept in the mysteries really must not
laugh at them.

MOMUS

A lot we need mysteries, Zeus, to know that gods
are gods, and dogheads are dogheads!

ZEUS

Never mind, I say, about the Egyptians. Some
other time we shall discuss their case at leisure.
Go on and name the others.

MOMUS

Trophonius, Zeus, and (what sticks in my gorge
beyond everything) Amphilochus, who, though the
son of an outcast and matricide,[1] gives prophecies,
the miscreant, in Cilicia, telling lies most of the time
and playing charlatan for the sake of his two obols.
That is why you, Apollo, are no longer in favour;
at present, oracles are delivered by every stone and
every altar that is drenched with oil and has garlands
and can provide itself with a charlatan—of whom
there are plenty. Already the statue of Polydamas
the athlete heals those who have fevers in Olympia,

---

[1] Alcmaeon, son of Amphiaraus; he slew his mother
Eriphyle, fled from Argos in frenzy, and never returned.

433

Ὀλυμπίᾳ καὶ ὁ Θεαγένους ἐν Θάσῳ, καὶ Ἕκτορι
θύουσιν ἐν Ἰλίῳ καὶ Πρωτεσιλάῳ καταντικρὺ ἐν
Χερρονήσῳ. ἀφ᾽ οὗ δ᾽ οὖν τοσοῦτοι γεγόναμεν,
ἐπιδέδωκε μᾶλλον ἡ ἐπιορκία καὶ ἱεροσυλία, καὶ
ὅλως καταπεφρονήκασιν ἡμῶν—εὖ ποιοῦντες.

13 Καὶ ταῦτα μὲν περὶ τῶν νόθων καὶ παρεγ-
γράπτων. ἐγὼ δὲ καὶ ξένα ὀνόματα πολλὰ
ἤδη ἀκούων οὔτε ὄντων τινῶν παρ᾽ ἡμῖν οὔτε
συστῆναι ὅλως δυναμένων, πάνυ, ὦ Ζεῦ, καὶ ἐπὶ
τούτοις γελῶ. ἢ ποῦ γάρ ἐστιν ἡ πολυθρύλητος
ἀρετὴ καὶ φύσις καὶ εἱμαρμένη καὶ τύχη, ἀνυπό-
στατα καὶ κενὰ πραγμάτων ὀνόματα ὑπὸ βλακῶν
ἀνθρώπων τῶν φιλοσόφων ἐπινοηθέντα; καὶ
ὅμως αὐτοσχέδια ὄντα οὕτω τοὺς ἀνοήτους πέπει-
κεν, ὥστε οὐδεὶς ἡμῖν οὐδὲ θύειν βούλεται, εἰδὼς
ὅτι, κἂν μυρίας ἑκατόμβας παραστήσῃ, ὅμως τὴν
τύχην πράξουσαν τὰ μεμοιραμένα καὶ ἃ ἐξ ἀρχῆς
ἑκάστῳ ἐπεκλώσθη. ἡδέως ἂν οὖν ἐροίμην σε,

---

[1] Polydamas, a gigantic pancratiast, was said to have killed
lions with his bare hands and stopped chariots at full speed
by laying hold of them. Pausanias (VI, 5, 1) mentions his
statue at Olympia, made by Lysippus, but does not speak
of its healing the sick. But about the Thasian statue of
Theagenes, who won 1400 crowns as boxer, pancratiast,
and runner, and was reputed to be a son of Heracles, we hear
not only from Pausanias (VI, 11, 6-9) but from Oenomaus (in
Euseb., *Praep. Evang.*, V, 34, 6-9) and Dio Chrysostom in
his *Rhodiaeus* (XXXI, 95-97). After his death, when an
enemy whipped the statue at night, it fell on him and killed
him; so it was tried for murder, and flung into the sea. Har-

THE PARLIAMENT OF THE GODS

and the statue of Theagenes does likewise in Thasos ;[1]
they sacrifice to Hector in Troy and to Protesilaus
on the opposite shore, in the Chersonese. So, ever
since we became so numerous, perjury and sacrilege
have been increasing, and in general they have
despised us—quite rightly.

Let this suffice on the subject of those who are
base-born and fraudulently registered. But there
are many outlandish names that have come to my
ears, of beings not to be found among us and
unable to exist at all as realities ; and over these
too, Zeus, I make very merry. Where is that famous
Virtue, and Nature, and Destiny, and Chance ? They
are unsubstantial, empty appellations, excogitated by
those dolts, the philosophers. All the same, arti-
ficial as they are, they have so imposed upon the
witless that nobody is willing to do as much as
sacrifice to us, knowing that though he offer ten
thousand hecatombs, nevertheless " Chance " will
effect what is " fated " and what has been " spun "
for every man from the beginning. So I should like

vests then failed, and after the reason had been elicited from
Delphi, the statue, miraculously recovered by fishermen in
their net, was set up where it had stood before, and sacrifices
were thereafter offered before it " as to a god." Pausanias
adds that he knows that Theagenes had many other statues
both in Greece and in " barbarian " parts, and that he healed
sicknesses and received honours from the natives of those
places. A very similar tale about the statue of another
Olympic victor, the Locrian Euthycles, previously known only
from Oenomaus (*ibid.*, 10–11), can now be traced to the *Iambi*
of Callimachus (*Diegeseis*, ed. Vitelli-Norsa, i, 37–ii, 8).
And in Lucian's *Lover of Lies*, 18–20 (III, 346, ff.) there is an
amusing account of activities imputed to the statue of Pellichus,
a Corinthian general.

435

ὦ Ζεῦ, εἴ που εἶδες ἢ ἀρετὴν ἢ φύσιν ἢ εἱμαρμένην ;
ὅτι μὲν γὰρ ἀεὶ καὶ σὺ ἀκούεις ἐν ταῖς τῶν φιλοσόφων διατριβαῖς, οἶδα,[1] εἰ μὴ καὶ κωφός τις
εἶ,[2] ὡς βοώντων αὐτῶν μὴ ἐπαίειν.

Πολλὰ ἔτι ἔχων εἰπεῖν καταπαύσω τὸν λόγον·
ὁρῶ γοῦν πολλοὺς ἀχθομένους μοι λέγοντι καὶ
συρίττοντας, ἐκείνους μάλιστα ὧν καθήψατο ἡ
14 παρρησία τῶν λόγων. πέρας γοῦν, εἰ ἐθέλεις,
ὦ Ζεῦ, ψήφισμά τι περὶ τούτων ἀναγνώσομαι ἤδη
ξυγγεγραμμένον.

ΖΕΥΣ

Ἀνάγνωθι· οὐ πάντα γὰρ ἀλόγως ᾐτιάσω.
καὶ δεῖ τὰ πολλὰ αὐτῶν ἐπισχεῖν, ὡς μὴ ἐπὶ πλεῖον
ἂν γίγνηται.

ΜΩΜΟΣ[3]

Ἀγαθῇ τύχῃ. Ἐκκλησίας ἐννόμου ἀγομένης
ἑβδόμῃ ἱσταμένου[4] ὁ Ζεὺς ἐπρυτάνευε καὶ προή-
δρευε Ποσειδῶν, ἐπεστάτει Ἀπόλλων, ἐγραμ-
μάτευε Μῶμος Νυκτὸς καὶ ὁ Ὕπνος τὴν γνώμην
εἶπεν.

[1] οἶδα N, edd.: οἶδας ΓΡ.
[2] εἶ vulg.: ἐστιν ΓΡΝ.
[3] Ψήφισμα MSS.
[4] ἑβδόμῃ Μεταγειτνιῶνος ἱσταμένου Γ[2] only; probably by
conjecture.

---

[1] Obtaining from fourth-century Athens a formula for
decrees of the senate and people, Olympus has filled in the
blanks as best it could. At Athens, the name of a *phyle*, or
tribe, would go in the first blank of the preamble, as " exercising the *prytany*"; but Olympus has no tribes, and anyhow
Zeus should come first. So his name is set down there. The
next two offices might now be crossed off; for as Zeus presides

THE PARLIAMENT OF THE GODS

to ask you, Zeus, if you have anywhere seen either Virtue or Nature or Destiny. I know that you too are always hearing of them in the discussions of the philosophers, unless you are deaf, so as not to be able to hear them screaming.

I still have plenty to say, but I will bring my speech to an end, for I notice that many are annoyed with me for my remarks, and are hissing, particularly those who have been touched to the quick by my frankness. To conclude, then, with your consent, Zeus, I shall read a motion on this subject which has already been committed to writing.

ZEUS

Read it, for not all your criticisms were unreasonable, and we must put a stop to most of this, so that it may not increase.

MOMUS (*reads*)

" With the blessing of Heaven! In a regular session of the assembly, held on the seventh of the month, Zeus presiding, Poseidon first vice-president, Apollo second vice-president, Momus, son of Night, recorder, the following resolution was proposed by Sleep : [1]

at assemblies, there is no function left for the *proedros*, or chairman of the board of presidents, and the office of *epistatês*, or chairman of the *prytanies*, is already filled, since Zeus can hardly be " exercising the *prytany* " in any other capacity. However, there are the blanks !—and Poseidon, second in the Olympian hierarchy, will do all the better for *proedros* if it is a sinecure, while the duties actually performed by Apollo as Zeus' right-hand man and more or less a factotum, are not too dissimilar to those of an Athenian *epistatês* in the fourth century B.C. These problems solved, the remaining blanks were easy to fill.

437

THE WORKS OF LUCIAN

Ἐπειδὴ πολλοὶ τῶν ξένων, οὐ μόνον Ἕλληνες
ἀλλὰ καὶ βάρβαροι, οὐδαμῶς ἄξιοι ὄντες κοινωνεῖν
ἡμῖν τῆς πολιτείας, παρεγγραφέντες οὐκ οἶδα
ὅπως καὶ θεοὶ δόξαντες ἐμπεπλήκασι μὲν τὸν
οὐρανὸν ὡς μεστὸν εἶναι τὸ συμπόσιον ὄχλου
ταραχώδους πολυγλώσσων τινῶν καὶ ξυγκλύδων
ἀνθρώπων, ἐπιλέλοιπε δὲ ἡ ἀμβροσία καὶ τὸ
νέκταρ, ὥστε μνᾶς ἤδη τὴν κοτύλην εἶναι διὰ τὸ
πλῆθος τῶν πινόντων· οἱ δὲ ὑπὸ αὐθαδείας παρωσά-
μενοι τοὺς παλαιούς τε καὶ ἀληθεῖς θεοὺς προεδρίας
ἠξιώκασιν αὑτοὺς παρὰ πάντα τὰ πάτρια καὶ ἐν
τῇ γῇ προτιμᾶσθαι θέλουσι·

15 Δεδόχθαι[1] τῇ βουλῇ καὶ τῷ δήμῳ ξυλλεγῆναι μὲν
ἐκκλησίαν ἐν τῷ Ὀλύμπῳ περὶ τροπὰς χειμε-
ρινάς, ἑλέσθαι δὲ ἐπιγνώμονας τελείους θεοὺς
ἑπτά, τρεῖς μὲν ἐκ τῆς παλαιᾶς βουλῆς τῆς ἐπὶ
Κρόνου, τέτταρας δὲ ἐκ τῶν δώδεκα, καὶ ἐν
αὐτοῖς τὸν Δία· τούτους δὲ τοὺς ἐπιγνώμονας
αὐτοὺς μὲν καθέζεσθαι ὀμόσαντας τὸν νόμιμον
ὅρκον τὴν Στύγα, τὸν Ἑρμῆν δὲ κηρύξαντα
ξυναγαγεῖν ἅπαντας ὅσοι ἀξιοῦσι ξυντελεῖν ἐς
τὸ ξυνέδριον, τοὺς δὲ ἥκειν μάρτυρας ἐπαγομέ-
νους ἐνωμότους καὶ ἀποδείξεις τοῦ γένους. τοὐν-
τεῦθεν δὲ οἱ μὲν παρίτωσαν καθ' ἕνα, οἱ δὲ ἐπιγνώ-
μονες ἐξετάζοντες ἢ θεοὺς εἶναι ἀποφανοῦνται
ἢ καταπέμψουσιν ἐπὶ τὰ σφέτερα ἠρία καὶ τὰς
θήκας τὰς προγονικάς. ἢν δέ τις ἁλῷ τῶν ἀδο-
κίμων καὶ ἅπαξ ὑπὸ τῶν ἐπιγνωμόνων ἐκκριθέντων
ἐπιβαίνων τοῦ οὐρανοῦ, ἐς τὸν Τάρταρον ἐμπε-
σεῖν τοῦτον.

16 Ἐργάζεσθαι δὲ τὰ αὑτοῦ ἕκαστον, καὶ μήτε

[1] δεδόχθω MSS.

438

THE PARLIAMENT OF THE GODS

" WHEREAS many aliens, not only Greeks but barbarians, in nowise worthy of admission to our body
politic, by obtaining fraudulent registration in one
way or another and coming to be accounted gods
have so filled heaven that our festal board is packed
with a noisy rabble of polyglot flotsam; and
WHEREAS the ambrosia and the nectar have run low,
so that a cup now costs a mina, on account of the
vast number of drinkers; and WHEREAS in their
boorishness they have thrust aside the ancient and
genuine gods, have claimed precedence for themselves, contrary to all the institutions of our fathers,
and want to be pre-eminently honoured on earth:
therefore

" BE IT RESOLVED by the senate and the commons
that a meeting of the assembly be convoked on
Olympus at the time of the winter solstice; that
seven gods of full standing be chosen as deputies, three
to be from the old senate of the time of Cronus, and
four from the Twelve, including Zeus; that these
deputies before convening take the regular oath,
invoking the Styx; that Hermes by proclamation
assemble all who claim to belong to our body; that
these present themselves with witnesses prepared to
take oath, and with birth-certificates; that they then
appear individually, and the deputies after investigation of each case either declare them to be gods
or send them down to their sepulchres and the
graves of their ancestors; and that if any one of
those who shall fail of approval and shall have
been expelled once for all by the deputies be
caught setting foot in heaven, he be thrown into
Tartarus;

" AND BE IT FURTHER RESOLVED that each ply

439

τὴν Ἀθηνᾶν ἰᾶσθαι μήτε τὸν Ἀσκληπιὸν χρη-
σμῳδεῖν μήτε τὸν Ἀπόλλω τοσαῦτα μόνον[1]
ποιεῖν, ἀλλὰ ἕν τι ἐπιλεξάμενον μάντιν ἢ κιθαρῳ-
17 δὸν ἢ ἰατρὸν εἶναι. τοῖς δὲ φιλοσόφοις προειπεῖν
μὴ ἀναπλάττειν κενὰ[2] ὀνόματα μηδὲ ληρεῖν περὶ
18 ὧν οὐκ ἴσασιν. ὁπόσοι δὲ ἤδη ναῶν ἢ θυσιῶν
ἠξιώθησαν, ἐκείνων μὲν καθαιρεθῆναι τὰ ἀγάλ-
ματα, ἐντεθῆναι δὲ ἢ Διὸς ἢ Ἥρας ἢ Ἀπόλλωνος
ἢ τῶν ἄλλων τινός, ἐκείνοις δὲ τάφον χῶσαι τὴν
πόλιν καὶ στήλην ἐπιστῆσαι ἀντὶ βωμοῦ. ἢν δέ
τις παρακούσῃ τοῦ κηρύγματος καὶ μὴ ἐθελήσῃ
ἐπὶ τοὺς ἐπιγνώμονας ἐλθεῖν, ἐρήμην αὐτοῦ κατα-
διαιτησάτωσαν.

Τοῦτο μὲν ὑμῖν[3] τὸ ψήφισμα.

ΖΕΥΣ

19 Δικαιότατον, ὦ Μῶμε· καὶ ὅτῳ δοκεῖ, ἀνατει-
νάτω τὴν χεῖρα· μᾶλλον δέ, οὕτω γιγνέσθω,
πλείους γὰρ οἶδ' ὅτι ἔσονται οἱ μὴ χειροτονήσοντες.[4] ἀλλὰ νῦν μὲν ἄπιτε· ὁπόταν δὲ κηρύξῃ
ὁ Ἑρμῆς, ἥκετε κομίζοντες ἕκαστος ἐναργῆ τὰ
γνωρίσματα καὶ σαφεῖς τὰς ἀποδείξεις, πατρὸς
ὄνομα καὶ μητρός, καὶ ὅθεν καὶ ὅπως θεὸς ἐγένετο,
καὶ φυλὴν καὶ φράτορας. ὡς ὅστις ἂν μὴ ταῦτα
παράσχηται, οὐδὲν μελήσει τοῖς ἐπιγνώμοσιν εἰ
νεών τις μέγαν ἐν τῇ γῇ ἔχει καὶ οἱ[5] ἄνθρωποι
θεὸν αὐτὸν εἶναι νομίζουσιν.

[1] μόνον not in N. Equivalent to ἕνα ὄντα.
[2] κενά Par. 2956: καινά ΓΝΡΖΑ. Cf. § 13.
[3] ὑμῖν ΓΡ: ἡμῖν ΖΝ (but N gives τοῦτο . . . ψήφισμα to
Zeus, wrongly).
[4] χειροτονήσοντες Z (apparently by correction) edd.: -σαντες
ΓΡΝ.

his own trade; that Athena shall not heal the sick or Asclepius give oracles or Apollo combine in himself so many activities; he shall select one and be either seer or singer or physician; that the philosophers be warned not to make up empty names or talk nonsense about matters of which they know nothing; that in the case of those who already have been vouchsafed temples or sacrifices, their images be pulled down and those of Zeus or Hera or Apollo or one of the others be substituted; but the city shall raise a funeral-mound for them and set a gravestone upon it instead of an altar; that if anyone shall fail to comply with this proclamation and shall be unwilling to appear before the deputies, judgement by default shall be rendered against him."

There you have the resolution.

ZEUS

It is most equitable, Momus; so let everyone who is in favour of the resolution hold up his hand—but no! I declare it carried, as those who will not vote for it will be the majority, I know. Well, you may go now; but when Hermes makes the proclamation, present yourselves, and let each of you bring unmistakable means of identification and clear proofs—his father's name and his mother's, why and how he became a god, and his tribe and clan. For if anyone shall fail to put all this in evidence, it will make no difference to the deputies that he has a huge temple on earth and that men believe him to be a god.

καὶ οἱ ΓΖ : καὶ εἰ οἱ NP.

THE TYRANNICIDE

THIS piece and the next are typical productions of the rhetorical school, where fictitious cases, often highly imaginative and improbable, were debated. The themes were common property, transmitted from one rhetorician to another. The one that underlies this declamation, outlined in the argument which precedes it, was later employed by Libanius (Or. VII) and still later by Choricius (XXVI). Erasmus, who was the author of the Latin translation of *Tyrannicide* and *Disowned* in its original form, wrote in Latin a companion-piece to *Tyrannicide*, a mock pleading in opposition to it, which is to be found in several of the old editions of Lucian.

If Lucian abandoned rhetoric at forty, as he says in the *Double Indictment* (32 : III, 142), both these declamations should be early works. Of the two, *Tyrannicide* seems the earlier, as *Disowned* more closely approximates the style of his maturity.

ΤΥΡΑΝΝΟΚΤΟΝΟΣ

Ἀνῆλθέν τις ἐς τὴν ἀκρόπολιν ἀποκτενῶν τὸν τύραννον· αὐτὸν
μὲν οὐχ εὗρεν, τὸν δὲ υἱὸν αὐτοῦ ἀποκτείνας κατέλιπε τὸ ξίφος ἐν
τῷ σώματι. ἐλθὼν ὁ τύραννος καὶ τὸν υἱὸν ἰδὼν ἤδη νεκρὸν τῷ
αὐτῷ ξίφει ἑαυτὸν ἀπέκτεινεν. αἰτεῖ ὁ ἀνελθὼν καὶ τὸν τοῦ
τυράννου υἱὸν ἀνελὼν γέρας ὡς τυραννοκτόνος.

1 Δύο τυράννους ἀποκτείνας, ὦ ἄνδρες δικασταί,
μιᾶς ἡμέρας, τὸν μὲν ἤδη παρηβηκότα, τὸν δὲ
ἀκμάζοντα καὶ πρὸς διαδοχὴν τῶν ἀδικημάτων
ἑτοιμότερον, ἥκω μίαν ὅμως ἐπ᾽ ἀμφοτέροις
αἰτήσων δωρεὰν μόνος τῶν πώποτε τυραννοκτόνων
πληγῇ μιᾷ δύο πονηροὺς ἀποσκευασάμενος καὶ
φονεύσας τὸν μὲν παῖδα τῷ ξίφει, τὸν πατέρα δὲ
τῇ πρὸς τὸν υἱὸν φιλοστοργίᾳ. ὁ μὲν οὖν τύραννος
ἀνθ᾽ ὧν ἐποίησεν ἱκανὴν ἡμῖν δέδωκε τιμωρίαν,
ζῶν μὲν τὸν υἱὸν ἐπιδὼν προανῃρημένον παρὰ τὴν
τελευτήν, τελευταῖον δὲ ἠναγκασμένος, τὸ παραδοξότατον, αὐτὸς αὑτοῦ γενέσθαι τυραννοκτόνος.
ὁ παῖς δὲ ὁ ἐκείνου τέθνηκεν μὲν ὑπ᾽ ἐμοῦ, ὑπηρέτησε δέ μοι καὶ ἀποθανὼν πρὸς ἄλλον φόνον,
ζῶν[1] μὲν συναδικῶν τῷ πατρί, μετὰ θάνατον δὲ
πατροκτονήσας, ὡς ἐδύνατο.

[1] ζῶν Jensius: ζῶντι MSS.

444

THE TYRANNICIDE

A MAN went to the Acropolis to slay the tyrant. He did not find him, but slew his son and left his sword in the body. When the tyrant came and saw his son already dead, he slew himself with the same sword. The man who went up and slew the tyrant's son claims the reward for slaying the tyrant.

Two tyrants, gentlemen of the jury,[1] have been done to death by me in a single day, one already past his prime, the other in the ripeness of his years and in better case to take up wrongdoing in his turn. Yet I have come to claim but one reward for both, as the only tyrant-slayer of all time who has done away with two malefactors at a single blow, killing the son with the sword and the father by means of his affection for his son. The tyrant has paid us a sufficient penalty for what he did, for while he still lived he saw his son, prematurely slain, in the toils of death, and at last (a thing incomparably strange) he himself was constrained to become his own executioner. And his son not only met death at my hands, but even after death assisted me to slay another; for though while he still lived he shared his father's crimes, after his death he slew his father as best he might.

[1] The form of procedure posited is analogous to *dokimasia* at Athens. The claimant's right to the reward offered by the state has been challenged by one of his fellow-citizens, and the authorities have referred the question to a jury. The adversary, as plaintiff, has already spoken.

445

2 Τὴν μὲν οὖν τυραννίδα ὁ παύσας εἰμὶ ἐγὼ καὶ
τὸ ξίφος ὃ πάντα εἴργασται ἐμόν, τὴν δὲ τάξιν
ἐνήλλαξα τῶν φόνων καὶ τὸν τρόπον ἐκαινοτό-
μησα τῆς τῶν πονηρῶν τελευτῆς, τὸν μὲν ἰσχυρό-
τερον καὶ ἀμύνασθαι δυνάμενον αὐτὸς ἀνελών,
τὸν γέροντα δὲ μόνῳ παραχωρήσας τῷ ξίφει.

3 Ἐγὼ μὲν οὖν καὶ περιττότερόν τι ἐπὶ τούτοις
ᾤμην γενήσεσθαί μοι παρ᾽ ὑμῶν καὶ δωρεὰς
λήψεσθαι ἰσαρίθμους τοῖς ἀνῃρημένοις, ὡς ἂν
οὐ τῶν παρόντων ἀπαλλάξας ὑμᾶς μόνον, ἀλλὰ
καὶ τῆς τῶν μελλόντων κακῶν ἐλπίδος, καὶ τὴν
ἐλευθερίαν βέβαιον παρασχών, οὐδενὸς παραλελειμ-
μένου[1] κληρονόμου τῶν ἀδικημάτων· μεταξὺ δὲ
κινδυνεύω τοσαῦτα κατορθώσας ἀγέραστος ἀπελθεῖν παρ᾽ ὑμῶν καὶ μόνος στερέσθαι τῆς παρὰ τῶν
νόμων ἀμοιβῆς, οὓς διεφύλαξα.

Ὁ μὲν οὖν ἀντιλέγων οὑτοσὶ δοκεῖ μοι οὐ κηδό-
μενος, ὥς φησι, τῶν κοινῶν αὐτὸ[2] ποιεῖν, ἀλλ᾽
ἐπὶ τοῖς τετελευτηκόσι λελυπημένος καὶ ἀμυνό-
μενος τὸν ἐκείνοις τοῦ θανάτου αἴτιον γεγενη-

4 μένον. ὑμεῖς δὲ ἀνάσχεσθέ μου, ὦ ἄνδρες δικασταί, πρὸς ὀλίγον τὰ ἐν τῇ τυραννίδι καίπερ εἰδόσιν
ὑμῖν ἀκριβῶς διηγουμένου· καὶ γὰρ τὸ μέγεθος
οὕτω μάθοιτ᾽ ἂν τῆς εὐεργεσίας τῆς ἐμῆς, καὶ αὐτοὶ
μᾶλλον εὐφρανεῖσθε λογιζόμενοι ὧν ἀπηλλάγητε.

Οὐ γὰρ ὥσπερ ἄλλοις τισὶν ἤδη συνέβη πολλάκις,
ἁπλῆν καὶ ἡμεῖς τυραννίδα καὶ μίαν δουλείαν
ὑπεμείναμεν, οὐδὲ ἑνὸς ὑπηνέγκαμεν ἐπιθυμίαν
δεσπότου, ἀλλὰ μόνοι τῶν πώποτε τὰ ὅμοια
δυστυχησάντων δύο ἀνθ᾽ ἑνὸς τυράννους εἴχομεν

---

[1] περιλελειμμένου N (K. G. P. Schwartz).
[2] αὐτὸ Shorey: τὸ αὐτὸ Γ: τοῦτο BNZUC.

THE TYRANNICIDE

It was I, then, who put an end to the tyranny, and the sword that accomplished everything was mine. But I inverted the order of executions, and made an innovation in the method of putting criminals to death, for I myself destroyed the stronger, the one capable of self-defence, and resigned the old man to my unaided sword.

It was my thought, therefore, that I should get for this a still more generous gift from you, and should receive rewards to match the number of the slain, because I had freed you not only from your present ills, but from your expectation of those that were to come, and had accorded you established liberty, since no successor in wrongdoing had been left alive. But now there is danger that after all these achievements I may come away from you unrewarded and may be the only one to be excluded from the recompense afforded by those laws which I maintained.

My adversary here seems to me to be taking this course, not, as he says, because of his concern for the interests of the state, but because of his grief over the dead men, and in the endeavour to avenge them upon the man who caused their death. On your part, however, gentlemen of the jury, bear with me for a moment while I recount the history of their tyranny, although you know it well; for then you can appreciate the greatness of my benefaction and you yourselves will be more exultant, thinking of all that you have escaped.

It is not as it has often before been with others; it is not a simple tyranny and a single slavery that we have endured, nor a single master's caprice that we have borne. Nay, of all those who have ever experienced such adversity we alone had two masters

447

καὶ πρὸς διττὰ οἱ δυστυχεῖς ἀδικήματα διῃρού-
μεθα. μετριώτερος δὲ ὁ πρεσβύτης ἦν παρὰ πολὺ
καὶ πρὸς τὰς ὀργὰς ἠπιώτερος καὶ πρὸς τὰς
κολάσεις ἀμβλύτερος καὶ πρὸς τὰς ἐπιθυμίας
βραδύτερος, ὡς ἂν ἤδη τῆς ἡλικίας τὸ μὲν σφοδρό-
τερον τῆς ὁρμῆς ἐπεχούσης, τὰς δὲ τῶν ἡδονῶν
ὀρέξεις χαλιναγωγούσης. καὶ πρός γε τὴν ἀρχὴν
τῶν ἀδικημάτων ὑπὸ τοῦ παιδὸς ἄκων προσῆχθαι
ἐλέγετο, οὐ πάνυ τυραννικὸς αὐτὸς ὤν, ἀλλ'
εἴκων ἐκείνῳ· φιλότεκνος γὰρ ἐς ὑπερβολὴν
ἐγένετο, ὡς ἔδειξεν, καὶ πάντα ὁ παῖς ἦν αὐτῷ
καὶ ἐκείνῳ ἐπείθετο καὶ ἠδίκει ὅσα κελεύοι καὶ
ἐκόλαζεν οὓς προστάττοι καὶ πάντα ὑπηρέτει,
καὶ ὅλως ἐτυραννεῖτο ὑπ' αὐτοῦ καὶ δορυφόρος
τῶν τοῦ παιδὸς ἐπιθυμιῶν ἦν.

5 Ὁ νεανίας δὲ τῆς μὲν τιμῆς παρεχώρει καθ'
ἡλικίαν ἐκείνῳ καὶ μόνου ἐξίστατο τοῦ τῆς
ἀρχῆς ὀνόματος, τὸ δ' ἔργον τῆς τυραννίδος
καὶ τὸ κεφάλαιον αὐτὸς ἦν, καὶ τὸ μὲν πιστὸν
καὶ ἀσφαλὲς ἀπ' αὐτοῦ παρεῖχε τῇ δυναστείᾳ,
τὴν δὲ ἀπόλαυσιν μόνος ἐκαρποῦτο τῶν ἀδικημάτων. ἐκεῖνος ἦν ὁ τοὺς δορυφόρους συνέχων,
ὁ τὴν φρουρὰν κρατύνων, ὁ τοὺς τυραννουμένους
φοβῶν,[1] ὁ τοὺς ἐπιβουλεύοντας ἐκκόπτων,[2] ἐκεῖνος
ὁ τοὺς ἐφήβους ἀνασπῶν, ὁ ἐνυβρίζων τοῖς γά-
μοις· ἐκείνῳ αἱ παρθένοι ἀνήγοντο, καὶ εἴ τινες
σφαγαὶ καὶ εἴ τινες φυγαὶ καὶ χρημάτων ἀφαιρέσεις
καὶ βάσανοι καὶ ὕβρεις, πάντα ταῦτα τολμήματα
ἦν νεανικά. ὁ γέρων δὲ ἐκείνῳ[3] ἠκολούθει καὶ

[1] φοβῶν Jacobitz: ἐκκόπτων MSS. Cf. n. 2.
[2] ἐκκόπτων Jacobitz: φοβῶν MSS.

instead of one and were torn asunder, unlucky folk! between two sets of wrongs. The elder man was more moderate by far, less acrimonious in his fits of anger, less hasty in his punishments, and less headlong in his desires, because by now his age was staying the excessive violence of his impulses and curbing his appetite for pleasures. It was said, indeed, that he was reluctantly impelled to begin his wrongdoings by his son, since he himself was not at all tyrannical but yielded to the other. For he was excessively devoted to his children, as he has shown, and his son was all the world to him; so he gave way to him, did the wrongs that he bade, punished the men whom he designated, served him in all things, and in a word was tyrannised by him, and was mere minister to his son's desires.

The young man conceded the honour to him by right of age and abstained from the name of sovereignty, but only from that; he was the substance and the mainspring of the tyranny. He gave the government its assurance and security, and he alone reaped the profit of its crimes. It was he who kept their guardsmen together, who maintained their defences in strength, who terrorised their subjects and extirpated conspirators; it was he who plucked lads from their homes, who made a mockery of marriages; it was for him that maids were carried off; and whatever deeds of blood there were, whatever banishments, confiscations of property, applications of torture, and outrages—all these were a young man's emprises. The old man followed him and shared his

---

3 ἐκείνῳ Struve : ἐκεῖνος MSS.

συνηδίκει καὶ ἐπήνει μόνον τὰ τοῦ παιδὸς ἀδικήματα, καὶ τὸ πρᾶγμα ἡμῖν ἀφόρητον καθειστήκει·
ὅταν γὰρ αἱ τῆς γνώμης ἐπιθυμίαι τὴν ἐκ τῆς
ἀρχῆς ἐξουσίαν προσλάβωσιν, οὐδένα ὅρον ποιοῦν-
ται τῶν ἀδικημάτων.

6   Μάλιστα δὲ ἐκεῖνο ἐλύπει, τὸ εἰδέναι μακράν,
μᾶλλον δὲ ἀΐδιον, τὴν δουλείαν ἐσομένην καὶ ἐκ
διαδοχῆς παραδοθησομένην τὴν πόλιν ἄλλοτε
ἄλλῳ δεσπότῃ καὶ πονηρῶν [1] κληρονόμημα γενη-
σόμενον τὸν δῆμον· ὡς τοῖς γε ἄλλοις οὐ μικρά
τις ἐλπὶς αὕτη, τὸ λογίζεσθαι καὶ πρὸς αὑτοὺς
λέγειν, " Ἀλλ' ἤδη παύσεται," " Ἀλλ' ἤδη τεθνήξεται καὶ μετ' ὀλίγον ἐλεύθεροι γενησόμεθα." ἐπ'
ἐκείνων δὲ οὐδὲν τοιοῦτον ἠλπίζετο, ἀλλὰ ἑωρῶμεν ἤδη ἕτοιμον τὸν τῆς ἀρχῆς διάδοχον. τοιγαροῦν οὐδ' ἐπιχειρεῖν τις ἐτόλμα τῶν γεννικῶν
καὶ τὰ αὐτὰ ἐμοὶ προαιρουμένων, ἀλλ' ἀπέγνωστο
παντάπασιν ἡ ἐλευθερία καὶ ἄμαχος ἡ τυραννὶς
ἐδόκει, πρὸς τοσούτους ἐσομένης τῆς ἐπιχειρήσεως.

7   Ἀλλ' οὐκ ἐμὲ ταῦτα ἐφόβησεν οὐδὲ τὸ δυσχερὲς
τῆς πράξεως λογισάμενος ἀπώκνησα οὐδὲ πρὸς
τὸν κίνδυνον ἀπεδειλίασα, μόνος δέ, μόνος πρὸς
οὕτως ἰσχυρὰν καὶ πολλὴν τυραννίδα, μᾶλλον δὲ
οὐ μόνος, ἀλλὰ μετὰ τοῦ ξίφους ἀνήειν τοῦ συμ-
μεμαχημένου καὶ τὸ μέρος συντετυραννοκτονη-
κότος, πρὸ ὀφθαλμῶν μὲν τὴν τελευτὴν ἔχων,
ἀλλαξόμενος δὲ ὅμως τὴν κοινὴν ἐλευθερίαν τῆς
σφαγῆς τῆς ἐμῆς. ἐντυχὼν δὲ τῇ πρώτῃ φρουρᾷ
καὶ τρεψάμενος οὐ ῥᾳδίως τοὺς δορυφόρους καὶ
τὸν ἐντυγχάνοντα κτείνων καὶ τὸ ἀνθιστάμενον
πᾶν διαφθείρων ἐπὶ τὸ κεφάλαιον αὐτὸ τῶν
ἔργων ἱέμην, ἐπὶ τὴν μόνην τῆς τυραννίδος ἰσχύν,

THE TYRANNICIDE

wrongdoing, and had but praise for his son's misdeeds.
So the thing became unendurable to us; for when the
desires of the will acquire the licence of sovereignty,
they recognise no limit to wrongdoing.

What hurt us most was to know that our slavery
would be long, nay unending, that our city would be
handed down by succession from despot to despot,
and that our folk would be the heritage of villains.
To other peoples it is no slight comfort to think, and
to tell one another, " But it will stop soon," " But
he will die soon, and in a little while we shall be
free." In their case, however, there was no such
comfort; we saw the successor to the sovereignty
already at hand. Therefore not one of the brave
men who entertained the same purpose as myself
even ventured to make an attempt. Liberty was
wholly despaired of, and the tyranny was thought
invincible, because any attempt would be directed
against so many.

This, however, did not frighten me; I did not
draw back when I estimated the difficulty of the
achievement, nor play the coward in the face of
danger. Alone, alone, I climbed the hill to front the
tyranny that was so strong and many-headed—yet,
not alone but with my sword that shared the fray
with me and in its turn was tyrant-slayer too. I had
my death in prospect, but sought to purchase our
common liberty with the shedding of my own blood.
I met the first guard-post, routed the guardsmen with
no little difficulty, slew whomsoever I encountered,
destroyed whatsoever blocked my path. Then I
assailed the very forefront of my tasks, the sole

THE WORKS OF LUCIAN

ἐπὶ τὴν ὑπόθεσιν τῶν ἡμετέρων συμφορῶν· καὶ
ἐπιστὰς τῷ τῆς ἀκροπόλεως φρουρίῳ καὶ ἰδὼν
γεννικῶς ἀμυνόμενον καὶ ἀνθιστάμενον πολλοῖς
τραύμασιν ὅμως ἀπέκτεινα.

8   Καὶ ἡ μὲν τυραννὶς ἤδη καθῄρητο, καὶ πέρας
εἶχέ μοι τὸ τόλμημα, καὶ τὸ ἀπ᾽ ἐκείνου πάντες
ἦμεν ἐλεύθεροι, ἐλείπετο δὲ γέρων ἔτι μόνος,
ἄνοπλος, ἀποβεβληκὼς τοὺς φύλακας, ἀπολωλεκὼς
τὸν μέγαν ἐκεῖνον ἑαυτοῦ δορυφόρον, ἔρημος,
οὐδὲ γενναίας ἔτι χειρὸς ἄξιος.

Ἐνταῦθα τοίνυν πρὸς ἐμαυτόν, ὦ ἄνδρες δικασταί,
τὰ τοιαῦτα ἐλογιζόμην· " Πάντ᾽ ἔχει μοι καλῶς,
πάντα πέπρακται, πάντα κατώρθωται. τίνα ἂν ὁ
περίλοιπος κολασθείη τρόπον ; ἐμοῦ μὲν γὰρ
ἀνάξιός ἐστι καὶ τῆς ἐμῆς δεξιᾶς, καὶ μάλιστα ἐπ᾽
ἔργῳ λαμπρῷ καὶ νεανικῷ καὶ γενναίῳ ἀνῃρημένος,[1] καταισχύνων κἀκείνην τὴν σφαγήν·
ἄξιον δέ τινα δεῖ ζητῆσαι δήμιον, ἀλλαγὴν συμφορᾶς,[2] μηδὲ τὴν αὐτὴν κερδαίνειν. ἰδέτω, κολα-
σθήτω, παρακείμενον ἐχέτω τὸ ξίφος· τούτῳ τὰ
λοιπὰ ἐντέλλομαι." ταῦτα βουλευσάμενος αὐτὸς
μὲν ἐκποδὼν ἀπηλλαττόμην, ὁ[3] δέ, ὅπερ ἐγὼ
προυμαντευσάμην, διεπράξατο καὶ ἐτυραννο-
κτόνησεν καὶ τέλος ἐπέθηκε τῷ ἐμῷ δράματι.

9   Πάρειμι οὖν κομίζων ὑμῖν τὴν δημοκρατίαν καὶ
θαρρεῖν ἤδη προκηρύττων ἅπασι καὶ τὴν ἐλευθερίαν εὐαγγελιζόμενος. ἤδη οὖν ἀπολαύετε τῶν
ἔργων τῶν ἐμῶν. κενὴ μέν, ὡς ὁρᾶτε, πονηρῶν ἡ

[1] ἀνῃρημένος Γ (late hand) vulg. : ἀνῃρημένῳ ΓUNZBC.
[2] ἀλλαγὴν συμφορᾶς Harmon : ἀλλὰ μὰ τὴν συμφορὰν ΓBN :
ἀλλ᾽ ἅμα τὴν συμφορὰν Z : ἀλλὰ μετὰ τὴν συμφορὰν UC. The
corruption appears to come from glossing ἀλλαγὴν as ἄλλαγμα

strength of the tyranny, the cause of our calamities. I came upon the warden of the citadel, I saw him offer a brave defence and hold out against many wounds; and yet I slew him.

The tyranny, therefore, had at last been overthrown, my undertaking had attained fulfilment, and from that moment we all were free. Only an old man still remained, unarmed, his guards lost, that mighty henchman of his gone, deserted, no longer even worthy of a valiant arm.

Thereupon, gentlemen of the jury, I thus reasoned with myself; " All has gone well for me, everything is accomplished, my success is complete. How shall the survivor be punished? Of me and my right hand he is unworthy, particularly if his slaying were to follow a glorious, daring, valiant deed, dishonouring that other mortal thrust. He must seek a fitting executioner, a change of fate, and not profit by having the same one. Let him behold, suffer his punishment, have the sword lying at hand; I commit the rest to him." This plan formed, I myself withdrew, and he, as I had presaged, carried through with it, slew the tyrant, supplied the ending to my play.

I am here, then, to bring you democracy, to notify all that they may now take heart, and to herald the glad tidings of liberty. Even now you are enjoying the results of my achievements. The acropolis, as you see, is empty of malefactors, and nobody issues

---

by writing μa over $\eta\nu$; in consequence of which those two letters were mistakenly admitted into the text, as often happens in the Lucianic tradition.

[3] τὸ A, editors since Jacobitz. But see § 20.

ἀκρόπολις, ἐπιτάττει δὲ οὐδείς, ἀλλὰ καὶ τιμᾶν
ἔξεστι καὶ δικάζειν καὶ ἀντιλέγειν κατὰ τοὺς
νόμους, καὶ πάντα ταῦτα γεγένηται δι' ἐμὲ ὑμῖν
καὶ διὰ τὴν τόλμαν τὴν ἐμήν, κἀκ τοῦ ἑνὸς ἐκείνου
φόνου, μεθ' ὃν οὐκέτι ζῆν πατὴρ ἐδύνατο. ἀξιῶ
δ' οὖν ἐπὶ τούτοις τὴν ὀφειλομένην δοθῆναί μοι
παρ' ὑμῶν δωρεάν, οὐ φιλοκερδὴς οὐδὲ μικρολόγος
τις ὢν οὐδὲ ἐπὶ μισθῷ τὴν πατρίδα εὐεργετεῖν
προηρημένος, ἀλλὰ βεβαιωθῆναί μοι βουλόμενος
τὰ κατορθώματα τῇ δωρεᾷ καὶ μὴ διαβληθῆναι
μηδὲ ἄδοξον γενέσθαι τὴν ἐπιχείρησιν τὴν ἐμὴν ὡς
ἀτελῆ καὶ γέρως ἀναξίαν κεκριμένην.

10   Οὑτοσὶ δὲ ἀντιλέγει καὶ φησὶν οὐκ εὔλογον
ποιεῖν με τιμᾶσθαι θέλοντα καὶ δωρεὰν λαμβάνειν·
οὐ γὰρ εἶναι τυραννοκτόνον οὐδὲ πεπρᾶχθαί μοί
τι κατὰ τὸν νόμον, ἀλλ' ἐνδεῖν τι τῷ ἔργῳ τῷ ἐμῷ
πρὸς ἀπαίτησιν τῆς δωρεᾶς. πυνθάνομαι τοίνυν
αὐτοῦ, "Τί λοιπὸν ἀπαιτεῖς παρ' ἡμῶν; οὐκ
ἠβουλήθην; οὐκ ἀνῆλθον; οὐκ ἐφόνευσα; οὐκ
ἠλευθέρωσα; μή τις ἐπιτάττει; μή τις κελεύει;
μή τις ἀπειλεῖ δεσπότης; μή τίς με τῶν κακούρ-
γων διέφυγεν; οὐκ ἂν εἴποις. ἀλλὰ πάντα
εἰρήνης μεστὰ καὶ πάντες οἱ νόμοι καὶ ἐλευθερία
σαφὴς καὶ δημοκρατία βέβαιος καὶ γάμοι ἀνύ-
βριστοι καὶ παῖδες ἀδεεῖς καὶ παρθένοι ἀσφαλεῖς
καὶ ἑορτάζουσα τὴν κοινὴν εὐτυχίαν ἡ πόλις.
τίς οὖν ὁ τούτων ἁπάντων αἴτιος; τίς ὁ ἐκεῖνα
μὲν παύσας, τὰ δὲ παρεσχημένος; εἰ γάρ τίς ἐστι
πρὸ ἐμοῦ[1] τιμᾶσθαι δίκαιος, παραχωρῶ τοῦ

---

[1] πρὸ ἐμοῦ Gesner: τῶν πρὸ ἐμοῦ MSS., except Z (τῶν
πάντων πρὸ ἐμοῦ).

orders; you may bestow honours, sit in judgement, and plead your cases in accordance with the laws. All this has come about for you through me and my bold deed, and in consequence of slaying that one man, after which his father could no longer continue in life. Therefore I request that you give me the reward which is my due, not because I am greedy or avaricious, or because it was my purpose to benefit my native land for hire, but because I wish that my achievements should be confirmed by the donative and that my undertaking should escape misrepresentation and loss of glory on the ground that it was not fully executed and has been pronounced unworthy of a reward.

This man, however, opposes my plea, and says that I am acting unreasonably in desiring to be honoured and to receive the gift, since I am not a tyrant-slayer, and have not accomplished anything in the eyes of the law; that my achievement is in some respect insufficient for claiming the reward. I ask him, therefore: "What more do you demand of me? Did I not form the purpose? Did I not climb the hill? Did I not slay? Did I not bring liberty? Does anyone issue orders? Does anyone give commands? Does any lord and master utter threats? Did any of the malefactors escape me? You cannot say so. No, everything is full of peace, we have all our laws, liberty is manifest, democracy is made safe, marriages are free from outrage, boys are free from fear, maidens are secure, and the city is celebrating its common good fortune. Who, then, is responsible for it all? Who stopped all that and caused all this? If there is anyone who deserves to be honoured in preference to me, I yield the guerdon, I resign the

γέρως, ἐξίσταμαι τῆς δωρεᾶς. εἰ δὲ μόνος ἐγὼ
πάντα διεπραξάμην τολμῶν καὶ[1] κινδυνεύων,
ἀνιών, ἀναιρῶν, κολάζων, δι᾽ ἀλλήλων τιμωρού-
μενος, τί μου διαβάλλεις τὰ κατορθώματα;
τί δὲ ἀχάριστον πρός με τὸν δῆμον ποιεῖς εἶναι;"

11 " Οὐ γὰρ αὐτὸν ἐφόνευσας τὸν τύραννον· ὁ δὲ
νόμος τυραννοκτόνῳ δίδωσιν τὴν δωρεάν." διαφέρει δέ, εἰπέ μοι, τί ἢ αὐτὸν ἀνελεῖν ἢ τοῦ θανάτου
παρασχεῖν τὴν αἰτίαν; ἐγὼ μὲν γὰρ οὐδὲν
οἶμαι· ἀλλὰ τοῦτο μόνον ὁ νομοθέτης εἶδεν, τὴν
ἐλευθερίαν, τὴν δημοκρατίαν, τὴν τῶν δεινῶν
ἀπαλλαγήν. τοῦτ᾽ ἐτίμησεν, τοῦτ᾽ ἄξιον ἀμοιβῆς
ὑπέλαβεν, ὅπερ οὐκ ἂν εἴποις μὴ δι᾽ ἐμὲ γεγενῆσθαι. εἰ γὰρ ἐφόνευσα δι᾽ ὃν ἐκεῖνος ζῆν οὐκ ἐδύνατο, αὐτὸς εἴργασμαι τὴν σφαγήν. ἐμὸς ὁ φόνος,
ἡ χεὶρ ἐκείνου. μὴ τοίνυν ἀκριβολογοῦ ἔτι περὶ
τοῦ τρόπου τῆς τελευτῆς μηδὲ ἐξέταζε ὅπως
ἀπέθανεν, ἀλλ᾽ εἰ μηκέτ᾽ ἐστίν, εἰ δι᾽ ἐμὲ τὸ
μηκέτ᾽ εἶναι ἔχει· ἐπεὶ κάκεῖνο προσεξετάσειν
μοι δοκεῖς καὶ συκοφαντήσειν τοὺς εὐεργέτας,
εἴ τις μὴ ξίφει, ἀλλὰ λίθῳ ἢ ξύλῳ ἢ ἄλλῳ τῳ
τρόπῳ ἀπέκτεινεν.

Τί δέ, εἰ λιμῷ ἐξεπολιόρκησα τὸν τύραννον
τὴν ἀνάγκην τῆς τελευτῆς παρέχων, ἀπήτεις ἂν
καὶ τότε[2] παρ᾽ ἐμοῦ αὐτόχειρα τὴν σφαγήν, ἢ
ἐνδεῖν ἔλεγές μοί τι πρὸς τὸν νόμον, καὶ ταῦτα
χαλεπώτερον τοῦ κακούργου πεφονευμένου; ἓν
μόνον ἐξέταζε, τοῦτο ἀπαίτει, τοῦτο πολυπραγ-
μόνει, τίς τῶν πονηρῶν λείπεται, ἢ τίς ἐλπὶς τοῦ

---

[1] καὶ not in N.
[2] τότε Z : τὸ ΓΝUB.

gift. But if I alone accomplished it all, making the venture, incurring the risks, going up to the citadel, taking life, inflicting punishment, wreaking vengeance upon them through one another, why do you misrepresent my achievements? Why, pray, do you make the people ungrateful towards me?"

"Because you did not slay the tyrant himself; and the law bestows the reward upon the slayer of a tyrant!" Is there any difference, tell me, between slaying him and causing his death? For my part I think there is none. All that the lawgiver had in view was simply liberty, democracy, freedom from dire ills. He bestowed honour upon this, he considered this worthy of compensation; and you cannot say that it has come about otherwise than through me. For if I caused a death which made it impossible for that man to live, I myself accomplished his slaying. The deed was mine, the hand was his. Then quibble no longer about the manner of his end; do not enquire how he died, but whether he no longer lives, whether his no longer living is due to me. Otherwise, it seems to me that you will be likely to carry your enquiry still further, to the point of carping at your benefactors if one of them should do the killing with a stone or a staff or in some other way, and not with a sword.

What if I had starved the tyrant out of his hold and thus occasioned the necessity of his death? Would you in that case require me to have killed him with my own hand, or say that I failed in any respect of satisfying the law, even though the malefactor had been done to death more cruelly? Enquire into one thing only, demand this alone, disturb yourself about this alone, whether any one of the villains is left, any

φόβου ἢ τί ὑπόμνημα τῶν συμφορῶν; εἰ δὲ
καθαρὰ πάντα καὶ εἰρηνικά, συκοφαντοῦντός ἐστιν
τῷ τρόπῳ τῶν πεπραγμένων χρώμενον [1] ἀποστερεῖν
ἐθέλειν τὴν ἐπὶ τοῖς πεπονημένοις δωρεάν.

12 Ἐγὼ δὲ [2] καὶ τοῦτο μέμνημαι διηγορευμένον
ἐν τοῖς νόμοις (ἐκτὸς εἰ μὴ διὰ τὴν πολλὴν δουλείαν
ἐπιλέλησμαι τῶν ἐν αὐτοῖς εἰρημένων) αἰτίας
θανάτου εἶναι διττάς, καὶ [3] εἴ τις μὴ αὐτὸς μὲν
ἀπέκτεινε μηδὲ τῇ χειρὶ ἔδρασεν τὸ ἔργον,
ἠνάγκασεν δὲ καὶ παρέσχεν ἀφορμὴν τοῦ φόνου,
τὰ ἴσα καὶ τοῦτον ἀξιοῖ ὁ νόμος αὐτὸν ἀντικολά-
ζεσθαι—μάλα δικαίως· οὐ γὰρ ἠβούλετο τοῦ
πεπραγμένου ἥσσων [4] γίνεσθαι τῷ τῆς ἀδείας·
καὶ περιττὴ λοιπὸν ἡ ἐξέτασις τοῦ τρόπου τῆς
σφαγῆς.

Εἶτα τὸν μὲν οὕτως ἀποκτείναντα κολάζειν ὡς
ἀνδροφόνον δικαιοῖς καὶ οὐδαμῶς ἀφεῖσθαι θέλεις,
τὸν δὲ κατὰ τὸν αὐτὸν τούτῳ τρόπον εὖ πεποιηκότα
τὴν πόλιν οὐ τῶν ὁμοίων ἀξιώσεις τοῖς εὐεργέ-
13 ταις; οὐδὲ γὰρ ἐκεῖνο ἂν ἔχοις λέγειν, ὡς ἐγὼ μὲν
ἁπλῶς αὐτὸ ἔπραξα, ἠκολούθησε δέ τι τέλος
ἄλλως χρηστόν, ἐμοῦ μὴ θελήσαντος. τί γὰρ ἔτι
ἐδεδίειν τοῦ ἰσχυροτέρου πεφονευμένου; τί δὲ
κατέλιπον τὸ ξίφος ἐν τῇ σφαγῇ, εἰ μὴ πάντως
τὸ ἐσόμενον αὐτὸ προεμαντευόμην; ἐκτὸς εἰ μὴ
τοῦτο φῇς, ὡς οὐ τύραννος ὁ τεθνεὼς ἦν οὐδὲ

---

[1] χρώμενον Dindorf: χρωμένου MSS.
[2] δὲ N: not in ΓZUB.
[3] καὶ Harmon: ἢ MSS. All editions follow the Florentine:
διττάς, εἴ τις αὐτὸς ἀπέκτεινεν ἢ. The clause εἰ . . . ἀπέκτεινεν
is not in ΓNUZBFA, and its admission creates asyndeton
below (τὰ ἴσα, etc.).

THE TYRANNICIDE

expectation of fearfulness, any reminder of our woes. If everything is uncontaminated and peaceful, only a cheat would wish to utilise the manner of accomplishing what has been done in order to take away the gratuity for the hard-won results.

I remember, moreover, this statement in the laws (unless, by reason of our protracted slavery, I have forgotten what is said in them), that there are two sorts of responsibility for manslaughter, and if, without taking life himself or doing the deed with his own hand, a man has necessitated and given rise to the killing, the law requires that in this case too he himself receive the same punishment—quite justly, for it was unwilling to be worsted by his deed through his immunity. It would be irrelevant, therefore, to enquire into the manner of the killing.

Can it, then, be that you think fit to punish as a murderer one who has taken life in this manner, and are not willing under any circumstances to acquit him, yet when a man has conferred a boon upon the city in the same way, you do not propose to hold him worthy of the same treatment as your benefactors? For you cannot even say that I did it at haphazard, and that a result followed which chanced to be beneficial, without my having intended it. What else did I fear after the stronger was slain, and why did I leave the sword in my victim if I did not absolutely prefigure exactly what would come to pass! You have no answer, unless you maintain that the dead man was not a tyrant and did not have that

---

[a] ἥσσων γίνεσθαι τῷ τῆς ἀδείας (*i.e.*, διὰ τὴν ἀδείαν) Harmon: ἴσον γίνεσθαι (γενέσθαι N) τὸ τῆς ἀδείας MSS. ἥσσον is a Renaissance conjecture. ἥσσον γίνεσθαι τὸ τῆς αἰτίας Markland.

ταύτην εἶχε τὴν προσηγορίαν, οὐδὲ δωρεὰς ἐπ᾽ αὐτῷ πολλάς, εἰ ἀποθάνοι, ἡδέως ἂν ὑμεῖς ἐδώκατε. ἀλλ᾽ οὐκ ἂν εἴποις.

Εἶτα τοῦ τυράννου πεφονευμένου[1] τῷ τὴν αἰτίαν παρασχόντι τῆς σφαγῆς οὐκ ἀποδώσεις τὴν δωρεάν; ὦ τῆς πολυπραγμοσύνης. μέλει δέ σοι, πῶς ἀπέθανεν, ἀπολαύοντι τῆς ἐλευθερίας, ἢ τὸν τὴν δημοκρατίαν ἀποδεδωκότα περιττότερόν τι προσαπαιτεῖς; "Καίτοι ὅ γε νόμος," ὡς φῄς, "τὸ κεφάλαιον ἐξετάζει τῶν πεπραγμένων, τὰ διὰ μέσου δὲ πάντα ἐᾷ καὶ οὐκέτι πολυπραγμονεῖ." τί γάρ; οὐχὶ καὶ[2] ἐξελάσας τις τύραννον ἤδη τιμὴν ἔλαβεν τυραννοκτόνου; καὶ μάλα δικαίως· ἐλευθερίαν γὰρ κἀκεῖνος ἀντὶ δουλείας παρέσχηται. τὸ δ᾽ ὑπ᾽ ἐμοῦ γεγενημένον οὐ φυγὴ οὐδὲ δευτέρας ἐπαναστάσεως ἐλπίς, ἀλλὰ παντελὴς καθαίρεσις καὶ πανωλεθρία παντὸς τοῦ γένους καὶ ῥιζόθεν τὸ δεινὸν ἅπαν ἐκκεκομμένον.

14 Καί μοι πρὸς θεῶν ἤδη ἀπ᾽ ἀρχῆς ἐς τέλος, εἰ δοκεῖ, πάντα ἐξετάσατε, εἴ τι τῶν πρὸς τὸν νόμον παραλέλειπται καὶ εἰ ἐνδεῖ τι τῶν προσεῖναι ὀφειλόντων τυραννοκτόνῳ. πρῶτα μὲν δὴ γνώμην προϋπάρχειν χρὴ γενναίαν καὶ φιλόπολιν καὶ πρὸ τῶν[3] κοινῶν κινδυνεύειν ἐθέλουσαν καὶ τῷ οἰκείῳ θανάτῳ τὴν τῶν πολλῶν σωτηρίαν ὠνησομένην. ἆρ᾽ οὖν πρὸς τοῦτο ἐνεδέησα, ἐμαλακίσθην, ἢ προελόμενός[4] τινα τῶν διὰ μέσου κινδύνων ἀπώκνησα; οὐκ ἂν εἴποις. μένε τοίνυν ἐπὶ τούτου

---

[1] πεφονευμένου ἀνεληλυθότος MSS.

[2] οὐχὶ καὶ Seager: καὶ οὐχὶ MSS.

[3] τῶν ΝΓ (late corr.): τούτων Γ¹Α, τοῦ τῶν ZUB.

[4] προελόμενος ΓUNZB(C)A: προειδόμενος (F) ed. Flor. προϊδόμενος recent edd. Cf. *Abd.*, 11.

name; and that the city would not have been glad to make many presents on his account if he should lose his life. But you cannot say so.

Can it be that, now the tyrant has been slain, you are going to refuse the reward to the man who caused his death? What pettiness! Does it concern you how he died, as long as you enjoy your liberty? Do you demand any greater boon of the man who gave back your democracy? "But the law," you say, "scrutinises only the main point in the facts of the case, ignoring all the incidentals and raising no further question!" What! was there not once a man who obtained the guerdon of a tyrannicide by just driving a tyrant into exile?[1] Quite rightly, too; for he bestowed liberty in exchange for slavery. But what I have wrought is not exile, or expectation of a second uprising, but complete abolition, extinction of the entire line, extirpation, root and branch, of the whole menace.

Do, in the name of the gods, make a full enquiry, if you like, from beginning to end, and see whether anything that affects the law has been left undone, and whether any qualification is wanting that a tyrant-slayer ought to have. In the first place, one must have at the outset a will that is valiant, patriotic, disposed to run risks for the common weal, and ready to purchase by its own extinction the deliverance of the people. Then did I fall short of that, play the weakling, or, my purpose formed, shrink from any of the risks that lay ahead? You cannot say so. Then confine your attention for a moment to this

[1] The allusion is to Harmodius, who slew Hipparchus, the brother of the tyrant Hippias.

ἔτι μόνου καὶ νόμιζε τοῦ θελῆσαι μόνον καὶ τοῦ
βουλεύσασθαι ταῦτα, εἰ καὶ μὴ χρηστὸν ἀποβεβήκει,
ἔκ γε τῆς γνώμης αὐτῆς καταστάντα με γέρας
ἀξιοῦν ὡς εὐεργέτην λαμβάνειν. ἐμοῦ μὲν οὐ
δυνηθέντος, ἄλλου δὲ μετ᾽ ἐμὲ τετυραννοκτονηκότος,
ἄλογον, εἰπέ μοι, ἢ ἀγνῶμον ἦν παρασχεῖν; καὶ
μάλιστα εἰ ἔλεγον, "Ἄνδρες, ἐβουλόμην, ἠθέλησα,
ἐπεχείρησα, ἐπειράθην· τῆς γνώμης μόνης¹ ἄξιός
εἰμι τιμᾶσθαι," τί ἂν ἀπεκρίνω τότε;

15   Νῦν δὲ οὐ τοῦτό φημι, ἀλλὰ καὶ ἀνῆλθον καὶ
ἐκινδύνευσα καὶ μυρία πρὸ τῆς τοῦ νεανίσκου σφαγῆς ἐπόνησα.² μὴ γὰρ οὕτω ῥᾷστον μηδὲ εὐχερὲς
ὑπολάβητε εἶναι τὸ πρᾶγμα, φρουρὰν ὑπερβῆναι
καὶ δορυφόρων κρατῆσαι καὶ τρέψασθαι τοσούτους μόνον, ἀλλὰ σχεδὸν τὸ μέγιστον ἐν τῇ τυραν-
νοκτονίᾳ καὶ τὸ κεφάλαιον τῶν ἔργων τοῦτό ἐστιν.
οὐ γὰρ δὴ αὐτός γε ὁ τύραννος μέγα καὶ δυσάλωτον
καὶ δυσκατέργαστόν ἐστιν, ἀλλὰ τὰ φρουροῦντα
καὶ συνέχοντα τὴν τυραννίδα, ἅ τις ἂν νικήσῃ,
πάντα οὗτος κατώρθωσεν, καὶ τὸ λοιπὸν ὀλίγον.
τὸ δὴ ἄχρι τῶν τυράννων προελθεῖν³ οὐκ ἂν ὑπῆρξέ
μοι, μὴ οὐχὶ τῶν περὶ αὐτοὺς φυλάκων καὶ δορυφόρων ἁπάντων κεκρατηκότι κἀκείνους ἅπαντας
προνενικηκότι. οὐδὲν ἔτι προστίθημι, ἀλλ᾽ ἐπὶ
τούτων αὖθις μένω· φυλακῆς ἐκράτησα, δορυφόρους ἐνίκησα, τὸν τύραννον ἀφύλακτον, ἄνοπλον,
γυμνὸν ἀπέδωκα. τιμῆς ἄξιος ἐπὶ τούτοις εἶναί
σοι δοκῶ, ἢ ἔτι ἀπαιτεῖς παρ᾽ ἐμοῦ τὸν φόνον;

¹ ἐπειράθην τῆς γνώμης· μόνος MSS.: corrected by du
Soul.
² ἐπόνησα Wyttenbach: ἐποίησα MSS.
³ προελθεῖν ΓΝΖ: προσελθεῖν UB.

THE TYRANNICIDE

point, and imagine that simply on account of my willing and planning all this, even if the result had not been favourable, I presented myself and demanded that in consequence of the intention itself I should receive a guerdon as a benefactor. Because I myself had not the power and someone else, coming after me, had slain the tyrant, would it be unreasonable, tell me, or absurd to give it me? Above all, if I said: "Gentlemen, I wanted it, willed it, undertook it, essayed it; simply for my intention I deserve to be honoured," what answer would you have made in that case?

But as things are, that is not what I say; no, I climbed the acropolis, I put myself in peril, I accomplished untold labours before I slew the young man. For you must not suppose that the affair was so easy and simple—to pass a guard, to overpower men-at-arms, to rout so many by myself; no, this is quite the mightiest obstacle in the slaying of a tyrant, and the principal of its achievements. For of course it is not the tyrant himself that is mighty and impregnable and indomitable, but what guards and maintains his tyranny; if anyone conquers all this, he has attained complete success, and what remains is trivial. Of course the approach to the tyrants would not have been open to me if I had not overpowered all the guards and henchmen about them, conquering all these to begin with. I add nothing further, but once more confine myself to this point: I overpowered the outposts, conquered the body-guards, rendered the tyrant unprotected, unarmed, defenceless. Does it seem to you that I deserve honour for that, or do you further demand of me the shedding of his blood?

16 Ἀλλ᾿ εἰ καὶ φόνον ζητεῖς, οὐδὲ τοῦτο ἐνδεῖ,
οὐδὲ ἀναίμακτός εἰμι, ἀλλ᾿ εἴργασμαι μεγάλην
καὶ γενναίαν σφαγὴν νεανίσκου ἀκμάζοντος καὶ
πᾶσι φοβεροῦ, δι᾿ ὃν ἀνεπιβούλευτος κἀκεῖνος ἦν,
ᾧ μόνῳ ἐθάρρει, ὃς ἀντὶ πολλῶν ἧκει δορυφόρων.
ἆρ᾿ οὖν οὐκ ἄξιος, ὦ οὗτος, δωρεᾶς, ἀλλὰ ἄτιμος
ἐπὶ τηλικούτοις γένωμαι ; τί γάρ, εἰ δορυφόρον
ἕνα, τί δ᾿ εἰ ὑπηρέτην τινὰ τοῦ τυράννου ἀπέκτεινα, τί δ᾿ εἰ οἰκέτην τίμιον, οὐ μέγα ἂν ἔδοξεν καὶ
τοῦτο, ἀνελθόντα ἐν μέσῃ τῇ ἀκροπόλει, ἐν μέσοις
τοῖς ὅπλοις φόνον τινὸς ἐργάσασθαι τῶν τοῦ
τυράννου φίλων ; νῦν δὲ καὶ τὸν πεφονευμένον
αὐτὸν ἰδέ. υἱὸς ἦν τυράννου, μᾶλλον δὲ τύραννος
χαλεπώτερος καὶ δεσπότης ἀπαραίτητος καὶ κολα-
στὴς ὠμότερος καὶ ὑβριστὴς βιαιότερος, τὸ δὲ
μέγιστον, κληρονόμος τῶν ὅλων καὶ διάδοχος καὶ
ἐπὶ πολὺ παρατεῖναι τὰ τῆς ἡμετέρας συμφορᾶς
δυνάμενος.

17 Βούλει τοῦτο μόνον πεπρᾶχθαί μοι, ζῆν δὲ ἔτι
τὸν τύραννον διαπεφευγότα; γέρας δὴ ἐπὶ τούτοις
αἰτῶ. τί φατέ ; οὐ δώσετε ; οὐχὶ κἀκεῖνον
ὑφεωρᾶσθε ; οὐ δεσπότης ; οὐ βαρύς ; οὐκ
ἀφόρητος ἦν ;

Νῦν δὲ καὶ τὸ κεφάλαιον αὐτὸ ἐννοήσατε·
ὃ γὰρ οὗτος ἀπαιτεῖ παρ᾿ ἐμοῦ, τοῦτο ὡς ἐνῆν
ἄριστα διεπραξάμην, καὶ τὸν τύραννον ἀπέκτεινα
ἑτέρῳ φόνῳ, οὐχ ἁπλῶς οὐδὲ πληγῇ μιᾷ, ὅπερ
εὐκταιότατον ἦν αὐτῷ ἐπὶ τηλικούτοις ἀδικήμασιν,
ἀλλὰ λύπῃ προβασανίσας πολλῇ καὶ ἐν ὀφθαλμοῖς
δείξας τὰ φίλτατα οἰκτρῶς προκείμενα, υἱὸν ἐν

THE TYRANNICIDE

But even if you require bloodshed, that is not wanting either, and I am not unstained with blood; on the contrary, I have done a great and valiant deed in that I slew a young man in the fullness of his strength, terrible to all, through whom that other was unassailed by plots, on whom alone he relied, who sufficed him instead of many guardsmen. Then am I not deserving of a reward, man? Am I to be devoid of honours for such deeds? What if I had killed a bodyguard, or some henchman of the tyrant, or a valued slave? Would not even this have seemed a great thing, to go up and slay one of the tyrant's friends in the midst of the citadel, in the midst of arms? But as it is, look at the slain man himself! He was a tyrant's son, nay more, a harsher tyrant, an inexorable despot, a more cruel chastiser, a more violent oppressor; what is most important, he was heir and successor to everything, and capable of prolonging vastly the duration of our misery.

Suppose, if you will, that this was my sole achievement—that the tyrant has made his escape and is still alive. Well and good, I demand a guerdon for this. What do you all say? Will you not vouchsafe it? Did you not view the son, too, with concern? Was he not a despot? Was he not cruel, unendurable?

As it is, however, think of the crowning feat itself. What this man requires of me I accomplished in the best possible way. I killed the tyrant by killing someone else, not directly nor at a single blow, which would have been his fondest prayer after misdeeds so monstrous. No, first I tortured him with profound grief, displayed full in his view all that was dearest

465

ἡλικίᾳ, εἰ καὶ πονηρόν, ἀλλ᾽ οὖν καὶ ἀκμάζοντα
καὶ ὅμοιον τῷ πατρί, αἵματος καὶ λύθρου ἐμπεπλησμένον. ταῦτ᾽ ἔστι πατέρων τὰ τραύματα,
ταῦτα ξίφη δικαίων τυραννοκτόνων, οὗτος θάνατος
ἄξιος ὠμῶν τυράννων, αὕτη τιμωρία πρέπουσα
τοσούτοις ἀδικήμασιν· τὸ δ᾽ εὐθὺς ἀποθανεῖν, τὸ
δ᾽ ἀγνοῆσαι,[1] τὸ δὲ μηδὲν τοιοῦτο θέαμα ἰδεῖν,
οὐδὲν ἔχει τυραννικῆς κολάσεως ἄξιον.

18 Οὐ γὰρ ἠγνόουν, ὦ οὗτος, οὐκ ἠγνόουν, οὐδὲ
τῶν ἄλλων οὐδείς, ὅσην ἐκεῖνος εὔνοιαν πρὸς τὸν
υἱὸν εἶχεν καὶ ὡς οὐκ ἂν ἠξίωσεν ἐπιβιῶναι
οὐδ᾽ ὀλίγον αὐτῷ χρόνον. πάντες μὲν γὰρ πατέ-
ρες ἴσως πρὸς τοὺς παῖδας τοιοῦτοι, ὁ δὲ καὶ
περιττότερόν τι τῶν ἄλλων εἶχεν, εἰκότως, ὁρῶν
μόνον ἐκεῖνον κηδεμόνα καὶ φύλακα τῆς τυραννίδος καὶ μόνον προκινδυνεύοντα τοῦ πατρὸς καὶ
τὴν ἀσφάλειαν τῇ ἀρχῇ παρεχόμενον. ὥστε εἰ καὶ
μὴ διὰ τὴν εὔνοιαν, ἀλλὰ διὰ τὴν ἀπόγνωσιν
εὐθὺς ἠπιστάμην τεθνηξόμενον αὐτὸν καὶ λογιού-
μενον ὡς οὐδὲν ἔτι τοῦ ζῆν ὄφελος τῆς ἐκ τοῦ παιδὸς
ἀσφαλείας καθῃρημένης. ἅπαντα τοίνυν αὐτῷ
ἀθρόα περιέστησα, τὴν φύσιν, τὴν λύπην, τὴν
ἀπόγνωσιν, τὸν φόβον, τὰς ἐπὶ τῶν μελλόντων . . .[2]
ἐπ᾽ αὐτὸν ἐχρησάμην τοῖς συμμάχοις καὶ πρὸς[3]
τὴν τελευταίαν ἐκείνην σκέψιν κατηνάγκασα.
ἀπέθανεν ὑμῖν ἄτεκνος, λελυπημένος, ὀδυρό-
μενος, δακρύων, πεπενθηκὼς πένθος ὀλιγοχρόνιον
μέν, ἀλλ᾽ ἱκανὸν πατρί, καὶ τὸ δεινότατον, αὐτὸς

[1] τὸ δ᾽ εὐθὺς ἀγνοῆσαι MSS. : εὐθὺς excised by Fritzsche.
[2] τὰς ἐπὶ τῶν μελλόντων ΓΒUΖ : τὸν ἐπὶ τῶν μελλόντων Ν :
τὰς ἐπὶ τῶν μελλόντων ἐλπίδας χρόνων (C)AF, edd.—plausible,
but conjectural, for more is missing. Supply approximately

to him lying exposed in pitiable case, a son in his youth, wicked, to be sure, but in the fullness of his strength and the image of his sire, befouled with blood and gore. Those are the wounds of fathers, those the swords of tyrannicides who deal justly, that is the death deserved by savage tyrants, that the requital befitting misdeeds so great. To die forthwith, to know nothing, to see no such spectacle has in it nothing worthy of a tyrant's punishment.

For I was not unaware, man—I was not unaware, nor was anyone else, how much love he had for his son, and that he would not have wanted to outlive him even a little while. To be sure, all fathers no doubt have such feelings toward their children; but in his case there was something more than in the case of others; naturally, for he discerned that it was his son who alone cherished and guarded the tyranny, who alone faced danger in his father's stead, and gave security to his rule. Consequently I knew that he would lay down his life at once, if not through his love, then at all events through his despair, considering that there was no profit in life now that the security derived from his son had been abolished. I encompassed him, therefore, with all manner of toils at once—his nature, his grief, his despair, his misgivings about the future; I used these allies against him, and forced him to that final decision. He has gone to his death childless, grief-stricken, in sorrow and in tears, after mourning but a little while, it is true, yet long enough for a father; gone (and that is most horrible) by his own

---

ἐλπίδας πονηράς. τούτοις οὖν. This is the reading followed in the translation.

[3] πρὸς Pellet: περὶ MSS., perhaps a variant on ἐπὶ above.

ὑφ᾽ αὑτοῦ, ὅσπερ θανάτων οἴκτιστος καὶ πολλῷ
χαλεπώτερος ἢ εἰ ὑπ᾽ ἄλλου γίγνοιτο.

19 Ποῦ μοι τὸ ξίφος; μή τις ἄλλος τοῦτο γνωρίζει;
μή τινος ἄλλου ὅπλον τοῦτο ἦν ; τίς αὐτὸ ἐς τὴν
ἀκρόπολιν ἀνεκόμισε ; πρὸ τοῦ τυράννου τίς[1]
ἐχρήσατο ; τίς αὐτὸ ἐπ᾽ ἐκεῖνον ἀπέστειλεν ;
ὦ ξίφος κοινωνὸν καὶ διάδοχον τῶν ἐμῶν κατορθω-
μάτων, μετὰ τοσούτους κινδύνους, μετὰ τοσούτους
φόνους ἀμελούμεθα καὶ ἀνάξιοι δοκοῦμεν δωρεᾶς.
εἰ γὰρ ὑπὲρ μόνου τούτου τὴν τιμὴν ᾔτουν παρ᾽
ὑμῶν, εἰ γὰρ ἔλεγον, " Ἄνδρες, ἀποθανεῖν ἐθελή-
σαντι τῷ τυράννῳ καὶ ἀνόπλῳ ἐπὶ τοῦ καιροῦ
κατειλημμένῳ ξίφος τοῦτο ἐμὸν ὑπηρέτησε καὶ
πρὸς τὸ τέλος τῆς ἐλευθερίας συνήργησε πάντη,[2]
τοῦτο[3] τιμῆς τε καὶ δωρεᾶς ἄξιον νομίσατε,"
δεσπότην οὕτω δημοτικοῦ κτήματος οὐκ ἂν
ἠμείψασθε ; οὐκ ἂν ἐν τοῖς εὐεργέταις ἀνεγρά-
ψατε ; οὐκ ἂν τὸ ξίφος ἐν τοῖς ἱεροῖς ἀνεθήκατε ;
οὐκ ἂν μετὰ τῶν θεῶν κἀκεῖνο προσεκυνήσατε ;

20 Νῦν μοι ἐννοήσατε οἷα πεποιηκέναι εἰκὸς τὸν
τύραννον, οἷα δὲ εἰρηκέναι πρὸ τῆς τελευτῆς·
ἐπεὶ γὰρ ὑπ᾽ ἐμοῦ φονευόμενος καὶ τιτρωσκόμενος
πολλοῖς τραύμασιν ἐς τὰ φανερὰ τοῦ σώματος,
ὡς ἂν μάλιστα λυπήσειν ἔμελλον τὸν γεγεννηκότα,
ὡς ἂν ἐκ τῆς πρώτης θέας διασπαράξειν, ὁ μὲν
ἀνεβόησεν οἰκτρόν, ἐπιβοώμενος τὸν γεγεννηκότα
οὐ βοηθὸν οὐδὲ σύμμαχον—ᾔδει γὰρ πρεσβύτην
ὄντα καὶ ἀσθενῆ—ἀλλὰ θεατὴν τῶν οἰκείων κακῶν·
ἐγὼ γὰρ[4] ἀπηλλαττόμην ποιητὴς μὲν τῆς ὅλης

---

[1] τίς N, cod. Graevii : not in other MSS.
[2] πάντη Guyet : παντὶ MSS.
[3] τοῦ ΓΖ.

hand, the most pitiable of deaths, far more bitter than as if it should come about at the hand of another.

Where is my sword? Does anyone else recognise this? Was this any other man's weapon? Who carried it up to the citadel? Who preceded the tyrant in its use? Who commissioned it against him? Good sword, partner and promoter of my successes, after so many perils, after so many slayings, we are disregarded and thought unworthy of a reward! If it were for the sword alone that I sought the meed of honour from you—if I were pleading: " Gentlemen, when the tyrant wished to die and at the moment found himself unarmed, this sword of mine served him and did its part in every way towards the attainment of liberty—account it worthy of honour and reward," would you not have requited the owner of a possession so valuable to the state? Would you not have recorded him among your benefactors? Would you not have enshrined the sword among your hallowed treasures? Would you not have worshipped it along with the gods?

Now then, imagine, I beg you, what the tyrant no doubt did and what he said before his end. When I sought to slay the son and wounded him again and again in those parts of his body which could be seen, that so I might grieve the parent most, that so I might rend his heart through the first sight, he raised a doleful cry, calling his parent to him, not to aid him or share the conflict—for he knew him to be old and weak—but to behold his own calamities. Before I slipped away, I had myself composed the

---

⁴ γὰρ not in ΓΖ.

τραγῳδίας γεγενημένος, καταλιπὼν δὲ τῷ ὑπο-
κριτῇ τὸν νεκρὸν καὶ τὴν σκηνὴν καὶ τὸ ξίφος
καὶ τὰ λοιπὰ τοῦ δράματος· ἐπιστὰς δὲ ἐκεῖνος
καὶ ἰδὼν υἱὸν ὃν εἶχεν μόνον ὀλίγον ἐμπνέοντα,
ἡμαγμένον, ἐμπεπλησμένον τοῦ φόνου καὶ τὰ
τραύματα συνεχῆ καὶ πολλὰ καὶ καίρια, ἀνεβόησεν
τοῦτο· " Τέκνον, ἀνῃρήμεθα, πεφονεύμεθα, τετυ-
ραννοκτονήμεθα, ποῦ ὁ σφαγεύς ; τίνι με τηρεῖ ;
τίνι με φυλάττει διὰ σοῦ, τέκνον, προανῃρημένον ;
ἢ μή τι ὡς γέροντος ὑπερφρονεῖ, καὶ τῇ βραδυτῆτι,
κολάζειν δέον, καὶ παρατείνει μοι τὸν φόνον καὶ
μακροτέραν μοι τὴν σφαγὴν ποιεῖ ; "

21   Καὶ ταῦτα λέγων ἐζήτει τὸ ξίφος· αὐτὸς γὰρ
ἄνοπλος ἦν διὰ τὸ πάντα τῷ παιδὶ θαρρεῖν. ἀλλ'
οὐδὲ τοῦτο ἐνεδέησεν, πάλαι δὲ ἦν ὑπ' ἐμοῦ καὶ
τοῦτο προπαρεσκευασμένον καὶ πρὸς τὸ μέλλον
τόλμημα καταλελειμμένον. ἀποσπάσας δὴ τῆς
σφαγῆς καὶ τοῦ τραύματος ἐξελὼν τὸ ξίφος
φησί, " Πρὸ μικροῦ μέν με ἀπέκτεινας, νῦν δὲ
ἀνάπαυσον, ξίφος. πατρὶ πενθοῦντι παραμύθιον
ἐλθὲ καὶ πρεσβυτικῇ χειρὶ δυστυχούσῃ συνα-
γώνισαι. ἀπόσφαξον, τυραννοκτόνησον καὶ τοῦ
πενθεῖν ἀπάλλαξον. εἴθε πρῶτός σοι ἐνέτυχον,
εἴθε τὴν τάξιν προὔλαβον τοῦ φόνου. ἀπέθανον
ἄν, ἀλλ' ὡς[1] τύραννος μόνον, ἀλλ' ἔτι νομίζων
ἕξειν ἔκδικον· νῦν δὲ ὡς ἄτεκνος, νῦν δὲ ὡς οὐδὲ
φονέως εὐπορῶν." Καὶ ταῦτα ἅμα λέγων ἐπῆγε
τὴν σφαγὴν τρέμων, οὐ δυνάμενος, ἐπιθυμῶν μέν,
ἀσθενῶν δὲ πρὸς τὴν ὑπηρεσίαν τοῦ τολμήματος.

---

[1] ὡς du Soul: ἢ ὡς MSS.

whole plot of the tragedy, but had left to the actor the body, the stage-setting, the sword, and the remainder of the play. When the other made his appearance and saw his only son with but little breath in him, bloodied, covered with gore, his wounds close together, numerous, and vital, he raised this cry: " My child, we are destroyed, assassinated, fallen victims to the tyrant-slayer! Where is the executioner? For what purpose is he keeping me, for what purpose reserving me, now that I am already destroyed through you, my child? Or is it perhaps that he contemns me as an old man, and also by his dilatoriness (since I must be punished) protracts my death and makes my execution longer? "

With these words he sought a sword; for he was unarmed on account of his complete reliance upon his son. But that too was not wanting; long beforehand, that too had been provided by me and left behind for the bold deed that was to come. So, withdrawing the sword from the victim, plucking it from the wound, he said: " A little while ago you gave me death; now give me repose, O sword. Come to console a mourning father; lighten the task of an aged hand beset by adversity; let my blood; be tyrant-slayer to me; quit me of my woe. Had I but encountered you first! had I but inverted the order of deaths! I should have perished; but simply as tyrant—but thinking still that I should have an avenger, while now I die as one who is childless, as one who can hardly so much as find a man to take his life! " Thereupon he hastened his despatch, trembling, incapable, craving it, to be sure, but lacking the strength to serve his bold purpose.

22 Πόσαι κολάσεις ταῦτα ; πόσα τραύματα ; πόσοι
θάνατοι ; πόσαι τυραννοκτονίαι ; πόσαι δωρεαί ;
καὶ τέλος ἑωράκατε πάντες τὸν μὲν νεανίαν προκεί-
μενον, οὐδὲ μικρὸν οὐδ' εὐκαταγώνιστον ἔργον, τὸν
πρεσβύτην δὲ αὐτῷ περικεχυμένον καὶ τὸ αἷμα
ἀμφοῖν ἀνακεκραμένον, τὴν ἐλευθέριον ἐκείνην καὶ
ἐπινίκιον σπονδήν, καὶ τὰ ἔργα τοῦ ξίφους τοῦ ἐμοῦ,
αὐτὸ δὲ τὸ ξίφος ἐν μέσῳ ἀμφοτέρων, ἐπιδεικνύμενον
ὡς οὐκ ἀνάξιον γεγένηται τοῦ δεσπότου καὶ μαρτυ-
ρόμενον ὅτι μοι πιστῶς διηκονήσατο. τοῦτο ὑπ'
ἐμοῦ γενόμενον μικρότερον ἦν· νῦν δὲ λαμπρό-
τερόν ἐστι τῇ καινότητι. καὶ ὁ μὲν καθελὼν τὴν
τυραννίδα πᾶσαν εἰμὶ ἐγώ· μεμέρισται δὲ ἐς
πολλοὺς τὸ ἔργον ὥσπερ ἐν δράματι· καὶ τὰ μὲν
πρῶτα ἐγὼ ὑπεκρινάμην, τὰ δεύτερα δὲ ὁ παῖς,
τὰ τρίτα δὲ ὁ τύραννος αὐτός, τὸ ξίφος δὲ πᾶσιν
ὑπηρέτησεν.

THE TYRANNICIDE

How many punishments were there in all this? How many wounds? How many deaths? How many tyrant-slayings? How many rewards? And at the end you have all seen not only the young man exposed in death (no slight accomplishment or easy to achieve), but the old man prostrate upon him, you have seen the blood of both intermingled (that thank-offering for liberty and for victory), and the havoc of my sword; aye, the sword itself between them both, evincing that it has not been unworthy of its owner and testifying that it served me faithfully. Had this been done by me, it would be less of an achievement; but now it is more splendid by reason of its novelty. It is I, to be sure, who overthrew the entire tyranny; but the performance has been distributed among many people as in a play; the leading part was played by me, the second by the son, the third by the tyrant himself, and the sword served all.

DISOWNED

THE fictitious case which underlies this declamation is
outlined in the argument that precedes the text. An earlier
treatment of the same theme is to be found in the *Controversiae*
of Seneca Rhetor (IV, 5). In the Lucianic piece, the speaker's
references to his stepmother constitute a notable example of
sustained irony as a rhetorical device.

ΑΠΟΚΗΡΥΤΤΟΜΕΝΟΣ

’Αποκηρυχθείς τις ἰατρικὴν ἐξέμαθεν. μανέντα τὸν πατέρα
καὶ ὑπὸ τῶν ἄλλων ἰατρῶν ἀπεγνωσμένον ἰασάμενος φαρμάκου
δόσει ἀνελήφθη αὖθις ἐς τὸ γένος. μετὰ ταῦτα μεμηνυῖαν τὴν
μητρυιὰν ἰάσασθαι κελευόμενος . . . ἀποκηρύττεται.[1]

1 Οὐ καινὰ μὲν ταῦτα, ὦ ἄνδρες δικασταί, οὐδὲ
παράδοξα τὰ[2] ὑπὸ τοῦ πατρὸς ἐν τῷ παρόντι
γιγνόμενα, οὐδὲ νῦν πρῶτον τὰ τοιαῦτα ὀργίζεται,
ἀλλὰ πρόχειρος οὗτος ὁ νόμος αὐτῷ καὶ συνήθως
ἐπὶ τοῦτ’ ἀφικνεῖται τὸ δικαστήριον. ἐκεῖνο δὲ
καινότερον νῦν δυστυχῶ, ὅτι ἔγκλημα μὲν ἴδιον
οὐκ ἔχω, κινδυνεύω δὲ τιμωρίαν ὑποσχεῖν ὑπὲρ
τῆς τέχνης εἰ μὴ πάντα δύναται πείθεσθαι τούτῳ
κελεύοντι, οὗ τί γένοιτ’ ἂν ἀτοπώτερον, θεραπεύειν ἐκ προστάγματος, οὐκέθ’ ὡς ἡ τέχνη
δύναται, ἀλλ’ ὡς ὁ πατὴρ βούλεται; ἐβουλόμην
μὲν οὖν τὴν ἰατρικὴν καὶ τοιοῦτόν τι ἔχειν

---

[1] κελευόμενος ἀποκηρύττεται ΓΝUBC. The lacuna is
variously filled by conjectural supplements: μὴ βουλόμενος
ΖΜ : καὶ μὴ βουλόμενος διὰ τὸ λέγειν μὴ δύνασθαι Β marg.;
καὶ λέγων μὴ δύνασθαι ς, edd.

[2] τὰ Γ²(Fritzsche): not in other MSS.

---

[1] The words in italics are supplied to give the approximate
sense of those lost in the Greek text.

[2] The law permitting a father to disown his son, and the
court before which his complaint had to be presented. No

DISOWNED

A son who had been disowned studied medicine. When his father became insane and had been given up by the other doctors, he cured him by administering a remedy, and was again received into the family. After that, he was ordered to cure his stepmother, who was insane, and *as he refused to do so*, he is now being disowned *again*.[1]

There is nothing novel or surprising, gentlemen of the jury, in my father's present course, and this is not the first time that he has displayed such anger; on the contrary, he keeps this law always in readiness and resorts to this court by habit.[2] There is, however, something of novelty in my present plight, in that I am under no personal charge, but am in jeopardy of punishment on behalf of my profession because it cannot in every particular obey his behests. But what could be more absurd than to give treatment under orders, in accordance, not with the powers of the profession, but with the desires of my father? I could wish, to be sure, that medical science had a remedy

certain case of disownment at Athens is known; but Dionysius of Halicarnassus (*Arch.*, II, 26) says that provisions for it were included in the codes of Solon, Pittacus, and Charondas, there is one in Plato's *Laws* (XI, 928 D; it involves a family council), and Egyptian documents attest it. P. M. Meyer, in publishing one of them (*Juristische Papyri*, No. XI) cites Cod. Just., VIII, 46, 6: abdicatio, quae Graeco more ad alienandos liberos usurpatur et apoceryxis dicebatur, Romanis legibus non comprobatur.

φάρμακον ὃ μὴ μόνον τοὺς μεμηνότας ἀλλὰ καὶ
τοὺς ἀδίκως ὀργιζομένους παύειν ἐδύνατο, ἵνα καὶ
τοῦτο τοῦ πατρὸς τὸ νόσημα ἰασαίμην. νυνὶ
δὲ τὰ μὲν τῆς μανίας αὐτῷ τέλεον πέπαυται,
τὰ δὲ τῆς ὀργῆς μᾶλλον ἐπιτείνεται, καὶ τὸ
δεινότατον, τοῖς μὲν ἄλλοις ἅπασιν σωφρονεῖ,
κατ' ἐμοῦ δὲ τοῦ θεραπεύσαντος μόνου μαίνεται.
τὸν μὲν οὖν μισθὸν τῆς θεραπείας ὁρᾶτε οἷον
ἀπολαμβάνω, ἀποκηρυττόμενος ὑπ' αὐτοῦ πάλιν
καὶ τοῦ γένους ἀλλοτριούμενος δεύτερον, ὥσπερ
διὰ τοῦτ' ἀναληφθεὶς πρὸς ὀλίγον ἵν' ἀτιμότερος
γένωμαι πολλάκις ἐκπεσὼν τῆς οἰκίας.

2   Ἐγὼ δὲ ἐν μὲν τοῖς δυνατοῖς οὐδὲ [1] κελευσθῆναι
περιμένω· πρῴην γοῦν ἄκλητος ἧκον ἐπὶ τὴν
βοήθειαν. ὅταν δέ τι ᾖ τελέως ἀπεγνωσμένον,
οὐδ' ἐπιχειρεῖν βούλομαι. ἐπὶ δὲ τῆς γυναικὸς
ταύτης εἰκότως καὶ ἀτολμότερός εἰμι· λογίζομαι
γὰρ οἷα πάθοιμ' ἂν ὑπὸ τοῦ πατρὸς ἀποτυχών,
ὃς οὐδὲ ἀρξάμενος τῆς θεραπείας ἀποκηρύτ-
τομαι. ἄχθομαι μὲν οὖν, ὦ ἄνδρες δικασταί,
ἐπὶ τῇ μητρυιᾷ χαλεπῶς ἐχούσῃ (χρηστὴ γὰρ
ἦν) καὶ ἐπὶ τῷ πατρὶ δι' ἐκείνην ἀνιωμένῳ, τὸ
δὲ μέγιστον, ἐπ' ἐμαυτῷ ἀπειθεῖν δοκοῦντι καὶ
ἃ προστάττομαι ὑπουργεῖν οὐ δυναμένῳ καὶ δι'
ὑπερβολὴν τῆς νόσου καὶ ἀσθένειαν τῆς τέχνης.
πλὴν οὐ δίκαιον οἶμαι ἀποκηρύττεσθαι τὸν ἃ
μὴ δύναται ποιεῖν μηδὲ τὴν ἀρχὴν ὑπισχνούμενον.

3   Δι' ἃς μὲν οὖν αἰτίας καὶ πρότερον ἀπεκήρυξέ με
ῥᾴδιον συνιδεῖν ἐκ τῶν παρόντων. ἐγὼ δὲ καὶ
πρὸς ἐκείνας μέν, ὡς οἴομαι, ἱκανῶς τῷ μετὰ

---

[1] οὐδὲ UΓ²: οὐδὲν ΓΝΖ(ΒC).

DISOWNED

of such sort that it could check not only insanity but unjust anger, in order that I might cure my father of this disorder also. As things are, his madness has been completely assuaged, but his anger is growing worse, and (what is hardest of all) he is sane to everyone else and insane towards me alone, his physician. You see, therefore, what fee I receive for my attendance—I am disowned by him once more and put away from my family a second time, as if I had been taken back for a brief space merely that I might be more disgraced by being turned out of the household repeatedly.

For my part, in cases which can be cured I do not wait to be summoned; on the previous occasion, for instance, I came to his relief uncalled. But when a case is perfectly desperate, I am unwilling even to essay it. And in respect to this woman I am with good reason even less venturesome, since I take into consideration how I should be treated by my father if I were to fail, when without having so much as begun treating her I am disowned. I am indeed pained, gentlemen of the jury, at my stepmother's serious condition (for she was a good woman), at my father's distress on her account, and most of all at my own apparent disobedience and real inability to do the service which is enjoined upon me, both because of the extraordinary violence of the illness and the ineffectiveness of the art of healing. I do not think, however, that it is just to disown a man who declines at the outset to promise what he cannot perform.

The charges on which he disowned me before can be readily understood from the present situation. To those charges I have made a sufficient answer, I

ταῦτα βίῳ ἀπελογησάμην, καὶ ταυτὶ δὲ ἃ νῦν
ἐγκαλεῖ ὡς ἂν οἷός τε ὦ ἀπολύσομαι, μικρὰ ὑμῖν
διηγησάμενος τῶν ἐμῶν.

Ὁ γὰρ δυσάγωγος καὶ δυσπειθὴς ἐγώ, ὁ καταισχύνων τὸν πατέρα καὶ ἀνάξια πράττων τοῦ
γένους, τότε μὲν αὐτῷ τὰ πολλὰ ἐκεῖνα βοῶντι καὶ
διατεινομένῳ ὀλίγα χρῆναι ἀντιλέγειν ᾠόμην.
ἀπελθὼν δὲ τῆς οἰκίας ἐνόμιζόν μοι δικαστήριον
ἔσεσθαι μέγα καὶ ψῆφον ἀληθῆ τὸν μετὰ ταῦτα
βίον καὶ τὸ φαίνεσθαι πάμπολυ τῶν τοῦ πατρὸς
ἐγκλημάτων ἐκείνων ἀφεστηκότα καὶ περὶ τὰ κάλλιστα τῶν ἐπιτηδευμάτων ἐσπουδακότα καὶ τοῖς
ἀρίστοις συνόντα. προεωρώμην δὲ καὶ τοιοῦτό τι
καὶ ὑπώπτευον ἤδη [1] ὡς οὐ σφόδρα καθεστηκότος
πατρὸς [2] ἀδίκως ὀργίζεσθαι καὶ ἐγκλήματα ψευδῆ
καθ' υἱοῦ συντιθέναι· καὶ ἦσάν τινες οἱ μανίας ἀρχὴν
ταῦτα εἶναι νομίζοντες καὶ ἀπειλὴν καὶ ἀκροβο-
λισμὸν οὐκ ἐς μακρὰν ἐπιπεσουμένου τοῦ κακοῦ,
μῖσος ἄλογον καὶ νόμον ἀπηνῆ καὶ βλασφημίας
προχείρους καὶ δικαστήριον σκυθρωπὸν καὶ βοὴν
καὶ ὀργὴν καὶ ὅλως χολῆς μεστὰ πάντα. διὸ δὴ
τάχα μοι καὶ ἰατρικῆς δεήσειν ποτὲ προσεδόκων.

4 Ἀποδημήσας οὖν καὶ τοῖς εὐδοκιμωτάτοις τῶν
ἐπὶ τῆς ἀλλοδαπῆς ἰατρῶν συγγενόμενος καὶ πόνῳ
πολλῷ καὶ προθυμίᾳ λιπαρεῖ χρησάμενος ἐξέμαθον τὴν τέχνην. ἐπανελθὼν δὲ καταλαμβάνω
τὸν πατέρα σαφῶς ἤδη μεμηνότα καὶ ὑπὸ τῶν

---

[1] ἤδη Pellet : μὴ δὴ MSS.

think, by my subsequent life, and these accusations which he now brings I shall dispose of to the best of my ability; but first I shall tell you a little about my position.

I who am so difficult and disobedient, who so disgrace my father and act so unworthily of my family, on the former occasion thought it behoved me to make little opposition to him when he was making all that clamour and straining his lungs. On leaving the house, I expected to have a grand jury and a true verdict in my subsequent life, with its disclosure that I was at a very great remove from those offences with which I had been charged by my father, that I had devoted myself to the noblest of pursuits, and that I was frequenting the best company. I foresaw, too, something like this, suspecting even then that it indicated no great sanity in a father to be angry unjustly and to concoct false accusations against a son. And there were those who held all that to be the beginning of madness, the hostile demonstration and skirmish-fire of the disease that was soon to fall upon him—the insensate hatred, the cruel law, the ready abusiveness, the grim tribunal, the clamour, the anger, and in general the atrabiliousness which impregnated the whole proceedings. Therefore I expected that perhaps I should some day need a knowledge of medicine.

I went abroad, then, studied with the most famous physicians in foreign parts, and by dint of great labour and insistent zeal thoroughly mastered the art. On my return I found my father by then defin-

---

[2] τοῦ πατρὸς (Dindorf, Jacobitz), F only, and mistakenly; cf. υἱοῦ.

THE WORKS OF LUCIAN

ἐπιχωρίων ἰατρῶν ἀπεγνωσμένον, οὐκ ἐς βάθος
ὁρώντων οὐδ' ἀκριβῶς φυλοκρινούντων[1] τὰς νό-
σους. πλὴν ὅπερ γε εἰκὸς ἦν ποιεῖν χρηστὸν
υἱόν, οὔτε ἐμνησικάκησα τῆς ἀποκηρύξεως οὔτε
μετάπεμπτος γενέσθαι περιέμεινα· οὐδὲ γὰρ εἶχόν
τι αὐτῷ ἴδιον ἐγκαλεῖν, ἀλλὰ πάντα ἐκεῖνα ἦν
ἀλλότρια τὰ ἁμαρτήματα καὶ ὥσπερ ἔφην ἤδη,
τῆς νόσου. παρελθὼν οὖν ἄκλητος οὐκ εὐθὺς
ἰασάμην· οὐ γὰρ οὕτω ποιεῖν ἔθος ἐστὶν ἡμῖν
οὐδὲ ταῦτα ἡ τέχνη παραινεῖ, ἀλλὰ πάντων πρῶτον
τοῦτο διδασκόμεθα συνορᾶν εἴτε ἰάσιμόν ἐστι τὸ
νόσημα εἴτε ἀνήκεστον καὶ ὑπερβεβηκὸς τοὺς
ὅρους τῆς τέχνης. καὶ τηνικαῦτα, ἢν μὲν εὐμετα-
χείριστον ᾖ, ἐπιχειροῦμεν καὶ πᾶσαν σπουδὴν
ἐσφερόμεθα σῶσαι τὸν νοσοῦντα· ἢν δὲ κεκρατηκὸς
ἤδη καὶ νενικηκὸς τὸ πάθος ἴδωμεν, οὐδὲ τὴν
ἀρχὴν προσαπτόμεθα, νόμον τινὰ παλαιὸν τῶν
προπατόρων τῆς τέχνης ἰατρῶν φυλάττοντες,
οἵ φασι μὴ δεῖν ἐπιχειρεῖν τοῖς κεκρατημένοις.

Ἰδὼν οὖν τὸν πατέρα ἔτι ἐντὸς τῆς ἐλπίδος καὶ
τὸ πάθος οὐχ ὑπὲρ τὴν τέχνην, ἐπὶ πολὺ τηρήσας
καὶ ἀκριβῶς ἐξετάσας ἕκαστα ἐπεχείρουν ἤδη καὶ
τὸ φάρμακον τεθαρρηκότως ἐνέχεον, καίτοι πολλοὶ
τῶν παρόντων ὑπώπτευον τὴν δόσιν καὶ τὴν
ἴασιν διέβαλλον καὶ πρὸς κατηγορίας παρεσκευά-
5 ζοντο. παρῆν δὲ καὶ ἡ μητρυιὰ φοβουμένη καὶ
ἀπιστοῦσα, οὐ τῷ μισεῖν ἐμέ, ἀλλὰ τῷ δεδιέναι
καὶ ἀκριβῶς εἰδέναι πονηρῶς ἐκεῖνον διακεί-
μενον· ἠπίστατο γὰρ μόνη τὰ πάντα συνοῦσα καὶ

[1] φυλοκρινούντων ΓΥΝ: φιλοκρινούντων Ζ(ΒC); cf. Phal.
II, 9.

482

itively insane and given up by the local physicians, who
had not profound insight and could not accurately distinguish different forms of disease. Yet I did as was
natural for an upright son to do, neither cherishing
a grudge because of my being disowned, nor waiting
to be sent after; for I had no fault to find with him
personally, but all those offences were of extraneous
origin and, as I have said already, peculiar to the
disease. So I came without being called, but did
not begin the treatment at once. It is not our
custom to do so, and the art of medicine does not re-
commend that course; we are taught first of all to
observe whether the disease is curable or irremediable
and beyond the limits of medical skill. Then, if it
is manageable, we put our hands to it and make
every effort to save the patient; but if we see that
the ailment already has the upper hand and is victori-
ous, we do not touch it at all, observing an ancient
law of the progenitors of the art of medicine, who
say that one must not lay hand to those who are
overmastered.[1]

Since I saw that my father was still within hope
and his ailment not beyond professional skill, after
long observation and accurate investigation of all
details I set my hand to it at last and compounded
my remedy confidently, although many of those
present were suspicious of my prescription, critical of
my treatment of the case, and ready to bring charges
against me. My stepmother was present also,
panic-stricken and distrustful, not because she hated
me but because she was fearful and well aware that
he was in a bad way; she knew it because she alone
associated exclusively with him and lived side by

[1] Hippocrates, *de Arte*, 3.

THE WORKS OF LUCIAN

ὁμοδίαιτος τῇ νόσῳ. πλὴν ἀλλ' ἔγωγε οὐδὲν
ἀποδειλιάσας—ἠπιστάμην γὰρ οὐ ψευσόμενά με
τὰ σημεῖα οὐδὲ προδώσουσαν τὴν τέχνην—ἐπῆγον
τὴν ἴασιν ἐν καιρῷ τῆς ἐπιχειρήσεως, καίτοι
κἀμοί τινες τῶν φίλων συνεβούλευον μὴ θρασύ-
νεσθαι, μὴ καὶ διαβολήν τινα μείζω ἐνέγκῃ μοι
τὸ ἀποτυχεῖν ὡς ἀμυνομένῳ τὸν πατέρα φαρμάκῳ καὶ μνησικακήσαντι ὧν ἐπεπόνθειν ὑπ'
αὐτοῦ.

Καὶ τὸ κεφάλαιον, σῶος μὲν οὗτος εὐθὺς ἦν καὶ
ἐσωφρόνει πάλιν καὶ πάντα διεγίγνωσκεν· οἱ
παρόντες δὲ ἐθαύμαζον, ἐπῄνει δὲ καὶ ἡ μητρυιὰ
καὶ φανερὰ πᾶσιν ἦν χαίρουσα κἀμοὶ εὐδοκιμοῦντι
κἀκείνῳ σωφρονοῦντι. οὗτος δ' οὖν (μαρτυρεῖν
γὰρ αὐτῷ ἔχω) μήτε μελλήσας μήτε σύμβουλόν
τινα περὶ τούτων προσλαβών, ἐπειδὴ τὸ πᾶν
ἤκουσε τῶν παρόντων, ἔλυε μὲν τὴν ἀποκήρυξιν,
υἱὸν δὲ ἐξ ὑπαρχῆς ἐποιεῖτό με, σωτῆρα καὶ
εὐεργέτην ἀποκαλῶν καὶ ἀκριβῆ πεῖραν εἰληφέναι
ὁμολογῶν καὶ περὶ τῶν ἔμπροσθεν ἐκείνων ἀπολογούμενος. τοῦτο γενόμενον εὔφραινε μὲν πολλούς,
ὅσοι παρῆσαν χρηστοί, ἐλύπει δὲ ἐκείνους ὅσοις
ἀποκήρυξις υἱοῦ ἡδίων ἀναλήψεως. εἶδον γοῦν
τότε οὐ πάντας ὁμοίως ἡδομένους τῷ πράγματι,
ἀλλ' εὐθύς τινος καὶ χρόαν τρεπομένην καὶ βλέμμα
τεταραγμένον καὶ πρόσωπον ὠργισμένον, οἷον ἐκ
φθόνου καὶ μίσους γίνεται.

Ἡμεῖς μὲν οὖν, ὡς τὸ εἰκός, ἐν εὐφροσύναις καὶ
6 θυμηδίαις ἦμεν, ἀλλήλους ἀπειληφότες· ἡ μητρυιὰ
δὲ μετὰ μικρὸν εὐθὺς νοσεῖν ἤρξατο νόσον, ὦ
ἄνδρες δικασταί, χαλεπὴν καὶ παράλογον· ἀρχό-

side with his disorder. Nevertheless, without any timidity (for I knew that the symptoms would not cheat me or the medical art betray me) I applied the treatment at the nick of time for the attempt, although some of my friends advised me not to be overbold for fear that failure bring upon me a more serious imputation of avenging myself upon my father with poison, having conceived a grudge against him for what I had suffered at his hands.

To sum it up, he became well at once, recovered his sanity, and was thoroughly in command of his faculties. Those present were amazed, and my stepmother was full of praise, making it plain to all that she was delighted with my success and his sanity. And as for my father here (for I am able to testify on his behalf) without delay and without asking any advice in this matter, as soon as he had heard the whole story from those who were there, he annulled the disownment and made me his son once more, calling me his saviour and benefactor, admitting that he had tested me thoroughly, and defending himself for his former charges. This event gave joy to many, the men of rectitude who were there, and pain to those who preferred the disownment of a son to his resumption. I saw, anyhow, at the time that not all were equally pleased with the affair, but at once one or another showed changed colour, disturbed eyes, and an angry face, such as comes from jealousy and hatred.

Well, we were rejoicing and making merry, as was natural, since we had regained each other, when after a short time my stepmother suddenly began to be afflicted, gentlemen of the jury, with an ailment which was severe and unusual. I observed the

485

THE WORKS OF LUCIAN

μενον γὰρ εὐθὺς τὸ δεινὸν παρεφύλαξα.[1] οὐ γὰρ
ἁπλοῦν οὐδὲ ἐπιπόλαιον τῆς μανίας τὸ εἶδος,
ἀλλά τι παλαιὸν ὑποικουροῦν ἐν τῇ ψυχῇ κακὸν
ἀπέρρηξε καὶ ἐς τοὐμφανὲς ἐξενίκησε. πολλὰ
μὲν οὖν καὶ ἄλλα ἡμῖν ἐστι σημεῖα τῶν ἀνιάτως
μεμηνότων, ἓν δὲ ἐκεῖνο καινὸν ἐπὶ τῆς γυναικὸς ταύτης παρεφύλαξα· πρὸς μὲν γὰρ τοὺς
ἄλλους ἡμερωτέρα καὶ πραεῖά ἐστι καὶ παρόντων
εἰρήνην ἄγει ἡ νόσος, ἂν δέ τινα ἰατρὸν ἴδῃ καὶ
τοῦτ᾿ ἀκούσῃ μόνον, κατ᾿ ἐκείνου μάλιστα παρο-
ξύνεται, ὅπερ καὶ αὐτὸ τοῦ πονηρῶς καὶ ἀνηκέστως
ἔχειν ἐστὶ τεκμήριον.

Ταῦτα ὁρῶν ἐγὼ μὲν ἠνιώμην καὶ τὴν γυναῖκα
ᾤκτειρον ἀξίαν οὖσαν καὶ παρὰ τὸ προσῆκον
7 δυστυχοῦσαν. ὁ πατὴρ δὲ ὑπὸ ἰδιωτείας (οὐ
γὰρ οἶδεν οὔτε ἀρχὴν τοῦ κατέχοντος κακοῦ
οὔτε τὴν αἰτίαν οὔτε τὸ μέτρον τοῦ πάθους)
ἐκέλευεν ἰᾶσθαι καὶ τὸ ὅμοιον ἐκχέαι φάρμακον·
οἴεται[2] γὰρ ἓν εἶναι μανίας εἶδος καὶ μίαν τὴν
νόσον καὶ τἀρρώστημα ταὐτὸν καὶ παραπλησίαν
τὴν θεραπείαν δεχόμενον.[3] ἐπεὶ δέ, ὅπερ ἀληθέστατον, ἀδύνατον εἶναί φημι σώζεσθαι τὴν γυναῖκα
καὶ ἡττῆσθαι ὑπὸ τῆς νόσου ὁμολογῶ, ἀγανακτεῖ
καὶ ὀργίζεται καί φησιν ἑκόντα καθυφίεσθαι
καὶ προδιδόναι τὴν ἄνθρωπον, ἐγκαλῶν ἐμοὶ τὴν
ἀσθένειαν τῆς τέχνης. καὶ πάσχει μὲν σύνηθες
τοῖς λυπουμένοις· ὀργίζονται γοῦν ἅπαντες τοῖς
μετὰ παρρησίας τἀληθῆ λέγουσιν. πλὴν ἔγωγε
ὡς ἂν οἷός τε ὦ δικαιολογήσομαι πρὸς αὐτὸν καὶ
ὑπὲρ ἐμαυτοῦ καὶ τῆς τέχνης.

[1] παρεφύλαξα (CM)AF : παρεφυλάξατο ΓΝΖUB.
[2] οἴεται ΓUZCM : ᾤετο BN, edd.

486

affliction constantly from the moment when it began.
Her form of insanity was not simple or superficial;
some trouble of long ago, lurking in the soul, had
broken out and won its way into the open. We have,
of course, many symptoms of incurable madness,
but in the case of this woman I have observed one
that is novel; towards everyone else she is very
civil and gentle, and in their presence the disease is
peaceful, but if she sees any physician and simply
hears that he is one, she is beyond all things exas-
perated against him, and this in itself is proof that
her condition is bad and incurable.

Seeing this, I was distressed and pitied the woman,
who was worthy of it and unfortunate beyond her
deserts. My father, in his inexperience (for he
does not know either the origin of the trouble that
holds her in its grip, or its cause, or the extent of the
infirmity), bade me treat her and give her the same
medicine; for he thinks that madness has but one
form, that the ailment is simple, and that her illness
is identical with his, permitting the same treatment.
When I say what is as true as true can be, that it is
impossible to save his wife and confess that I am
worsted by the disorder, he is indignant and angry,
and says that I am deliberately shirking and giving
the woman up, thus making the ineffectiveness of
the art of medicine a reproach against me. He does,
indeed, what is habitually done by people who are
offended; all are angry at those who speak the
truth in frankness. In spite of that, I shall plead to
the best of my ability against him, not only for myself
but for my art.

---

[3] ἐνδεχόμενον BC.

THE WORKS OF LUCIAN

8 Καὶ πρῶτόν γε ἀπὸ τοῦ νόμου ἄρξομαι καθ᾽
ὃν οὗτός με ἀποκηρῦξαι βούλεται, ἵν᾽ εἰδῇ οὐκέθ᾽
ὁμοίαν οὖσαν αὐτῷ νῦν τε καὶ πρότερον τὴν
ἐξουσίαν. οὐ γὰρ ἅπασιν, ὦ πάτερ, ὁ νομοθέτης
οὐδὲ πάντας υἱέας οὐδὲ ὁσάκις ἂν ἐθέλωσιν
ἀποκηρύττειν συγκεχώρηκεν οὐδ᾽ ἐπὶ πάσαις
αἰτίαις, ἀλλ᾽ ὥσπερ τοῖς πατράσιν τὰ τηλικαῦτα
ὀργίζεσθαι ἐφῆκεν, οὕτω καὶ τῶν παίδων προὐ-
νόησεν, ὡς μὴ ἀδίκως αὐτὸ πάσχωσιν· καὶ διὰ
τοῦτο οὐκ ἐλευθέραν ἐφῆκε γίγνεσθαι οὐδὲ ἄκριτον
τὴν τιμωρίαν, ἀλλ᾽ ἐς δικαστήριον ἐκάλεσε καὶ
δοκιμαστὰς ἐκάθισε τοὺς μήτε πρὸς ὀργὴν μήτε
διαβολὴν [1] τὸ δίκαιον κρινοῦντας. ᾔδει γὰρ πολλοῖς
πολλάκις ἀλόγους αἰτίας ὀργῆς παρισταμένας,
καὶ τὸν μὲν ψευδεῖ τινι διαβολῇ πειθόμενον,
τὸν δὲ οἰκέτῃ πιστεύοντα ἢ γυναίῳ ἐχθρῷ. οὔκουν
ἡγεῖτο ἀδίκαστον γίγνεσθαι τὸ πρᾶγμα οὐδ᾽ ἐξ
ἐρήμης τοὺς παῖδας εὐθὺς ἁλίσκεσθαι, ἀλλὰ καὶ
ὕδωρ ἐγχεῖται καὶ λόγος ἀποδίδοται καὶ ἀνεξέταστον οὐδὲν καταλείπεται.

9 Ἐπεὶ τοίνυν ἔξεστιν, καὶ τοῦ μὲν ἐγκαλεῖν
μόνου ὁ πατὴρ κύριος, τοῦ κρῖναι δὲ εἰ εὔλογα
αἰτιᾶται ὑμεῖς οἱ δικάζοντες, αὐτὸ μὲν ὅ μοι
ἐπιφέρει καὶ ἐφ᾽ ᾧ νῦν ἀγανακτεῖ μηδέπω σκοπεῖτε,
πρότερον δὲ ἐκεῖνο ἐξετάσατε, εἰ ἔτι δοτέον
ἀποκηρύττειν αὐτῷ ἅπαξ ἀποκηρύξαντι καὶ χρησαμένῳ τῇ παρὰ τοῦ νόμου ἐξουσίᾳ καὶ ἀποπληρώ-
σαντι τὴν πατρικὴν ταύτην δυναστείαν, εἶτ᾽

[1] διαβολὴν ΓΥΝ(Β): πρὸς διαβολὴν ΖCMF.

DISOWNED

First, I shall begin with the law under which he
wishes to disown me, in order that he may discover
that his power is now no longer what it was before.
The lawgiver, father, has not permitted all to exercise
the privilege of disownment, or upon all sons, or as
often as they choose, or upon all manner of grounds.
On the contrary, just as he has conceded to fathers
the right to exercise such anger, just so he has made
provision in behalf of sons, that they may not suffer it
unjustly; and for that reason he has not allowed the
punishment to be inflicted freely or without trial,
but has ordered men to be summoned to court and
empanelled as investigators who will not be influenced
either by anger or by malice in determining what is
just. For he knew that many people on many
occasions are obsessed by senseless reasons for
anger; that one believes a malicious falsehood, while
another relies upon a servant or an unfriendly female.
It was not his idea, therefore, that the thing should
go untried or that sons should at once lose their case
by default. Water is measured,[1] a hearing is given,
and nothing is left uninvestigated.

Accordingly, since it is within your powers, since
my father controls only the charge, and you who sit
in judgement control the decision whether his accusation is reasonable, do not yet consider his specific
allegation against me and the ground of his present
indignation, but first examine that other point,
whether he should still be allowed to disown a son
when, after once for all disowning him, using the
privilege that derives from the law and exercising to
the full this paternal suzerainty, he has subsequently

[1] Time for speaking is apportioned to each side by the water-
clock (κλέψυδρα).

αὖθις ἀναλαβόντι καὶ λύσαντι τὴν ἀποκήρυξιν.
ἐγὼ μὲν γὰρ ἀδικώτατον εἶναί φημι τὸ τοιοῦτον,
ἀπεράντους γίνεσθαι καὶ[1] τῶν παίδων τὰς
τιμωρίας καὶ πολλὰς τὰς καταδίκας καὶ τὸν
φόβον ἀίδιον καὶ τὸν νόμον ἄρτι μὲν συνοργί-
ζεσθαι, μετὰ μικρὸν δὲ λύεσθαι, καὶ πάλιν ὁμοίως
ἰσχυρὸν εἶναι, καὶ ὅλως ἄνω καὶ κάτω στρέφεσθαι
τὰ δίκαια πρὸς τὸ ἐπὶ καιροῦ δοκοῦν πατράσιν.
ἀλλὰ τὸ μὲν πρῶτον ἄξιον ἐφιέναι καὶ ἀγανα-
κτοῦντι συναγανακτεῖν καὶ κύριον τῆς τιμωρίας
ποιεῖν τὸν γεγεννηκότα· ἢν δὲ ἅπαξ ἀναλώσῃ
τὴν ἐξουσίαν καὶ καταχρήσηται τῷ νόμῳ καὶ
ἐμπλησθῇ τῆς ὀργῆς, εἶτα μετὰ ταῦτα ἀναλάβῃ,
χρηστὸν εἶναι μεταπεισθείς, ἐπὶ τούτων ἀνάγκη
μένειν[2] καὶ μηκέτι μεταπηδᾶν μηδὲ μεταβουλεύε-
σθαι μηδὲ μεταποιεῖν τὴν κρίσιν.

Τοῦ[3] μὲν γὰρ τὸν γεννηθέντα πονηρὸν ἢ χρηστὸν
ἀποβήσεσθαι οὐδέν, οἶμαι, γνώρισμα ἦν, καὶ διὰ
τοῦτο τοὺς ἀναξίους τοῦ γένους παραιτεῖσθαι
συγκεχώρηται τοῖς ὅτε ἠγνόουν ἀναθρεψαμένοις·
10 ὅταν δὲ μὴ κατ᾽ ἀνάγκην ἀλλ᾽ ἐπ᾽ ἐξουσίας
αὐτός τις ἀφ᾽ ἑαυτοῦ[4] καὶ δοκιμάσας ἀναλάβῃ,
τίς ἔτι μηχανὴ μεταβάλλεσθαι, ἢ τίς ἔτι χρῆσις
ὑπόλοιπος τοῦ νόμου; φαίη γὰρ ἂν πρὸς σὲ ὁ
νομοθέτης, " Εἰ πονηρὸς οὗτος ἦν καὶ τοῦ ἀποκη-
ρυχθῆναι ἄξιος, τί παθὼν ἀνεκάλεις ; τί δ᾽
αὖθις ἐπανῆγες ἐς τὴν οἰκίαν ; τί δ᾽ ἔλυες τὸν
νόμον ; ἐλεύθερος γὰρ ἦσθα καὶ τοῦ μὴ ποιεῖν
ταῦτα κύριος. οὐ γὰρ δὴ ἐντρυφᾶν σοι δοτέον

---

[1] καὶ ΓUZNB : κατὰ (C)A, not in F.
[2] μένειν N(Fritzsche) : μὲν μένειν ΓUZ cett.; cf. p. 494, n. 1.
[3] τοῦ N(CM) : τοῦτο ΓUZB.

taken him back again and annulled the disownment.
I say that such a thing is most unjust—for punishments, precisely in the case of children, to be inter-
minable, their condemnations numerous, and their
fear eternal; for the law at one moment to share
the prosecutor's anger, only soon afterward to relax,
and then again to be as severe as before; in a word,
for justice to be altered this way and that to conform
to the momentary opinion of fathers. No, the first
time it is right to give the parent free rein, to share
his anger with him, to make him arbiter of the
punishment; but if, once for all, he expends his
privilege, makes full use of the law, satisfies his anger,
and then afterwards takes back his son, persuaded
that he deserves it, he must abide by it, and not keep
shifting, changing his mind, and altering his decision.

When that son was born there was no way, of
course, to ascertain whether he would turn out to be
bad or good, and on that account the privilege of
repudiating children who are unworthy of their
family has been allowed to their parents, since they
determined to bring them up at a time when they
were unaware of this. When, however, under no con-
straint but able to do as he pleases, a man himself,
of his own motion and after putting his son to
the test, takes him back, what pretext for change of
mind remains, or what further recourse to the law?
The legislator would say to you: " If he was bad and
deserved to be disowned, what made you ask him
back? Why did you readmit him to your house?
Why did you nullify the law? You were free and
at liberty not to do this. Surely it cannot be conceded that you should make sport of the laws and that

---

[4] ἀφ' ἑαυτοῦ Schaefer: ὑφ' ἑαυτοῦ MSS.

τοῖς νόμοις οὐδὲ πρὸς τὰς σὰς μεταβολὰς συνά-
γεσθαι τὰ δικαστήρια, οὐδὲ ἄρτι μὲν λύεσθαι
ἄρτι δὲ κυρίους εἶναι τοὺς νόμους καὶ τοὺς
δικαστὰς καθῆσθαι μάρτυρας, μᾶλλον δὲ ὑπηρέτας,
τῶν σοὶ δοκούντων, ὁτὲ μὲν κολάζοντας ὁτὲ δὲ
διαλλάττοντας, ὁπόταν σοι δοκῇ. ἅπαξ γεγέν-
νηκας, ἅπαξ ἀνατέτραφας, ἅπαξ καὶ τὸ ἀποκηρύττειν ἀντὶ τούτων ἔχεις, καὶ τότε, ἢν δικαίως αὐτὸ
ποιεῖν δοκῇς· τὸ δ' ἄπαυστον τοῦτο καὶ ἀΐδιον
καὶ πολὺ ῥᾴδιον[1] μεῖζον ἤδη τῆς πατρικῆς ἐστιν
ἐξουσίας."

11 Μὴ δή, πρὸς Διός, ὦ ἄνδρες δικασταί, συγχωρή-
σητε αὐτῷ ἑκούσιον τὴν ἀνάληψιν πεποιημένῳ
καὶ λύσαντι τὴν γνῶσιν τοῦ πάλαι δικαστηρίου
καὶ ἀκυρώσαντι τὴν ὀργὴν αὖθις τὴν[2] αὐτὴν
τιμωρίαν ἀνακαλεῖν καὶ ἐπὶ τὴν ἐξουσίαν τὴν
πατρικὴν ἀνατρέχειν, ἧς ἔξωρος ἤδη καὶ ἔωλος
ἡ προθεσμία καὶ μόνῳ τούτῳ ἄκυρος καὶ προδεδα-
πανημένη. ὁρᾶτε γάρ που καὶ ἐν τοῖς ἄλλοις
δικαστηρίοις ὡς ἀπὸ μὲν τῶν κλήρῳ λαχόντων
δικαστῶν, ἤν τις ἄδικον οἴηται γεγενῆσθαι τὴν
κρίσιν, δίδωσιν ὁ νόμος ἐς ἕτερον ἐφεῖναι δικαστή-
ριον· ἢν δέ τινες ἑκόντες αὐτοὶ σύνθωνται δικαστὰς καὶ προελόμενοι ἐπιτρέψωσιν διαιτᾶν, οὐκέτι.
οἷς γὰρ ἐξῆν μηδὲ τὴν ἀρχὴν ἐμμένειν,[3] εἰ τούτους
τις αὐθαίρετος εἵλετο, στέργειν ἐστὶ δίκαιος τοῖς
ἐγνωσμένοις. οὕτω δὴ καὶ σύ, ὃν ἐξῆν μηκέτ'
ἀναλαμβάνειν εἰ ἀνάξιος[4] ἐδόκει τοῦ γένους,
τοῦτον εἰ χρηστὸν ἡγησάμενος εἶναι πάλιν ἀνείλη-

---

[1] πολὺ ῥᾴδιον ΓΖ: πολὺ καὶ ῥᾴδιον other MSS.; cf. Dial.
Mer., 9, 3, πολὺ ἀφόρητος.
[2] αὖθις ἐπὶ τὴν MSS.: ἐπὶ excised by Fritzsche.

the courts should be convened to suit your changes
of mind, that the laws should be relaxed one moment
and enforced the next and the jurors sit to register,
or rather to execute, your decisions, inflicting a
penalty at one time, bringing you together at another,
as often as it shall please you. You begat him
once for all, you brought him up once for all, and
have once for all, in return for this, the power to
disown him, and then only if you are held to be
doing it justly. This persistence, this interminability, this prodigious casualness is beyond the legal
right of a father."

In Heaven's name, gentlemen of the jury, do not
permit him, once he has effected the reinstatement
of his own free will, set aside the decision of the
former court, and nullified his anger, to reinvoke the
same penalty and to recur to the right of a father
when its term by now is over and done with, inoperative in his case alone because it is already used
up. You perceive, surely, that in all courts where
jurors are drawn by lot, if a man thinks that the
verdict is unjust, the law allows him to appeal from
them to another tribunal; but if people have themselves of their own accord agreed upon jurors and
willingly committed the arbitrament to them, that is
not then the case. For there was no need to consult
them at all; but if a man has selected them of his own
choice, he ought to remain content with their decision.
So it is with you : a son who seemed to you unworthy
of his lineage need never have been taken back, but
one whom you have pronounced good and taken

---

[3] The sense seems to require ἐπιτρέψαι.
[4] εἰ ἀνάξιος N : εἰ μὴ ἀνάξιος other MSS.

φας, οὐκέτ᾽ ἀποκηρύττειν ἕξεις· ὅτι γὰρ οὐκ
ἄξιος αὖθις παθεῖν ταῦτα, ὑπ᾽ αὐτοῦ σοῦ μεμαρ-
τύρηται καὶ χρηστὸς ἤδη ἀνωμολόγηται. ἀμετα-
νόητον οὖν τὴν ἀνάληψιν καὶ τὴν διαλλαγὴν βέβαιον
εἶναι προσήκει μετὰ κρίσιν οὕτω πολλὴν καὶ δύο
δικαστήρια, ἐν μὲν¹ τὸ πρῶτον, ἐφ᾽ οὗ παρῃτήσω,
δεύτερον δὲ τὸ σόν, ὅτε μετεβουλεύσω καὶ ἀνά-
δαστον ἐποίησας· τὰ πρότερον ἐγνωσμένα λύσας
βεβαιοῖς τὰ μετ᾽ ἐκεῖνα βεβουλευμένα. μένε
τοίνυν ἐπὶ τῶν τελευταίων καὶ φύλαττε τὴν σαυτοῦ
κρίσιν· πατέρα σε εἶναι δεῖ· τοῦτο γὰρ ἔδοξέ
σοι, τοῦτ᾽ ἐδοκίμασας, τοῦτ᾽ ἐκύρωσας.

12 Ἐγὼ μὲν οὐδ᾽ εἰ μὴ φύσει παῖς ἦν, θέμενος
δὲ ἀποκηρύττειν ἤθελες, ἐξεῖναι ἄν σοι ᾠόμην·
ὃ γὰρ τὴν ἀρχὴν μὴ ποιεῖν δυνατὸν ἦν, τοῦτ᾽
ἄδικον λύειν ἅπαξ γενόμενον. τὸν δὲ καὶ φύσει
καὶ αὖθις προαιρέσει καὶ γνώμῃ ἐσπεποιημένον,
πῶς εὔλογον αὖθις ἀπωθεῖσθαι καὶ πολλάκις τῆς
μιᾶς οἰκειότητος ἀποστερεῖν ; εἰ δ᾽ οἰκέτης ὢν
ἐτύγχανον, καὶ τὸ μὲν πρῶτον πονηρὸν οἰόμενος
ἐπέδησας, μεταπεισθεὶς δὲ ὡς οὐδὲν ἠδίκουν
ἐλεύθερον ἀφῆκας εἶναι, ἆρ᾽ ἄν σοι πρὸς καιρὸν
ὀργισθέντι αὖθις ἐξῆν ἐς τὴν ὁμοίαν δουλείαν
ἐπανάγειν ; οὐδαμῶς. τὰ γὰρ τοιαῦτα βέβαια καὶ
διὰ παντὸς κύρια ὑπάρχειν οἱ νόμοι ἀξιοῦσιν.

Ὑπὲρ μὲν οὖν τοῦ μηκέτι ἐξεῖναι τούτῳ ἀποκηρύττειν ὃν ἅπαξ ἀποκηρύξας ἑκὼν ἀνέλαβεν
13 ἔτι πολλὰ εἰπεῖν ἔχων ὅμως παύσομαι. σκέψασθε
δὲ ἤδη ὅντινα ὄντα καὶ ἀποκηρύξει² καὶ οὐ δή

---

¹ μὲν N(BCM) : μὲν εἰ ΓΖ, μένει U.
² MSS. have με either after ὄντα (A) or after ἀποκηρύξει :
it is better out.

back again you will not thereafter be able to disown;
for you yourself have borne witness that he does not
deserve to undergo this again, and have acknowledged
that he is good. It is fitting, therefore, that his
reinstatement should be irrevocable and the re-
conciliation binding after deliberation so oft-repeated,
and two sessions of court, one (the first) in which
you repudiated him, the other (your own) when you
changed your mind and undid it. By setting aside
the earlier decision you have guaranteed your later
determination. Abide, then, by your latest purpose
and maintain your own verdict; you must be a
father, for that is what you decided, what you
approved, what you ratified.

Even if I were not your own son, but adopted, and
you wished to disown me, I should not think you
could; for what it was possible not to do at all, it is
unjust to undo once it has taken place. But when
a son has been got by birth, and then again by choice
and decision, how is it reasonable to put him away
again and deprive him repeatedly of that single
relationship? If I happened to be a slave, and at
first, thinking me vicious, you had put me in irons,
but on becoming convinced that I was not a wrong-
doer you had let me go and set me free, would it be
in your power, if you became angry on occasion, to
bring me back into the same condition of slavery? By
no means, for the laws require that such pacts should
be permanent and under all circumstances valid.

Upon the point that it is no longer in his power to
disown one whom he has once disowned and then of
his own accord taken back I still have much to say;
nevertheless, I shall make an end. But consider
what manner of man he will now be disowning. I do

THE WORKS OF LUCIAN

που τοῦτό φημι, ὡς τότε μὲν ἰδιώτην, νῦν δὲ
ἰατρόν· οὐδὲν γὰρ ἂν πρὸς τοῦτο ἡ τέχνη συναγω-
νίσαιτο· οὐδ' ὅτι τότε μὲν νέον, νῦν δὲ ἤδη καὶ
προβεβηκότα καὶ τὸ πιστὸν τοῦ μηδὲν ἀδικῆσαι
ἂν παρὰ τῆς ἡλικίας ἔχοντα· μικρὸν γὰρ ἴσως καὶ
τοῦτο. ἀλλὰ τότε μέν, εἰ καὶ μηδὲν ἠδικημένος,
ὡς ἂν ἔγωγε φαίην, ἀλλ' οὐδὲ εὖ πεπονθὼς παρῃ-
τεῖτο τῆς οἰκίας, νῦν δὲ σωτῆρα ἔναγχος καὶ εὐεργέτην γεγενημένον. οὗ τί γένοιτ' ἂν ἀχαριστότερον,
σωθέντα δι' ἐμὲ καὶ τηλικοῦτον κίνδυνον διαπεφευγότα τοῖς τοιούτοις εὐθὺς ἀμείβεσθαι, τῆς
θεραπείας ἐκείνης οὐδένα λόγον ἔχοντα, ἀλλ'
οὕτω ῥᾳδίως ἐπιλελῆσθαι καὶ ἐπὶ τὴν ἐρημίαν
ἐλαύνειν τὸν ἐφησθέντ' ἂν δικαίως ἐφ' οἷς ἀδίκως
ἐξεβέβλητο, μὴ μόνον δ' οὐ[1] μνησικακήσαντα,
ἀλλὰ καὶ σώσαντα καὶ σωφρονεῖν παρασκευά-
σαντα;

14 Οὐ γὰρ σμικρόν, ὦ ἄνδρες δικασταί, οὐδὲ τὸ
τυχὸν εὖ πεποιηκὼς αὐτόν, ὅμως τῶν τοιούτων
νῦν ἀξιοῦμαι. ἀλλ' εἰ καὶ οὗτος ἀγνοεῖ τὰ τότε,
πάντες ὑμεῖς ἴστε οἷα ποιοῦντα αὐτὸν καὶ πάσχοντα καὶ ὅπως διακείμενον ἐγὼ παραλαβών,
τῶν μὲν ἄλλων ἰατρῶν ἀπεγνωκότων, τῶν δὲ
οἰκείων φευγόντων καὶ μηδὲ πλησίον προσιέναι
τολμώντων, τοιοῦτον ἀπέφηνα ὡς καὶ κατηγορεῖν
δύνασθαι καὶ περὶ τῶν νόμων διαλέγεσθαι. μᾶλλον
δέ, ὁρᾷς, ὦ πάτερ, τὸ παράδειγμα· τοιοῦτον ὄντα
σε παρ' ὀλίγον οἷα νῦν ἡ γυνή ἐστιν, πρὸς τὴν
ἀρχαίαν φρόνησιν ἐπανήγαγον. οὐ δὴ δίκαιον
τοιαύτην μοι γενέσθαι ἀντ' ἐκείνων τὴν ἀμοιβὴν

[1] δ' οὐ ed. Flor., οὐ MSS.

496

not mean that then I was but a layman, whereas
now I am a physician, for my profession would avail
me nothing in this respect. Nor that then I was
young, whereas now I am well on in years and
derive from my age the right to have it believed
that I would do no wrong; for that too is perhaps
trivial. But at that time, even if he had suffered
no wrong, as I should maintain, yet he had received
no benefit from me when he excluded me from the
house; whereas now I have recently been his saviour
and benefactor. What could be more ungrateful
than that, after he had been saved through me and
had escaped so great a danger, he should at once
make return in this way, taking no account of that
cure; nay, should so easily forget and try to drive
into loneliness a man who, when he might justly
have exulted over those who had unjustly cast
him out, not only had borne him no grudge but
actually had saved his life and made him sound of
mind?

It is no trifling or commonplace benefit, gentlemen
of the jury, that I have conferred upon him; and
yet I am accounted worthy of treatment like this.
Although he himself does not know what happened
then, you all know how he acted and felt and what his
condition was when, taking him in hand after the
other doctors had given up, while the members of
the family were avoiding him and not venturing
even to approach him, I made him what you see him,
so that he is able to bring charges and argue about the
laws. Stay! you can see your counterpart, father;
you were nearly as your wife is now, when I brought
you back to your former sanity. Truly it is not just
that I should receive such a recompense for it, or that

οὐδὲ κατ' ἐμοῦ σε μόνου σωφρονεῖν· ὅτι γὰρ μὴ
μικρὰ ὑπ' ἐμοῦ εὐηργέτησαι, καὶ ἀπ' αὐτῶν ὧν
ἐγκαλεῖς δῆλόν ἐστιν· ὃν [1] γὰρ ὡς ἐν ἐσχάτοις
οὖσαν τὴν γυναῖκα καὶ παμπονήρως ἔχουσαν
οὐκ ἰώμενον μισεῖς, πῶς οὐ πολὺ μᾶλλον ὅτι σε
τῶν ὁμοίων ἀπήλλαξα ὑπεραγαπᾷς καὶ χάριν
ὁμολογεῖς, τῶν οὕτω δεινῶν ἀπηλλαγμένος ; σὺ
δέ, ὅπερ ἀγνωμονέστατον, σωφρονήσας εὐθὺς ἐς
δικαστήριον ἄγεις καὶ σεσωσμένος κολάζεις καὶ ἐπὶ
τὸ ἀρχαῖον ἐκεῖνο μῖσος ἀνατρέχεις καὶ τὸν αὐτὸν
ἀναγινώσκεις νόμον. καλὸν γοῦν τὸν μισθὸν
ἀποδίδως τῇ τέχνῃ καὶ ἀξίας ἀμοιβὰς τῶν φαρμάκων ἐπὶ τὸν ἰατρὸν ὑγιαίνων μόνον.

15 Ὑμεῖς δέ, ὦ ἄνδρες δικασταί, τὸν εὐεργέτην
τούτῳ κολάζειν ἐπιτρέψετε καὶ τὸν σώσαντα
ἐξελαύνειν καὶ τὸν σωφρονίσαντα μισεῖν καὶ τὸν
ἀναστήσαντα τιμωρεῖσθαι ; οὔκ, ἤν γε τὰ δίκαια
ποιῆτε. καὶ γὰρ εἰ τὰ μέγιστα νῦν ἁμαρτάνων
ἐτύγχανον, ἦν μοί τις οὐ μικρὰ προσοφειλομένη
χάρις, ἐς ἣν ἀποβλέποντα τοῦτον καὶ ἧς μεμνη-
μένον καλῶς εἶχε τῶν μὲν παρόντων καταφρονεῖν,
δι' ἐκεῖνα δὲ πρόχειρον τὴν συγγνώμην ἔχειν,
καὶ μάλιστα εἰ τηλικαύτη τις ἡ εὐεργεσία τυγχάνοι
ὡς πάντα ὑπερπαίειν τὰ μετὰ ταῦτα. ὅπερ
οἶμαι κἀμοὶ πρὸς τοῦτον ὑπάρχειν, ὃν ἔσωσα,
καὶ ὃς τοῦ βίου παντὸς χρεώστης ἐστί μοι, καὶ
ᾧ τὸ εἶναι καὶ τὸ σωφρονεῖν καὶ τὸ συνιέναι
παρέσχημαι, καὶ μάλιστα ὅτε οἱ ἄλλοι πάντες
ἤδη ἀπεγνώκεσαν καὶ ἥττους εἶναι ὡμολόγουν τῆς
νόσου.

16 Τοῦτο γὰρ μείζω οἶμαι ποιεῖν τὴν ἐμὴν εὐερ-

[1] ὃν N : ὃς ΓUZB.

you should employ your reason only against me. That I have done you no little good is clear from the very charges which you bring; you hate me because I do not cure your wife when she is at the end of everything and in an utterly wretched plight. Since I freed you from a similar condition, why are you not far rather overjoyed and thankful to have been liberated from a state so terrible? Instead, and it is most ungrateful—you no sooner recover your sanity than you bring me to court and after your life has been saved, seek to punish me, reverting to that old-time hatred and citing the self-same law. It is a handsome fee, in truth, that you pay in this manner to the art of healing, and a fitting price for your medicines, to employ your sanity only to attack your physician!

Will you, gentlemen of the jury, empower this man to punish his benefactor, to banish his saviour, to hate the one who made him sane, to take vengeance on the one who set him on his feet? Not if you do what is just. For if I were really now guilty of the greatest offences, there was no slight gratitude owing me previously; keeping this in sight and in mind, he would have done well to ignore the present and to be prompt to forgive for the sake of the past, especially if the benefaction were so great as to overtop everything subsequent. That, I think, is true of mine toward this man, whom I saved, who is my debtor for the whole of his life, to whom I have given existence, sanity, and intelligence, and that at a time when all the others had finally given up and were confessing themselves defeated by the malady.

My benefaction, I think, is the greater because,

γεσίαν, ὃς οὔτε υἱὸς ὢν τότε οὔτε ἀναγκαίαν τῆς
θεραπείας ἔχων αἰτίαν ἀλλὰ ἐλεύθερος καθεστὼς
καὶ ἀλλότριος, τῆς φυσικῆς αἰτίας ἀφειμένος, ὅμως
οὐ περιεῖδον, ἀλλ' ἐθελοντής, ἄκλητος, αὐτεπάγ-
γελτος ἧκον· ἐβοήθησα, προσελιπάρησα, ἰασά-
μην, ἀνέστησα, καὶ τὸν πατέρα ἐμαυτῷ διεφύλαξα,
καὶ ὑπὲρ τῆς ἀποκηρύξεως ἀπελογησάμην, καὶ
τῇ εὐνοίᾳ τὴν ὀργὴν ἔπαυσα, καὶ τὸν νόμον ἔλυσα
τῇ φιλοστοργίᾳ, καὶ μεγάλῃ σεὐεργεσίας τὴν ἐς τὸ
γένος ἐπάνοδον ἐπριάμην, καὶ ἐν οὕτως ἐπισφαλεῖ
καιρῷ τὴν πρὸς τὸν πατέρα πίστιν ἐπεδειξάμην,
καὶ μετὰ τῆς τέχνης ἐμαυτὸν ἐσεποίησα, καὶ
γνήσιος υἱὸς ἐν τοῖς δεινοῖς ἀνεφάνην.

Πόσα γὰρ οἴεσθε παθεῖν με, πόσα καμεῖν
παρόντα, ὑπηρετοῦντα, καιροφυλακοῦντα, νῦν μὲν
εἴκοντα τῇ τοῦ πάθους ἀκμῇ, νῦν δὲ τὴν τέχνην
ἐπάγοντα πρὸς ὀλίγον ἐνδιδόντος τοῦ κακοῦ;
ἔστιν δὲ τῶν ὄντων ἁπάντων τούτων ἐν τῇ ἰατρικῇ
τὸ ἐπισφαλέστατον τοὺς τοιούτους ἰᾶσθαι καὶ
πλησιάζειν οὕτω διακειμένοις· ἐς γὰρ τοὺς
πλησίον πολλάκις ἀφιᾶσι τὴν λύτταν, ἐπιζέσαντος
τοῦ πάθους. καὶ ὅμως πρὸς οὐδὲν τούτων ἀπώκνησα οὐδὲ ἀπεδειλίασα, συνὼν δὲ καὶ πάντα
τρόπον ἀντεξεταζόμενος τῇ νόσῳ τὸ τελευταῖον
ἐκράτησα τῷ φαρμάκῳ.

17 Μὴ γὰρ τοῦτ' ἀκούσας εὐθὺς ὑπολάβῃ τις
" Ποῖος δὲ ἢ πόσος ὁ κάματος ἐγχέαι φάρμακον; "
πολλὰ γὰρ πρὸ τούτου γενέσθαι δεῖ, καὶ προοδο-
ποιῆσαι τῇ πόσει καὶ προπαρασκευάσαι ῥᾴδιον

although I was not his son at that time and had no
imperative reason to take the case but was free
and independent, having been released from the
responsibility imposed by nature, nevertheless I was
not indifferent but came voluntarily, unsummoned,
on my own initiative ; I gave my assistance, lavished
my attentions, brought about a cure, and set my
father on his feet, preserving him for myself, pleading
my own cause against his disownment, stilling his
anger by my friendliness, annulling the law by my
love, purchasing by a great benefaction my re-
entrance into the family, demonstrating my loyalty
to my father at a crisis so dangerous, bringing about
my own adoption with the help of my profession, and
proving myself a legitimate son in his time of dire
need.

What do you suppose my sufferings were, what my
exertions, to be with him, to wait upon him, to watch
my opportunity, now yielding to the full force of the
ailment, now bringing my professional skill to bear
when the disorder abated a little ? And truly, of all
these duties that are included in medical science,
the most dangerous is to treat such patients and to
approach people in that condition, for often they
loose their frenzy upon those who are near them,
when their ailment has become severe. And yet
none of these considerations made me hesitant or
faint-hearted. I joined battle with the disease and
measured myself against it in every way, and so at
last prevailed by means of my remedy.

Let no one, hearing this, be quick to remark :
" What sort of feat is it, and how great, to give a
remedy ? " Many things must precede this ; one
must prepare the way for the medicine, make the

ἐς ἴασιν τὸ σῶμα καὶ τῆς ἁπάσης ἕξεως φροντίσαι
κενοῦντα καὶ ἰσχναίνοντα καὶ οἷς χρὴ τρέφοντα καὶ
κινοῦντα ἐς ὅσον χρήσιμον καὶ ὕπνους ἐπινοοῦντα
καὶ ἠρεμίας μηχανώμενον, ἅπερ οἱ μὲν ἄλλο τι
νοσοῦντες ῥᾳδίως πεισθεῖεν ἄν, οἱ μεμηνότες δὲ
διὰ τὴν ἐλευθερίαν τοῦ νοῦ δυσάγωγοι καὶ δυσηνιό-
χητοι καὶ τῷ ἰατρῷ ἐπισφαλεῖς καὶ τῇ θεραπείᾳ
δυσκαταγώνιστοι. ὅταν γοῦν πολλάκις οἰήθωμεν [1]
ἤδη πλησίον γενέσθαι τοῦ τέλους καὶ ἐλπίσωμεν,
ἐμπεσόν τι μικρὸν ἁμάρτημα ἐπακμάσαντος τοῦ
πάθους ἅπαντα ῥᾳδίως ἐκεῖνα ἀνέτρεψε καὶ
ἐνεπόδισε [2] τὴν θεραπείαν καὶ τὴν τέχνην διέ-
σφηλε.

18 Τὸν οὖν ταῦτα πάντα ὑπομεμενηκότα καὶ
οὕτω χαλεπῷ νοσήματι προσπαλαίσαντα καὶ πάθος
ἁπάντων παθῶν τὸ δυσαλωτότατον νενικηκότα
ἔτι τούτῳ ἀποκηρύττειν ἐπιτρέψετε, καὶ τοὺς
νόμους ὡς βούλεται ἑρμηνεύειν κατ᾽ εὐεργέτου
συγχωρήσετε, καὶ τῇ φύσει πολεμεῖν αὐτὸν
ἐάσετε;

Ἐγὼ τῇ φύσει πειθόμενος, ὦ ἄνδρες δικασταί,
σώζω καὶ διαφυλάττω τὸν πατέρα ἐμαυτῷ
κἂν ἀδικῇ· οὑτοσὶ [3] δὲ τὸν εὐεργετηκότα παῖδα
τοῖς νόμοις, ὥς φησιν, ἀκολουθῶν διαφθείρει
καὶ τοῦ γένους ἀποστερεῖ. μισόπαις οὗτος, ἐγὼ
φιλοπάτωρ γίγνομαι· ἐγὼ τὴν φύσιν ἀσπάζομαι,
οὗτος τὰ τῆς φύσεως παρορᾷ καὶ [4] καθυβρίζει
δίκαια.[5] ὦ πατρὸς μισοῦντος ἀδίκως· ὦ παιδὸς
φιλοῦντος ἀδικώτερον. ἐγκαλῶ γὰρ ἐμαυτῷ, τοῦ

[1] οἰήθωμεν W. A. Hirschig: ποιήσωμεν MSS.
[2] ἐνεπόδισε NC: ἀνεπόδισε ΓUZ cett.

body easy to cure, and take thought for the patient's whole condition, purging him, reducing him, nourishing him with the proper foods, rousing him as much as is expedient, planning for periods of sleep, contriving periods of solitude. Those who have any other sickness can readily be persuaded to consent to all this, but the insane because of their independence of spirit are hard to influence and hard to direct, dangerous to the physician, and hard to conquer by the treatment. Often when we think we are near the goal at last and become hopeful, some trivial slip, occurring when the illness has reached its height, easily overturns everything that has been done, hampers the treatment, and thwarts our skill.

When a man has endured all this, has wrestled with an illness so serious, and has conquered the ailment of all ailments most difficult to master, will you empower the plaintiff to disown him again, permit him to interpret the laws in any way he will against a benefactor, and allow him to fight with nature?

I, obeying nature, save and preserve my father for my own sake, gentlemen of the jury, even if he wrongs me; but that father, following, he says, the laws, ruins the son that has done him a benefit, and deprives him of his family. He is his son's enemy, I am my father's friend. I cherish nature, he slights and insults her just claims. To think of a father who hates his son unjustly! To think of a son that loves his father still more unjustly! For I bring it as a charge

---

[3] ἀδικῇ· οὑτοσὶ δὲ Fritzsche: ἀδικῇ οὗτος· εἰ δὲ MSS. But U has a point before οὗτος as well as one after it.

[4] καὶ not in N. Very likely παρορᾷ is intrusive here; cf. p. 504, n. 1.

[5] δίκαια not in C.

πατρὸς ἀναγκάζοντος, ὅτι μισούμενος οὐ δέον
φιλῶ καὶ φιλῶ πλέον ἢ προσῆκεν. καίτοι γε ἡ
φύσις τοῖς πατράσιν τοὺς παῖδας μᾶλλον ἢ τοῖς
παισὶν τοὺς πατέρας ἐπιτάττει φιλεῖν. ἀλλ᾽ οὗτος
ἑκὼν καὶ τοὺς νόμους παρορᾷ,[1] οἳ τοὺς οὐδὲν
ἠδικηκότας παῖδας τῷ γένει φυλάττουσιν, καὶ
τὴν φύσιν, ἣ τοὺς γεννήσαντας ἕλκει πρὸς πόθον
τῶν γεγεννημένων πολύν. οὐχ ὅπως μείζους
ἀρχὰς εὐνοίας ἔχων πρὸς ἐμὲ μείζονα τὰ δίκαιά
μοι τῆς εὐνοίας ἐσφέρει καὶ ἐπιδίδωσιν, ἢ τό γε
ἔλαττον ἐμὲ μιμεῖται καὶ ζηλοῖ τοῦ φίλτρου·
ἀλλ᾽, οἴμοι τῆς συμφορᾶς, προσέτι καὶ μισεῖ
φιλοῦντα καὶ ἀγαπῶντα ἐλαύνει καὶ εὐεργετοῦντα
ἀδικεῖ καὶ ἀσπαζόμενον ἀποκηρύττει, καὶ τοὺς
φιλόπαιδας νόμους ὡς μισόπαιδας κατ᾽ ἐμοῦ
μεταχειρίζεται. ὢ μάχης ἣν ἐσάγεις, πάτερ, τοῖς
νόμοις κατὰ τῆς φύσεως.

19   Οὐκ ἔστι ταῦτα, οὐκ ἔστιν ὡς θέλεις· κακῶς
ἑρμηνεύεις, ὦ πάτερ, καλῶς κειμένους τοὺς
νόμους. οὐ πολεμεῖ φύσις καὶ νόμος ἐν ταῖς
εὐνοίαις, ἀλλ᾽ ἀκολουθοῦσιν ἀλλήλοις ἐνταῦθα καὶ
συναγωνίζονται τῇ λύσει τῶν ἀδικημάτων. ὑβρίζεις τὸν εὐεργέτην, ἀδικεῖς τὴν φύσιν. τί καὶ
τοὺς νόμους συναδικεῖς τῇ φύσει ; οὓς καλοὺς
καὶ δικαίους καὶ φιλόπαιδας εἶναι θέλοντας οὐ
συγχωρεῖς, καθ᾽ ἑνὸς παιδὸς ὡς κατὰ πολλῶν
κινῶν πολλάκις καὶ ἡσυχάζειν οὐκ ἐῶν ἐν ταῖς
τιμωρίαις τοὺς ἐν ταῖς τῶν παίδων πρὸς τοὺς
πατέρας εὐνοίαις ἡσυχάζειν ἐθέλοντας, καίτοι
γε ἐπὶ τοῖς μηδὲν ἡμαρτηκόσιν μηδὲ κειμένους.
καὶ μὴν οἵ γε νόμοι καὶ ἀχαριστίας δικάζεσθαι

----

[1] παρορᾷ omitted in ΓΖ.

against myself, since my father constrains me to do so, that I who am hated love when I should not and love more than I ought. Yet it is nature's behest that fathers love their sons more than sons their fathers. He, however, deliberately slights even the laws, which preserve for the family sons who have done no wrong, as well as nature, who draws parents into great affection for their children. It cannot be said that, having exceptional grounds for good-will towards me, he pays me exceptional dues of good-will and runs the measure over, or that at least he imitates and rivals me in my love; no, alas! he even hates one who loves him, repels one who cherishes him, injures one who helps him, and disowns one who clings to him. Aye, though the laws are kindly to children, he employs them against me as if they were unkindly. Ah, what a conflict you wish to precipitate, father, between the laws and nature!

Truly, truly, this matter is not as you will have it to be. You ill interpret the laws, father, for they are well made. Nature and law are not at war in the matter of good-will; they go hand in hand there, and work together for the righting of wrongs. You mistreat your benefactor; you wrong nature. Why wrong the laws, as well as nature? They mean to be good, and just, and kindly to children, but you will not allow it, inciting them repeatedly against one son as if his name were legion, and not suffering them to rest contented with punishments when they are willing to rest contented with demonstrations of filial affection; and yet they were not made, surely, as a menace to those who have done no wrong. Indeed, the laws permit suit to be brought on the charge of ingratitude against persons who do

διδόασιν κατὰ τῶν τοὺς εὐεργέτας μὴ ἀντευ-
ποιούντων. ὁ δὲ πρὸς τῷ μὴ ἀμείβεσθαι καὶ ἐπ'
αὐτοῖς οἷς πέπονθε[1] κολάζειν ἀξιῶν, σκέψασθε
εἴ τινα ὑπερβολὴν ἀδικίας ἀπολέλοιπεν.

Ὡς μὲν οὖν οὔτε ἀποκηρύττειν ἔτι τούτῳ
ἔξεστιν ἅπαξ ἤδη τὴν πατρικὴν ἐξουσίαν ἀποπληρώ-
σαντι καὶ χρησαμένῳ τοῖς νόμοις, οὔτε ἄλλως
δίκαιον εὐεργέτην ἐς τὰ τηλικαῦτα γεγενημένον
ἀπωθεῖσθαι καὶ τῆς οἰκίας παραιτεῖσθαι, ἱκανῶς,
20 οἶμαι, δέδεικται. ἤδη δὲ καὶ ἐπ' αὐτὴν τὴν
αἰτίαν ἔλθωμεν τῆς ἀποκηρύξεως καὶ τὸ ἔγκλημα ἐξετάσωμεν ὁποῖόν ἐστιν. ἀνάγκη δὲ αὖθις
ἐπὶ τὴν γνώμην ἀναδραμεῖν τοῦ νομοθέτου· ἵνα
γάρ σοι τοῦτο πρὸς ὀλίγον δῶμεν, τὸ ἐξεῖναι
ὁσάκις ἂν θέλῃς ἀποκηρύττειν, καὶ κατά γε τοῦ
εὐεργέτου προσέτι τὴν ἐξουσίαν ταύτην συγχωρή-
σωμεν, οὐχ ἁπλῶς, οἶμαι, οὐδὲ ἐπὶ πάσαις αἰτίαις
ἀποκηρύξεις. οὐδὲ τοῦθ' ὁ νομοθέτης φησίν,
ὅ τι ἂν τύχῃ ὁ πατὴρ αἰτιασάμενος, ἀποκηρυτ-
τέτω, καὶ ἀπόχρη θελῆσαι μόνον καὶ μέμψασθαι.
τί γὰρ ἂν ἔδει δικαστηρίου ; ἀλλ' ἐν ὑμῖν[2] ποιεῖ
τοῦτο, ὦ ἄνδρες δικασταί, σκοπεῖν εἴτε ἐπὶ μεγά-
λοις καὶ δικαίοις ὁ πατὴρ ὀργίζεται εἴτε καὶ μή.
οὐκοῦν τοῦτο ἤδη ἐξετάσατε. ἄρξομαι δὲ ἀπὸ
τῶν μετὰ τὴν μανίαν εὐθύς.

---

[1] οἷς εὖ πέπονθε (MF) edd.
[2] ἐν ὑμῖν Harmon (ἐφ' ὑμῖν Madvig): ὑμῖν MSS. (ὑμᾶς N).

---

[1] The existence of a law making ingratitude (ἀχαριστία)
actionable was part of the accepted tradition of the Greek
rhetorical schools (Sopater in Walz, *Rhetores Graeci*, VIII,
175 and 239; Cyrus, *ibid.*, 391; cf. Seneca, *de Benef.*, III, 6, 1).
For its existence outside the schools the evidence is conflict-

not help those who have helped them.[1]   But when a
man, besides failing to render like for like, even
deems it right to inflict punishment in return for
the very benefits that he has received, think whether
there is any exaggeration of injustice which he has
overlooked!

That it is neither possible for him to disown a
son after having already once for all exhausted his
paternal right and made use of the laws, nor yet just
to thrust away one who has shown himself so great
a benefactor and exclude him from the house has
been, I think, sufficiently established.   Therefore
let us now come to the ground of disownment and
let us see what the nature of the charge is.   It is
necessary to recur once more to the intent of the
lawgiver; for, suppose we grant you briefly the
right to disown as often as you wish and also concede
you this right even against your benefactor, you are
not to disown casually, I take it, or for any and every
cause.   The lawgiver does not say that the father
may disown for any reason that he may chance to
allege—that it is enough just to express the wish
and find a fault.   Else why should we need a court?
No, he commits it to you, gentlemen of the jury,
to consider whether the father's anger is based upon
just and sufficient grounds or not.   This, then, is
what you should now look into.   And I shall begin
with what immediately followed his insanity.

ing.   The name of the action is included in the list given by
Pollux, VIII, 31, and Valerius Maximus (V, 3, ext. 3) says that
Athens had such a law.   On the other hand, Xenophon
puts into the mouth of Socrates (*Mem.*, II, 2, 13; cf. *Cyrop.* I,
2, 7) the statement that Athens took no cognisance of ingratitude except toward parents, and Seneca (*loc. cit.*) says that
no nation except the Macedonians had a law against it.

21 Τὰ μὲν δὴ πρῶτα τῆς σωφροσύνης τοῦ πατρὸς
λύσις ἦν τῆς ἀποκηρύξεως, καὶ σωτὴρ καὶ εὐεργέτης
καὶ πάντα ἦν ἐγώ. καὶ οὐδέν, οἶμαι, τούτοις
ἔγκλημα προσεῖναι ἐδύνατο. τὰ μετὰ ταῦτα δέ, τί
τῶν πάντων αἰτιᾷ; τίνα θεραπείαν, τίνα ἐπιμέλειαν
υἱοῦ παρῆκα; πότε ἀπόκοιτος ἐγενόμην; τίνας
πότους ἀκαίρους, τίνας κώμους ἐγκαλεῖς; τίς
ἀσωτία; τίς πορνοβοσκὸς ὕβρισται; τίς ᾐτιάσατο; οὐδὲ εἷς. καὶ μὴν ταῦτ' ἐστὶν ἐφ' οἷς
μάλιστα ὁ νόμος ἀποκηρύττειν ἐφίησιν.

" Ἀλλὰ νοσεῖν ἤρξατο ἡ μητρυιά." τί οὖν;
ἐμοὶ τοῦτ' ἐγκαλεῖς καὶ νόσου δίκην ἀπαιτεῖς;
22 " οὔ," φησίν. ἀλλὰ τί; " θεραπεύειν προστατ-
τόμενος οὐ θέλεις, καὶ διὰ τοῦτ' ἄξιος ἂν εἴης
ἀποκηρύξεως ἀπειθῶν τῷ πατρί." ἐγὼ δὲ τὸ
μὲν οἷα προστάττοντι αὐτῷ ὑπακούειν οὐ δυνάμενος ἀπειθεῖν δοκῶ πρὸς ὀλίγον ὑπερθήσομαι·
πρότερον δὲ ἁπλῶς ἐκεῖνό φημι, ὡς οὐ πάντα
προστάττειν οὔτε τούτῳ δίδωσιν ὁ νόμος οὔτ'
ἐμοὶ τὸ πείθεσθαι πᾶσιν πάντως ἀναγκαῖον. ἐν
δ' οὖν τοῖς τῶν προσταγμάτων τὰ μὲν ἀνεύθυνά
ἐστιν, τὰ δὲ ὀργῆς καὶ τιμωρίας ἄξια. ἐὰν νοσῇς
αὐτός, ἐγὼ δὲ ἀμελῶ· ἐὰν τῶν κατ' οἶκον ἐπι-
μελεῖσθαι κελεύῃς, ἐγὼ δὲ ὀλιγωρῶ· ἐὰν τὰ κατ'
ἀγρὸν ἐπισκοπεῖν προστάττῃς, ἐγὼ δὲ ὀκνῶ·
πάντα ταῦτα καὶ τὰ τοιαῦτα εὐλόγους ἔχει τὰς
προφάσεις καὶ τὰς μέμψεις πατρικάς. τὰ δὲ
ἄλλα ἐφ' ἡμῖν ἐστιν τοῖς παισίν, ὄντα τῶν τεχνῶν
καὶ τῆς τούτων χρήσεως, καὶ μάλιστα εἰ μηδὲν ὁ
πατὴρ αὐτὸς ἀδικοῖτο. ἐπεί τοι ἂν τῷ γραφεῖ[1]

[1] τῷ γραφεῖ (MC)A, ed. Flor.: τῳ γράφειν ΓUZNB.

DISOWNED

The first act of his sanity was to set aside the disownment, and I was a saviour, a benefactor, all in all to him. No charge, I take it, could go with that. And as to what followed, what do you censure in all of it? What service, what attention proper to a son did I omit? When did I sleep away from home? Of what ill-timed carouses, of what riotous revels do you accuse me? What licentiousness has there been? What pander have I assaulted? Who has filed any charges? Nobody at all. Yet these are the deeds for which the law especially sanctions disownment.

" No, but your stepmother began to be ill." Well, do you accuse me of that, and demand satisfaction for the illness? "No," he says. What, then? " That when you are ordered to treat her, you do not consent; and on that account would merit disownment for disobeying your father." Deferring for a moment the question what sort of orders on his part, when I cannot obey them, cause me to be considered disobedient, I first assert simply that the law does not allow him to issue all orders, and that I am not obliged to obey all orders under all circumstances. In the matter of commands, sometimes disobedience is unexceptionable, sometimes it justifies anger and punishment. If you yourself are ill, and I am indifferent; if you bid me manage the household, and I am neglectful; if you direct me to oversee the estate, and I am indiligent—all this and the like of it affords reasonable grounds for a father's censure. But these other matters are within the discretion of us children, belonging as they do to our callings and the exercise of them; particularly if the father himself is in no way wronged. For

THE WORKS OF LUCIAN

πατὴρ προστάττῃ, "ταῦτα μέν, τέκνον, γράφε,
ταυτὶ δὲ μή," καὶ τῷ μουσικῷ, "τήνδε μὲν τὴν
ἁρμονίαν κροῦε, ταύτην δὲ μή," καὶ τῷ χαλ-
κεύοντι, "τοιαῦτα μὲν χάλκευε, τοιαῦτα δὲ μή,"
ἆρ' ἄν τις ἀνάσχοιτο ἀποκηρύττοντα, ὅτι μὴ κατὰ
τὰ ἐκείνῳ δοκοῦντα ὁ παῖς χρῆται τῇ τέχνῃ;
οὐδὲ εἷς, οἶμαι.

23 Τὸ δὲ τῆς ἰατρικῆς ὅσῳ σεμνότερόν ἐστιν καὶ
τῷ βίῳ χρησιμώτερον, τοσούτῳ καὶ ἐλευθεριώ-
τερον εἶναι προσήκει τοῖς χρωμένοις, καί τινα
προνομίαν ἔχειν τὴν τέχνην δίκαιον τῇ ἐξουσίᾳ
τῆς χρήσεως, ἀναγκάζεσθαι δὲ μηδὲν μηδὲ προσ-
τάττεσθαι πρᾶγμα ἱερὸν καὶ θεῶν παίδευμα καὶ
ἀνθρώπων σοφῶν ἐπιτήδευμα, μηδ' ὑπὸ δουλείαν
γενέσθαι νόμου μηδ' ὑπὸ ψῆφον[1] καὶ τιμωρίαν
δικαστηρίου, μηδὲ ὑπὸ φόβον[2] καὶ πατρὸς ἀπειλὴν
καὶ ὀργὴν ἰδιωτικήν. ὥστε καὶ εἰ τοῦτό σοι
σαφῶς οὑτωσὶ καὶ διαρρήδην ἔλεγον, "Οὐ βούλομαι οὐδὲ θεραπεύω δυνάμενος, ἀλλ' ἐμαυτῷ
μόνῳ τὴν τέχνην οἶδα καὶ πατρί, τοῖς δὲ ἄλλοις
ἅπασιν ἰδιώτης εἶναι βούλομαι," τίς τύραννος
οὕτω βίαιος ὡς ἀναγκάσαι ἂν καὶ ἄκοντα χρῆσθαι
τῇ τέχνῃ; τὰ γὰρ τοιαῦτα ἱκετείαις καὶ δεήσεσιν,
οὐ νόμοις καὶ ὀργαῖς καὶ δικαστηρίοις ὑπάγειν,
οἶμαι, προσήκει· πείθεσθαι τὸν ἰατρὸν χρή,
οὐ κελεύεσθαι· βούλεσθαι, οὐ φοβεῖσθαι· ἐπὶ τὴν
θεραπείαν οὐκ ἄγεσθαι, ἑκόντα δὲ ἐρχόμενον
ἥδεσθαι.[3] πατρικῆς δὲ ἀνάγκης ἄμοιρος ἡ τέχνη,[4]

[1] ψῆφον K. G. P. Schwarz: φόβον MSS.
[2] φόβον K. G. P. Schwarz: ψῆφον MSS.
[3] εὐχόμενον ἰδέσθαι Γ¹Ζ¹.

510

really, if a scribe's father gives him the order,
"Write this, my boy, not that," or a musician's
father, "Play this tune, not that," or a copper-
smith's father, "Forge things like this, not like that,"
would anyone put up with his disowning his son
because the son does not exercise his calling in
accordance with the views of the father? No one,
I think.

In the case of the medical profession, the more
distinguished it is and the more serviceable to the
world, the more unrestricted it should be for those
who practise it. It is only just that the art of healing should carry with it some privilege in respect to
the liberty of practising it; that no compulsion and
no commands should be put upon a holy calling,
taught by the gods and exercised by men of learning; that it should not be subject to enslavement
by the law, or to voting and judicial punishment, or
to fear and a father's threats and a layman's wrath.
Consequently, if I were to say to you, as clearly and
expressly as this: "I am unwilling to give treatment,
and I do not do so, although I can; my knowledge of
the profession is for my benefit alone and my father's,
and to others I wish to be a layman," what tyrant
so high-handed that he would constrain me to practise
my calling against my will? Such things should, in
my opinion, be amenable to entreaties and suppli-
cations, not to laws and fits of anger and courts: the
physician ought to be persuaded, not ordered; he
ought to be willing, not fearful; he ought not to be
haled to the bedside, but to take pleasure in coming
of his own accord. Surely his calling is exempt
from paternal compulsion in view of the fact that

---

⁴ ἄμοιρος ἀτελὴς ἡ τέχνη MSS. ἀτελὴς is clearly a gloss.

THE WORKS OF LUCIAN

ὅπου γε τοῖς ἰατροῖς καὶ δημοσίᾳ αἱ πόλεις τιμὰς
καὶ προεδρίας καὶ ἀτελείας καὶ προνομίας διδόασιν.
24 Ταῦτα μὲν οὖν ἁπλῶς ἂν εἶχον εἰπεῖν ὑπὲρ τῆς
τέχνης, εἰ καὶ σοῦ διδαξαμένου με καὶ πολλὰ
ἐπιμεληθέντος καὶ ἀναλώσαντος ὡς μάθοιμι πρὸς
μίαν ὅμως θεραπείαν ταύτην, δυνατὴν οὖσαν,
ἀντέλεγον. νυνὶ δὲ κἀκεῖνο ἐννόησον, ὡς παντάπασιν ἄγνωμον ποιεῖς οὐκ ἐῶν με χρῆσθαι μετ'
ἐλευθερίας ἐμῷ κτήματι. ταύτην ἐγὼ τὴν τέχνην οὐχ υἱὸς ὢν σὸς ἐξέμαθον οὐδὲ τῷ σῷ νόμῳ
ὑποκείμενος, καὶ ὅμως αὐτὴν μεμάθηκά σοι—καὶ
πρῶτος αὐτῆς ἀπολέλαυκας—οὐδὲν παρὰ σοῦ πρὸς
τὸ μαθεῖν ἔχων. τίνα διδάσκαλον ἐμισθώσω;
τίνα φαρμάκων παρασκευήν; οὐδ' ἡντιναοῦν·
ἀλλὰ πενόμενος ἐγὼ καὶ τῶν ἀναγκαίων ἀπορού-
μενος καὶ ὑπὸ τῶν διδασκάλων ἐλεούμενος ἐπαι-
δευόμην, καί μοι τοιαῦτα παρὰ τοῦ πατρὸς
ἦν πρὸς τὸ μαθεῖν ἐφόδια, λύπη καὶ ἐρημία καὶ
ἀπορία καὶ μῖσος οἰκείων καὶ ἀποστροφὴ συγγενῶν.
ἀντὶ τούτων τοίνυν χρῆσθαί μου τῇ τέχνῃ ἀξιοῖς
καὶ δεσπότης εἶναι θέλεις τῶν ὅτ' οὐκ ἦσθα
δεσπότης πεπορισμένων; ἀγάπα εἴ τί σε καὶ
πρότερον ἑκὼν οὐ προοφείλων εὖ ἐποίησα, μηδε-
μίαν μηδὲ τότε [1] χάριν ἀπαιτεῖσθαι δυνάμενος.
25 Οὐ δὴ δεῖ τὴν εὐποιΐαν τὴν ἐμὴν ἀνάγκην ἐς τὸ
λοιπόν μοι γενέσθαι, οὐδὲ τὸ ἑκόντα εὐεργετῆσαι
ἀφορμὴν τοῦ ἄκοντα κελεύεσθαι καταστῆναι, οὐδὲ
ἔθος ὑπάρξαι τοῦτο, τὸ ἅπαξ τινὰ ἰασάμενον πάντας
ἐς ἀεὶ θεραπεύειν ὁπόσους ἂν ὁ θεραπευθεὶς θέλῃ·
ἐπεὶ δεσπότας ἂν οὕτως καθ' ἡμῶν εἴημεν τοὺς

[1] τότε N : τὸ ΓΖUBC (του F).

512

physicians have honours, precedence, immunities, and privileges publicly bestowed on them by states.

This, then, is what I might say without circumlocution in behalf of my profession if you had had me taught and had been at much pains and expense that I might learn, and I were nevertheless reluctant to undertake this one cure, which was possible. But as things stand, consider how absolutely unreasonable a thing you are doing in not allowing me to use my own possession freely. I did not learn this profession while I was your son or subject to your jurisdiction, and yet I learned it for you (aye, you were the first to profit by it) though I had no help from you towards learning it. What teacher did you furnish money for? What supply of drugs? None at all. No, poor as I was, in want of necessities, and pitied by my teachers, I got myself educated, and the assistance towards learning which I had from my father was grief, loneliness, poverty, the hatred of my family, and the aversion of my kinsmen. In return for this, do you now think fit to utilize my profession and wish to be master of all that I acquired when you were not my master? Be content if I have already done you a good turn of my own accord, without previous indebtedness to you, for then as now nothing could have been required of me as an expression of gratitude.

Surely my act of kindness should not become an obligation for the future, nor should the fact that I conferred a benefit of my own free will constitute a reason that I should be ordered to do it against my will; neither should it become customary that once a man has cured anybody, he must for ever treat all those whom his former patient wishes him to treat. Under those conditions we should have elected our

θεραπευομένους κεχειροτονηκότες καὶ μισθὸν τὸ
δουλεύειν αὐτοῖς καὶ τὸ πάντα κελεύουσιν ὑπηρετεῖν
προσδεδωκότες,[1] οὗ τί γένοιτ' ἂν ἀδικώτερον ;
διότι σε νοσήσαντα χαλεπῶς οὕτως ἀνέστησα,
διὰ τοῦτο νομίζεις ἐξεῖναί σοι καταχρῆσθαί μου
τῇ τέχνῃ ;

26 Ταῦτα μὲν οὖν εἶχον ἂν λέγειν, εἰ καὶ δυνατὰ
μὲν οὗτος προσέταττεν, ἐγὼ δὲ μὴ πάντως ἅπασι
μηδὲ πρὸς ἀνάγκην ὑπήκουον. νῦν δὲ ἤδη σκέψασθε καὶ οἷά ἐστιν αὐτοῦ τὰ ἐπιτάγματα· "Ἐπεὶ
γὰρ ἐμὲ ἰάσω," φησίν, " μεμηνότα, μέμηνεν δὲ
καὶ ἡ γυνὴ καὶ ὅμοια πάσχει "—τοῦτο γὰρ οἴεται—
" καὶ ὑπὸ τῶν ἄλλων ὁμοίως ἀπέγνωσται, δύνασαι
δὲ σὺ πάντα ὡς ἔδειξας, ἰῶ καὶ ταύτην καὶ ἀπάλ-
λαττε ἤδη τῆς νόσου." τοῦτο δέ, οὑτωσὶ μὲν ἁπλῶς
ἀκοῦσαι, πάνυ εὔλογον ἂν δόξειεν, καὶ μάλιστα
ἰδιώτῃ καὶ ἀπείρῳ ἰατρικῆς· εἰ δέ μου ἀκούσαιτε[2]
ὑπὲρ τῆς τέχνης δικαιολογουμένου, μάθοιτ' ἂν ὡς
οὔτε πάντα ἡμῖν δυνατά ἐστιν οὔθ' αἱ τῶν νοσημάτων φύσεις παραπλήσιοι οὔτ' ἴασις ἡ αὐτὴ οὔτε
φάρμακα τὰ αὐτὰ ἐπὶ πάντων ἰσχυρά, καὶ τότ'
ἔσται δῆλον ὡς πάμπολυ τοῦ μὴ βούλεσθαί τι τὸ
μὴ δύνασθαι διαφέρει. ἀνάσχεσθε δέ μου τὰ περὶ
τούτων φιλοσοφοῦντος, καὶ μὴ ἀπειρόκαλον μηδὲ
ἐξαγώνιον μηδὲ ἀλλότριον ἢ ἄκαιρον ἡγήσησθε
τὸν περὶ τῶν τοιούτων λόγον.

27 Πρῶτα μὲν δὴ σωμάτων φύσεις καὶ κράσεις
οὐχ αἱ αὐταί, κἂν ὅτι μάλιστα ἐκ τῶν ὁμοίων

patients to be our masters, paying them, too, by
playing slave to them and executing all their orders.
What could be more inequitable than this? Because
I restored you to health in this way when you had
fallen severely ill, do you think that you are therefore
empowered to abuse my skill?

That is what I might have said if what he enjoined
upon me were possible, and I were refusing to obey
him in absolutely everything, and under compulsion.
But as things are, consider now what his commands
are like. " Since you have cured me," says he,
" from insanity, since my wife too is insane and has
the same symptoms " (for so he thinks), " and has
been given up by others in the same way, and since
you can do everything, as you have shown, cure her
too and free her forthwith from the disorder." That,
to hear it so simply put, might seem very reasonable,
particularly to a layman, inexperienced in matters
of medicine. But if you will listen to my plea on
behalf of my profession, you will discover that all
things are not possible to us, that the natures of
ailments are not alike, that the cure is not the same
or the same medicines effective in all cases; and
then it will be clear that there is a great difference
between not wishing to do a thing and not being
able. Suffer me to indulge in scientific discourse
about these matters, and do not consider my discussion of them tactless, beside the point, or alien
and unseasonable.

In the first place, the natures and temperaments of
human bodies are not the same, although they are

---

[1] προσδεδωκότες Wesseling's marginalia: προδεδωκότες
MSS.
[2] ἀκούσαιτε ed. Flor.: ἀκούσεται Γ, ἀκούσετε NZUB.

συνεστάναι ὁμολογῶνται, ἀλλὰ τὰ μὲν τῶνδε,
τὰ δὲ τῶνδε μᾶλλον [1] ἢ ἔλαττον μετέχει. καὶ λέγω
τοῦτο ἔτι περὶ τῶν ἀνδρείων, ὡς οὐδὲ ταῦτα
πᾶσιν ἴσα ἢ ὅμοια οὔτε τῇ κράσει οὔτε τῇ συστάσει.
διάφορα δὴ [2] καὶ μεγέθει καὶ εἴδει ἀνάγκη καὶ τὰ
νοσήματα ἐγγίγνεσθαι αὐτοῖς, καὶ τὰ μὲν εὔιατα
εἶναι καὶ πρὸς τὴν θεραπείαν ἀναπεπταμένα,
τὰ δὲ τέλεον ἀπεγνωσμένα καὶ ῥᾳδίως ἁλισκόμενα
καὶ κατὰ κράτος ὑπὸ τῶν νοσημάτων λαμβανό-
μενα. τὸ τοίνυν οἴεσθαι πάντα πυρετὸν ἢ πᾶσαν
φθόην ἢ περιπλευμονίαν ἢ μανίαν μίαν καὶ τὴν
αὐτὴν οὖσαν τῷ γένει ὁμοίαν ἐπὶ παντὸς εἶναι
σώματος, οὐ σωφρονούντων οὐδὲ λελογισμένων
οὐδὲ τὰ τοιαῦτα ἐξητακότων ἐστὶν ἀνθρώπων,
ἀλλὰ τὸ αὐτὸ ἐν μὲν τῷδε ῥᾴδιον ἰᾶσθαι, ἐν δὲ
τῷδε οὐκέτι. ὥσπερ οἶμαι καὶ πυρὸν ἢν τὸν
αὐτὸν ἐς διαφόρους χώρας ἐμβάλῃς, ἄλλως μὲν
ἐν τῇ πεδινῇ καὶ βαθείᾳ καὶ ποτιζομένῃ καὶ
εὐηλίῳ καὶ εὐηνέμῳ καὶ ἐξειργασμένῃ ἀναφύσεται,
εὐθαλὴς οἶμαι καὶ εὔτροφος καὶ πολύχους καρπός,
ἄλλως δὲ ἐν ὄρει καὶ ὑπολίθῳ γηδίῳ, ἄλλως δὲ
ἐν δυσηλίῳ, ἄλλως δὲ ἐν ὑπωρείᾳ, καὶ ὅλως διαφό-
ρως καθ᾽ ἑκάστους τόπους. οὕτω δὲ καὶ τὰ
νοσήματα παρὰ τοὺς ὑποδεξαμένους τόπους ἢ
εὔφορα καὶ [3] εὔτροφα ἢ ἐλάττω γίγνεται. τοῦτο
τοίνυν ὑπερβὰς ὁ πατὴρ καὶ ὅλον ἀνεξέταστον
καταλιπὼν ἀξιοῖ πᾶσαν μανίαν τὴν ἐν ἅπαντι
σώματι ὁμοίαν εἶναι καὶ τὴν θεραπείαν ἴσην.

28   Πρὸς δὲ τούτοις τοσούτοις οὖσιν, ὅτι τὰ γυναικεῖα σώματα πάμπολυ τῶν ἀνδρείων διαφέρει πρός

---

[1] μᾶλλον N vulg.: omitted in ΓZUB(C)A.
[2] διάφορα δὴ ΓΖ: διάφορα γὰρ δὴ NUB.

admittedly composed of the same elements, but some contain more, or perhaps less, of this, others of that. And I say further that even the bodies of males are not all equal or alike either in temperament or in constitution. So it is inevitable that the diseases which arise in them should be different both in intensity and in kind, and that some bodies should be easy to cure and amenable to treatment, while others are completely hopeless, being easily affected and quickly overcome. Therefore, to think that all fevers or consumptions or inflammations of the lungs or madnesses, if of one and the same kind, are alike in all bodies is not what one expects of sound-minded, sensible men who have investigated such matters. No, the same ailment is easy to cure in this person but not in that. Just so, I take it, with wheat; if you cast the same seed into different plots of ground, it will grow in one way in the ground that is level, deep-soiled, well watered, blessed with sunshine and breezes, and thoroughly tilled, yielding a full, rich, abundant harvest, no doubt, but otherwise in a stony farm on a mountain, or in ground with little sun, or in the foothills; to put it generally, in different ways according to the various soils. So too diseases become prolific and luxuriant or less so through the soils which receive them. Omitting this point and leaving it entirely uninvestigated, my father expects all attacks of insanity in all bodies to be alike and their treatment the same.

In addition to these important distinctions, it is easy to grasp the fact that the bodies of women differ very widely from those of men, both in respect to

---

³ καὶ Fritzsche: ἢ MSS.

τε νόσου διαφορὰν καὶ πρὸς θεραπείας ἐλπίδα ἢ
ἀπόγνωσιν ῥᾴδιον καταμαθεῖν· τὰ μὲν γὰρ τῶν
ἀνδρῶν εὐπαγῆ καὶ εὔτονα, πόνοις καὶ κινήσεσιν
καὶ ὑπαιθρίῳ διαίτῃ γεγυμνασμένα, τὰ δὲ ἔκλυτα καὶ
ἀσυμπαγῆ, ἐνσκιατροφημένα [1] καὶ λευκὰ αἵματος
ἐνδείᾳ καὶ θερμοῦ ἀπορίᾳ καὶ ὑγροῦ περιττοῦ [2]
ἐπιρροίᾳ. εὐαλωτότερα τοίνυν τῶν ἀνδρείων καὶ
ταῖς νόσοις ἐκκείμενα καὶ τὴν ἴασιν οὐ περιμέ-
νοντα καὶ μάλιστα πρὸς μανίας εὐχερέστερα· ἅτε
γὰρ πολὺ μὲν τὸ ὀργίλον καὶ κοῦφον καὶ ὀξυ-
κίνητον ἔχουσαι, ὀλίγην δὲ τὴν τοῦ σώματος αὐτοῦ
δύναμιν, ῥᾳδίως ἐς τὸ πάθος τοῦτο κατολισ-
θάνουσιν.

29   Οὐ δίκαιον τοίνυν παρὰ τῶν ἰατρῶν τὴν ὁμοίαν
ἐπ' ἀμφοῖν θεραπείαν ἀπαιτεῖν, εἰδότας ὡς πολὺ
τοὐν μέσῳ, βίῳ παντὶ καὶ πράξεσιν ὅλαις καὶ
πᾶσιν ἐπιτηδεύμασιν ἐξ ἀρχῆς εὐθὺς κεχωρισμένων.
ὅταν τοίνυν λέγῃς ὅτι μέμηνε, προστίθει καὶ
ὅτι γυνὴ οὖσα μέμηνε, καὶ μὴ σύγχει πάντα ταῦτα
τῷ τῆς μανίας ὑπάγων ὀνόματι ἑνὶ καὶ τῷ αὐτῷ
δοκοῦντι, ἀλλὰ χωρίσας, ὥσπερ ἐστὶ δίκαιον,[3]
τῇ φύσει, τὸ δυνατὸν ἐφ' ἑκάστου σκόπει. καὶ
γὰρ ἡμεῖς, ὅπερ ἐν ἀρχῇ τῶν λόγων εἰπὼν μέμνημαι, τοῦτο πρῶτον ἐπισκοποῦμεν, φύσιν σώματος
τοῦ νοσοῦντος καὶ κρᾶσιν, καὶ τίνος πλείονος
μετέχει, καὶ εἰ θερμότερον ἢ ψυχρότερον, καὶ [4]

---

[1] ἐνσκιατροφημένα U : ἐν σκιᾷ τροφημένα Γ ; cf. Plut. Mor.
476 θ. ἐν σκιᾷ τραφημένα B, ἐν σκιᾷ τετραφημένα N, ἐσκιατραφη-
μένα Z[1] : ἐσκιατροφημένα CMF vulg.

DISOWNED

the dissimilarity of their diseases and in respect to
one's hopefulness or despair of a cure. For the
bodies of men are well-knit and sinewy, since they
have been trained by toils and exercises, and by an
open-air life ; but those of women are weak and
soft from being reared indoors, and white for lack of
blood, deficiency of heat, and an excessive supply
of the moist humour. They are therefore more
susceptible than those of men, prone to diseases,
intolerant of medical treatment, and above all, more
liable to attacks of insanity; for since women have
much bad temper, frivolity, and instability, but little
physical strength, they easily fall into this affection.

It is not right, then, to ask of the physicians the
same treatment for both, when we know that there
is a great gulf between them, dissociated as they have
been from the very first in their entire mode of life,
and in all their activities and all their pursuits. So
when you say " It is a case of insanity," add, " insanity in a woman," and do not confuse all these
variations by subsuming them under the title of
insanity, which seems always one and the same
thing, but distinguish them, as is right, in their
nature and see what can be done in each case. That
is what we do, for, as I remember telling you in the
beginning of my speech, the first thing that we consider is the constitution and temperament of the
patient's body, what quality predominates in it,
whether it is inclined to be hot or cold, whether it is

² περιττοῦ omitted in Z¹CMF.

³ ἐστὶ δίκαιον Hemsterhuys: ἐστὶν καὶ ὂν ΓΝΖC (ἐστὶ ΝΖC);
ἐστὶ καὶ ἐν UB vulg.

⁴ καὶ ed. Flor.: ἢ MSS.

ἀκμάζον ἢ παρηβηκός, καὶ μέγα ἢ μικρόν, καὶ
πιμελὲς ἢ ὀλιγόσαρκον, καὶ πάντα τὰ τοιαῦτα. καὶ
ὅλως ἄν τις αὐτὰ προεξετάσῃ, πάνυ ἀξιόπιστος ἂν
εἴη ἀπογιγνώσκων τι ἢ ὑπισχνούμενος.

30 Ἐπεὶ καὶ τῆς μανίας αὐτῆς μυρία εἴδη ἐστὶν καὶ
παμπόλλας ἔχει τὰς αἰτίας καὶ οὐδὲ τὰς προσηγορίας αὐτὰς ὁμοίας· οὐ γὰρ ταὐτὸν παρανοεῖν καὶ
παραπαίειν καὶ λυττᾶν καὶ μεμηνέναι, ἀλλὰ ταῦτα
πάντα τοῦ μᾶλλον ἢ ἧττον ἔχεσθαι τῇ νόσῳ ὀνόματά
ἐστιν. αἰτίαι τε τοῖς μὲν ἀνδράσιν ἄλλαι, ταῖς δὲ
γυναιξὶν ἕτεραι, καὶ τῶν ἀνδρῶν αὐτῶν τοῖς μὲν νέοις
ἄλλαι, τοῖς δὲ γεγηρακόσιν διάφοροι, οἷον νέοις
μὲν πλῆθος[1] ὡς τὸ πολύ, γέροντας δὲ καὶ διαβολὴ
ἄκαιρος καὶ ὀργὴ ἄλογος πολλάκις κατ' οἰκείων
ἐμπεσοῦσα τὸ μὲν πρῶτον διετάραξεν, εἶτα κατ'
ὀλίγον ἐς μανίαν περιέτρεψεν. γυναικῶν δὲ πολλὰ
καθικνεῖται καὶ ῥᾳδίως ἐς τὴν νόσον ἐπάγεται,
μάλιστα δὲ μῖσος κατά τινος πολὺ ἢ φθόνος ἐπ'
ἐχθρῷ εὐτυχοῦντι ἢ λύπη τις ἢ ὀργή· κατ' ὀλίγον
ταῦτα ὑποτυφόμενα καὶ μακρῷ χρόνῳ ἐντρεφόμενα
μανίαν ἀποτελεῖ.

31 Τοιαῦτά σοι, ὦ πάτερ, καὶ ἡ γυνὴ πέπονθεν καὶ
ἴσως τι λελύπηκεν αὐτὴν ἔναγχος· οὐδὲν[2] γὰρ
ἐκείνη ἐμίσει. πλὴν ἔχεταί γε καὶ οὐκ ἂν ἐκ τῶν
παρόντων ὑπ' ἰατροῦ θεραπευθῆναι δύναιτο· ὡς
εἴ γε ἄλλος τις ὑπόσχοιτο, εἴ τις ἀπαλλάξειε,
μίσει τότε ὡς ἀδικοῦντα ἐμέ. καὶ μὴν κἀκεῖνο,

---

[1] This word, which has perhaps elicited more conjectures
than any other in Lucian, is right. Its use as a synonym
of πληθώρα, though not recognised in the dictionaries, is
abundantly documented in Galen; e.g., *De San. Tuenda,*
IV, 2, 13: τοῦ τοιούτου πλήθους ὃ δὴ καὶ πληθώραν ὀνομάζουσι.

vigorous or senile, tall or short, fat or lean, and everything of that sort. In short, if a man examines into these matters to begin with, he will be very trustworthy when he expresses any doubt or makes any promise.

To be sure, of madness itself there are countless varieties, with many causes and even dissimilar names; for perversity, eccentricity, delirium, and lunacy are not the same thing, but are all names that signify whether one is more or less in the grip of the disease. The causes, too, are of one sort with men, another with women, and even among men they are of one sort with the young and different with the aged; for instance, with the young usually excess of humours, whereas in the case of the old, groundless prejudice and insensate anger against members of the family, attacking them frequently, disturbs them at first, then gradually deranges them to the point of insanity. Women are affected by many things which easily incline them to this ailment, especially by excessive hatred of someone, or jealousy of an enemy who is prospering, or grief of some sort, or anger; these passions, slowly smouldering and acquiring strength in a long lapse of time, produce madness.

That, father, is what has happened to your wife, and it may be that something has grieved her recently, for she, of course, hated nothing at all. However that may be, she has a seizure, at all events, and in the circumstances cannot be cured by a physician. If anyone else should engage to do it, if anyone should relieve her, you may then hate me as offending

---

[2] οὐδένα (C)A, perhaps right.

ὦ πάτερ, οὐκ ἂν ὀκνήσαιμι εἰπεῖν, ὅτι εἰ καὶ μὴ
τελέως οὕτως ἀπέγνωστο, ἀλλά τις ἔτι σωτηρίας
ἐλπὶς ὑπεφαίνετο, οὐκ ἂν οὐδὲ οὕτω ῥᾳδίως
προσηψάμην οὐδ' αὖ προχείρως φάρμακον ἐγχέαι
ἐτόλμησα, δεδιὼς τὴν τύχην καὶ τὴν παρὰ τῶν
πολλῶν δυσφημίαν. ὁρᾷς ὡς οἴονται πάντες
εἶναί τι μῖσος πρὸς τοὺς προγόνους πάσαις μη-
τρυιαῖς, κἂν ὦσι χρησταί, καί τινα κοινὴν μανίαν
ταύτην[1] γυναικείαν αὐτὰς μεμηνέναι. τάχ' ἂν
οὖν[2] τις ὑπώπτευσεν, ἄλλως χωρήσαντος τοῦ
κακοῦ καὶ τῶν φαρμάκων οὐ δυνηθέντων, κακοήθη
καὶ δολερὰν τὴν θεραπείαν γεγονέναι.

32   Καὶ τὰ μὲν τῆς γυναικός, ὦ πάτερ, οὕτως ἔχει,
καὶ πάνυ σοι τετηρηκὼς λέγω—οὔ ποτε ῥᾷον ἕξει,
κἂν μυριάκις πίῃ τοῦ φαρμάκου. διὰ τοῦτ'
ἐπιχειρεῖν οὐκ ἄξιον, εἰ μὴ πρὸς μόνον τὸ ἀποτυχεῖν
με κατεπείγεις καὶ κακοδοξίᾳ περιβαλεῖν θέλεις.
ἔασον ὑπὸ τῶν ὁμοτέχνων φθονεῖσθαι. ἐὰν δέ
με ἀποκηρύξῃς πάλιν, ἐγὼ μὲν καίτοι πάντων
ἔρημος γενόμενος οὐδὲν κατὰ σοῦ δεινὸν εὔξομαι·
τί δ' ἄν, ὅπερ μὴ γένοιτο, αὖθις ἡ νόσος ἐπανέλ-
θῃ; φιλεῖ γάρ πως τὰ τοιαῦτα ἐρεθιζόμενα παλιν-
δρομεῖν. τί με πρᾶξαι δεήσει; θεραπεύσω μὲν
εὖ ἴσθι καὶ τότε καὶ οὔ ποτε λείψω τὴν τάξιν
ἣν τοὺς παῖδας ἔταξεν ἡ φύσις, οὐδὲ τοῦ γένους τὸ
ἐπ' ἐμαυτῷ ἐπιλήσομαι. εἶτ' ἂν σωφρονήσῃς,
αὖθις ἀναλαμβάνειν πώποτε πιστεῦσαί με δεῖ;
ὁρᾷς; ἤδη καὶ ταῦτα ποιῶν ἐπισπᾷ τὴν νόσον καὶ

---

[1] ταύτην Z(MFC) edd. : ταύτῃ ΓUNB.
[2] τάχ' ἂν οὖν Jacobitz: τάχα οὖν ΓUNBAZ², τάχα ἂν
Z¹M.

against you. Indeed, father, I shall not hesitate to say further that even if her case were not so wholly desperate, but some hope of saving her still were in sight, even then I should not have undertaken her case lightly or ventured to prescribe for her out of hand, fearing mischance and the slanderous tongues of the common sort. You are aware that everybody thinks that all stepmothers entertain some hatred of their stepsons, even if they are good women, and that in this they suffer from a sort of insanity affecting women in common. Perhaps someone would have suspected, if the ailment had gone badly and the remedies had not been effective, that the treatment had been malevolent and treacherous.

As regards your wife, father, the case stands thus, and I tell you so after careful observation—she will never be better, even if she takes medicine a thousand times. For that reason it is not proper to make any attempt, unless you are trying to force me into sheer failure and wish to give me a bad name. Let me continue to be envied by my fellow-practitioners! If, however, you disown me again, I certainly, though totally alone in the world, will not pray that any adversity may befall you; but what if (Heaven forfend!) your affliction returns once more? Somehow it often happens that such afflictions, under irritation, do recur. What shall I be required to do? I will treat you even then, you may be sure, and shall never desert the post which Nature has commanded sons to hold, nor ever, so far as in me lies, forget my origin. And then, if you recover your mind, may I expect you some day to take me back again? Look! even now by these actions of yours you are bringing on the disorder and provoking the

ὑπομιμνήσκεις τὸ πάθος. χθὲς καὶ πρώην ἐκ
τηλικούτων κακῶν ἀνασφήλας διατείνῃ καὶ βοᾷς,
καὶ τὸ μέγιστον, ὀργίζῃ καὶ πρὸς μῖσος τρέπῃ
καὶ τοὺς νόμους ἀνακαλεῖς. οἴμοι, πάτερ, ταῦτ'
ἦν σου καὶ τῆς πάλαι μανίας τὰ προοίμια.

ailment. You have only just recovered from that terrible plight, and yet you strain your lungs shouting; more than that, you are angry, you take to hatred, and you invoke the laws. Ah, father, that is the way your former seizure began!

INDEX

INDEX

Amphion, who with the aid of a lyre given him by Hermes, built the wall of Thebes by making the stones move of their own accord, 253 (*see note* 2)

Anaximenes of Lampsacus, writer of the time of Alexander the Great, probable author of the work "Tricaranus" (*p.* 96, *note* 1)

Anchises, beloved of Aphrodite, by whom he had Aeneas, 429

Androgeos, son of Minos, for whose death in Attica the Athenians had to send each year seven youths and seven maids to Crete, 259

Andromache, wife of Hector, who became the slave of Neoptolemus, 241

Andromeda, saved from the sea-monster by Perseus, 255

Antigone, 255

Antioch, 277 *sq.*, 397

Antipater (son of Cassander?), 263 *and note*

Antiphilus of Alopece, an Athenian, 149 *sqq.*

Antisthenes, pupil of Gorgias and of Socrates, founder of the Cynic school, 9, 67, 73, 77

Antoninus Pius, 21, *note*

Anubideum (temple of Anubis), 149 *sq.*, 151

Anubis, dog-headed god of Egypt, equated with Hermes by the Greeks, 155, 431

Anytus, wealthy Athenian tanner and politician, prosecutor of Socrates, 59

Apelles, famous painter, contemporary of Alexander the Great, 247

Aphrodite, 227, 249, 267, 277, 363, 365, (A. Pandemus) 387, (A. Genetyllis) 386, *note* 2

Apis, Egyptian god, incarnated in the sacred bull of Memphis, 353, 431

Apollo, 237, 365, 433, 437, 441; *character in " The Runaways,"* 55 *sq.*

Apsyrtus, brother of Medea, taken with her on her flight with Jason, dismembered and thrown overboard to delay their pursuers, 261

Arabia, 55

Arcadia, Arcadian, 259, 367

Archemorus, 255 (*see note* 3)

Archilochus, 373, 375

Areopagus of Athens (first trial on), 251; *see* Halirrhothius

Ares, 183, 233, 235, 267, 363, 365, 367

Aretaeus of Corinth, 141 *sq.*

Argo, Argonauts, 87, 107, 261

Argos, 109, 357, 359

Argus, of the many eyes, set by Hera to watch Io; lulled to sleep and slain by Hermes, 255

Ariadne, daughter of Minos, whose clue helped Theseus escape from the labyrinth; abandoned by him at Naxos, and carried off by Dionysus, 227, 259, 425

Aries (Ram), sign of the Zodiac, 353, 357

Ariphrades of Athens, 377 (*see note* 3)

Aristo, son of (Plato), 293, 295

Aristophanes, 97 *note*

Aristotle, 213, 273, 335, 341

Armenia, 11

Arsacomas, a Scythian, 173–195

Artemidore, 311 *and note*

Artemis, 27, 105, 311

Ascalaphus, son of Ares, a hero of the Trojan war, 363

Asclepius (*see p.* 6, *note* 1), 7, 29, 257, 425, 441; scion of (physician), 301

Asia, 261; (province of) 11, 15, (governor of), 133

Aspasia, 239, 339

Assyrian (*i.e.*, Syrian; *see Vol. IV., p.* 339, *note* 2), 263

Astyanax, infant son of Hector, 279

Atalanta, virgin huntress, shared in the killing of the Calydonian boar, and was given the hide by Meleager, 259

Atarneus, city in Mysia, opposite Lesbos, 341

Athamas, King of Orchomenus, father of Phrixus and Helle by Nephele, and of Learchus and Melicertes by Ino, went mad and slew Learchus, 253, 271, 359

Athena, 251, 317, 365, 405, 441

Athenian, 253, 327, 359, 381, 387, 405

Athens, 135, 139, 197, 391, (Agora), 331

Attic, 81, 251, 253, 325, 326, 387, 389

Attica, 251, 387, 391

Atticion, name in the *Banquet* of Lexiphanes, 299

Atticism, 313

Atimarchus, a nickname, 405 (*see note* 1 *and p.* 371, *note*)

527

INDEX

INDEX

INDEX

INDEX

INDEX

Lazi, 175

Learchus, son of Ino and Athamas, killed by Athamas gone mad, 429

Lecythium (Pomander), 95

Lemnos, incidents at, 261 (*see* p. 255, note 3)

Lesbonax, of Mytilene, sophist somewhat prior to Lucian, author of three extant declamations, 273

Lesbos, 407

Leto, mother of Apollo and Artemis whom she bore on Delos, 251

Leucanor, King of Bosporus, 173–187 (*see* p. 173, note 2)

Lexiphanes, an Atticist, 293–327

Libyans, 353 *sq.*

Lonchates, a Scythian, 173 *sqq.*

Lotus-Eaters (Lotophagi), 215

Lucian, 7 note, 8 note 2, 371 note

Lycambes, father of Neobule, attacked by Archilochus for not allowing him to marry her, 375 (*see* note 1)

Lyceum, enclosure at Athens, dedicated to Apollo, 297

Lycinus, nom-de-plume of Lucian. (*The Dance*; *Lexiphanes*; *Eunuch*), 211 *sqq.*, 293 *sqq.*, 331 *sqq.*

Lycophron, the poet, 327

Lycurgus, of Thrace, driven mad by Dionysus, whom he refused to receive, and killed by his subjects, 261

Lycurgus, Spartan lawgiver, 367

Lyde, typical courtesan of the New Comedy, 213

Lydians, 235

Lyson, an Ephesian, 125, 131

Macedonian, 263

Macentes, a Scythian, 173 *sqq.*

Machlyene, Machlyans, district in Scythia known only from Lucian, 175 *sqq.*, 185, 189, 191

Maenads, 5

Maeotis, Lake, 109, 177, 189

Magi, 65

Marcus Aurelius, 333 (*see* p. 329, note)

Mariantes, a Scythian, father of Arsacomas, 183

Mars, *see* Ares

Massaliote, 145, 149

Massilia, 143

Masteira, an Alan woman, wife of Leucanor, King of Bosporus, 187

Mazaea, daughter of Leucanor, King of Bosporus, 173 *sqq.*, 187 *sq.*

Mede, 431

Medea, reception of (by Aegeus, at Athens), 251; dream of, 261 (*see* note 1)

Megalonymus, name in the *Banquet* of Lexiphanes, 305

Megara, 135, 253

Meleager, hero of the hunting of the Caledonian boar, 259

Melicertes (Palaemon), son of Athamas and Ino (*see* Ino), 253

Memnon, statue of, in Egypt, 149

Memphis, city in Egypt, 431

Menander, 379

Menecrates of Massilia, 145 *sq.*

Menippus, of Gadara, Cynic satirist, 67 (*see* note 1)

Menoeceus, son of Creon, of Thebes, betrothed of Antigone, whom Creon's condemnation of her drives to suicide, 255

Mentor, silversmith, 305 (*see* note 1)

Mercury, *see* Hermes

Meriones, 223

Metiochus, the Phrygian, hero of a Greek romance, 403 (*see* note 1)

Minerva, *see* Athena

Minos, King of Crete, 253 (*see* note 1), 363

Minotaur, 259 note

Mithras, Persian sun-god, 431

Mitraeans, mountains of the (imaginary?), 189

Mnemosyne (Memory), the mother of the Muses, 247

Mnesarchus, son of (Pythagoras), 317

Mnesippus, a Greek, takes part in the dialogue *Toxaris*, 103 *sqq.*

Momus, god of mockery, chief speaker in *The Parliament of the Gods*, 419 *sqq.*

Musaeus, half-mythical early singer, composer of hymns and religious poetry, 229

Muses, 79, 225

Musonius (Gaius Musonius Rufus), Stoic philosopher of the time of Nero, banished by him, whose writings (Greek) survive in excerpts, 21

Mycenae, 109, 225

Myropnus (Stinkadore), 95

Myrrha (Smyrna), mother of Adonis, 263

INDEX

INDEX

INDEX

Pytho, the dragon that originally inhabited the site of the Delphic oracle, slain by Apollo, 251

Rhea, 221, 249
Rhodes, unknown sophist from, 149
Rhododaphne, a nickname, 405
Rhodope, heroine, sister of Haemus (see p. 212, note 1) and mountain in Thrace, 81, 213, 261
Rome, Romans, 7, 21, 383, 399; Roman dance (Salii), 233

Sabazius, 429 (see note 3)
Salii (Roman priesthood), 233
Samos, Samian, 65, 123, 131, 261, 317
Saturn, see Cronus
Satyrs, 235, 281, 423
Sauromatae (Sarmatians), 165 sqq., 191
Scarabee, see Cantharus
Scopadean (masterpiece), a work by the sculptor Scopas, 311
Scylla, betrayed her father Nisus by stealing his purple lock of hair, out of love for Minos, 253
Scyros, island of, 257
Scythia, Scythians, 65, 257, 375, 387, 431, and "Toxaris" passim (103–121, 161–203)
Selene, goddess of the moon, 55
Seleucus Nicator, 263 (see note 4)
Semele, beloved of Zeus, burnt up by his lightnings when he appeared to her at her request in all his majesty, 251, 283
Serpent, constellation, 365
Seven Captains, leaders of the host that unsuccessfully attempted to take Thebes and restore Polynices, 255
Sibyl, the, 33, 35
Sicily, 57, 137
Sicyon, 141
Silenus, 423
Simonides (Semonides) of Amorgos, 375
Simylus, a Megarian sea-captain, 135 sqq.
Sindians, neighbours of the Scythians, east of the Straits of Kertsch, 193
Sinope, city of Paphlagonia, 85; the man of (Diogenes), 9, 397
Siphae, 303
Sirens, 215, 259 (see note 3)

Sisinnes, a Scythian, 195–201
Six Hundred, the, of Massilia, 145, 147
Socrates, 9, 43, 59, 237, 341; Socrates, "the new" (Peregrinus), 13
Sophists, 65 sqq., 323, 379, 381
Sophocles, 5
Sopolis, a physician, 317 sqq.
Sparta, Spartan, 85, 225, 255, 257, 367, 391
Spartae (Sown Men), 253
Stheneboea, wife of Proetus, King of Corinth, whose advances were repulsed by Bellerophon, 253
Stoics, 333, 339
Stratonice, wife of Seleucus Nicator, 263 (see note 4)
Struthias, parasite in Menander's Colax, 75
Styx, river by which the gods swear, 439
Sun, see Helius
Sunium, 149
Sybarite, 377
Synanche (Quinsy), a nickname, 405
Syria, Syrian, 7, 15, 49, 149, 263, 385, 397, 405
Syrophoenician (Cadmus), 423
Syrus, a slave, 149, 151, 157, 159

Talus, son of Minos, a man of bronze who guarded the shores of Crete, making the rounds three times a day, 259
Tanais (Don), 167
Tantalus, admitted to the society of the gods, was expelled from it because he could not control his tongue, 261
Tarsus, 397
Tartarus, 363, 439
Taurus (Bull), sign of the Zodiac, 353, 359
Telegonus, son of Odysseus and Circe, 257 (see note 3)
Telemachus (punned on), 311
Termerian, 309 (see note 4)
Thargelia of Miletus, 339 (see note 1)
Thasos, 435
Theagenes, athlete, 435 (see note)
Theagenes, a Cynic, of Patras, (see p. 7, note 2), 5, 7, 9, 25, 29, 33, 35, 41
Thebes, Thebans, 253, 279, 395
Theodore, play on the name, 311
Theopompus(see p. 96, note 1) 97, 409

535

INDEX